vault

WESTERN WORLD - MANAGING EDITOR

NATHAN C. GOODEN - DESIGN ARTIST

TIM DANIEL - EVP BRANDING & DESIGN

IAN BALDESSARI - PRODUCTION MANAGER

SONJA SYNAK - SENIOR DESIGNER

DAVID DISSANAYAKE - VP SALES & MARKETING

SYNDEE BARWICK - BOOK TRADE SALES & MARKETING

DANIEL ERABY - COMMERCE & COMMUNICATION

ALEX SCOLA - SOCIAL MEDIA COORDINATOR

WRITER
CHRISTOPHER CANTWELL

ARTIST
ADAM GORHAM

COLORIST
KURT MICHAEL RUSSELL

LETTERER
HASSAN OTSMANE-ELHAOU

SERIES COVERS BY **ADAM GORHAM** & **KURT MICHAEL RUSSELL**
YOSHI YOSHITANI

ORIGINAL SCORE BY **AARON FISCHER**
USE THE QR CODE TO LISTEN

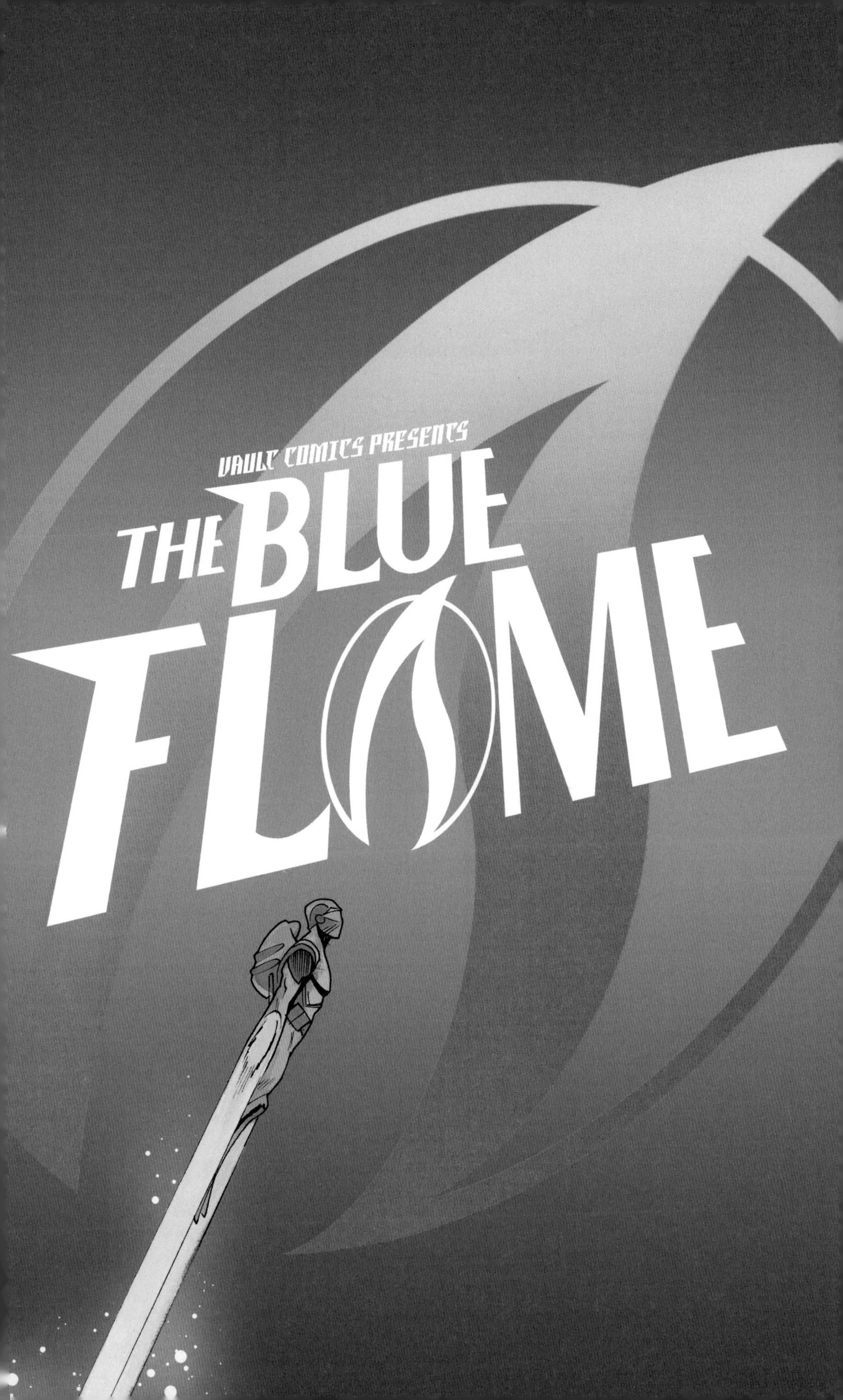
VAULT COMICS PRESENTS
THE BLUE
FLAME

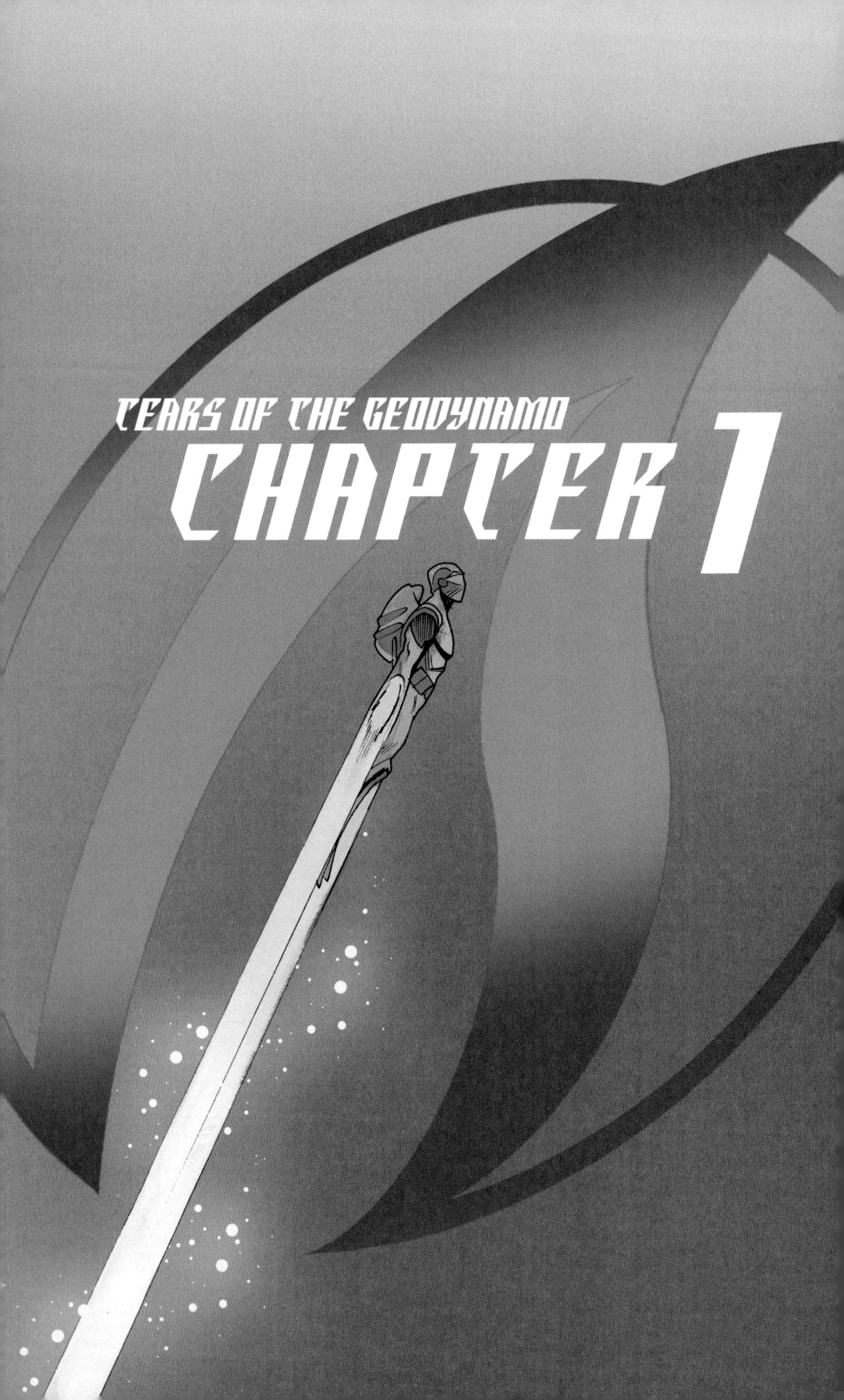
TEARS OF THE GEODYNAMO
CHAPTER 1

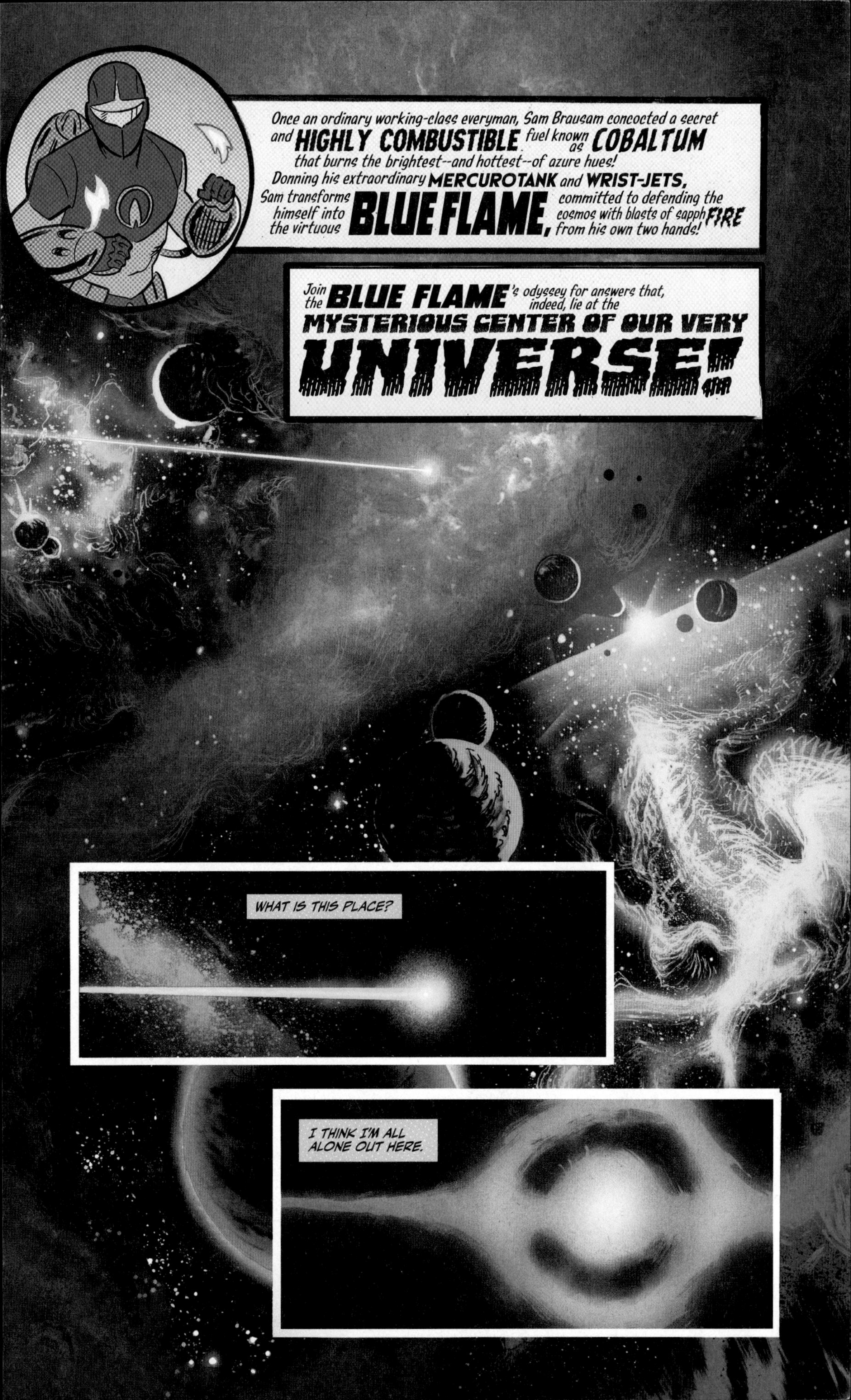

Once an ordinary working-class everyman, Sam Brausam concocted a secret and HIGHLY COMBUSTIBLE fuel known as COBALTUM that burns the brightest--and hottest--of azure hues!
Donning his extraordinary MERCUROTANK and WRIST-JETS, Sam transforms himself into the virtuous BLUE FLAME, committed to defending the cosmos with blasts of sapphFIRE from his own two hands!
Join the BLUE FLAME's odyssey for answers that, indeed, lie at the MYSTERIOUS CENTER OF OUR VERY UNIVERSE!
WHAT IS THIS PLACE?
I THINK I'M ALL ALONE OUT HERE.

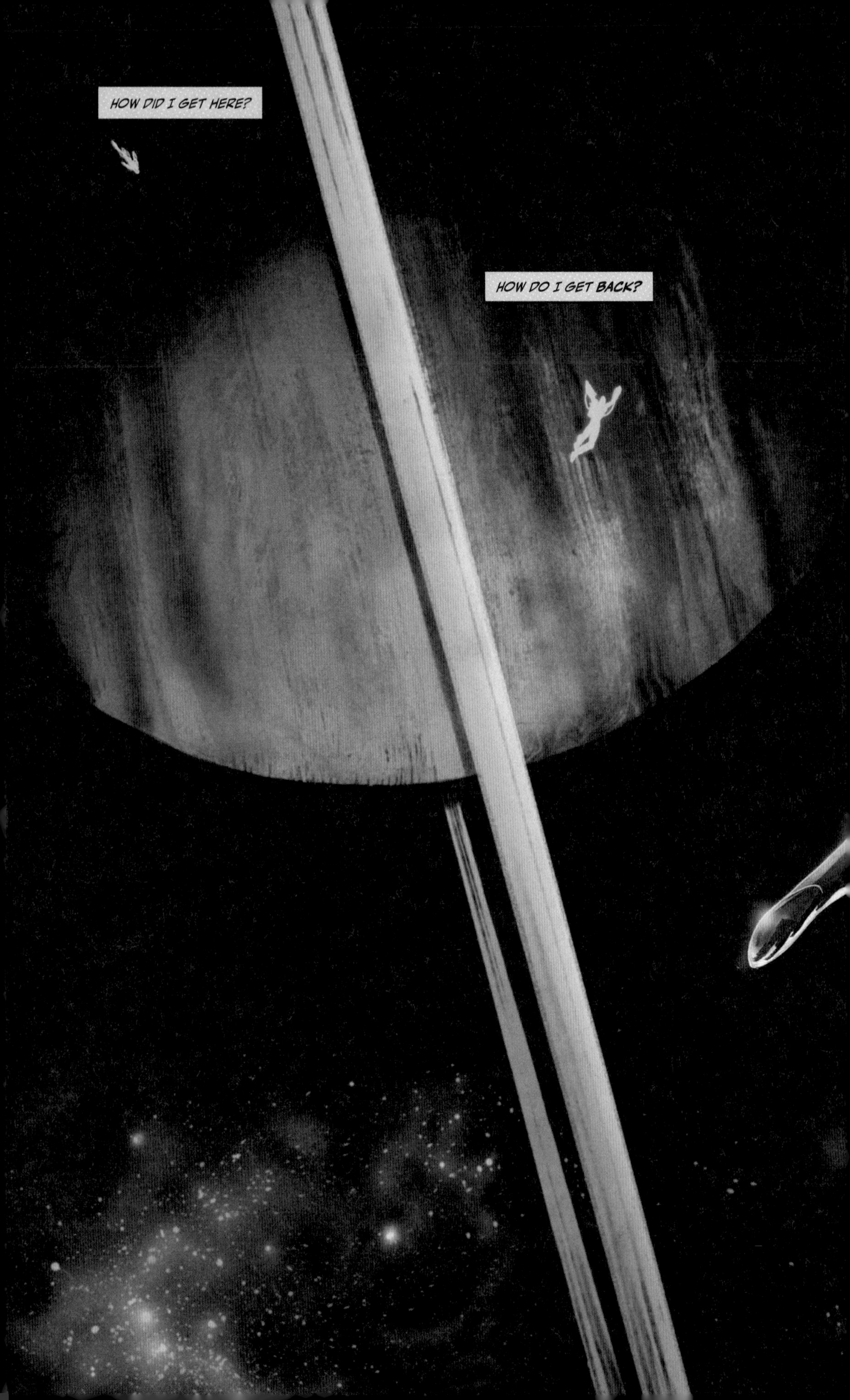
HOW DID I GET HERE?
HOW DO I GET BACK?

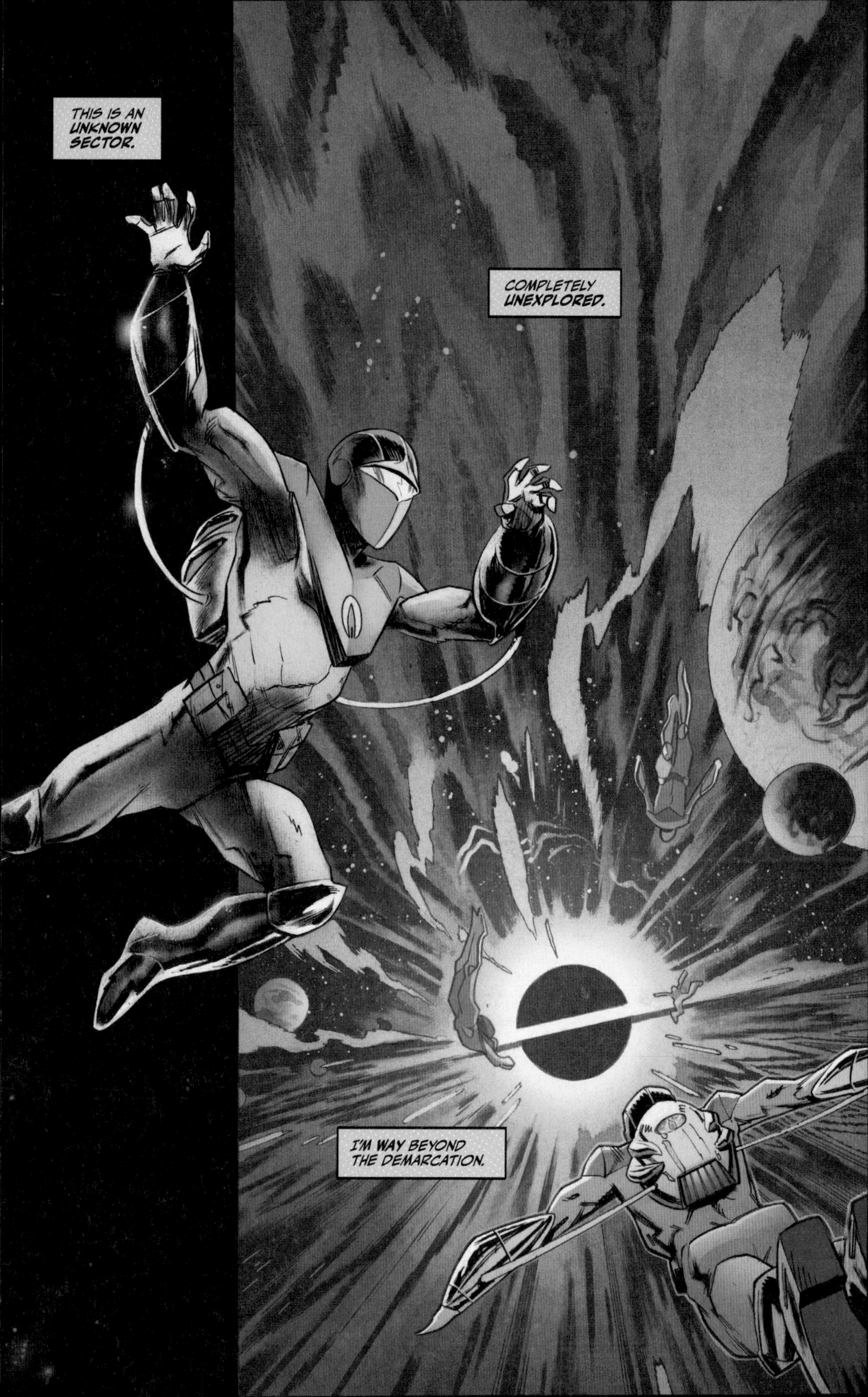
THIS IS AN UNKNOWN SECTOR.
COMPLETELY UNEXPLORED.
I'M WAY BEYOND THE DEMARCATION.

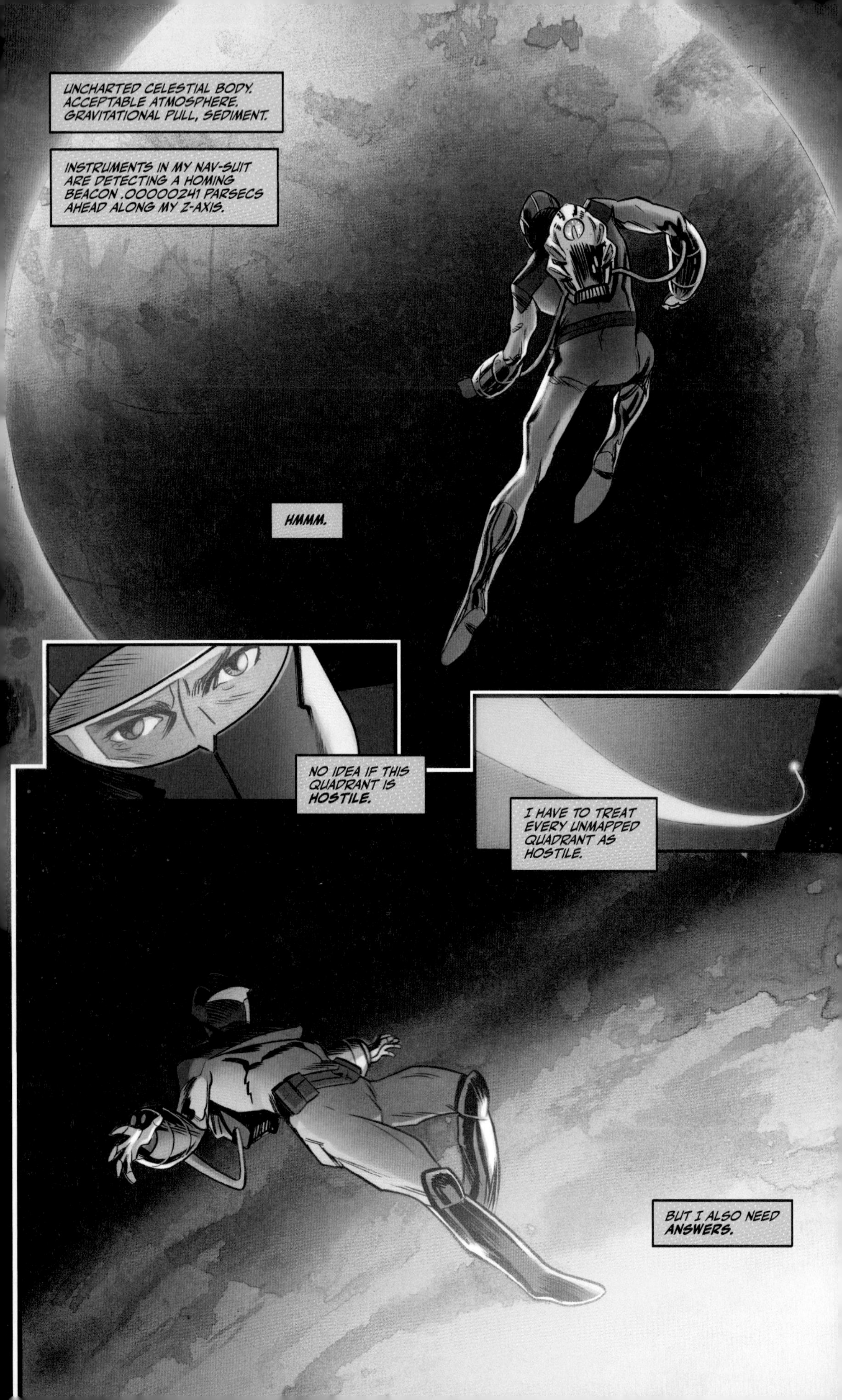
UNCHARTED CELESTIAL BODY. ACCEPTABLE ATMOSPHERE. GRAVITATIONAL PULL, SEDIMENT.
INSTRUMENTS IN MY NAV-SUIT ARE DETECTING A HOMING BEACON .00000241 PARSECS AHEAD ALONG MY Z-AXIS.
HMMM.
NO IDEA IF THIS QUADRANT IS HOSTILE.
I HAVE TO TREAT EVERY UNMAPPED QUADRANT AS HOSTILE.
BUT I ALSO NEED ANSWERS.

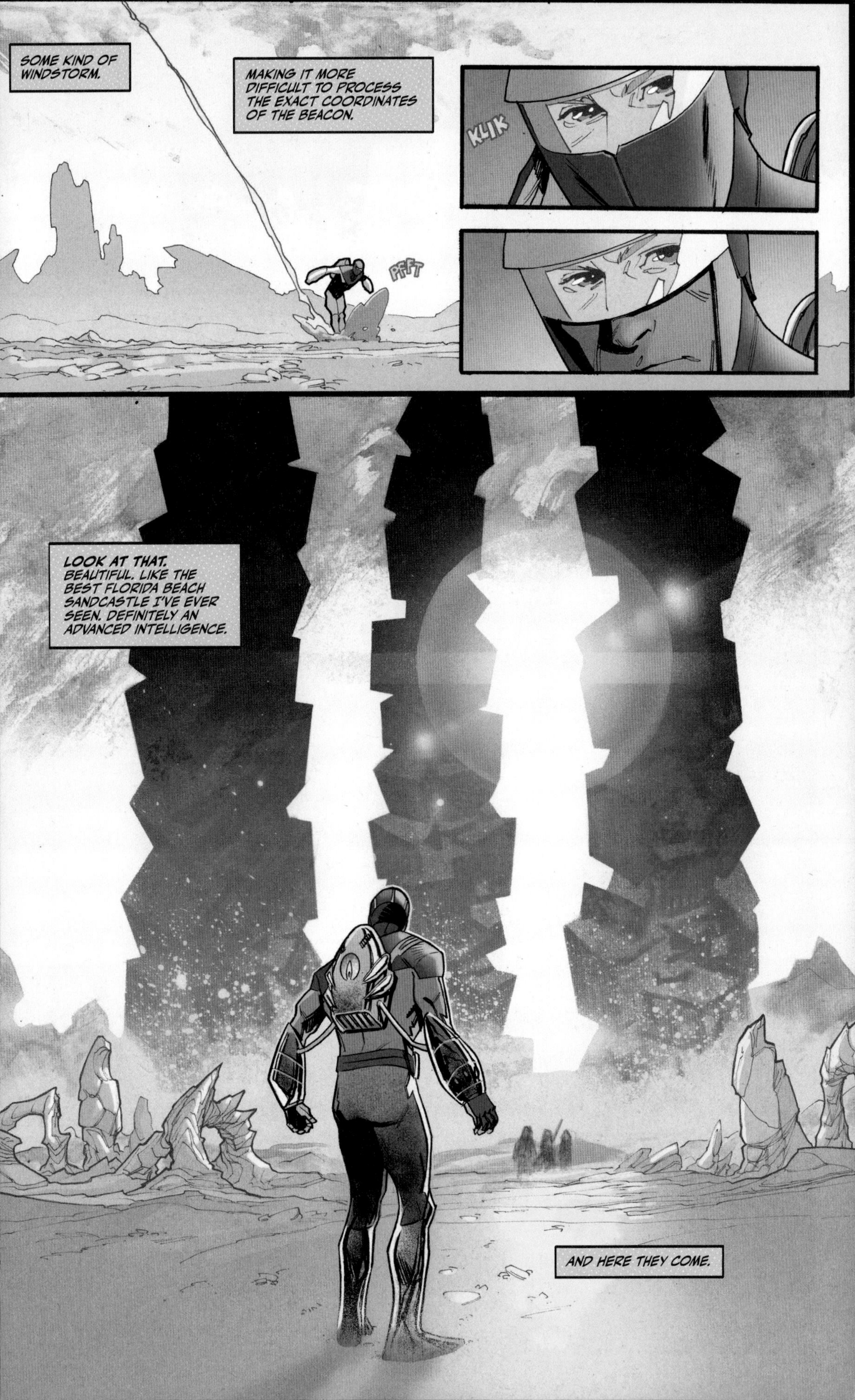
SOME KIND OF WINDSTORM.
MAKING IT MORE DIFFICULT TO PROCESS THE EXACT COORDINATES OF THE BEACON.
PFFT
KLIK
LOOK AT THAT. BEAUTIFUL. LIKE THE BEST FLORIDA BEACH SANDCASTLE I'VE EVER SEEN. DEFINITELY AN ADVANCED INTELLIGENCE.
AND HERE THEY COME.

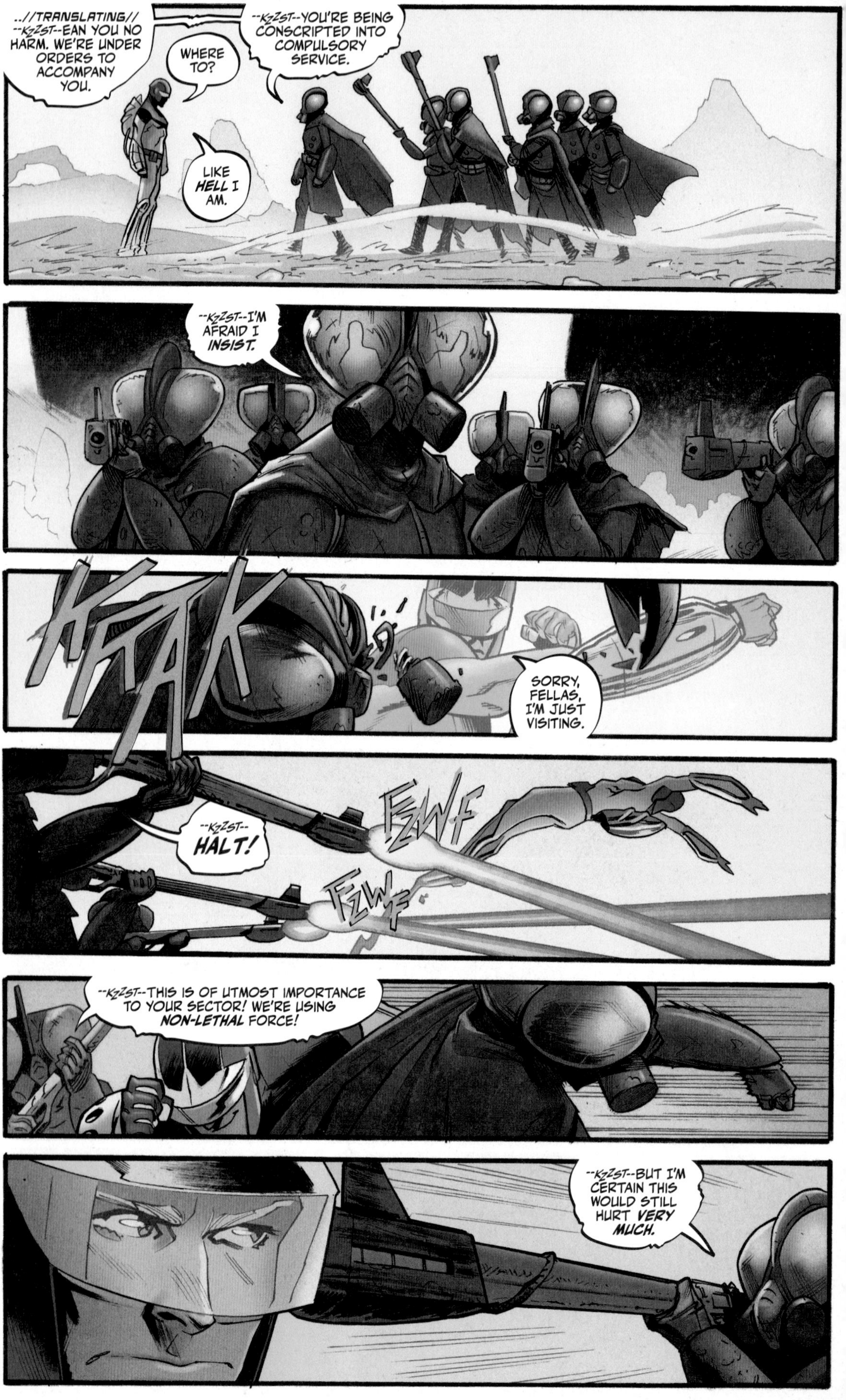

..//TRANSLATING// --KZZST--EAN YOU NO HARM. WE'RE UNDER ORDERS TO ACCOMPANY YOU.
WHERE TO?
--KZZST--YOU'RE BEING CONSCRIPTED INTO COMPULSORY SERVICE.
LIKE HELL I AM.
--KZZST--I'M AFRAID I INSIST.
KTAK
SORRY, FELLAS, I'M JUST VISITING.
--KZZST-- HALT!
FZWF
FZWF
--KZZST--THIS IS OF UTMOST IMPORTANCE TO YOUR SECTOR! WE'RE USING NON-LETHAL FORCE!
--KZZST--BUT I'M CERTAIN THIS WOULD STILL HURT VERY MUCH.

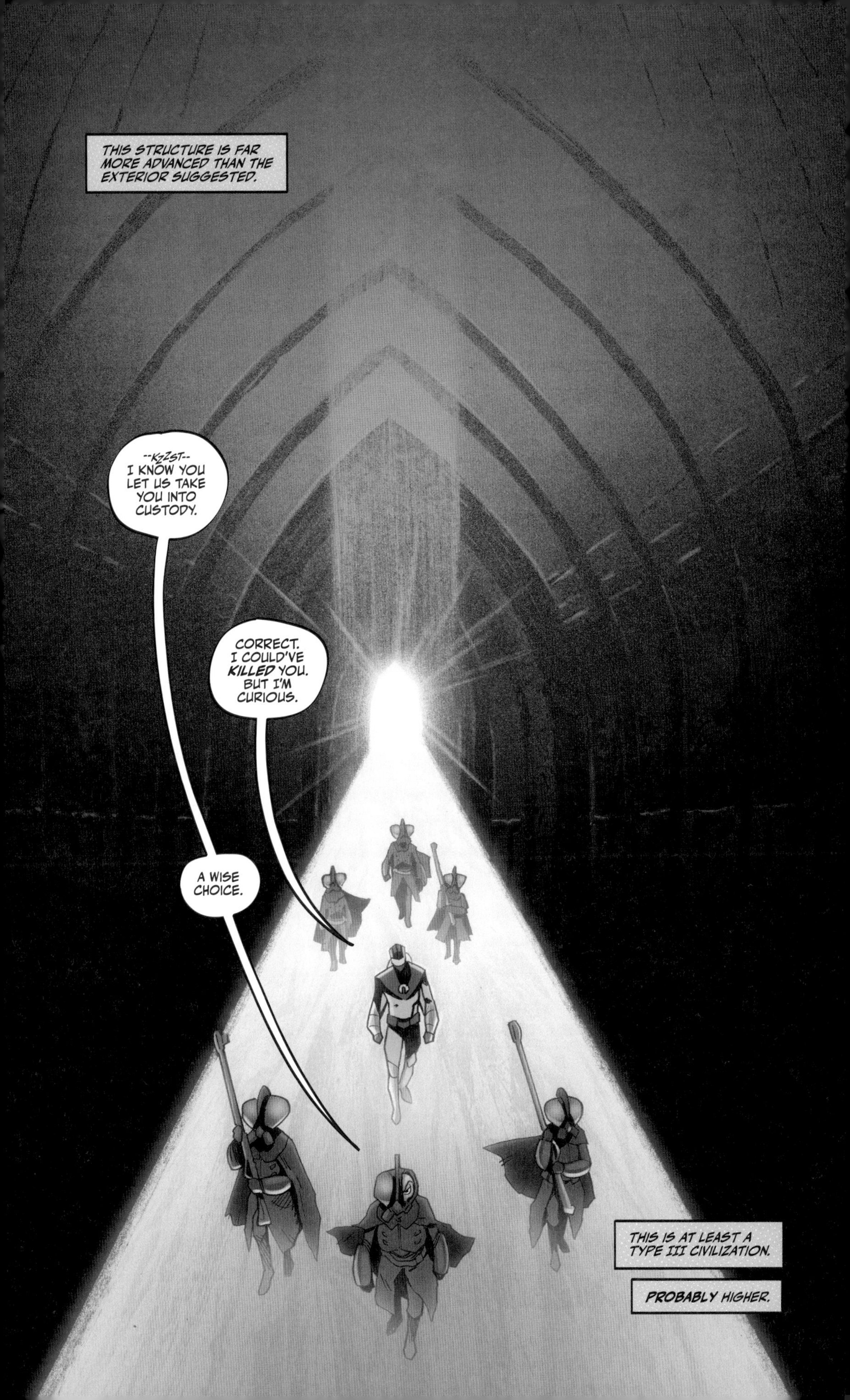
THIS STRUCTURE IS FAR MORE ADVANCED THAN THE EXTERIOR SUGGESTED.
--KZZST-- I KNOW YOU LET US TAKE YOU INTO CUSTODY.
CORRECT. I COULD'VE KILLED YOU. BUT I'M CURIOUS.
A WISE CHOICE.
THIS IS AT LEAST A TYPE III CIVILIZATION.
PROBABLY HIGHER.

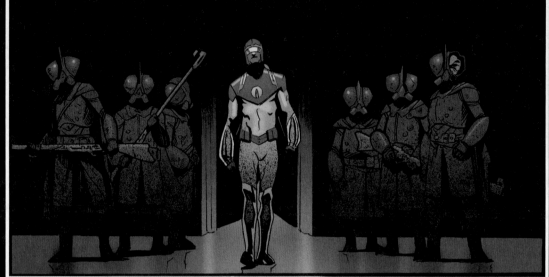

TCHUNK

HELLO?

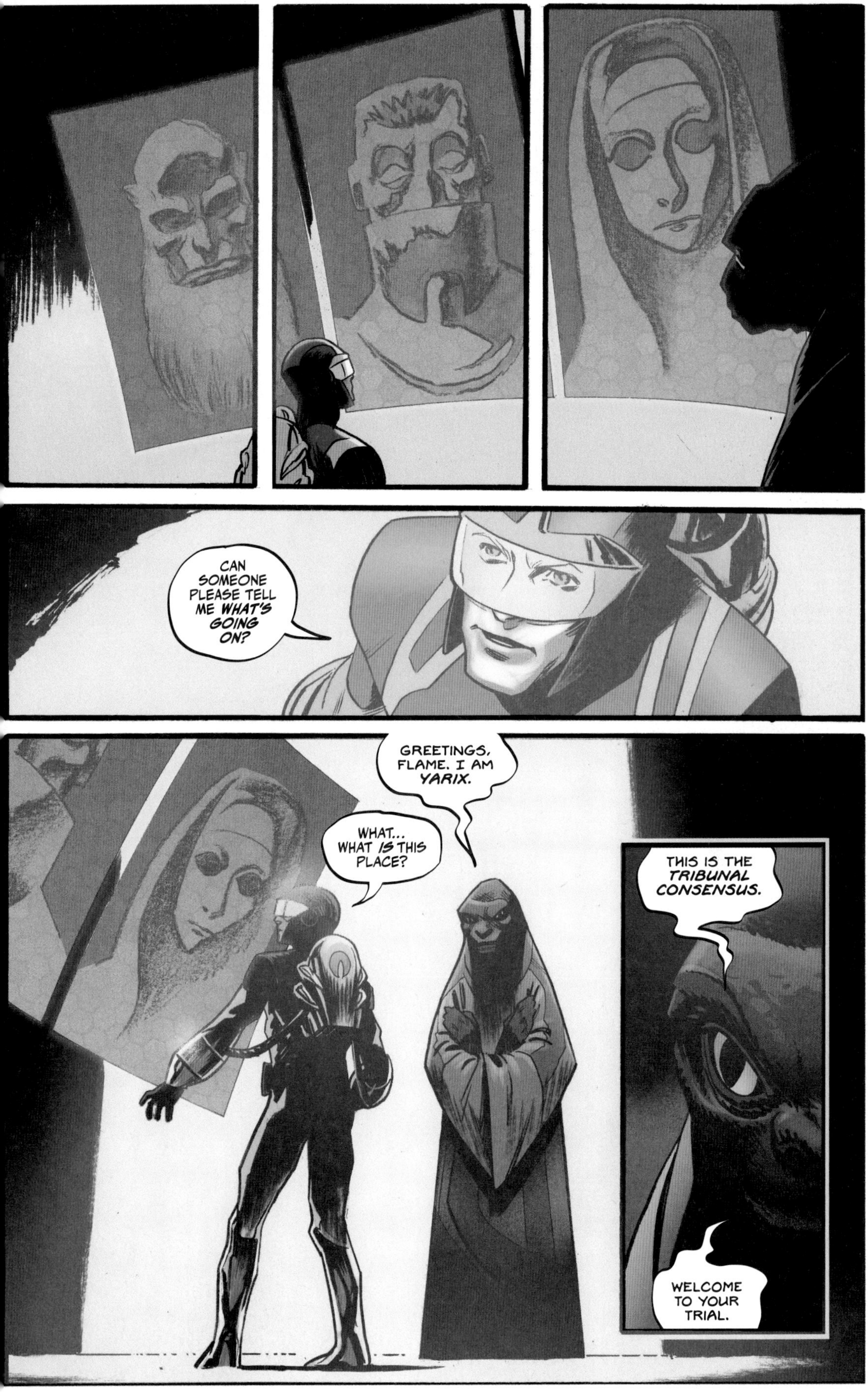
CAN SOMEONE PLEASE TELL ME WHAT'S GOING ON?
GREETINGS, FLAME. I AM YARIX.
WHAT... WHAT IS THIS PLACE?
THIS IS THE TRIBUNAL CONSENSUS.
WELCOME TO YOUR TRIAL.

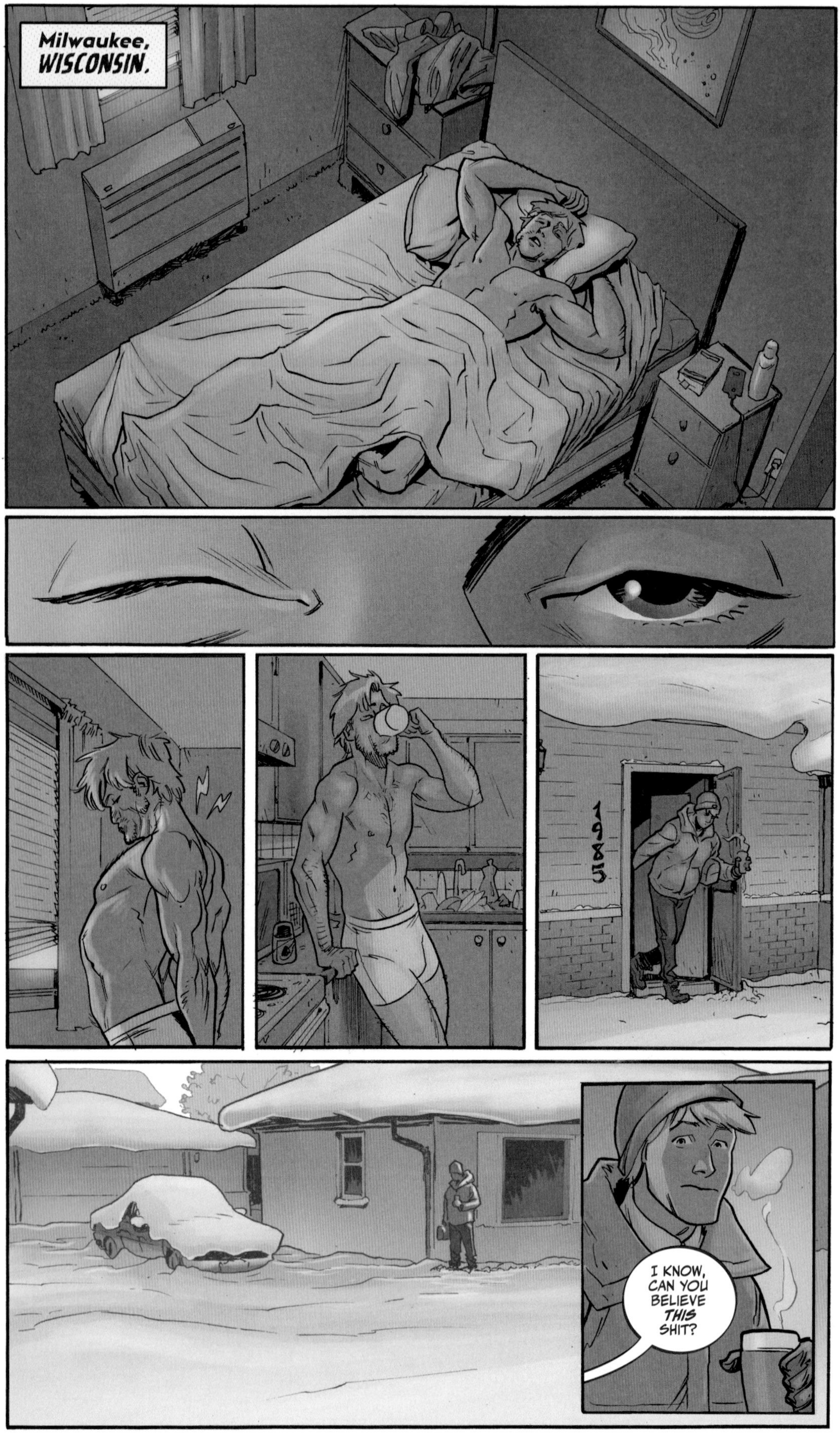
Milwaukee, WISCONSIN.
I KNOW, CAN YOU BELIEVE THIS SHIT?

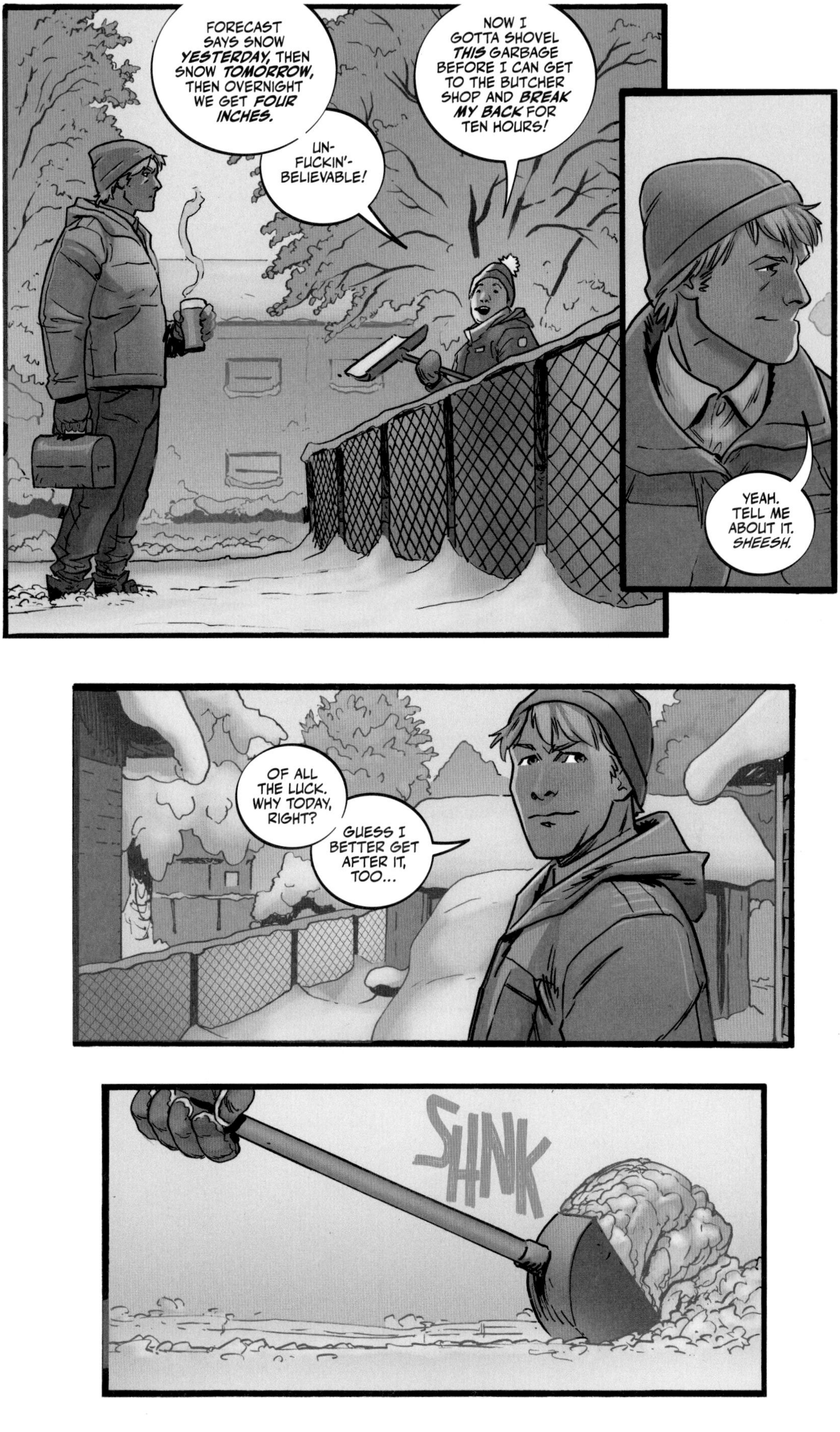
FORECAST SAYS SNOW YESTERDAY, THEN SNOW TOMORROW, THEN OVERNIGHT WE GET FOUR INCHES.
UN-FUCKIN'-BELIEVABLE!
NOW I GOTTA SHOVEL THIS GARBAGE BEFORE I CAN GET TO THE BUTCHER SHOP AND BREAK MY BACK FOR TEN HOURS!
YEAH. TELL ME ABOUT IT. SHEESH.
OF ALL THE LUCK. WHY TODAY, RIGHT?
GUESS I BETTER GET AFTER IT, TOO...
SHNK

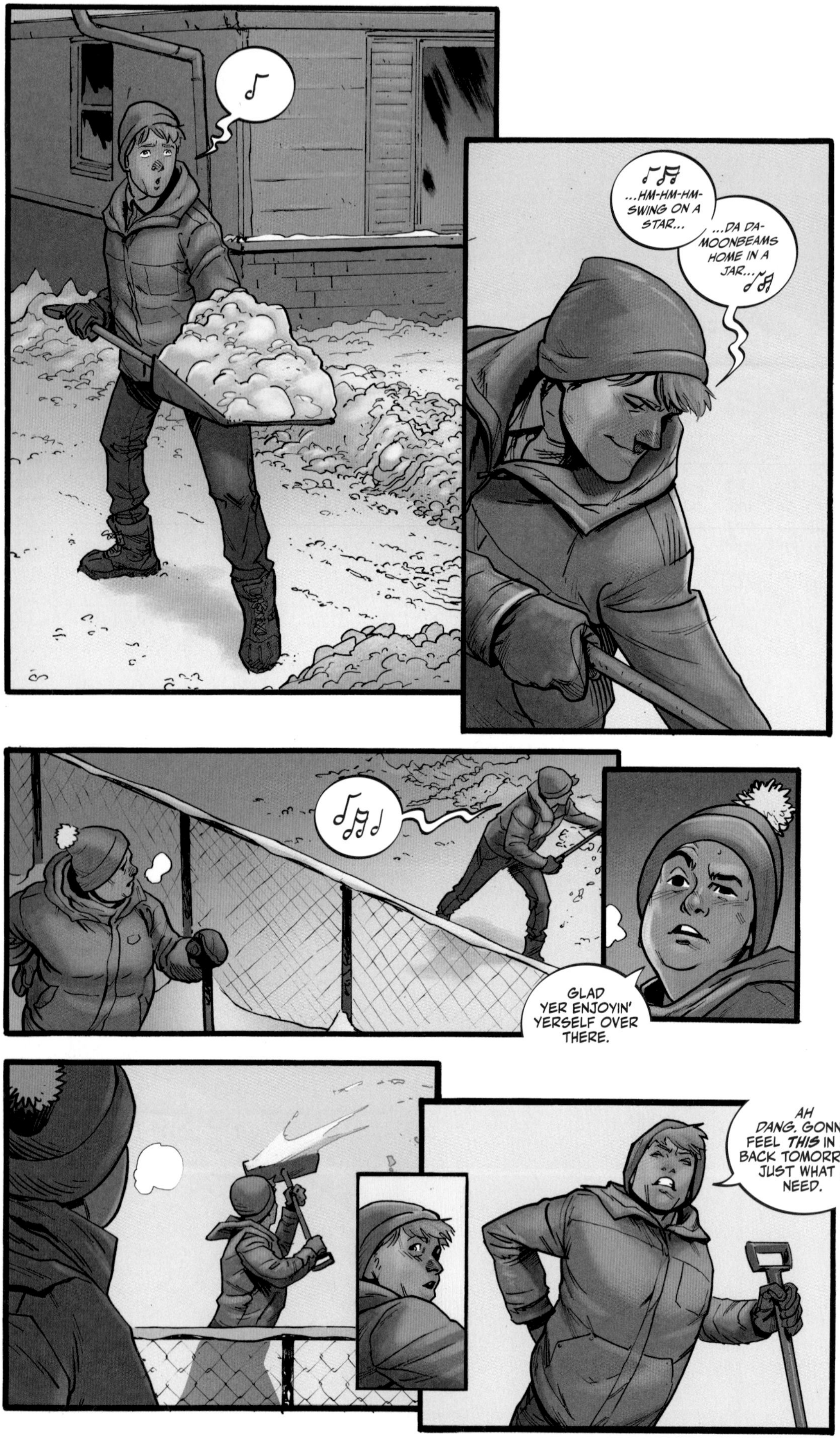
...HM-HM-HM-SWING ON A STAR...
...DA DA-MOONBEAMS HOME IN A JAR...
GLAD YER ENJOYIN' YERSELF OVER THERE.
AH DANG. GONNA FEEL *THIS* IN MY BACK TOMORROW. JUST WHAT I NEED.

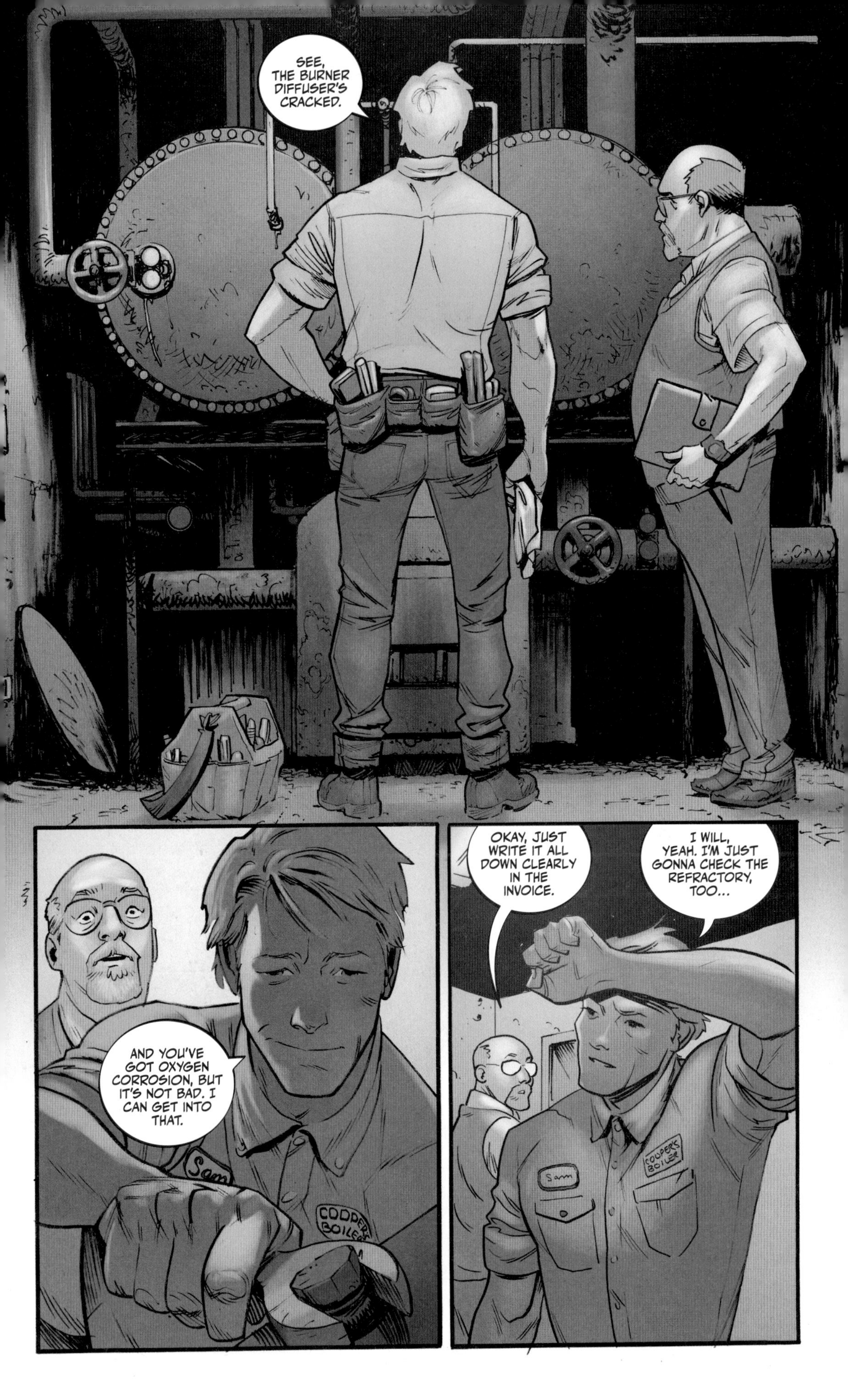
SEE, THE BURNER DIFFUSER'S CRACKED.
AND YOU'VE GOT OXYGEN CORROSION, BUT IT'S NOT BAD. I CAN GET INTO THAT.
Sam
COOPER'S BOILER
OKAY, JUST WRITE IT ALL DOWN CLEARLY IN THE INVOICE.
I WILL, YEAH. I'M JUST GONNA CHECK THE REFRACTORY, TOO...
Sam
COOPER'S BOILER

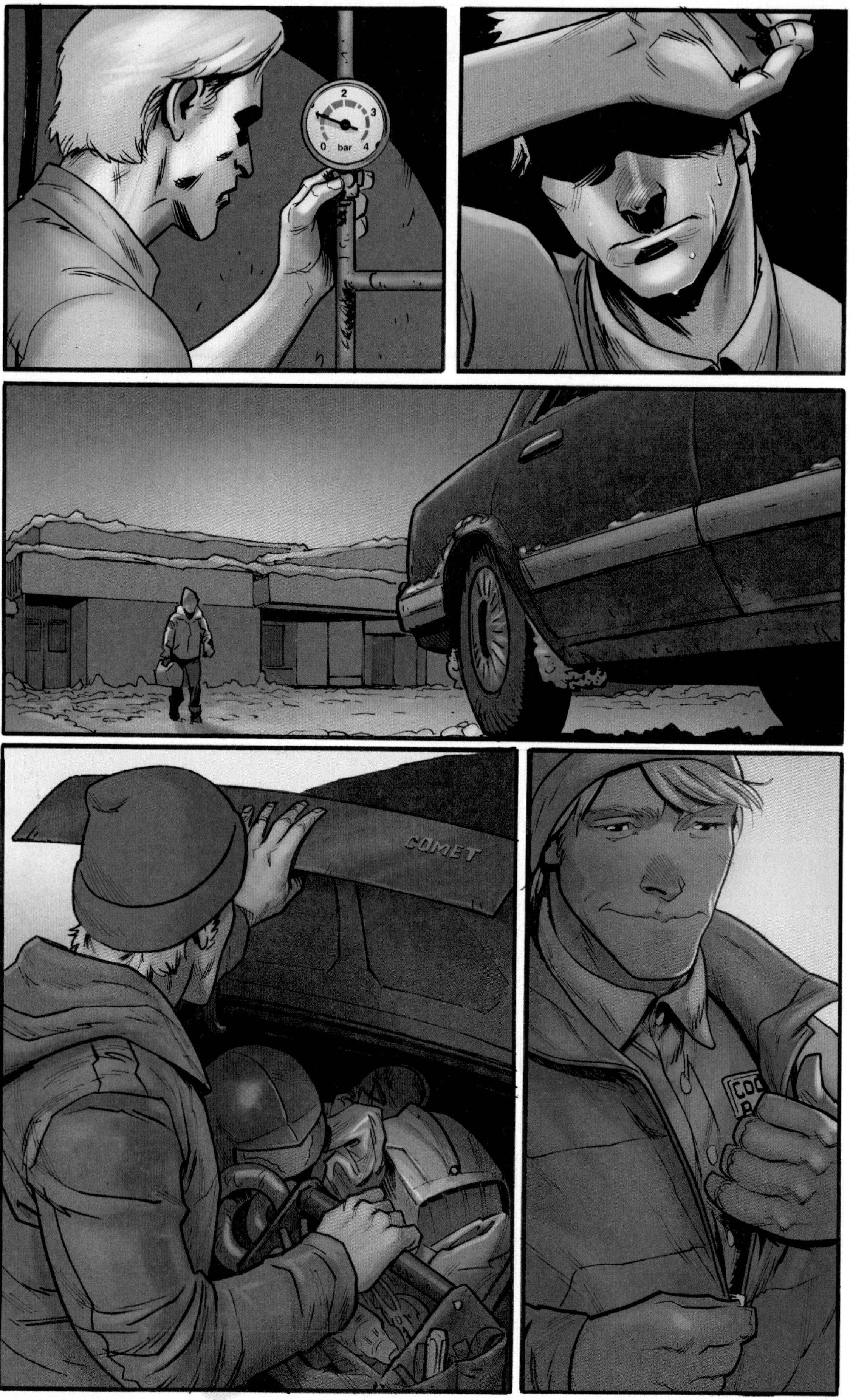
2
3
0 bar 4
COMET

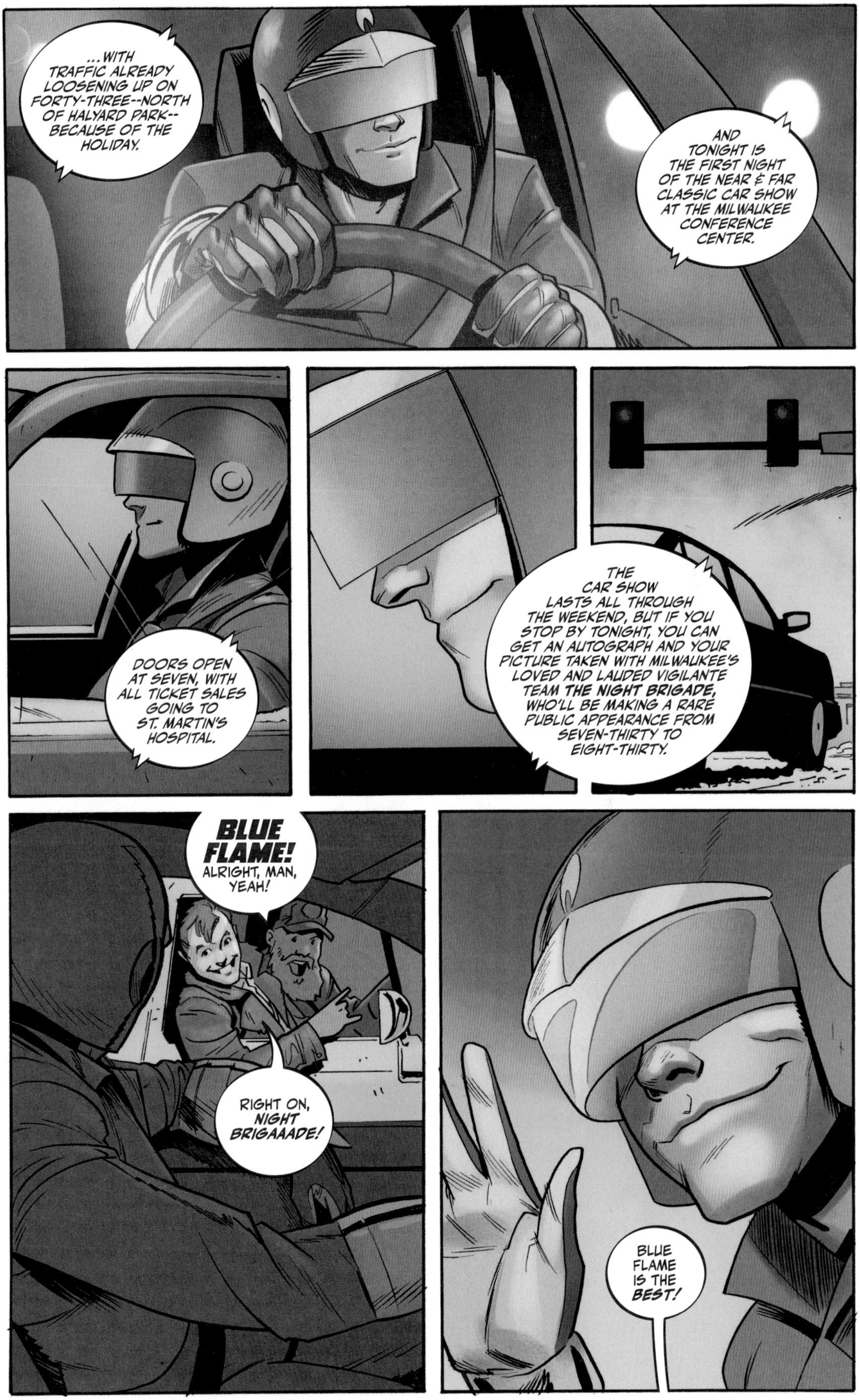
...WITH TRAFFIC ALREADY LOOSENING UP ON FORTY-THREE--NORTH OF HALYARD PARK--BECAUSE OF THE HOLIDAY.
AND TONIGHT IS THE FIRST NIGHT OF THE NEAR & FAR CLASSIC CAR SHOW AT THE MILWAUKEE CONFERENCE CENTER.
DOORS OPEN AT SEVEN, WITH ALL TICKET SALES GOING TO ST. MARTIN'S HOSPITAL.
THE CAR SHOW LASTS ALL THROUGH THE WEEKEND, BUT IF YOU STOP BY TONIGHT, YOU CAN GET AN AUTOGRAPH AND YOUR PICTURE TAKEN WITH MILWAUKEE'S LOVED AND LAUDED VIGILANTE TEAM THE NIGHT BRIGADE, WHO'LL BE MAKING A RARE PUBLIC APPEARANCE FROM SEVEN-THIRTY TO EIGHT-THIRTY.
BLUE FLAME! ALRIGHT, MAN, YEAH!
RIGHT ON, NIGHT BRIGAAADE!
BLUE FLAME IS THE BEST!

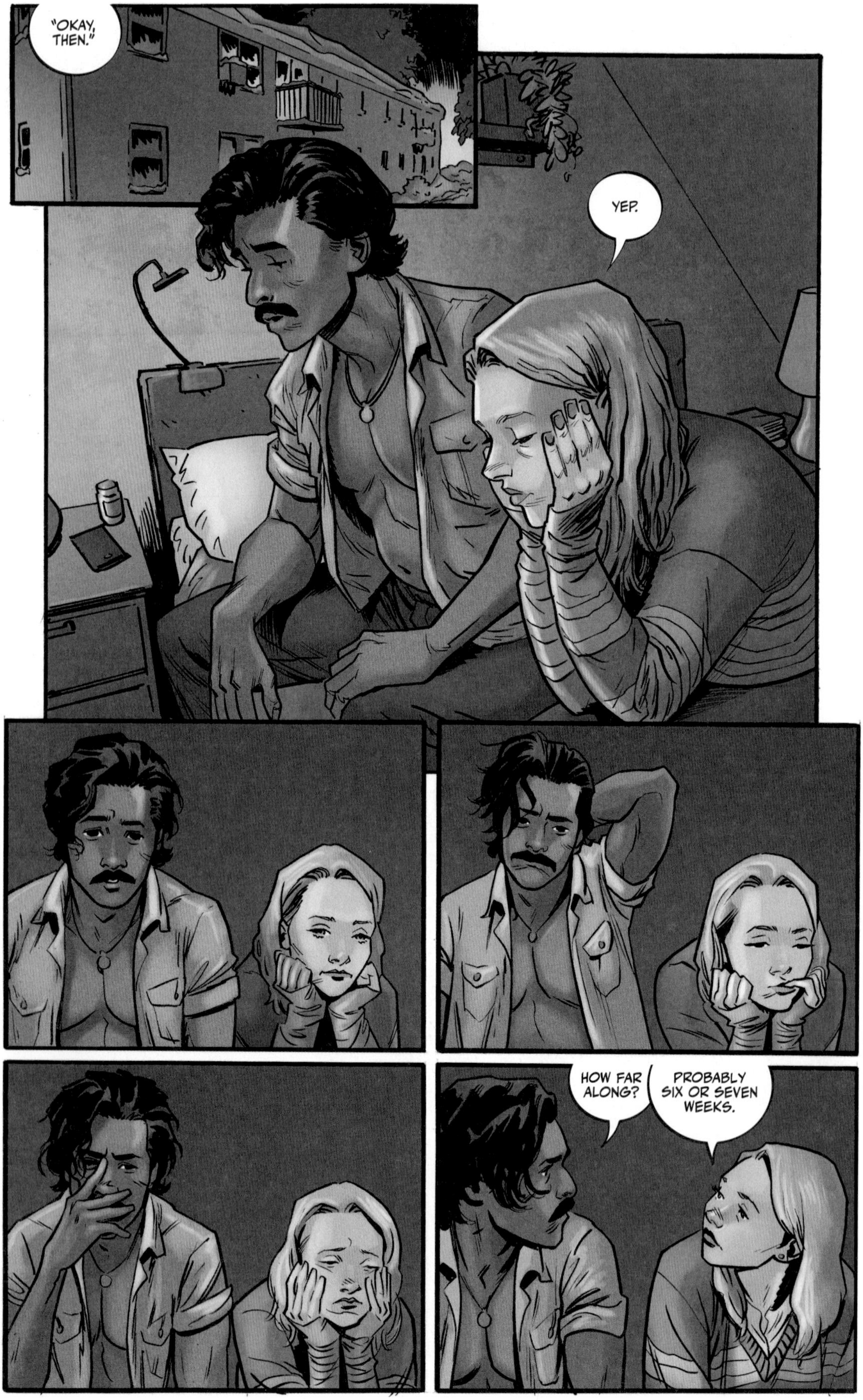
"OKAY, THEN."
YEP.
HOW FAR ALONG?
PROBABLY SIX OR SEVEN WEEKS.

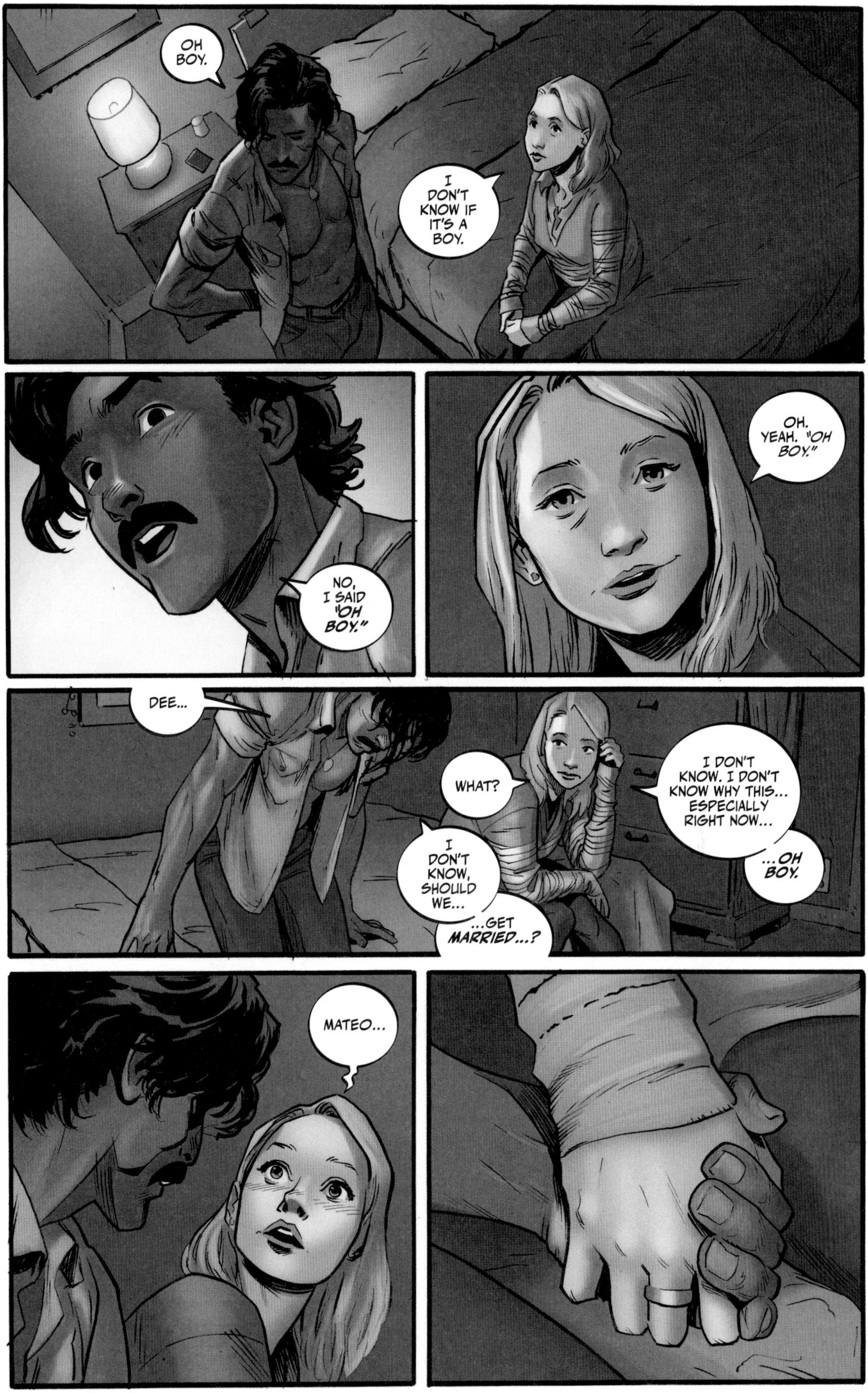
OH BOY.
I DON'T KNOW IF IT'S A BOY.
NO, I SAID "OH BOY."
OH. YEAH. "OH BOY."
DEE...
WHAT?
I DON'T KNOW, SHOULD WE...
...GET MARRIED...?
I DON'T KNOW. I DON'T KNOW WHY THIS... ESPECIALLY RIGHT NOW...
...OH BOY.
MATEO...

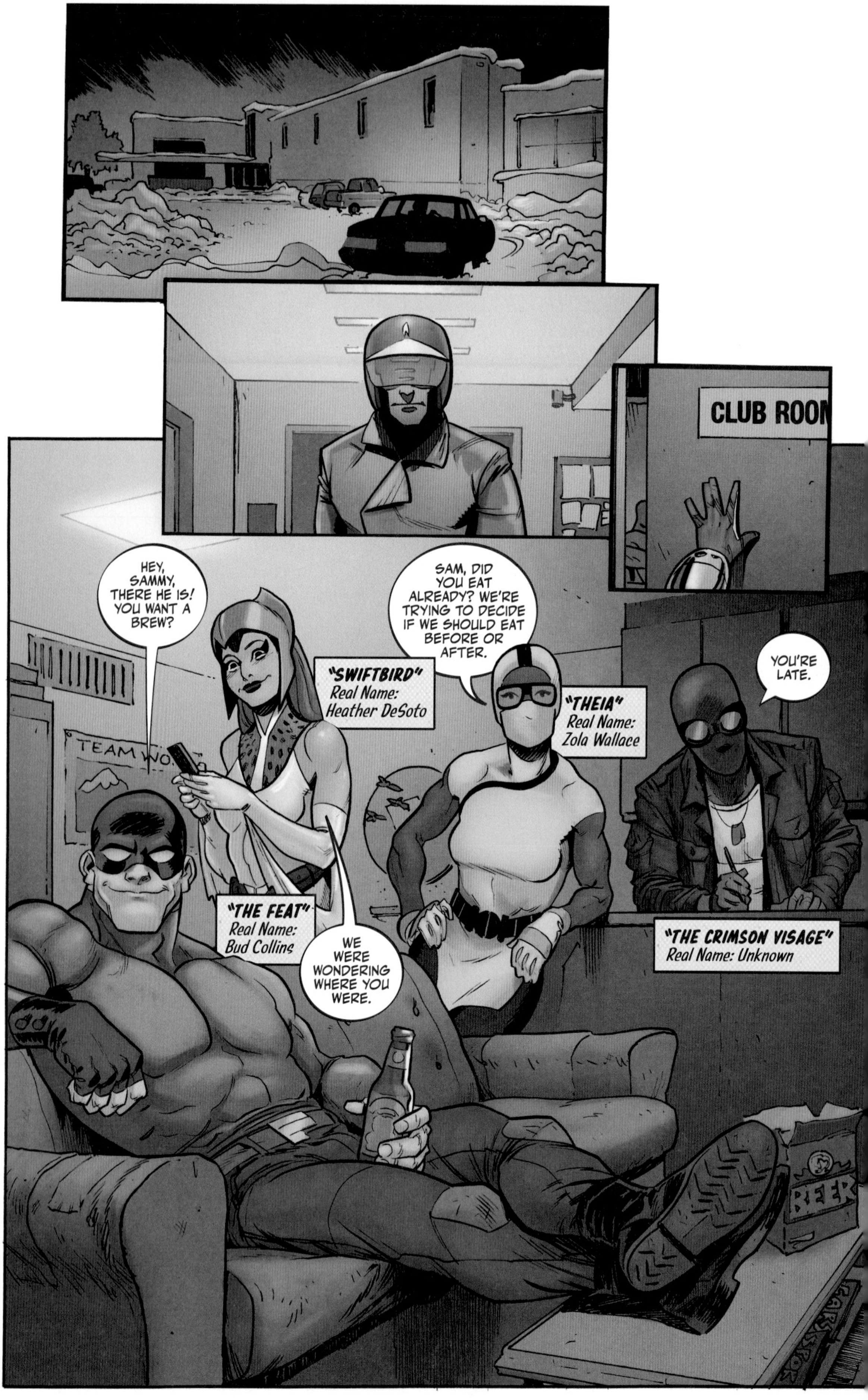
CLUB ROOM
HEY, SAMMY, THERE HE IS! YOU WANT A BREW?
"SWIFTBIRD" Real Name: Heather DeSoto
SAM, DID YOU EAT ALREADY? WE'RE TRYING TO DECIDE IF WE SHOULD EAT BEFORE OR AFTER.
"THEIA" Real Name: Zola Wallace
YOU'RE LATE.
"THE FEAT" Real Name: Bud Collins
WE WERE WONDERING WHERE YOU WERE.
"THE CRIMSON VISAGE" Real Name: Unknown
BEER

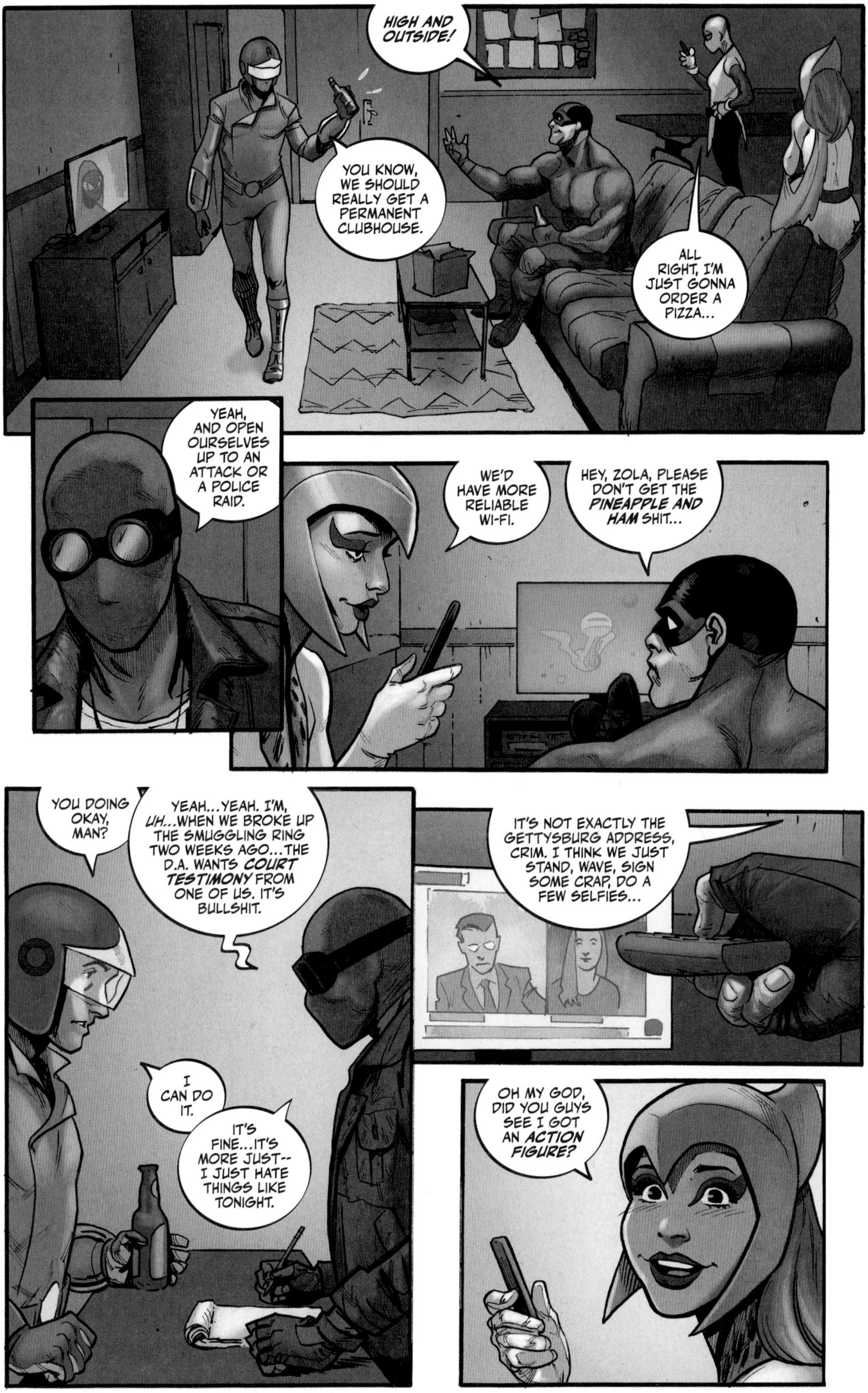

HIGH AND OUTSIDE!
YOU KNOW, WE SHOULD REALLY GET A PERMANENT CLUBHOUSE.
ALL RIGHT, I'M JUST GONNA ORDER A PIZZA...
YEAH, AND OPEN OURSELVES UP TO AN ATTACK OR A POLICE RAID.
WE'D HAVE MORE RELIABLE WI-FI.
HEY, ZOLA, PLEASE DON'T GET THE PINEAPPLE AND HAM SHIT...
YOU DOING OKAY, MAN?
YEAH...YEAH. I'M, UH...WHEN WE BROKE UP THE SMUGGLING RING TWO WEEKS AGO...THE D.A. WANTS COURT TESTIMONY FROM ONE OF US. IT'S BULLSHIT.
I CAN DO IT.
IT'S FINE...IT'S MORE JUST-- I JUST HATE THINGS LIKE TONIGHT.
IT'S NOT EXACTLY THE GETTYSBURG ADDRESS, CRIM. I THINK WE JUST STAND, WAVE, SIGN SOME CRAP, DO A FEW SELFIES...
OH MY GOD, DID YOU GUYS SEE I GOT AN ACTION FIGURE?

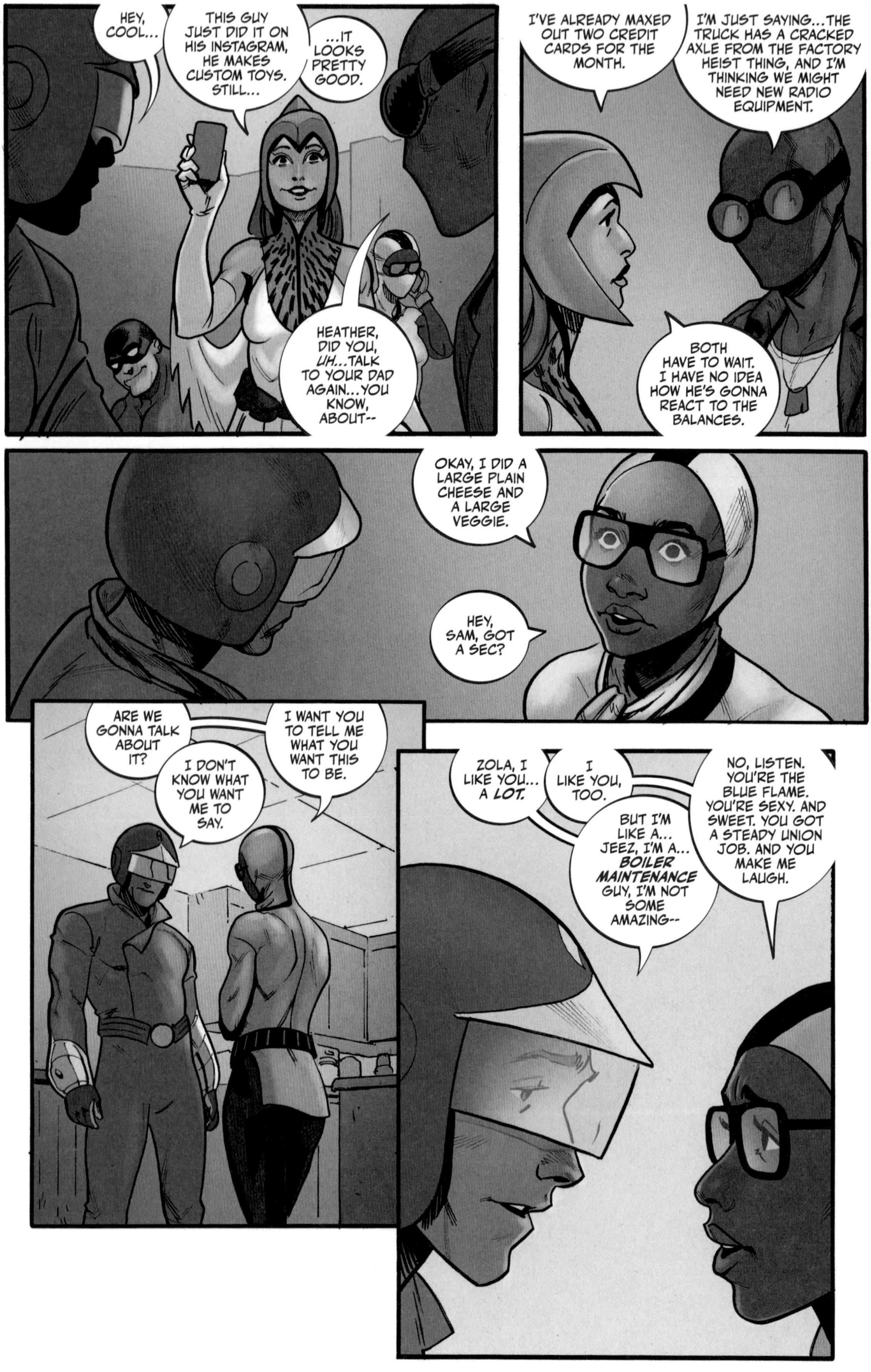
HEY, COOL...
THIS GUY JUST DID IT ON HIS INSTAGRAM, HE MAKES CUSTOM TOYS. STILL...
...IT LOOKS PRETTY GOOD.
HEATHER, DID YOU, *UH*...TALK TO YOUR DAD AGAIN...YOU KNOW, ABOUT--
I'VE ALREADY MAXED OUT TWO CREDIT CARDS FOR THE MONTH.
I'M JUST SAYING...THE TRUCK HAS A CRACKED AXLE FROM THE FACTORY HEIST THING, AND I'M THINKING WE MIGHT NEED NEW RADIO EQUIPMENT.
BOTH HAVE TO WAIT. I HAVE NO IDEA HOW HE'S GONNA REACT TO THE BALANCES.
OKAY, I DID A LARGE PLAIN CHEESE AND A LARGE VEGGIE.
HEY, SAM, GOT A SEC?
ARE WE GONNA TALK ABOUT IT?
I DON'T KNOW WHAT YOU WANT ME TO SAY.
I WANT YOU TO TELL ME WHAT YOU WANT THIS TO BE.
ZOLA, I LIKE YOU... A *LOT.*
I LIKE YOU, TOO.
BUT I'M LIKE A... JEEZ, I'M A... ***BOILER MAINTENANCE*** GUY, I'M NOT SOME AMAZING--
NO, LISTEN. YOU'RE THE BLUE FLAME. YOU'RE SEXY. AND SWEET. YOU GOT A STEADY UNION JOB. AND YOU MAKE ME LAUGH.

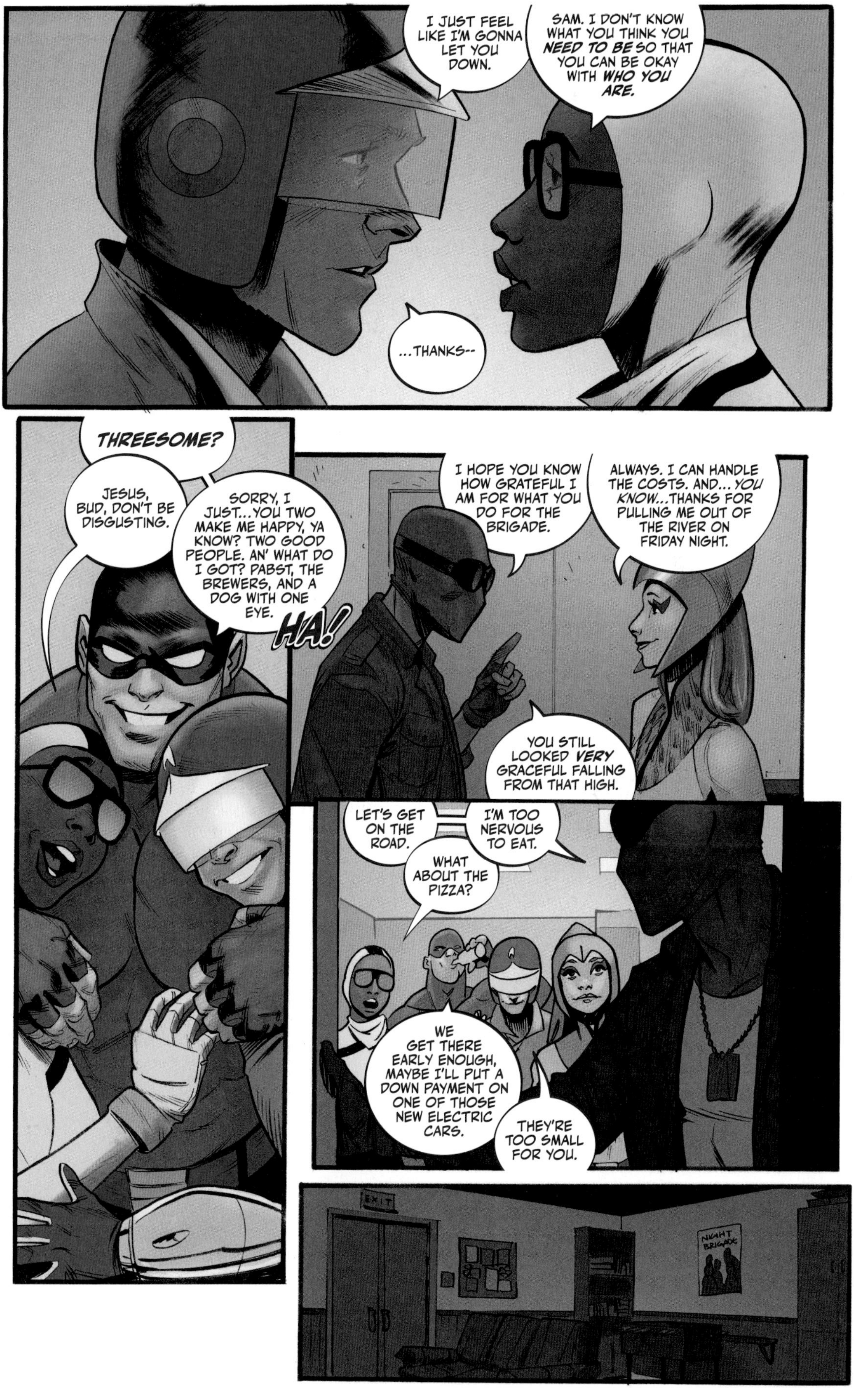
I JUST FEEL LIKE I'M GONNA LET YOU DOWN.
SAM. I DON'T KNOW WHAT YOU THINK YOU NEED TO BE SO THAT YOU CAN BE OKAY WITH WHO YOU ARE.
...THANKS--
THREESOME?
JESUS, BUD, DON'T BE DISGUSTING.
SORRY, I JUST...YOU TWO MAKE ME HAPPY, YA KNOW? TWO GOOD PEOPLE. AN' WHAT DO I GOT? PABST, THE BREWERS, AND A DOG WITH ONE EYE.
HA!
I HOPE YOU KNOW HOW GRATEFUL I AM FOR WHAT YOU DO FOR THE BRIGADE.
ALWAYS. I CAN HANDLE THE COSTS. AND... YOU KNOW...THANKS FOR PULLING ME OUT OF THE RIVER ON FRIDAY NIGHT.
YOU STILL LOOKED VERY GRACEFUL FALLING FROM THAT HIGH.
LET'S GET ON THE ROAD.
I'M TOO NERVOUS TO EAT.
WHAT ABOUT THE PIZZA?
WE GET THERE EARLY ENOUGH, MAYBE I'LL PUT A DOWN PAYMENT ON ONE OF THOSE NEW ELECTRIC CARS.
THEY'RE TOO SMALL FOR YOU.
EXIT
NIGHT BRIGADE

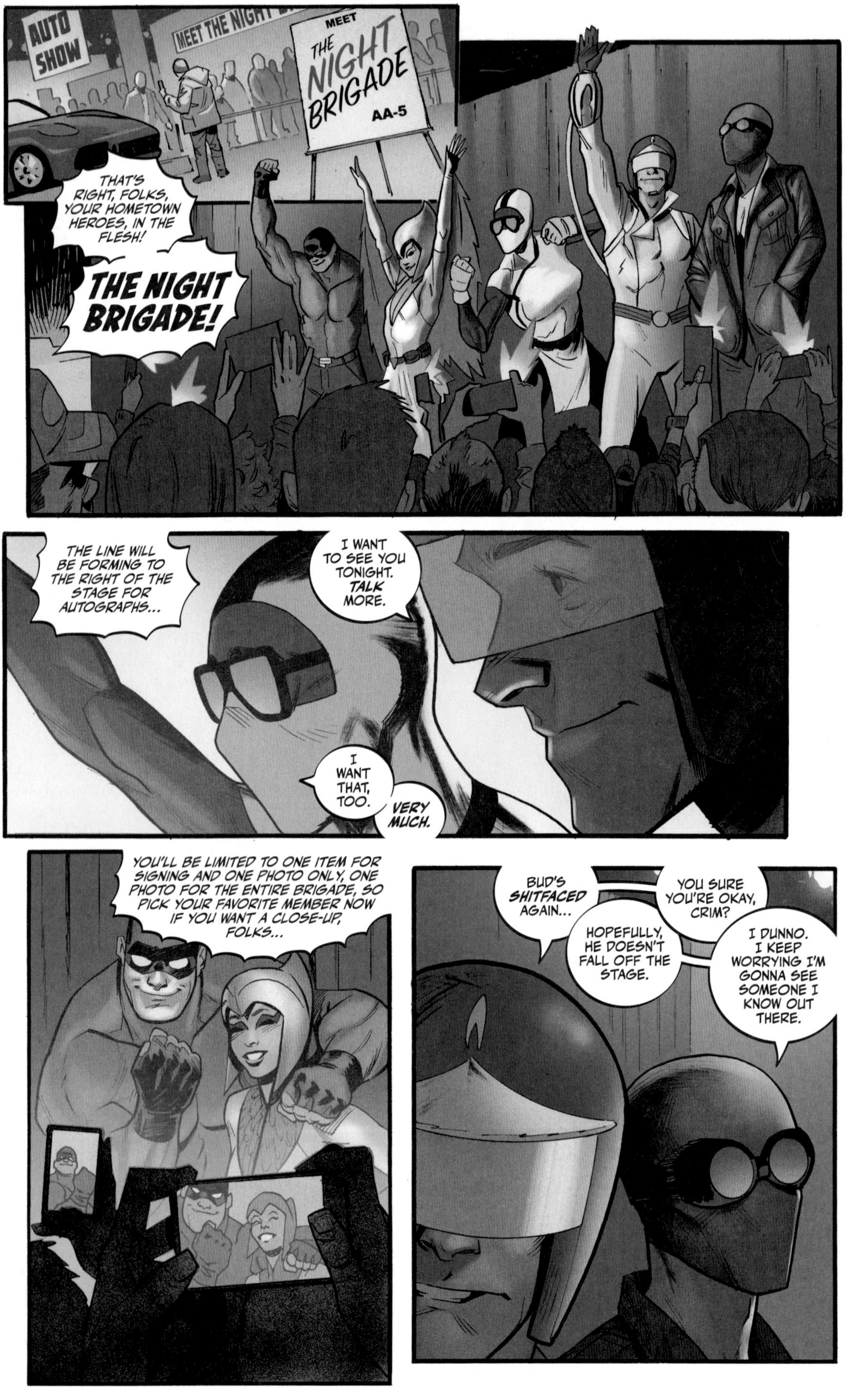

AUTO SHOW
MEET THE NIGHT
MEET THE NIGHT BRIGADE AA-5
THAT'S RIGHT, FOLKS, YOUR HOMETOWN HEROES, IN THE FLESH!
THE NIGHT BRIGADE!
THE LINE WILL BE FORMING TO THE RIGHT OF THE STAGE FOR AUTOGRAPHS...
I WANT TO SEE YOU TONIGHT. TALK MORE.
I WANT THAT, TOO.
VERY MUCH.
YOU'LL BE LIMITED TO ONE ITEM FOR SIGNING AND ONE PHOTO ONLY, ONE PHOTO FOR THE ENTIRE BRIGADE, SO PICK YOUR FAVORITE MEMBER NOW IF YOU WANT A CLOSE-UP, FOLKS...
BUD'S SHITFACED AGAIN...
YOU SURE YOU'RE OKAY, CRIM?
HOPEFULLY, HE DOESN'T FALL OFF THE STAGE.
I DUNNO. I KEEP WORRYING I'M GONNA SEE SOMEONE I KNOW OUT THERE.

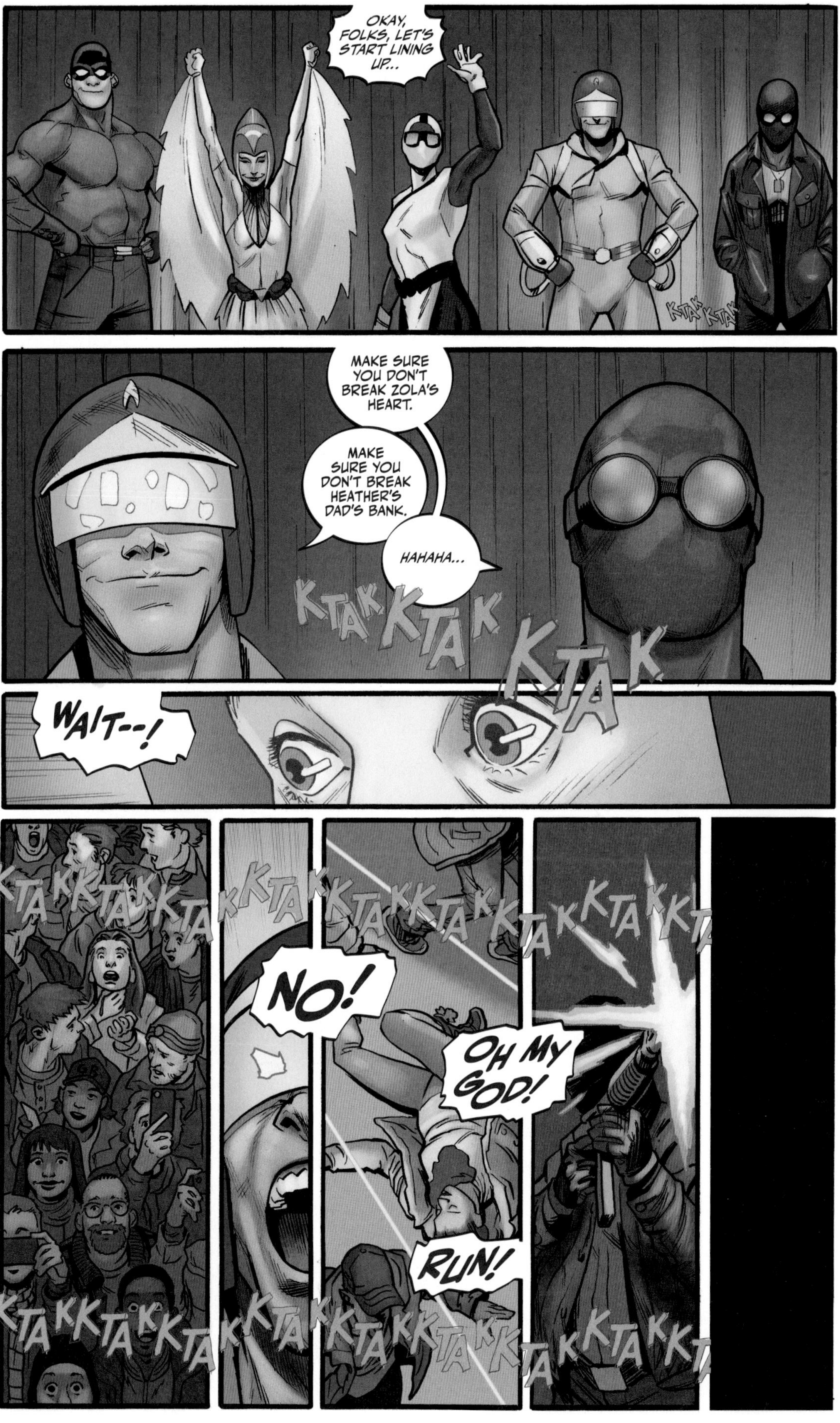
OKAY, FOLKS, LET'S START LINING UP...
KTAK KTAK
MAKE SURE YOU DON'T BREAK ZOLA'S HEART.
MAKE SURE YOU DON'T BREAK HEATHER'S DAD'S BANK.
HAHAHA...
KTAK KTAK KTAK
WAIT--!
NO!
OH MY GOD!
RUN!

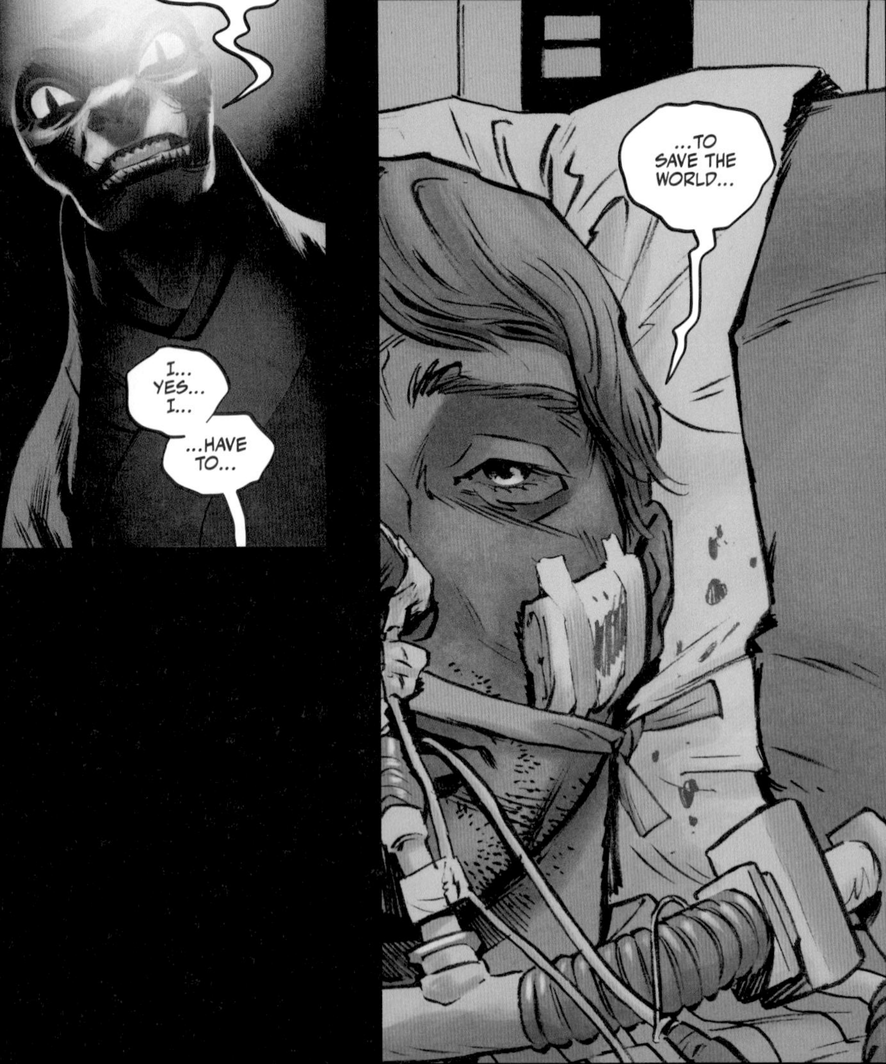
I... YES... I...
...HAVE TO...
...TO SAVE THE WORLD...

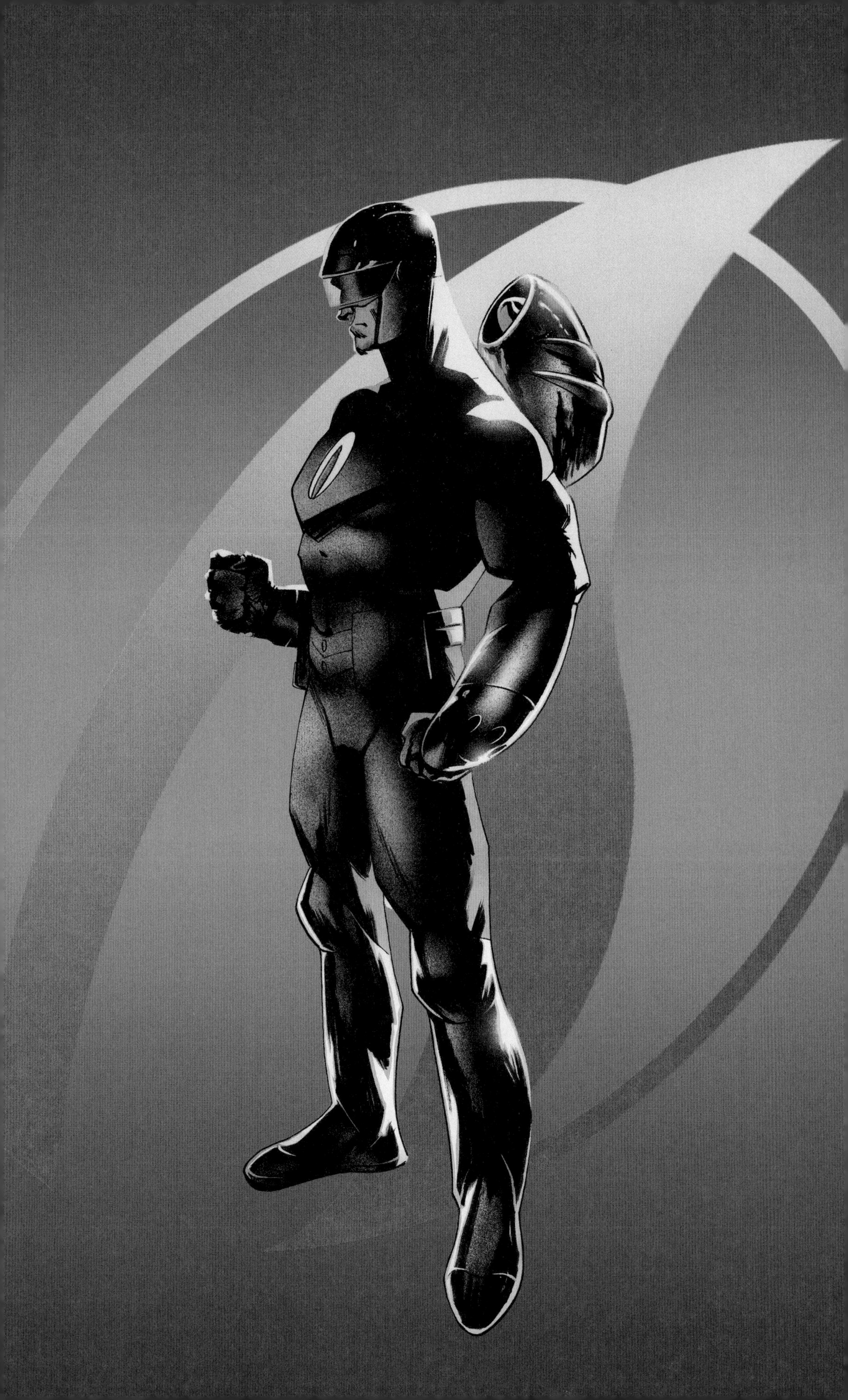

THE CELESTIAL BARGAIN

CHAPTER 2

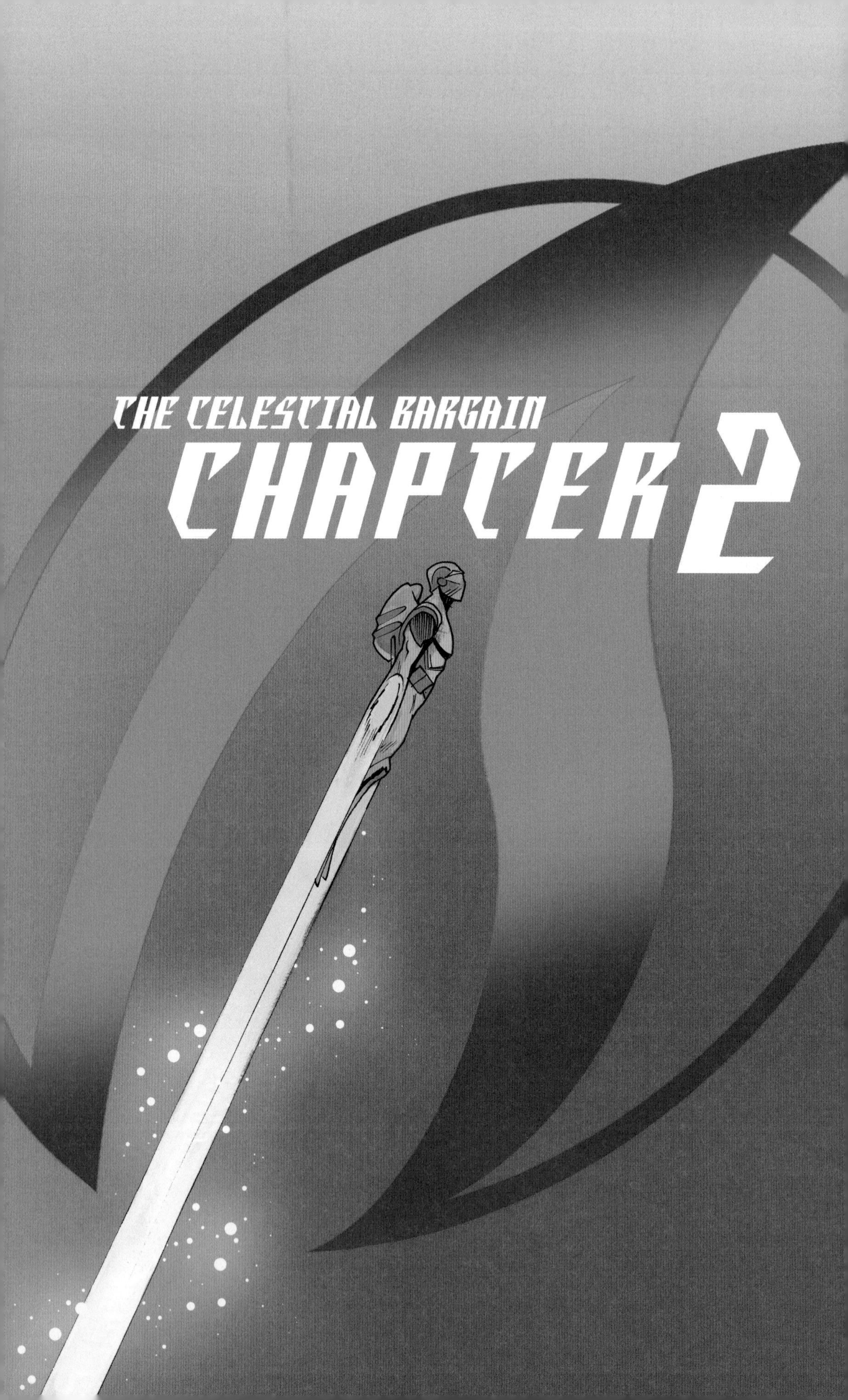

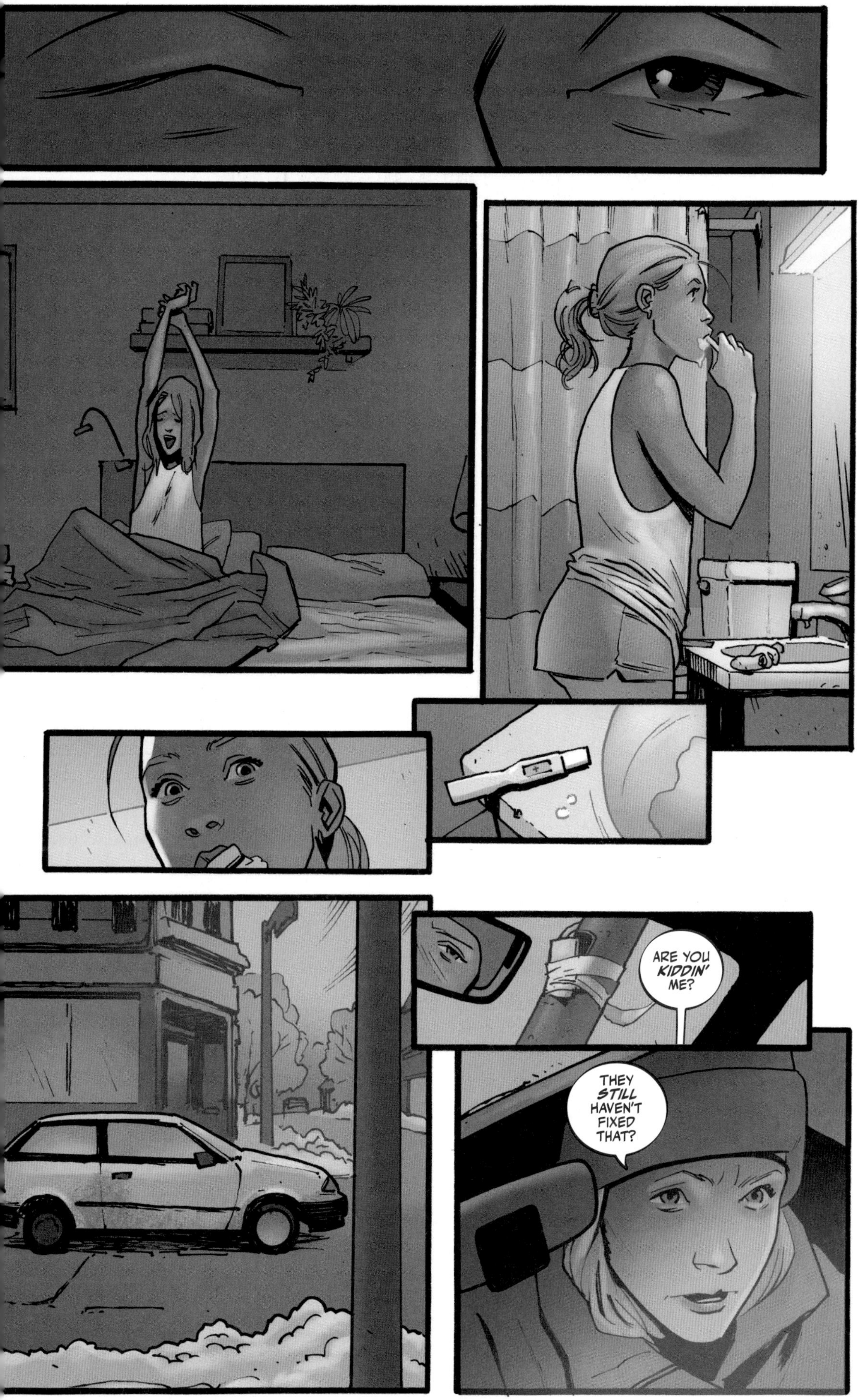
ARE YOU KIDDIN' ME?
THEY STILL HAVEN'T FIXED THAT?

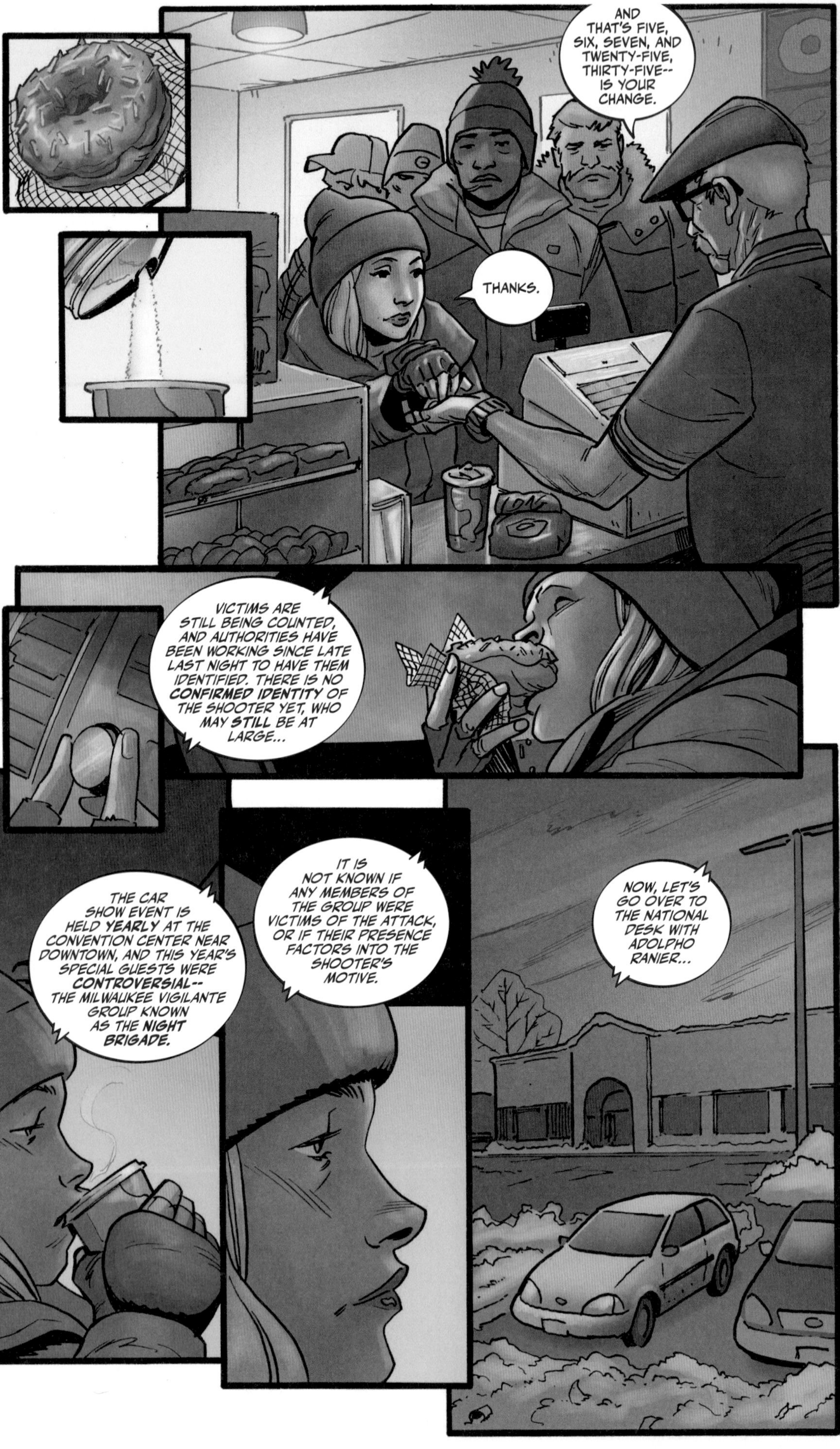
AND THAT'S FIVE, SIX, SEVEN, AND TWENTY-FIVE, THIRTY-FIVE-- IS YOUR CHANGE.
THANKS.
VICTIMS ARE STILL BEING COUNTED, AND AUTHORITIES HAVE BEEN WORKING SINCE LATE LAST NIGHT TO HAVE THEM IDENTIFIED. THERE IS NO CONFIRMED IDENTITY OF THE SHOOTER YET, WHO MAY STILL BE AT LARGE...
THE CAR SHOW EVENT IS HELD YEARLY AT THE CONVENTION CENTER NEAR DOWNTOWN, AND THIS YEAR'S SPECIAL GUESTS WERE CONTROVERSIAL-- THE MILWAUKEE VIGILANTE GROUP KNOWN AS THE NIGHT BRIGADE.
IT IS NOT KNOWN IF ANY MEMBERS OF THE GROUP WERE VICTIMS OF THE ATTACK, OR IF THEIR PRESENCE FACTORS INTO THE SHOOTER'S MOTIVE.
NOW, LET'S GO OVER TO THE NATIONAL DESK WITH ADOLPHO RANIER...

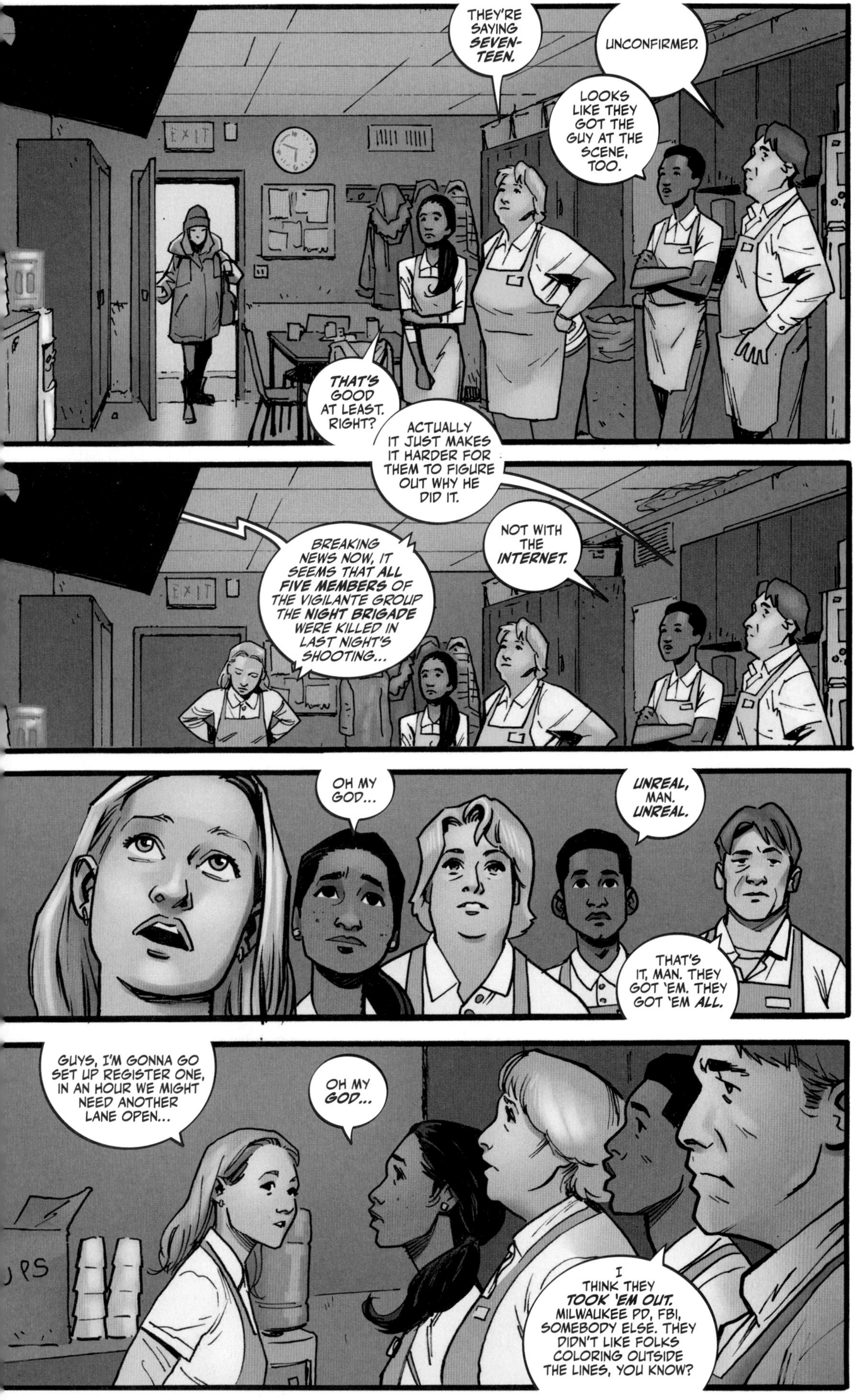
THEY'RE SAYING SEVENTEEN.
UNCONFIRMED.
LOOKS LIKE THEY GOT THE GUY AT THE SCENE, TOO.
THAT'S GOOD AT LEAST. RIGHT?
ACTUALLY IT JUST MAKES IT HARDER FOR THEM TO FIGURE OUT WHY HE DID IT.
NOT WITH THE INTERNET.
BREAKING NEWS NOW, IT SEEMS THAT ALL FIVE MEMBERS OF THE VIGILANTE GROUP THE NIGHT BRIGADE WERE KILLED IN LAST NIGHT'S SHOOTING...
OH MY GOD...
UNREAL, MAN. UNREAL.
THAT'S IT, MAN. THEY GOT 'EM. THEY GOT 'EM ALL.
GUYS, I'M GONNA GO SET UP REGISTER ONE, IN AN HOUR WE MIGHT NEED ANOTHER LANE OPEN...
OH MY GOD...
I THINK THEY TOOK 'EM OUT. MILWAUKEE PD, FBI, SOMEBODY ELSE. THEY DIDN'T LIKE FOLKS COLORING OUTSIDE THE LINES, YOU KNOW?

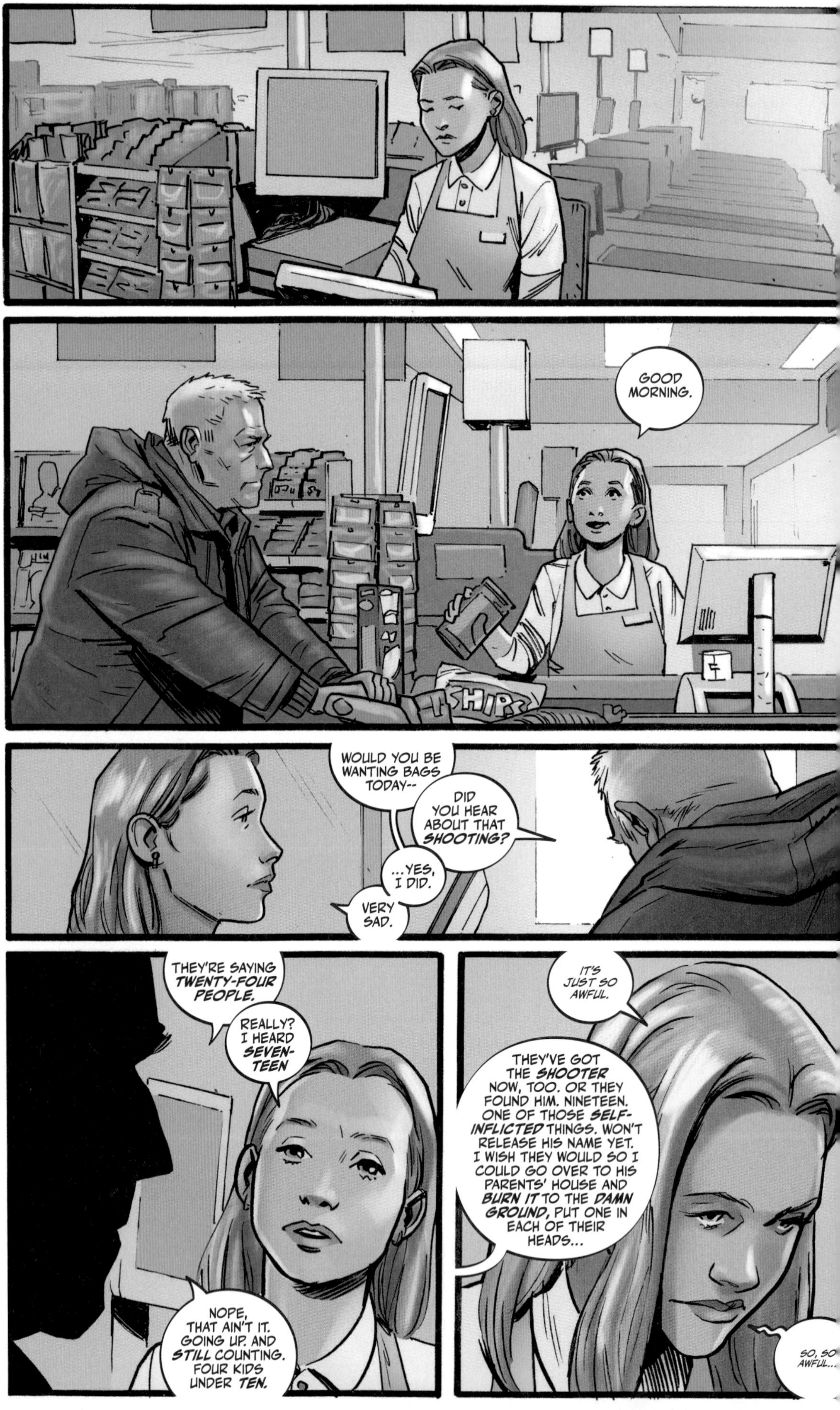
GOOD MORNING.
WOULD YOU BE WANTING BAGS TODAY--
DID YOU HEAR ABOUT THAT SHOOTING?
...YES, I DID.
VERY SAD.
THEY'RE SAYING TWENTY-FOUR PEOPLE.
REALLY? I HEARD SEVEN-TEEN
NOPE, THAT AIN'T IT. GOING UP. AND STILL COUNTING. FOUR KIDS UNDER TEN.
IT'S JUST SO AWFUL.
THEY'VE GOT THE SHOOTER NOW, TOO. OR THEY FOUND HIM. NINETEEN. ONE OF THOSE SELF-INFLICTED THINGS. WON'T RELEASE HIS NAME YET. I WISH THEY WOULD SO I COULD GO OVER TO HIS PARENTS' HOUSE AND BURN IT TO THE DAMN GROUND, PUT ONE IN EACH OF THEIR HEADS...
SO, SO AWFUL...

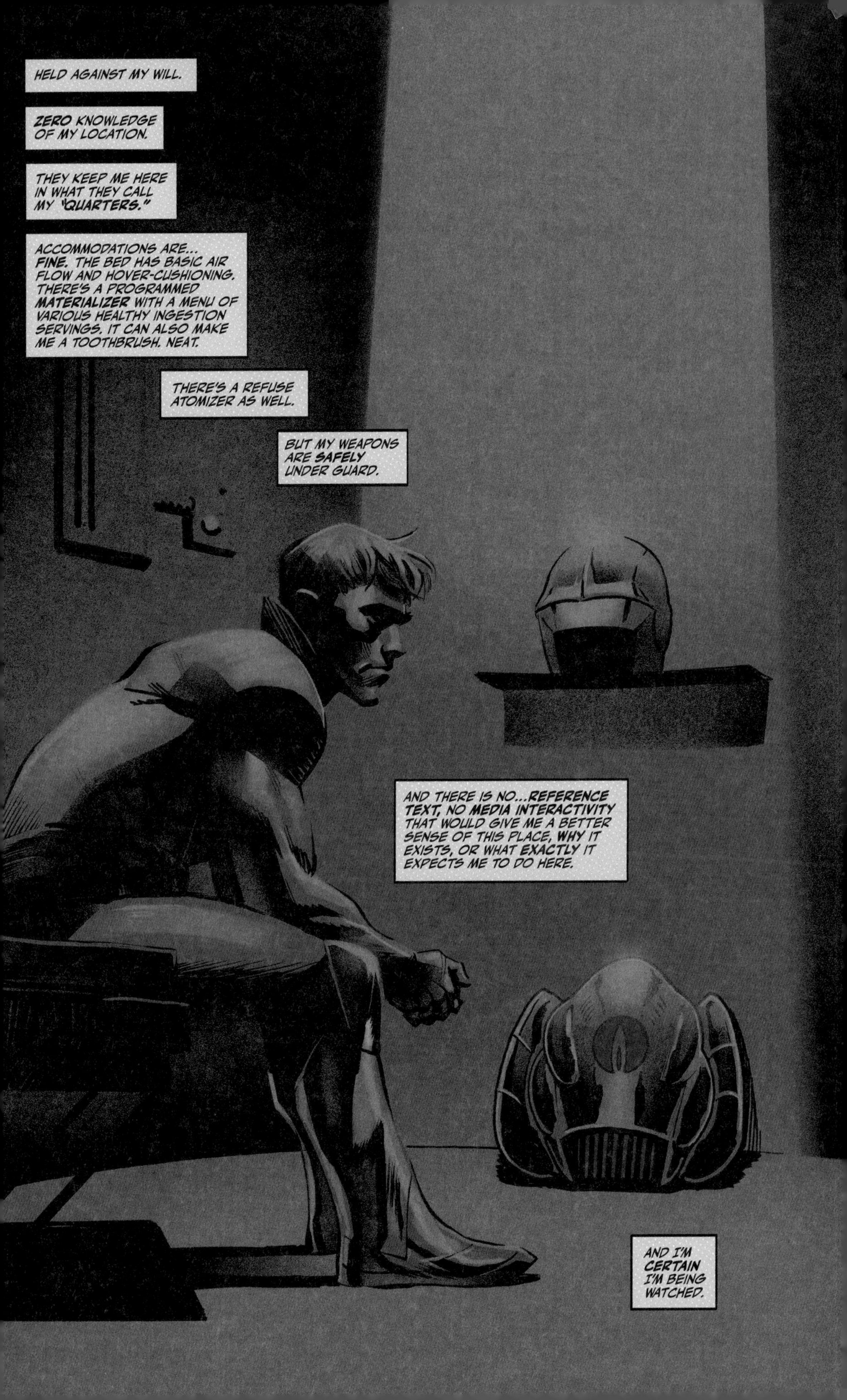
HELD AGAINST MY WILL.
ZERO KNOWLEDGE OF MY LOCATION.
THEY KEEP ME HERE IN WHAT THEY CALL MY "QUARTERS."
ACCOMMODATIONS ARE... FINE. THE BED HAS BASIC AIR FLOW AND HOVER-CUSHIONING. THERE'S A PROGRAMMED MATERIALIZER WITH A MENU OF VARIOUS HEALTHY INGESTION SERVINGS. IT CAN ALSO MAKE ME A TOOTHBRUSH. NEAT.
THERE'S A REFUSE ATOMIZER AS WELL.
BUT MY WEAPONS ARE SAFELY UNDER GUARD.
AND THERE IS NO...REFERENCE TEXT, NO MEDIA INTERACTIVITY THAT WOULD GIVE ME A BETTER SENSE OF THIS PLACE, WHY IT EXISTS, OR WHAT EXACTLY IT EXPECTS ME TO DO HERE.
AND I'M CERTAIN I'M BEING WATCHED.

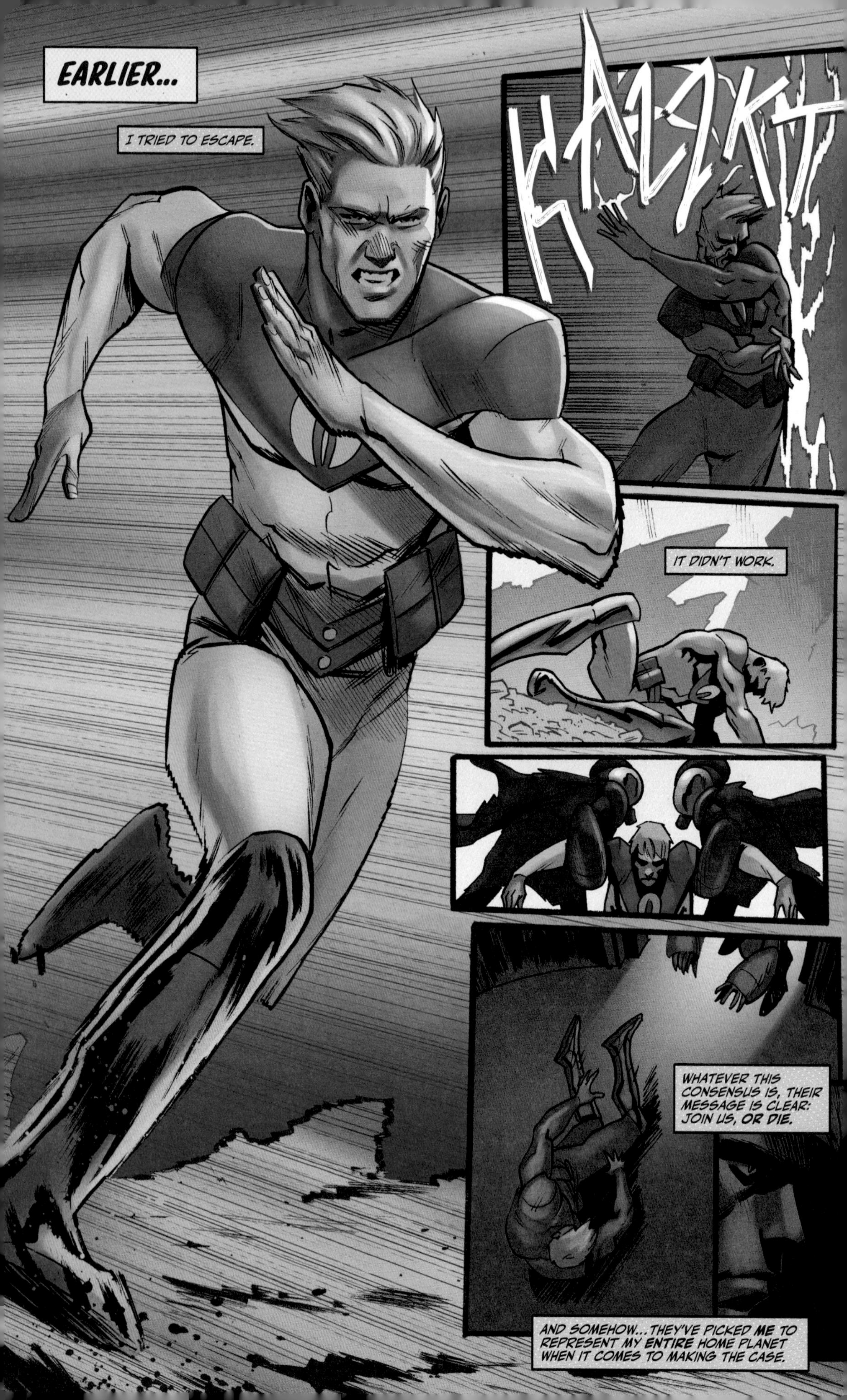
EARLIER...
I TRIED TO ESCAPE.
KAZZKT!
IT DIDN'T WORK.
WHATEVER THIS CONSENSUS IS, THEIR MESSAGE IS CLEAR: JOIN US, OR DIE.
AND SOMEHOW... THEY'VE PICKED ME TO REPRESENT MY ENTIRE HOME PLANET WHEN IT COMES TO MAKING THE CASE.

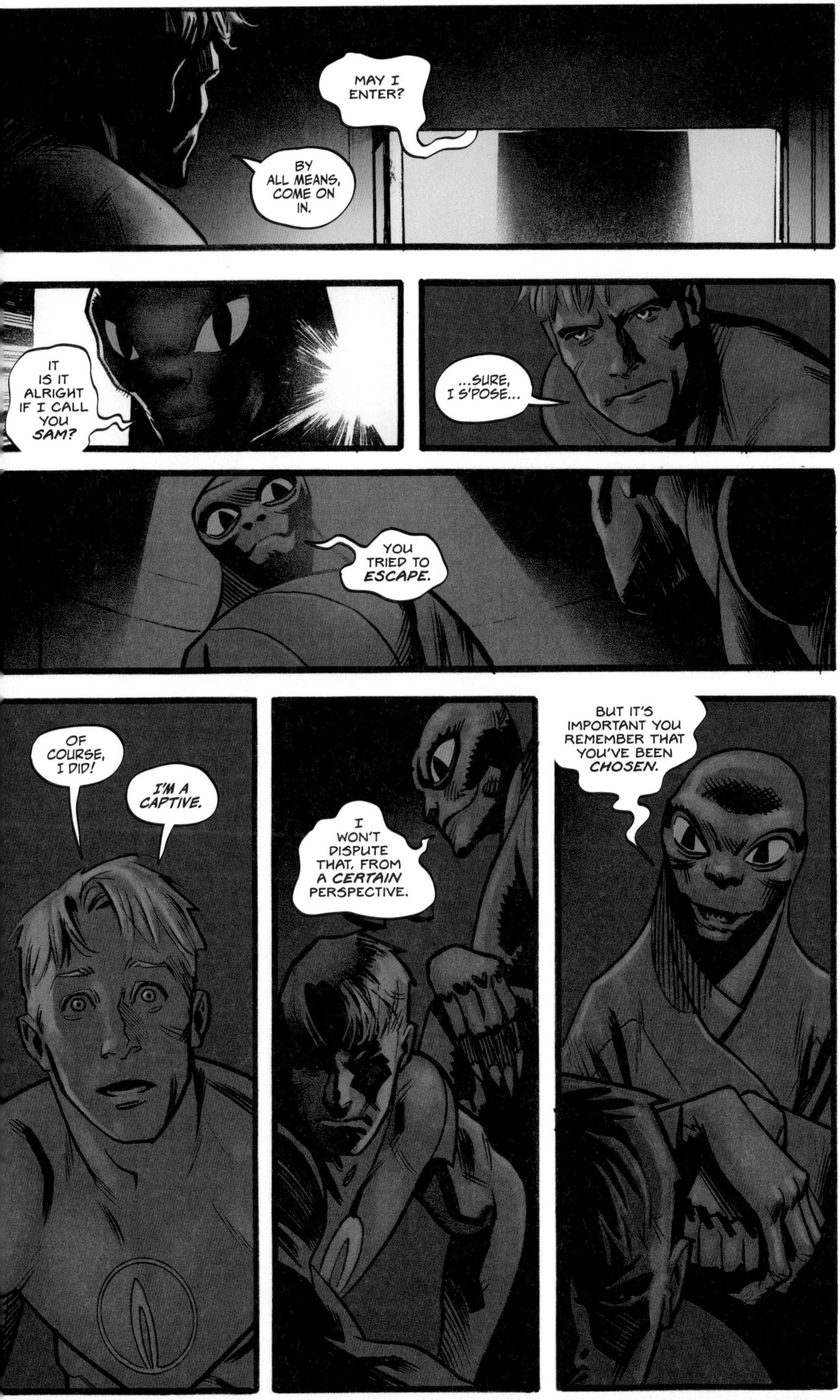
MAY I ENTER?
BY ALL MEANS, COME ON IN.
IT IS IT ALRIGHT IF I CALL YOU *SAM?*
...SURE, I S'POSE...
YOU TRIED TO *ESCAPE.*
OF COURSE, I DID!
I'M A CAPTIVE.
I WON'T DISPUTE THAT, FROM A *CERTAIN* PERSPECTIVE.
BUT IT'S IMPORTANT YOU REMEMBER THAT YOU'VE BEEN *CHOSEN.*

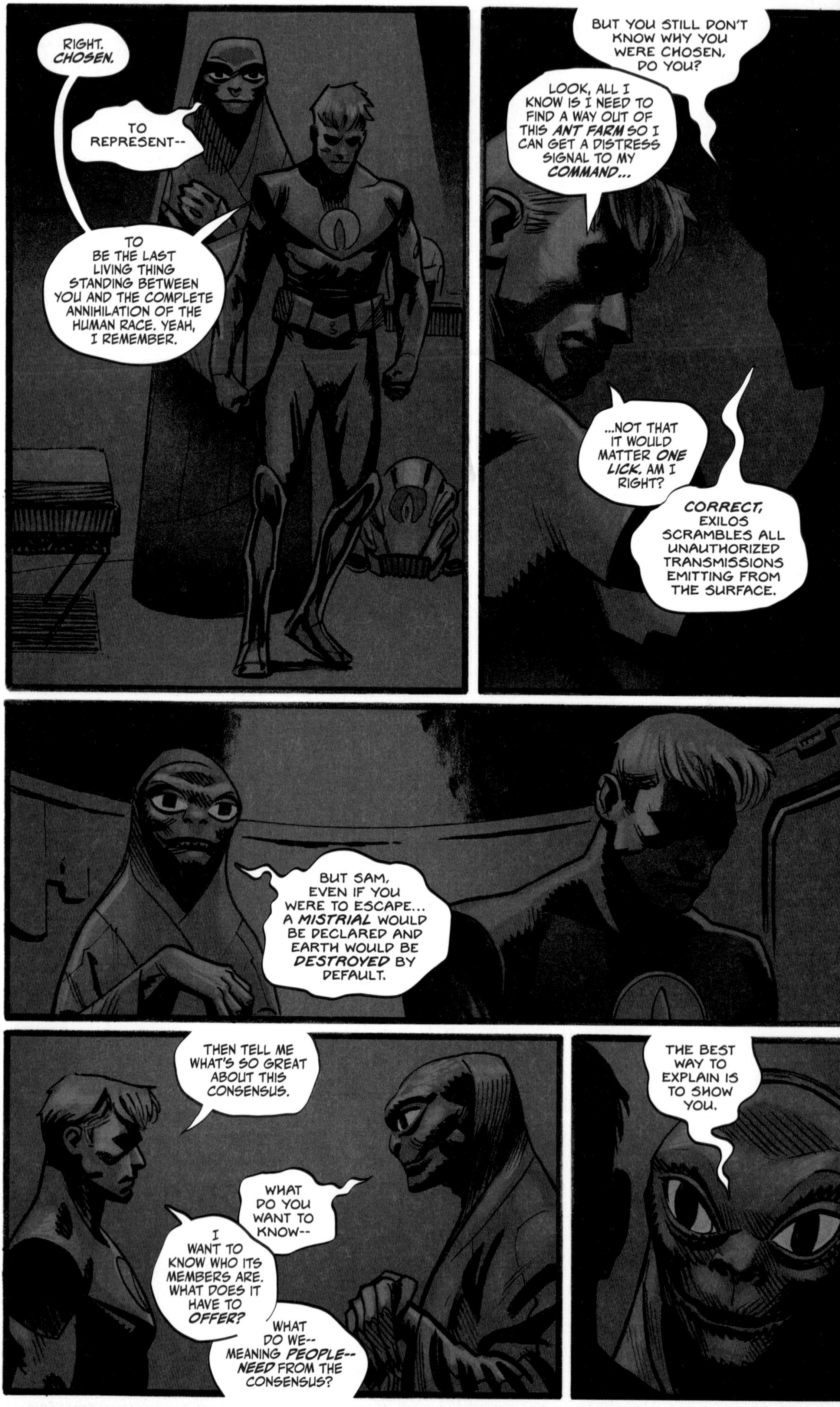
RIGHT. CHOSEN.
TO REPRESENT--
TO BE THE LAST LIVING THING STANDING BETWEEN YOU AND THE COMPLETE ANNIHILATION OF THE HUMAN RACE. YEAH, I REMEMBER.
BUT YOU STILL DON'T KNOW WHY YOU WERE CHOSEN, DO YOU?
LOOK, ALL I KNOW IS I NEED TO FIND A WAY OUT OF THIS ANT FARM SO I CAN GET A DISTRESS SIGNAL TO MY COMMAND...
...NOT THAT IT WOULD MATTER ONE LICK. AM I RIGHT?
CORRECT. EXILOS SCRAMBLES ALL UNAUTHORIZED TRANSMISSIONS EMITTING FROM THE SURFACE.
BUT SAM, EVEN IF YOU WERE TO ESCAPE... A MISTRIAL WOULD BE DECLARED AND EARTH WOULD BE DESTROYED BY DEFAULT.
THEN TELL ME WHAT'S SO GREAT ABOUT THIS CONSENSUS.
WHAT DO YOU WANT TO KNOW--
I WANT TO KNOW WHO ITS MEMBERS ARE. WHAT DOES IT HAVE TO OFFER?
WHAT DO WE-- MEANING PEOPLE-- NEED FROM THE CONSENSUS?
THE BEST WAY TO EXPLAIN IS TO SHOW YOU.

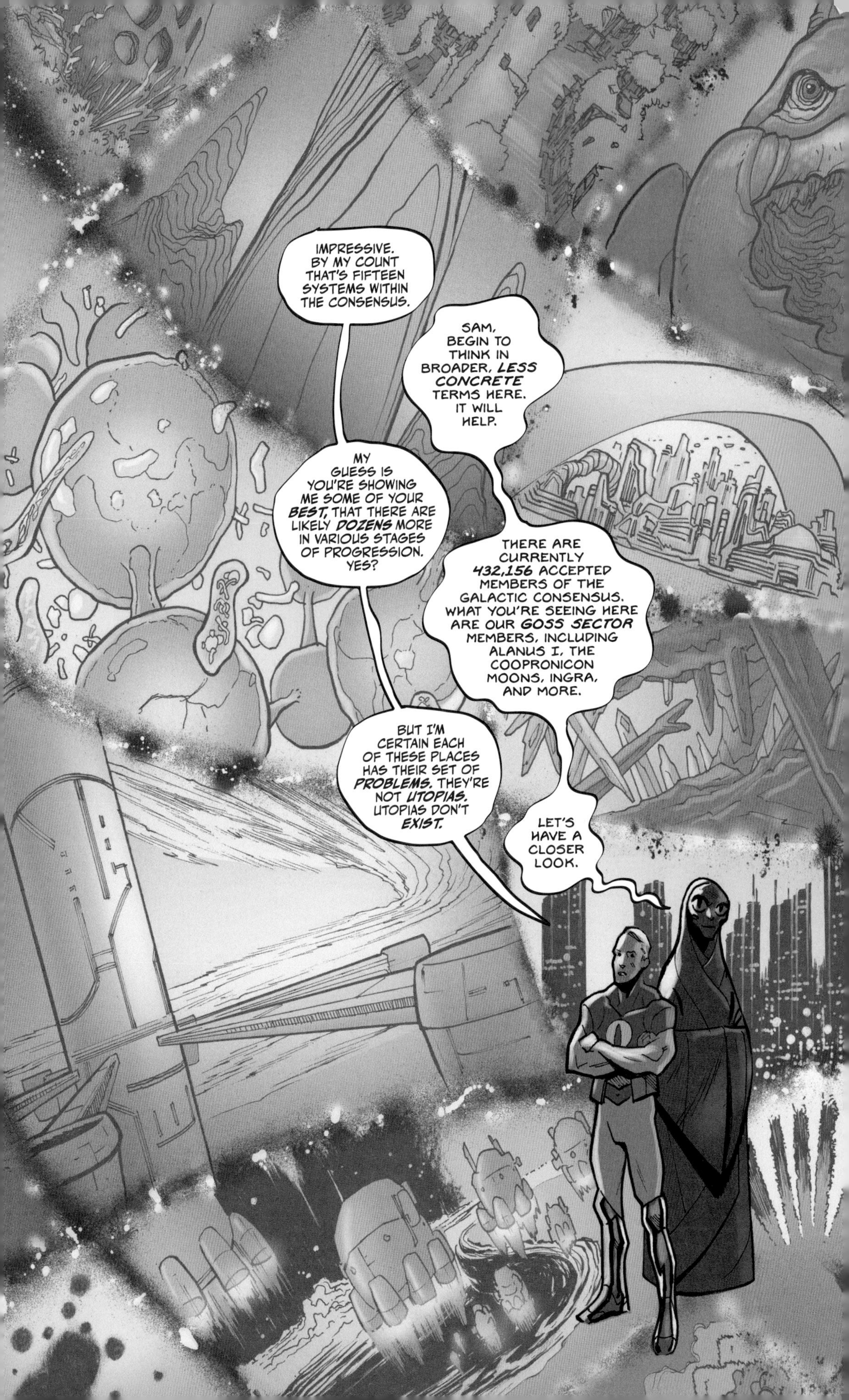
IMPRESSIVE. BY MY COUNT THAT'S FIFTEEN SYSTEMS WITHIN THE CONSENSUS.
SAM, BEGIN TO THINK IN BROADER, LESS CONCRETE TERMS HERE. IT WILL HELP.
MY GUESS IS YOU'RE SHOWING ME SOME OF YOUR BEST, THAT THERE ARE LIKELY DOZENS MORE IN VARIOUS STAGES OF PROGRESSION. YES?
THERE ARE CURRENTLY 432,156 ACCEPTED MEMBERS OF THE GALACTIC CONSENSUS. WHAT YOU'RE SEEING HERE ARE OUR GOSS SECTOR MEMBERS, INCLUDING ALANUS I, THE COOPRONICON MOONS, INGRA, AND MORE.
BUT I'M CERTAIN EACH OF THESE PLACES HAS THEIR SET OF PROBLEMS. THEY'RE NOT UTOPIAS. UTOPIAS DON'T EXIST.
LET'S HAVE A CLOSER LOOK.

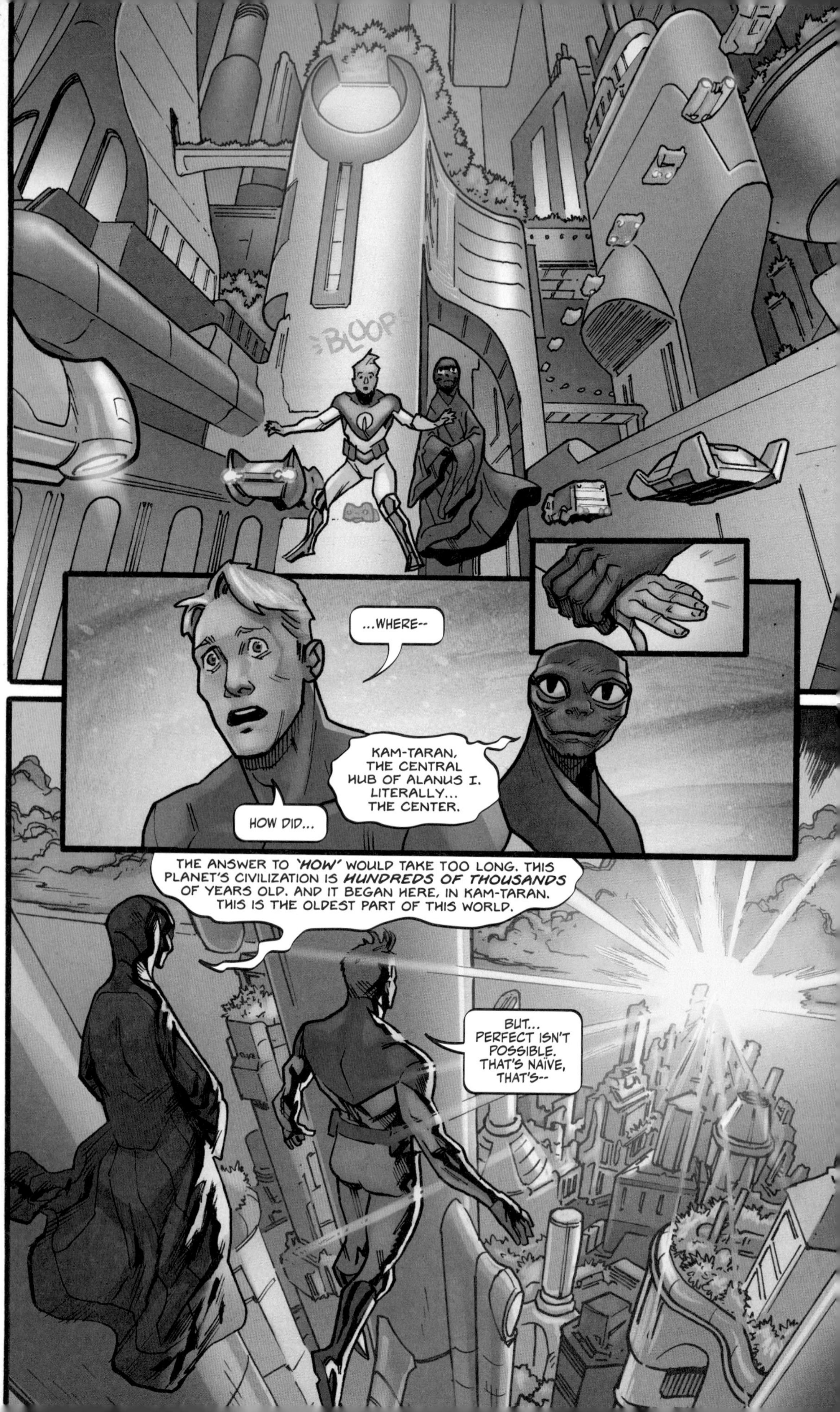
BLOOP
...WHERE--
HOW DID...
KAM-TARAN, THE CENTRAL HUB OF ALANUS I. LITERALLY... THE CENTER.
THE ANSWER TO 'HOW' WOULD TAKE TOO LONG. THIS PLANET'S CIVILIZATION IS HUNDREDS OF THOUSANDS OF YEARS OLD. AND IT BEGAN HERE, IN KAM-TARAN. THIS IS THE OLDEST PART OF THIS WORLD.
BUT... PERFECT ISN'T POSSIBLE. THAT'S NAÏVE, THAT'S--

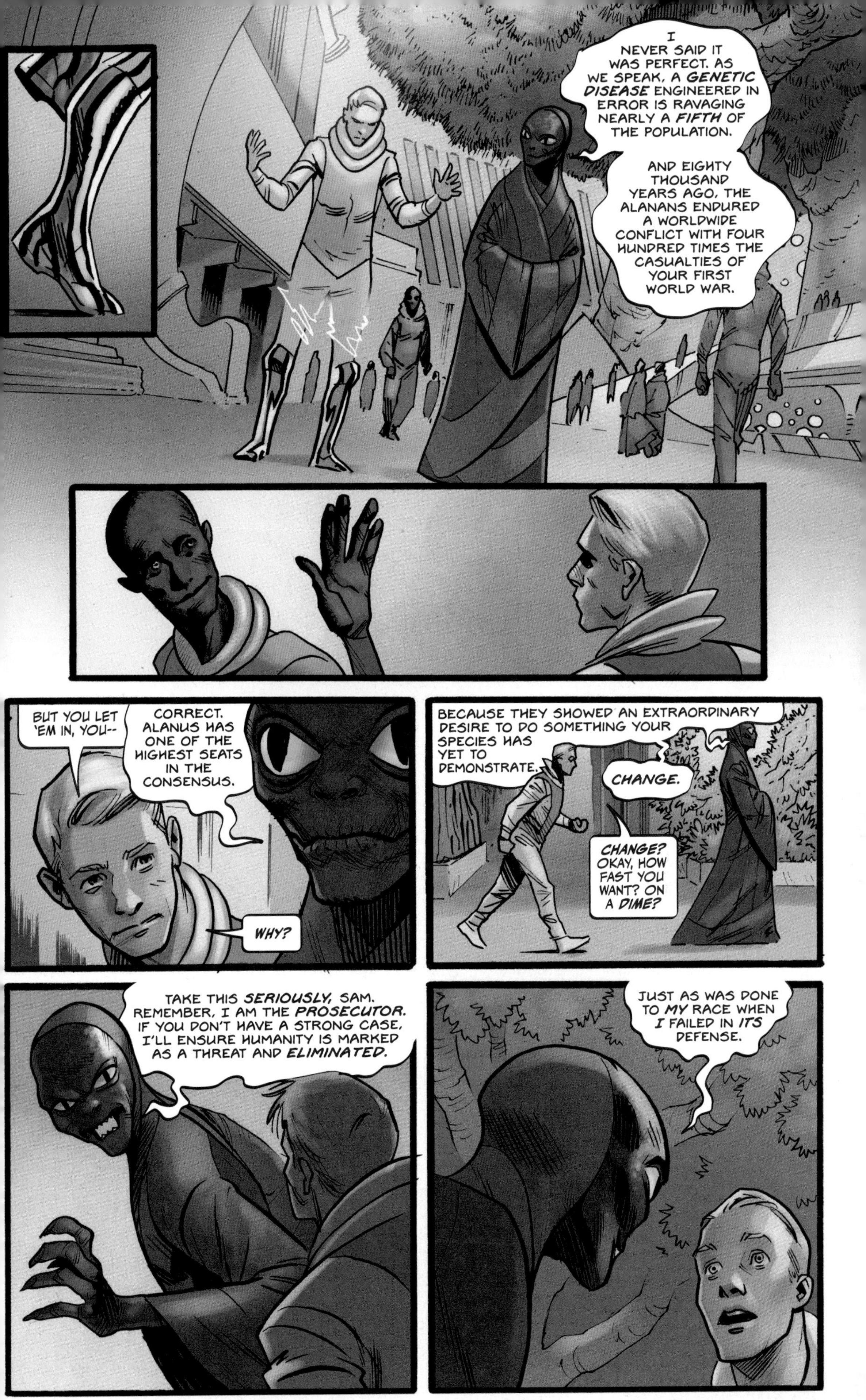
I NEVER SAID IT WAS PERFECT. AS WE SPEAK, A GENETIC DISEASE ENGINEERED IN ERROR IS RAVAGING NEARLY A FIFTH OF THE POPULATION.
AND EIGHTY THOUSAND YEARS AGO, THE ALANANS ENDURED A WORLDWIDE CONFLICT WITH FOUR HUNDRED TIMES THE CASUALTIES OF YOUR FIRST WORLD WAR.
BUT YOU LET 'EM IN, YOU--
CORRECT. ALANUS HAS ONE OF THE HIGHEST SEATS IN THE CONSENSUS.
WHY?
BECAUSE THEY SHOWED AN EXTRAORDINARY DESIRE TO DO SOMETHING YOUR SPECIES HAS YET TO DEMONSTRATE.
CHANGE.
CHANGE? OKAY, HOW FAST YOU WANT? ON A DIME?
TAKE THIS SERIOUSLY, SAM. REMEMBER, I AM THE PROSECUTOR. IF YOU DON'T HAVE A STRONG CASE, I'LL ENSURE HUMANITY IS MARKED AS A THREAT AND ELIMINATED.
JUST AS WAS DONE TO MY RACE WHEN I FAILED IN ITS DEFENSE.

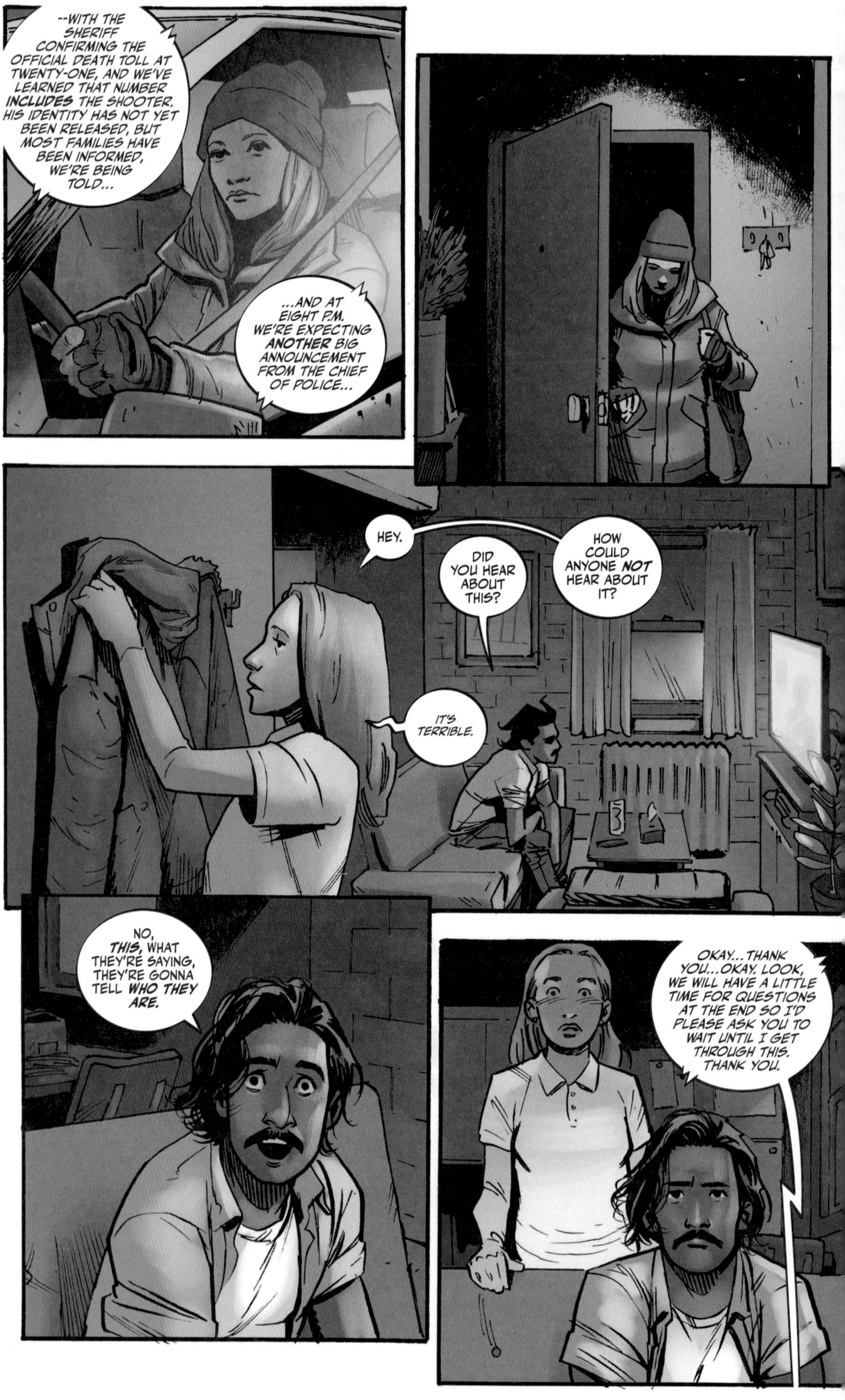
--WITH THE SHERIFF CONFIRMING THE OFFICIAL DEATH TOLL AT TWENTY-ONE, AND WE'VE LEARNED THAT NUMBER INCLUDES THE SHOOTER. HIS IDENTITY HAS NOT YET BEEN RELEASED, BUT MOST FAMILIES HAVE BEEN INFORMED, WE'RE BEING TOLD...
...AND AT EIGHT P.M. WE'RE EXPECTING ANOTHER BIG ANNOUNCEMENT FROM THE CHIEF OF POLICE...
HEY.
HOW COULD ANYONE NOT HEAR ABOUT IT?
DID YOU HEAR ABOUT THIS?
IT'S TERRIBLE.
NO, THIS, WHAT THEY'RE SAYING, THEY'RE GONNA TELL WHO THEY ARE.
OKAY...THANK YOU...OKAY. LOOK, WE WILL HAVE A LITTLE TIME FOR QUESTIONS AT THE END SO I'D PLEASE ASK YOU TO WAIT UNTIL I GET THROUGH THIS. THANK YOU.

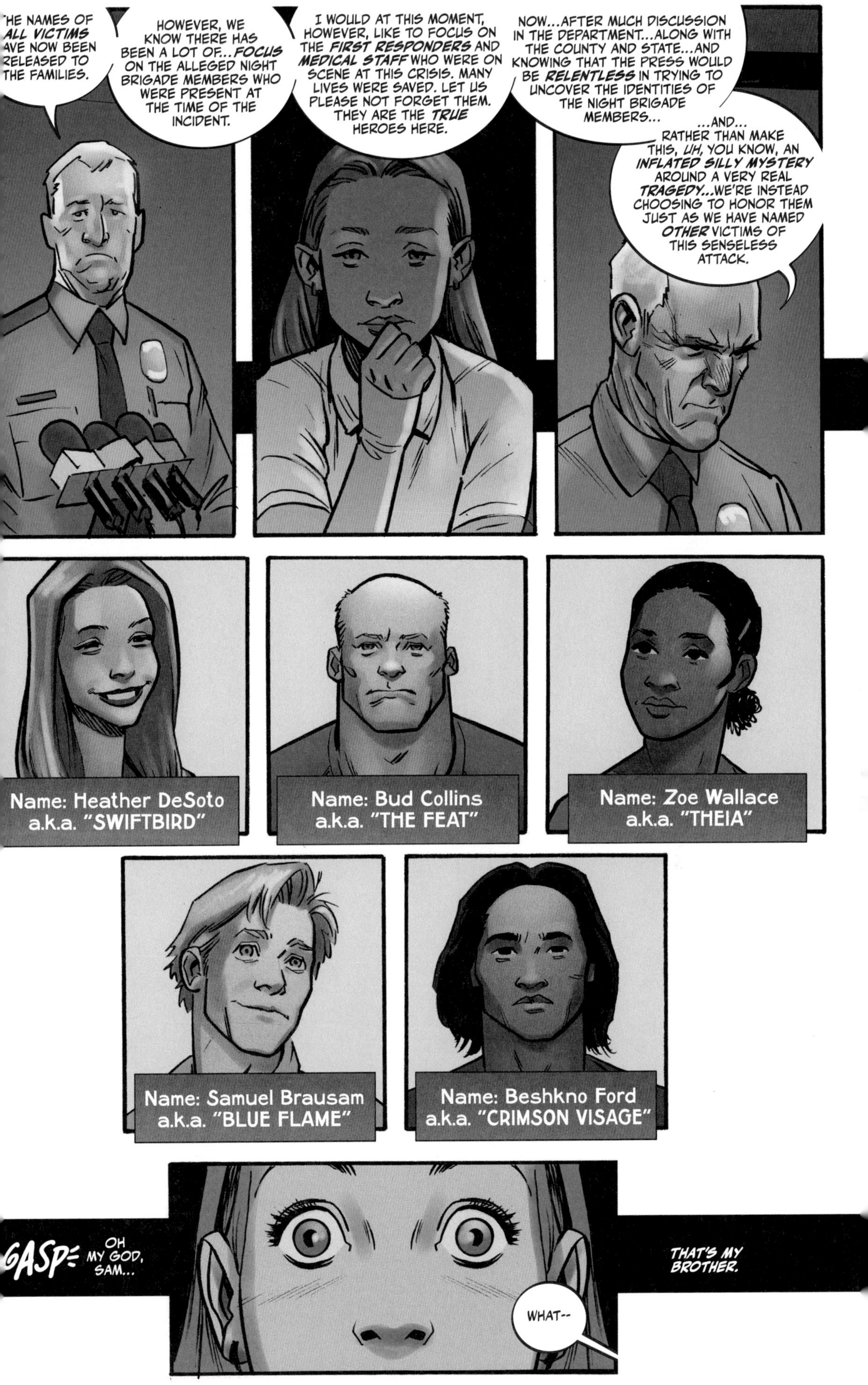
HE NAMES OF ALL VICTIMS AVE NOW BEEN RELEASED TO THE FAMILIES.
HOWEVER, WE KNOW THERE HAS BEEN A LOT OF...FOCUS ON THE ALLEGED NIGHT BRIGADE MEMBERS WHO WERE PRESENT AT THE TIME OF THE INCIDENT.
I WOULD AT THIS MOMENT, HOWEVER, LIKE TO FOCUS ON THE FIRST RESPONDERS AND MEDICAL STAFF WHO WERE ON SCENE AT THIS CRISIS. MANY LIVES WERE SAVED. LET US PLEASE NOT FORGET THEM. THEY ARE THE TRUE HEROES HERE.
NOW...AFTER MUCH DISCUSSION IN THE DEPARTMENT...ALONG WITH THE COUNTY AND STATE...AND KNOWING THAT THE PRESS WOULD BE RELENTLESS IN TRYING TO UNCOVER THE IDENTITIES OF THE NIGHT BRIGADE MEMBERS...
...AND... RATHER THAN MAKE THIS, UH, YOU KNOW, AN INFLATED SILLY MYSTERY AROUND A VERY REAL TRAGEDY...WE'RE INSTEAD CHOOSING TO HONOR THEM JUST AS WE HAVE NAMED OTHER VICTIMS OF THIS SENSELESS ATTACK.
Name: Heather DeSoto a.k.a. "SWIFTBIRD"
Name: Bud Collins a.k.a. "THE FEAT"
Name: Zoe Wallace a.k.a. "THEIA"
Name: Samuel Brausam a.k.a. "BLUE FLAME"
Name: Beshkno Ford a.k.a. "CRIMSON VISAGE"
GASP
OH MY GOD, SAM...
THAT'S MY BROTHER.
WHAT--

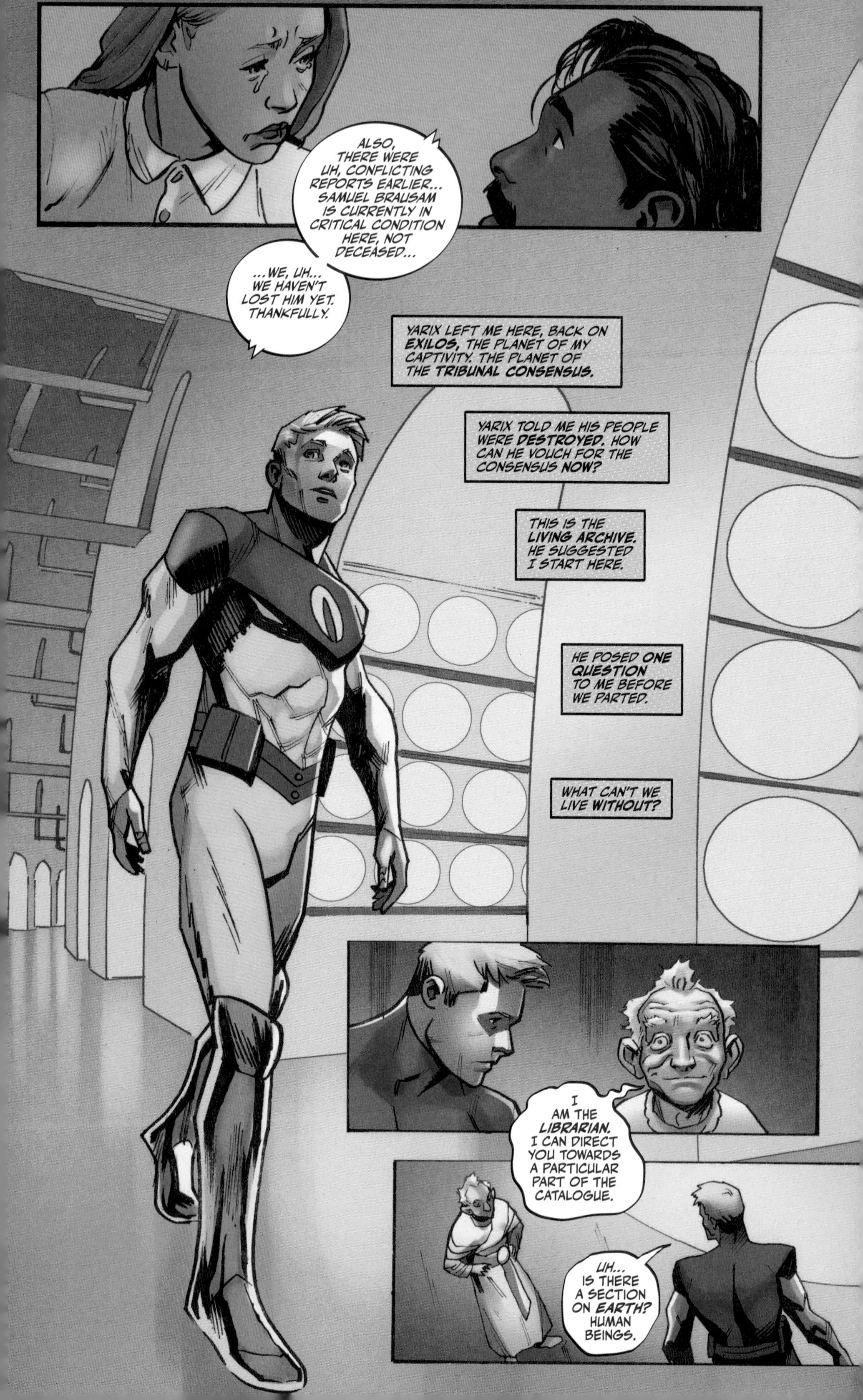
ALSO, THERE WERE UH, CONFLICTING REPORTS EARLIER... SAMUEL BRAUSAM IS CURRENTLY IN CRITICAL CONDITION HERE, NOT DECEASED...
...WE, UH... WE HAVEN'T LOST HIM YET. THANKFULLY.
YARIX LEFT ME HERE, BACK ON EXILOS, THE PLANET OF MY CAPTIVITY. THE PLANET OF THE TRIBUNAL CONSENSUS.
YARIX TOLD ME HIS PEOPLE WERE DESTROYED. HOW CAN HE VOUCH FOR THE CONSENSUS NOW?
THIS IS THE LIVING ARCHIVE. HE SUGGESTED I START HERE.
HE POSED ONE QUESTION TO ME BEFORE WE PARTED.
WHAT CAN'T WE LIVE WITHOUT?
I AM THE LIBRARIAN. I CAN DIRECT YOU TOWARDS A PARTICULAR PART OF THE CATALOGUE.
UH... IS THERE A SECTION ON EARTH? HUMAN BEINGS.

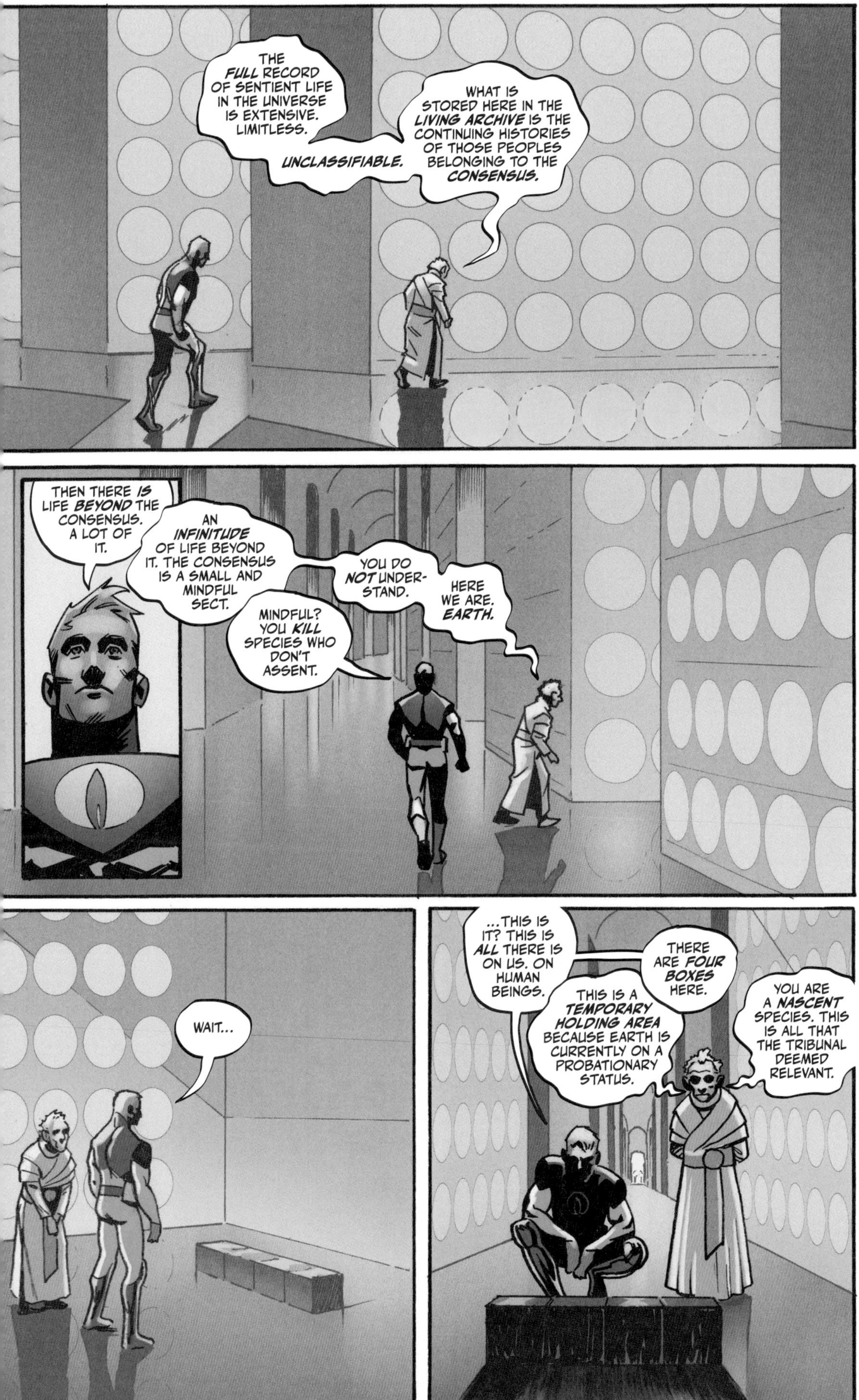
THE FULL RECORD OF SENTIENT LIFE IN THE UNIVERSE IS EXTENSIVE. LIMITLESS.
UNCLASSIFIABLE.
WHAT IS STORED HERE IN THE LIVING ARCHIVE IS THE CONTINUING HISTORIES OF THOSE PEOPLES BELONGING TO THE CONSENSUS.
THEN THERE IS LIFE BEYOND THE CONSENSUS. A LOT OF IT.
AN INFINITUDE OF LIFE BEYOND IT. THE CONSENSUS IS A SMALL AND MINDFUL SECT.
MINDFUL? YOU KILL SPECIES WHO DON'T ASSENT.
YOU DO NOT UNDER-STAND.
HERE WE ARE. EARTH.
WAIT...
...THIS IS IT? THIS IS ALL THERE IS ON US. ON HUMAN BEINGS.
THERE ARE FOUR BOXES HERE.
THIS IS A TEMPORARY HOLDING AREA BECAUSE EARTH IS CURRENTLY ON A PROBATIONARY STATUS.
YOU ARE A NASCENT SPECIES. THIS IS ALL THAT THE TRIBUNAL DEEMED RELEVANT.

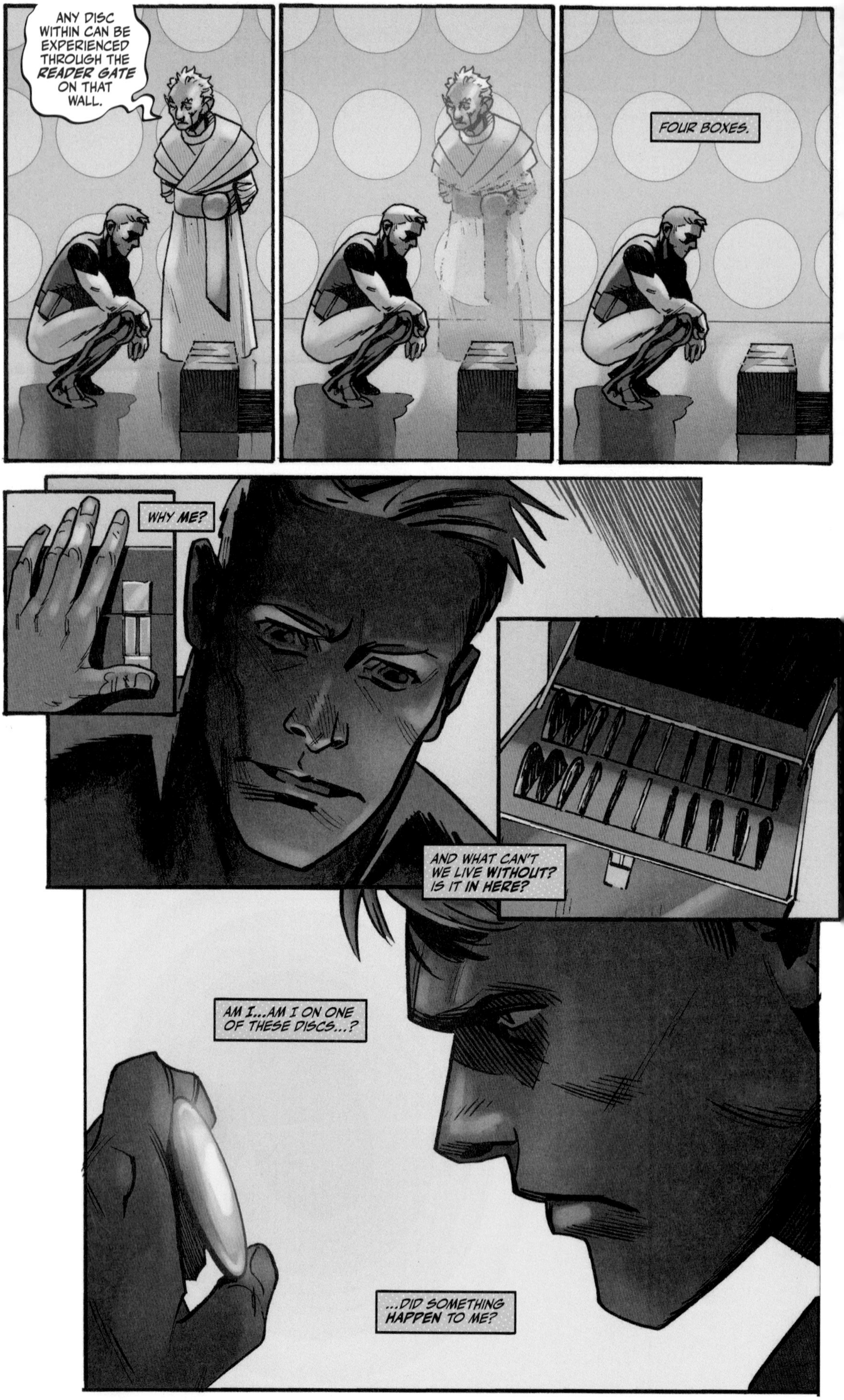
ANY DISC WITHIN CAN BE EXPERIENCED THROUGH THE READER GATE ON THAT WALL.
FOUR BOXES.
WHY ME?
AND WHAT CAN'T WE LIVE WITHOUT? IS IT IN HERE?
AM I...AM I ON ONE OF THESE DISCS...?
...DID SOMETHING HAPPEN TO ME?

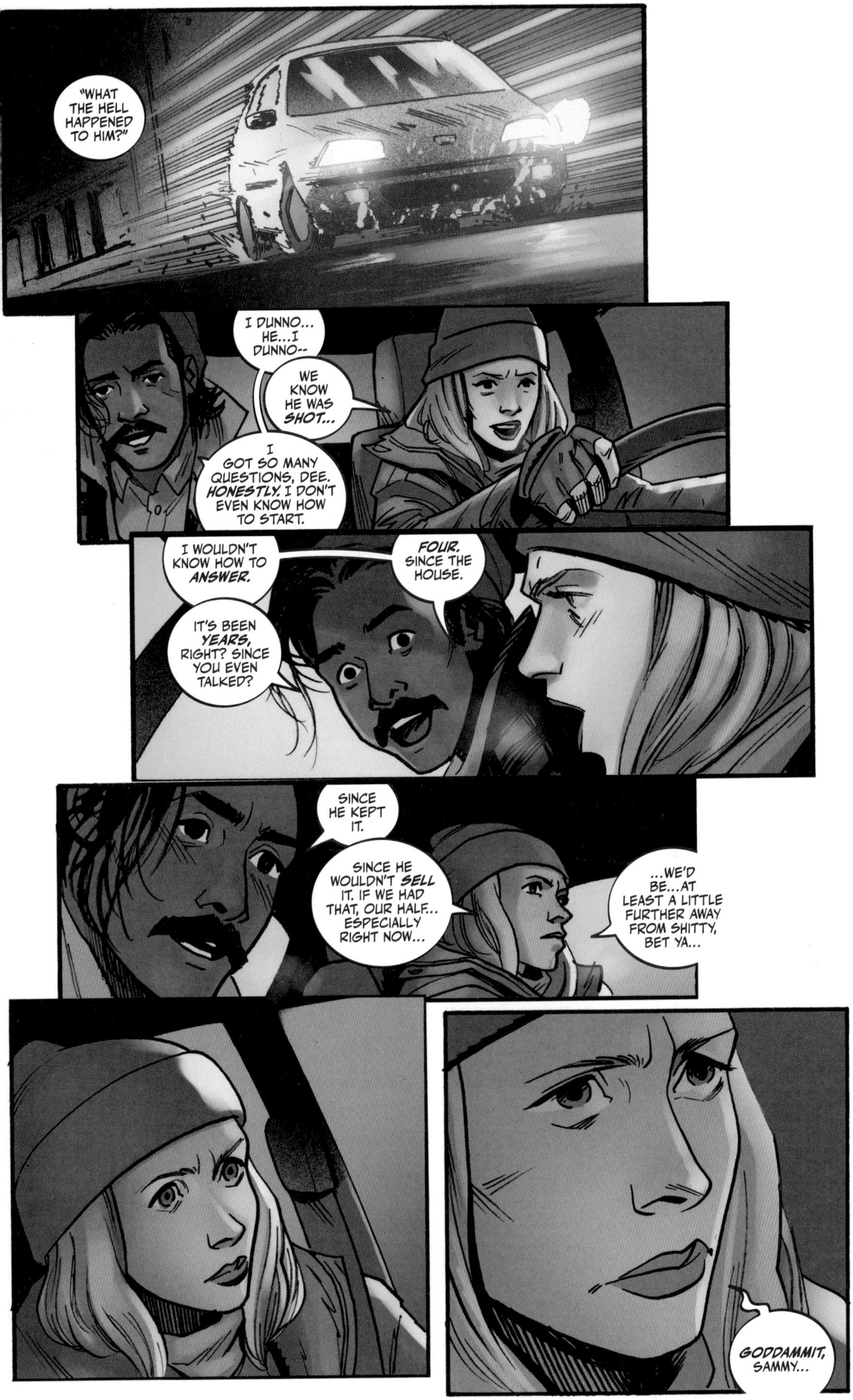
"WHAT THE HELL HAPPENED TO HIM?"
I DUNNO... HE...I DUNNO--
WE KNOW HE WAS SHOT...
I GOT SO MANY QUESTIONS, DEE. HONESTLY. I DON'T EVEN KNOW HOW TO START.
I WOULDN'T KNOW HOW TO ANSWER.
IT'S BEEN YEARS, RIGHT? SINCE YOU EVEN TALKED?
FOUR. SINCE THE HOUSE.
SINCE HE KEPT IT.
SINCE HE WOULDN'T SELL IT. IF WE HAD THAT, OUR HALF... ESPECIALLY RIGHT NOW...
...WE'D BE...AT LEAST A LITTLE FURTHER AWAY FROM SHITTY, BET YA...
GODDAMMIT, SAMMY...

WHERE IS--

ARE YOU FAMILY?

WE'RE LOOKING FOR--

FAMILY IS THIS WAY, PLEASE.

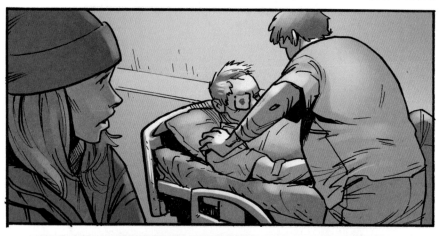

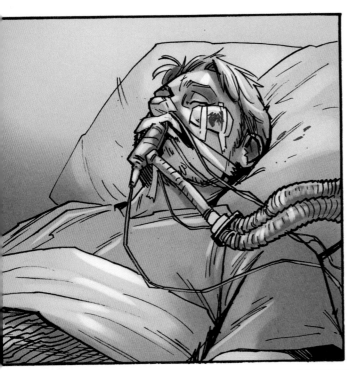

HE WAS SHOT TWICE IN THE SPINE, MIDDLE-LOWER BACK...WE BELIEVE IT'S AN *INCOMPLETE* INJURY BUT WE WON'T KNOW FOR SURE FOR A FEW DAYS--

THE TRUTH IS WE HAVE *NO IDEA.*

WHAT DOES THAT MEAN? CAN HE WALK?

BUT HE'LL LIVE?

YES. WE REMOVED THE BULLETS AND WE JUST HAVE TO PROTECT AGAINST INFECTION...

...HIS RECOVERY ROAD WILL BE...*LONG...* HE'LL LIKELY NEED IN-HOME CARE FOR... QUITE A WHILE.

WE'LL DO IT. WE'LL TAKE CARE OF HIM.

DEE--

MATEO. WE'RE GONNA TAKE CARE OF HIM.

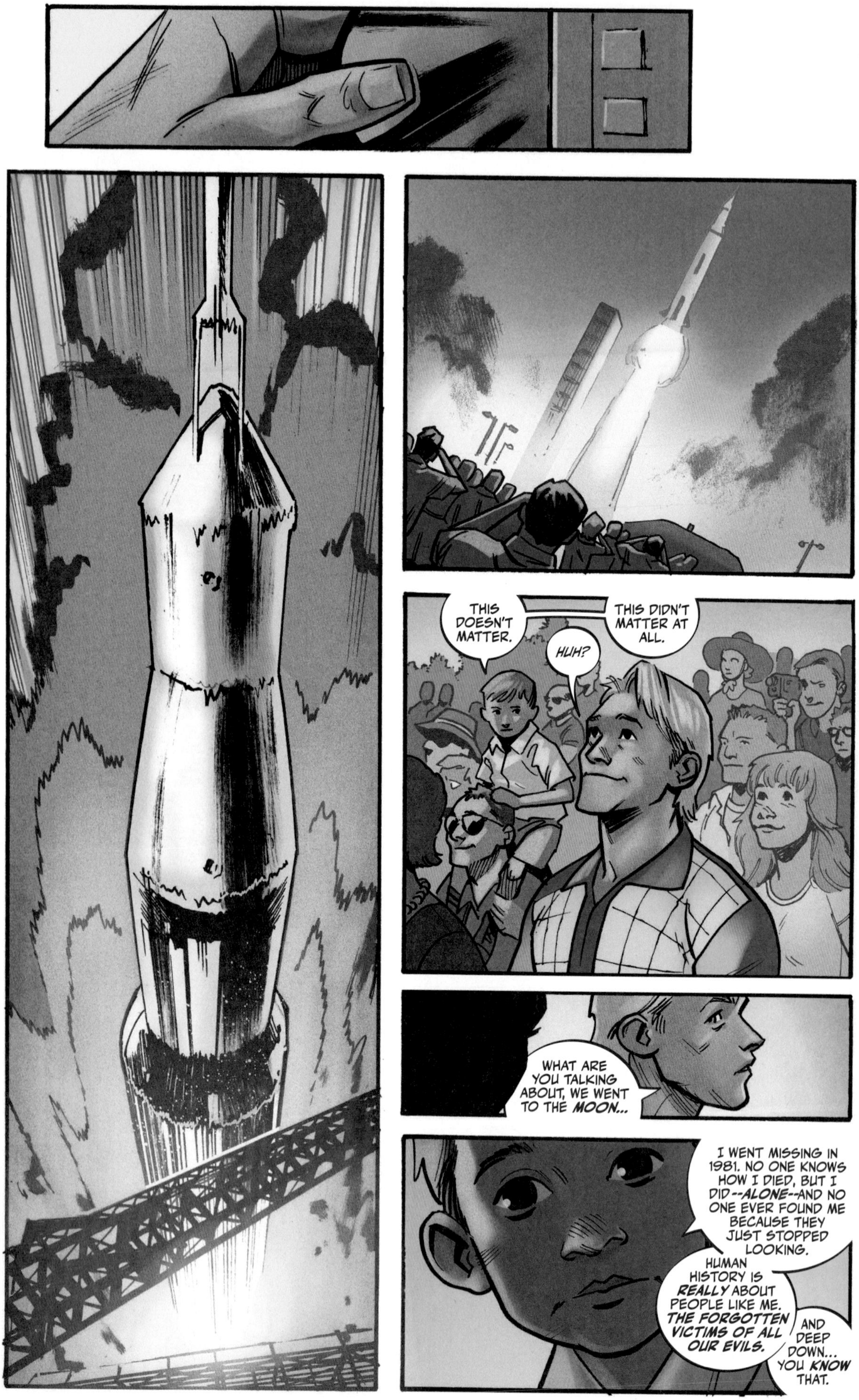
THIS DOESN'T MATTER.
THIS DIDN'T MATTER AT ALL.
HUH?
WHAT ARE YOU TALKING ABOUT, WE WENT TO THE MOON...
I WENT MISSING IN 1981. NO ONE KNOWS HOW I DIED, BUT I DID--ALONE--AND NO ONE EVER FOUND ME BECAUSE THEY JUST STOPPED LOOKING.
HUMAN HISTORY IS REALLY ABOUT PEOPLE LIKE ME. THE FORGOTTEN VICTIMS OF ALL OUR EVILS.
AND DEEP DOWN... YOU KNOW THAT.

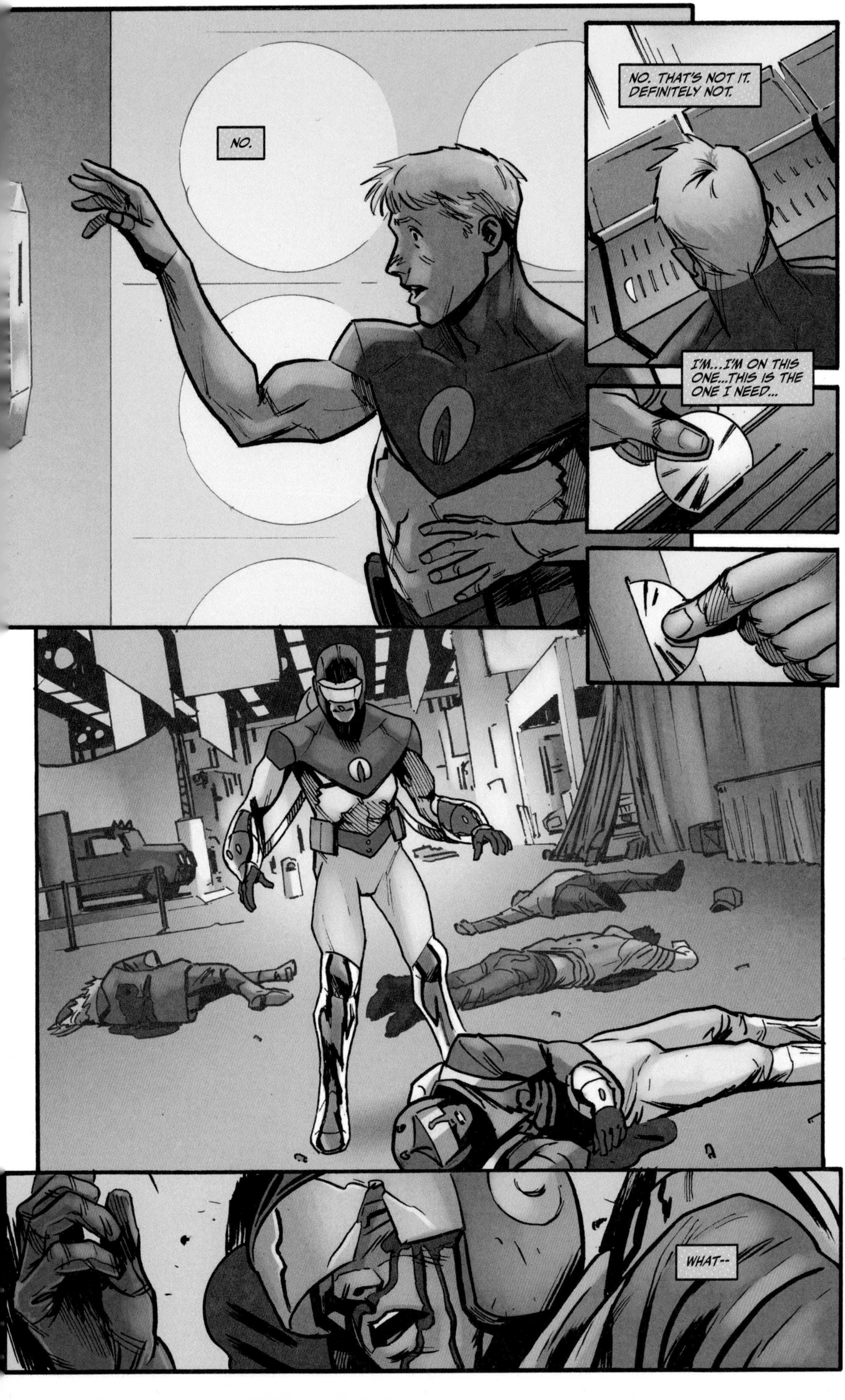
NO.
NO. THAT'S NOT IT. DEFINITELY NOT.
I'M...I'M ON THIS ONE...THIS IS THE ONE I NEED...
WHAT--

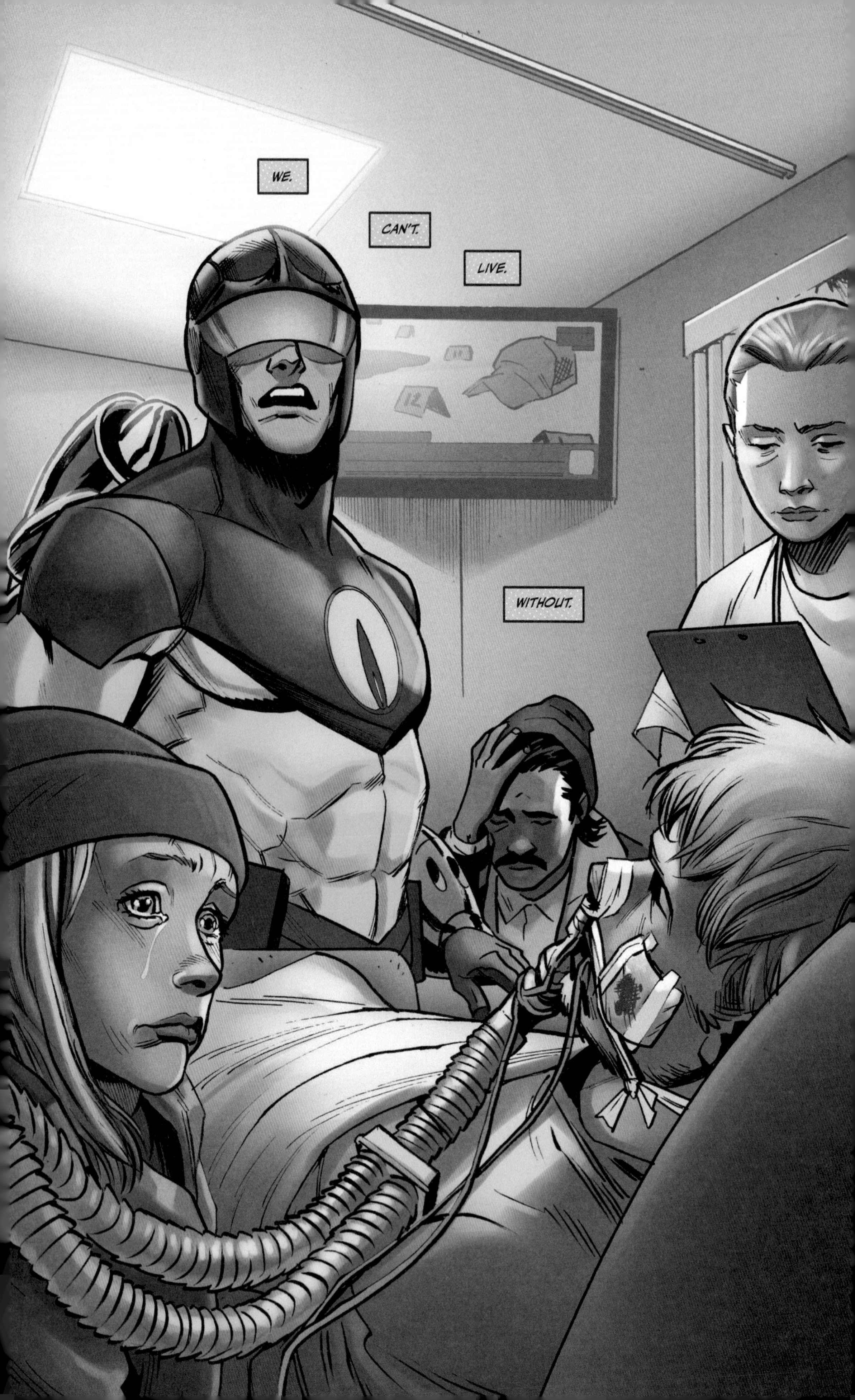
WE.
CAN'T.
LIVE.
WITHOUT.

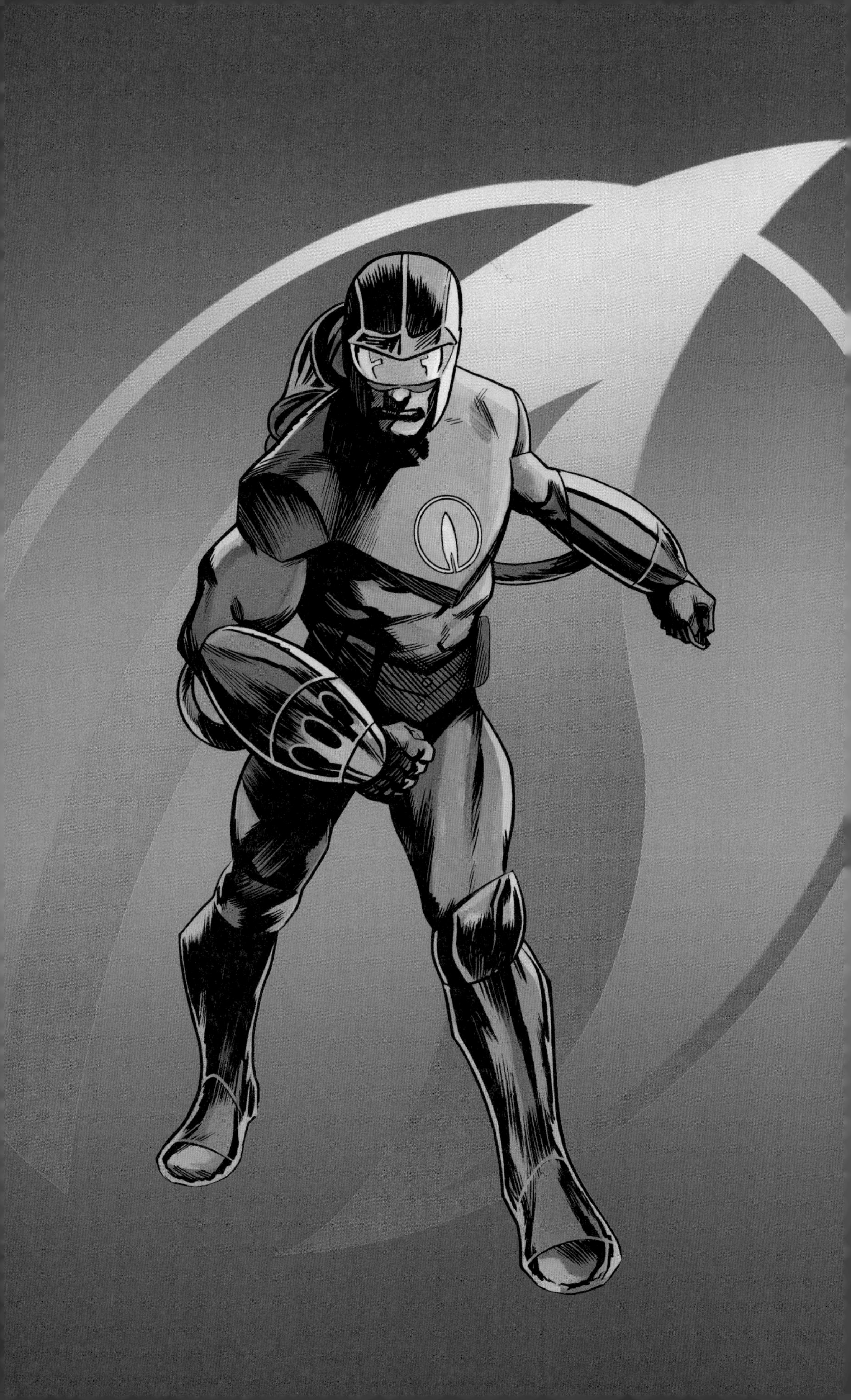

WEATHER SYSTEMS FAILURE
CHAPTER 3

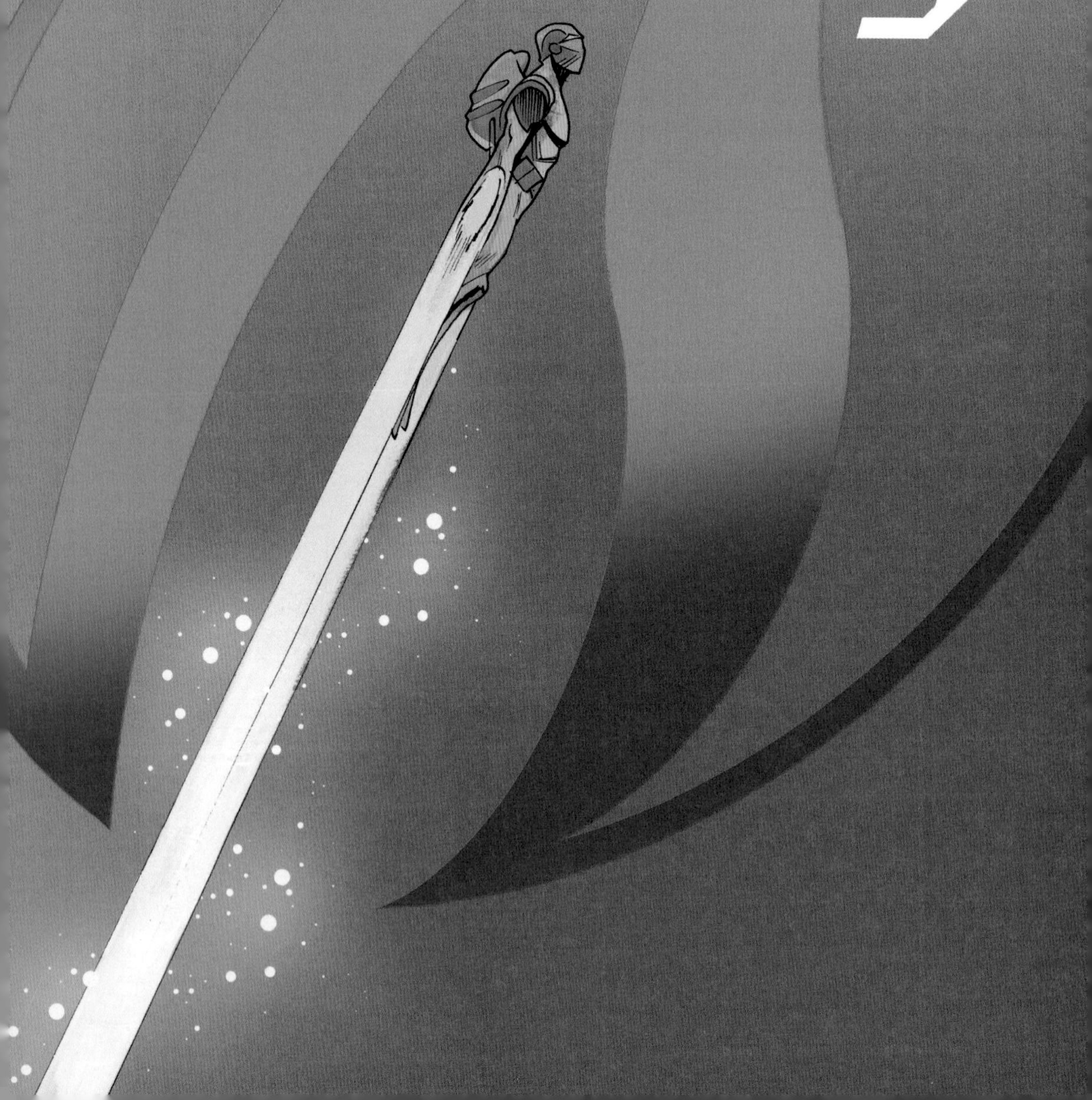

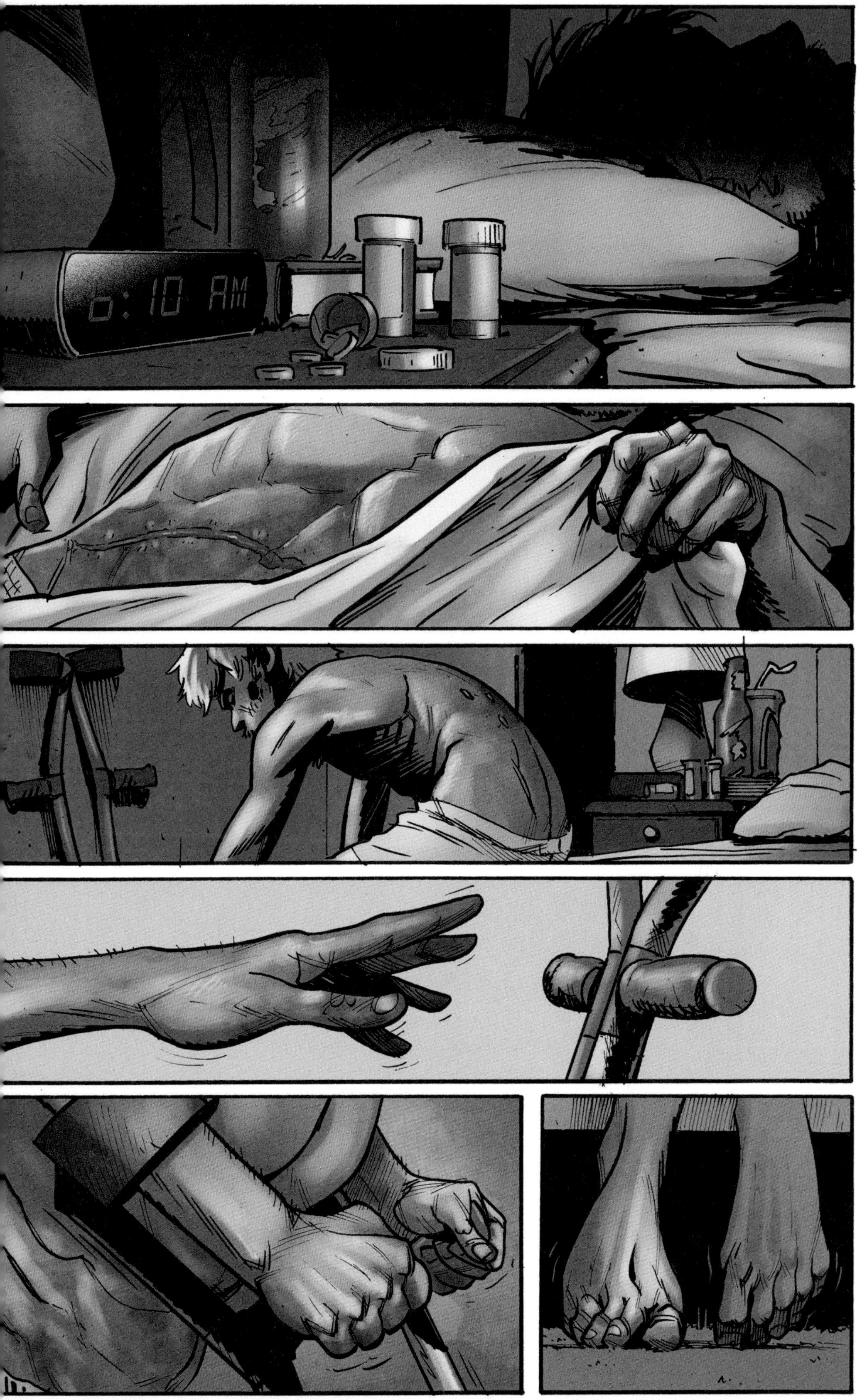
6:10 AM

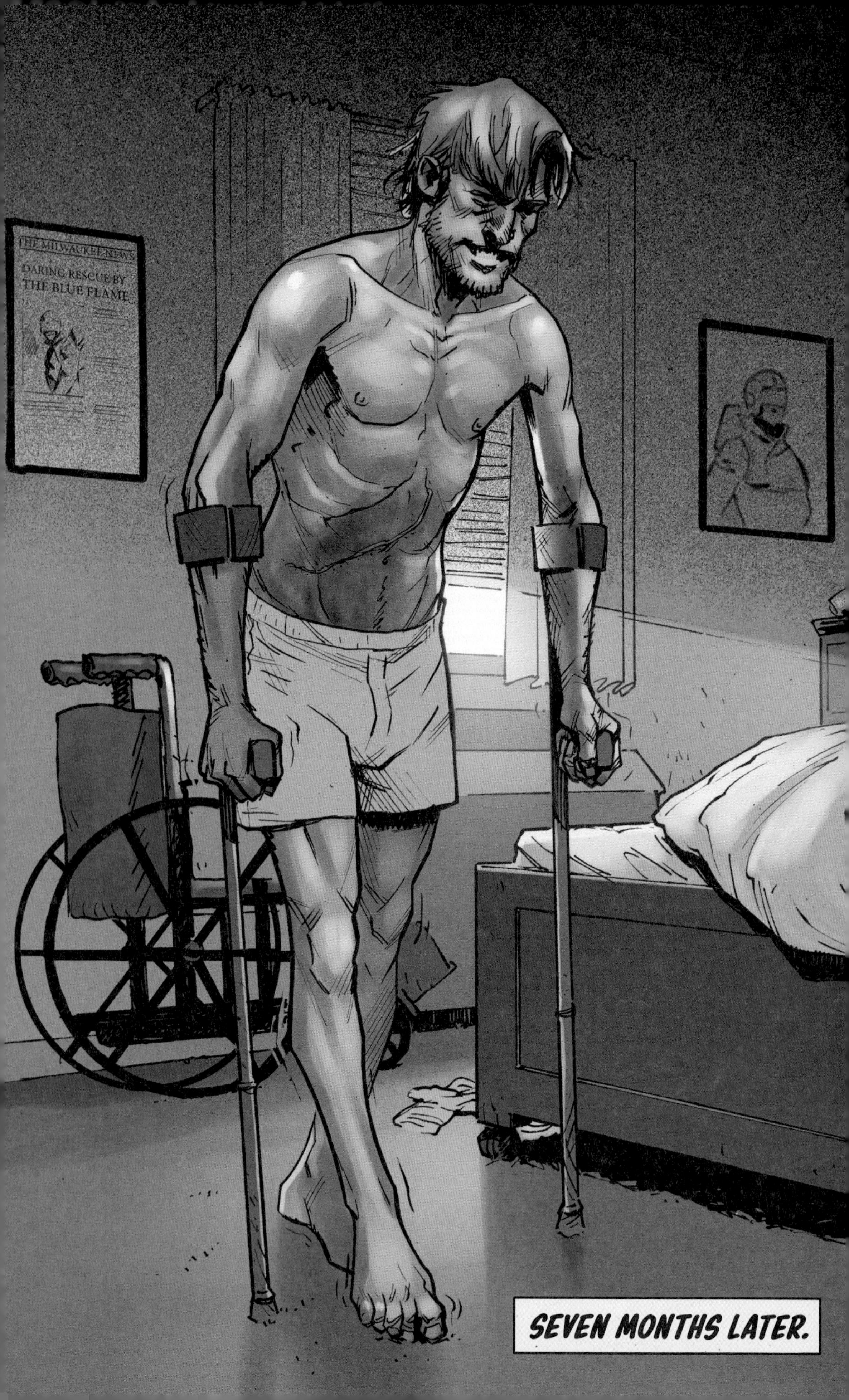
THE MILWAUKEE NEWS
DARING RESCUE BY THE BLUE FLAME
SEVEN MONTHS LATER.

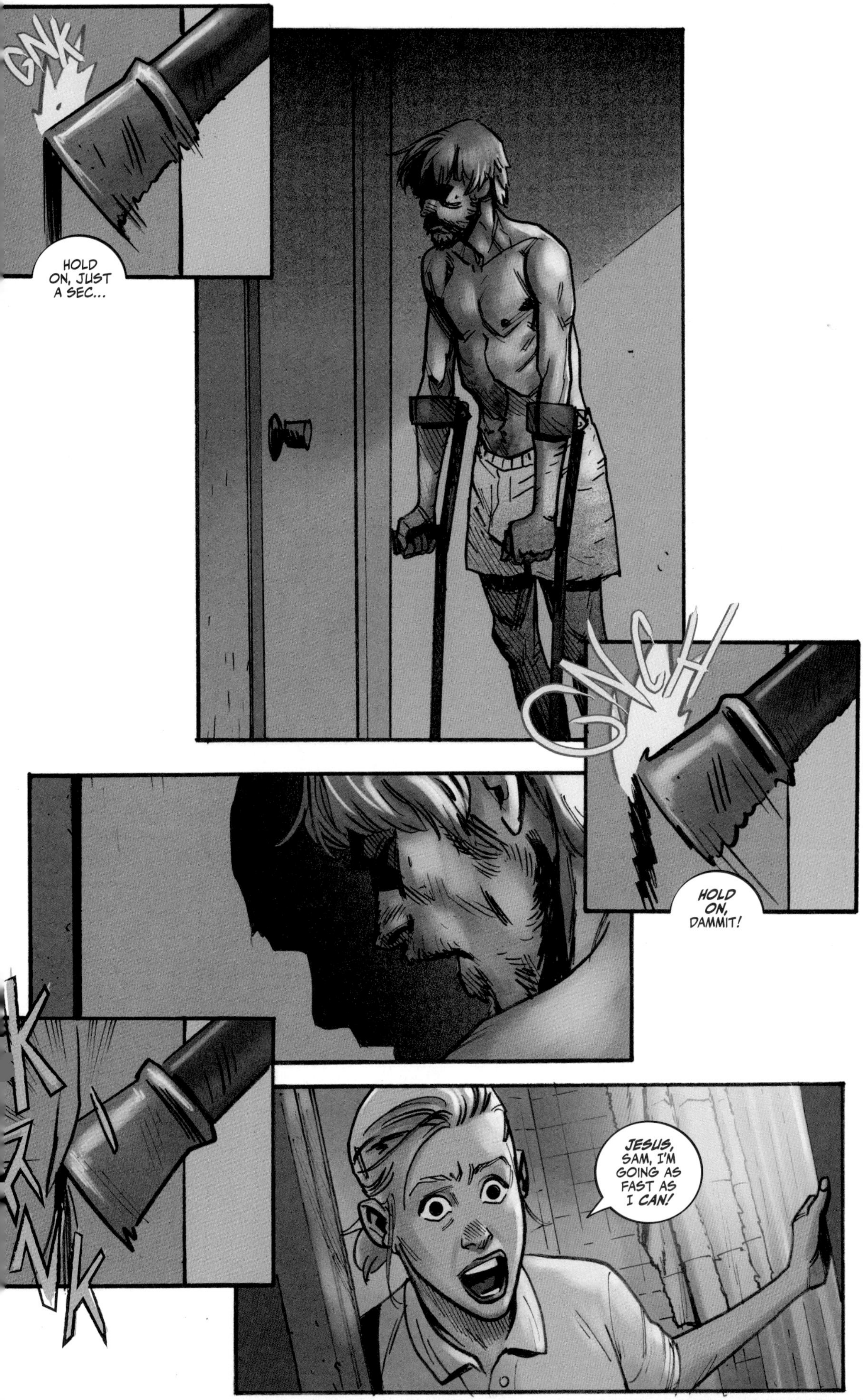
GNK
HOLD ON, JUST A SEC...
GNCH
HOLD ON, DAMMIT!
KRANK
JESUS, SAM, I'M GOING AS FAST AS I CAN!

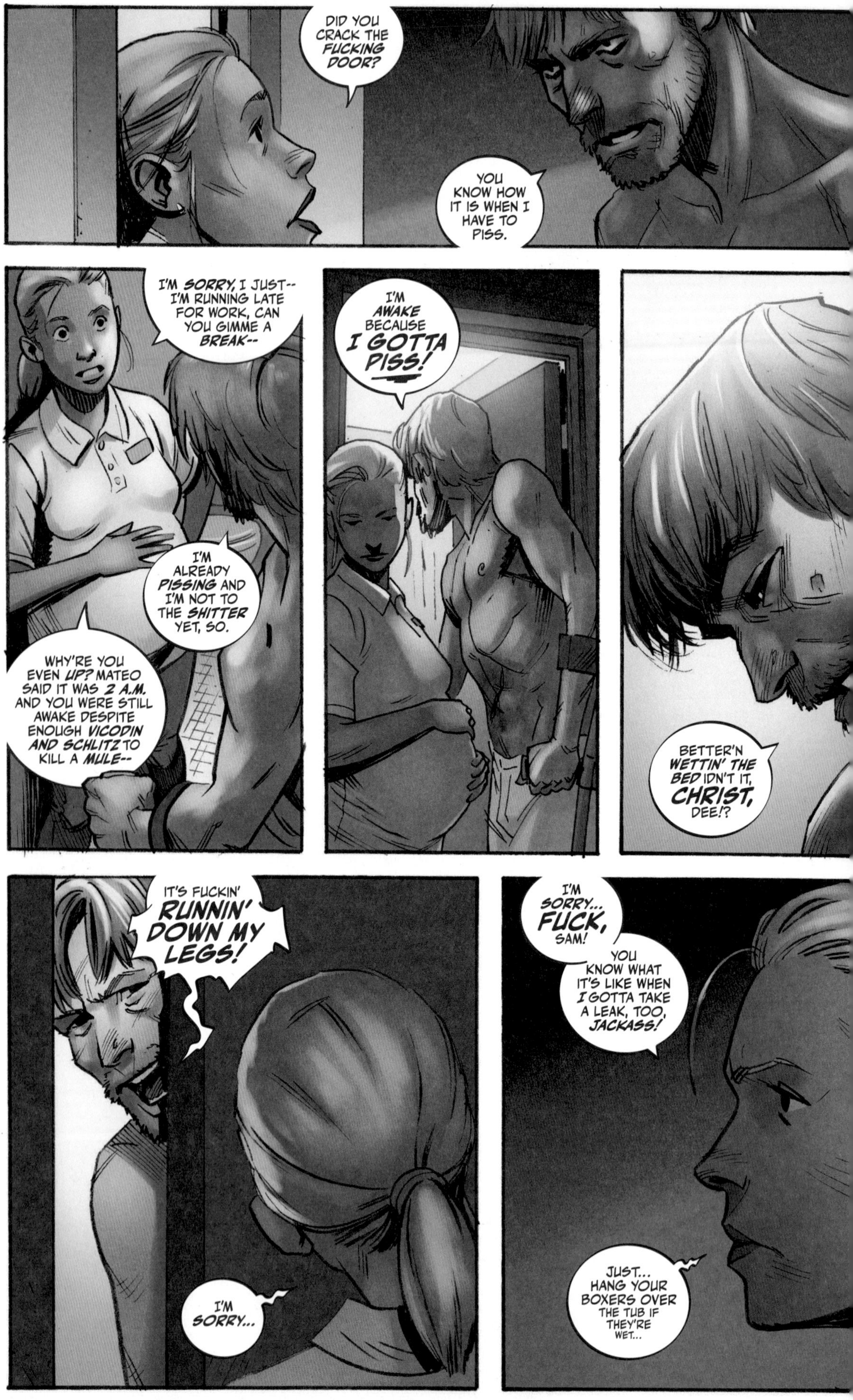
DID YOU CRACK THE FUCKING DOOR?
YOU KNOW HOW IT IS WHEN I HAVE TO PISS.
I'M SORRY, I JUST-- I'M RUNNING LATE FOR WORK, CAN YOU GIMME A BREAK--
I'M ALREADY PISSING AND I'M NOT TO THE SHITTER YET, SO.
WHY'RE YOU EVEN UP? MATEO SAID IT WAS 2 A.M. AND YOU WERE STILL AWAKE DESPITE ENOUGH VICODIN AND SCHLITZ TO KILL A MULE--
I'M AWAKE BECAUSE I GOTTA PISS!
BETTER'N WETTIN' THE BED IDN'T IT, CHRIST, DEE!?
IT'S FUCKIN' RUNNIN' DOWN MY LEGS!
I'M SORRY...
I'M SORRY... FUCK, SAM!
YOU KNOW WHAT IT'S LIKE WHEN I GOTTA TAKE A LEAK, TOO, JACKASS!
JUST... HANG YOUR BOXERS OVER THE TUB IF THEY'RE WET...

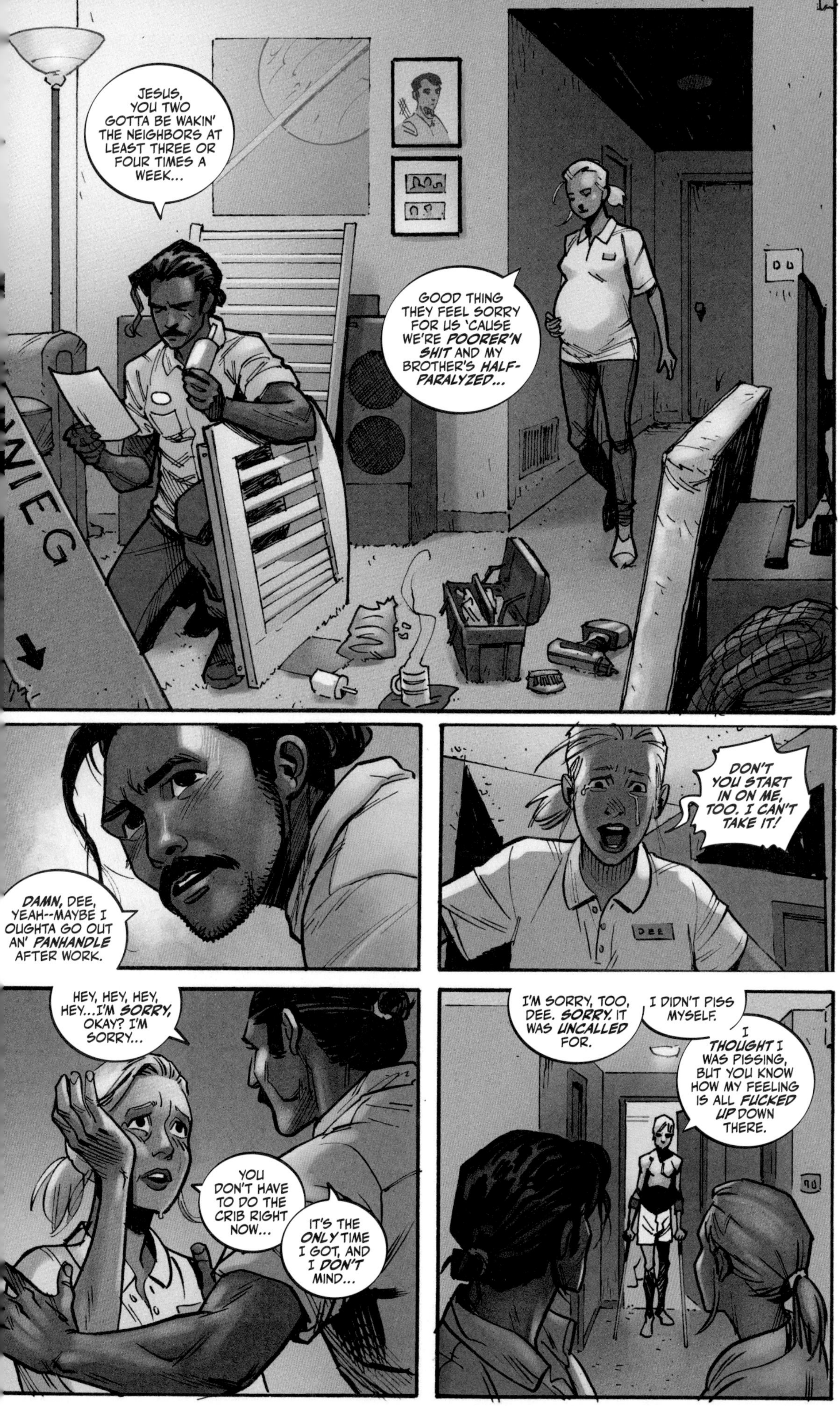
JESUS, YOU TWO GOTTA BE WAKIN' THE NEIGHBORS AT LEAST THREE OR FOUR TIMES A WEEK...
GOOD THING THEY FEEL SORRY FOR US 'CAUSE WE'RE POORER'N SHIT AND MY BROTHER'S HALF-PARALYZED...
DAMN, DEE, YEAH--MAYBE I OUGHTA GO OUT AN' PANHANDLE AFTER WORK.
DON'T YOU START IN ON ME, TOO. I CAN'T TAKE IT!
DEE
HEY, HEY, HEY, HEY...I'M SORRY, OKAY? I'M SORRY...
YOU DON'T HAVE TO DO THE CRIB RIGHT NOW...
IT'S THE ONLY TIME I GOT, AND I DON'T MIND...
I'M SORRY, TOO, DEE. SORRY. IT WAS UNCALLED FOR.
I DIDN'T PISS MYSELF.
I THOUGHT I WAS PISSING, BUT YOU KNOW HOW MY FEELING IS ALL FUCKED UP DOWN THERE.

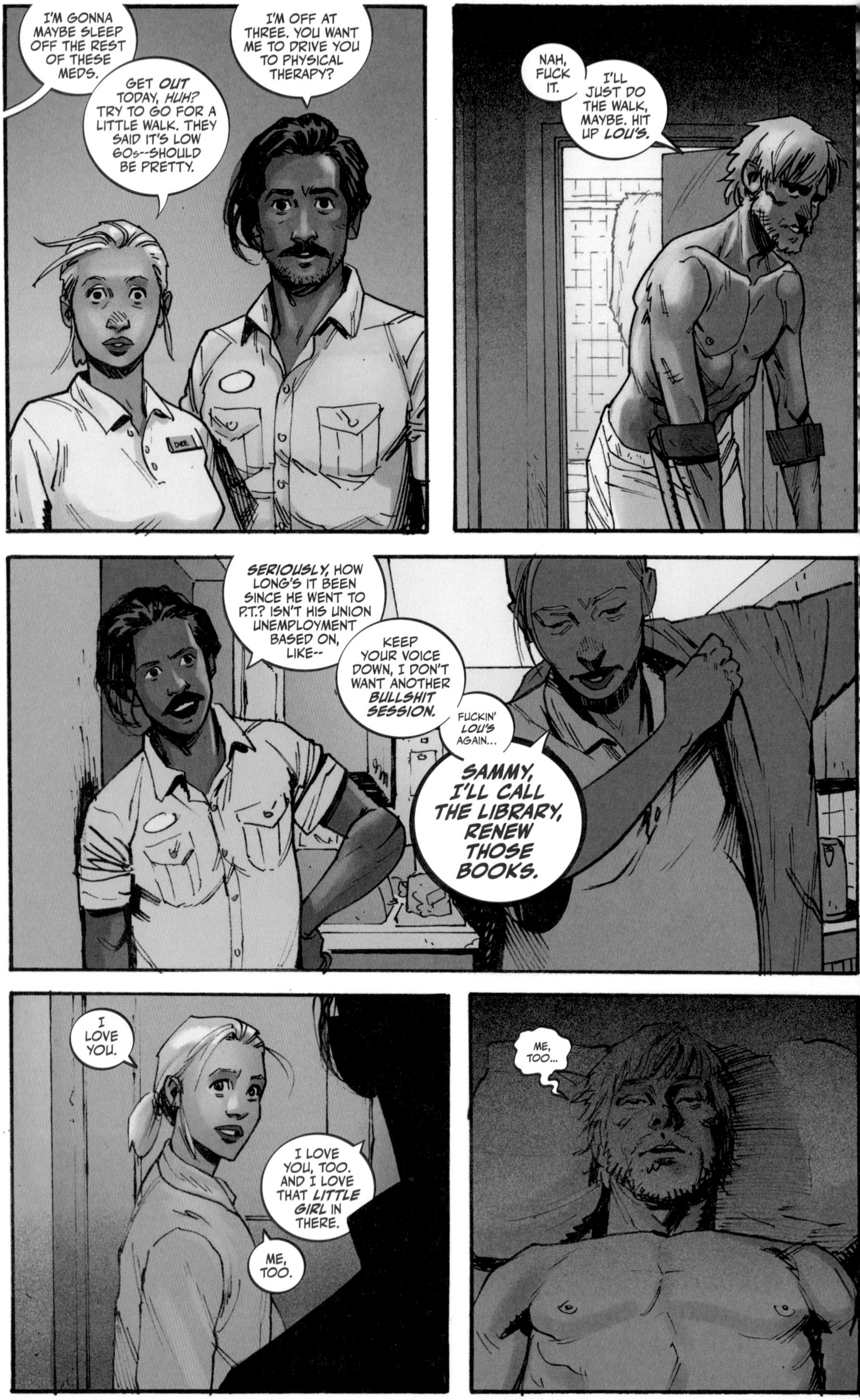
I'M GONNA MAYBE SLEEP OFF THE REST OF THESE MEDS.
GET OUT TODAY, HUH? TRY TO GO FOR A LITTLE WALK. THEY SAID IT'S LOW 60s--SHOULD BE PRETTY.
I'M OFF AT THREE. YOU WANT ME TO DRIVE YOU TO PHYSICAL THERAPY?
DEE
NAH, FUCK IT.
I'LL JUST DO THE WALK, MAYBE. HIT UP LOU'S.
SERIOUSLY, HOW LONG'S IT BEEN SINCE HE WENT TO P.T.? ISN'T HIS UNION UNEMPLOYMENT BASED ON, LIKE--
KEEP YOUR VOICE DOWN, I DON'T WANT ANOTHER BULLSHIT SESSION.
FUCKIN' LOU'S AGAIN...
SAMMY, I'LL CALL THE LIBRARY, RENEW THOSE BOOKS.
I LOVE YOU.
I LOVE YOU, TOO. AND I LOVE THAT LITTLE GIRL IN THERE.
ME, TOO.
ME, TOO...

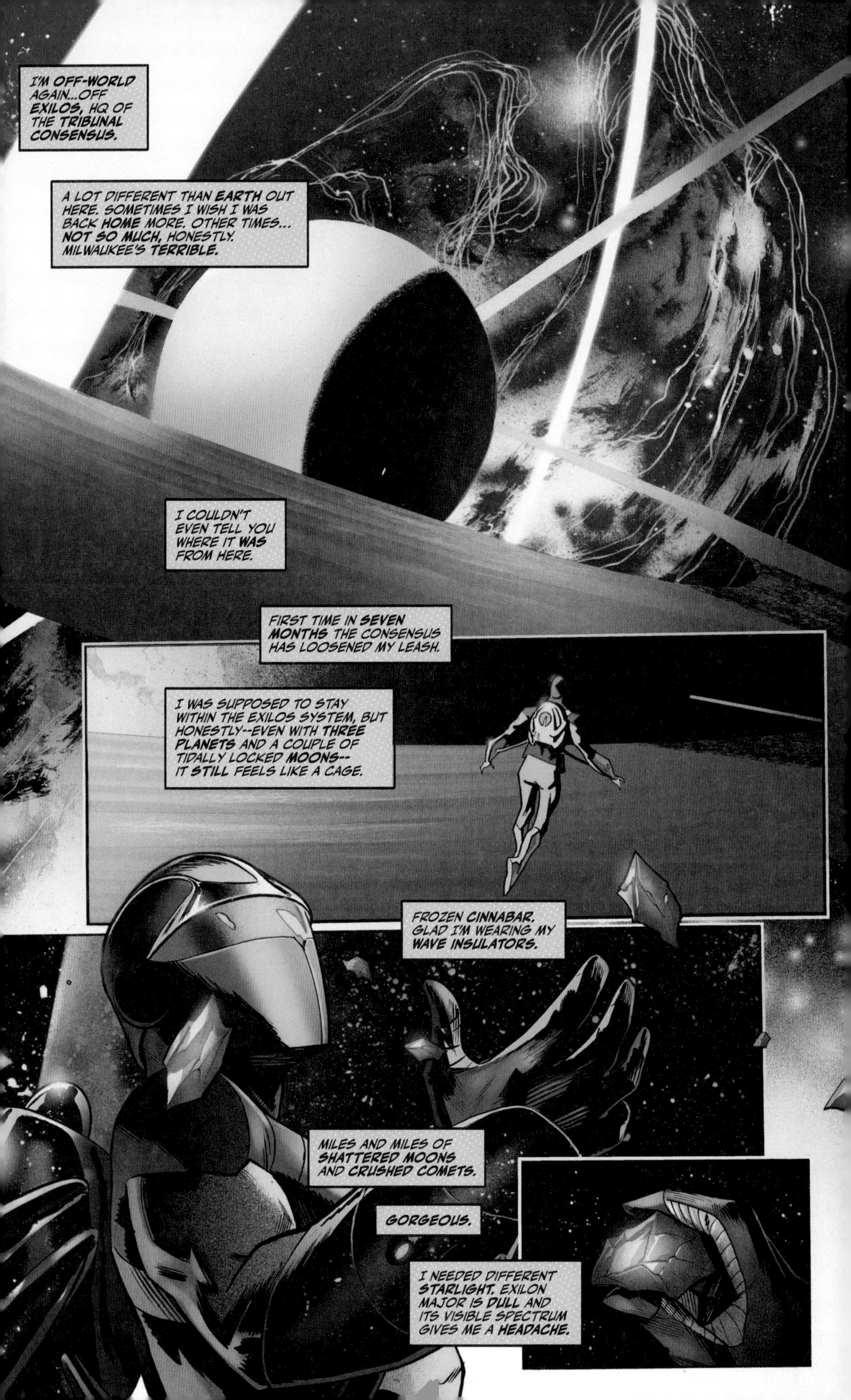

I'M OFF-WORLD AGAIN...OFF EXILOS, HQ OF THE TRIBUNAL CONSENSUS.
A LOT DIFFERENT THAN EARTH OUT HERE. SOMETIMES I WISH I WAS BACK HOME MORE. OTHER TIMES... NOT SO MUCH, HONESTLY. MILWAUKEE'S TERRIBLE.
I COULDN'T EVEN TELL YOU WHERE IT WAS FROM HERE.
FIRST TIME IN SEVEN MONTHS THE CONSENSUS HAS LOOSENED MY LEASH.
I WAS SUPPOSED TO STAY WITHIN THE EXILOS SYSTEM, BUT HONESTLY--EVEN WITH THREE PLANETS AND A COUPLE OF TIDALLY LOCKED MOONS--IT STILL FEELS LIKE A CAGE.
FROZEN CINNABAR. GLAD I'M WEARING MY WAVE INSULATORS.
MILES AND MILES OF SHATTERED MOONS AND CRUSHED COMETS.
GORGEOUS.
I NEEDED DIFFERENT STARLIGHT. EXILON MAJOR IS DULL AND ITS VISIBLE SPECTRUM GIVES ME A HEADACHE.

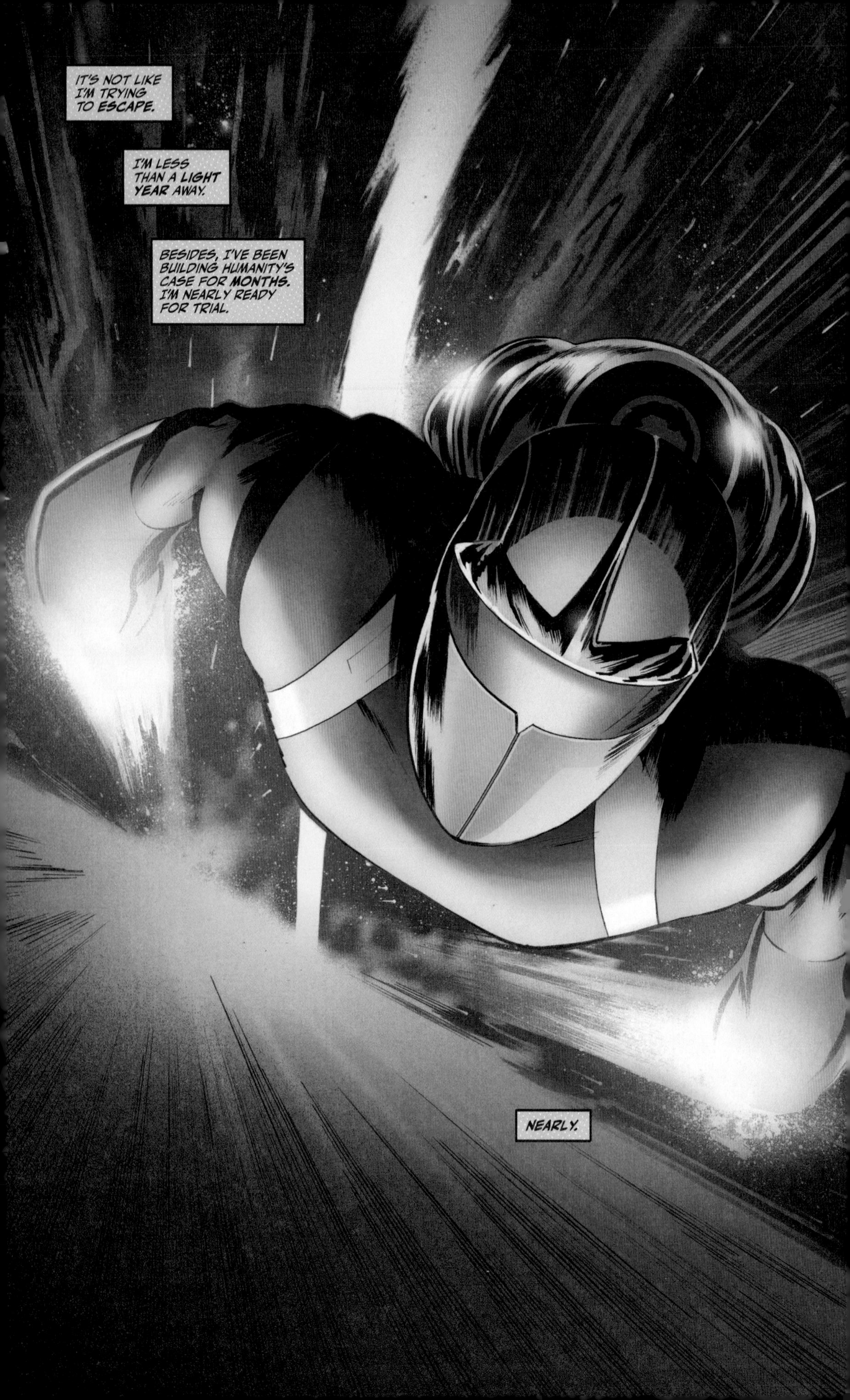
IT'S NOT LIKE I'M TRYING TO ESCAPE.
I'M LESS THAN A LIGHT YEAR AWAY.
BESIDES, I'VE BEEN BUILDING HUMANITY'S CASE FOR MONTHS. I'M NEARLY READY FOR TRIAL.
NEARLY.

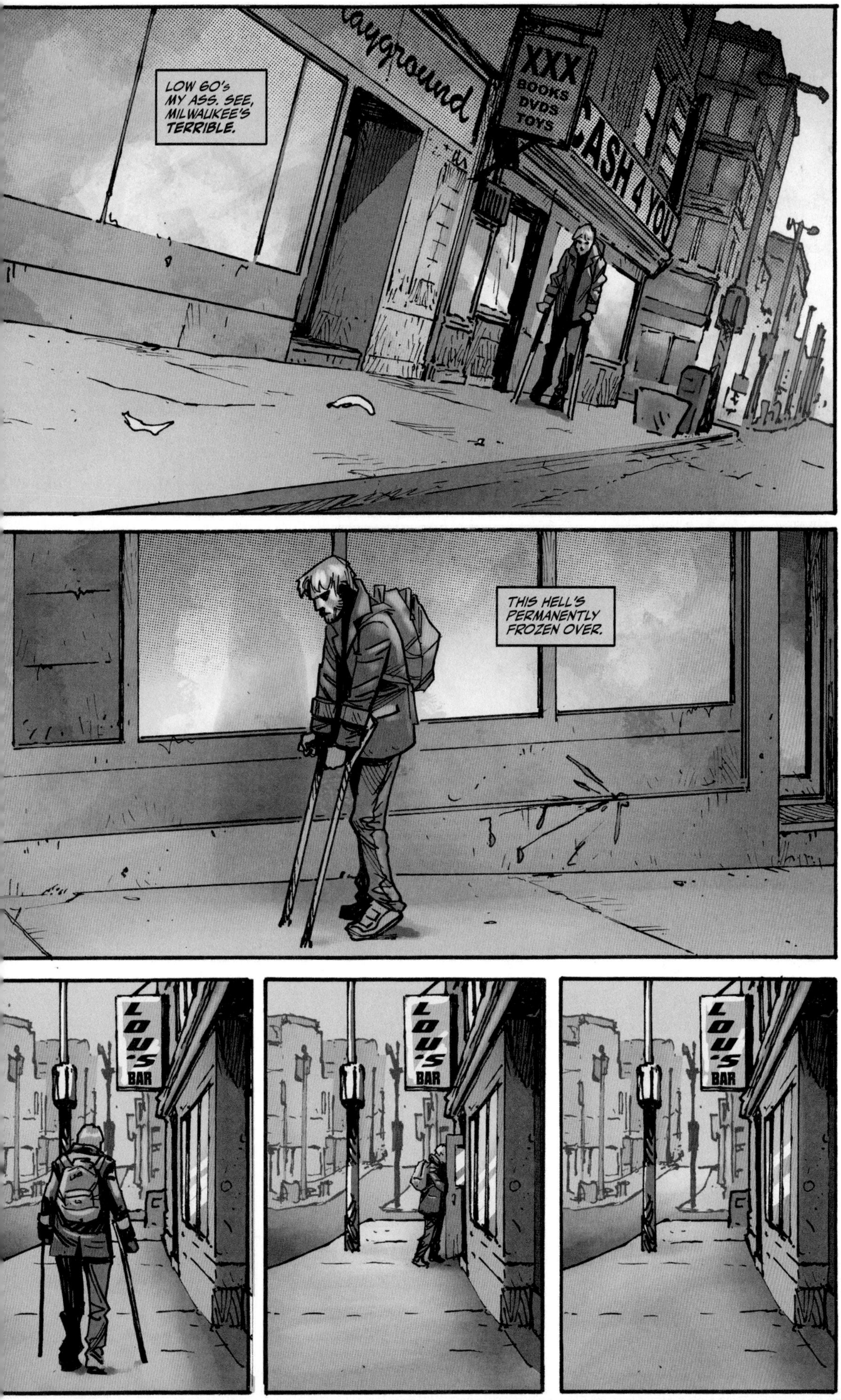
LOW 60's MY ASS. SEE, MILWAUKEE'S TERRIBLE.
XXX BOOKS DVDS TOYS
CASH 4 YOU
THIS HELL'S PERMANENTLY FROZEN OVER.
LOU'S BAR
LOU'S BAR
LOU'S BAR

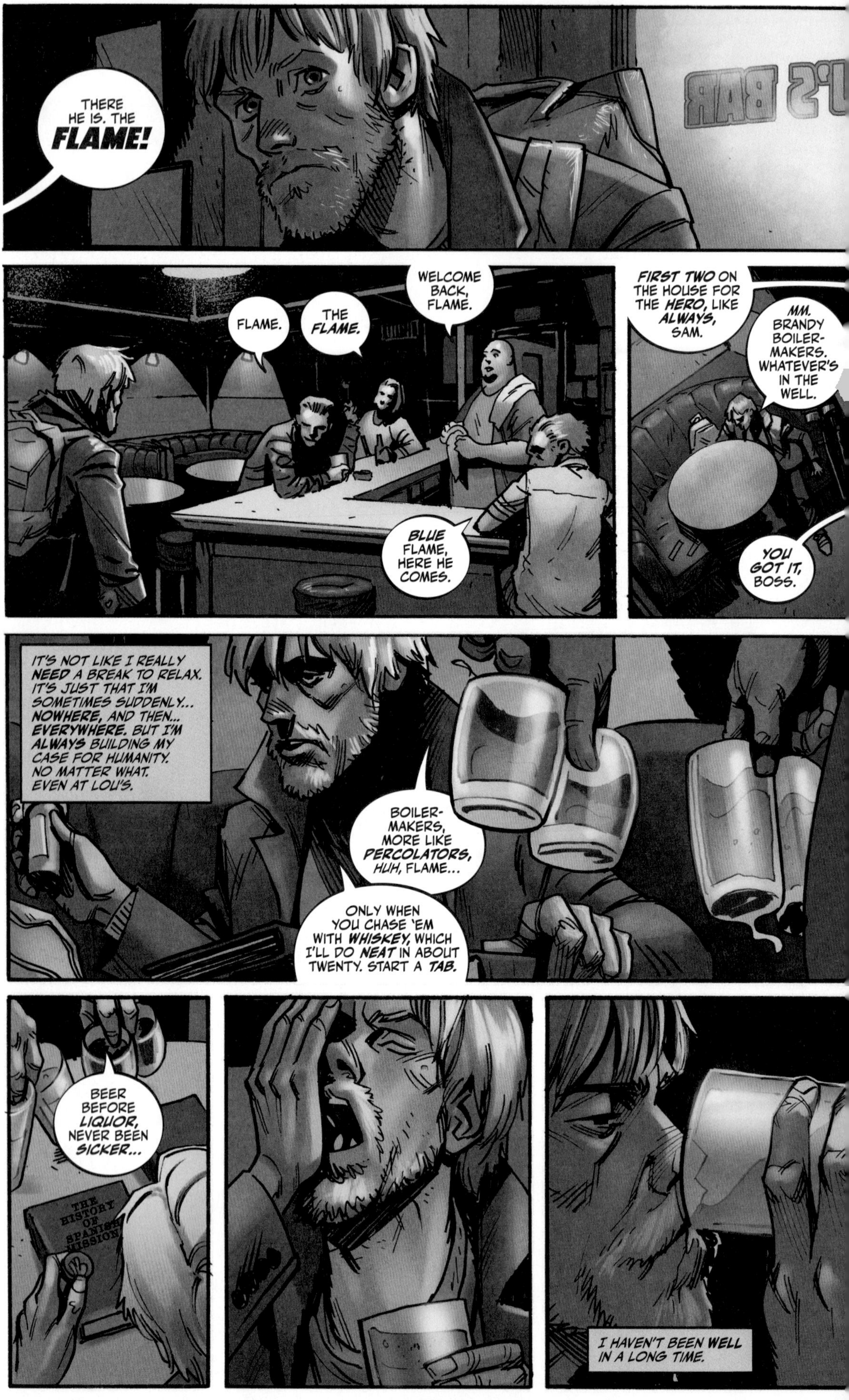
THERE HE IS. THE FLAME!
FLAME.
THE FLAME.
WELCOME BACK, FLAME.
BLUE FLAME, HERE HE COMES.
FIRST TWO ON THE HOUSE FOR THE HERO, LIKE ALWAYS, SAM.
MM. BRANDY BOILER-MAKERS. WHATEVER'S IN THE WELL.
YOU GOT IT, BOSS.
IT'S NOT LIKE I REALLY NEED A BREAK TO RELAX. IT'S JUST THAT I'M SOMETIMES SUDDENLY... NOWHERE, AND THEN... EVERYWHERE. BUT I'M ALWAYS BUILDING MY CASE FOR HUMANITY. NO MATTER WHAT. EVEN AT LOU'S.
BOILER-MAKERS, MORE LIKE PERCOLATORS, HUH, FLAME...
ONLY WHEN YOU CHASE 'EM WITH WHISKEY, WHICH I'LL DO NEAT IN ABOUT TWENTY. START A TAB.
BEER BEFORE LIQUOR, NEVER BEEN SICKER...
THE HISTORY OF SPANISH MISSION
I HAVEN'T BEEN WELL IN A LONG TIME.

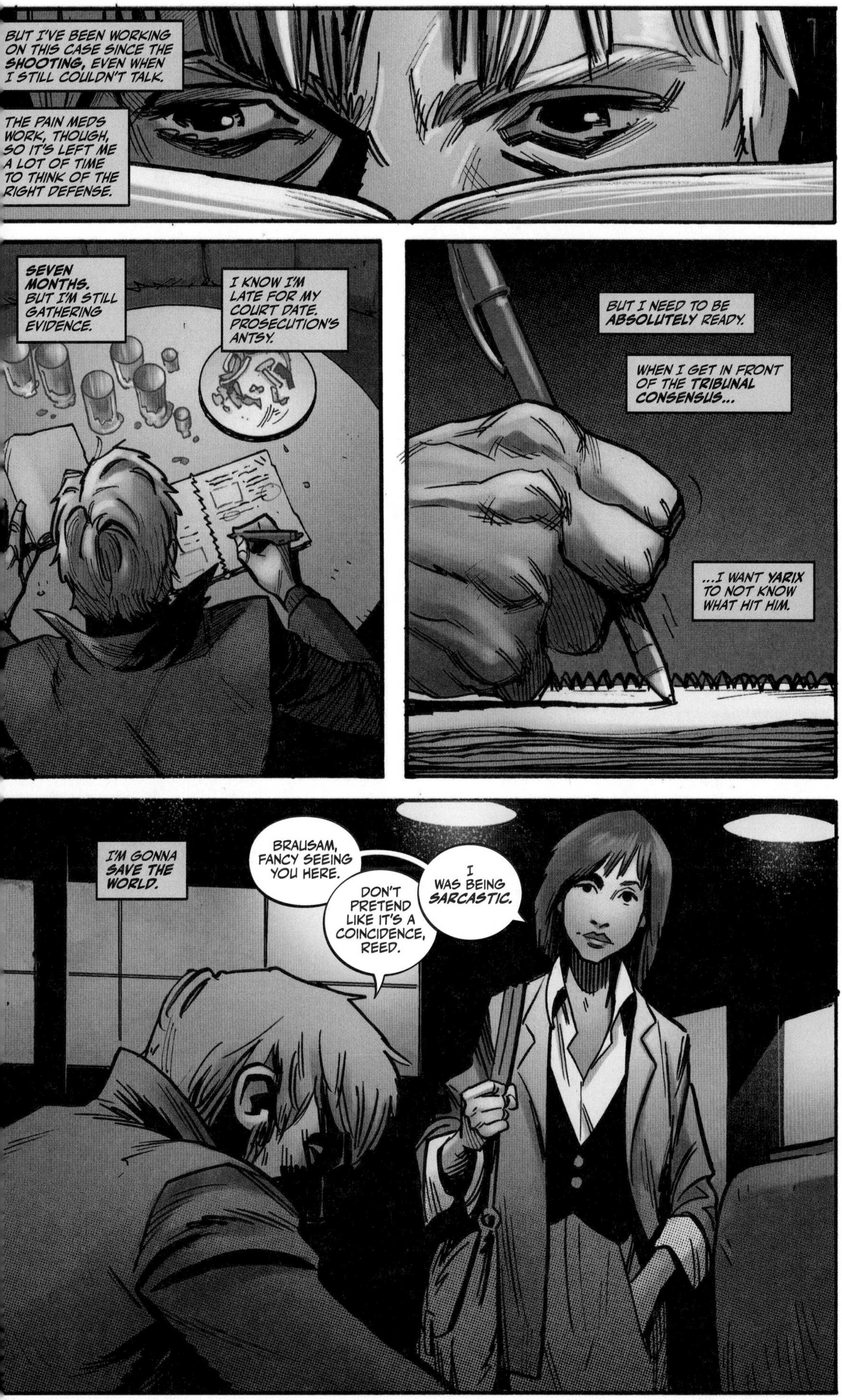
BUT I'VE BEEN WORKING ON THIS CASE SINCE THE SHOOTING, EVEN WHEN I STILL COULDN'T TALK.
THE PAIN MEDS WORK, THOUGH, SO IT'S LEFT ME A LOT OF TIME TO THINK OF THE RIGHT DEFENSE.
SEVEN MONTHS. BUT I'M STILL GATHERING EVIDENCE.
I KNOW I'M LATE FOR MY COURT DATE. PROSECUTION'S ANTSY.
BUT I NEED TO BE ABSOLUTELY READY.
WHEN I GET IN FRONT OF THE TRIBUNAL CONSENSUS...
...I WANT YARIX TO NOT KNOW WHAT HIT HIM.
I'M GONNA SAVE THE WORLD.
BRAUSAM, FANCY SEEING YOU HERE.
DON'T PRETEND LIKE IT'S A COINCIDENCE, REED.
I WAS BEING SARCASTIC.

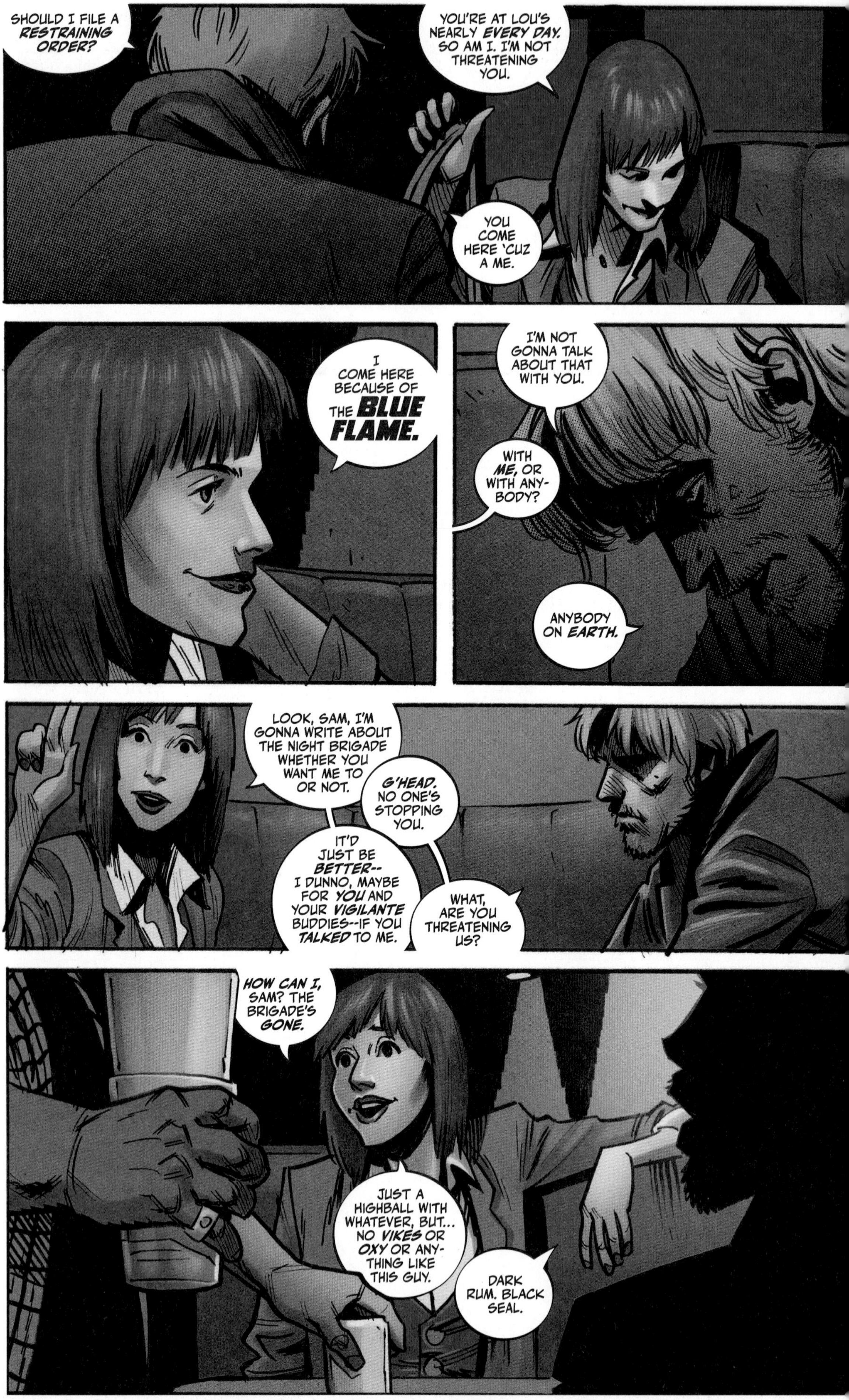
SHOULD I FILE A RESTRAINING ORDER?
YOU'RE AT LOU'S NEARLY EVERY DAY. SO AM I. I'M NOT THREATENING YOU.
YOU COME HERE 'CUZ A ME.
I COME HERE BECAUSE OF THE BLUE FLAME.
I'M NOT GONNA TALK ABOUT THAT WITH YOU.
WITH ME, OR WITH ANY-BODY?
ANYBODY ON EARTH.
LOOK, SAM, I'M GONNA WRITE ABOUT THE NIGHT BRIGADE WHETHER YOU WANT ME TO OR NOT.
G'HEAD. NO ONE'S STOPPING YOU.
IT'D JUST BE BETTER-- I DUNNO, MAYBE FOR YOU AND YOUR VIGILANTE BUDDIES--IF YOU TALKED TO ME.
WHAT, ARE YOU THREATENING US?
HOW CAN I, SAM? THE BRIGADE'S GONE.
JUST A HIGHBALL WITH WHATEVER, BUT... NO VIKES OR OXY OR ANY-THING LIKE THIS GUY.
DARK RUM. BLACK SEAL.

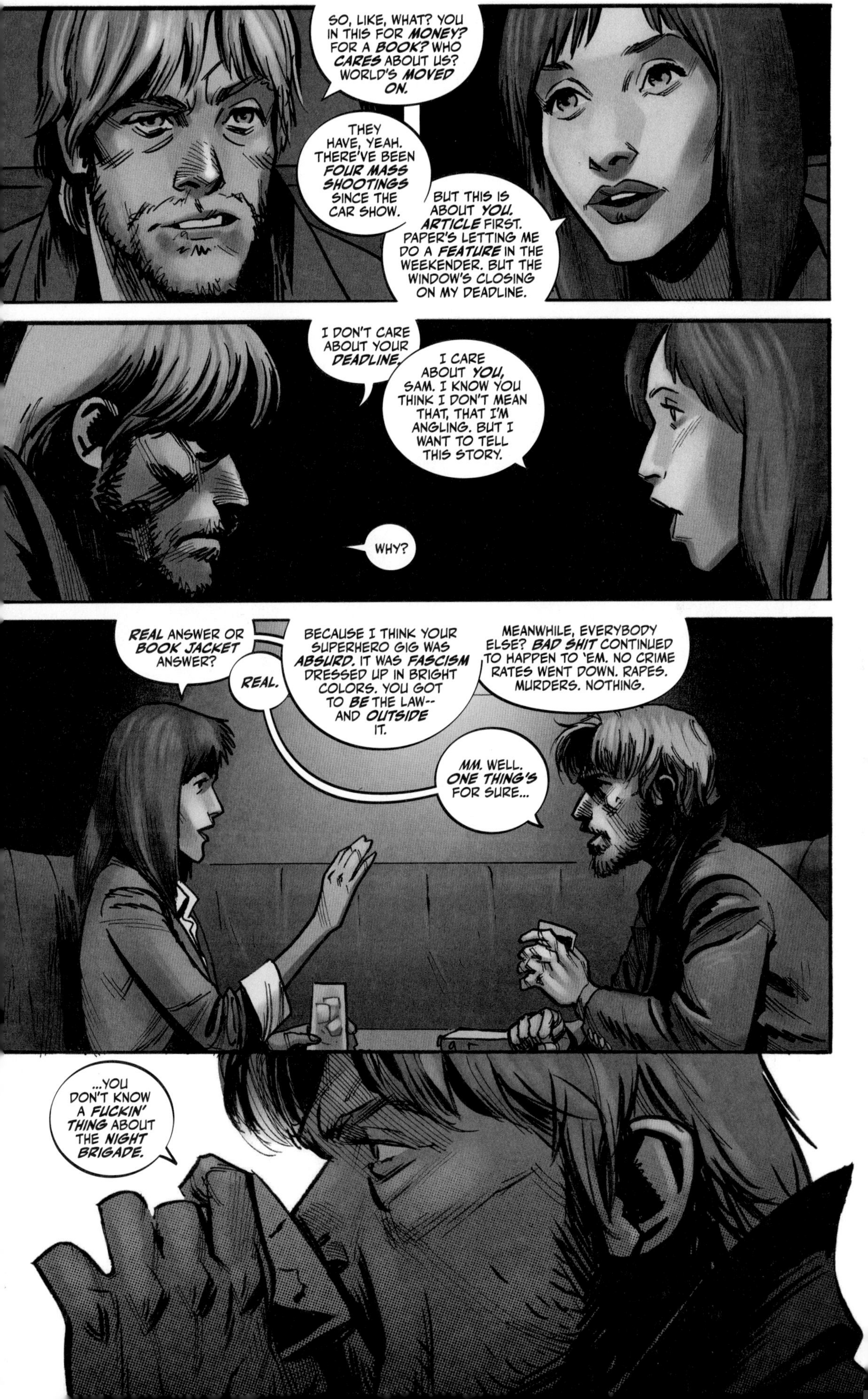
SO, LIKE, WHAT? YOU IN THIS FOR MONEY? FOR A BOOK? WHO CARES ABOUT US? WORLD'S MOVED ON.
THEY HAVE, YEAH. THERE'VE BEEN FOUR MASS SHOOTINGS SINCE THE CAR SHOW.
BUT THIS IS ABOUT YOU. ARTICLE FIRST. PAPER'S LETTING ME DO A FEATURE IN THE WEEKENDER. BUT THE WINDOW'S CLOSING ON MY DEADLINE.
I DON'T CARE ABOUT YOUR DEADLINE.
I CARE ABOUT YOU, SAM. I KNOW YOU THINK I DON'T MEAN THAT, THAT I'M ANGLING. BUT I WANT TO TELL THIS STORY.
WHY?
REAL ANSWER OR BOOK JACKET ANSWER?
REAL.
BECAUSE I THINK YOUR SUPERHERO GIG WAS ABSURD. IT WAS FASCISM DRESSED UP IN BRIGHT COLORS. YOU GOT TO BE THE LAW-- AND OUTSIDE IT.
MEANWHILE, EVERYBODY ELSE? BAD SHIT CONTINUED TO HAPPEN TO 'EM. NO CRIME RATES WENT DOWN. RAPES. MURDERS. NOTHING.
MM. WELL. ONE THING'S FOR SURE...
...YOU DON'T KNOW A FUCKIN' THING ABOUT THE NIGHT BRIGADE.

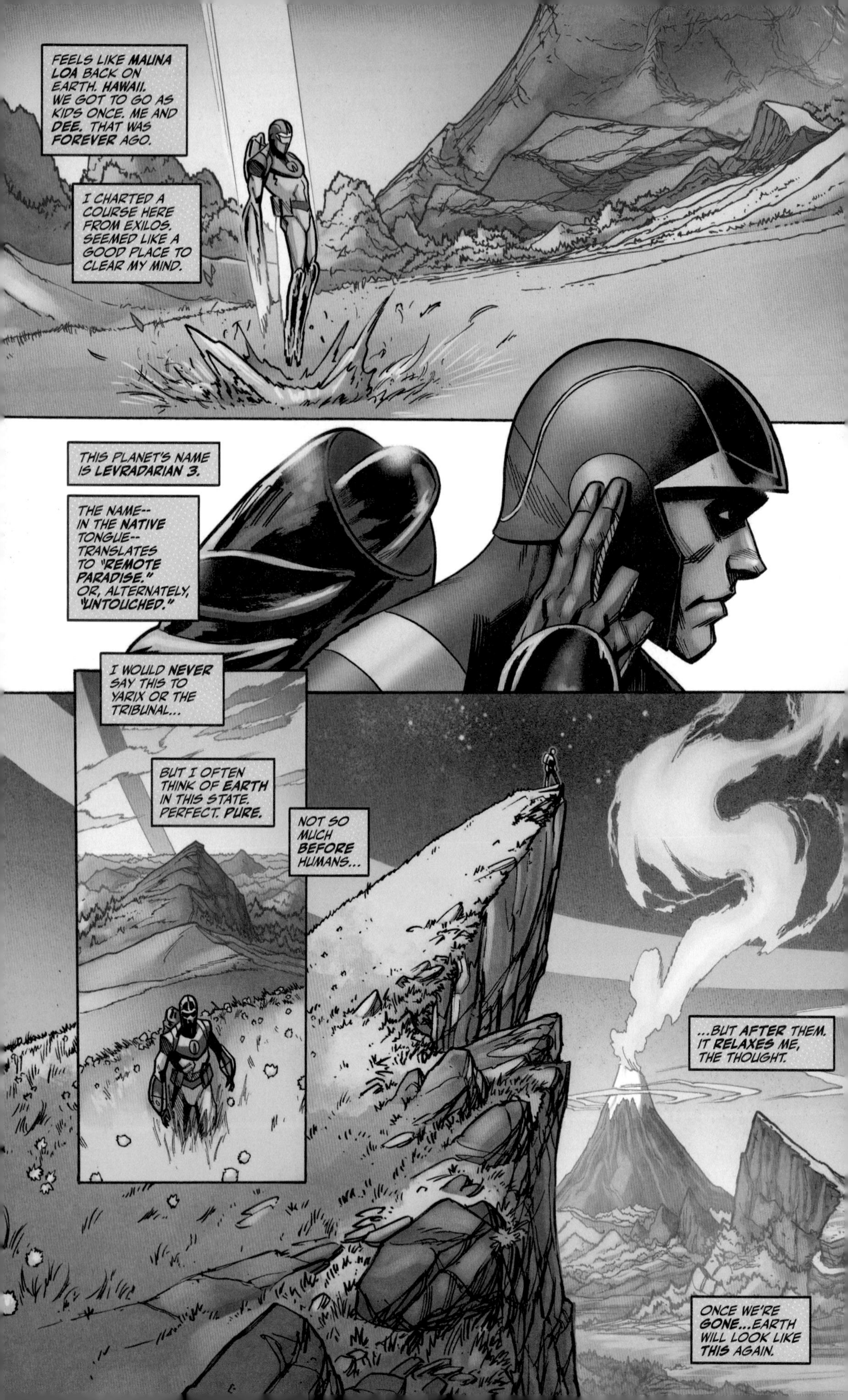
FEELS LIKE MAUNA LOA BACK ON EARTH. HAWAII. WE GOT TO GO AS KIDS ONCE. ME AND DEE. THAT WAS FOREVER AGO.
I CHARTED A COURSE HERE FROM EXILOS. SEEMED LIKE A GOOD PLACE TO CLEAR MY MIND.
THIS PLANET'S NAME IS LEVRADARIAN 3.
THE NAME-- IN THE NATIVE TONGUE-- TRANSLATES TO "REMOTE PARADISE." OR, ALTERNATELY, "UNTOUCHED."
I WOULD NEVER SAY THIS TO YARIX OR THE TRIBUNAL...
BUT I OFTEN THINK OF EARTH IN THIS STATE. PERFECT. PURE.
NOT SO MUCH BEFORE HUMANS...
...BUT AFTER THEM. IT RELAXES ME, THE THOUGHT.
ONCE WE'RE GONE...EARTH WILL LOOK LIKE THIS AGAIN.

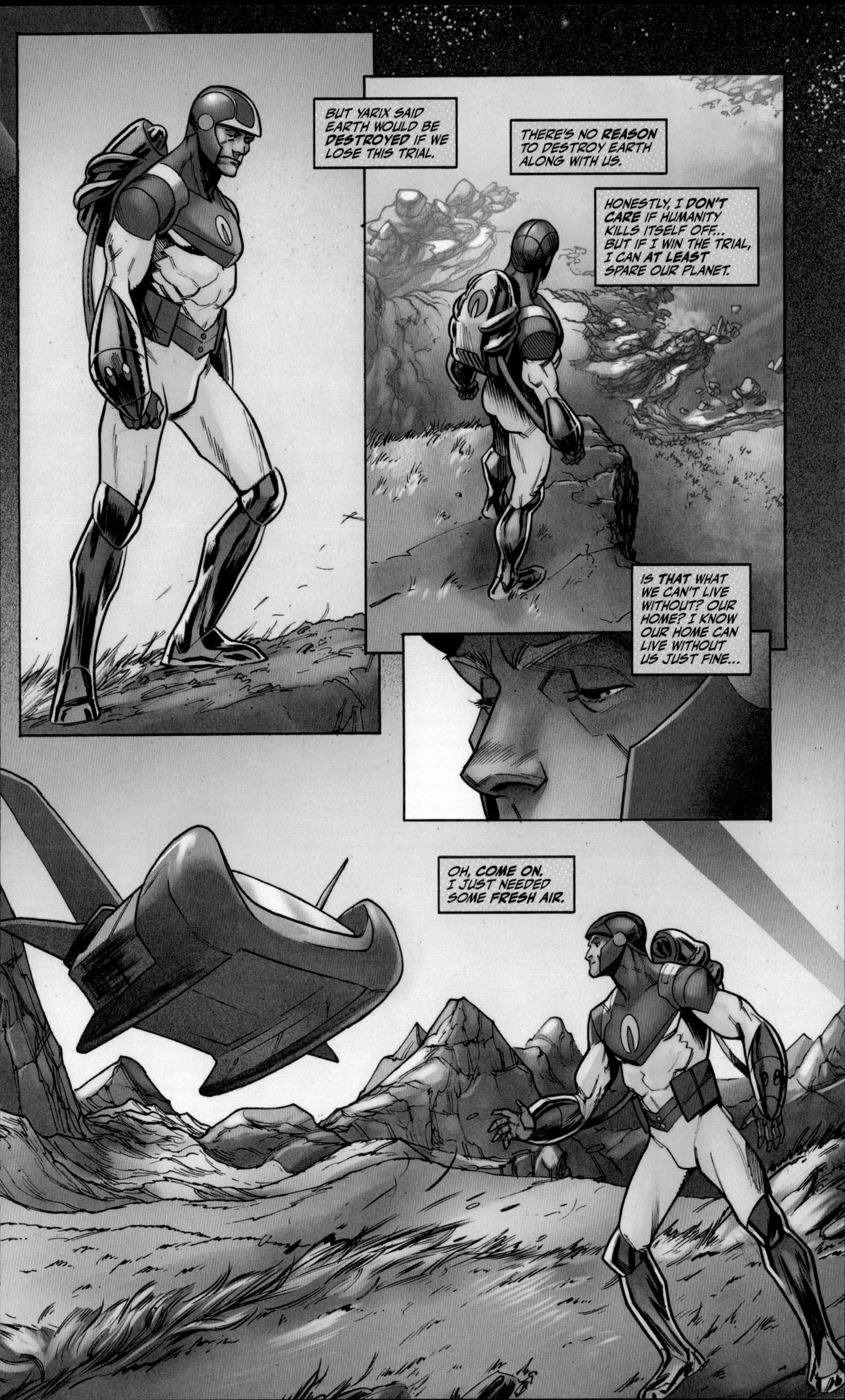
BUT YARIX SAID EARTH WOULD BE DESTROYED IF WE LOSE THIS TRIAL.
THERE'S NO REASON TO DESTROY EARTH ALONG WITH US.
HONESTLY, I DON'T CARE IF HUMANITY KILLS ITSELF OFF... BUT IF I WIN THE TRIAL, I CAN AT LEAST SPARE OUR PLANET.
IS THAT WHAT WE CAN'T LIVE WITHOUT? OUR HOME? I KNOW OUR HOME CAN LIVE WITHOUT US JUST FINE...
OH, COME ON. I JUST NEEDED SOME FRESH AIR.

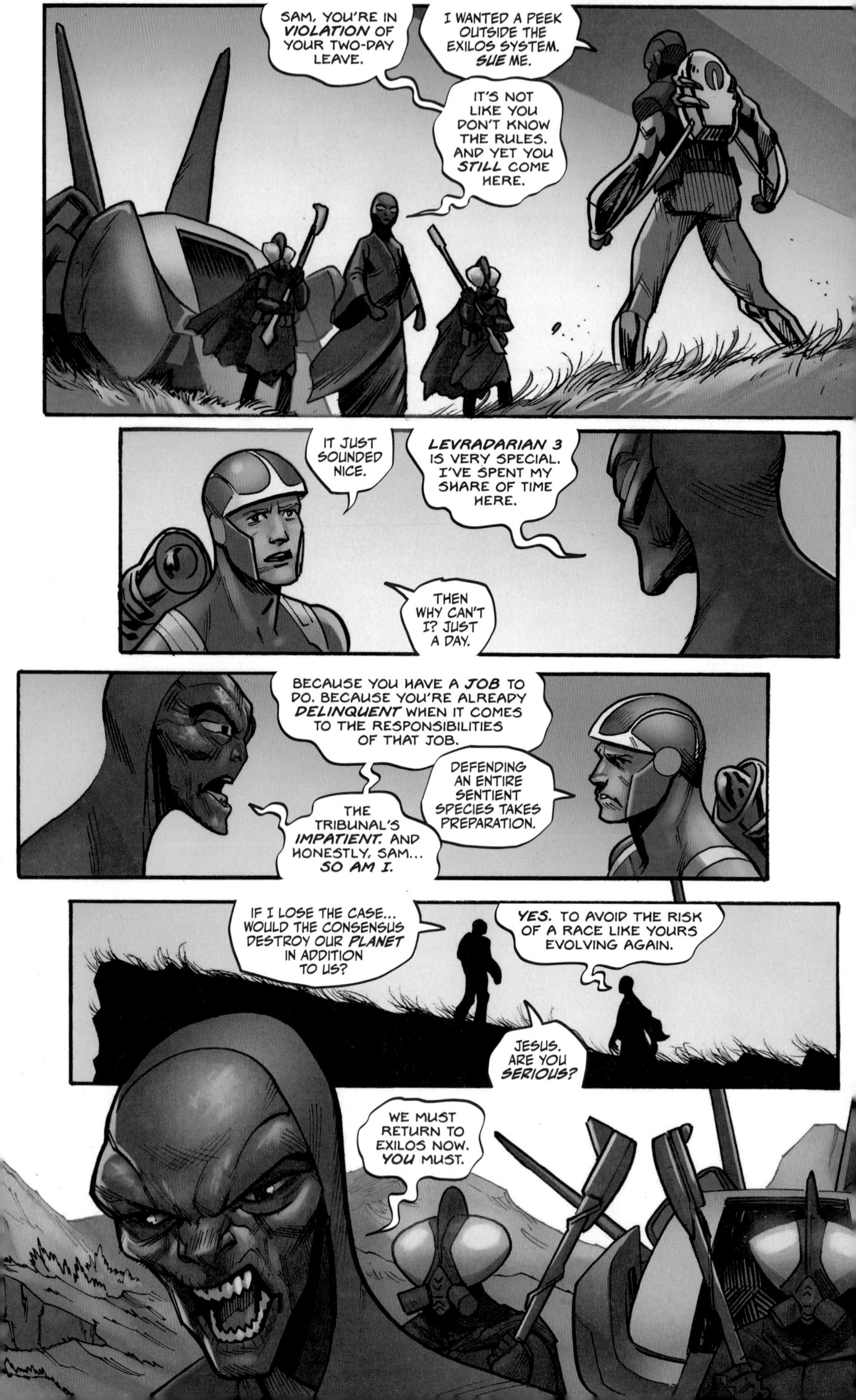
SAM, YOU'RE IN VIOLATION OF YOUR TWO-DAY LEAVE.
I WANTED A PEEK OUTSIDE THE EXILOS SYSTEM. SUE ME.
IT'S NOT LIKE YOU DON'T KNOW THE RULES. AND YET YOU STILL COME HERE.
IT JUST SOUNDED NICE.
LEVRADARIAN 3 IS VERY SPECIAL. I'VE SPENT MY SHARE OF TIME HERE.
THEN WHY CAN'T I? JUST A DAY.
BECAUSE YOU HAVE A JOB TO DO. BECAUSE YOU'RE ALREADY DELINQUENT WHEN IT COMES TO THE RESPONSIBILITIES OF THAT JOB.
DEFENDING AN ENTIRE SENTIENT SPECIES TAKES PREPARATION.
THE TRIBUNAL'S IMPATIENT. AND HONESTLY, SAM... SO AM I.
IF I LOSE THE CASE... WOULD THE CONSENSUS DESTROY OUR PLANET IN ADDITION TO US?
YES. TO AVOID THE RISK OF A RACE LIKE YOURS EVOLVING AGAIN.
JESUS. ARE YOU SERIOUS?
WE MUST RETURN TO EXILOS NOW. YOU MUST.

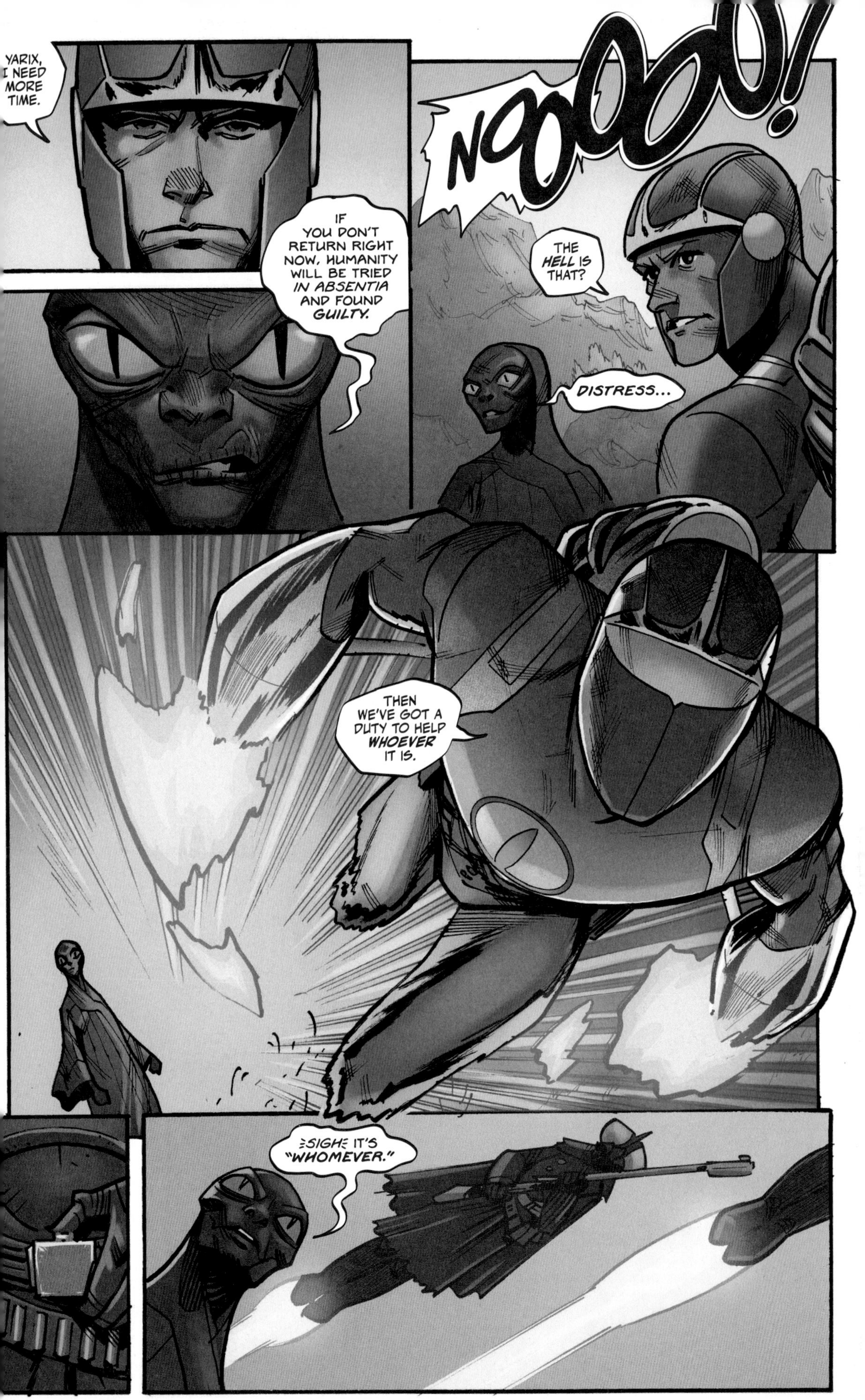
YARIX, I NEED MORE TIME.
IF YOU DON'T RETURN RIGHT NOW, HUMANITY WILL BE TRIED IN ABSENTIA AND FOUND GUILTY.
NOOOOOO!
THE HELL IS THAT?
DISTRESS...
THEN WE'VE GOT A DUTY TO HELP WHOEVER IT IS.
≡SIGH≡ IT'S "WHOMEVER."

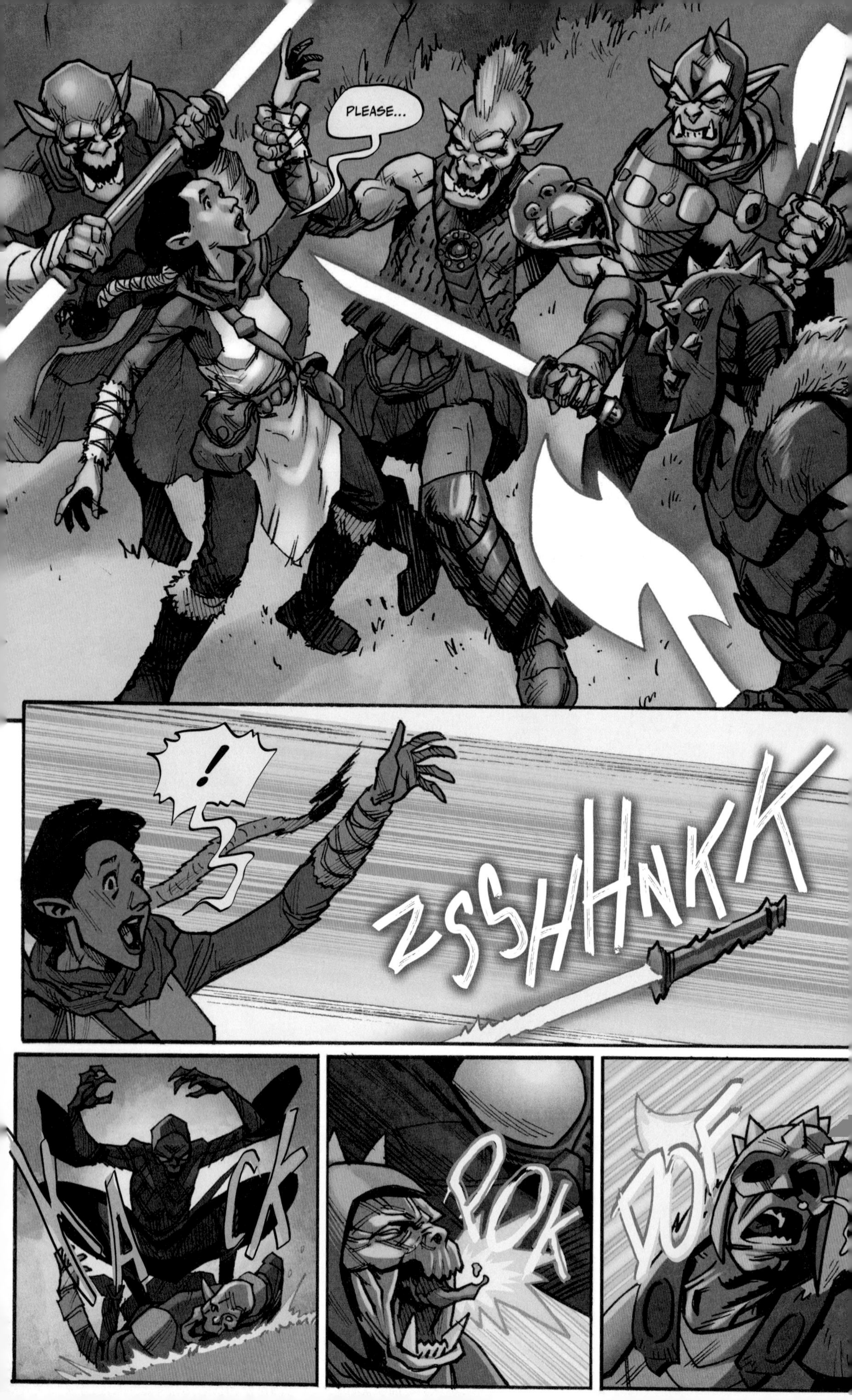

PLEASE...
!
ZSSHHNKK
KACK
POK
DOOF

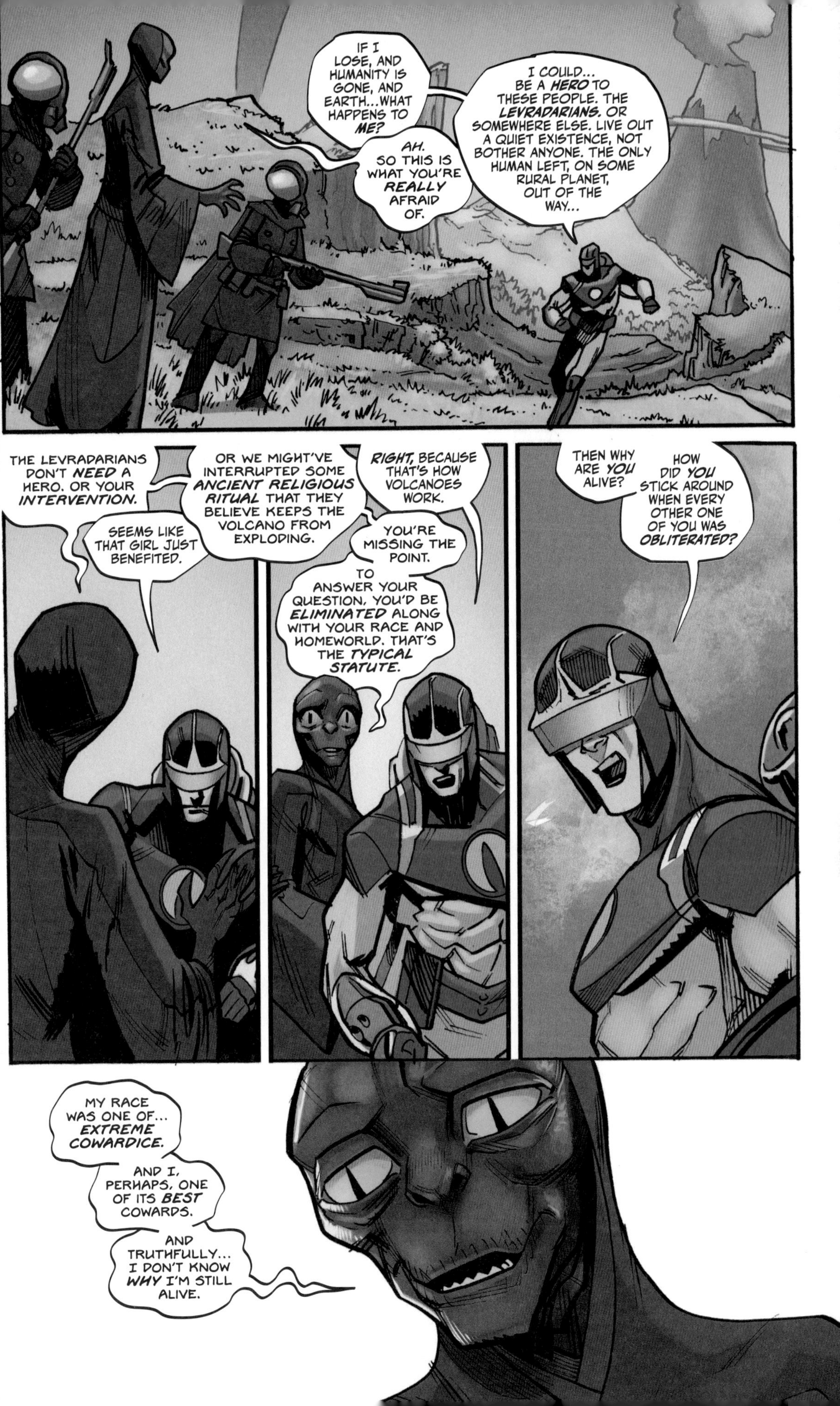
IF I LOSE, AND HUMANITY IS GONE, AND EARTH...WHAT HAPPENS TO ME?
AH. SO THIS IS WHAT YOU'RE REALLY AFRAID OF.
I COULD... BE A HERO TO THESE PEOPLE. THE LEVRADARIANS. OR SOMEWHERE ELSE. LIVE OUT A QUIET EXISTENCE, NOT BOTHER ANYONE. THE ONLY HUMAN LEFT, ON SOME RURAL PLANET, OUT OF THE WAY...
THE LEVRADARIANS DON'T NEED A HERO. OR YOUR INTERVENTION.
SEEMS LIKE THAT GIRL JUST BENEFITED.
OR WE MIGHT'VE INTERRUPTED SOME ANCIENT RELIGIOUS RITUAL THAT THEY BELIEVE KEEPS THE VOLCANO FROM EXPLODING.
RIGHT, BECAUSE THAT'S HOW VOLCANOES WORK.
YOU'RE MISSING THE POINT.
TO ANSWER YOUR QUESTION, YOU'D BE ELIMINATED ALONG WITH YOUR RACE AND HOMEWORLD. THAT'S THE TYPICAL STATUTE.
THEN WHY ARE YOU ALIVE?
HOW DID YOU STICK AROUND WHEN EVERY OTHER ONE OF YOU WAS OBLITERATED?
MY RACE WAS ONE OF... EXTREME COWARDICE.
AND I, PERHAPS, ONE OF ITS BEST COWARDS.
AND TRUTHFULLY... I DON'T KNOW WHY I'M STILL ALIVE.

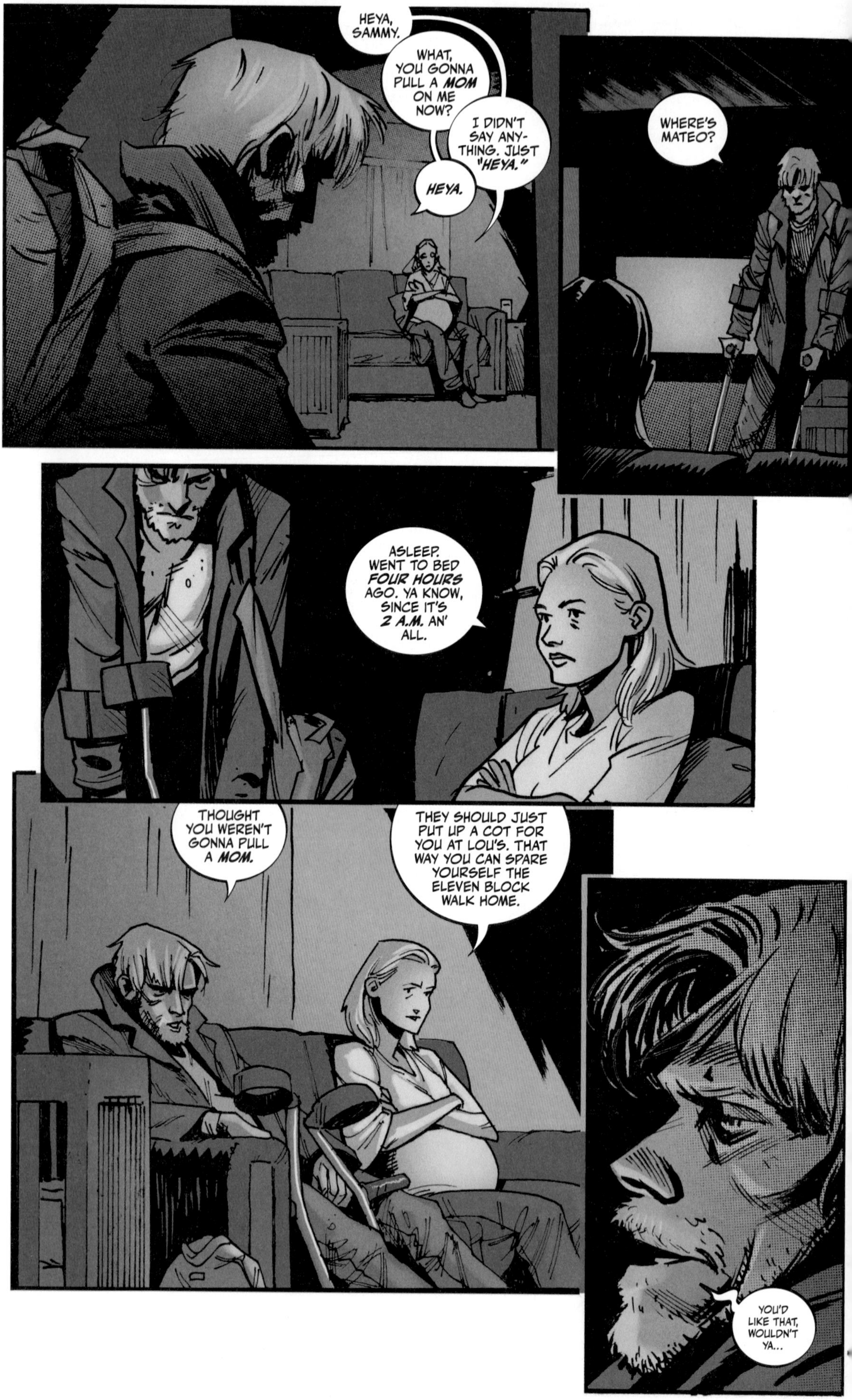
HEYA, SAMMY.
WHAT, YOU GONNA PULL A *MOM* ON ME NOW?
I DIDN'T SAY ANY-THING. JUST *"HEYA."*
HEYA.
WHERE'S MATEO?
ASLEEP. WENT TO BED *FOUR HOURS* AGO. YA KNOW, SINCE IT'S *2 A.M.* AN' ALL.
THOUGHT YOU WEREN'T GONNA PULL A *MOM.*
THEY SHOULD JUST PUT UP A COT FOR YOU AT LOU'S. THAT WAY YOU CAN SPARE YOURSELF THE ELEVEN BLOCK WALK HOME.
YOU'D LIKE THAT, WOULDN'T YA...

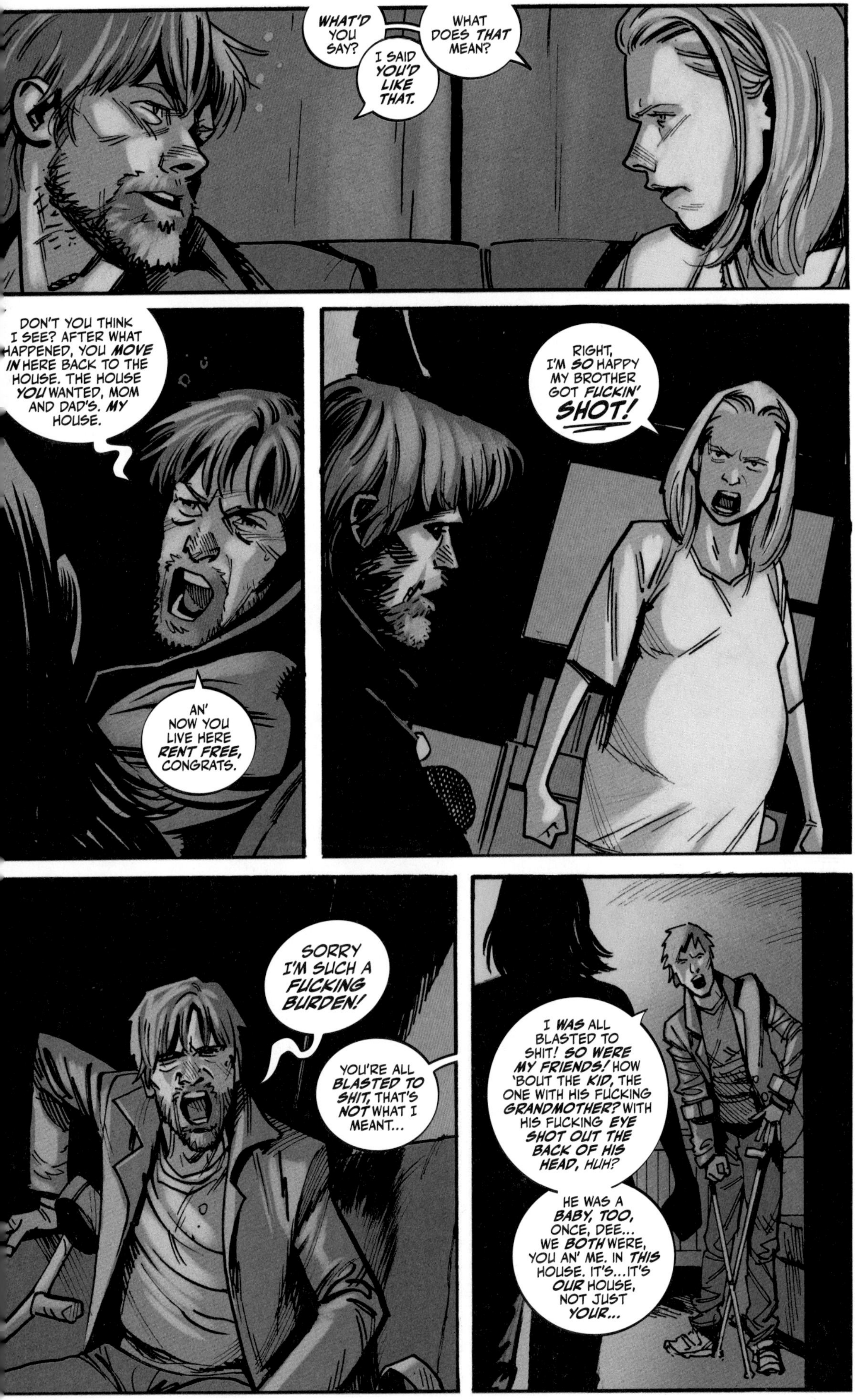
WHAT'D YOU SAY?
WHAT DOES THAT MEAN?
I SAID YOU'D LIKE THAT.
DON'T YOU THINK I SEE? AFTER WHAT HAPPENED, YOU MOVE IN HERE BACK TO THE HOUSE. THE HOUSE YOU WANTED, MOM AND DAD'S. MY HOUSE.
AN' NOW YOU LIVE HERE RENT FREE, CONGRATS.
RIGHT, I'M SO HAPPY MY BROTHER GOT FUCKIN' SHOT!
SORRY I'M SUCH A FUCKING BURDEN!
YOU'RE ALL BLASTED TO SHIT, THAT'S NOT WHAT I MEANT...
I WAS ALL BLASTED TO SHIT! SO WERE MY FRIENDS! HOW 'BOUT THE KID, THE ONE WITH HIS FUCKING GRANDMOTHER? WITH HIS FUCKING EYE SHOT OUT THE BACK OF HIS HEAD, HUH?
HE WAS A BABY, TOO, ONCE, DEE... WE BOTH WERE, YOU AN' ME. IN THIS HOUSE. IT'S...IT'S OUR HOUSE, NOT JUST YOUR...

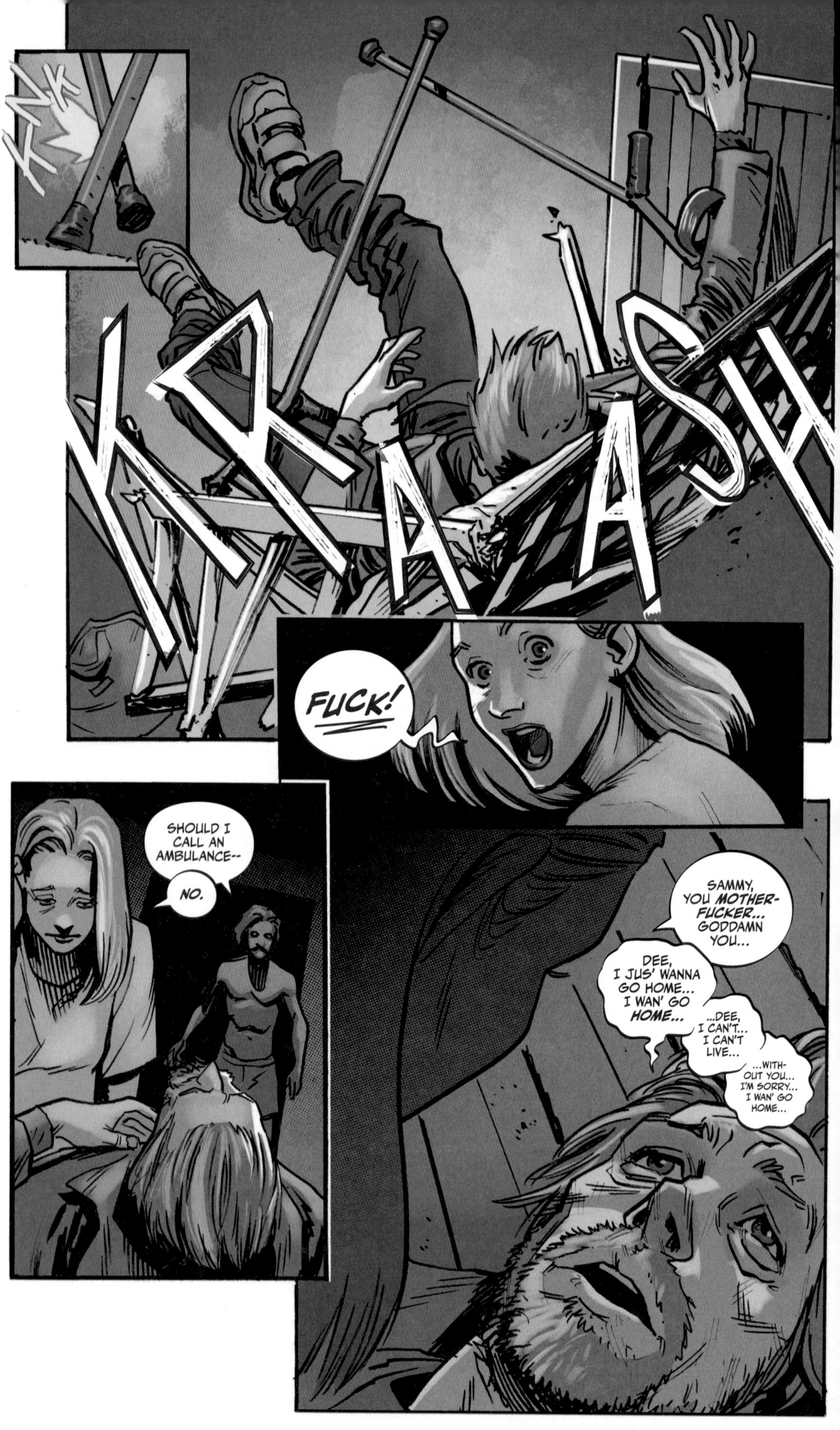

KRAASH
FUCK!
SHOULD I CALL AN AMBULANCE--
NO.
SAMMY, YOU MOTHER-FUCKER... GODDAMN YOU...
DEE, I JUS' WANNA GO HOME... I WAN' GO HOME...
...DEE, I CAN'T... I CAN'T LIVE...
...WITH-OUT YOU... I'M SORRY... I WAN' GO HOME...

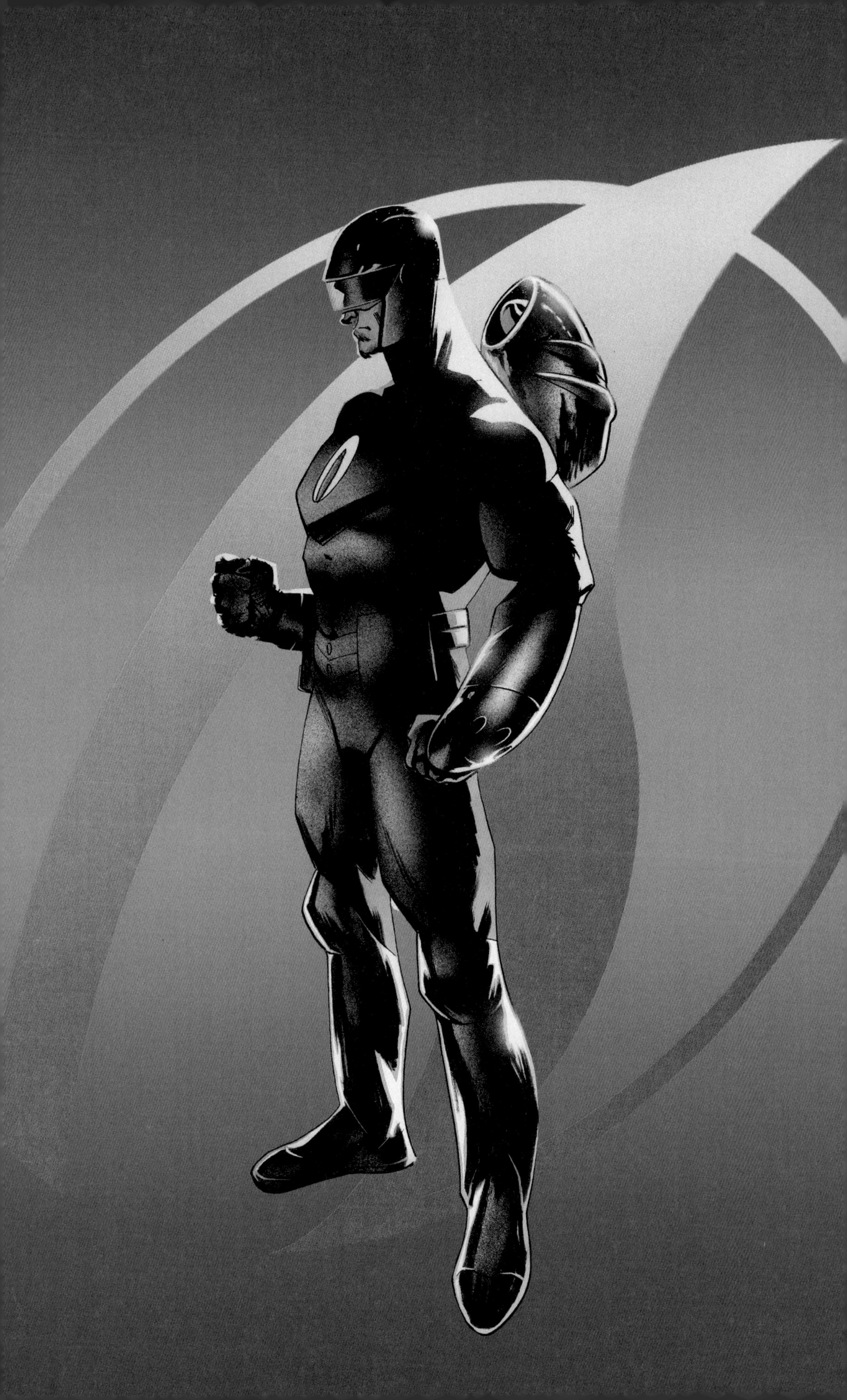

FUTURE IN PERIL

CHAPTER 4

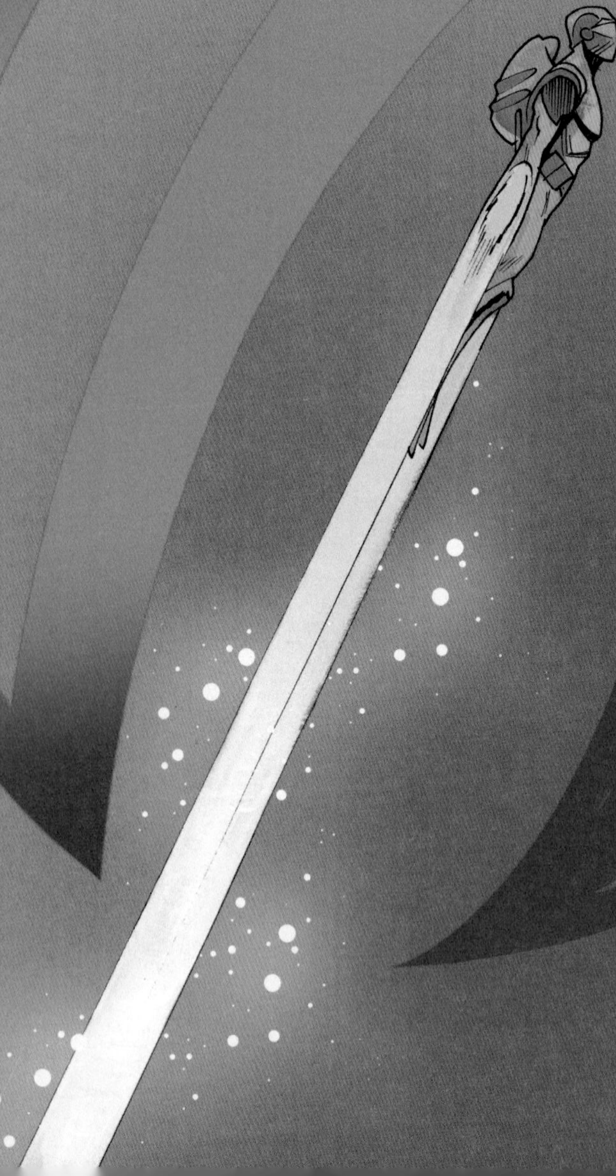

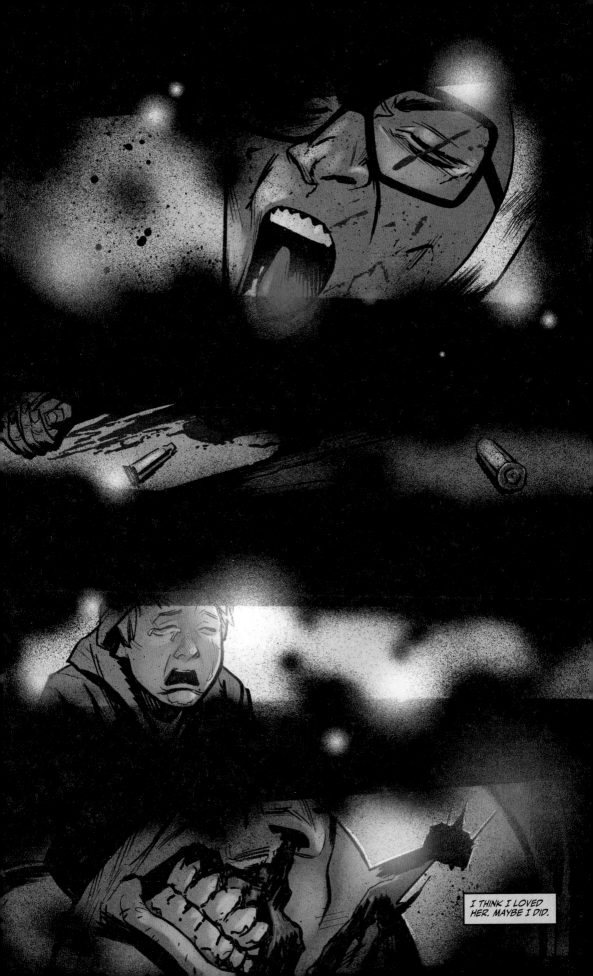

I THINK I LOVED
HER. MAYBE I DID.

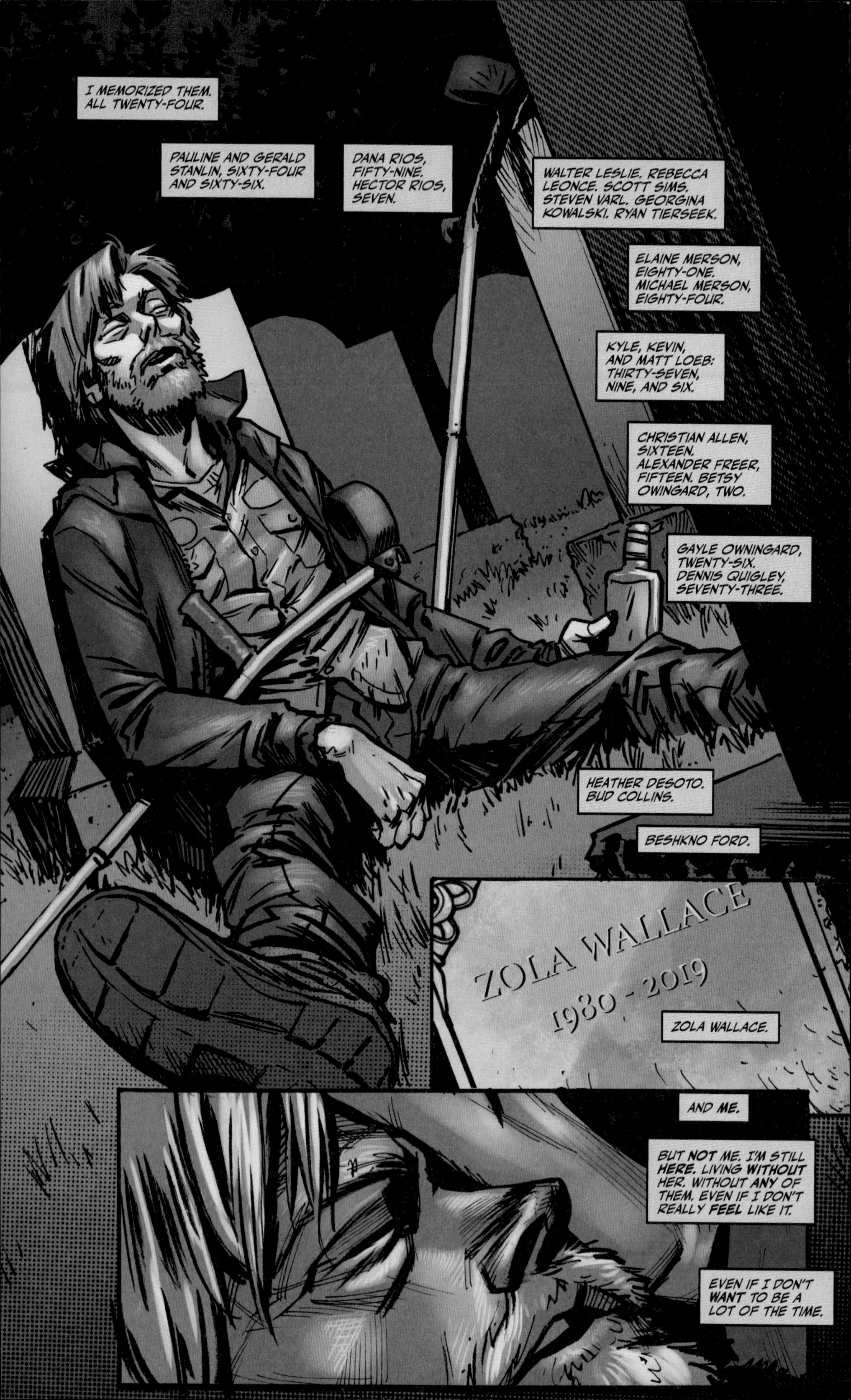
I MEMORIZED THEM. ALL TWENTY-FOUR.
PAULINE AND GERALD STANLIN, SIXTY-FOUR AND SIXTY-SIX.
DANA RIOS, FIFTY-NINE. HECTOR RIOS, SEVEN.
WALTER LESLIE. REBECCA LEONCE. SCOTT SIMS. STEVEN VARL. GEORGINA KOWALSKI. RYAN TIERSEEK.
ELAINE MERSON, EIGHTY-ONE. MICHAEL MERSON, EIGHTY-FOUR.
KYLE, KEVIN, AND MATT LOEB: THIRTY-SEVEN, NINE, AND SIX.
CHRISTIAN ALLEN, SIXTEEN. ALEXANDER FREER, FIFTEEN. BETSY OWINGARD, TWO.
GAYLE OWNINGARD, TWENTY-SIX. DENNIS QUIGLEY, SEVENTY-THREE.
HEATHER DESOTO. BUD COLLINS.
BESHKNO FORD.
ZOLA WALLACE
1980 - 2019
ZOLA WALLACE.
AND **ME**.
BUT **NOT ME**. I'M STILL **HERE**. LIVING **WITHOUT** HER. WITHOUT **ANY** OF THEM. EVEN IF I DON'T REALLY **FEEL** LIKE IT.
EVEN IF I DON'T **WANT** TO BE A LOT OF THE TIME.

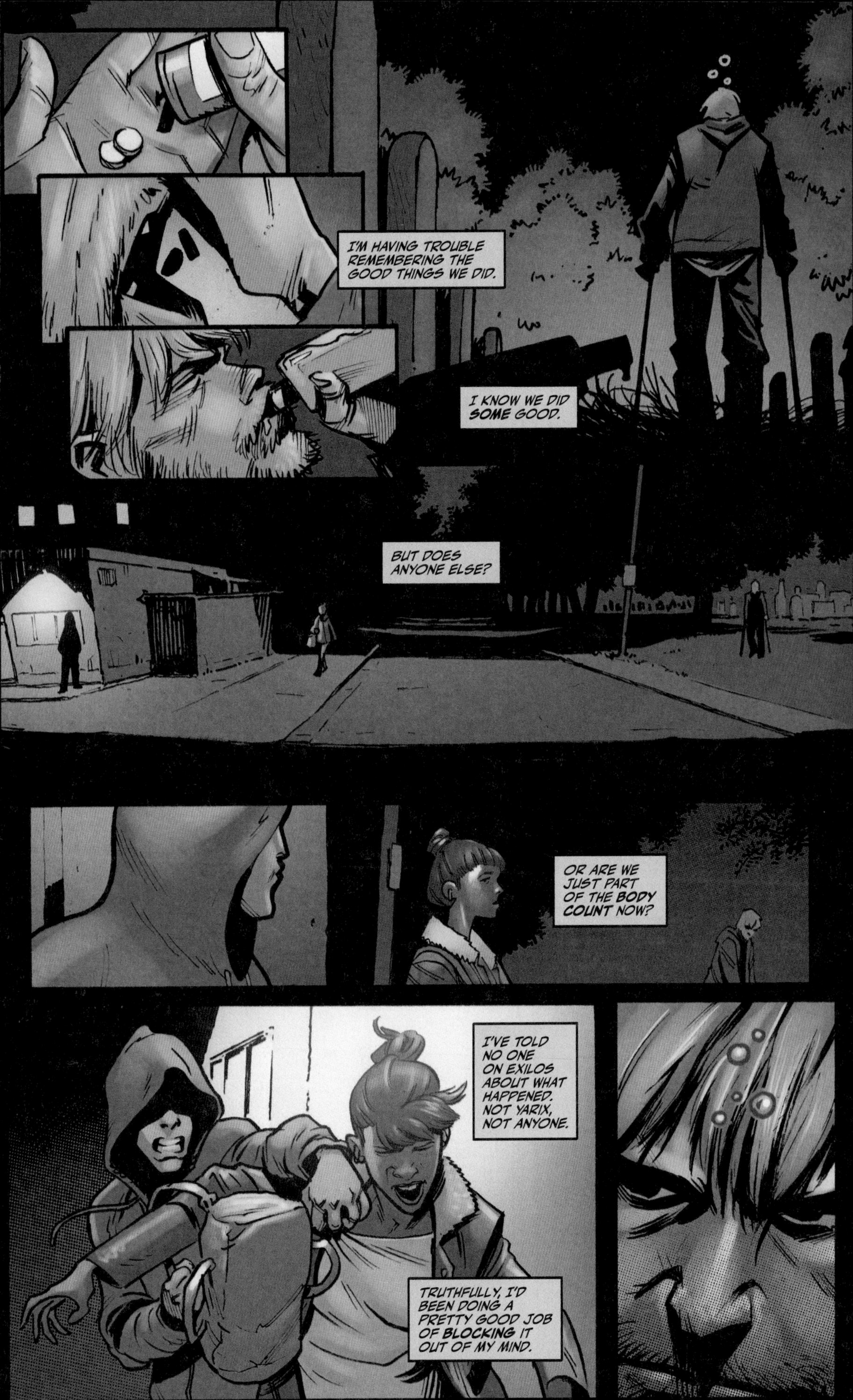
I'M HAVING TROUBLE REMEMBERING THE GOOD THINGS WE DID.
I KNOW WE DID SOME GOOD.
BUT DOES ANYONE ELSE?
OR ARE WE JUST PART OF THE BODY COUNT NOW?
I'VE TOLD NO ONE ON EXILOS ABOUT WHAT HAPPENED. NOT YARIX, NOT ANYONE.
TRUTHFULLY, I'D BEEN DOING A PRETTY GOOD JOB OF BLOCKING IT OUT OF MY MIND.

I THINK WE WERE HEROES.

I THOUGHT I WAS.

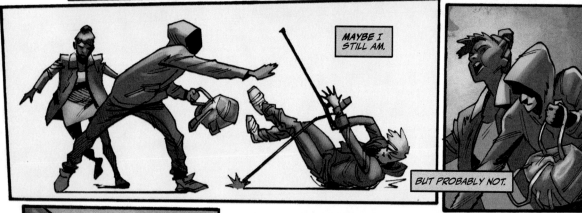

MAYBE I STILL AM.

BUT PROBABLY NOT.

I SHOULD'VE DIED WITH THEM.

WHY DIDN'T I DIE?

"IS THE PROSECUTION PREPARED?"

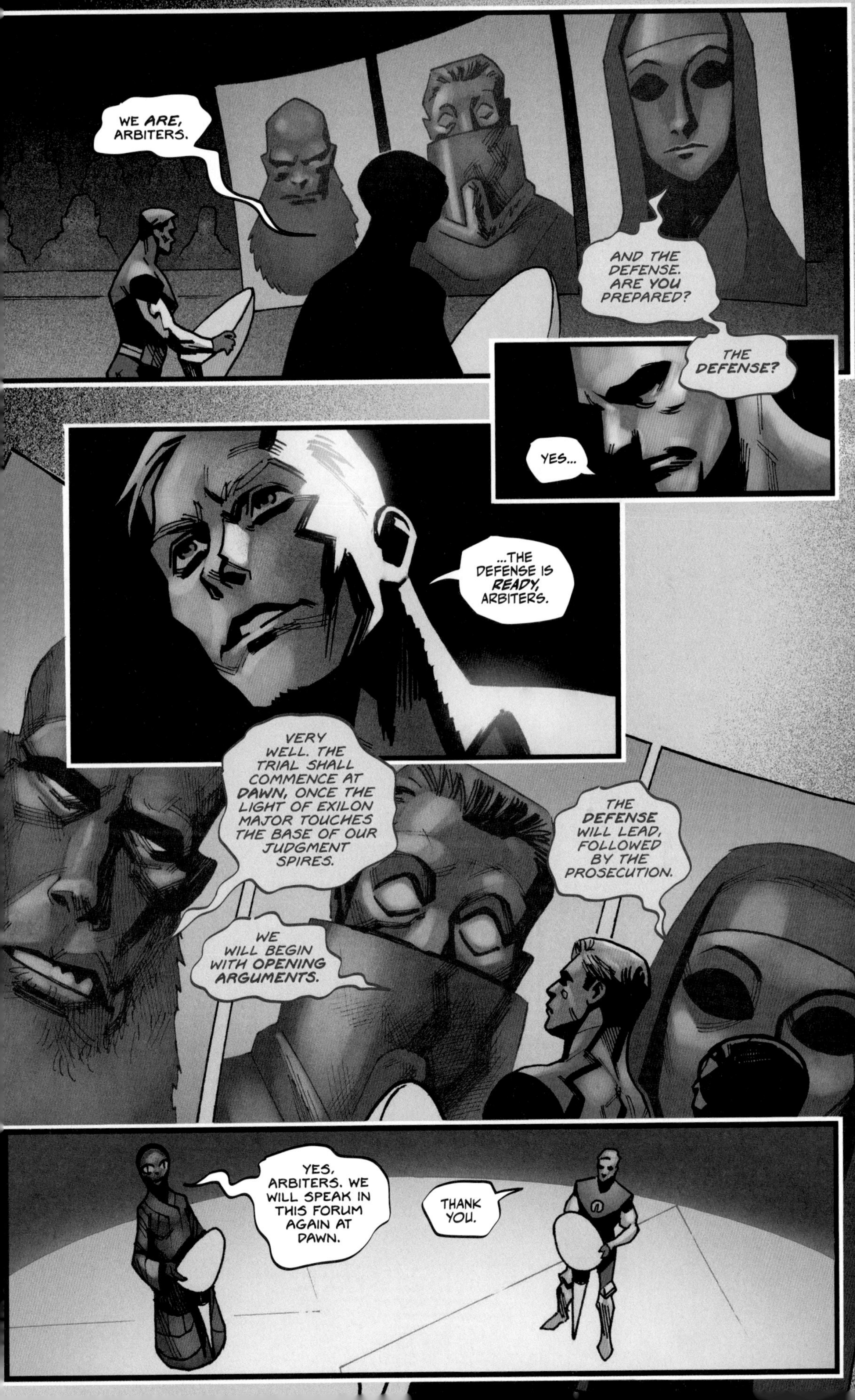
WE ARE, ARBITERS.
AND THE DEFENSE. ARE YOU PREPARED?
THE DEFENSE?
YES...
...THE DEFENSE IS READY, ARBITERS.
VERY WELL. THE TRIAL SHALL COMMENCE AT DAWN, ONCE THE LIGHT OF EXILON MAJOR TOUCHES THE BASE OF OUR JUDGMENT SPIRES.
THE DEFENSE WILL LEAD, FOLLOWED BY THE PROSECUTION.
WE WILL BEGIN WITH OPENING ARGUMENTS.
YES, ARBITERS. WE WILL SPEAK IN THIS FORUM AGAIN AT DAWN.
THANK YOU.

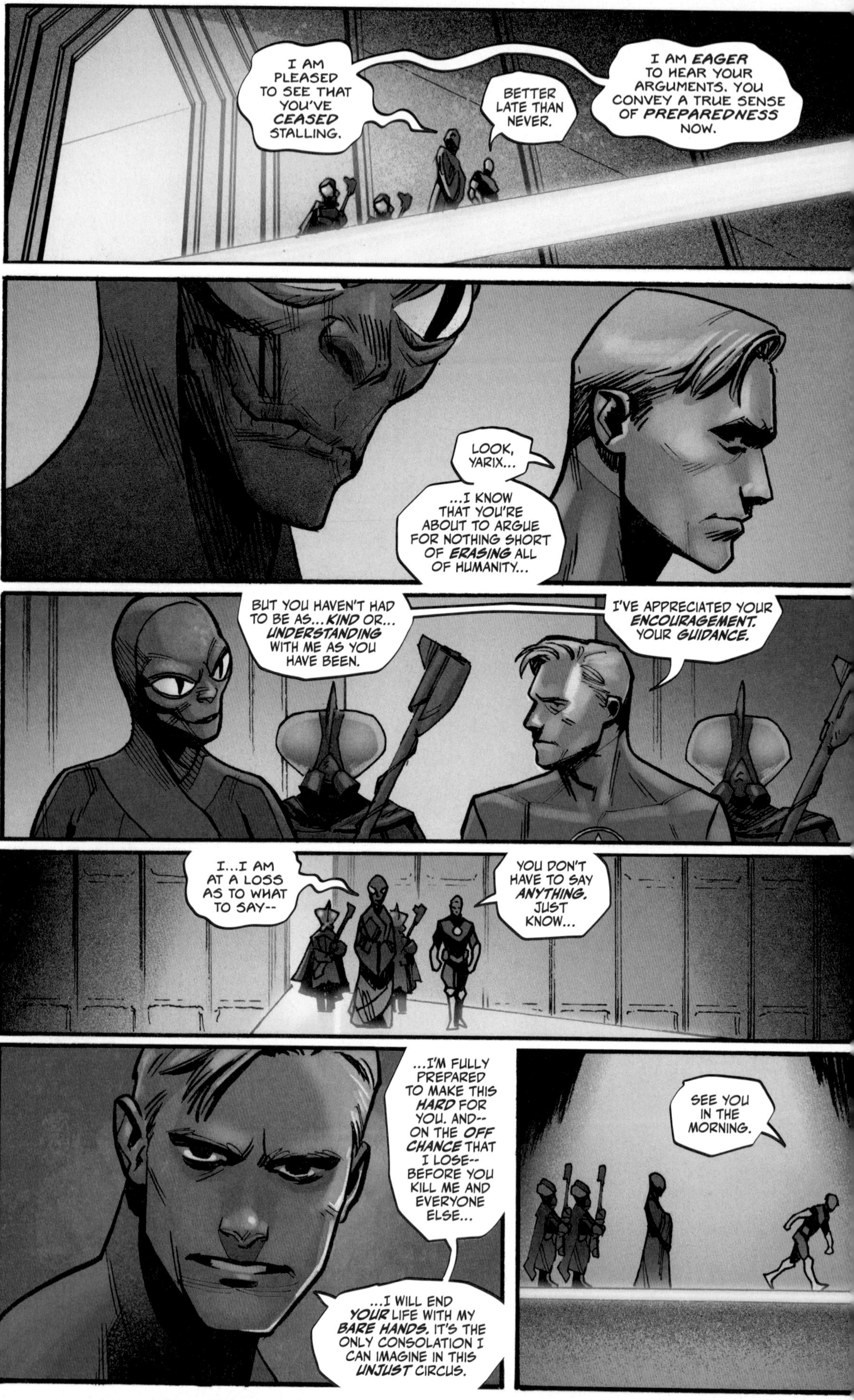
I AM PLEASED TO SEE THAT YOU'VE CEASED STALLING.
BETTER LATE THAN NEVER.
I AM EAGER TO HEAR YOUR ARGUMENTS. YOU CONVEY A TRUE SENSE OF PREPAREDNESS NOW.
LOOK, YARIX...
...I KNOW THAT YOU'RE ABOUT TO ARGUE FOR NOTHING SHORT OF ERASING ALL OF HUMANITY...
BUT YOU HAVEN'T HAD TO BE AS...KIND OR... UNDERSTANDING WITH ME AS YOU HAVE BEEN.
I'VE APPRECIATED YOUR ENCOURAGEMENT. YOUR GUIDANCE.
I...I AM AT A LOSS AS TO WHAT TO SAY--
YOU DON'T HAVE TO SAY ANYTHING. JUST KNOW...
...I'M FULLY PREPARED TO MAKE THIS HARD FOR YOU. AND-- ON THE OFF CHANCE THAT I LOSE-- BEFORE YOU KILL ME AND EVERYONE ELSE...
...I WILL END YOUR LIFE WITH MY BARE HANDS. IT'S THE ONLY CONSOLATION I CAN IMAGINE IN THIS UNJUST CIRCUS.
SEE YOU IN THE MORNING.

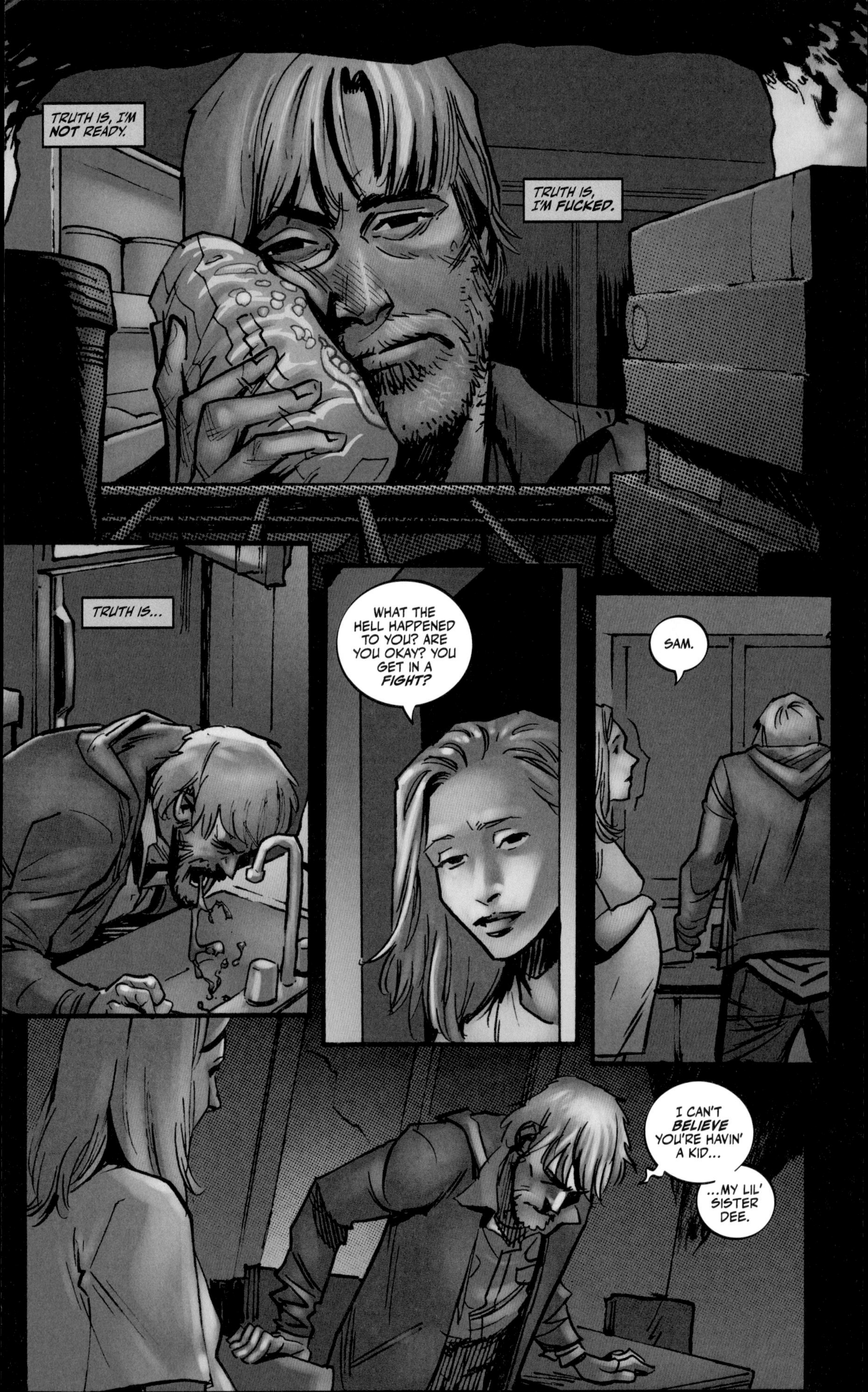
TRUTH IS, I'M NOT READY.
TRUTH IS, I'M FUCKED.
TRUTH IS...
WHAT THE HELL HAPPENED TO YOU? ARE YOU OKAY? YOU GET IN A FIGHT?
SAM.
I CAN'T BELIEVE YOU'RE HAVIN' A KID...
...MY LIL' SISTER DEE.

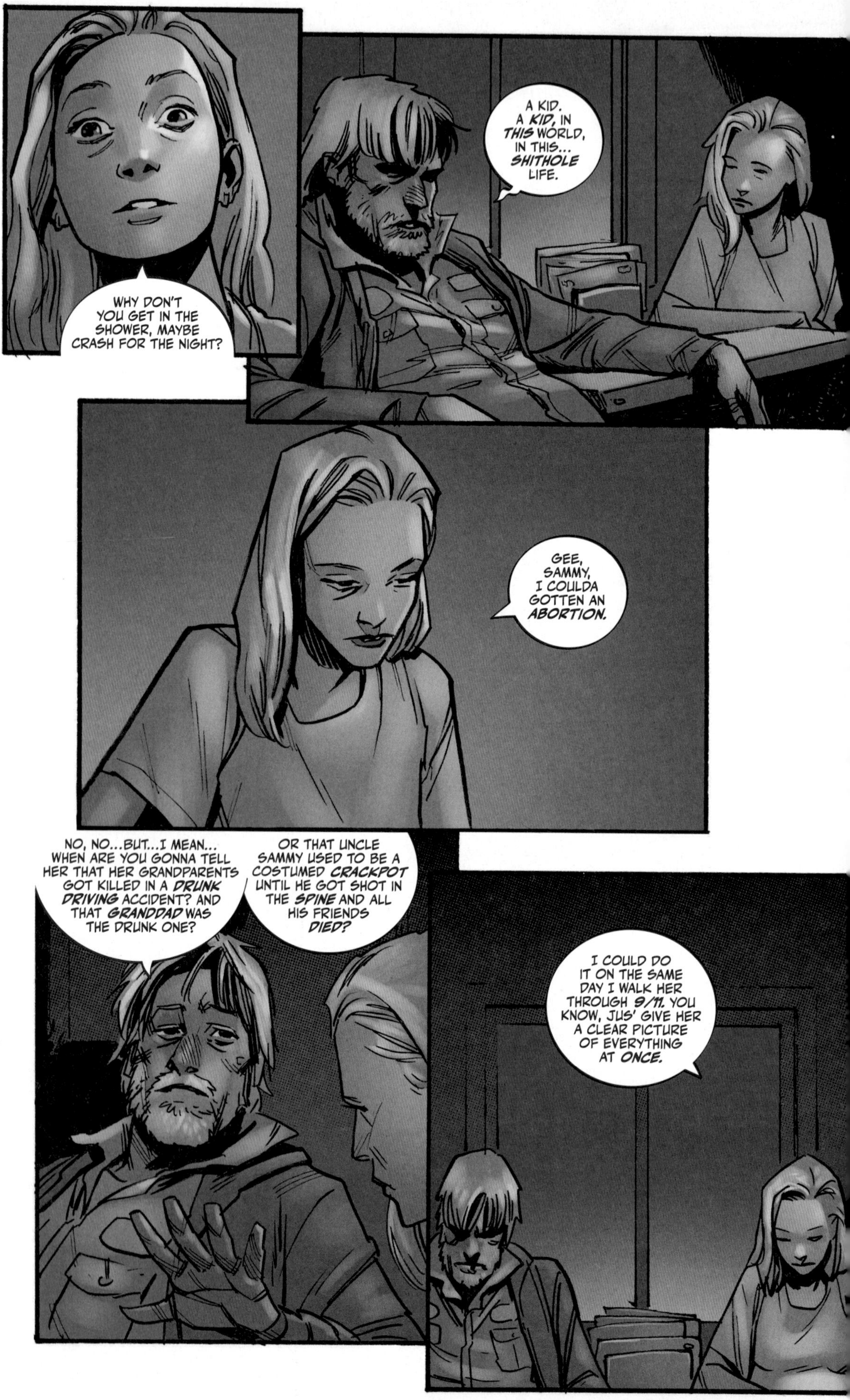
WHY DON'T YOU GET IN THE SHOWER, MAYBE CRASH FOR THE NIGHT?
A KID. A KID, IN THIS WORLD, IN THIS... SHITHOLE LIFE.
GEE, SAMMY, I COULDA GOTTEN AN ABORTION.
NO, NO...BUT...I MEAN... WHEN ARE YOU GONNA TELL HER THAT HER GRANDPARENTS GOT KILLED IN A DRUNK DRIVING ACCIDENT? AND THAT GRANDDAD WAS THE DRUNK ONE?
OR THAT UNCLE SAMMY USED TO BE A COSTUMED CRACKPOT UNTIL HE GOT SHOT IN THE SPINE AND ALL HIS FRIENDS DIED?
I COULD DO IT ON THE SAME DAY I WALK HER THROUGH 9/11. YOU KNOW, JUS' GIVE HER A CLEAR PICTURE OF EVERYTHING AT ONCE.

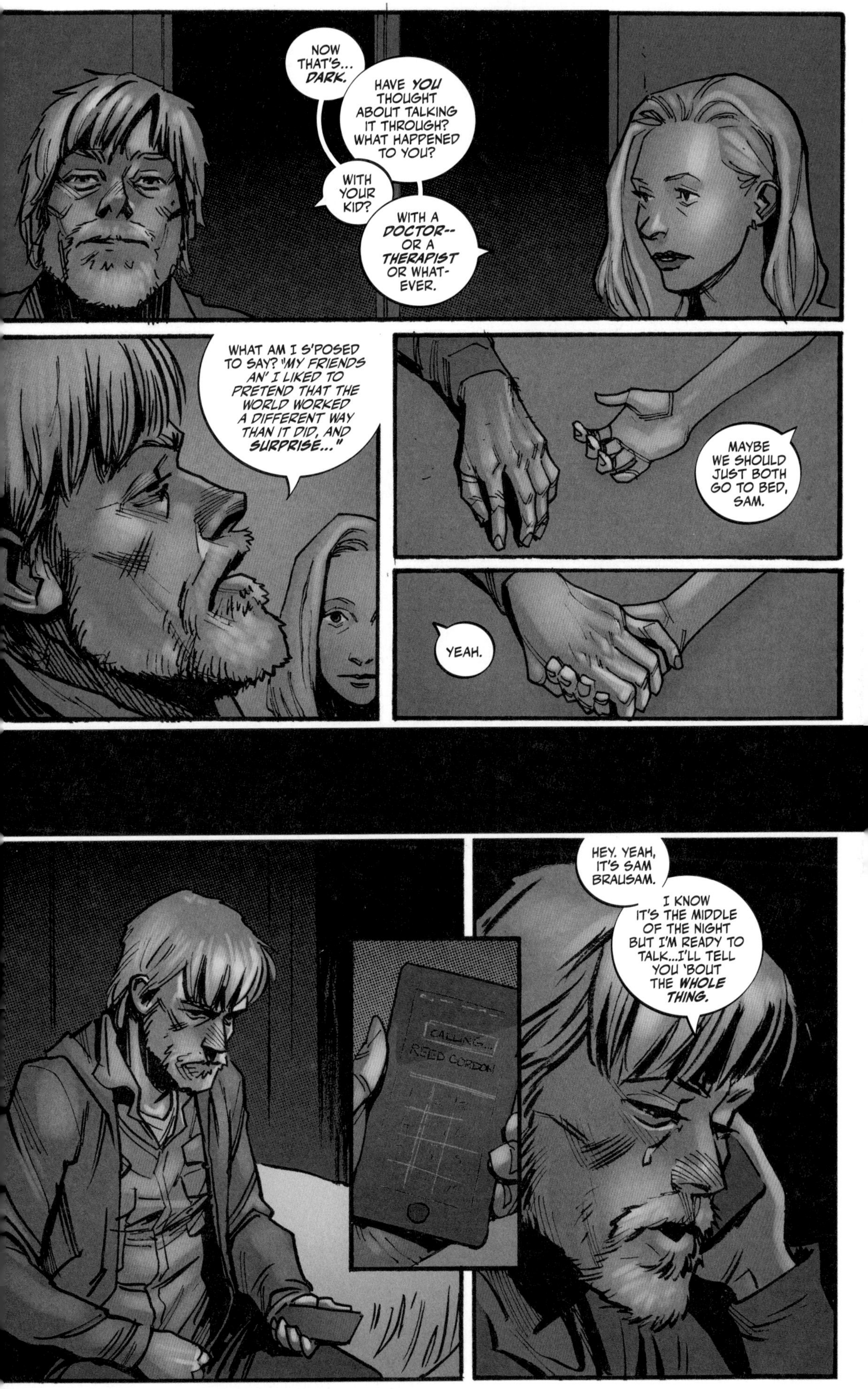
NOW THAT'S... DARK.
HAVE YOU THOUGHT ABOUT TALKING IT THROUGH? WHAT HAPPENED TO YOU?
WITH YOUR KID?
WITH A DOCTOR-- OR A THERAPIST OR WHAT-EVER.
WHAT AM I S'POSED TO SAY? "MY FRIENDS AN' I LIKED TO PRETEND THAT THE WORLD WORKED A DIFFERENT WAY THAN IT DID, AND SURPRISE..."
MAYBE WE SHOULD JUST BOTH GO TO BED, SAM.
YEAH.
CALLING...
REED GORDON
HEY. YEAH, IT'S SAM BRAUSAM.
I KNOW IT'S THE MIDDLE OF THE NIGHT BUT I'M READY TO TALK...I'LL TELL YOU 'BOUT THE WHOLE THING.

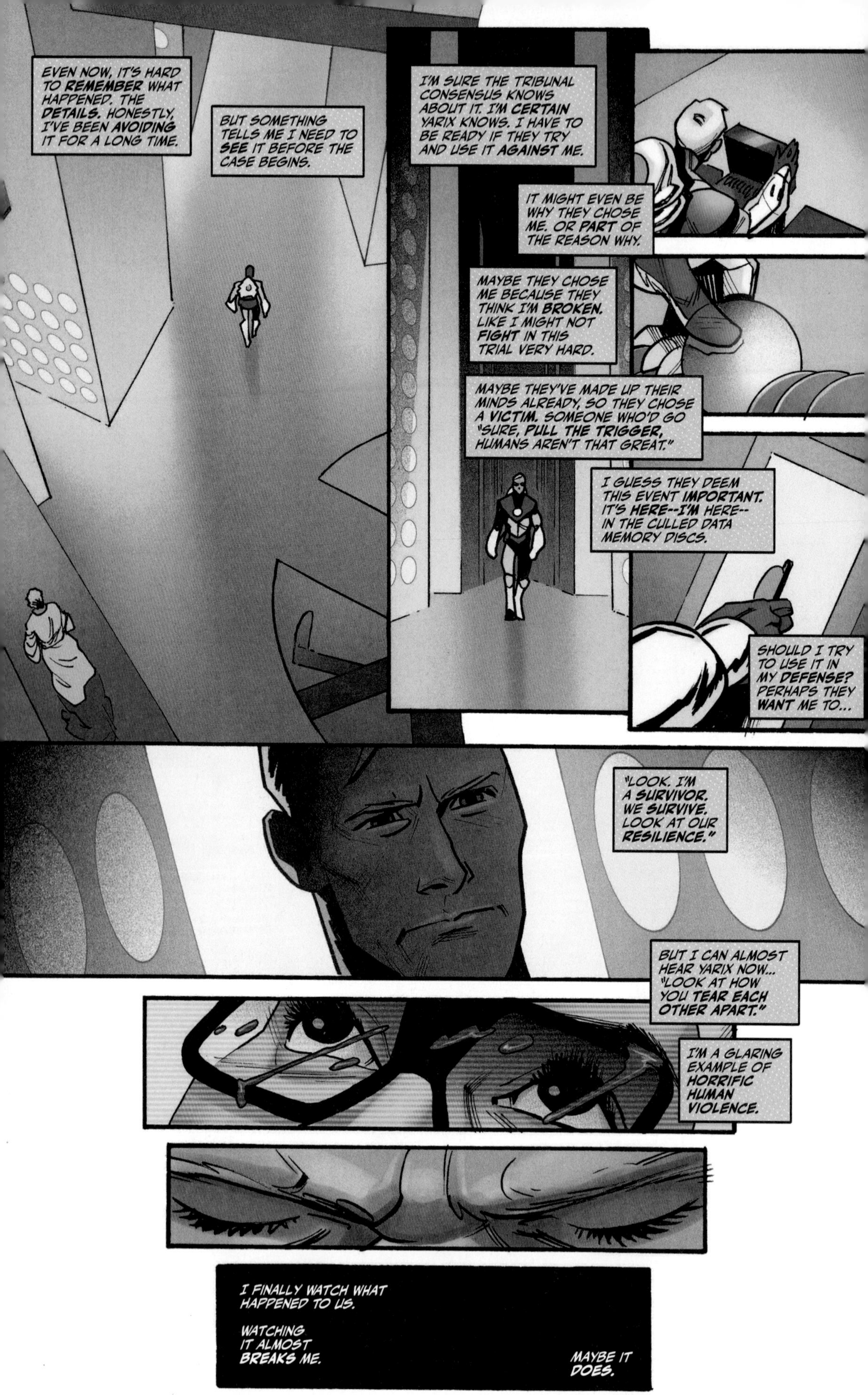
EVEN NOW, IT'S HARD TO REMEMBER WHAT HAPPENED. THE DETAILS. HONESTLY, I'VE BEEN AVOIDING IT FOR A LONG TIME.
BUT SOMETHING TELLS ME I NEED TO SEE IT BEFORE THE CASE BEGINS.
I'M SURE THE TRIBUNAL CONSENSUS KNOWS ABOUT IT. I'M CERTAIN YARIX KNOWS. I HAVE TO BE READY IF THEY TRY AND USE IT AGAINST ME.
IT MIGHT EVEN BE WHY THEY CHOSE ME. OR PART OF THE REASON WHY.
MAYBE THEY CHOSE ME BECAUSE THEY THINK I'M BROKEN. LIKE I MIGHT NOT FIGHT IN THIS TRIAL VERY HARD.
MAYBE THEY'VE MADE UP THEIR MINDS ALREADY, SO THEY CHOSE A VICTIM. SOMEONE WHO'D GO "SURE, PULL THE TRIGGER, HUMANS AREN'T THAT GREAT."
I GUESS THEY DEEM THIS EVENT IMPORTANT. IT'S HERE--I'M HERE-- IN THE CULLED DATA MEMORY DISCS.
SHOULD I TRY TO USE IT IN MY DEFENSE? PERHAPS THEY WANT ME TO...
"LOOK. I'M A SURVIVOR. WE SURVIVE. LOOK AT OUR RESILIENCE."
BUT I CAN ALMOST HEAR YARIX NOW... "LOOK AT HOW YOU TEAR EACH OTHER APART."
I'M A GLARING EXAMPLE OF HORRIFIC HUMAN VIOLENCE.
I FINALLY WATCH WHAT HAPPENED TO US.
WATCHING IT ALMOST BREAKS ME.
MAYBE IT DOES.

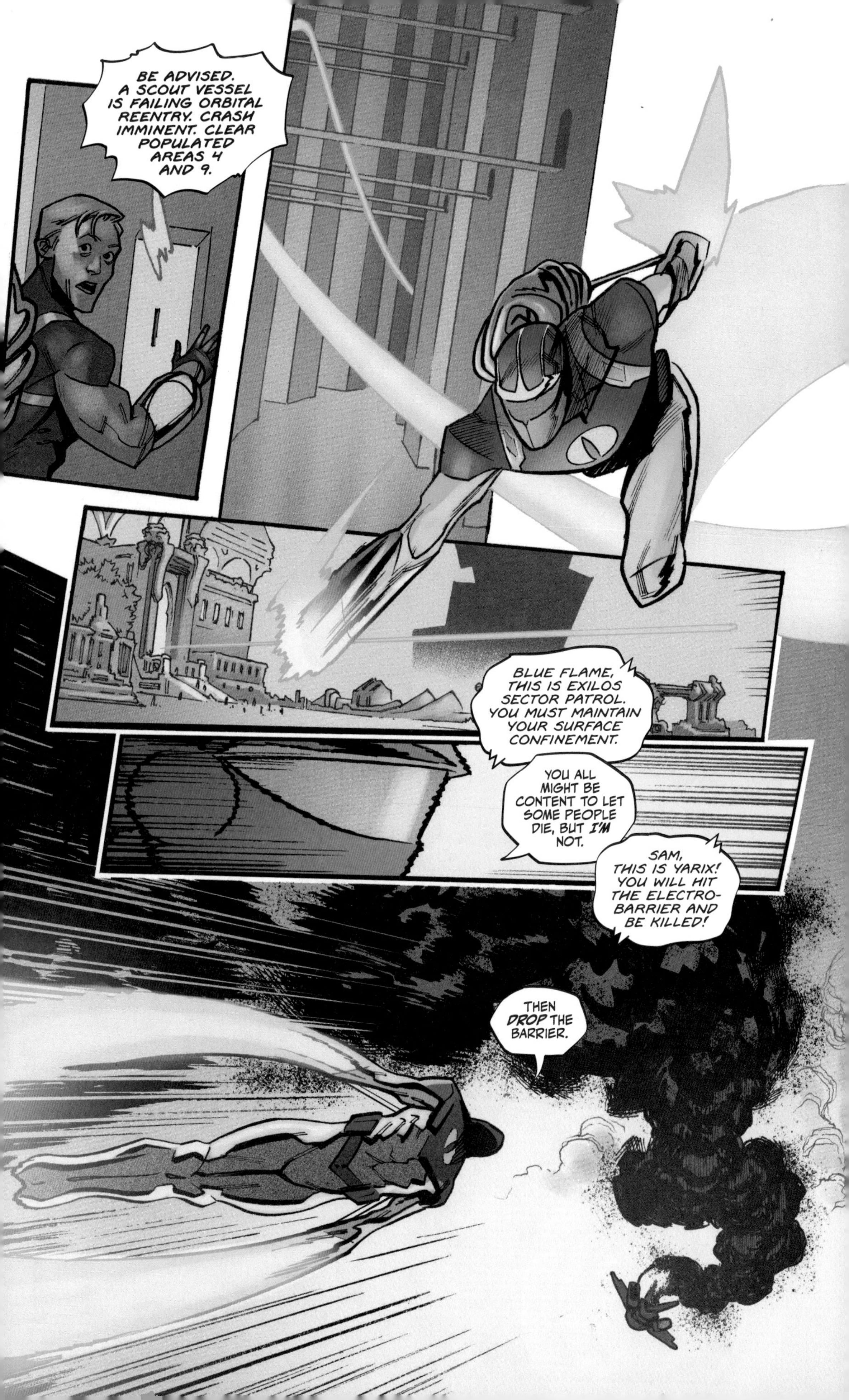
BE ADVISED. A SCOUT VESSEL IS FAILING ORBITAL REENTRY. CRASH IMMINENT. CLEAR POPULATED AREAS 4 AND 9.
BLUE FLAME, THIS IS EXILOS SECTOR PATROL. YOU MUST MAINTAIN YOUR SURFACE CONFINEMENT.
YOU ALL MIGHT BE CONTENT TO LET SOME PEOPLE DIE, BUT *I'M* NOT.
SAM, THIS IS YARIX! YOU WILL HIT THE ELECTRO-BARRIER AND BE KILLED!
THEN *DROP* THE BARRIER.

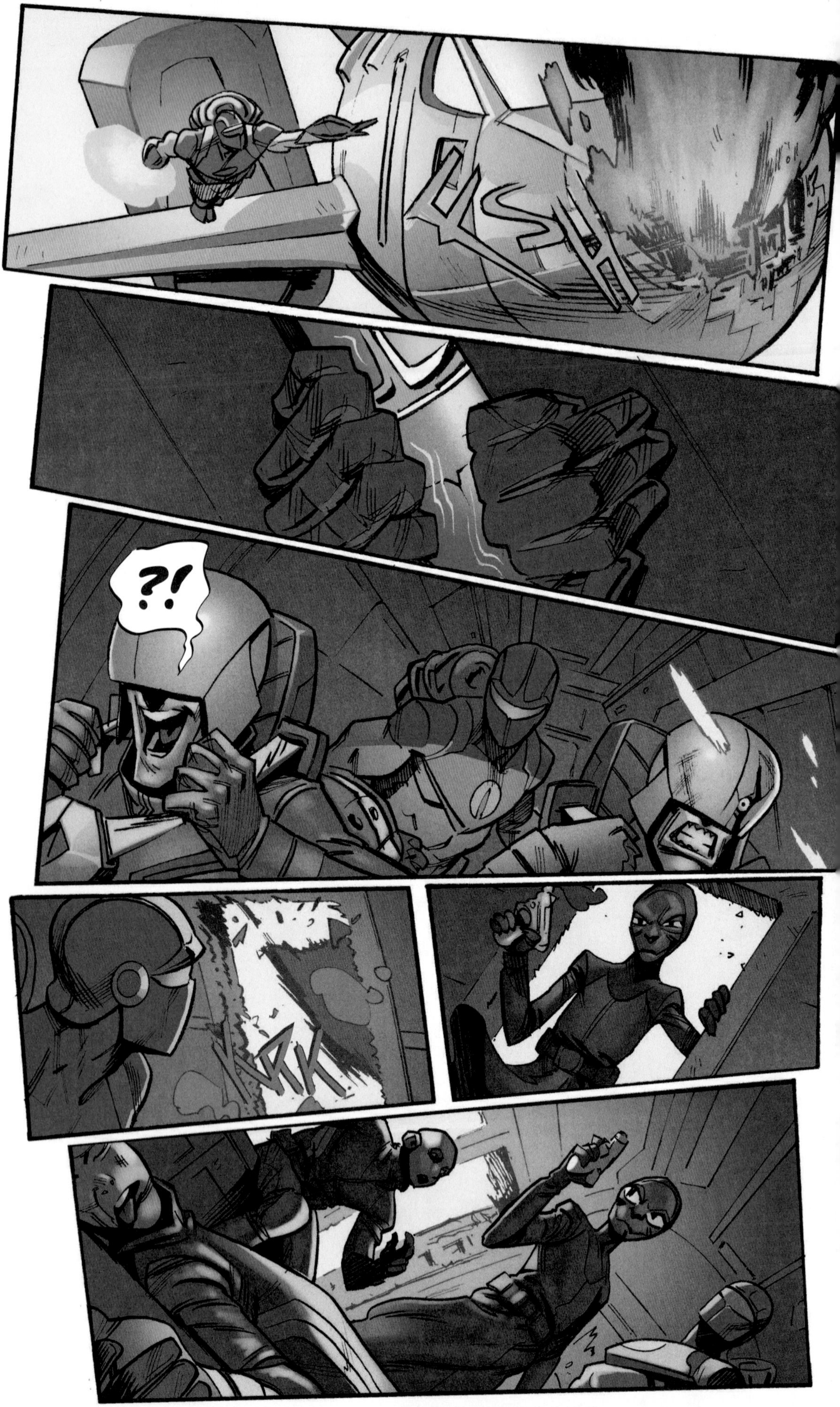
KSH
?!
KRK

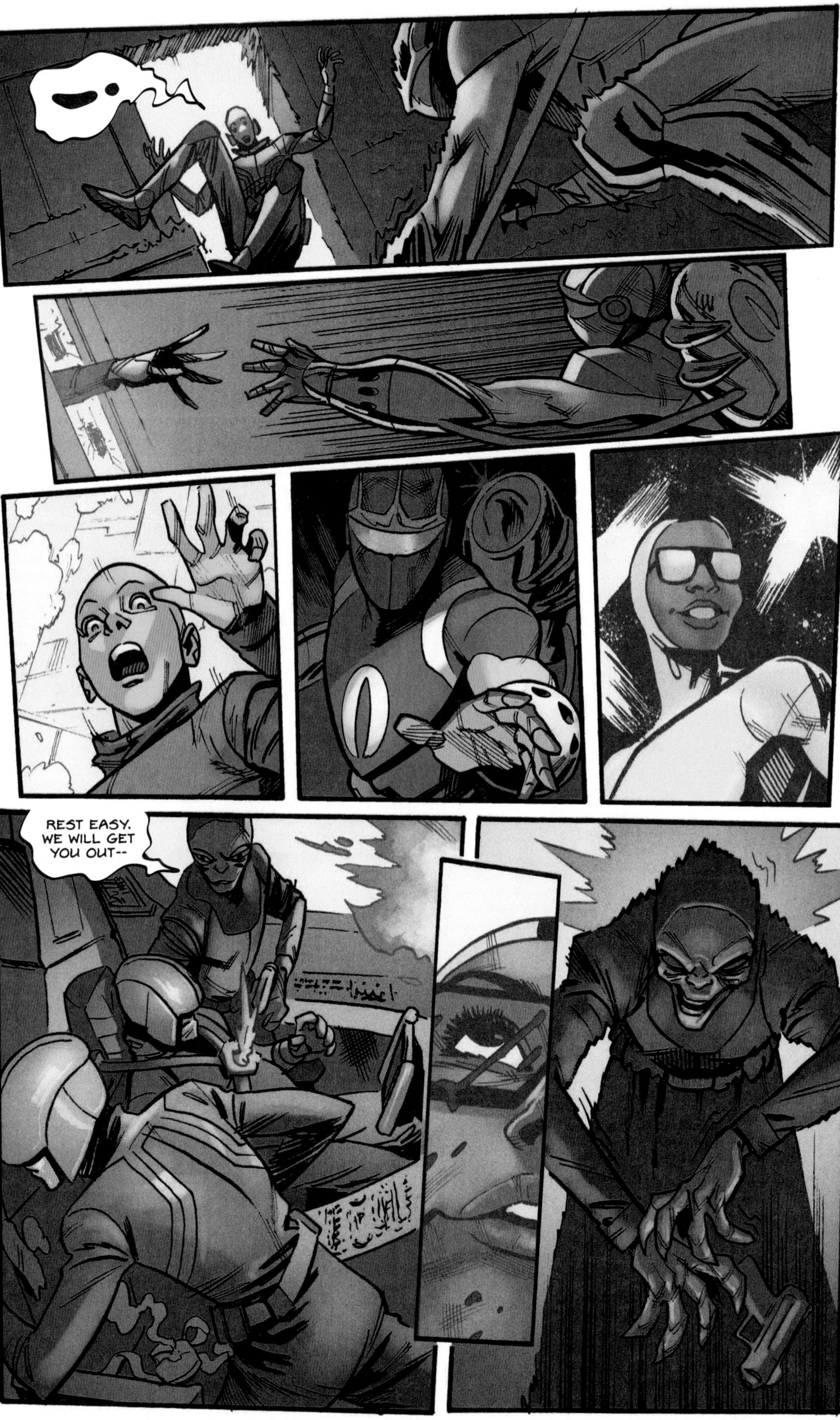
REST EASY. WE WILL GET YOU OUT--

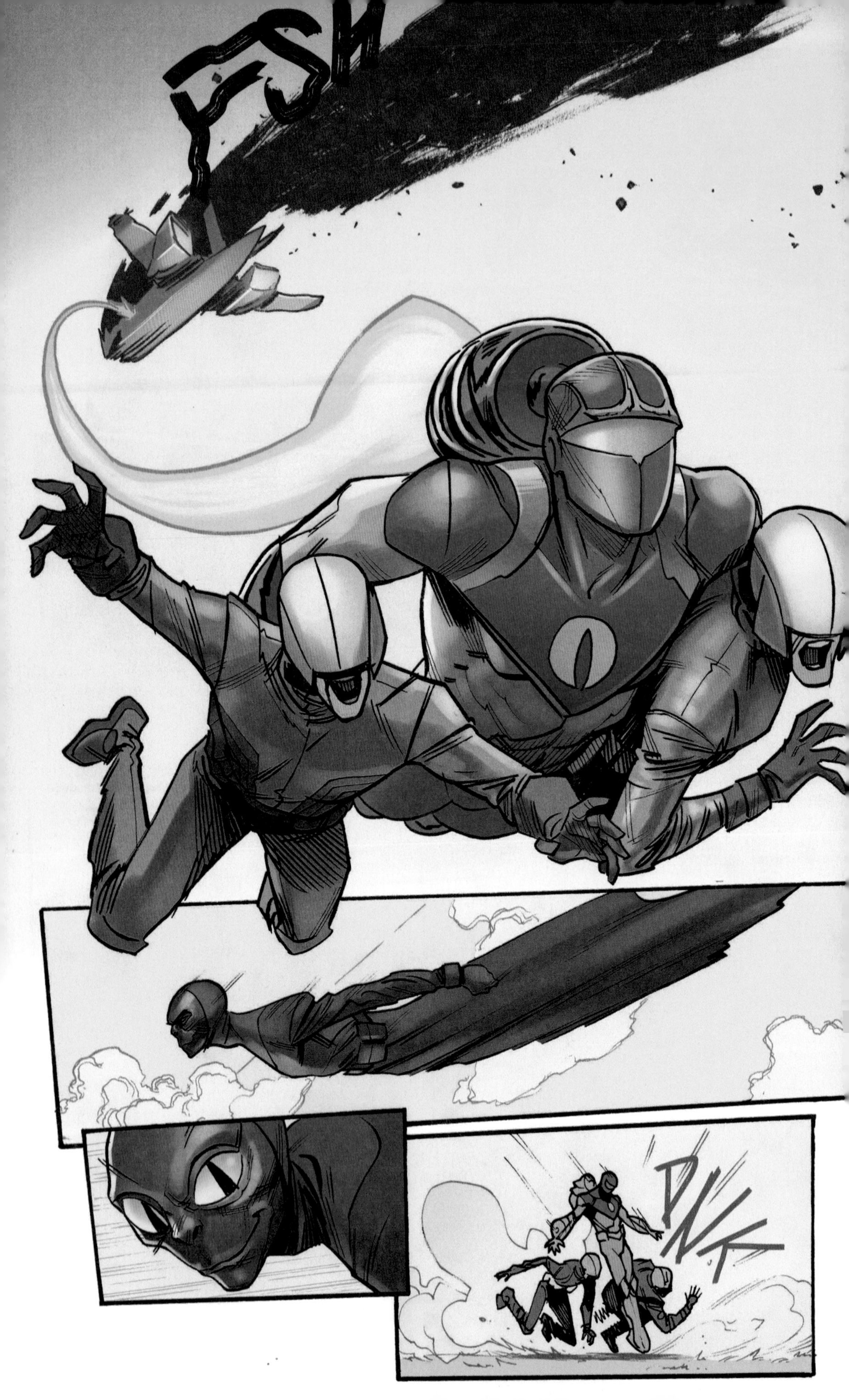

FSH
DNK

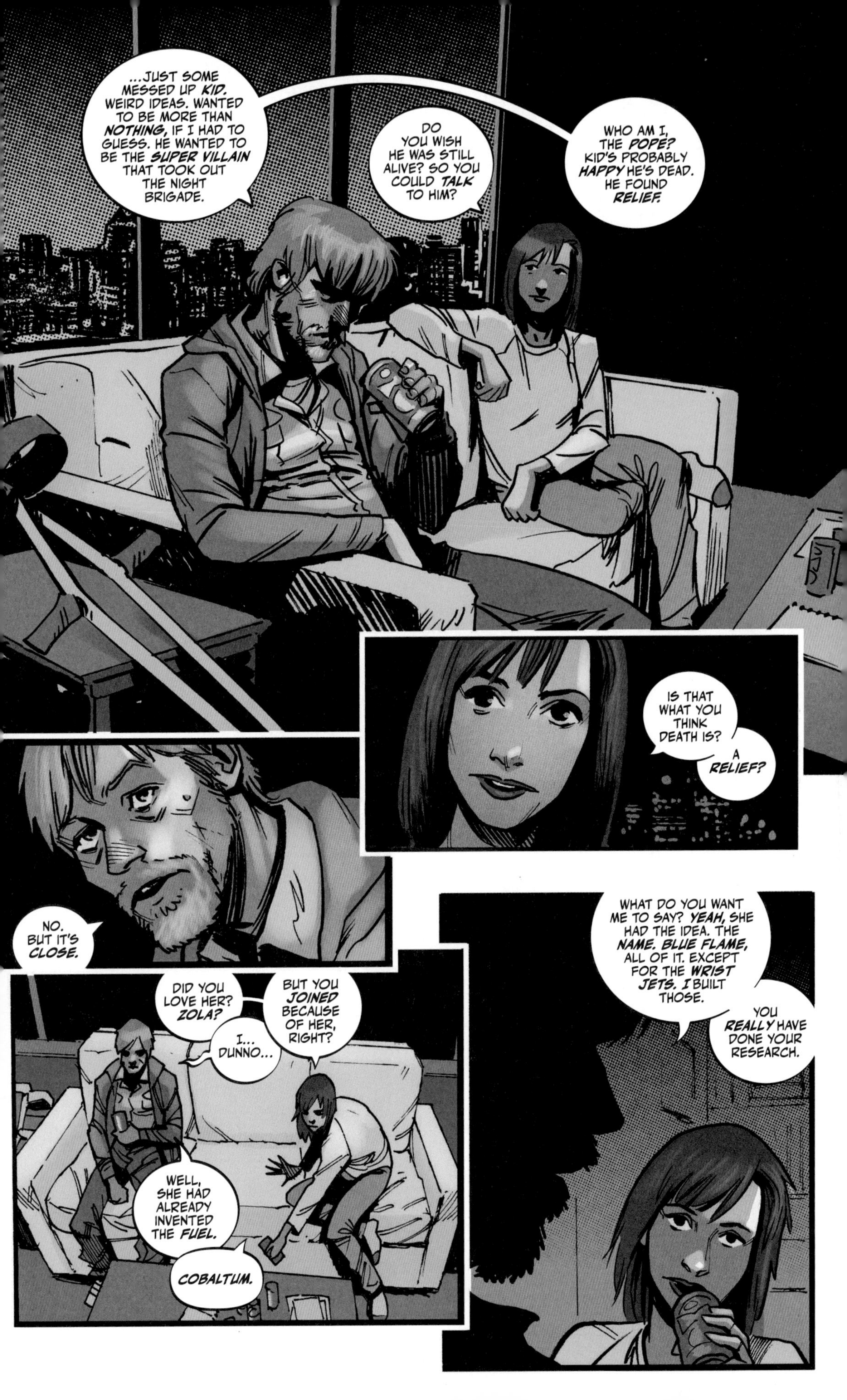
...JUST SOME MESSED UP KID. WEIRD IDEAS. WANTED TO BE MORE THAN NOTHING, IF I HAD TO GUESS. HE WANTED TO BE THE SUPER VILLAIN THAT TOOK OUT THE NIGHT BRIGADE.
DO YOU WISH HE WAS STILL ALIVE? SO YOU COULD TALK TO HIM?
WHO AM I, THE POPE? KID'S PROBABLY HAPPY HE'S DEAD. HE FOUND RELIEF.
IS THAT WHAT YOU THINK DEATH IS?
A RELIEF?
NO. BUT IT'S CLOSE.
DID YOU LOVE HER? ZOLA?
I... DUNNO...
BUT YOU JOINED BECAUSE OF HER, RIGHT?
WELL, SHE HAD ALREADY INVENTED THE FUEL.
COBALTUM.
WHAT DO YOU WANT ME TO SAY? YEAH, SHE HAD THE IDEA. THE NAME. BLUE FLAME, ALL OF IT. EXCEPT FOR THE WRIST JETS. I BUILT THOSE.
YOU REALLY HAVE DONE YOUR RESEARCH.

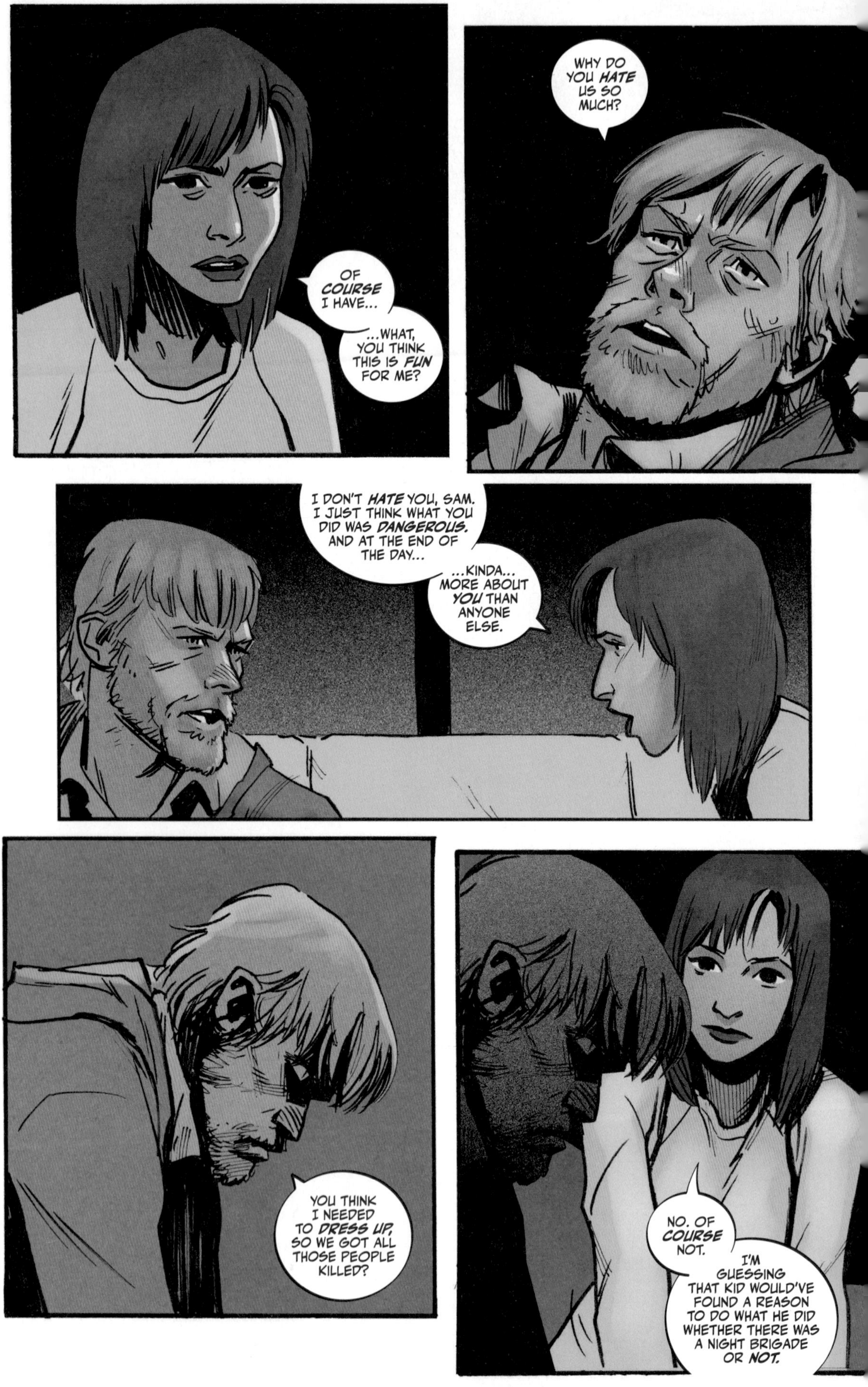
OF COURSE I HAVE...
...WHAT, YOU THINK THIS IS FUN FOR ME?
WHY DO YOU HATE US SO MUCH?
I DON'T HATE YOU, SAM. I JUST THINK WHAT YOU DID WAS DANGEROUS. AND AT THE END OF THE DAY...
...KINDA... MORE ABOUT YOU THAN ANYONE ELSE.
YOU THINK I NEEDED TO DRESS UP, SO WE GOT ALL THOSE PEOPLE KILLED?
NO. OF COURSE NOT.
I'M GUESSING THAT KID WOULD'VE FOUND A REASON TO DO WHAT HE DID WHETHER THERE WAS A NIGHT BRIGADE OR NOT.

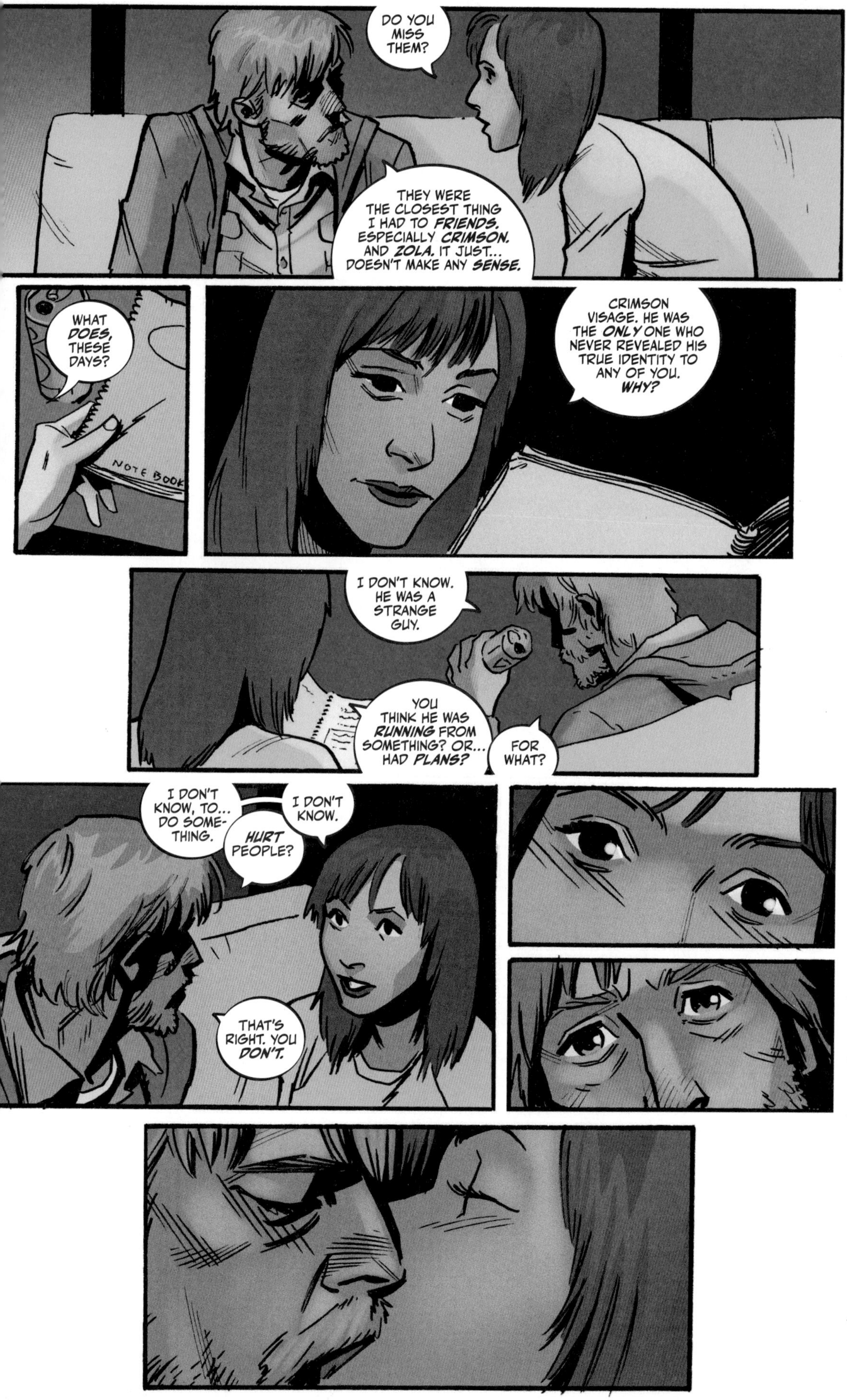
DO YOU MISS THEM?
THEY WERE THE CLOSEST THING I HAD TO FRIENDS. ESPECIALLY CRIMSON. AND ZOLA. IT JUST... DOESN'T MAKE ANY SENSE.
WHAT DOES, THESE DAYS?
NOTE BOOK
CRIMSON VISAGE. HE WAS THE ONLY ONE WHO NEVER REVEALED HIS TRUE IDENTITY TO ANY OF YOU. WHY?
I DON'T KNOW. HE WAS A STRANGE GUY.
YOU THINK HE WAS RUNNING FROM SOMETHING? OR... HAD PLANS?
FOR WHAT?
I DON'T KNOW, TO... DO SOME-THING.
I DON'T KNOW.
HURT PEOPLE?
THAT'S RIGHT. YOU DON'T.

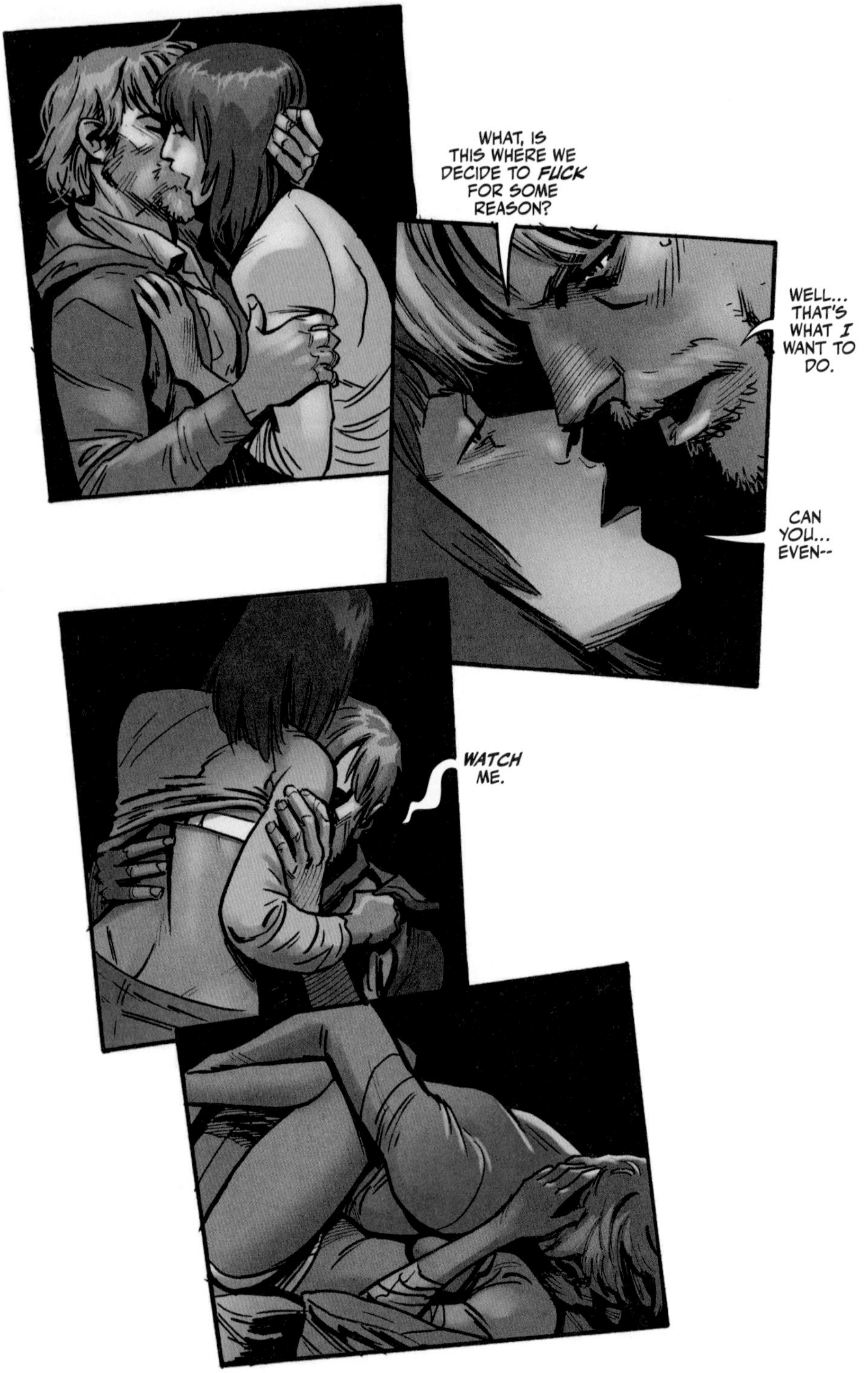
WHAT, IS THIS WHERE WE DECIDE TO FUCK FOR SOME REASON?
WELL... THAT'S WHAT I WANT TO DO.
CAN YOU... EVEN--
WATCH ME.

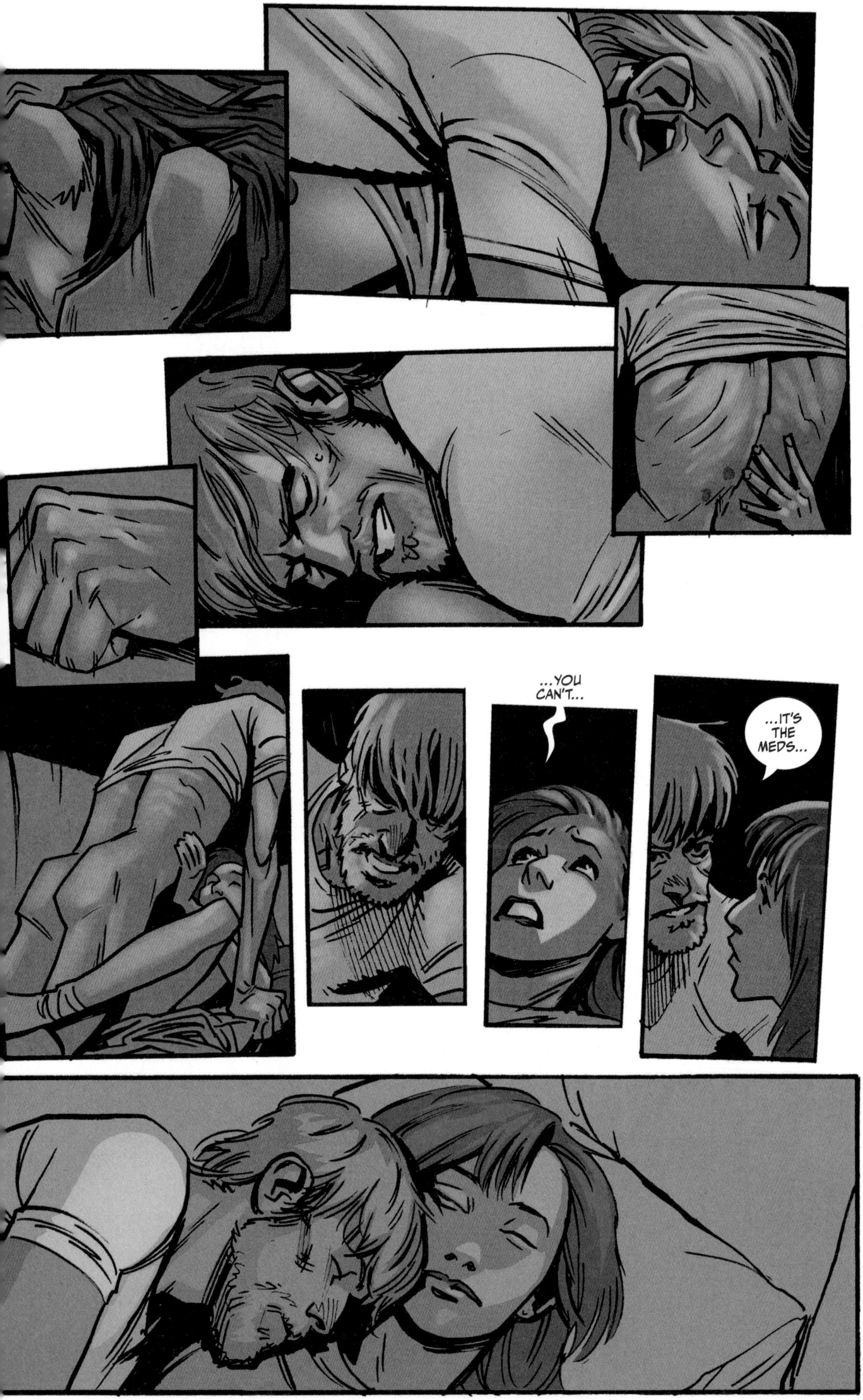
...YOU CAN'T...
...IT'S THE MEDS...

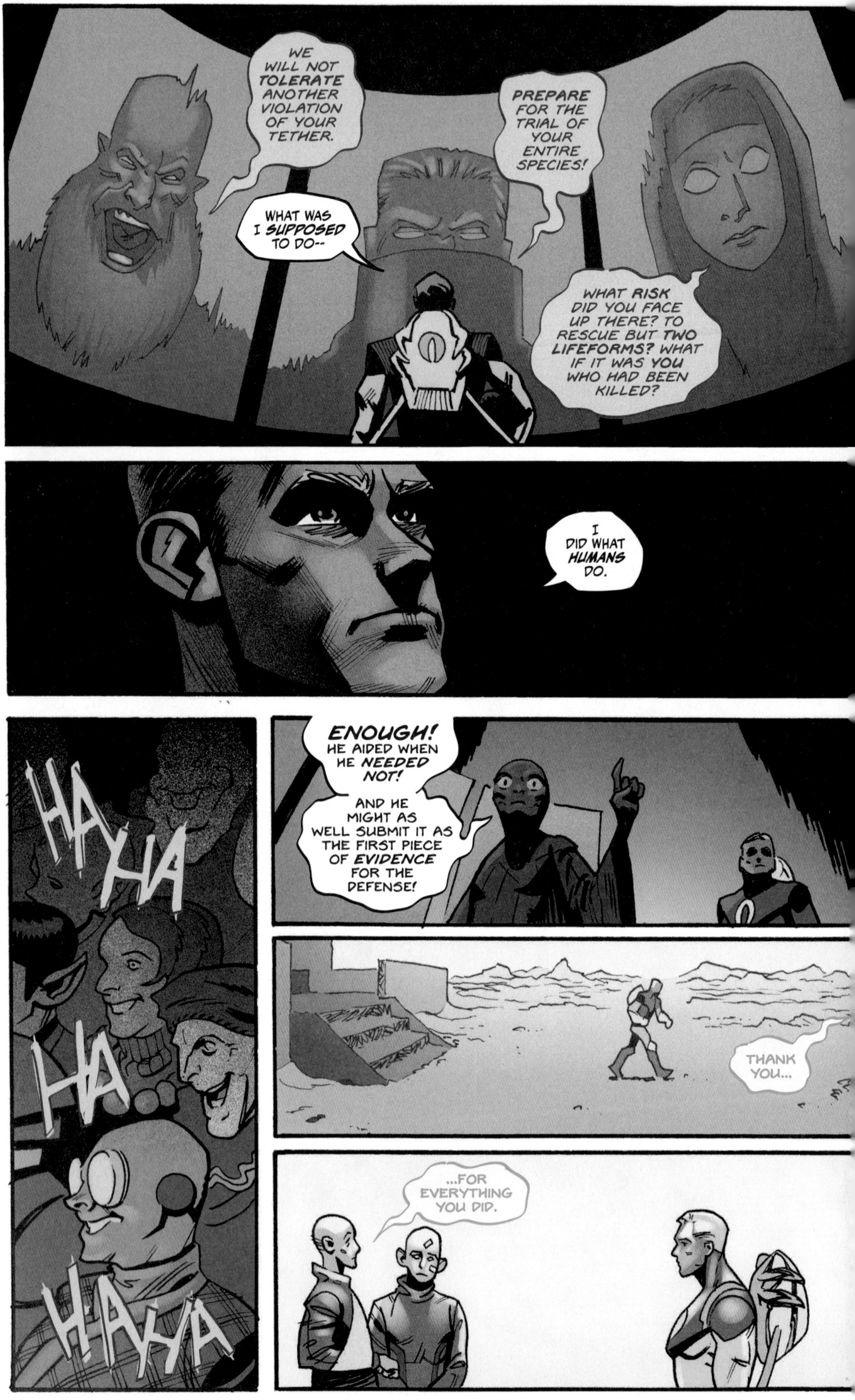
WE WILL NOT TOLERATE ANOTHER VIOLATION OF YOUR TETHER.
PREPARE FOR THE TRIAL OF YOUR ENTIRE SPECIES!
WHAT WAS I SUPPOSED TO DO--
WHAT RISK DID YOU FACE UP THERE? TO RESCUE BUT TWO LIFEFORMS? WHAT IF IT WAS YOU WHO HAD BEEN KILLED?
I DID WHAT HUMANS DO.
HA HA
HA...
HAHA
ENOUGH! HE AIDED WHEN HE NEEDED NOT!
AND HE MIGHT AS WELL SUBMIT IT AS THE FIRST PIECE OF EVIDENCE FOR THE DEFENSE!
THANK YOU...
...FOR EVERYTHING YOU DID.

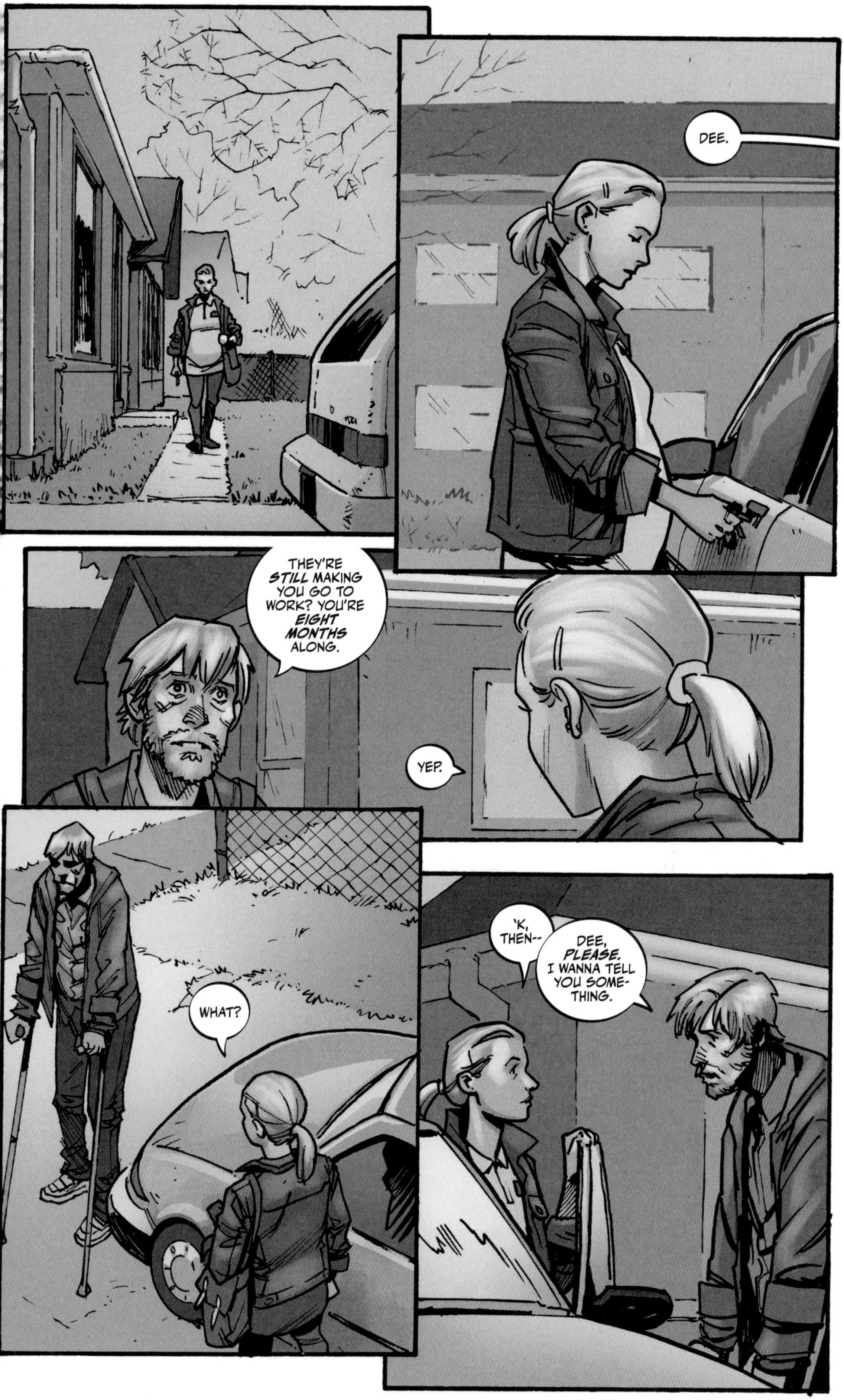
DEE.
THEY'RE *STILL* MAKING YOU GO TO WORK? YOU'RE *EIGHT MONTHS* ALONG.
YEP.
WHAT?
'K, THEN--
DEE, *PLEASE.* I WANNA TELL YOU SOME-THING.

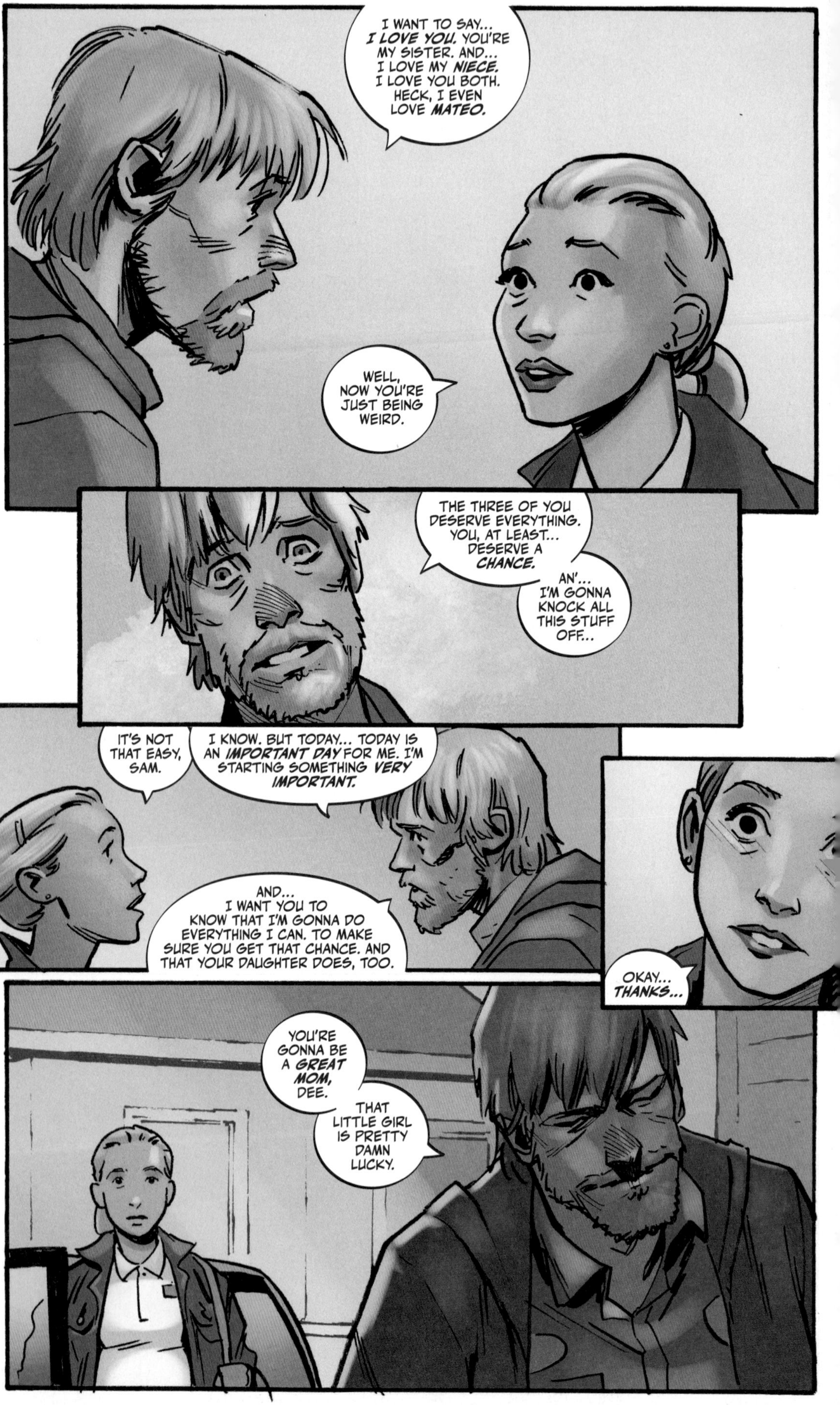

I WANT TO SAY... I LOVE YOU. YOU'RE MY SISTER. AND... I LOVE MY NIECE. I LOVE YOU BOTH. HECK, I EVEN LOVE MATEO.
WELL, NOW YOU'RE JUST BEING WEIRD.
THE THREE OF YOU DESERVE EVERYTHING. YOU, AT LEAST... DESERVE A CHANCE.
AN'... I'M GONNA KNOCK ALL THIS STUFF OFF...
IT'S NOT THAT EASY, SAM.
I KNOW. BUT TODAY... TODAY IS AN IMPORTANT DAY FOR ME. I'M STARTING SOMETHING VERY IMPORTANT.
AND... I WANT YOU TO KNOW THAT I'M GONNA DO EVERYTHING I CAN. TO MAKE SURE YOU GET THAT CHANCE. AND THAT YOUR DAUGHTER DOES, TOO.
OKAY... THANKS...
YOU'RE GONNA BE A GREAT MOM, DEE.
THAT LITTLE GIRL IS PRETTY DAMN LUCKY.

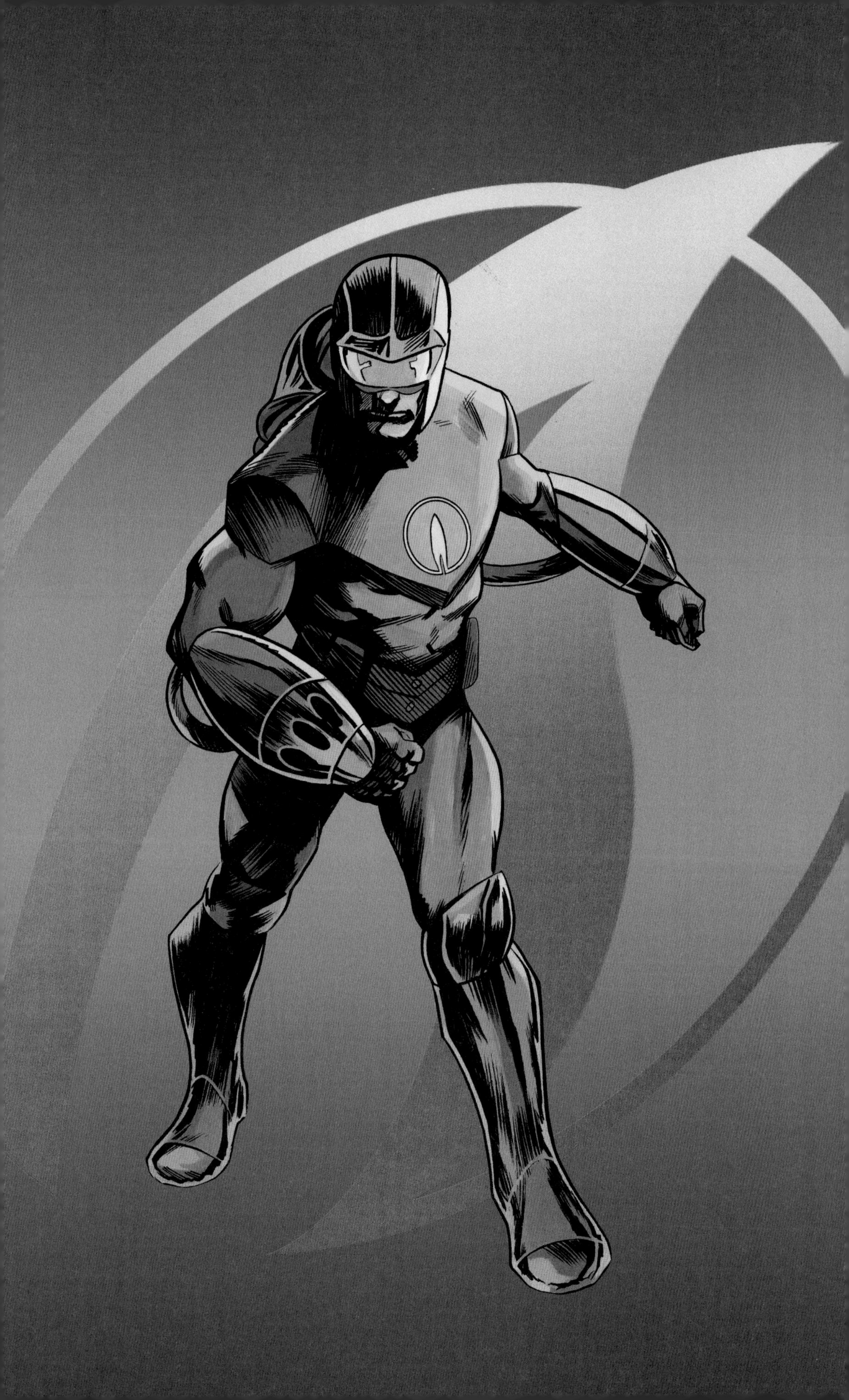

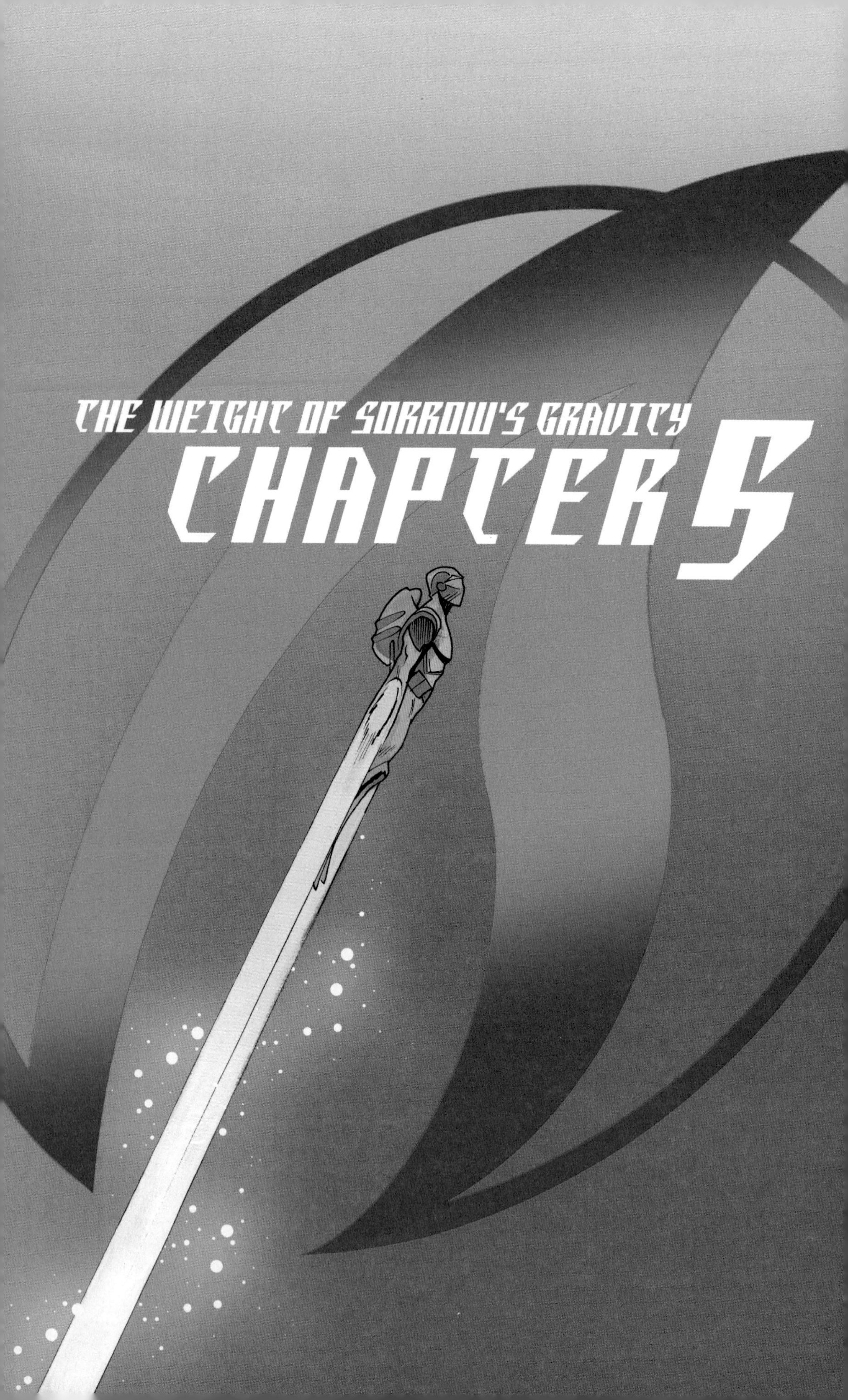
THE WEIGHT OF SORROW'S GRAVITY
CHAPTER 5

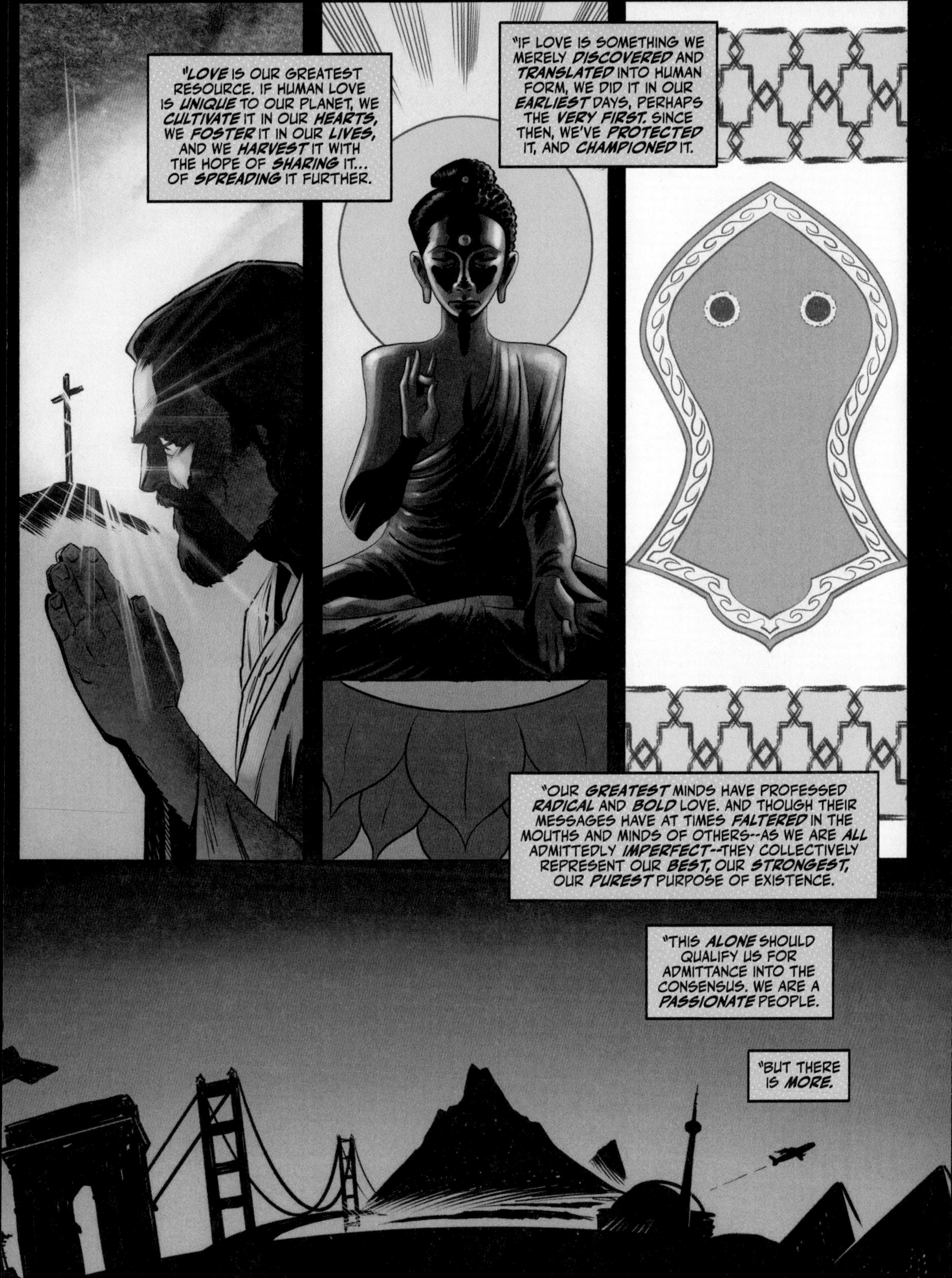
"LOVE IS OUR GREATEST RESOURCE. IF HUMAN LOVE IS UNIQUE TO OUR PLANET, WE CULTIVATE IT IN OUR HEARTS, WE FOSTER IT IN OUR LIVES, AND WE HARVEST IT WITH THE HOPE OF SHARING IT... OF SPREADING IT FURTHER.
"IF LOVE IS SOMETHING WE MERELY DISCOVERED AND TRANSLATED INTO HUMAN FORM, WE DID IT IN OUR EARLIEST DAYS, PERHAPS THE VERY FIRST. SINCE THEN, WE'VE PROTECTED IT, AND CHAMPIONED IT.
"OUR GREATEST MINDS HAVE PROFESSED RADICAL AND BOLD LOVE. AND THOUGH THEIR MESSAGES HAVE AT TIMES FALTERED IN THE MOUTHS AND MINDS OF OTHERS--AS WE ARE ALL ADMITTEDLY IMPERFECT--THEY COLLECTIVELY REPRESENT OUR BEST, OUR STRONGEST, OUR PUREST PURPOSE OF EXISTENCE.
"THIS ALONE SHOULD QUALIFY US FOR ADMITTANCE INTO THE CONSENSUS. WE ARE A PASSIONATE PEOPLE.
"BUT THERE IS MORE.

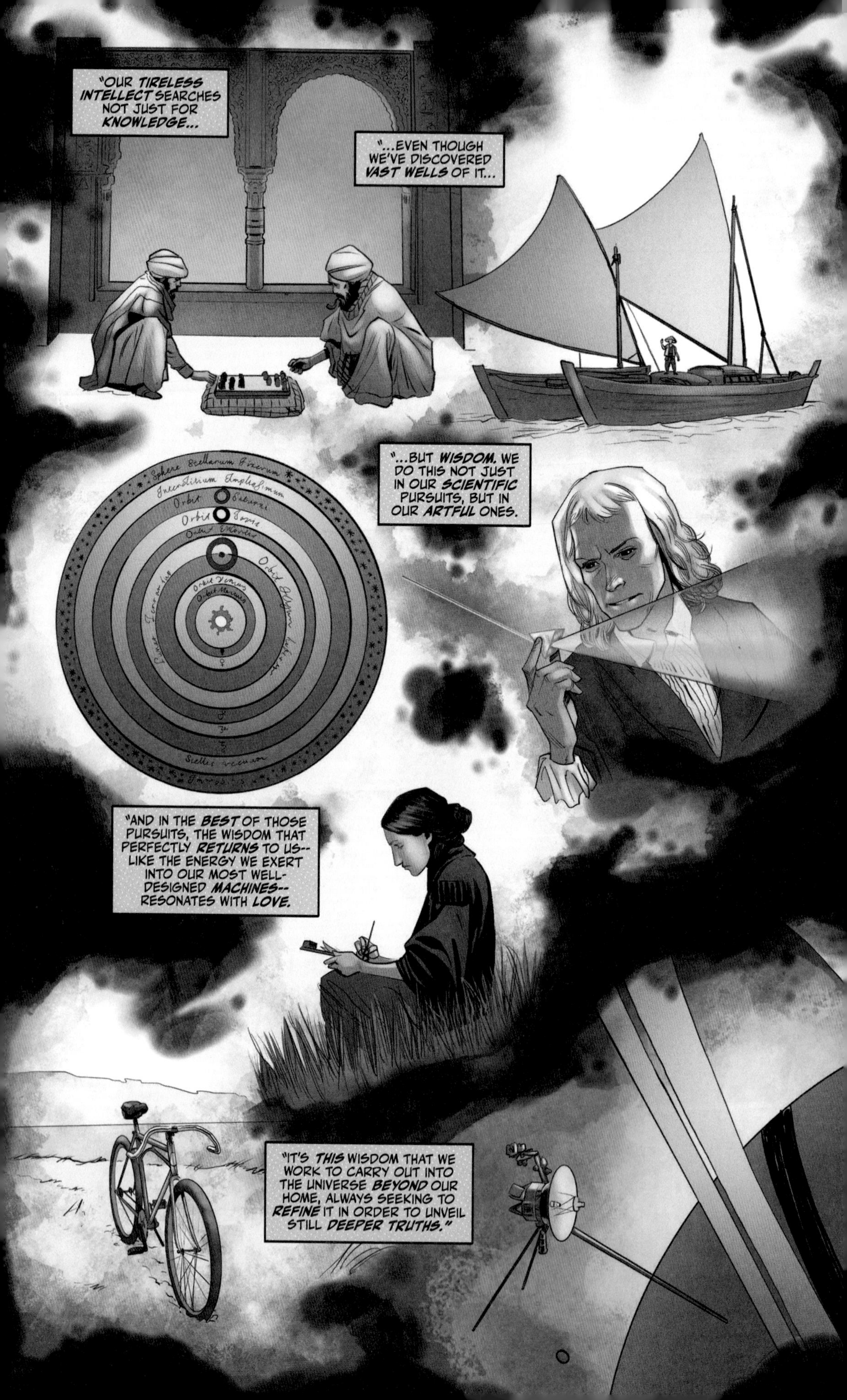
"OUR TIRELESS INTELLECT SEARCHES NOT JUST FOR KNOWLEDGE...
"...EVEN THOUGH WE'VE DISCOVERED VAST WELLS OF IT...
"...BUT WISDOM. WE DO THIS NOT JUST IN OUR SCIENTIFIC PURSUITS, BUT IN OUR ARTFUL ONES.
"AND IN THE BEST OF THOSE PURSUITS, THE WISDOM THAT PERFECTLY RETURNS TO US--LIKE THE ENERGY WE EXERT INTO OUR MOST WELL-DESIGNED MACHINES--RESONATES WITH LOVE.
"IT'S THIS WISDOM THAT WE WORK TO CARRY OUT INTO THE UNIVERSE BEYOND OUR HOME, ALWAYS SEEKING TO REFINE IT IN ORDER TO UNVEIL STILL DEEPER TRUTHS."

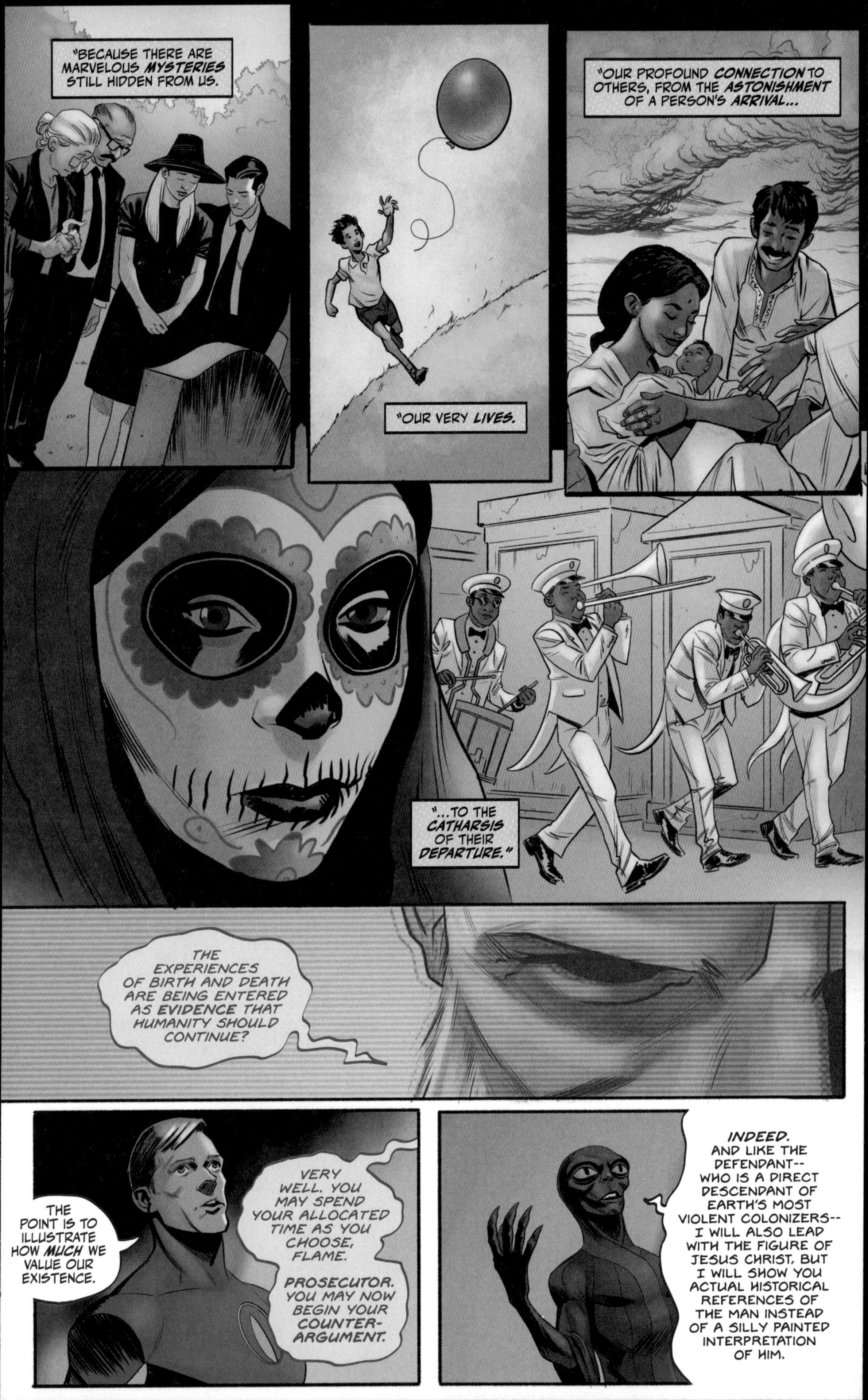
"BECAUSE THERE ARE MARVELOUS *MYSTERIES* STILL HIDDEN FROM US.
"OUR VERY *LIVES*.
"OUR PROFOUND *CONNECTION* TO OTHERS, FROM THE *ASTONISHMENT* OF A PERSON'S *ARRIVAL*...
"...TO THE *CATHARSIS* OF THEIR *DEPARTURE*."
THE EXPERIENCES OF BIRTH AND DEATH ARE BEING ENTERED AS **EVIDENCE** THAT HUMANITY SHOULD CONTINUE?
THE POINT IS TO ILLUSTRATE HOW *MUCH* WE VALUE OUR EXISTENCE.
VERY WELL. YOU MAY SPEND YOUR ALLOCATED TIME AS YOU CHOOSE, FLAME.
PROSECUTOR. YOU MAY NOW BEGIN YOUR COUNTER-ARGUMENT.
INDEED.
AND LIKE THE DEFENDANT-- WHO IS A DIRECT DESCENDANT OF EARTH'S MOST VIOLENT COLONIZERS-- I WILL ALSO LEAD WITH THE FIGURE OF JESUS CHRIST, BUT I WILL SHOW YOU ACTUAL HISTORICAL REFERENCES OF THE MAN INSTEAD OF A SILLY PAINTED INTERPRETATION OF HIM.

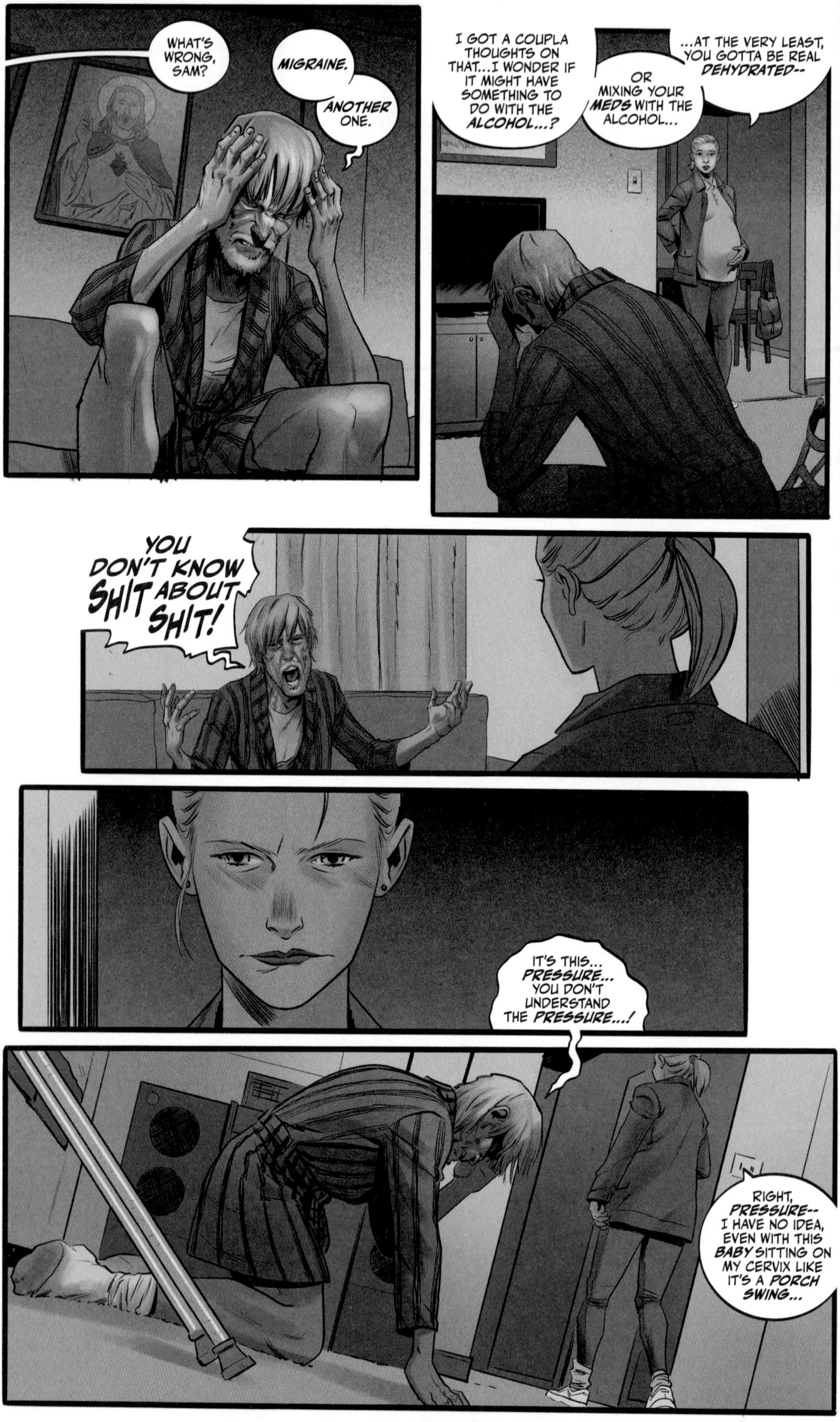

WHAT'S WRONG, SAM?
MIGRAINE.
ANOTHER ONE.
I GOT A COUPLA THOUGHTS ON THAT...I WONDER IF IT MIGHT HAVE SOMETHING TO DO WITH THE ALCOHOL...?
OR MIXING YOUR MEDS WITH THE ALCOHOL...
...AT THE VERY LEAST, YOU GOTTA BE REAL DEHYDRATED--
YOU DON'T KNOW SHIT ABOUT SHIT!
IT'S THIS... PRESSURE... YOU DON'T UNDERSTAND THE PRESSURE...!
RIGHT, PRESSURE-- I HAVE NO IDEA, EVEN WITH THIS BABY SITTING ON MY CERVIX LIKE IT'S A PORCH SWING...

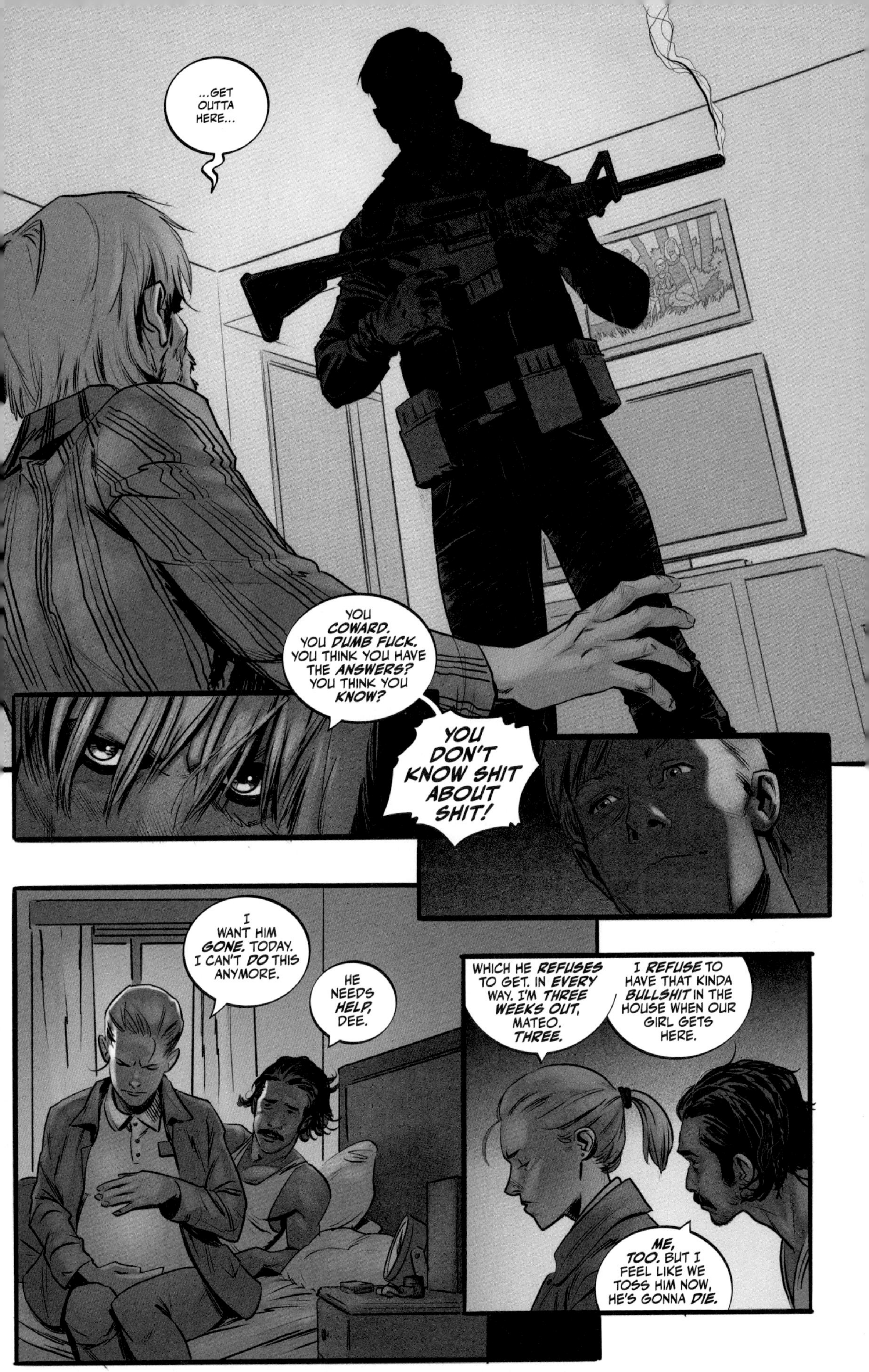
...GET OUTTA HERE...
YOU COWARD. YOU DUMB FUCK. YOU THINK YOU HAVE THE ANSWERS? YOU THINK YOU KNOW?
YOU DON'T KNOW SHIT ABOUT SHIT!
I WANT HIM GONE. TODAY. I CAN'T DO THIS ANYMORE.
HE NEEDS HELP, DEE.
WHICH HE REFUSES TO GET. IN EVERY WAY. I'M THREE WEEKS OUT, MATEO. THREE.
I REFUSE TO HAVE THAT KINDA BULLSHIT IN THE HOUSE WHEN OUR GIRL GETS HERE.
ME, TOO. BUT I FEEL LIKE WE TOSS HIM NOW, HE'S GONNA DIE.

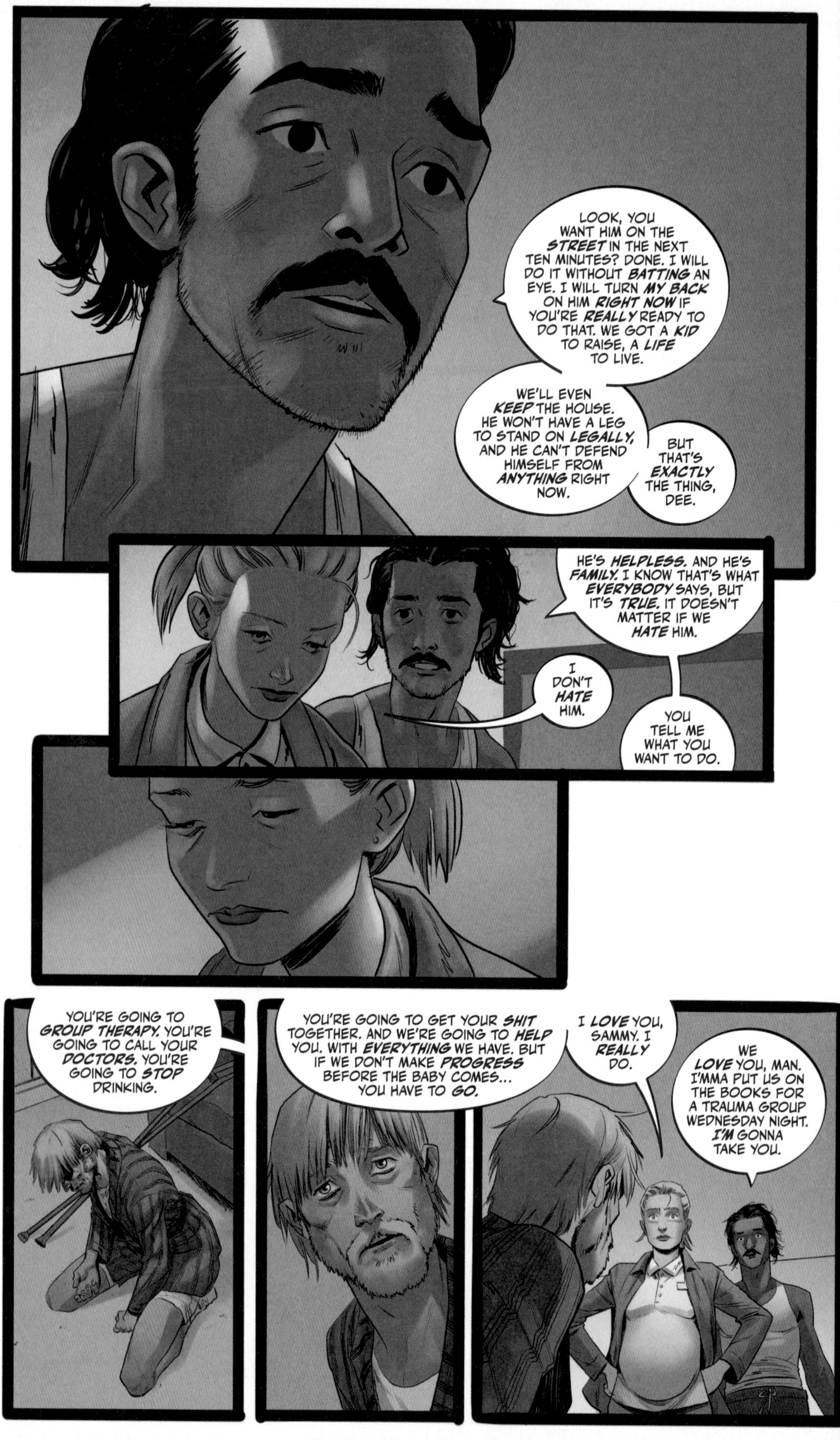
LOOK, YOU WANT HIM ON THE STREET IN THE NEXT TEN MINUTES? DONE. I WILL DO IT WITHOUT BATTING AN EYE. I WILL TURN MY BACK ON HIM RIGHT NOW IF YOU'RE REALLY READY TO DO THAT. WE GOT A KID TO RAISE, A LIFE TO LIVE.
WE'LL EVEN KEEP THE HOUSE. HE WON'T HAVE A LEG TO STAND ON LEGALLY, AND HE CAN'T DEFEND HIMSELF FROM ANYTHING RIGHT NOW.
BUT THAT'S EXACTLY THE THING, DEE.
HE'S HELPLESS. AND HE'S FAMILY. I KNOW THAT'S WHAT EVERYBODY SAYS, BUT IT'S TRUE. IT DOESN'T MATTER IF WE HATE HIM.
I DON'T HATE HIM.
YOU TELL ME WHAT YOU WANT TO DO.
YOU'RE GOING TO GROUP THERAPY. YOU'RE GOING TO CALL YOUR DOCTORS. YOU'RE GOING TO STOP DRINKING.
YOU'RE GOING TO GET YOUR SHIT TOGETHER. AND WE'RE GOING TO HELP YOU. WITH EVERYTHING WE HAVE. BUT IF WE DON'T MAKE PROGRESS BEFORE THE BABY COMES... YOU HAVE TO GO.
I LOVE YOU, SAMMY. I REALLY DO.
WE LOVE YOU, MAN. I'MMA PUT US ON THE BOOKS FOR A TRAUMA GROUP WEDNESDAY NIGHT. I'M GONNA TAKE YOU.

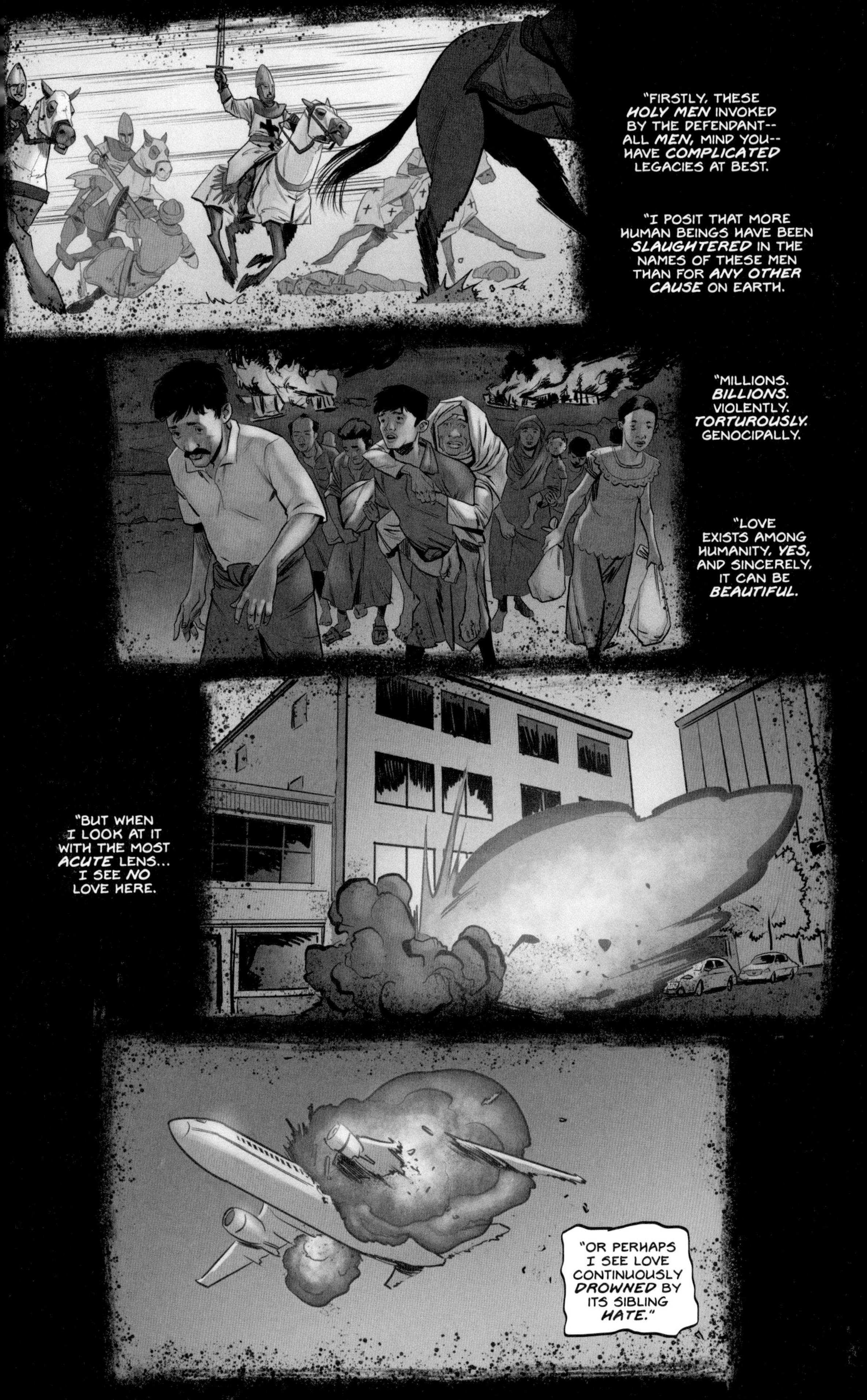
"FIRSTLY, THESE HOLY MEN INVOKED BY THE DEFENDANT-- ALL MEN, MIND YOU-- HAVE COMPLICATED LEGACIES AT BEST.
"I POSIT THAT MORE HUMAN BEINGS HAVE BEEN SLAUGHTERED IN THE NAMES OF THESE MEN THAN FOR ANY OTHER CAUSE ON EARTH.
"MILLIONS. BILLIONS. VIOLENTLY. TORTUROUSLY. GENOCIDALLY.
"LOVE EXISTS AMONG HUMANITY, YES, AND SINCERELY, IT CAN BE BEAUTIFUL.
"BUT WHEN I LOOK AT IT WITH THE MOST ACUTE LENS... I SEE NO LOVE HERE.
"OR PERHAPS I SEE LOVE CONTINUOUSLY DROWNED BY ITS SIBLING HATE."

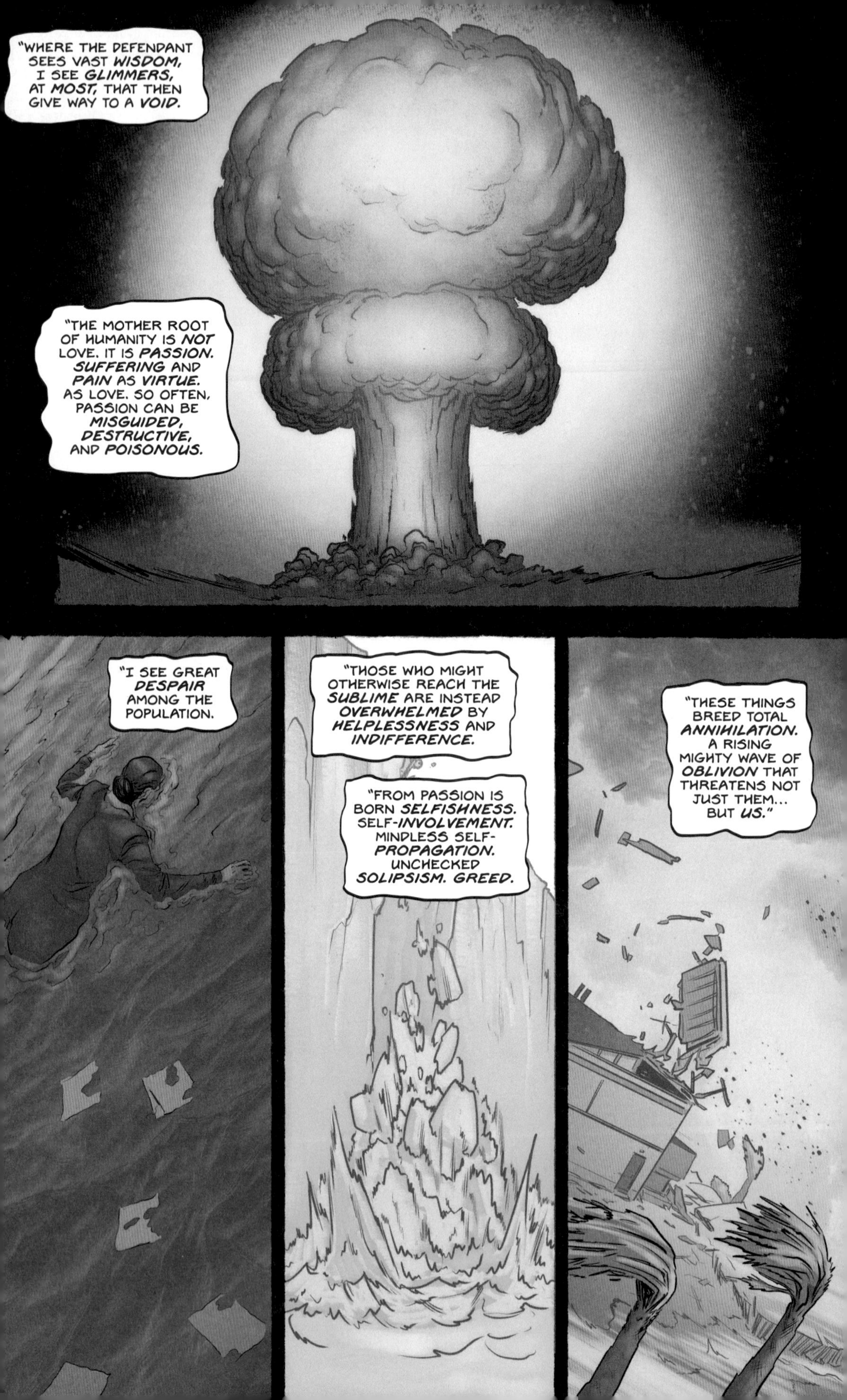
"WHERE THE DEFENDANT SEES VAST WISDOM, I SEE GLIMMERS, AT MOST, THAT THEN GIVE WAY TO A VOID.
"THE MOTHER ROOT OF HUMANITY IS NOT LOVE. IT IS PASSION. SUFFERING AND PAIN AS VIRTUE. AS LOVE. SO OFTEN, PASSION CAN BE MISGUIDED, DESTRUCTIVE, AND POISONOUS.
"I SEE GREAT DESPAIR AMONG THE POPULATION.
"THOSE WHO MIGHT OTHERWISE REACH THE SUBLIME ARE INSTEAD OVERWHELMED BY HELPLESSNESS AND INDIFFERENCE.
"FROM PASSION IS BORN SELFISHNESS. SELF-INVOLVEMENT. MINDLESS SELF-PROPAGATION. UNCHECKED SOLIPSISM. GREED.
"THESE THINGS BREED TOTAL ANNIHILATION. A RISING MIGHTY WAVE OF OBLIVION THAT THREATENS NOT JUST THEM... BUT US."

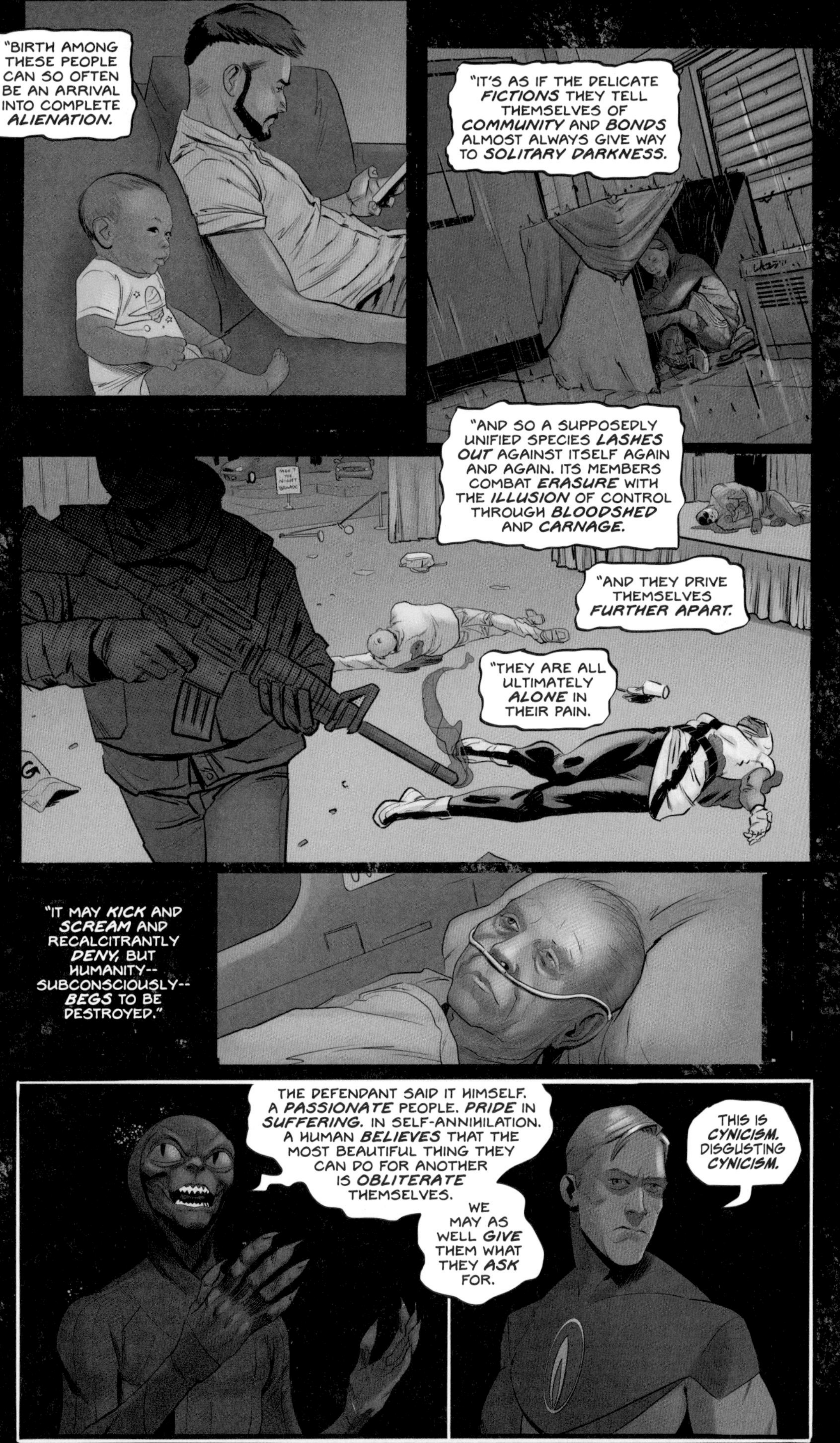

"BIRTH AMONG THESE PEOPLE CAN SO OFTEN BE AN ARRIVAL INTO COMPLETE *ALIENATION.*
"IT'S AS IF THE DELICATE *FICTIONS* THEY TELL THEMSELVES OF *COMMUNITY* AND *BONDS* ALMOST ALWAYS GIVE WAY TO *SOLITARY DARKNESS.*
"AND SO A SUPPOSEDLY UNIFIED SPECIES *LASHES OUT* AGAINST ITSELF AGAIN AND AGAIN. ITS MEMBERS COMBAT *ERASURE* WITH THE *ILLUSION* OF CONTROL THROUGH *BLOODSHED* AND *CARNAGE.*
"AND THEY DRIVE THEMSELVES *FURTHER APART.*
"THEY ARE ALL ULTIMATELY *ALONE* IN THEIR PAIN.
"IT MAY *KICK* AND *SCREAM* AND RECALCITRANTLY *DENY,* BUT HUMANITY-- SUBCONSCIOUSLY-- *BEGS* TO BE DESTROYED."
THE DEFENDANT SAID IT HIMSELF. A *PASSIONATE* PEOPLE. *PRIDE* IN *SUFFERING.* IN SELF-ANNIHILATION. A HUMAN *BELIEVES* THAT THE MOST BEAUTIFUL THING THEY CAN DO FOR ANOTHER IS *OBLITERATE* THEMSELVES.
WE MAY AS WELL *GIVE* THEM WHAT THEY *ASK* FOR.
THIS IS *CYNICISM.* DISGUSTING *CYNICISM.*

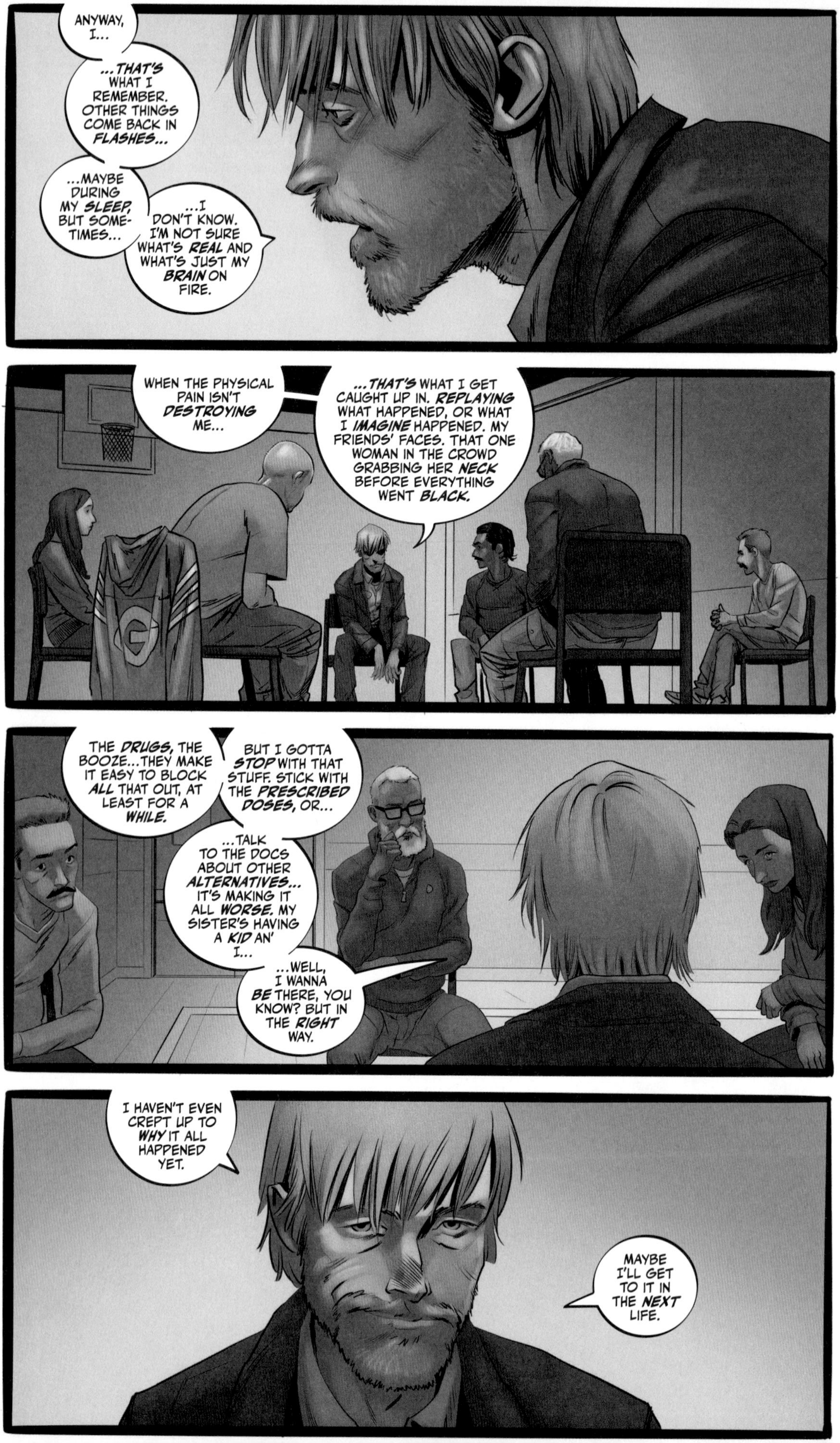
ANYWAY, I...
...THAT'S WHAT I REMEMBER. OTHER THINGS COME BACK IN FLASHES...
...MAYBE DURING MY SLEEP, BUT SOME-TIMES...
...I DON'T KNOW. I'M NOT SURE WHAT'S REAL AND WHAT'S JUST MY BRAIN ON FIRE.
WHEN THE PHYSICAL PAIN ISN'T DESTROYING ME...
...THAT'S WHAT I GET CAUGHT UP IN. REPLAYING WHAT HAPPENED, OR WHAT I IMAGINE HAPPENED. MY FRIENDS' FACES. THAT ONE WOMAN IN THE CROWD GRABBING HER NECK BEFORE EVERYTHING WENT BLACK.
THE DRUGS, THE BOOZE...THEY MAKE IT EASY TO BLOCK ALL THAT OUT, AT LEAST FOR A WHILE.
BUT I GOTTA STOP WITH THAT STUFF. STICK WITH THE PRESCRIBED DOSES, OR...
...TALK TO THE DOCS ABOUT OTHER ALTERNATIVES... IT'S MAKING IT ALL WORSE. MY SISTER'S HAVING A KID AN' I...
...WELL, I WANNA BE THERE, YOU KNOW? BUT IN THE RIGHT WAY.
I HAVEN'T EVEN CREPT UP TO WHY IT ALL HAPPENED YET.
MAYBE I'LL GET TO IT IN THE NEXT LIFE.

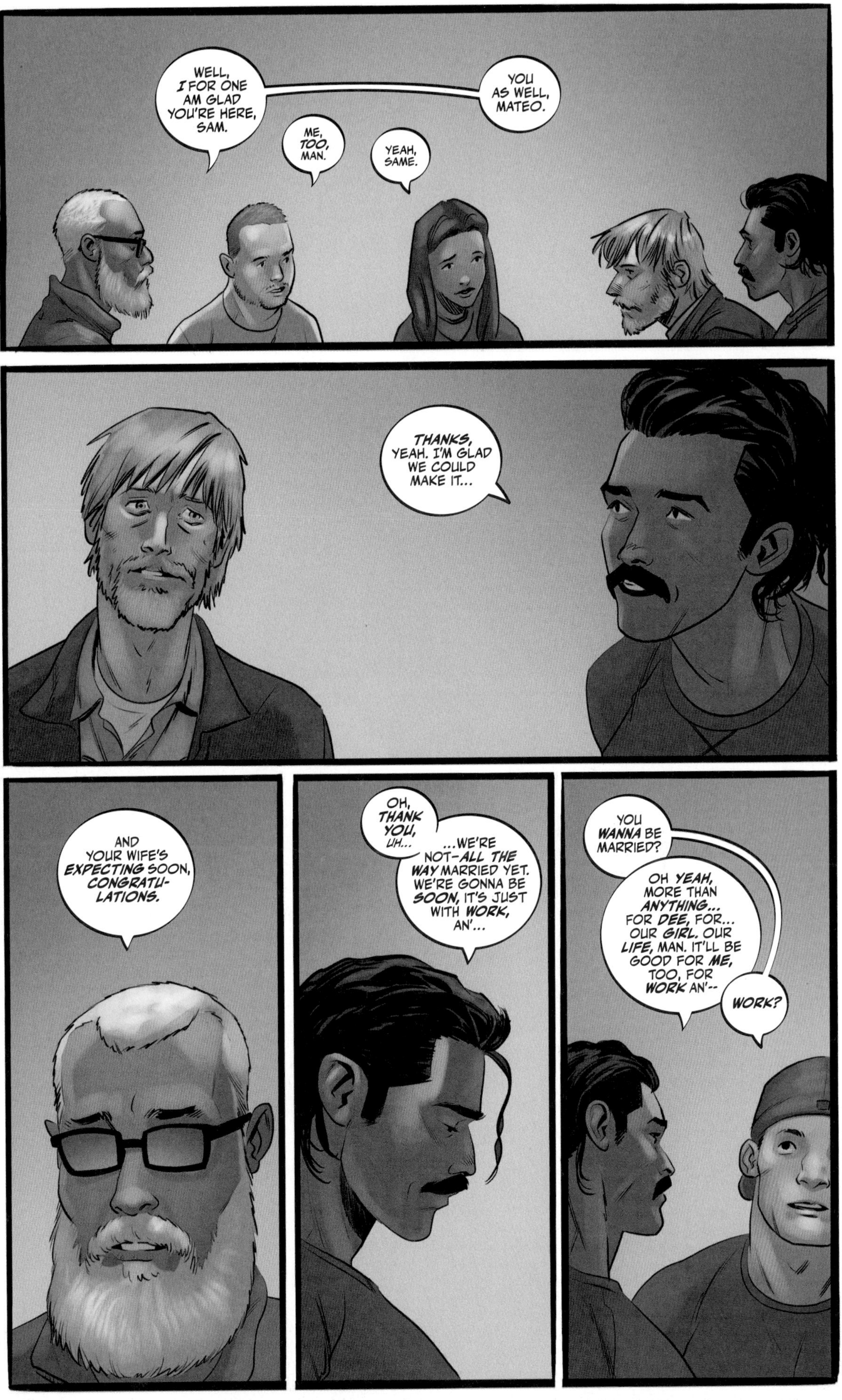
WELL, I FOR ONE AM GLAD YOU'RE HERE, SAM.
ME, TOO, MAN.
YEAH, SAME.
YOU AS WELL, MATEO.
THANKS, YEAH. I'M GLAD WE COULD MAKE IT...
AND YOUR WIFE'S EXPECTING SOON, CONGRATU-LATIONS.
OH, THANK YOU, UH...
...WE'RE NOT--ALL THE WAY MARRIED YET. WE'RE GONNA BE SOON, IT'S JUST WITH WORK, AN'...
YOU WANNA BE MARRIED?
OH YEAH, MORE THAN ANYTHING... FOR DEE, FOR... OUR GIRL. OUR LIFE, MAN. IT'LL BE GOOD FOR ME, TOO, FOR WORK AN'--
WORK?

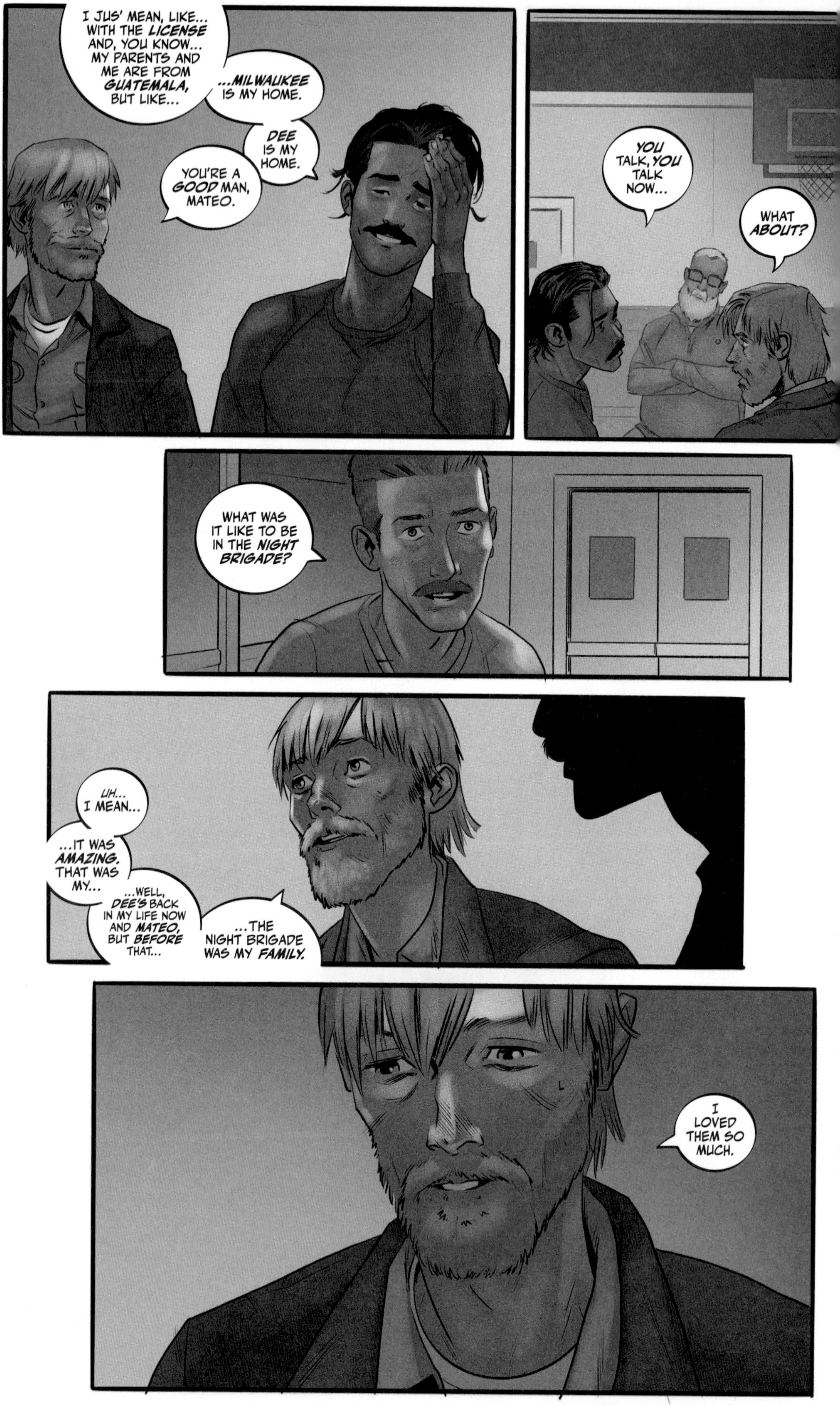
I JUS' MEAN, LIKE... WITH THE LICENSE AND, YOU KNOW... MY PARENTS AND ME ARE FROM GUATEMALA, BUT LIKE...
...MILWAUKEE IS MY HOME.
DEE IS MY HOME.
YOU'RE A GOOD MAN, MATEO.
YOU TALK, YOU TALK NOW...
WHAT ABOUT?
WHAT WAS IT LIKE TO BE IN THE NIGHT BRIGADE?
UH... I MEAN...
...IT WAS AMAZING. THAT WAS MY...
...WELL, DEE'S BACK IN MY LIFE NOW AND MATEO, BUT BEFORE THAT...
...THE NIGHT BRIGADE WAS MY FAMILY.
I LOVED THEM SO MUCH.

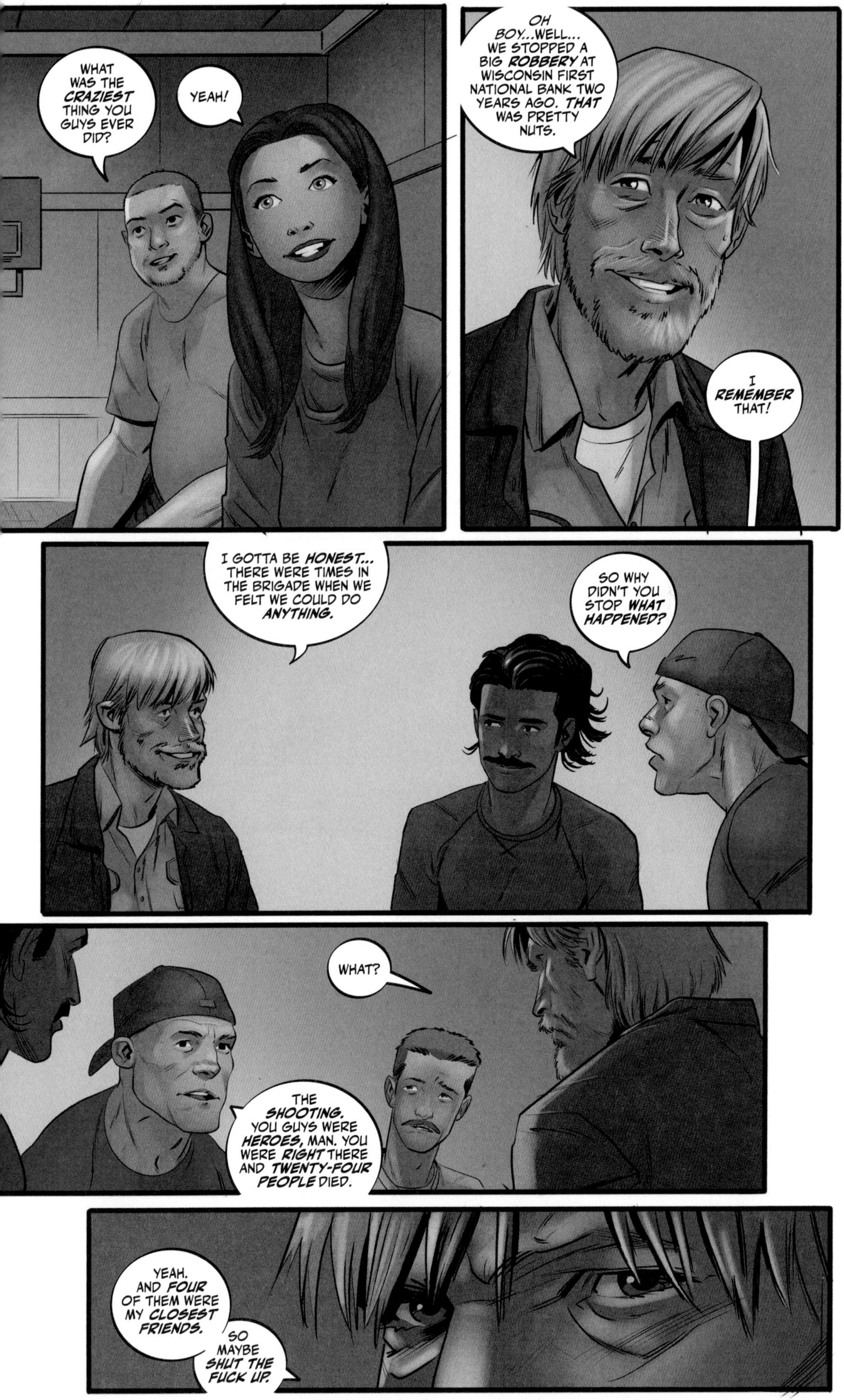
WHAT WAS THE CRAZIEST THING YOU GUYS EVER DID?
YEAH!
OH BOY...WELL... WE STOPPED A BIG ROBBERY AT WISCONSIN FIRST NATIONAL BANK TWO YEARS AGO. THAT WAS PRETTY NUTS.
I REMEMBER THAT!
I GOTTA BE HONEST... THERE WERE TIMES IN THE BRIGADE WHEN WE FELT WE COULD DO ANYTHING.
SO WHY DIDN'T YOU STOP WHAT HAPPENED?
WHAT?
THE SHOOTING. YOU GUYS WERE HEROES, MAN. YOU WERE RIGHT THERE AND TWENTY-FOUR PEOPLE DIED.
YEAH. AND FOUR OF THEM WERE MY CLOSEST FRIENDS.
SO MAYBE SHUT THE FUCK UP.

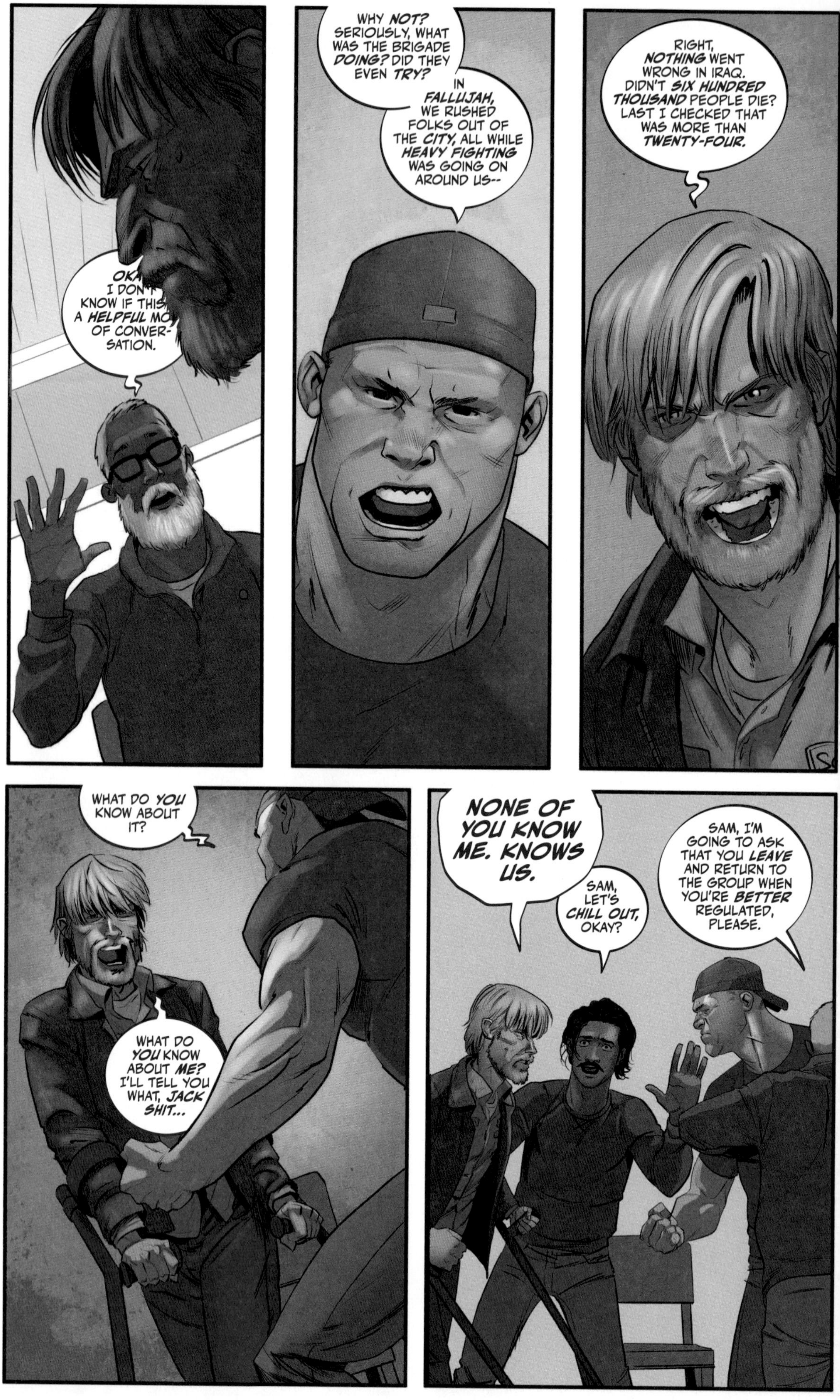
OKA
I DON'
KNOW IF THIS
A HELPFUL MO
OF CONVER-
SATION.
WHY NOT? SERIOUSLY, WHAT WAS THE BRIGADE DOING? DID THEY EVEN TRY?
IN FALLUJAH, WE RUSHED FOLKS OUT OF THE CITY, ALL WHILE HEAVY FIGHTING WAS GOING ON AROUND US--
RIGHT, NOTHING WENT WRONG IN IRAQ. DIDN'T SIX HUNDRED THOUSAND PEOPLE DIE? LAST I CHECKED THAT WAS MORE THAN TWENTY-FOUR.
WHAT DO YOU KNOW ABOUT IT?
WHAT DO YOU KNOW ABOUT ME? I'LL TELL YOU WHAT, JACK SHIT...
NONE OF YOU KNOW ME. KNOWS US.
SAM, LET'S CHILL OUT, OKAY?
SAM, I'M GOING TO ASK THAT YOU LEAVE AND RETURN TO THE GROUP WHEN YOU'RE BETTER REGULATED, PLEASE.

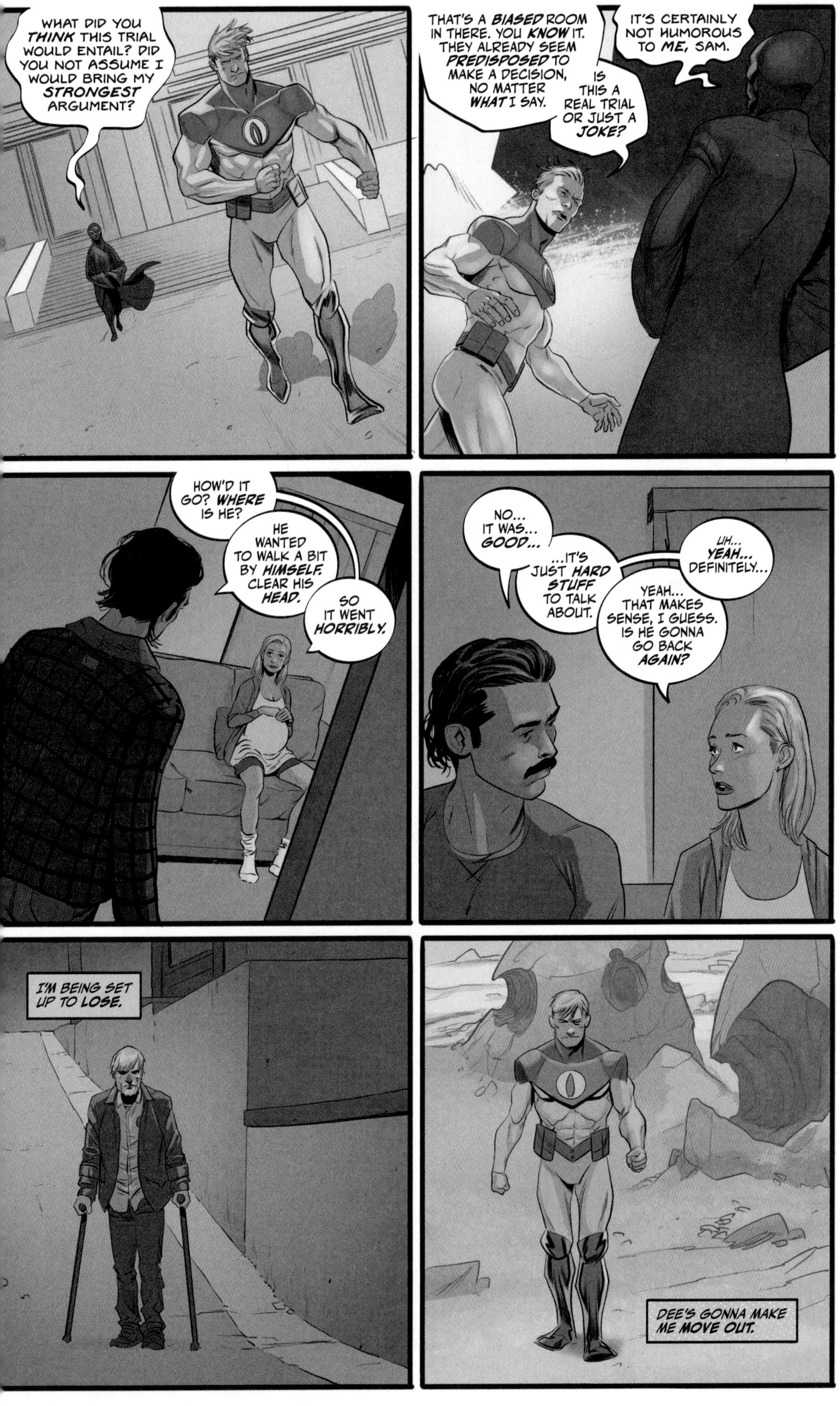
WHAT DID YOU THINK THIS TRIAL WOULD ENTAIL? DID YOU NOT ASSUME I WOULD BRING MY STRONGEST ARGUMENT?
THAT'S A BIASED ROOM IN THERE. YOU KNOW IT. THEY ALREADY SEEM PREDISPOSED TO MAKE A DECISION, NO MATTER WHAT I SAY.
IS THIS A REAL TRIAL OR JUST A JOKE?
IT'S CERTAINLY NOT HUMOROUS TO ME, SAM.
HOW'D IT GO? WHERE IS HE?
HE WANTED TO WALK A BIT BY HIMSELF. CLEAR HIS HEAD.
SO IT WENT HORRIBLY.
NO... IT WAS... GOOD...
...IT'S JUST HARD STUFF TO TALK ABOUT.
UH... YEAH... DEFINITELY...
YEAH... THAT MAKES SENSE, I GUESS. IS HE GONNA GO BACK AGAIN?
I'M BEING SET UP TO LOSE.
DEE'S GONNA MAKE ME MOVE OUT.

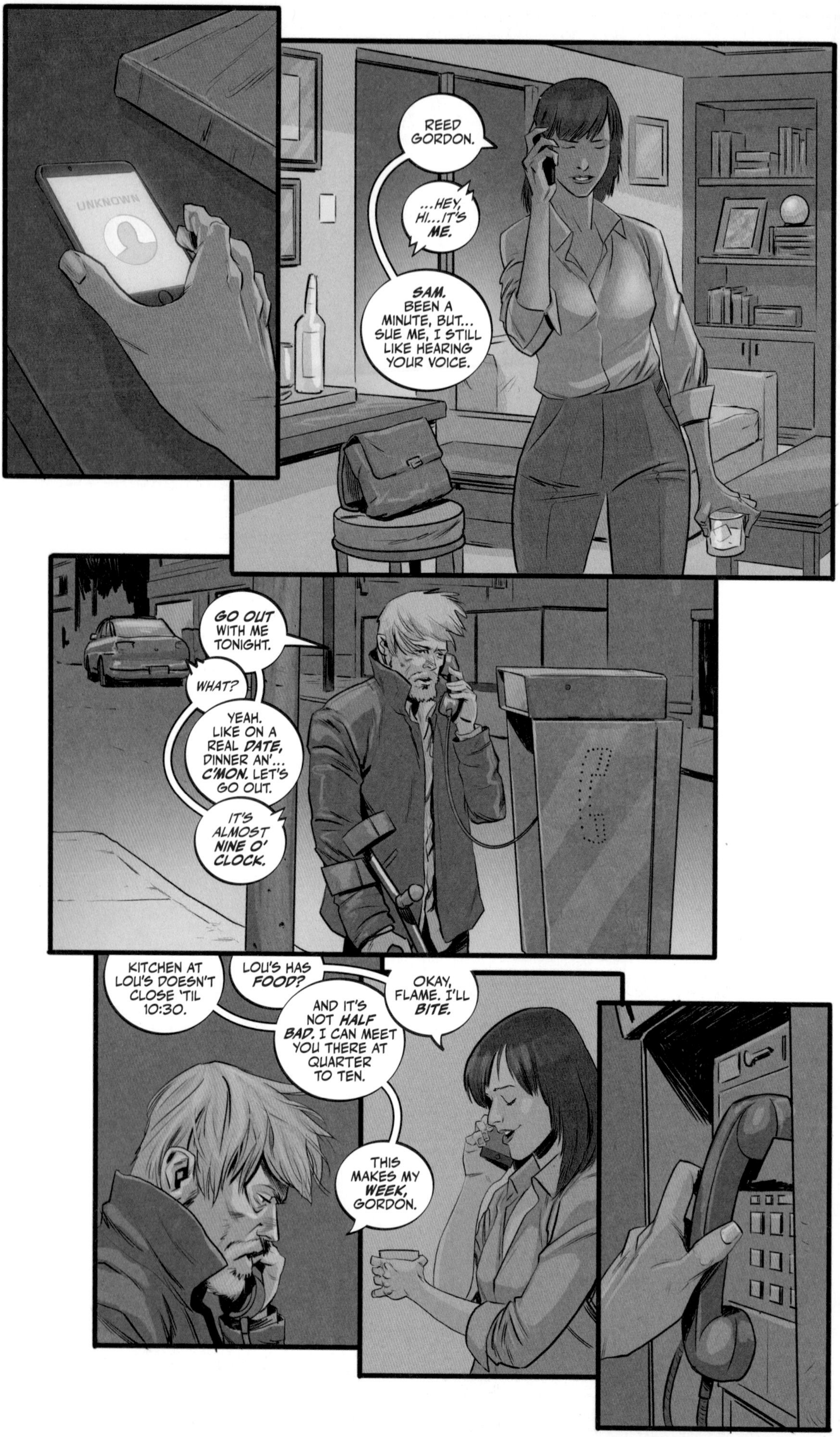
UNKNOWN
REED GORDON.
...HEY, HI...IT'S ME.
SAM. BEEN A MINUTE, BUT... SUE ME, I STILL LIKE HEARING YOUR VOICE.
GO OUT WITH ME TONIGHT.
WHAT?
YEAH. LIKE ON A REAL DATE, DINNER AN'... C'MON. LET'S GO OUT.
IT'S ALMOST NINE O' CLOCK.
KITCHEN AT LOU'S DOESN'T CLOSE 'TIL 10:30.
LOU'S HAS FOOD?
AND IT'S NOT HALF BAD. I CAN MEET YOU THERE AT QUARTER TO TEN.
OKAY, FLAME. I'LL BITE.
THIS MAKES MY WEEK, GORDON.

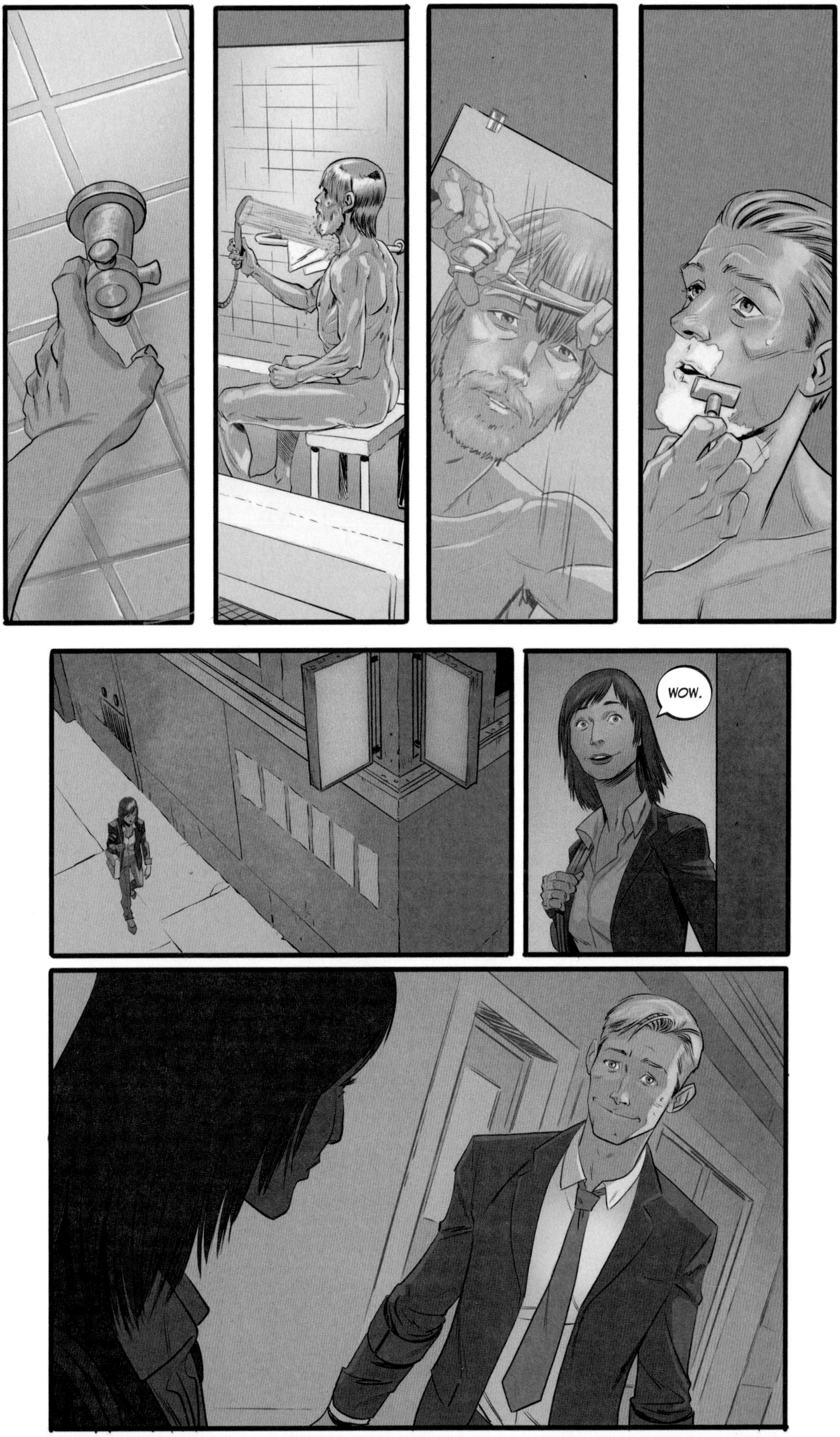
WOW.

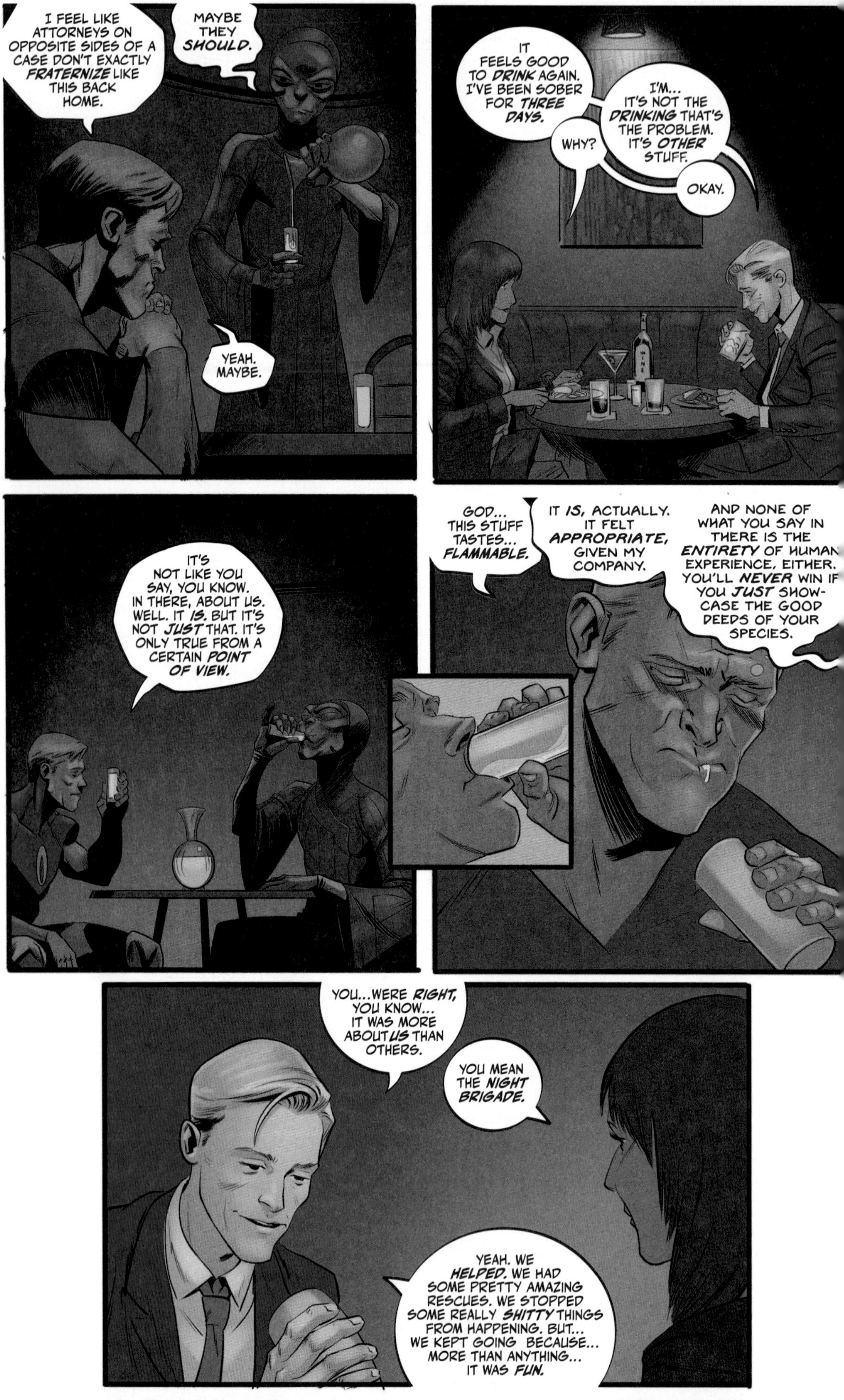
I FEEL LIKE ATTORNEYS ON OPPOSITE SIDES OF A CASE DON'T EXACTLY FRATERNIZE LIKE THIS BACK HOME.
MAYBE THEY SHOULD.
YEAH. MAYBE.
IT FEELS GOOD TO DRINK AGAIN. I'VE BEEN SOBER FOR THREE DAYS.
WHY?
I'M... IT'S NOT THE DRINKING THAT'S THE PROBLEM. IT'S OTHER STUFF.
OKAY.
IT'S NOT LIKE YOU SAY, YOU KNOW. IN THERE, ABOUT US. WELL. IT IS. BUT IT'S NOT JUST THAT. IT'S ONLY TRUE FROM A CERTAIN POINT OF VIEW.
GOD... THIS STUFF TASTES... FLAMMABLE.
IT IS, ACTUALLY. IT FELT APPROPRIATE, GIVEN MY COMPANY.
AND NONE OF WHAT YOU SAY IN THERE IS THE ENTIRETY OF HUMAN EXPERIENCE, EITHER. YOU'LL NEVER WIN IF YOU JUST SHOW-CASE THE GOOD DEEDS OF YOUR SPECIES.
YOU...WERE RIGHT, YOU KNOW... IT WAS MORE ABOUT US THAN OTHERS.
YOU MEAN THE NIGHT BRIGADE.
YEAH. WE HELPED. WE HAD SOME PRETTY AMAZING RESCUES. WE STOPPED SOME REALLY SHITTY THINGS FROM HAPPENING. BUT... WE KEPT GOING BECAUSE... MORE THAN ANYTHING... IT WAS FUN.

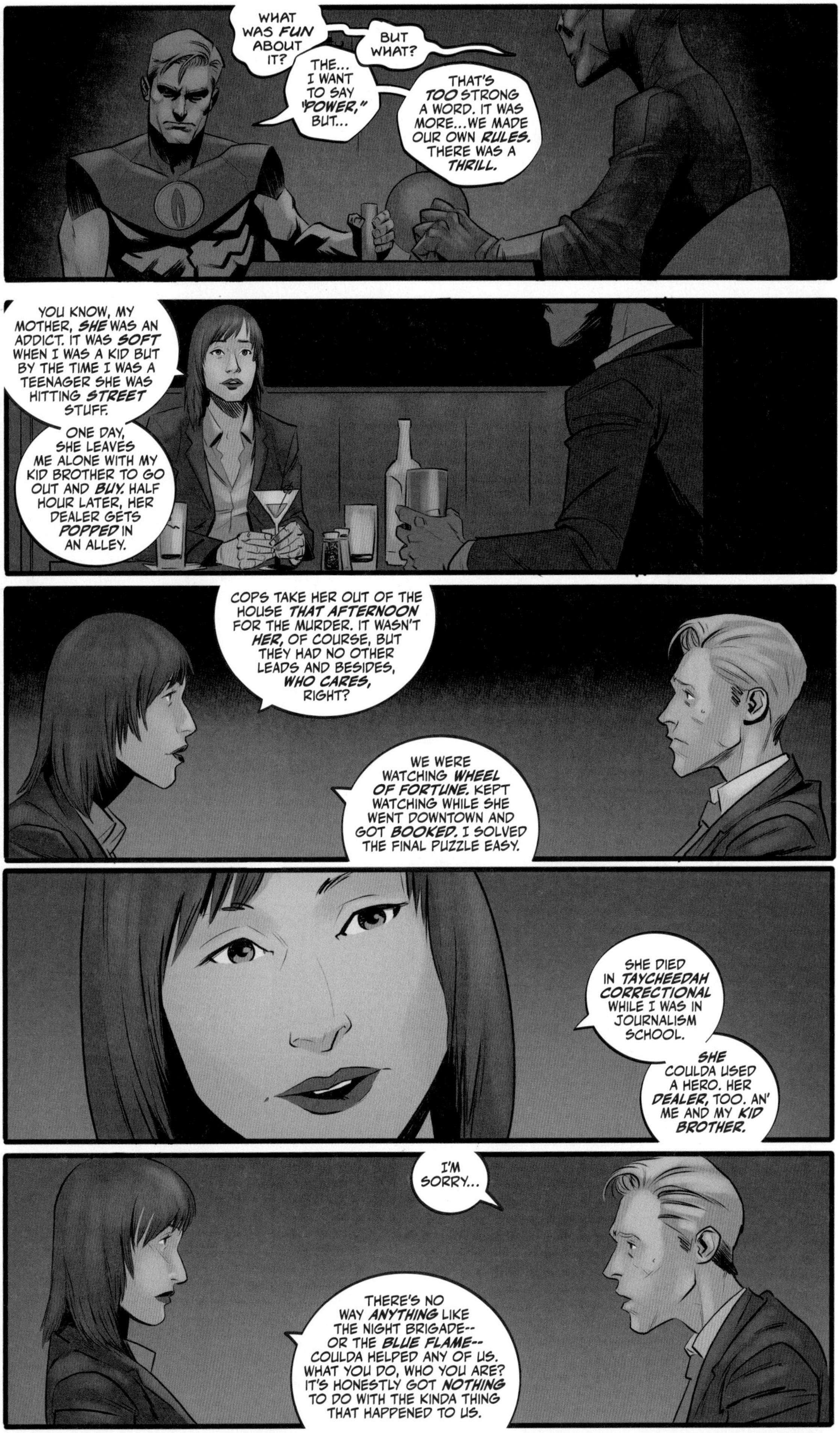
WHAT WAS FUN ABOUT IT?
BUT WHAT?
THE... I WANT TO SAY "POWER," BUT...
THAT'S TOO STRONG A WORD. IT WAS MORE...WE MADE OUR OWN RULES. THERE WAS A THRILL.
YOU KNOW, MY MOTHER, SHE WAS AN ADDICT. IT WAS SOFT WHEN I WAS A KID BUT BY THE TIME I WAS A TEENAGER SHE WAS HITTING STREET STUFF.
ONE DAY, SHE LEAVES ME ALONE WITH MY KID BROTHER TO GO OUT AND BUY. HALF HOUR LATER, HER DEALER GETS POPPED IN AN ALLEY.
COPS TAKE HER OUT OF THE HOUSE THAT AFTERNOON FOR THE MURDER. IT WASN'T HER, OF COURSE, BUT THEY HAD NO OTHER LEADS AND BESIDES, WHO CARES, RIGHT?
WE WERE WATCHING WHEEL OF FORTUNE. KEPT WATCHING WHILE SHE WENT DOWNTOWN AND GOT BOOKED. I SOLVED THE FINAL PUZZLE EASY.
SHE DIED IN TAYCHEEDAH CORRECTIONAL WHILE I WAS IN JOURNALISM SCHOOL.
SHE COULDA USED A HERO. HER DEALER, TOO. AN' ME AND MY KID BROTHER.
I'M SORRY...
THERE'S NO WAY ANYTHING LIKE THE NIGHT BRIGADE-- OR THE BLUE FLAME-- COULDA HELPED ANY OF US. WHAT YOU DO, WHO YOU ARE? IT'S HONESTLY GOT NOTHING TO DO WITH THE KINDA THING THAT HAPPENED TO US.

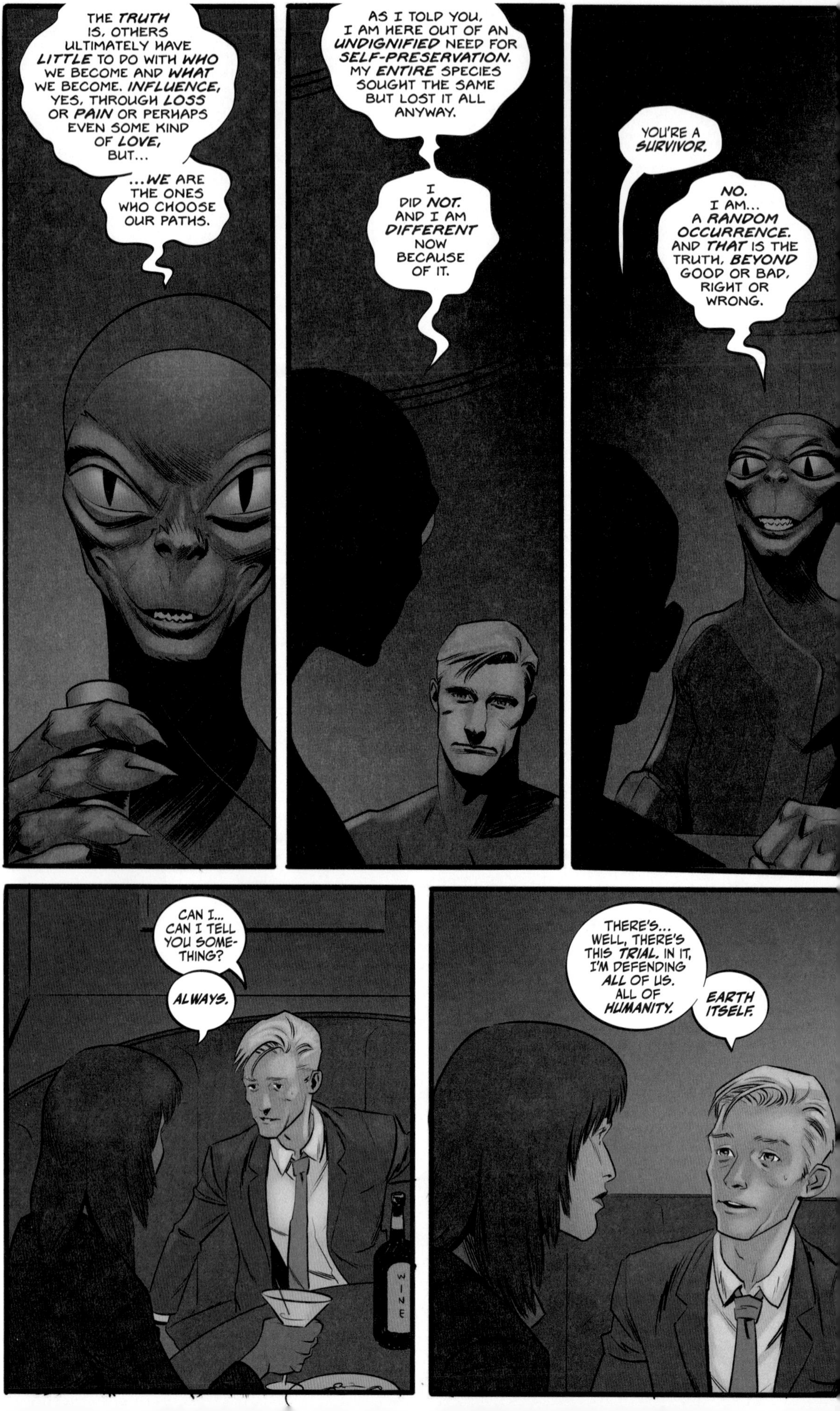

THE TRUTH IS, OTHERS ULTIMATELY HAVE LITTLE TO DO WITH WHO WE BECOME AND WHAT WE BECOME. INFLUENCE, YES, THROUGH LOSS OR PAIN OR PERHAPS EVEN SOME KIND OF LOVE, BUT...
...WE ARE THE ONES WHO CHOOSE OUR PATHS.
AS I TOLD YOU, I AM HERE OUT OF AN UNDIGNIFIED NEED FOR SELF-PRESERVATION. MY ENTIRE SPECIES SOUGHT THE SAME BUT LOST IT ALL ANYWAY.
I DID NOT. AND I AM DIFFERENT NOW BECAUSE OF IT.
YOU'RE A SURVIVOR.
NO. I AM... A RANDOM OCCURRENCE. AND THAT IS THE TRUTH, BEYOND GOOD OR BAD, RIGHT OR WRONG.
CAN I... CAN I TELL YOU SOME-THING?
ALWAYS.
WINE
THERE'S... WELL, THERE'S THIS TRIAL. IN IT, I'M DEFENDING ALL OF US. ALL OF HUMANITY.
EARTH ITSELF.

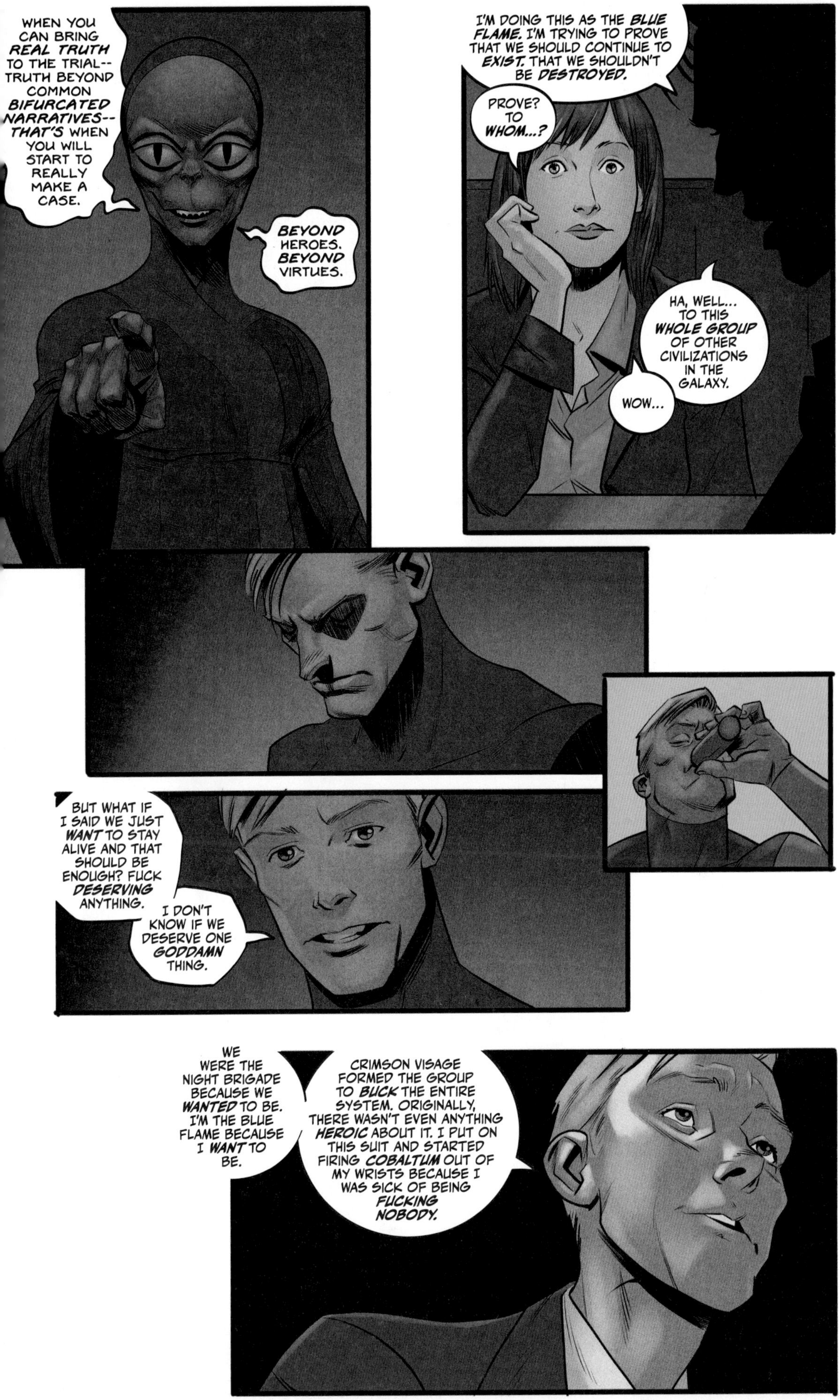
WHEN YOU CAN BRING REAL TRUTH TO THE TRIAL-- TRUTH BEYOND COMMON BIFURCATED NARRATIVES-- THAT'S WHEN YOU WILL START TO REALLY MAKE A CASE.
BEYOND HEROES. BEYOND VIRTUES.
I'M DOING THIS AS THE BLUE FLAME. I'M TRYING TO PROVE THAT WE SHOULD CONTINUE TO EXIST. THAT WE SHOULDN'T BE DESTROYED.
PROVE? TO WHOM...?
HA, WELL... TO THIS WHOLE GROUP OF OTHER CIVILIZATIONS IN THE GALAXY.
WOW...
BUT WHAT IF I SAID WE JUST WANT TO STAY ALIVE AND THAT SHOULD BE ENOUGH? FUCK DESERVING ANYTHING.
I DON'T KNOW IF WE DESERVE ONE GODDAMN THING.
WE WERE THE NIGHT BRIGADE BECAUSE WE WANTED TO BE. I'M THE BLUE FLAME BECAUSE I WANT TO BE.
CRIMSON VISAGE FORMED THE GROUP TO BUCK THE ENTIRE SYSTEM. ORIGINALLY, THERE WASN'T EVEN ANYTHING HEROIC ABOUT IT. I PUT ON THIS SUIT AND STARTED FIRING COBALTUM OUT OF MY WRISTS BECAUSE I WAS SICK OF BEING FUCKING NOBODY.

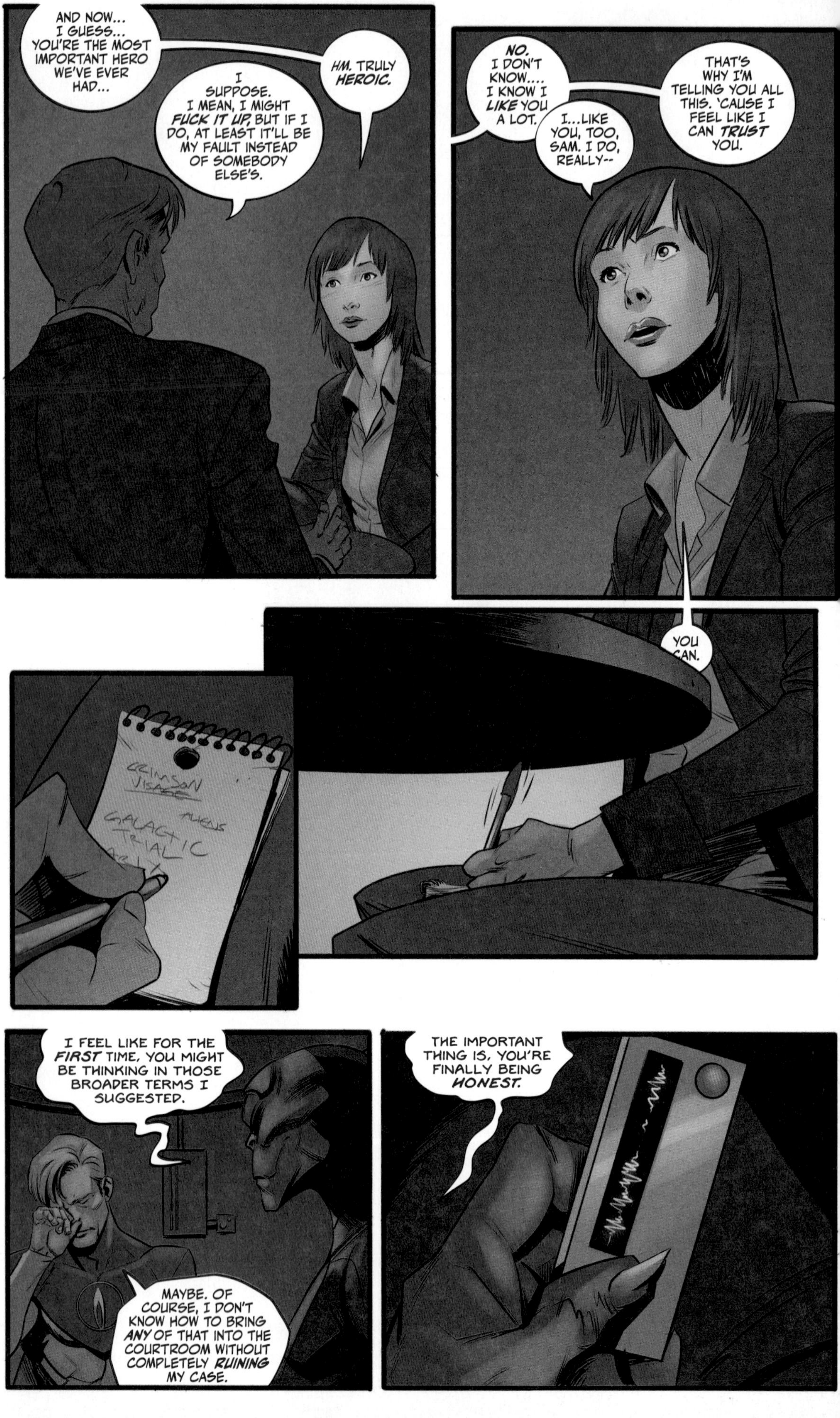
AND NOW... I GUESS... YOU'RE THE MOST IMPORTANT HERO WE'VE EVER HAD...
HM. TRULY HEROIC.
I SUPPOSE. I MEAN, I MIGHT FUCK IT UP, BUT IF I DO, AT LEAST IT'LL BE MY FAULT INSTEAD OF SOMEBODY ELSE'S.
NO. I DON'T KNOW.... I KNOW I LIKE YOU A LOT.
I...LIKE YOU, TOO, SAM. I DO, REALLY--
THAT'S WHY I'M TELLING YOU ALL THIS. 'CAUSE I FEEL LIKE I CAN TRUST YOU.
YOU CAN.
CRIMSON VISAGE
ALIENS
GALACTIC TRIAL
I FEEL LIKE FOR THE FIRST TIME, YOU MIGHT BE THINKING IN THOSE BROADER TERMS I SUGGESTED.
MAYBE. OF COURSE, I DON'T KNOW HOW TO BRING ANY OF THAT INTO THE COURTROOM WITHOUT COMPLETELY RUINING MY CASE.
THE IMPORTANT THING IS, YOU'RE FINALLY BEING HONEST.

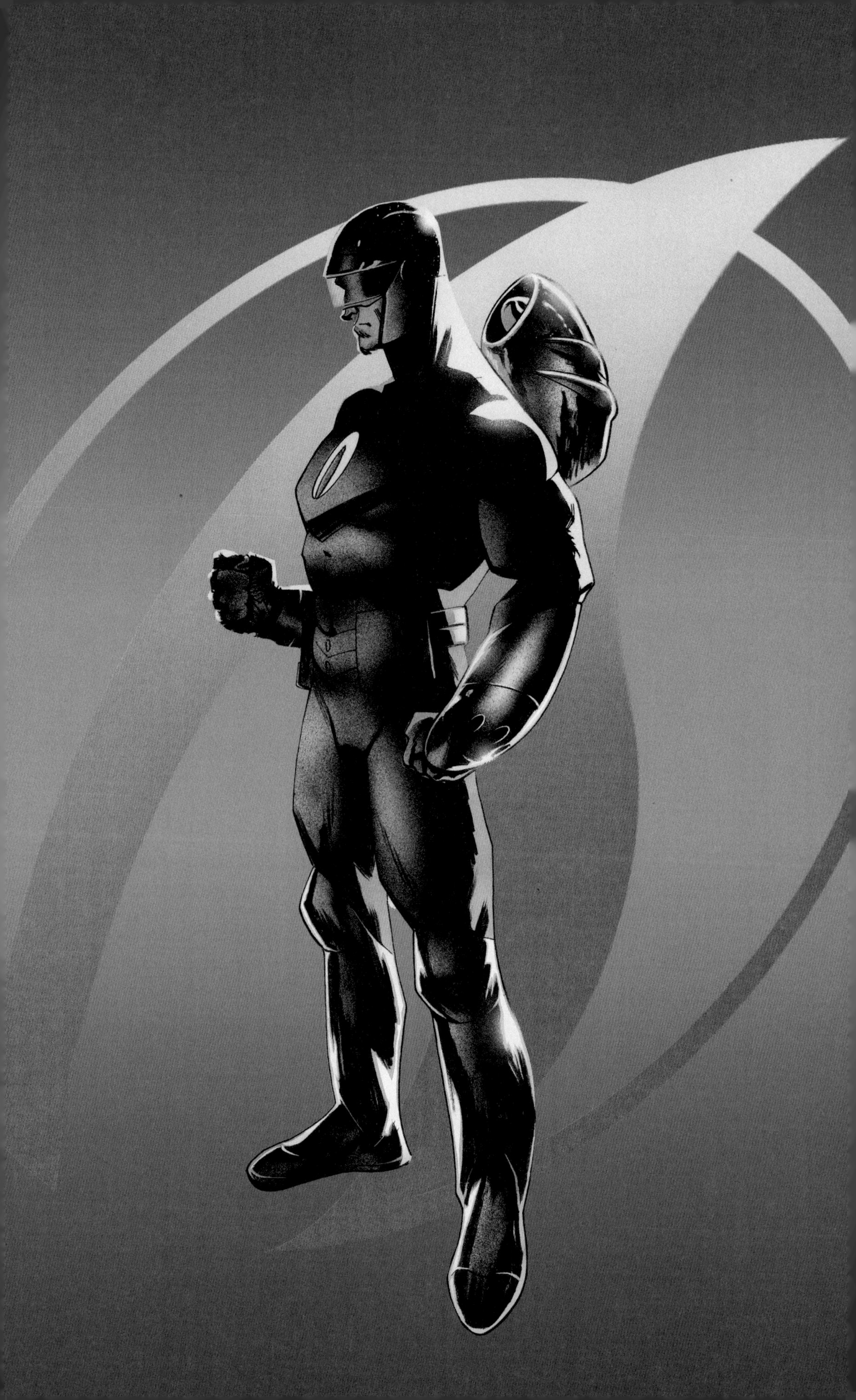

VENGEANCE NEEDS NO CHAMPION

CHAPTER 6

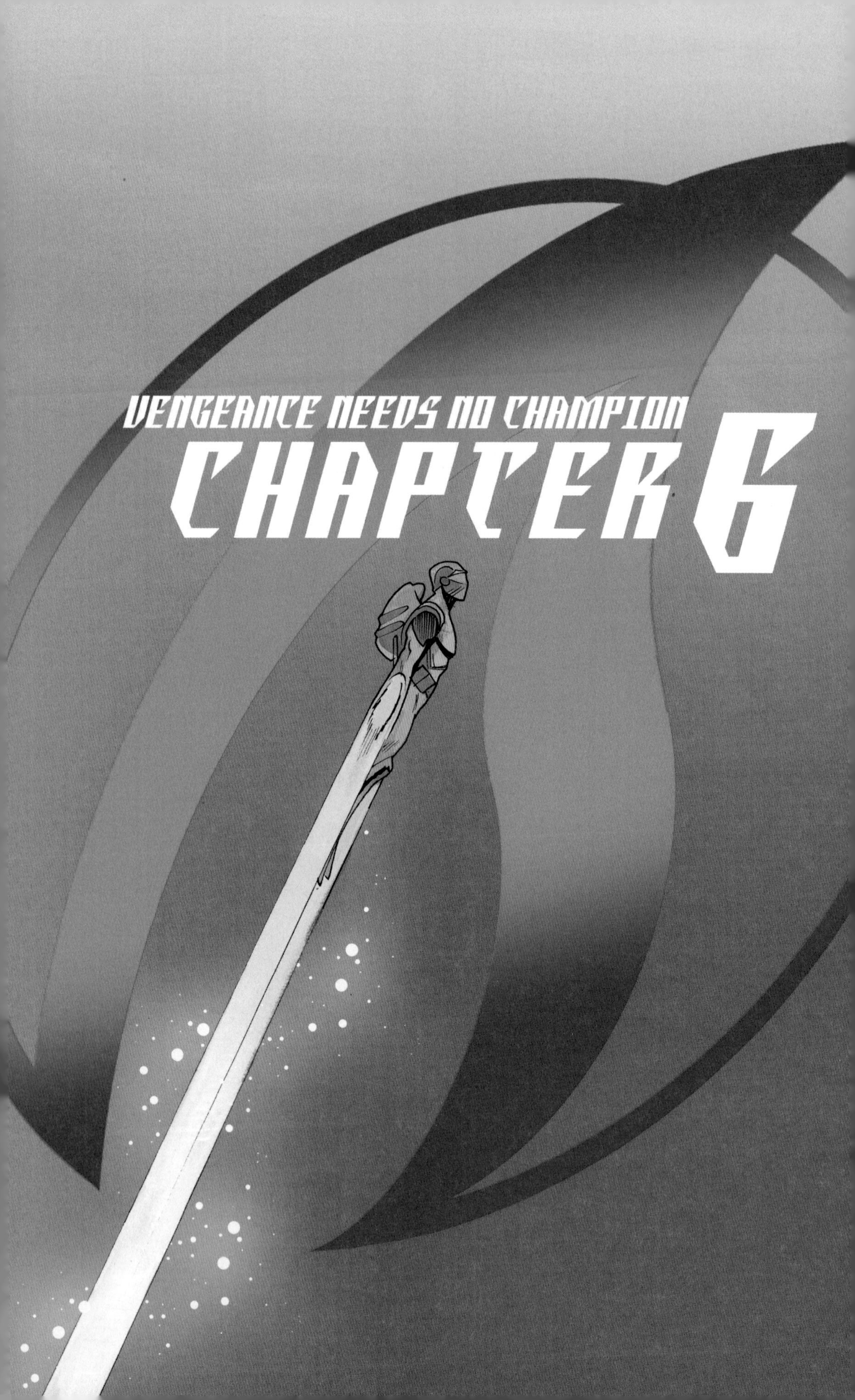

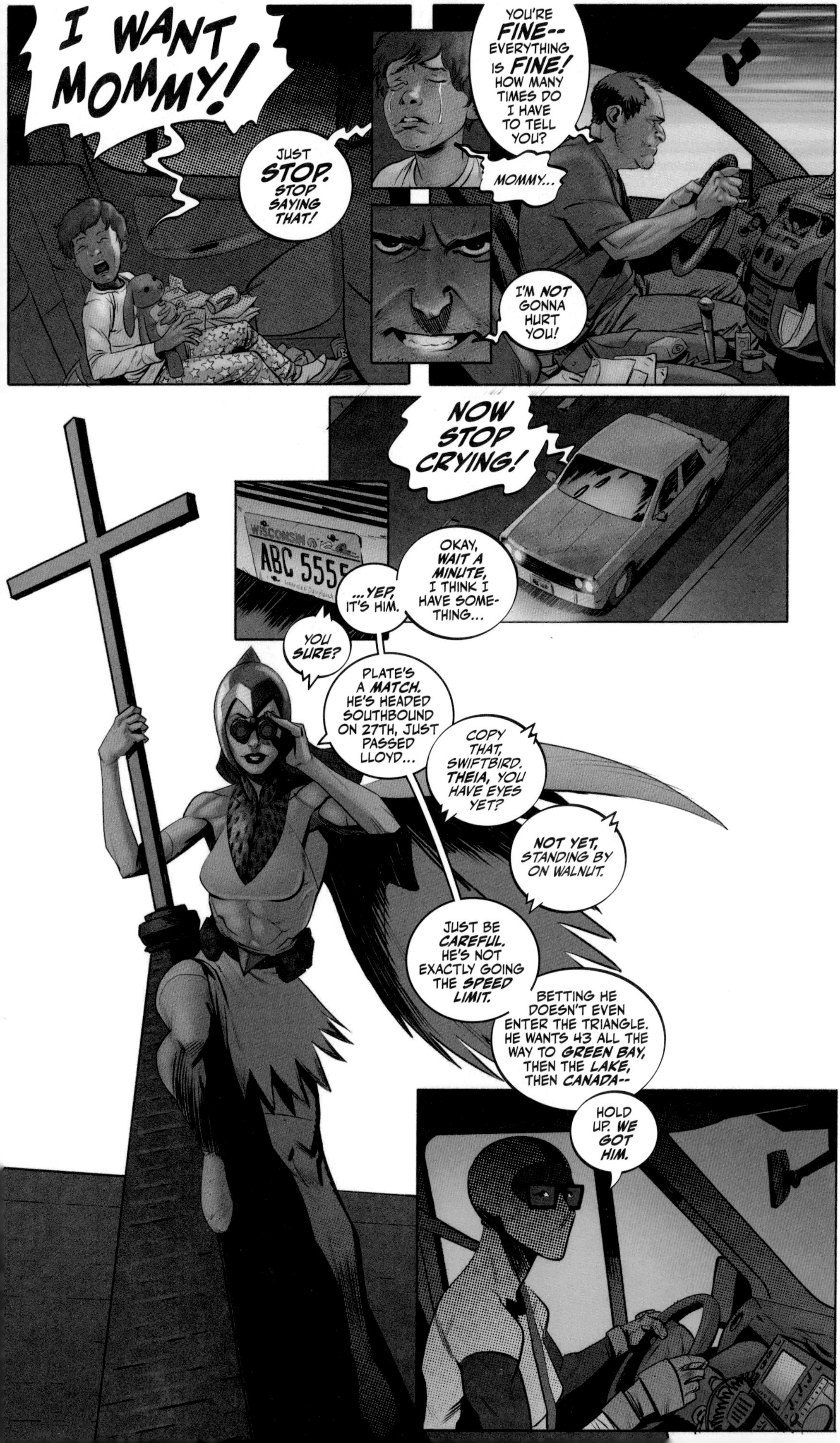
I WANT MOMMY!
JUST STOP. STOP SAYING THAT!
YOU'RE FINE-- EVERYTHING IS FINE! HOW MANY TIMES DO I HAVE TO TELL YOU?
MOMMY...
I'M NOT GONNA HURT YOU!
NOW STOP CRYING!
WISCONSIN
ABC 5555
OKAY, WAIT A MINUTE, I THINK I HAVE SOME-THING...
...YEP, IT'S HIM.
YOU SURE?
PLATE'S A MATCH. HE'S HEADED SOUTHBOUND ON 27TH, JUST PASSED LLOYD...
COPY THAT, SWIFTBIRD. THEIA, YOU HAVE EYES YET?
NOT YET, STANDING BY ON WALNUT.
JUST BE CAREFUL. HE'S NOT EXACTLY GOING THE SPEED LIMIT.
BETTING HE DOESN'T EVEN ENTER THE TRIANGLE. HE WANTS 43 ALL THE WAY TO GREEN BAY, THEN THE LAKE, THEN CANADA--
HOLD UP. WE GOT HIM.

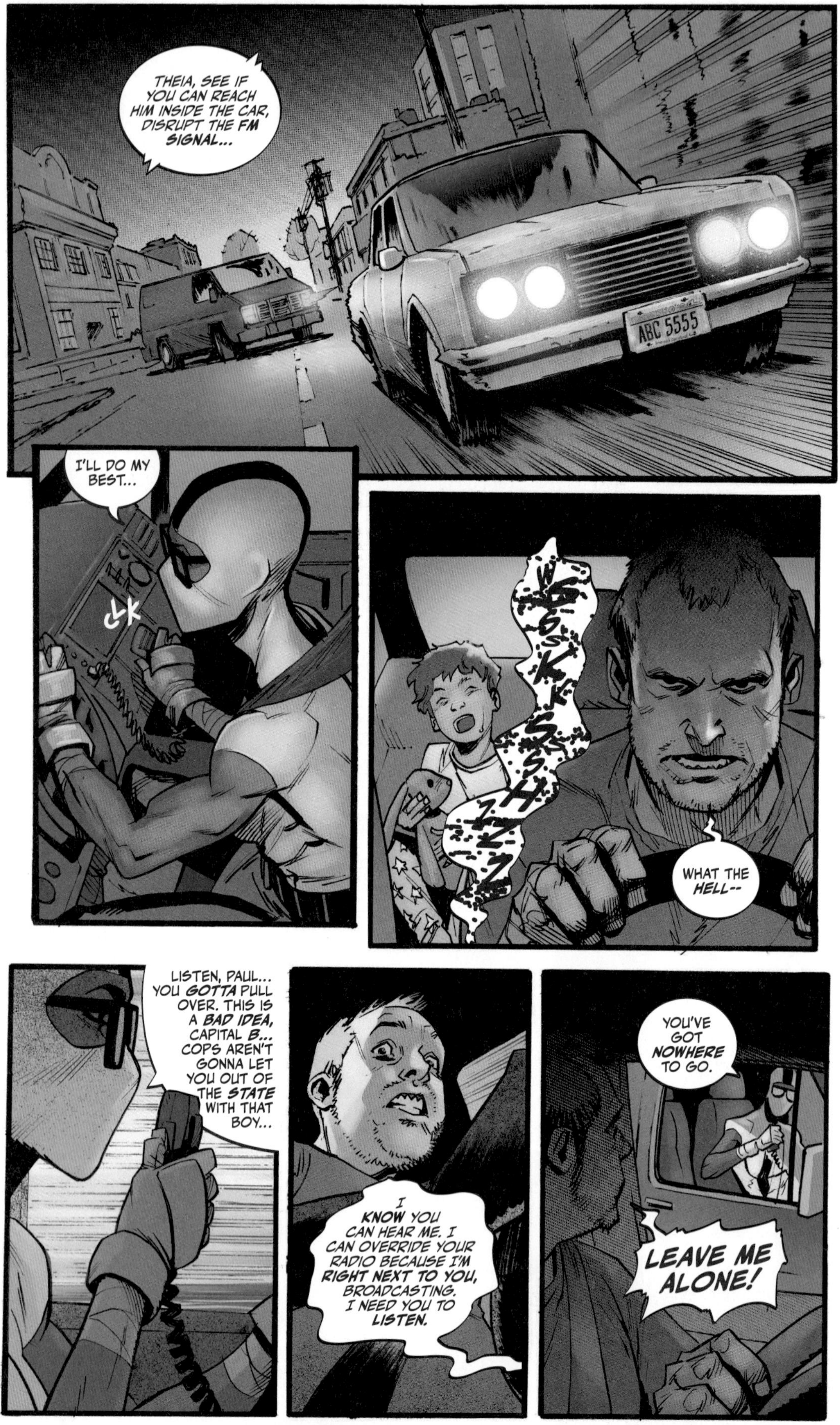
THEIA, SEE IF YOU CAN REACH HIM INSIDE THE CAR, DISRUPT THE FM SIGNAL...
ABC 5555
I'LL DO MY BEST...
CLK
WHAT THE HELL--
LISTEN, PAUL... YOU GOTTA PULL OVER. THIS IS A BAD IDEA, CAPITAL B... COPS AREN'T GONNA LET YOU OUT OF THE STATE WITH THAT BOY...
I KNOW YOU CAN HEAR ME. I CAN OVERRIDE YOUR RADIO BECAUSE I'M RIGHT NEXT TO YOU, BROADCASTING. I NEED YOU TO LISTEN.
YOU'VE GOT NOWHERE TO GO.
LEAVE ME ALONE!

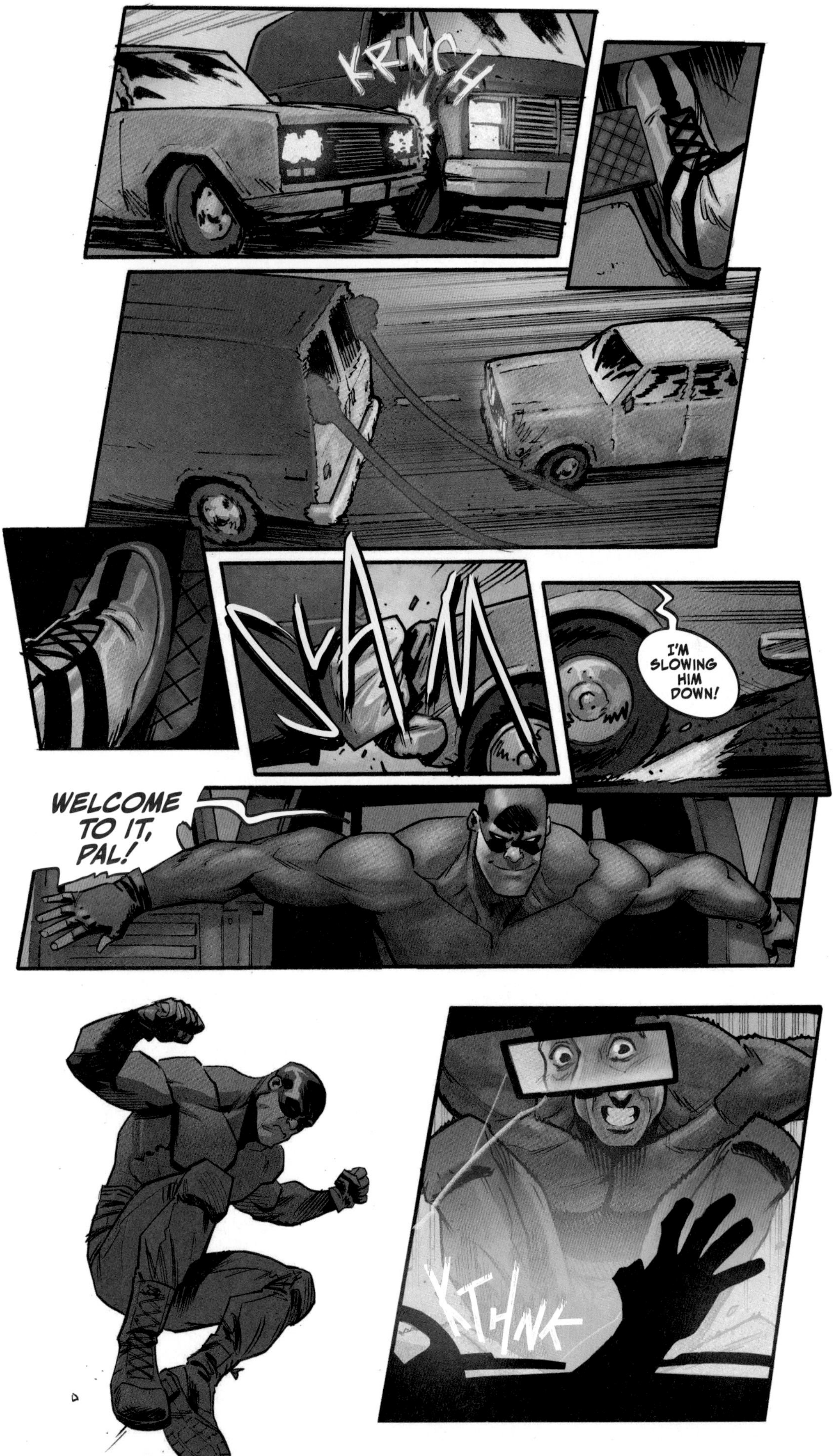
KRNCH
SLAM
I'M SLOWING HIM DOWN!
WELCOME TO IT, PAL!
KTHNK

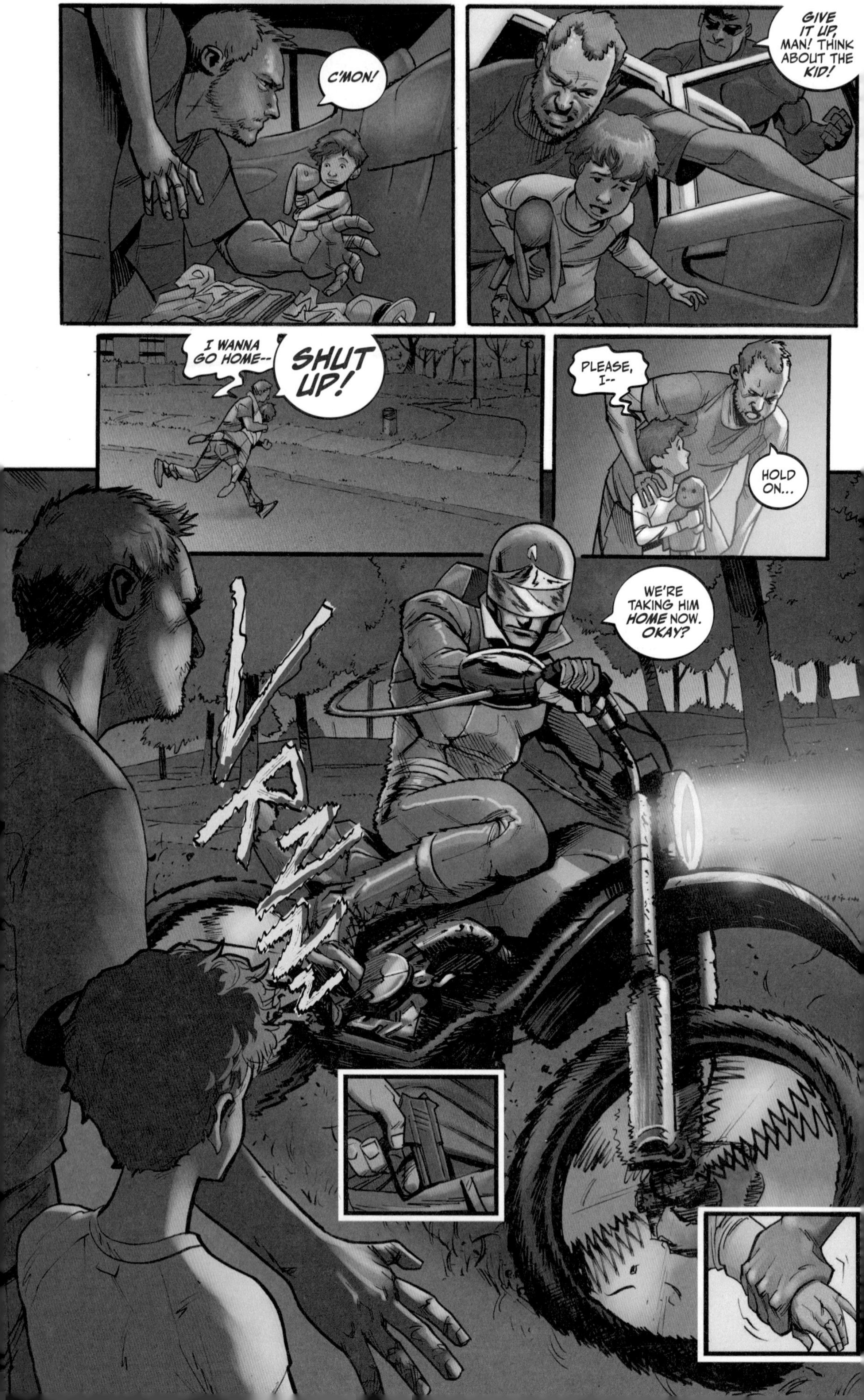
C'MON!
GIVE IT UP, MAN! THINK ABOUT THE KID!
I WANNA GO HOME--
SHUT UP!
PLEASE, I--
HOLD ON...
WE'RE TAKING HIM HOME NOW. OKAY?
VRRMMM

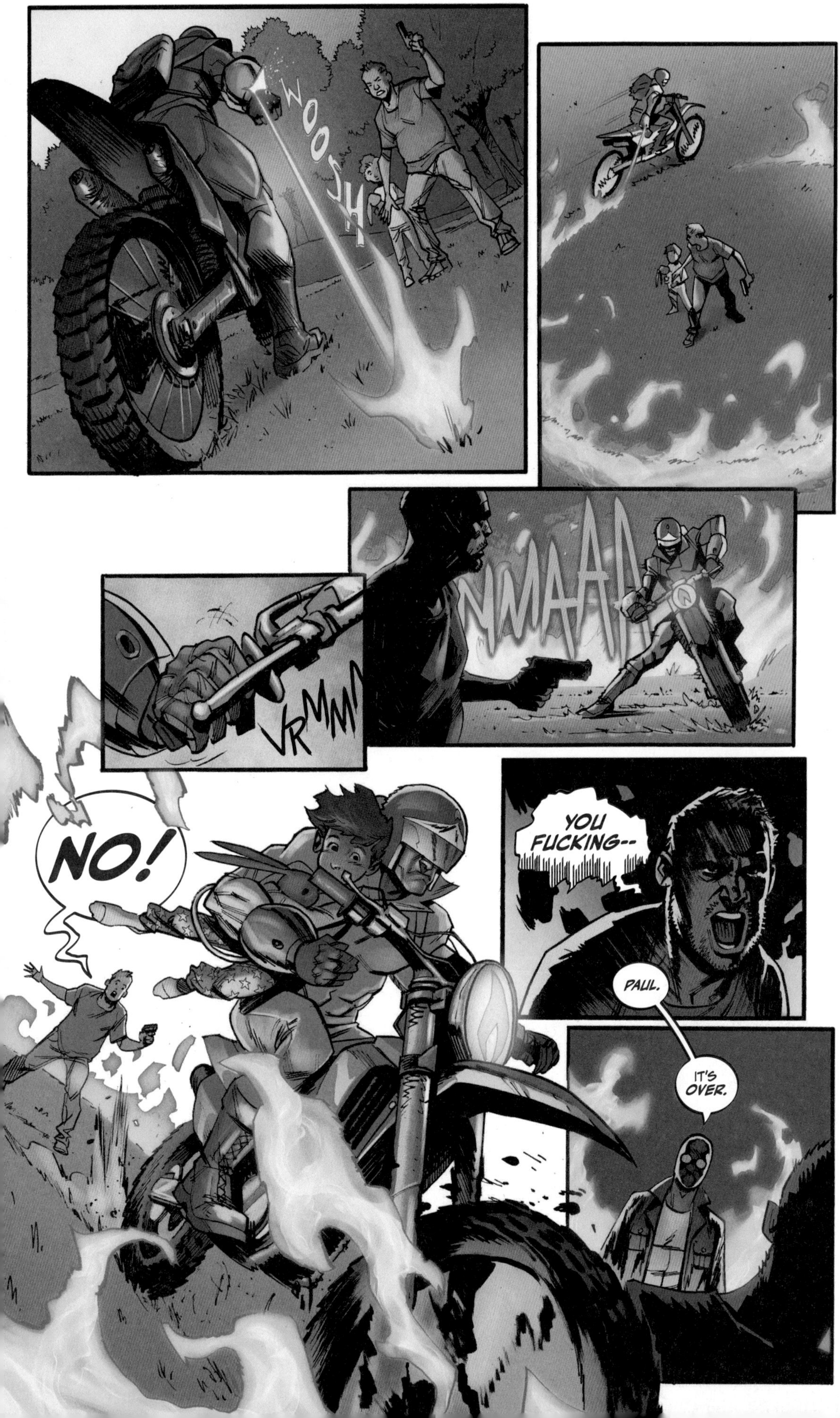
WOOOSH
VRMMM
NMAAA
NO!
YOU FUCKING--
PAUL.
IT'S OVER.

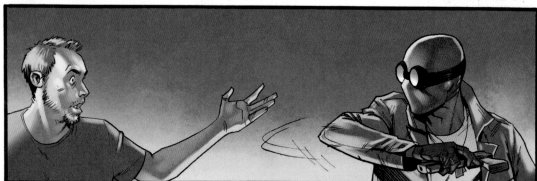

IT'S GONNA BE ALRIGHT.

THAT'S MY *SON*, MAN... I JUST WANNA BE WITH MY *SON*...

I *KNOW*. BUT *THIS* ISN'T THE WAY TO DO IT.

I...I *LOVE* HIM... I WOULD *NEVER*... HURT HIM...

YOU *DID*, THOUGH. NOT *BAD*. NOT *FOREVER*. BUT YOU *DID*. THIS-- WHAT YOU DID TODAY...

...THIS *HURT* HIM.

AND THEY'RE GOING TO TAKE YOU *AWAY* FOR A WHILE BECAUSE OF THAT.

POLICE ////

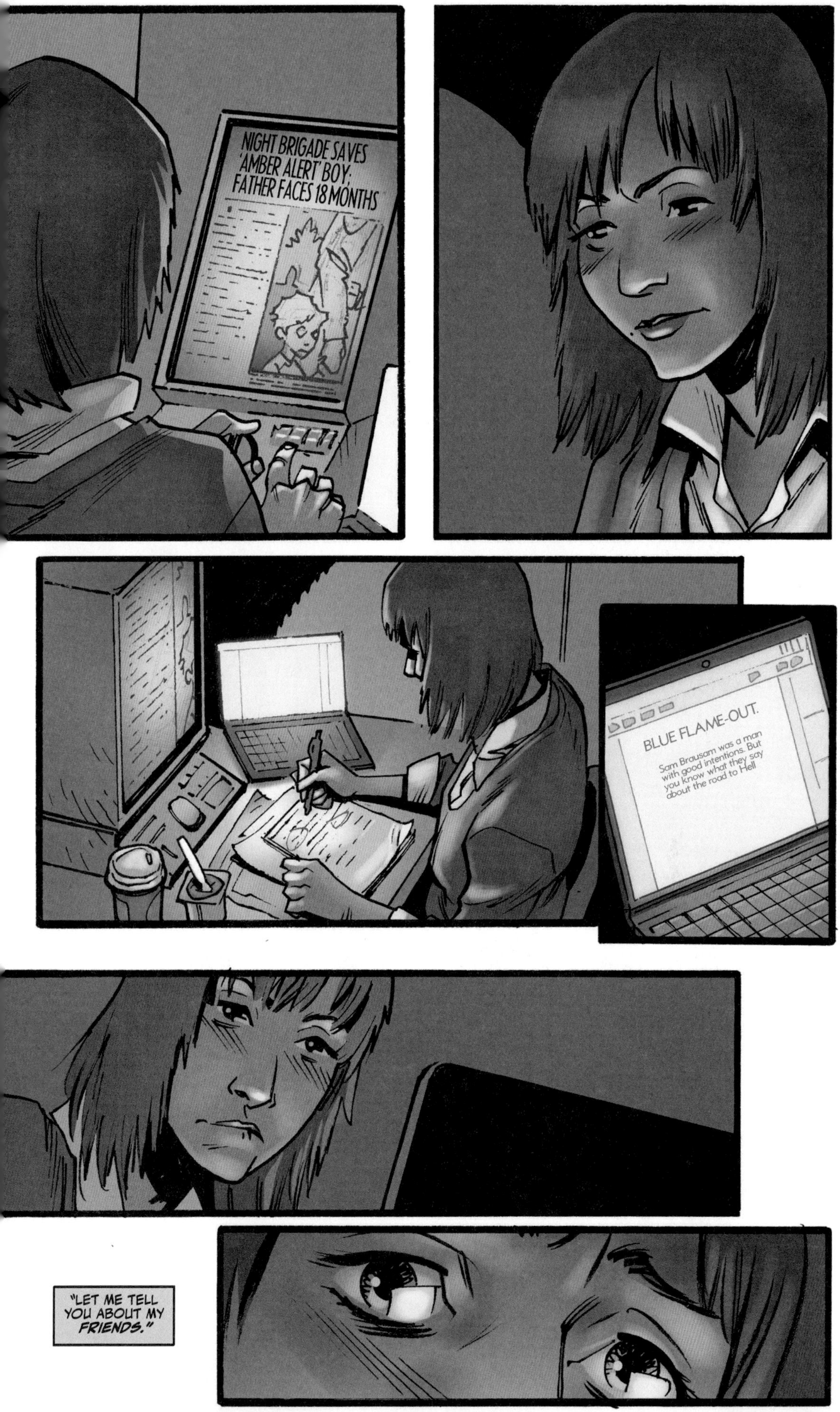
NIGHT BRIGADE SAVES 'AMBER ALERT' BOY; FATHER FACES 18 MONTHS
BLUE FLAME-OUT.
Sam Brausam was a man with good intentions. But you know what they say about the road to Hell
"LET ME TELL YOU ABOUT MY FRIENDS."

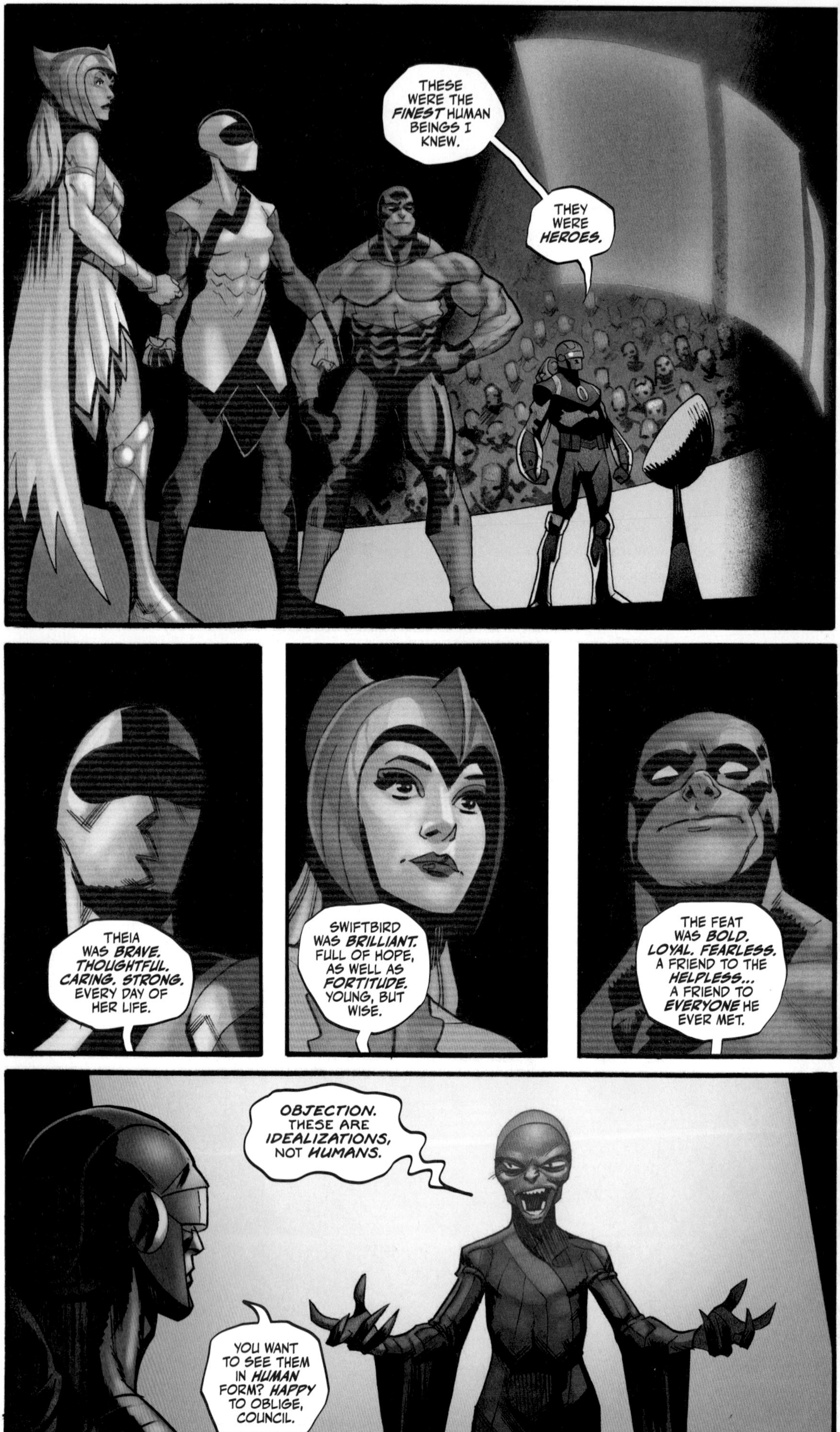
THESE WERE THE FINEST HUMAN BEINGS I KNEW.
THEY WERE HEROES.
THEIA WAS BRAVE. THOUGHTFUL. CARING. STRONG. EVERY DAY OF HER LIFE.
SWIFTBIRD WAS BRILLIANT. FULL OF HOPE, AS WELL AS FORTITUDE. YOUNG, BUT WISE.
THE FEAT WAS BOLD. LOYAL. FEARLESS. A FRIEND TO THE HELPLESS... A FRIEND TO EVERYONE HE EVER MET.
OBJECTION. THESE ARE IDEALIZATIONS, NOT HUMANS.
YOU WANT TO SEE THEM IN HUMAN FORM? HAPPY TO OBLIGE, COUNCIL.

HERE.

THIS IS WHO THEY WERE.

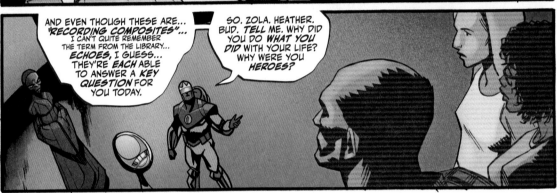

AND EVEN THOUGH THESE ARE... "RECORDING COMPOSITES"... I CAN'T QUITE REMEMBER THE TERM FROM THE LIBRARY... ECHOES, I GUESS... THEY'RE EACH ABLE TO ANSWER A KEY QUESTION FOR YOU TODAY.

SO. ZOLA. HEATHER. BUD. TELL ME. WHY DID YOU DO WHAT YOU DID WITH YOUR LIFE? WHY WERE YOU HEROES?

BECAUSE GROWING UP, IT FELT LIKE NO ONE ELSE WAS ONE. BUT I KNEW IT COULD BE DONE. I KNEW THERE WAS GOOD. AND IF I COULDN'T FIND IT... I COULD LOCATE IT... MAKE IT REAL... IN MYSELF.

SO MUCH IN LIFE IS TAKEN. MORE IS TAKEN THAN THERE IS TO BE TAKEN. I THOUGHT... IF I COULD GIVE... I COULD STEM THE TIDE.

I HAVE LEGS AND ARMS. I HAVE STRENGTH. I CAN LIFT UP. I CAN PUSH BACK. I CAN STAND AGAINST. I CAN PULL TO SAFETY.

SAM

HEY... WHAT'S UP--

REED, I NEED YOUR HELP. WELL, I--MY SISTER NEEDS HELP.

NO, *FUCK THAT,* WE NEED HELP. *BOTH* OF US. IT'S A *FAMILY THING*--

SAM, WHAT'S GOING ON--

MY BROTHER-IN-LAW MATEO... WELL, I MEAN... MY SISTER'S BOYFRIEND. WE CAN'T FIND HIM.

WHAT?

CAN YOU JUST *COME OVER?*

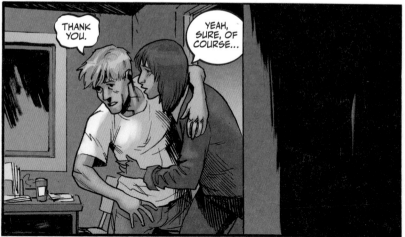

THANK YOU.

YEAH, SURE, OF COURSE...

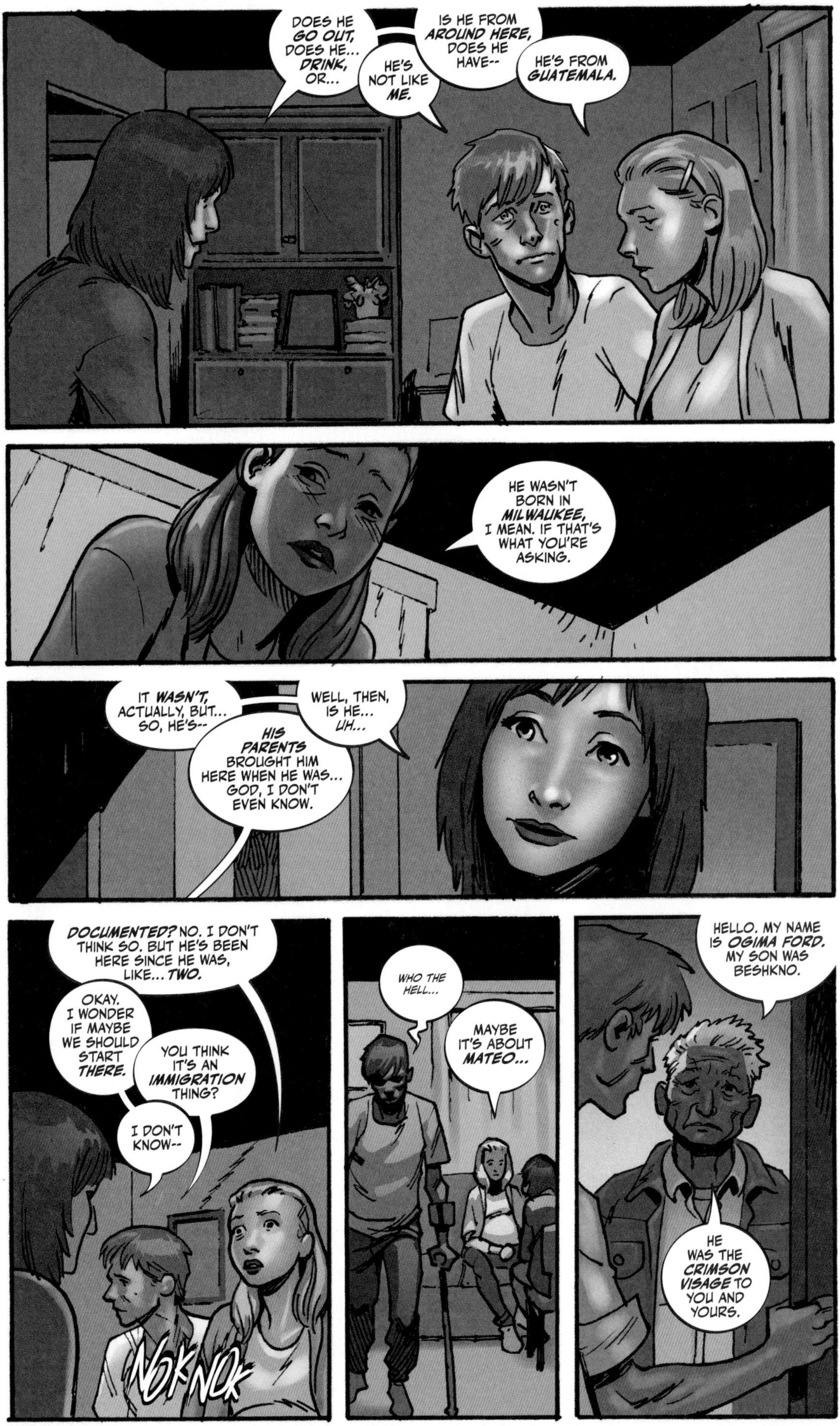
DOES HE GO OUT, DOES HE... DRINK, OR...
HE'S NOT LIKE ME.
IS HE FROM AROUND HERE, DOES HE HAVE--
HE'S FROM GUATEMALA.
HE WASN'T BORN IN MILWAUKEE, I MEAN. IF THAT'S WHAT YOU'RE ASKING.
IT WASN'T, ACTUALLY, BUT... SO, HE'S--
WELL, THEN, IS HE... UH...
HIS PARENTS BROUGHT HIM HERE WHEN HE WAS... GOD, I DON'T EVEN KNOW.
DOCUMENTED? NO. I DON'T THINK SO. BUT HE'S BEEN HERE SINCE HE WAS, LIKE... TWO.
OKAY. I WONDER IF MAYBE WE SHOULD START THERE.
YOU THINK IT'S AN IMMIGRATION THING?
I DON'T KNOW--
NOK NOK
WHO THE HELL...
MAYBE IT'S ABOUT MATEO...
HELLO. MY NAME IS OGIMA FORD. MY SON WAS BESHKNO.
HE WAS THE CRIMSON VISAGE TO YOU AND YOURS.

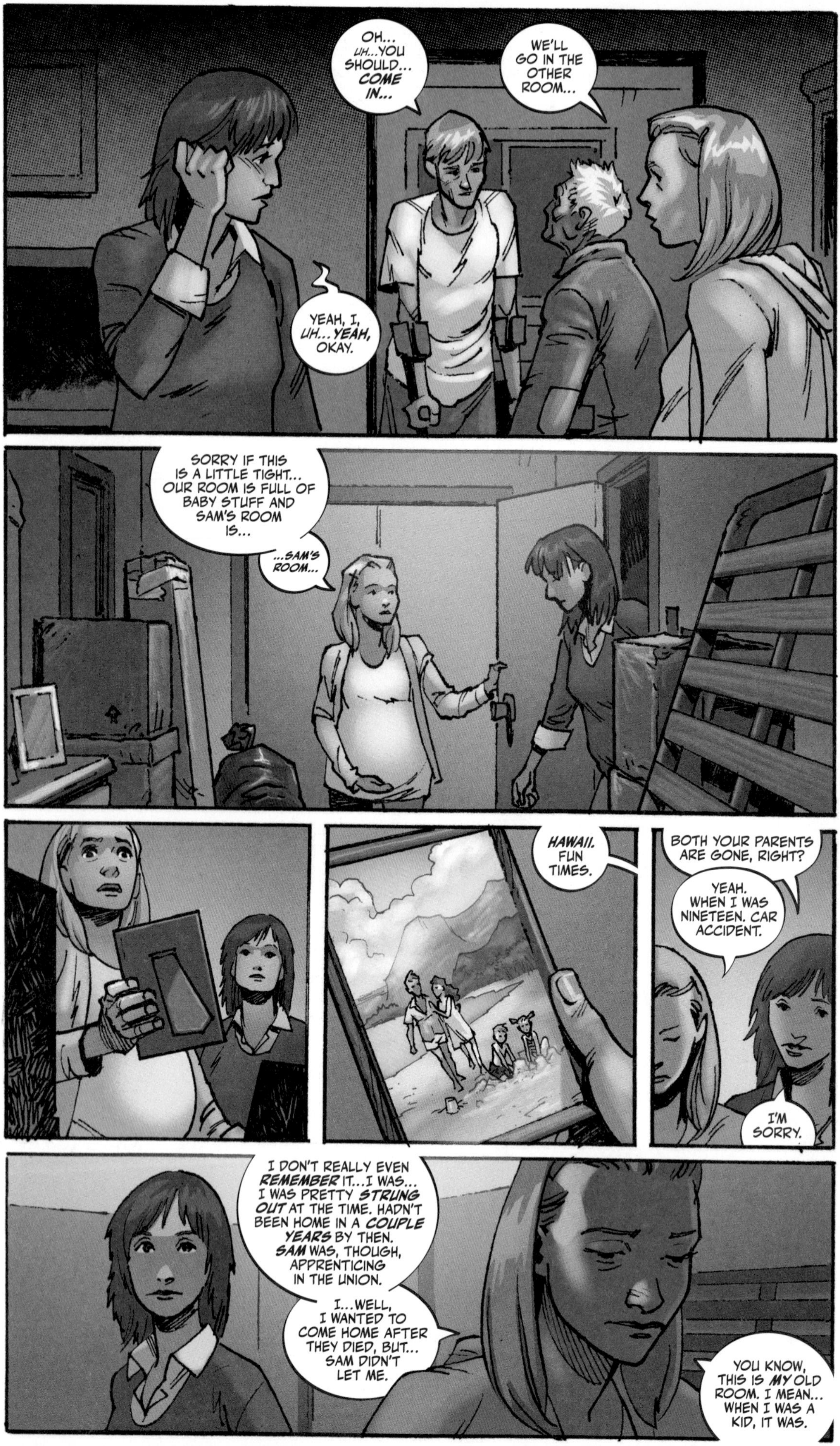

OH... UH... YOU SHOULD... COME IN...
WE'LL GO IN THE OTHER ROOM...
YEAH, I, UH... YEAH, OKAY.
SORRY IF THIS IS A LITTLE TIGHT... OUR ROOM IS FULL OF BABY STUFF AND SAM'S ROOM IS...
...SAM'S ROOM...
HAWAII. FUN TIMES.
BOTH YOUR PARENTS ARE GONE, RIGHT?
YEAH. WHEN I WAS NINETEEN. CAR ACCIDENT.
I'M SORRY.
I DON'T REALLY EVEN REMEMBER IT... I WAS... I WAS PRETTY STRUNG OUT AT THE TIME. HADN'T BEEN HOME IN A COUPLE YEARS BY THEN. SAM WAS, THOUGH, APPRENTICING IN THE UNION.
I... WELL, I WANTED TO COME HOME AFTER THEY DIED, BUT... SAM DIDN'T LET ME.
YOU KNOW, THIS IS MY OLD ROOM. I MEAN... WHEN I WAS A KID, IT WAS.

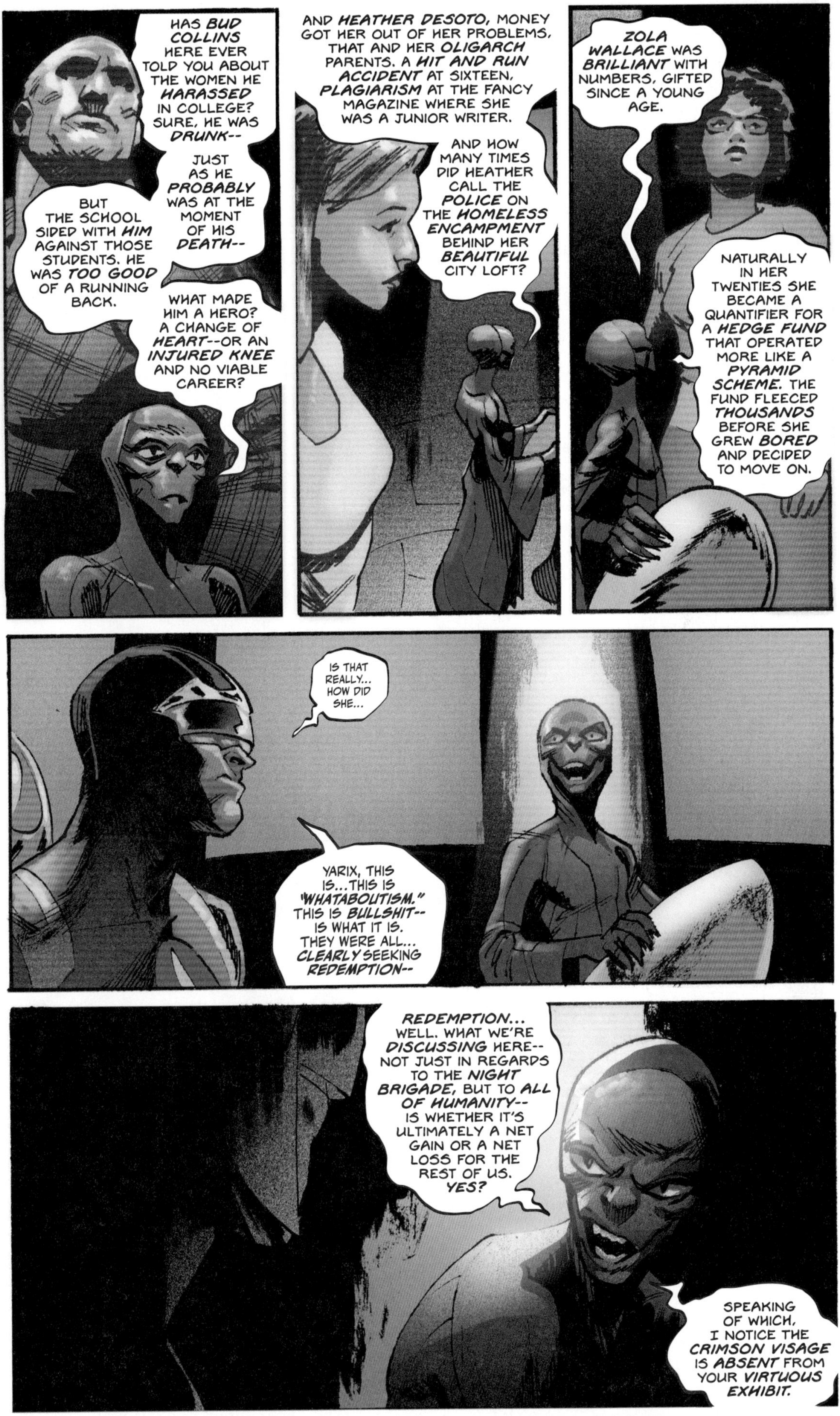
HAS BUD COLLINS HERE EVER TOLD YOU ABOUT THE WOMEN HE HARASSED IN COLLEGE? SURE, HE WAS DRUNK--
JUST AS HE PROBABLY WAS AT THE MOMENT OF HIS DEATH--
BUT THE SCHOOL SIDED WITH HIM AGAINST THOSE STUDENTS. HE WAS TOO GOOD OF A RUNNING BACK.
WHAT MADE HIM A HERO? A CHANGE OF HEART--OR AN INJURED KNEE AND NO VIABLE CAREER?
AND HEATHER DESOTO, MONEY GOT HER OUT OF HER PROBLEMS, THAT AND HER OLIGARCH PARENTS. A HIT AND RUN ACCIDENT AT SIXTEEN, PLAGIARISM AT THE FANCY MAGAZINE WHERE SHE WAS A JUNIOR WRITER.
AND HOW MANY TIMES DID HEATHER CALL THE POLICE ON THE HOMELESS ENCAMPMENT BEHIND HER BEAUTIFUL CITY LOFT?
ZOLA WALLACE WAS BRILLIANT WITH NUMBERS, GIFTED SINCE A YOUNG AGE.
NATURALLY IN HER TWENTIES SHE BECAME A QUANTIFIER FOR A HEDGE FUND THAT OPERATED MORE LIKE A PYRAMID SCHEME. THE FUND FLEECED THOUSANDS BEFORE SHE GREW BORED AND DECIDED TO MOVE ON.
IS THAT REALLY... HOW DID SHE...
YARIX, THIS IS...THIS IS "WHATABOUTISM." THIS IS BULLSHIT-- IS WHAT IT IS. THEY WERE ALL... CLEARLY SEEKING REDEMPTION--
REDEMPTION... WELL. WHAT WE'RE DISCUSSING HERE-- NOT JUST IN REGARDS TO THE NIGHT BRIGADE, BUT TO ALL OF HUMANITY-- IS WHETHER IT'S ULTIMATELY A NET GAIN OR A NET LOSS FOR THE REST OF US. YES?
SPEAKING OF WHICH, I NOTICE THE CRIMSON VISAGE IS ABSENT FROM YOUR VIRTUOUS EXHIBIT.

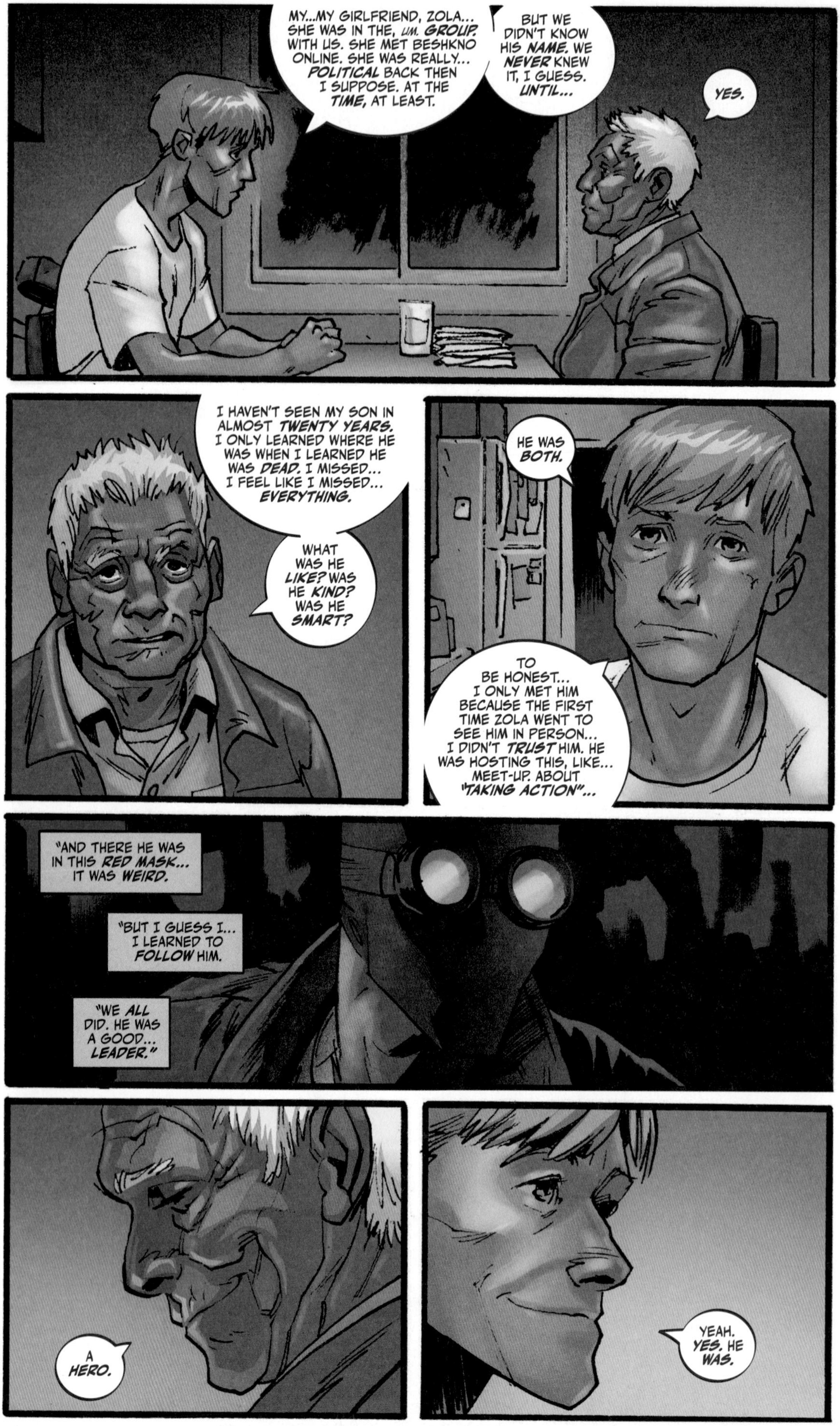
MY...MY GIRLFRIEND, ZOLA... SHE WAS IN THE, UM, GROUP. WITH US. SHE MET BESHKNO ONLINE. SHE WAS REALLY... POLITICAL BACK THEN I SUPPOSE. AT THE TIME, AT LEAST.
BUT WE DIDN'T KNOW HIS NAME. WE NEVER KNEW IT, I GUESS. UNTIL...
YES.
I HAVEN'T SEEN MY SON IN ALMOST TWENTY YEARS. I ONLY LEARNED WHERE HE WAS WHEN I LEARNED HE WAS DEAD. I MISSED... I FEEL LIKE I MISSED... EVERYTHING.
WHAT WAS HE LIKE? WAS HE KIND? WAS HE SMART?
HE WAS BOTH.
TO BE HONEST... I ONLY MET HIM BECAUSE THE FIRST TIME ZOLA WENT TO SEE HIM IN PERSON... I DIDN'T TRUST HIM. HE WAS HOSTING THIS, LIKE... MEET-UP. ABOUT "TAKING ACTION"...
"AND THERE HE WAS IN THIS RED MASK... IT WAS WEIRD.
"BUT I GUESS I... I LEARNED TO FOLLOW HIM.
"WE ALL DID. HE WAS A GOOD... LEADER."
A HERO.
YEAH. YES. HE WAS.

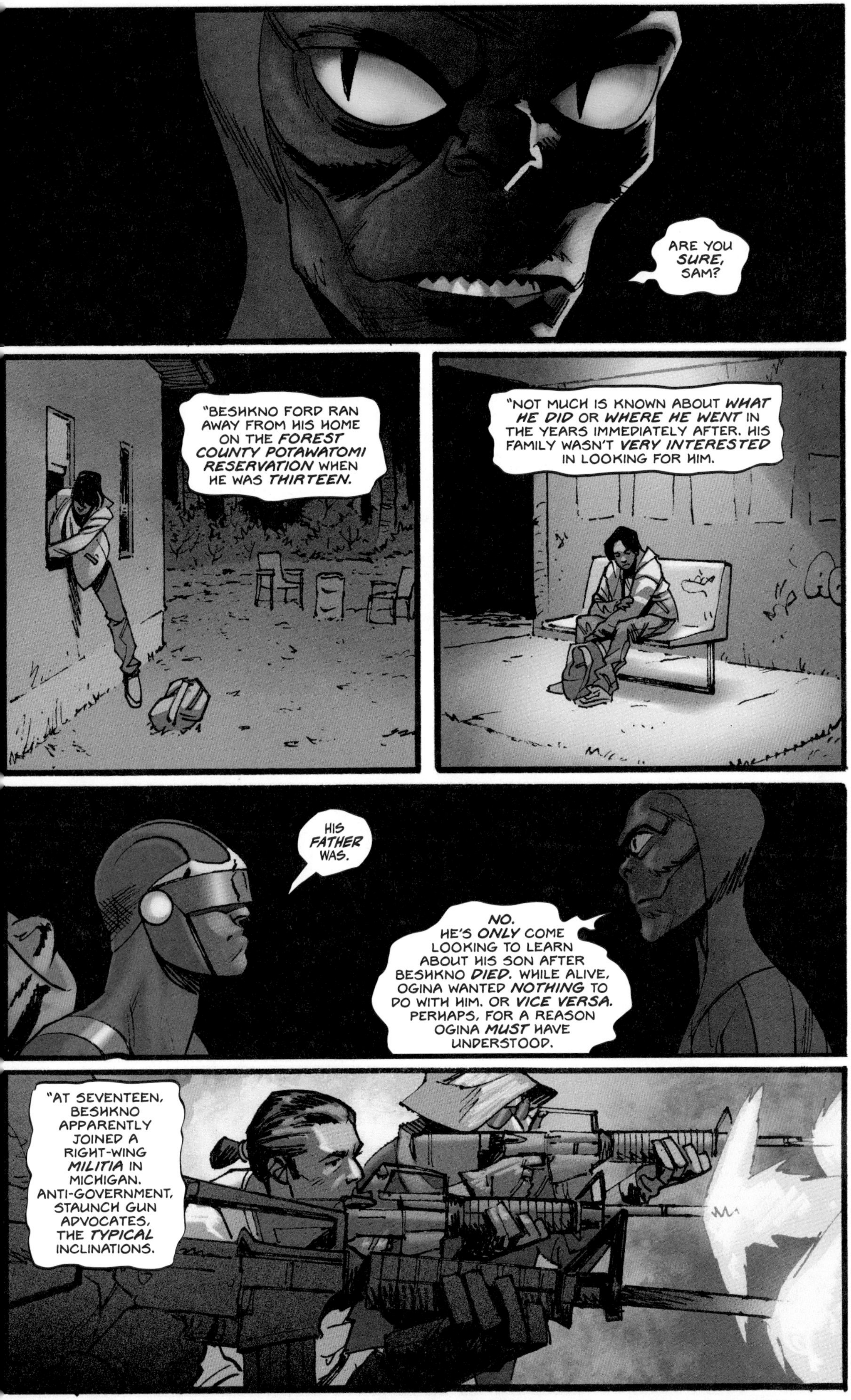
ARE YOU SURE, SAM?
"BESHKNO FORD RAN AWAY FROM HIS HOME ON THE FOREST COUNTY POTAWATOMI RESERVATION WHEN HE WAS THIRTEEN.
"NOT MUCH IS KNOWN ABOUT WHAT HE DID OR WHERE HE WENT IN THE YEARS IMMEDIATELY AFTER. HIS FAMILY WASN'T VERY INTERESTED IN LOOKING FOR HIM.
HIS FATHER WAS.
NO. HE'S ONLY COME LOOKING TO LEARN ABOUT HIS SON AFTER BESHKNO DIED. WHILE ALIVE, OGINA WANTED NOTHING TO DO WITH HIM. OR VICE VERSA. PERHAPS, FOR A REASON OGINA MUST HAVE UNDERSTOOD.
"AT SEVENTEEN, BESHKNO APPARENTLY JOINED A RIGHT-WING MILITIA IN MICHIGAN. ANTI-GOVERNMENT, STAUNCH GUN ADVOCATES, THE TYPICAL INCLINATIONS.

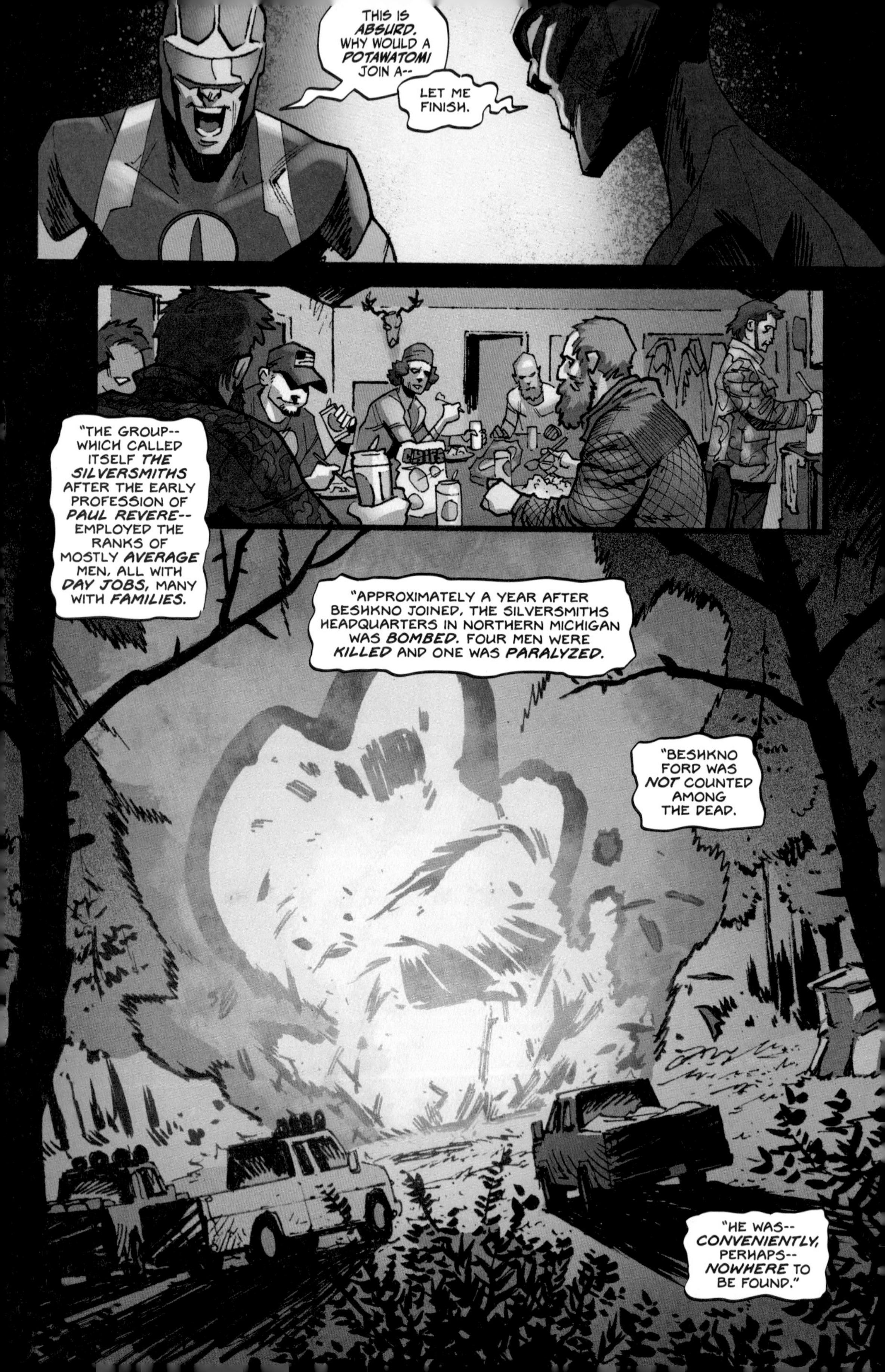

THIS IS *ABSURD.* WHY WOULD A *POTAWATOMI* JOIN A--
LET ME FINISH.
"THE GROUP-- WHICH CALLED ITSELF *THE SILVERSMITHS* AFTER THE EARLY PROFESSION OF *PAUL REVERE*-- EMPLOYED THE RANKS OF MOSTLY *AVERAGE* MEN, ALL WITH *DAY JOBS,* MANY WITH *FAMILIES.*
"APPROXIMATELY A YEAR AFTER BESHKNO JOINED, THE SILVERSMITHS HEADQUARTERS IN NORTHERN MICHIGAN WAS *BOMBED.* FOUR MEN WERE *KILLED* AND ONE WAS *PARALYZED.*
"BESHKNO FORD WAS *NOT* COUNTED AMONG THE DEAD.
"HE WAS-- *CONVENIENTLY,* PERHAPS-- *NOWHERE* TO BE FOUND."

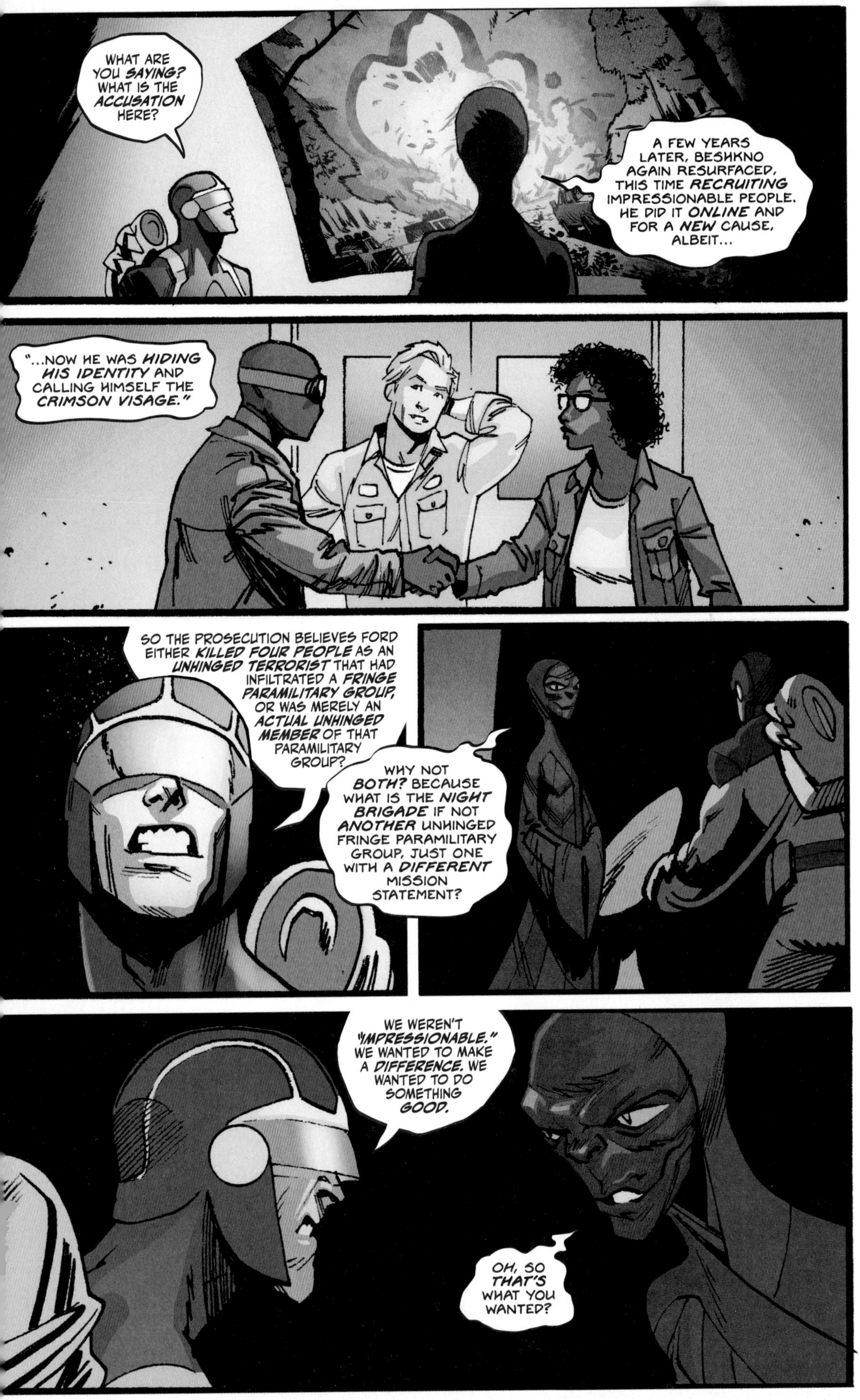
WHAT ARE YOU SAYING? WHAT IS THE ACCUSATION HERE?
A FEW YEARS LATER, BESHKNO AGAIN RESURFACED, THIS TIME RECRUITING IMPRESSIONABLE PEOPLE. HE DID IT ONLINE AND FOR A NEW CAUSE, ALBEIT...
"...NOW HE WAS HIDING HIS IDENTITY AND CALLING HIMSELF THE CRIMSON VISAGE."
SO THE PROSECUTION BELIEVES FORD EITHER KILLED FOUR PEOPLE AS AN UNHINGED TERRORIST THAT HAD INFILTRATED A FRINGE PARAMILITARY GROUP, OR WAS MERELY AN ACTUAL UNHINGED MEMBER OF THAT PARAMILITARY GROUP?
WHY NOT BOTH? BECAUSE WHAT IS THE NIGHT BRIGADE IF NOT ANOTHER UNHINGED FRINGE PARAMILITARY GROUP, JUST ONE WITH A DIFFERENT MISSION STATEMENT?
WE WEREN'T "IMPRESSIONABLE." WE WANTED TO MAKE A DIFFERENCE. WE WANTED TO DO SOMETHING GOOD.
OH, SO THAT'S WHAT YOU WANTED?

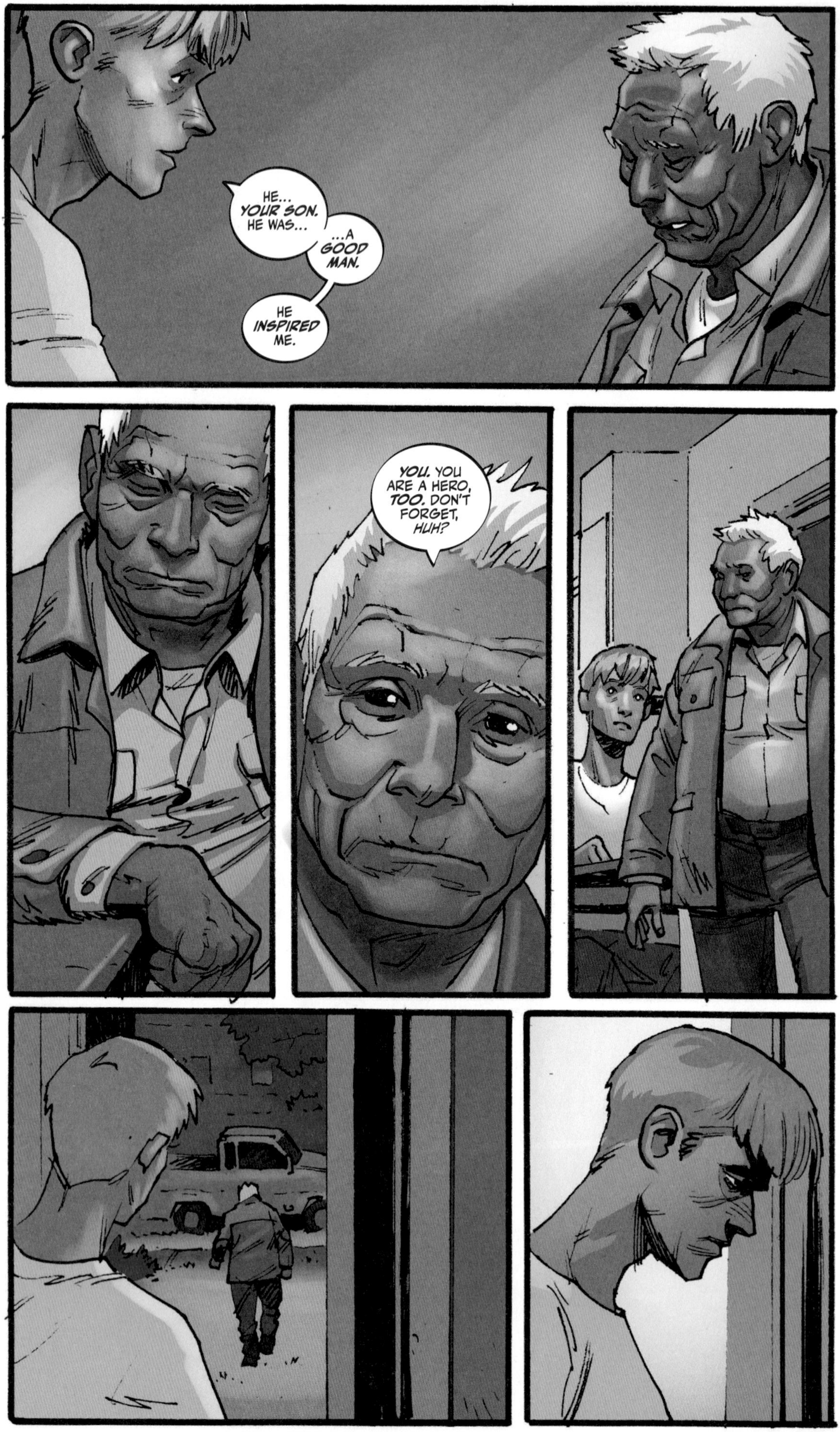
HE... YOUR SON. HE WAS...
...A GOOD MAN.
HE INSPIRED ME.
YOU. YOU ARE A HERO, TOO. DON'T FORGET, HUH?

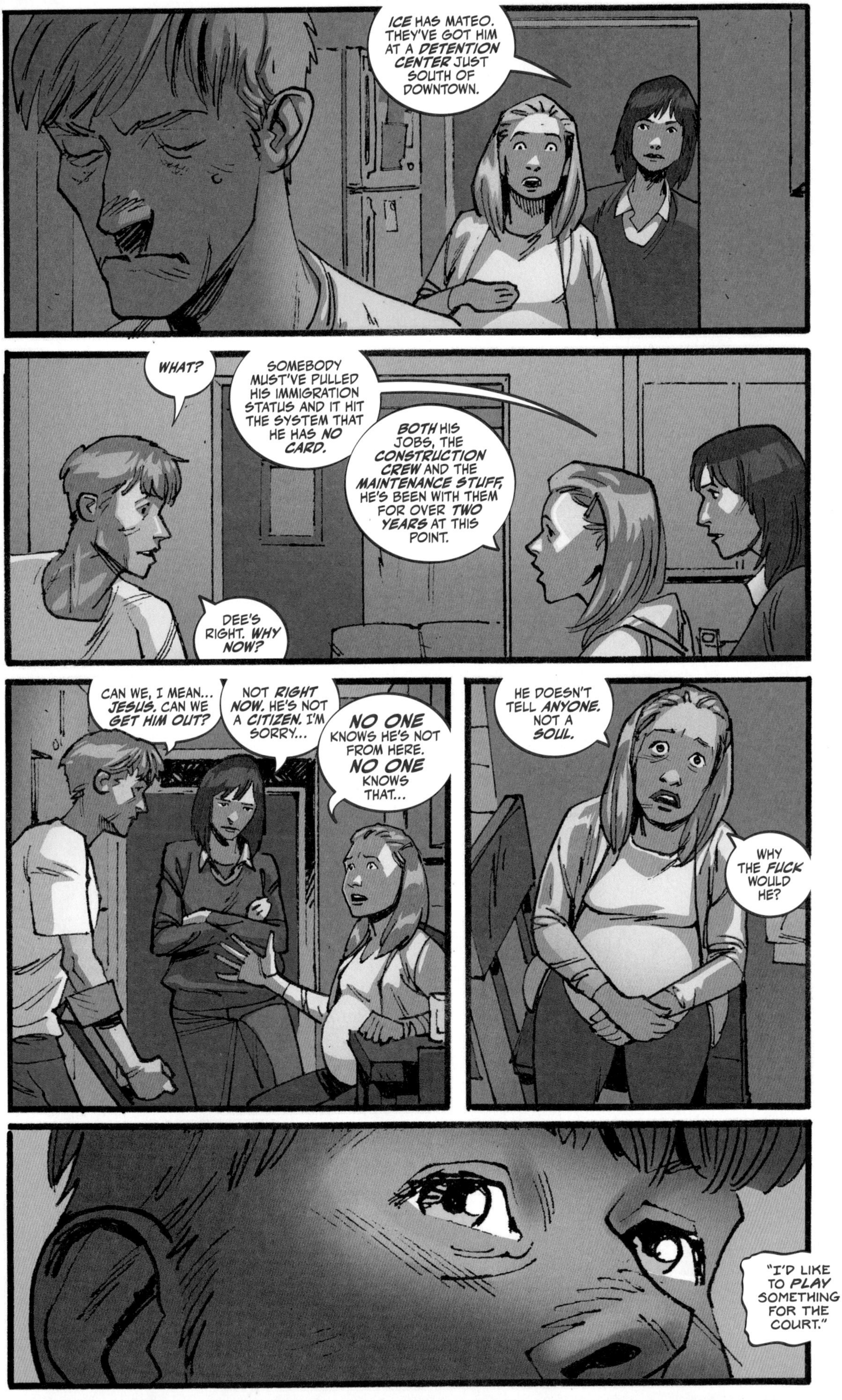
ICE HAS MATEO. THEY'VE GOT HIM AT A DETENTION CENTER JUST SOUTH OF DOWNTOWN.
WHAT?
SOMEBODY MUST'VE PULLED HIS IMMIGRATION STATUS AND IT HIT THE SYSTEM THAT HE HAS NO CARD.
BOTH HIS JOBS, THE CONSTRUCTION CREW AND THE MAINTENANCE STUFF, HE'S BEEN WITH THEM FOR OVER TWO YEARS AT THIS POINT.
DEE'S RIGHT. WHY NOW?
CAN WE, I MEAN... JESUS. CAN WE GET HIM OUT?
NOT RIGHT NOW. HE'S NOT A CITIZEN. I'M SORRY...
NO ONE KNOWS HE'S NOT FROM HERE. NO ONE KNOWS THAT...
HE DOESN'T TELL ANYONE. NOT A SOUL.
WHY THE FUCK WOULD HE?
"I'D LIKE TO PLAY SOMETHING FOR THE COURT."

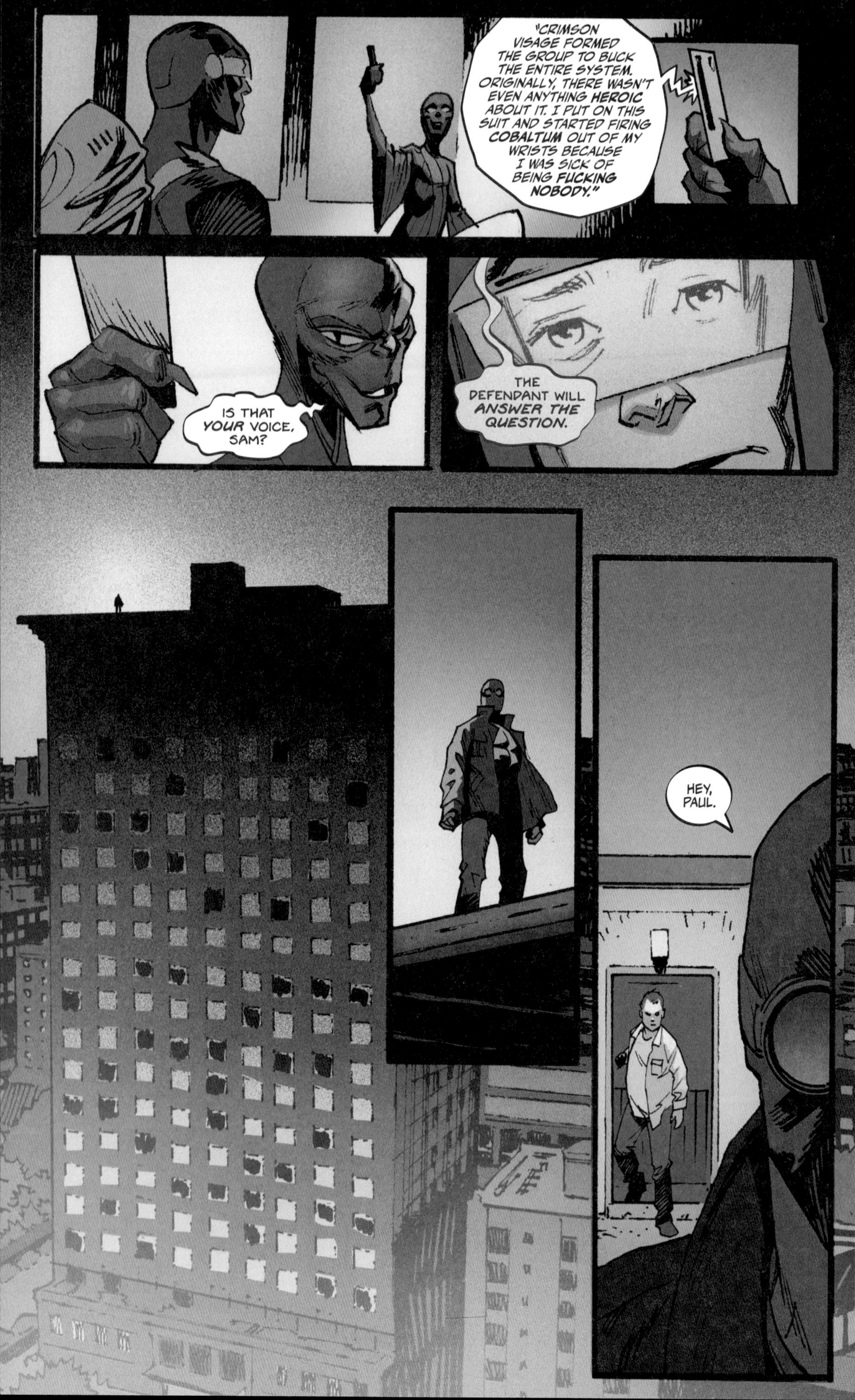
"CRIMSON VISAGE FORMED THE GROUP TO BUCK THE ENTIRE SYSTEM. ORIGINALLY, THERE WASN'T EVEN ANYTHING HEROIC ABOUT IT. I PUT ON THIS SUIT AND STARTED FIRING COBALTUM OUT OF MY WRISTS BECAUSE I WAS SICK OF BEING FUCKING NOBODY."
IS THAT YOUR VOICE, SAM?
THE DEFENDANT WILL ANSWER THE QUESTION.
HEY, PAUL.

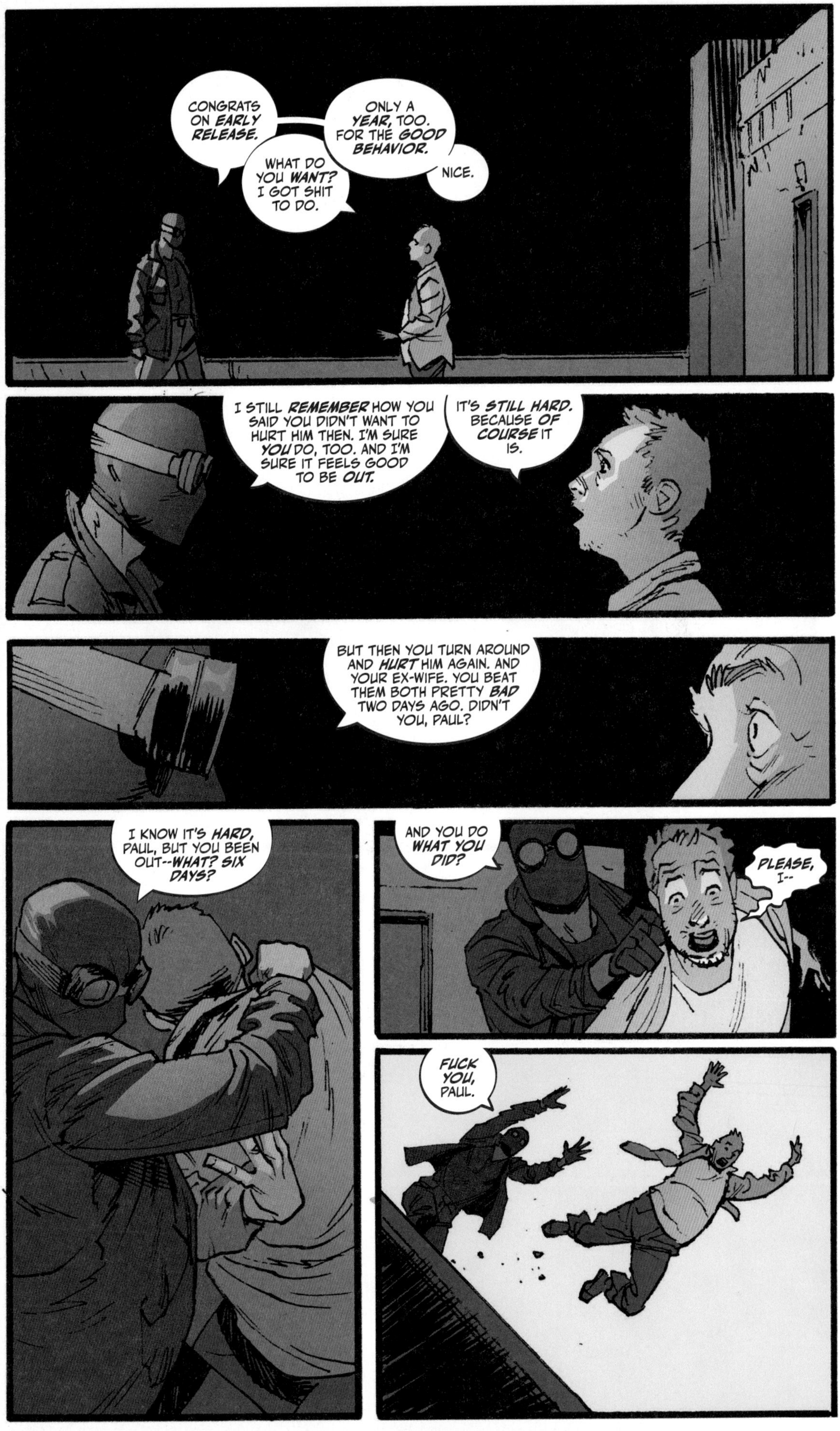
CONGRATS ON EARLY RELEASE.
ONLY A YEAR, TOO. FOR THE GOOD BEHAVIOR.
WHAT DO YOU WANT? I GOT SHIT TO DO.
NICE.
I STILL REMEMBER HOW YOU SAID YOU DIDN'T WANT TO HURT HIM THEN. I'M SURE YOU DO, TOO. AND I'M SURE IT FEELS GOOD TO BE OUT.
IT'S STILL HARD. BECAUSE OF COURSE IT IS.
BUT THEN YOU TURN AROUND AND HURT HIM AGAIN. AND YOUR EX-WIFE. YOU BEAT THEM BOTH PRETTY BAD TWO DAYS AGO. DIDN'T YOU, PAUL?
I KNOW IT'S HARD, PAUL, BUT YOU BEEN OUT--WHAT? SIX DAYS?
AND YOU DO WHAT YOU DID?
PLEASE, I--
FUCK YOU, PAUL.

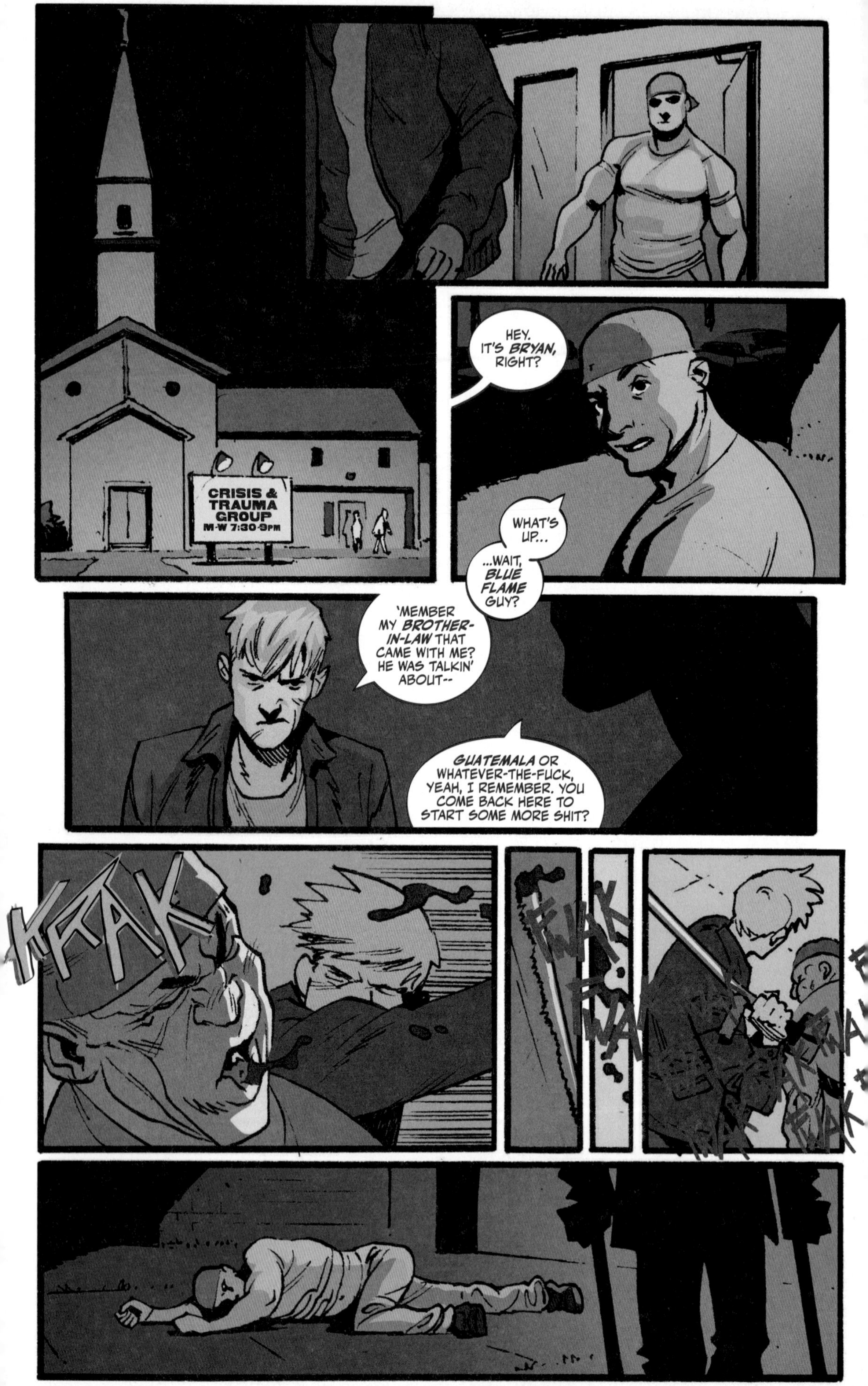
CRISIS & TRAUMA GROUP M-W 7:30-9PM
HEY. IT'S BRYAN, RIGHT?
WHAT'S UP...
...WAIT, BLUE FLAME GUY?
'MEMBER MY BROTHER-IN-LAW THAT CAME WITH ME? HE WAS TALKIN' ABOUT--
GUATEMALA OR WHATEVER-THE-FUCK, YEAH, I REMEMBER. YOU COME BACK HERE TO START SOME MORE SHIT?
KRAK
FWAK
FWAK

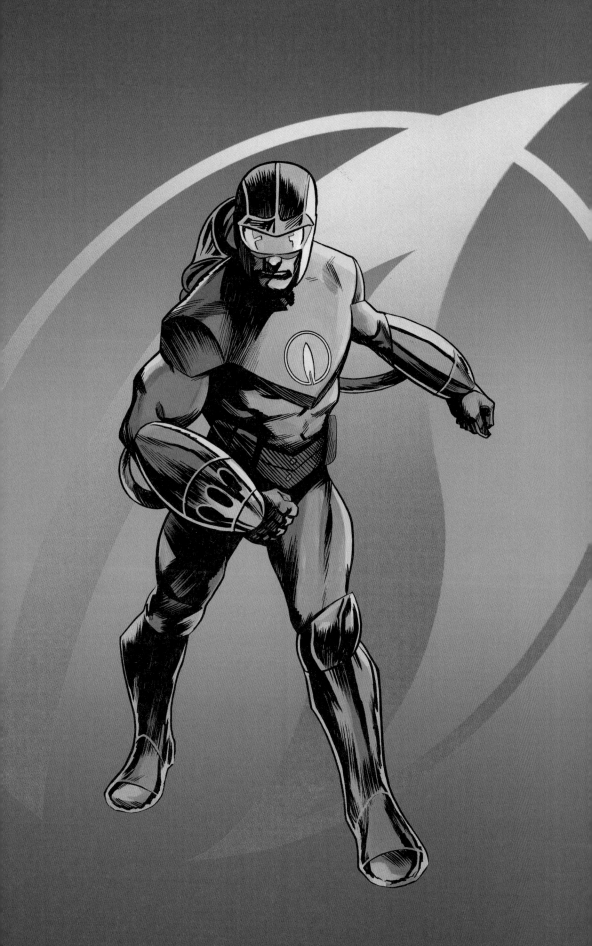

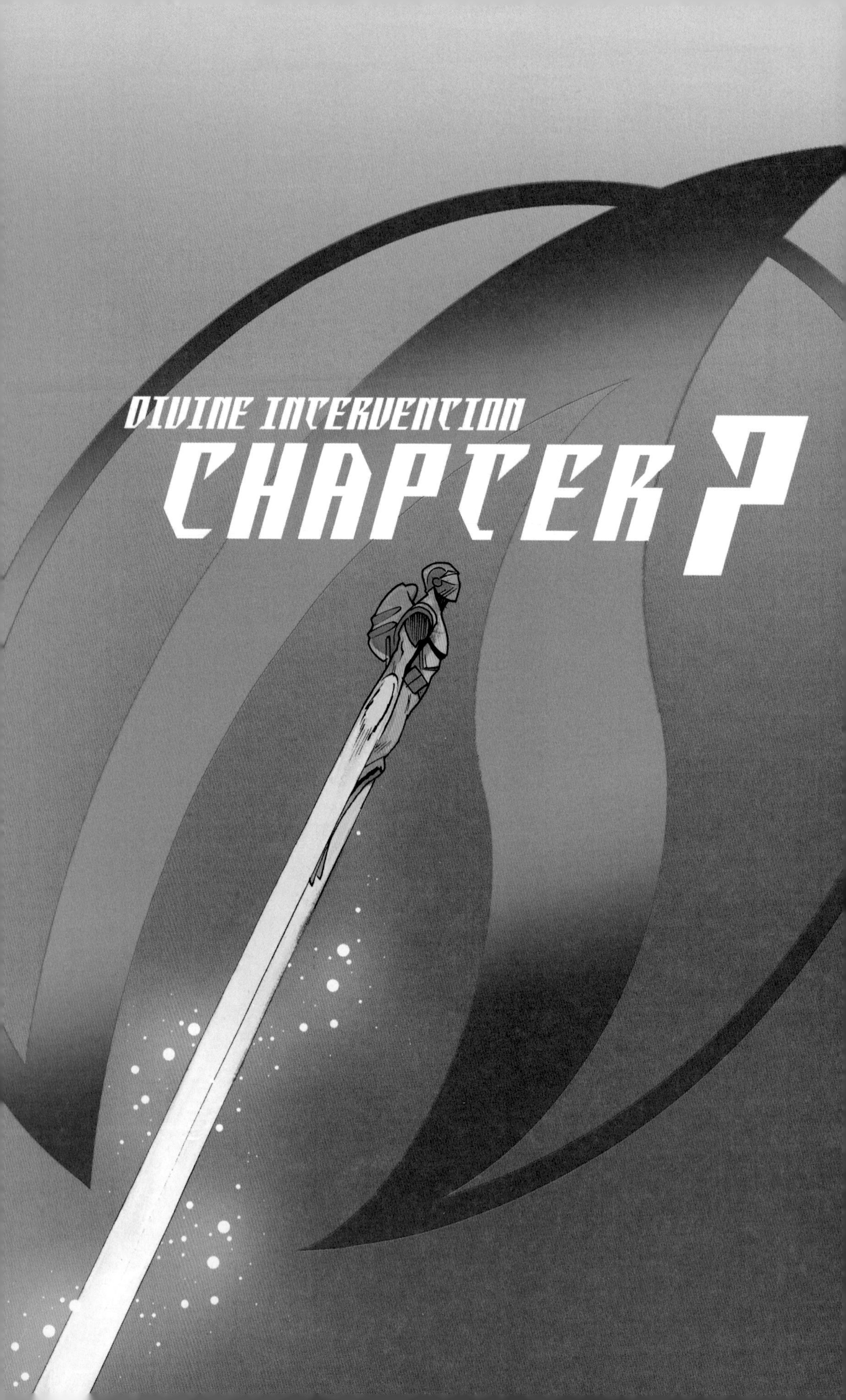
DIVINE INTERVENTION
CHAPTER 7

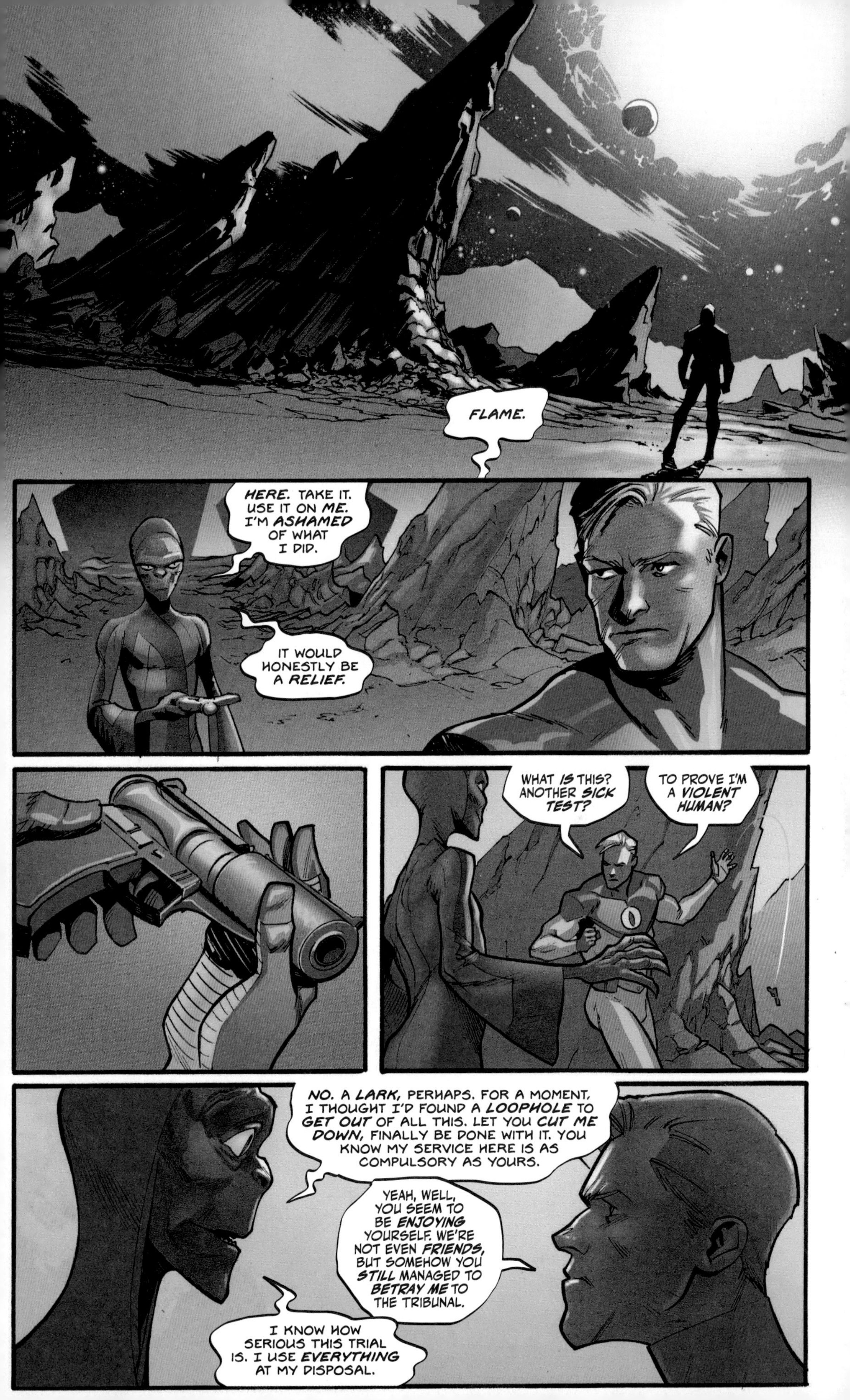
FLAME.
HERE. TAKE IT. USE IT ON ME. I'M ASHAMED OF WHAT I DID.
IT WOULD HONESTLY BE A RELIEF.
WHAT IS THIS? ANOTHER SICK TEST?
TO PROVE I'M A VIOLENT HUMAN?
NO. A LARK, PERHAPS. FOR A MOMENT, I THOUGHT I'D FOUND A LOOPHOLE TO GET OUT OF ALL THIS. LET YOU CUT ME DOWN, FINALLY BE DONE WITH IT. YOU KNOW MY SERVICE HERE IS AS COMPULSORY AS YOURS.
YEAH, WELL, YOU SEEM TO BE ENJOYING YOURSELF. WE'RE NOT EVEN FRIENDS, BUT SOMEHOW YOU STILL MANAGED TO BETRAY ME TO THE TRIBUNAL.
I KNOW HOW SERIOUS THIS TRIAL IS. I USE EVERYTHING AT MY DISPOSAL.

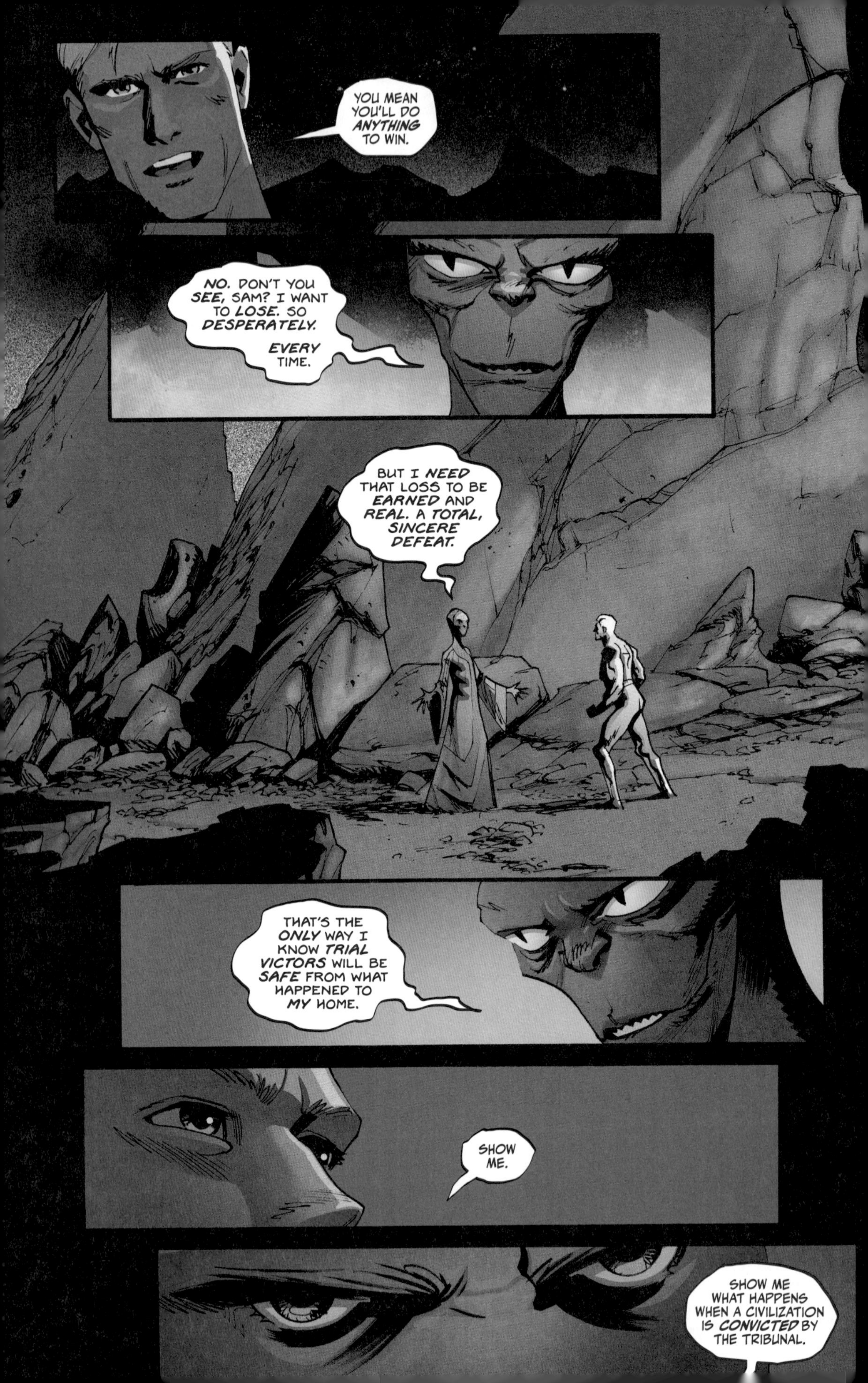
YOU MEAN YOU'LL DO ANYTHING TO WIN.
NO. DON'T YOU SEE, SAM? I WANT TO LOSE. SO DESPERATELY.
EVERY TIME.
BUT I NEED THAT LOSS TO BE EARNED AND REAL. A TOTAL, SINCERE DEFEAT.
THAT'S THE ONLY WAY I KNOW TRIAL VICTORS WILL BE SAFE FROM WHAT HAPPENED TO MY HOME.
SHOW ME.
SHOW ME WHAT HAPPENS WHEN A CIVILIZATION IS CONVICTED BY THE TRIBUNAL.

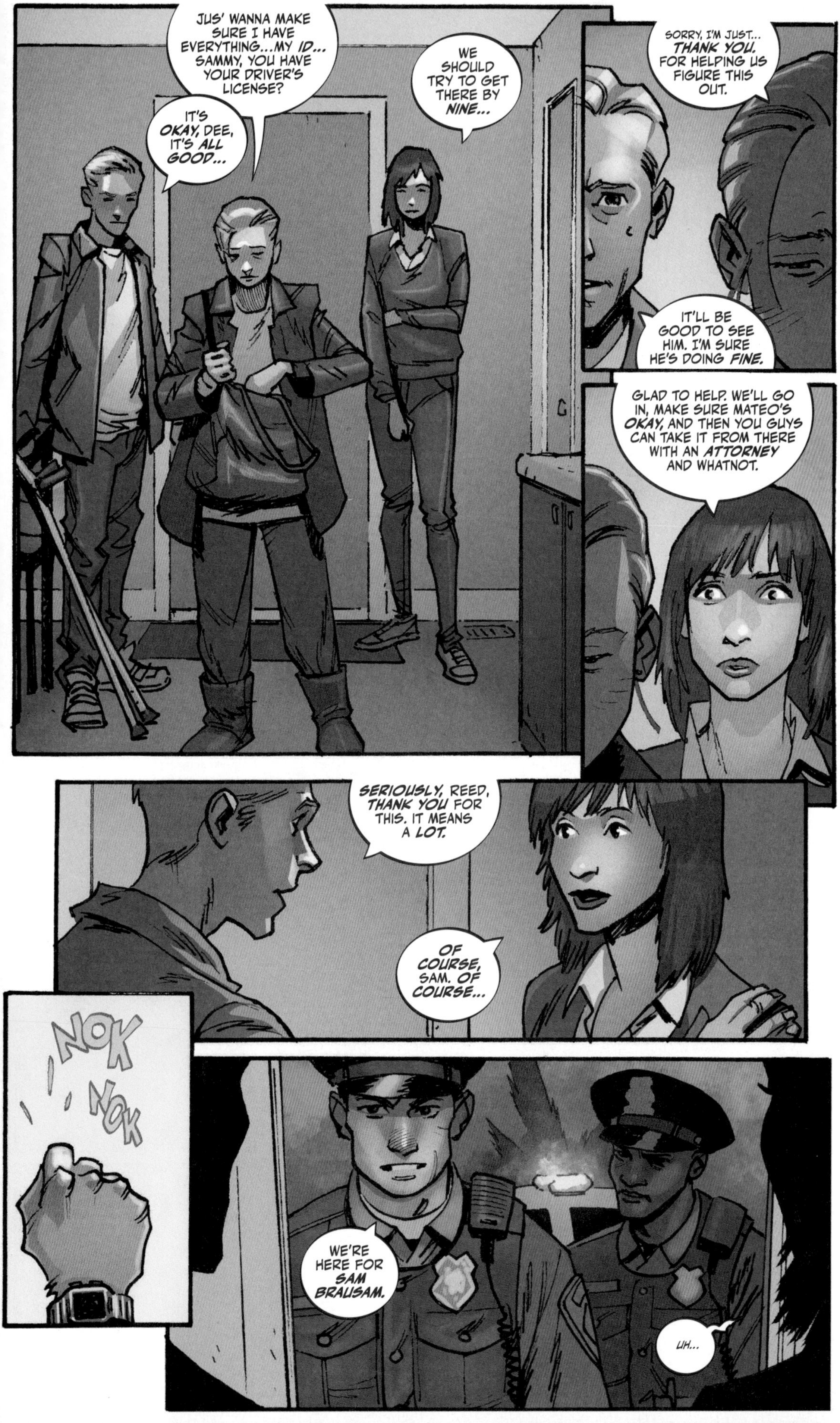
JUS' WANNA MAKE SURE I HAVE EVERYTHING...MY ID... SAMMY, YOU HAVE YOUR DRIVER'S LICENSE?
IT'S OKAY, DEE, IT'S ALL GOOD...
WE SHOULD TRY TO GET THERE BY NINE...
SORRY, I'M JUST... THANK YOU. FOR HELPING US FIGURE THIS OUT.
IT'LL BE GOOD TO SEE HIM. I'M SURE HE'S DOING FINE.
GLAD TO HELP. WE'LL GO IN, MAKE SURE MATEO'S OKAY, AND THEN YOU GUYS CAN TAKE IT FROM THERE WITH AN ATTORNEY AND WHATNOT.
SERIOUSLY, REED, THANK YOU FOR THIS. IT MEANS A LOT.
OF COURSE, SAM. OF COURSE...
NOK
NOK
WE'RE HERE FOR SAM BRAUSAM.
UH...

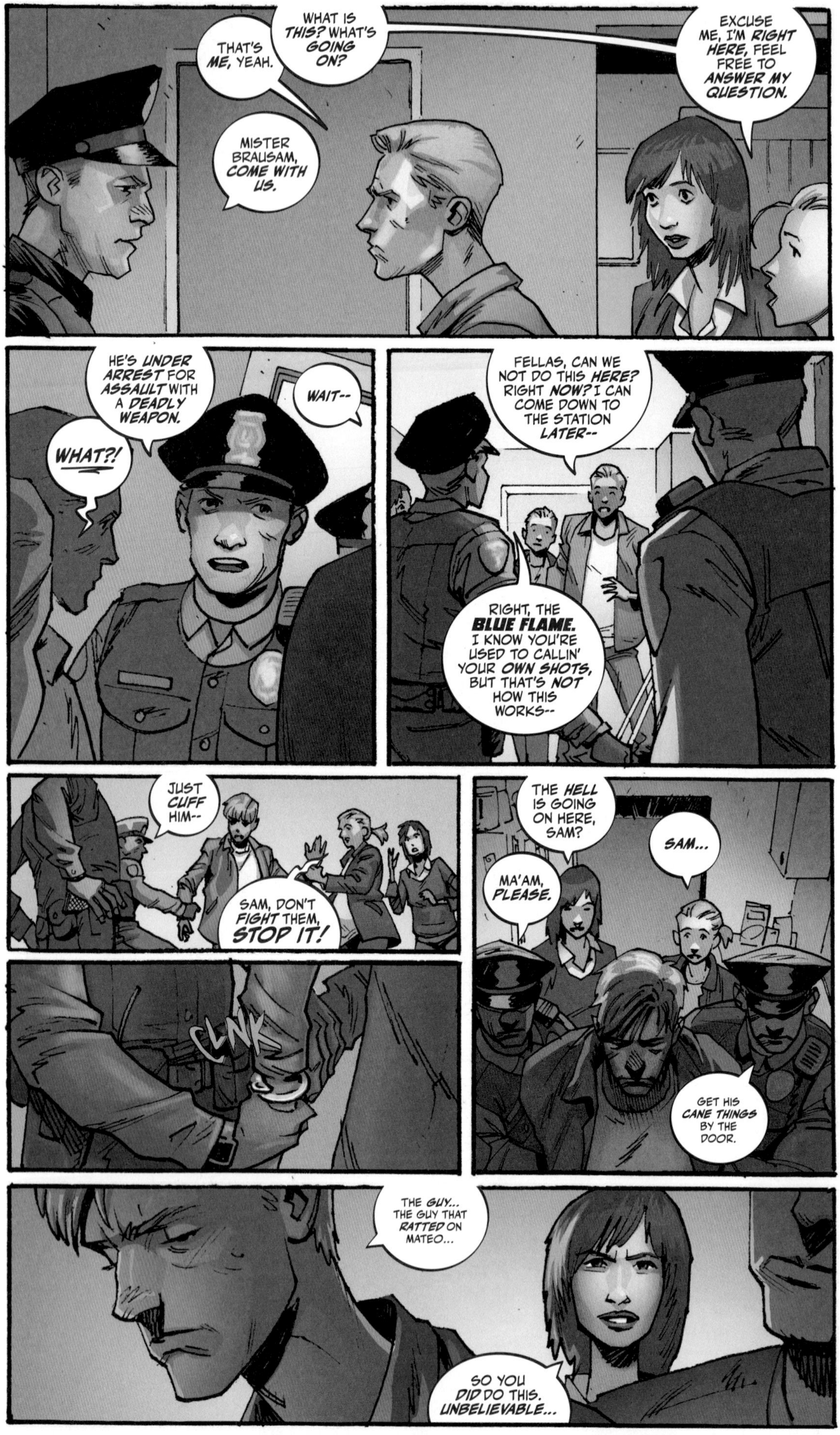

THAT'S ME, YEAH.
WHAT IS THIS? WHAT'S GOING ON?
EXCUSE ME, I'M RIGHT HERE, FEEL FREE TO ANSWER MY QUESTION.
MISTER BRAUSAM, COME WITH US.
HE'S UNDER ARREST FOR ASSAULT WITH A DEADLY WEAPON.
WHAT?!
WAIT--
FELLAS, CAN WE NOT DO THIS HERE? RIGHT NOW? I CAN COME DOWN TO THE STATION LATER--
RIGHT, THE BLUE FLAME. I KNOW YOU'RE USED TO CALLIN' YOUR OWN SHOTS, BUT THAT'S NOT HOW THIS WORKS--
JUST CUFF HIM--
SAM, DON'T FIGHT THEM, STOP IT!
THE HELL IS GOING ON HERE, SAM?
SAM...
MA'AM, PLEASE.
CLNK
GET HIS CANE THINGS BY THE DOOR.
THE GUY... THE GUY THAT RATTED ON MATEO...
SO YOU DID DO THIS. UNBELIEVABLE...

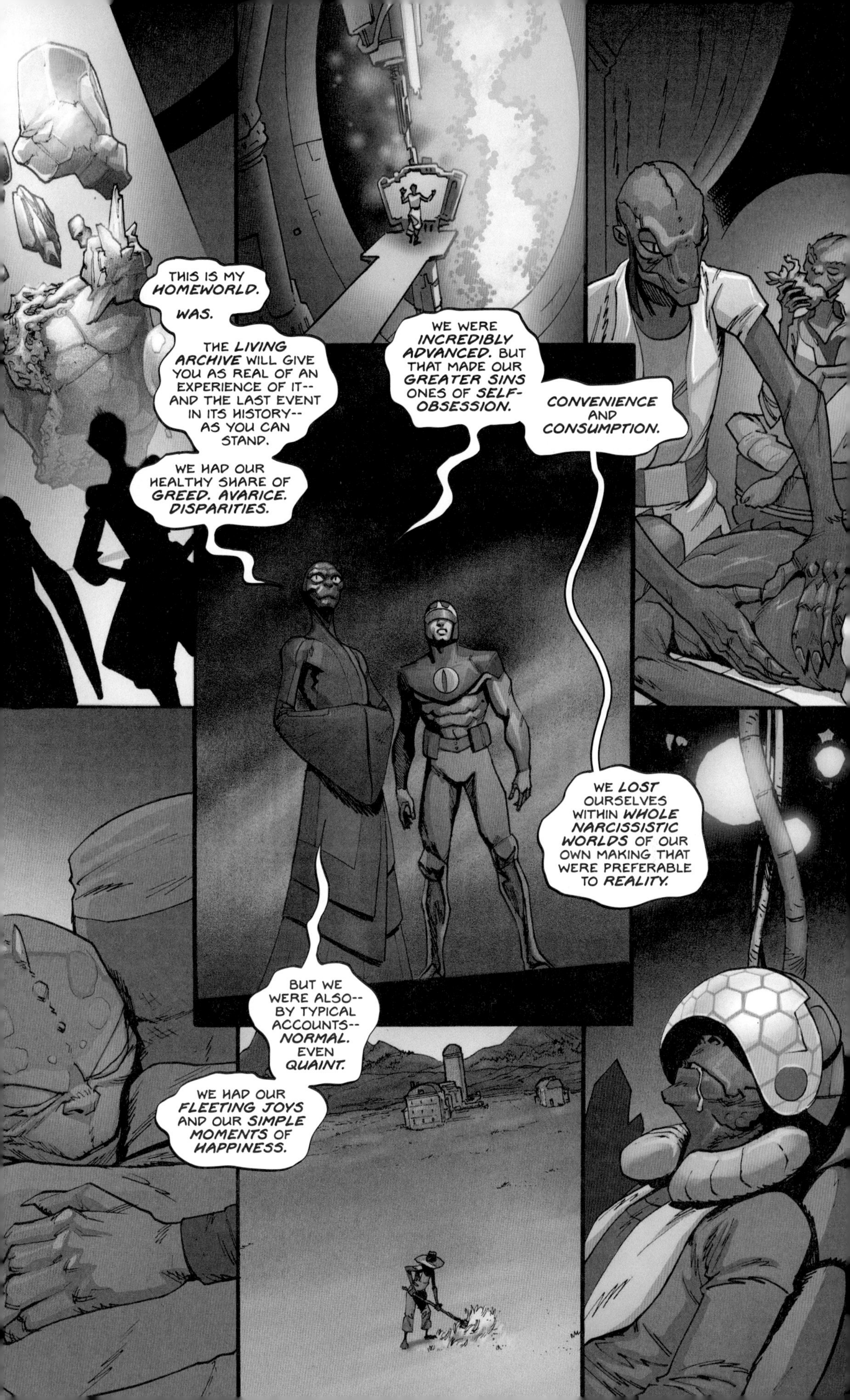
THIS IS MY *HOMEWORLD.*
WAS.
THE *LIVING ARCHIVE* WILL GIVE YOU AS REAL OF AN EXPERIENCE OF IT-- AND THE LAST EVENT IN ITS HISTORY-- AS YOU CAN STAND.
WE HAD OUR HEALTHY SHARE OF *GREED. AVARICE. DISPARITIES.*
WE WERE *INCREDIBLY ADVANCED.* BUT THAT MADE OUR *GREATER SINS* ONES OF *SELF-OBSESSION.*
CONVENIENCE AND *CONSUMPTION.*
WE *LOST* OURSELVES WITHIN *WHOLE NARCISSISTIC WORLDS* OF OUR OWN MAKING THAT WERE PREFERABLE TO *REALITY.*
BUT WE WERE ALSO-- BY TYPICAL ACCOUNTS-- *NORMAL.* EVEN *QUAINT.*
WE HAD OUR *FLEETING JOYS* AND OUR *SIMPLE MOMENTS* OF *HAPPINESS.*

"THE JUDGMENT CRAFT.
"NO WARNING IS EVER GIVEN TO A SENTENCED SPECIES. THE TRIBUNAL FEELS IT WOULD BE CRUEL TO INSTILL A SENSE OF HELPLESS CHAOS BEFORE MASS EXECUTION.
"THE TRIBUNAL USES A TORRENT OF STRONG STERILIZING ACID.
"WITHIN MINUTES, THE ENTIRE PLANET WILL BE DEAD.
"IT WILL BECOME NOTHING.
MY GOD--!
GET AWAY FROM IT! GET CLEAR!
"NO ONE IS SPARED.
NO...NO NO NO!
"NO ONE.

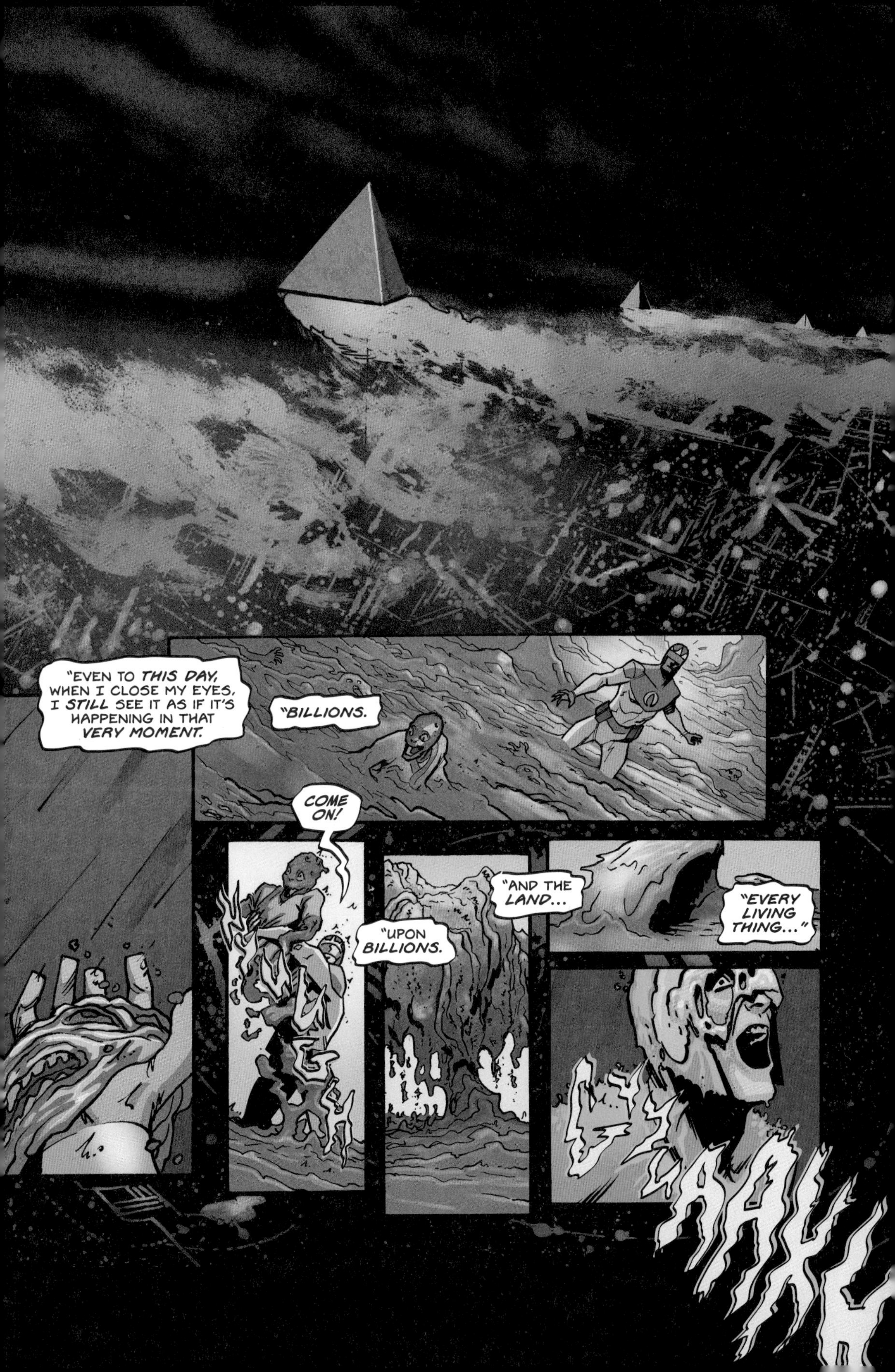
"EVEN TO THIS DAY, WHEN I CLOSE MY EYES, I STILL SEE IT AS IF IT'S HAPPENING IN THAT VERY MOMENT.
"BILLIONS.
COME ON!
"UPON BILLIONS.
"AND THE LAND...
"EVERY LIVING THING..."

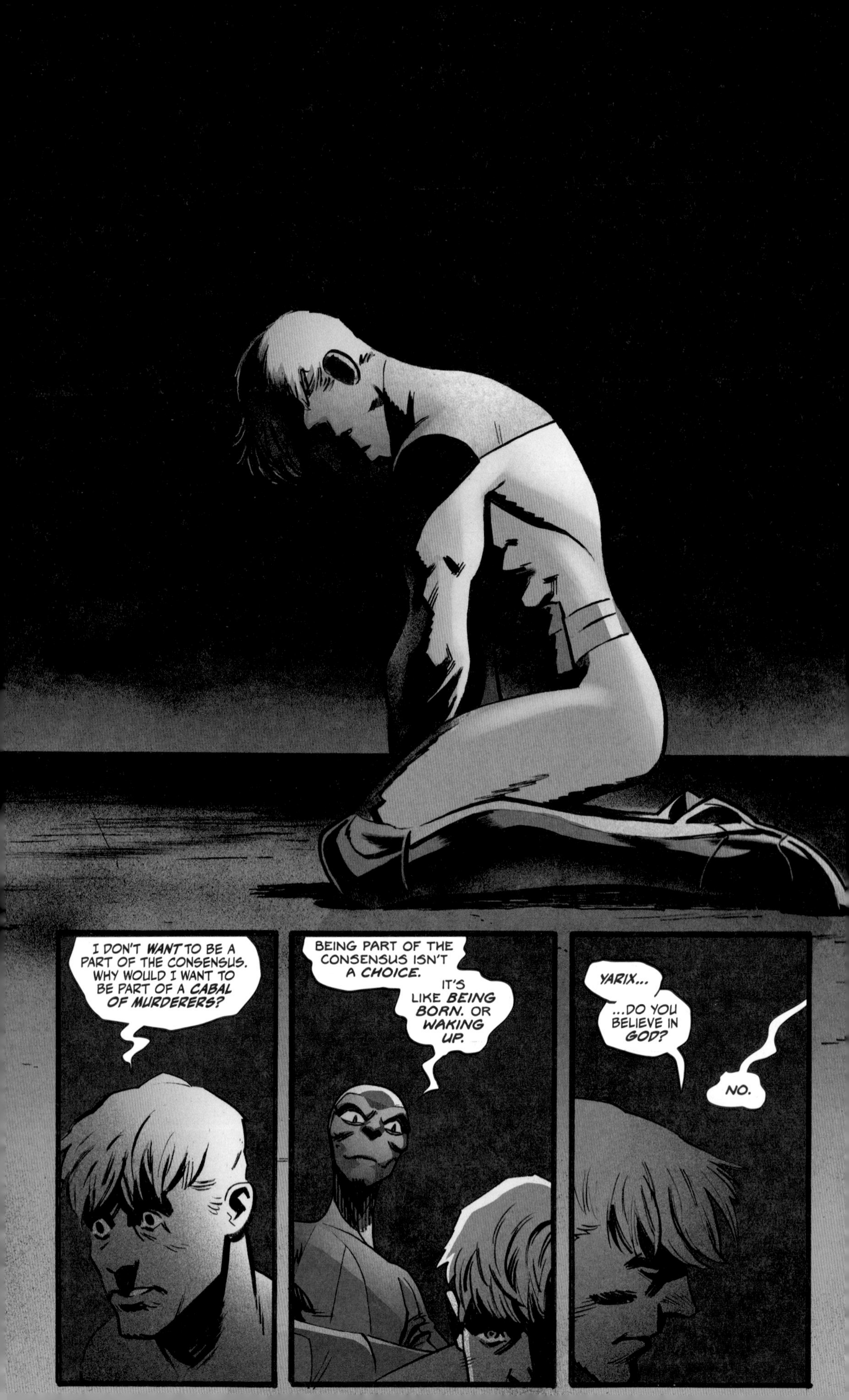
I DON'T WANT TO BE A PART OF THE CONSENSUS. WHY WOULD I WANT TO BE PART OF A CABAL OF MURDERERS?
BEING PART OF THE CONSENSUS ISN'T A CHOICE.
IT'S LIKE BEING BORN. OR WAKING UP.
YARIX...
...DO YOU BELIEVE IN GOD?
NO.

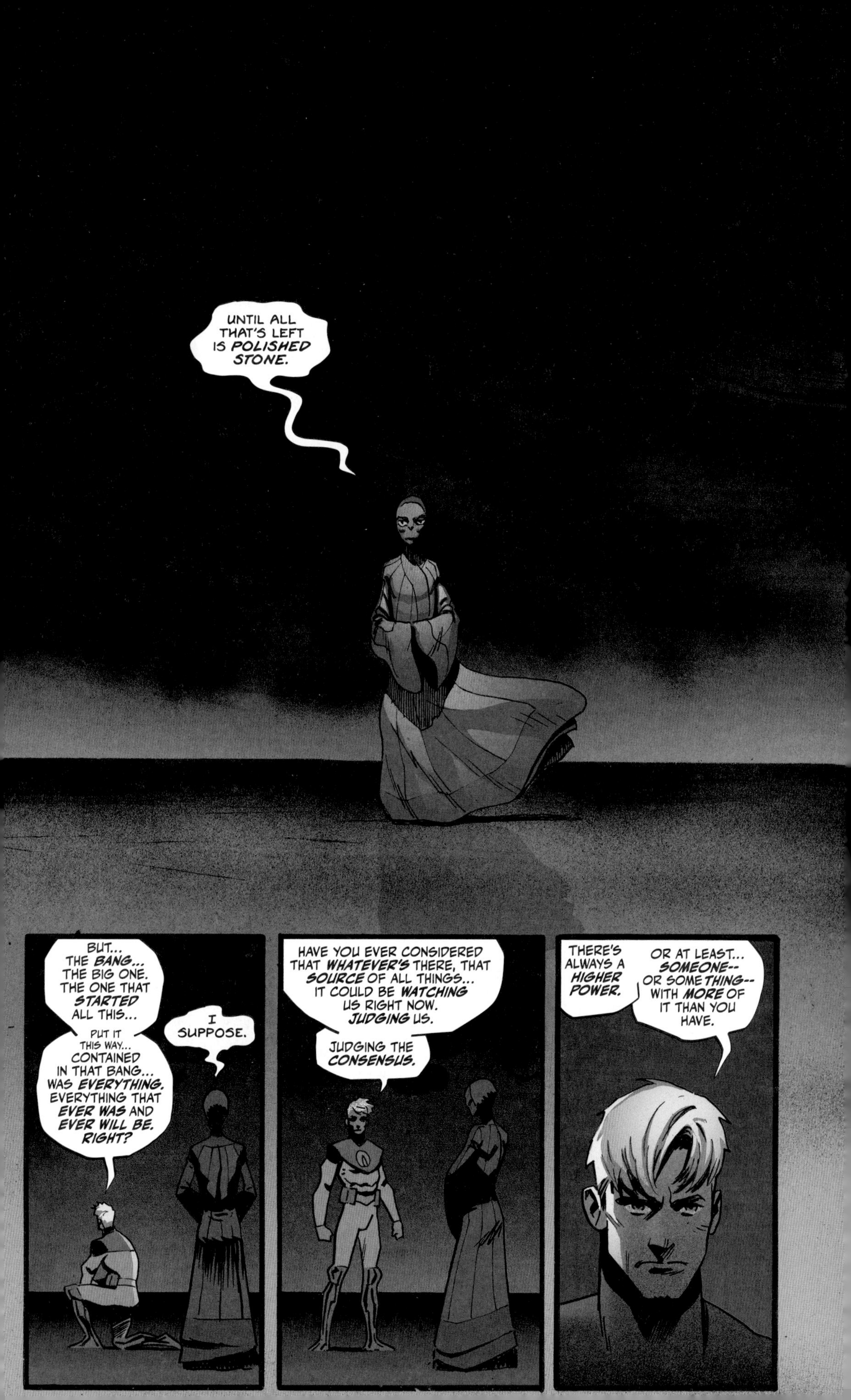
UNTIL ALL THAT'S LEFT IS POLISHED STONE.
BUT... THE BANG... THE BIG ONE. THE ONE THAT STARTED ALL THIS...
PUT IT THIS WAY... CONTAINED IN THAT BANG... WAS EVERYTHING. EVERYTHING THAT EVER WAS AND EVER WILL BE. RIGHT?
I SUPPOSE.
HAVE YOU EVER CONSIDERED THAT WHATEVER'S THERE, THAT SOURCE OF ALL THINGS... IT COULD BE WATCHING US RIGHT NOW. JUDGING US.
JUDGING THE CONSENSUS.
THERE'S ALWAYS A HIGHER POWER.
OR AT LEAST... SOMEONE-- OR SOMETHING-- WITH MORE OF IT THAN YOU HAVE.

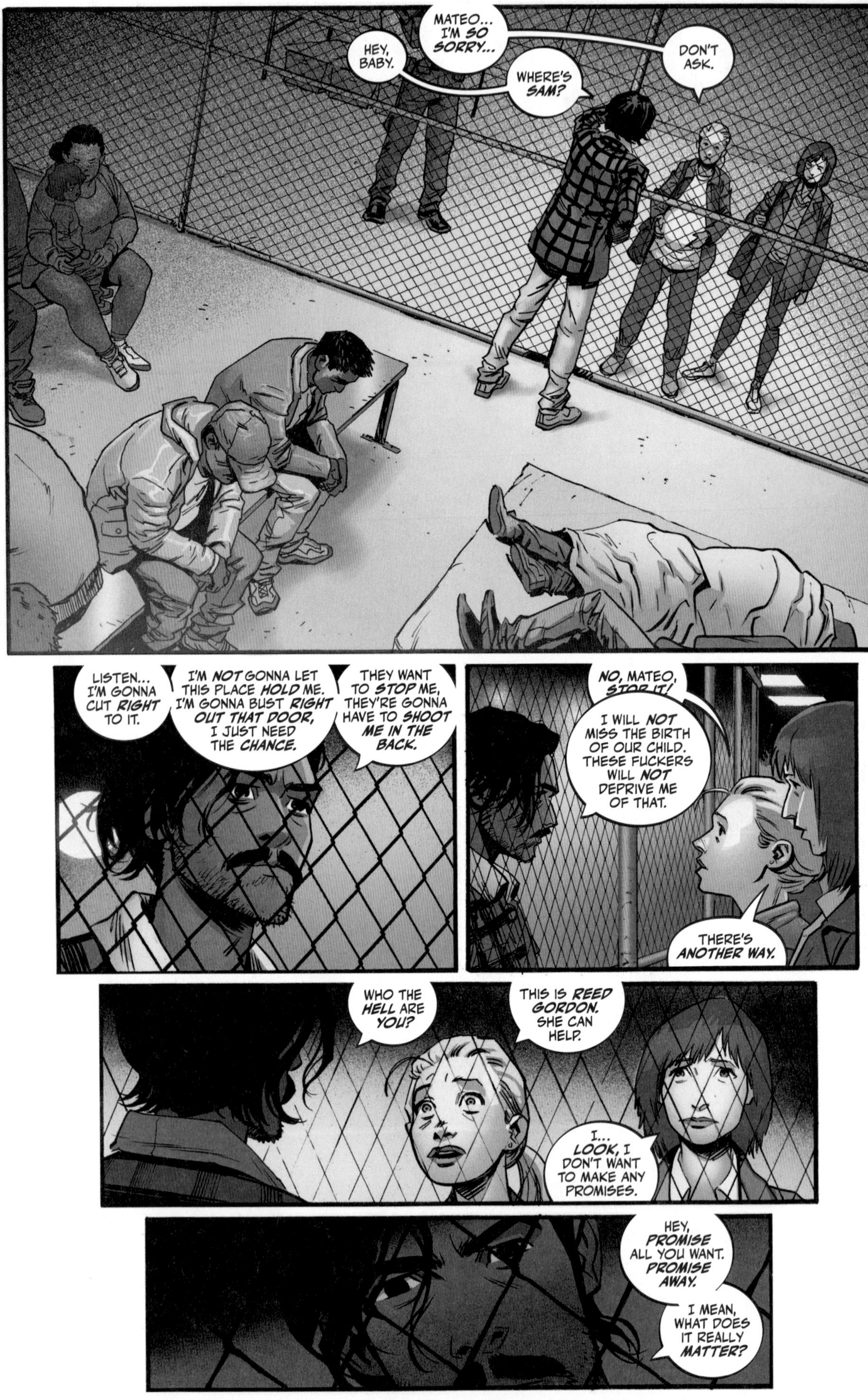
HEY, BABY.
MATEO... I'M SO SORRY...
WHERE'S SAM?
DON'T ASK.
LISTEN... I'M GONNA CUT RIGHT TO IT.
I'M NOT GONNA LET THIS PLACE HOLD ME. I'M GONNA BUST RIGHT OUT THAT DOOR, I JUST NEED THE CHANCE.
THEY WANT TO STOP ME, THEY'RE GONNA HAVE TO SHOOT ME IN THE BACK.
NO, MATEO, STOP IT!
I WILL NOT MISS THE BIRTH OF OUR CHILD. THESE FUCKERS WILL NOT DEPRIVE ME OF THAT.
THERE'S ANOTHER WAY.
WHO THE HELL ARE YOU?
THIS IS REED GORDON. SHE CAN HELP.
I... LOOK, I DON'T WANT TO MAKE ANY PROMISES.
HEY, PROMISE ALL YOU WANT. PROMISE AWAY.
I MEAN, WHAT DOES IT REALLY MATTER?

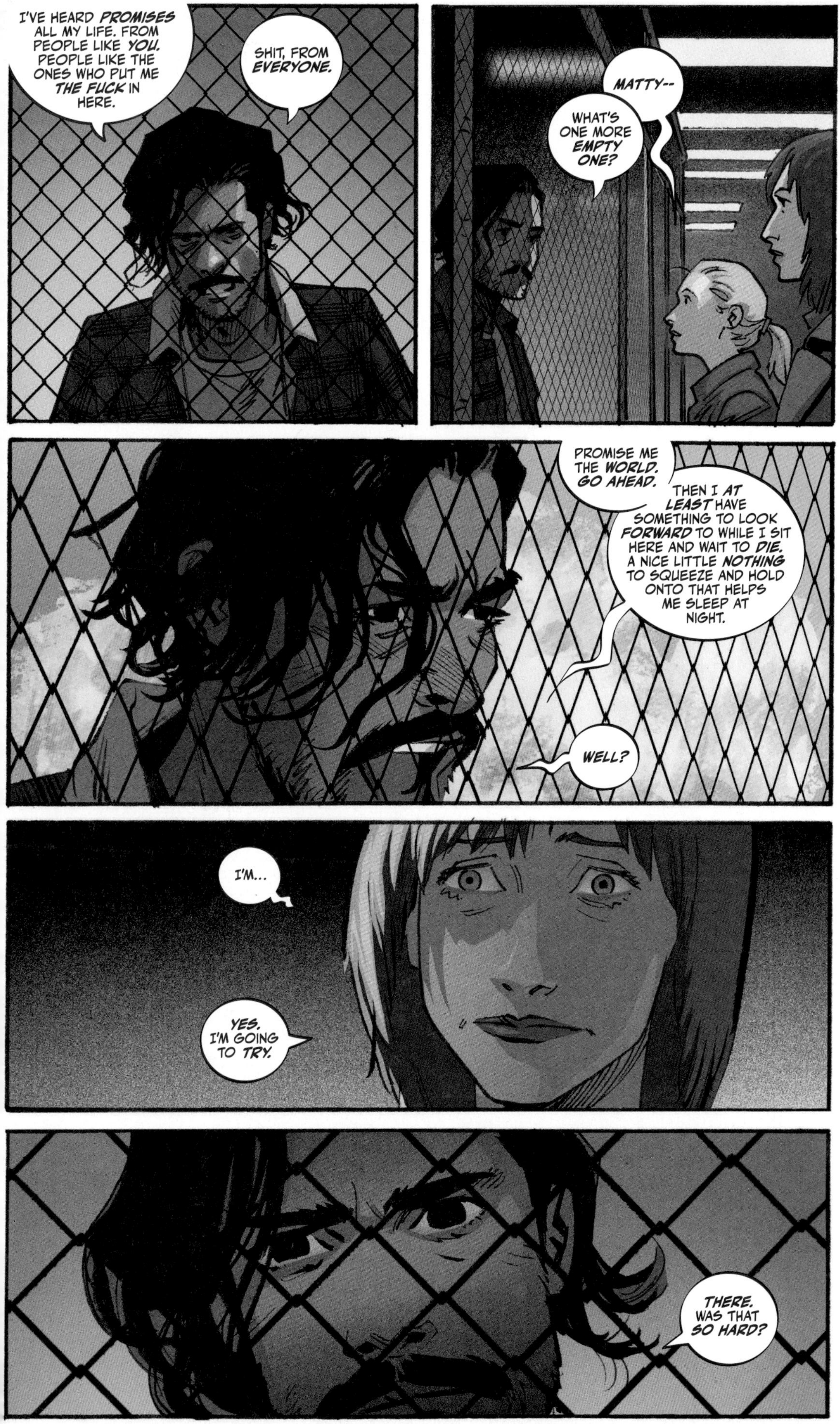
I'VE HEARD PROMISES ALL MY LIFE. FROM PEOPLE LIKE YOU. PEOPLE LIKE THE ONES WHO PUT ME THE FUCK IN HERE.
SHIT, FROM EVERYONE.
MATTY--
WHAT'S ONE MORE EMPTY ONE?
PROMISE ME THE WORLD. GO AHEAD.
THEN I AT LEAST HAVE SOMETHING TO LOOK FORWARD TO WHILE I SIT HERE AND WAIT TO DIE. A NICE LITTLE NOTHING TO SQUEEZE AND HOLD ONTO THAT HELPS ME SLEEP AT NIGHT.
WELL?
I'M...
YES. I'M GOING TO TRY.
THERE. WAS THAT SO HARD?

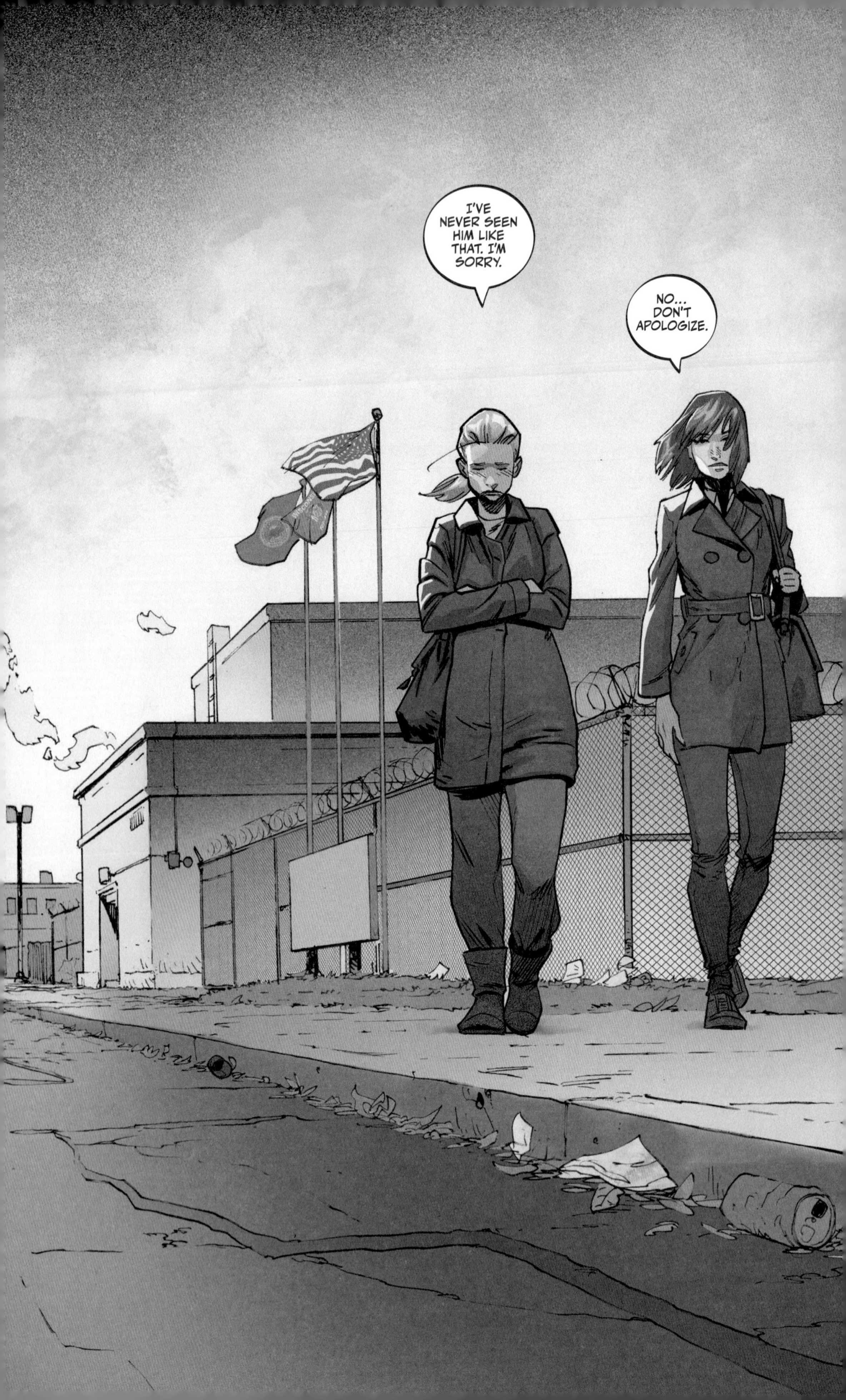
I'VE NEVER SEEN HIM LIKE THAT. I'M SORRY.
NO... DON'T APOLOGIZE.

POLISHED STONE AND YOU. ALL THAT WAS LEFT. POLISHED STONE...
...AND YOU.
WHY?
THE CONSENSUS NEEDED A PROSECUTOR. I WAS A GOOD CANDIDATE.
BECAUSE FOR ME, IT WASN'T ENOUGH PUNISHMENT TO WATCH MY OWN HOME BE ANNIHILATED. THE CONSENSUS FELT I SHOULD WATCH IT-- SOME NEW, HORRIBLE VERSION OF IT-- AGAIN AND AGAIN. EVEN HELP INSTIGATE IT. BE CULPABLE IN IT.
I'LL ASK AGAIN. WHY?
ON MY PLANET... I WAS WHAT YOU MIGHT CALL... A HERMIT. BY MY ADULTHOOD, I HAD REJECTED ALL OF MY SOCIETY. I...I HATED MY OWN PEOPLE. BECAUSE OF WHAT THEY DID. WHAT THEY LACKED. HOW THEY REPEATEDLY FAILED ONE ANOTHER, AND THEMSELVES.
SO I CHOSE TO WHILE AWAY MY TIME ALONE, CONTRIBUTING NOTHING, OFTEN CYNICALLY BELIEVING THAT THE BEST THING THAT COULD HAPPEN TO MY PLANET WAS ITS ULTIMATE DESTRUCTION.
WELL...

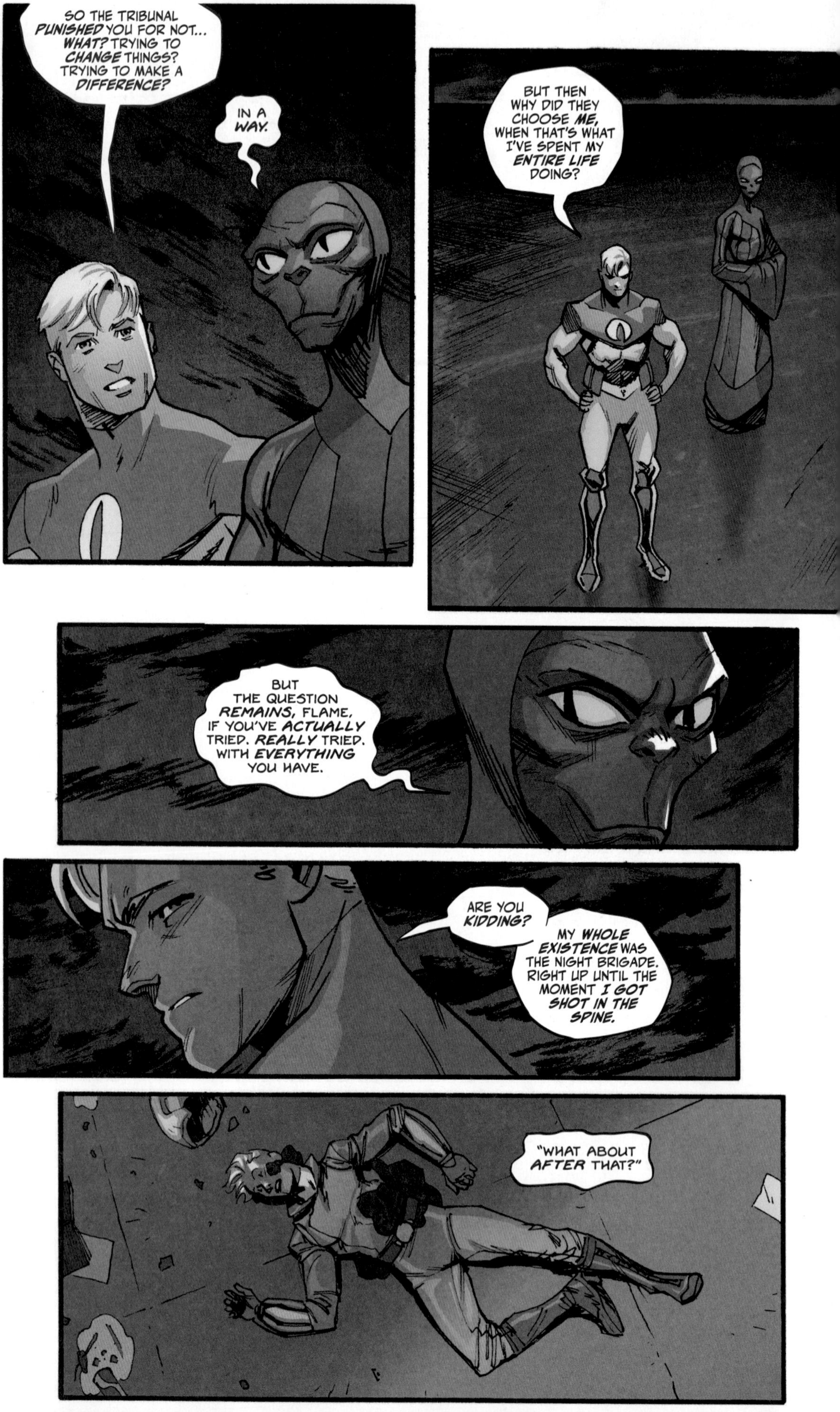
SO THE TRIBUNAL PUNISHED YOU FOR NOT... WHAT? TRYING TO CHANGE THINGS? TRYING TO MAKE A DIFFERENCE?
IN A WAY.
BUT THEN WHY DID THEY CHOOSE ME, WHEN THAT'S WHAT I'VE SPENT MY ENTIRE LIFE DOING?
BUT THE QUESTION REMAINS, FLAME, IF YOU'VE ACTUALLY TRIED. REALLY TRIED. WITH EVERYTHING YOU HAVE.
ARE YOU KIDDING?
MY WHOLE EXISTENCE WAS THE NIGHT BRIGADE. RIGHT UP UNTIL THE MOMENT I GOT SHOT IN THE SPINE.
"WHAT ABOUT AFTER THAT?"

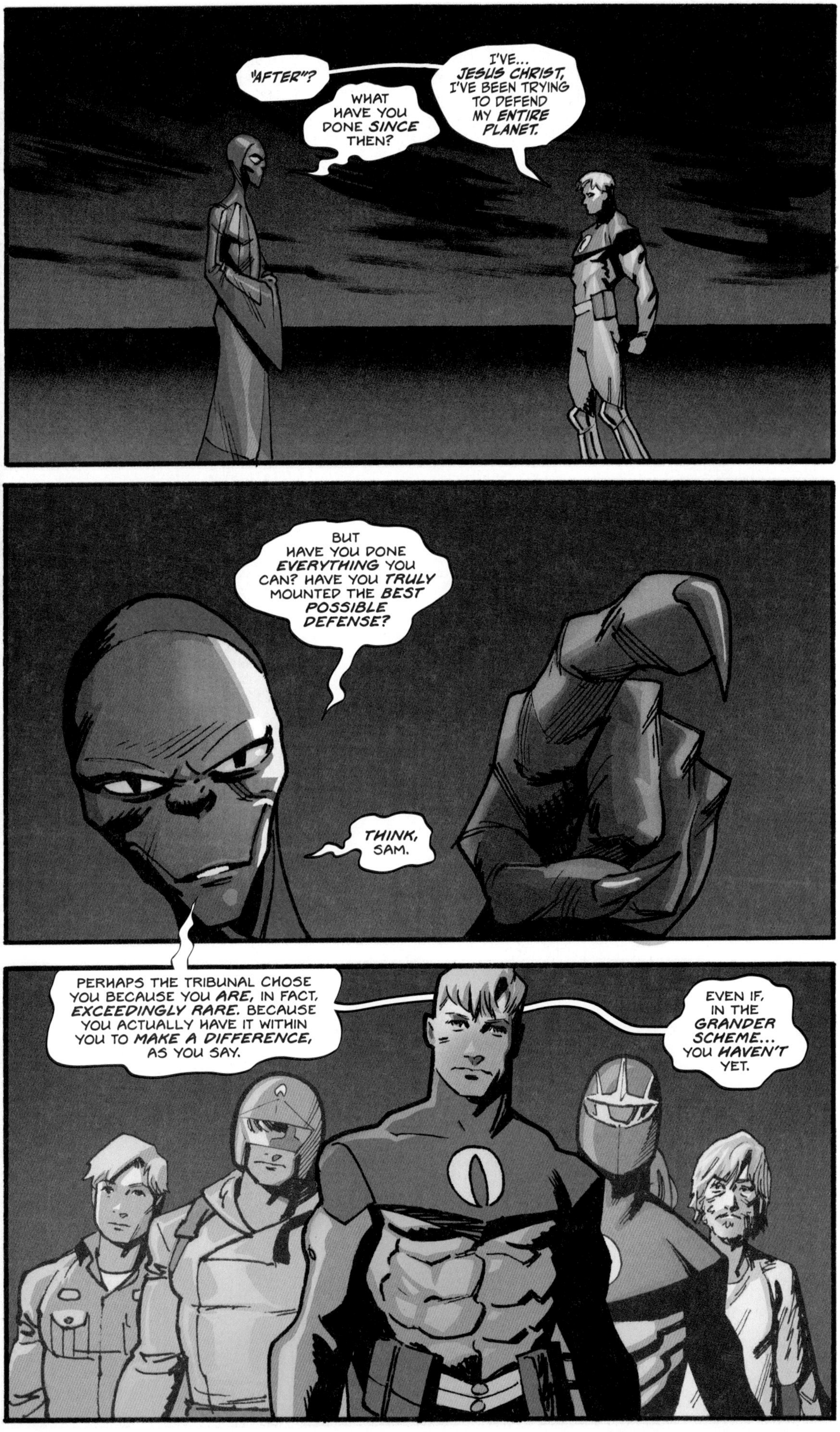
"AFTER"?
WHAT HAVE YOU DONE SINCE THEN?
I'VE... JESUS CHRIST, I'VE BEEN TRYING TO DEFEND MY ENTIRE PLANET.
BUT HAVE YOU DONE EVERYTHING YOU CAN? HAVE YOU TRULY MOUNTED THE BEST POSSIBLE DEFENSE?
THINK, SAM.
PERHAPS THE TRIBUNAL CHOSE YOU BECAUSE YOU ARE, IN FACT, EXCEEDINGLY RARE. BECAUSE YOU ACTUALLY HAVE IT WITHIN YOU TO MAKE A DIFFERENCE, AS YOU SAY.
EVEN IF, IN THE GRANDER SCHEME... YOU HAVEN'T YET.

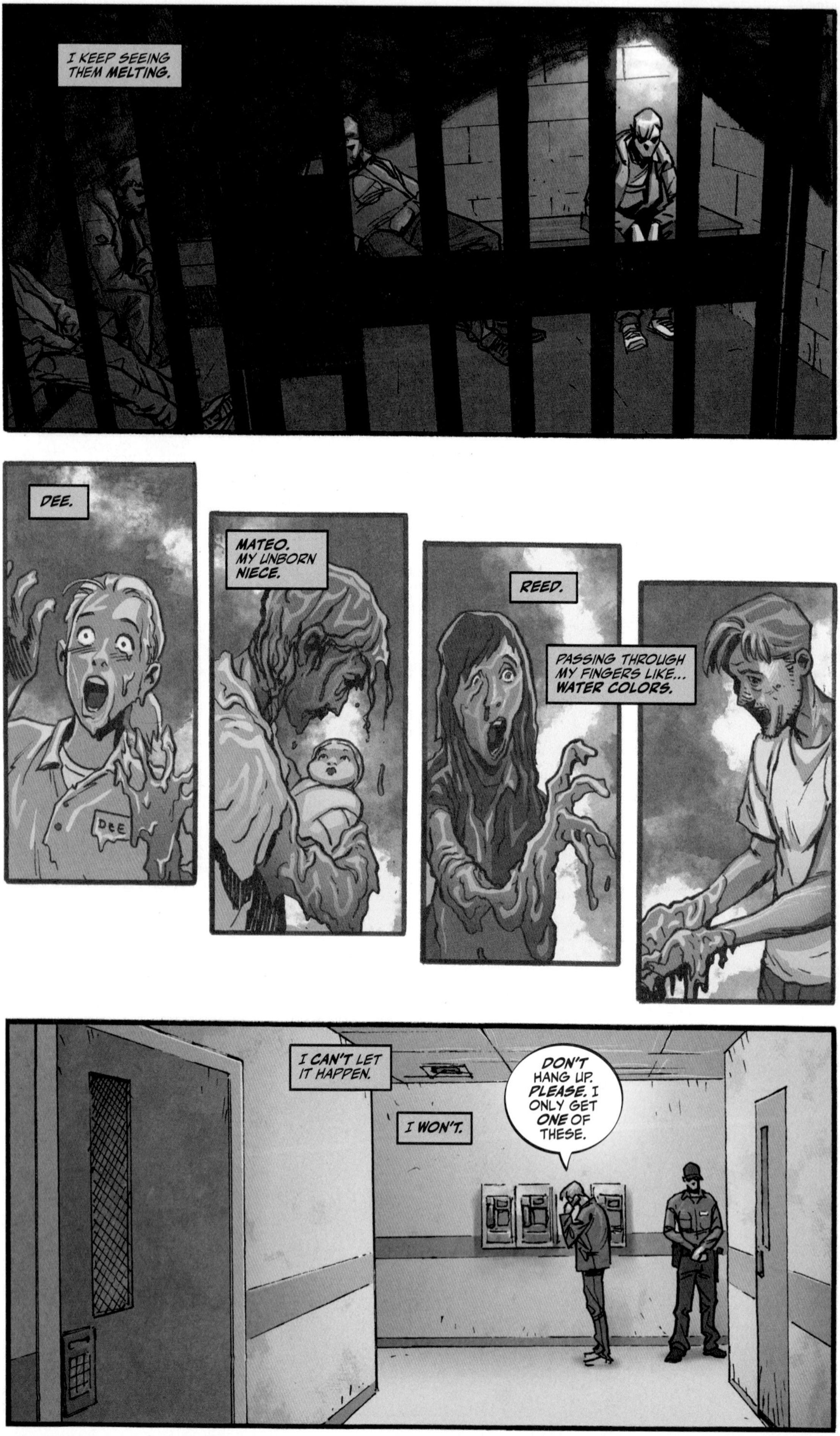
I KEEP SEEING THEM MELTING.
DEE.
MATEO. MY UNBORN NIECE.
REED.
PASSING THROUGH MY FINGERS LIKE... WATER COLORS.
I CAN'T LET IT HAPPEN.
I WON'T.
DON'T HANG UP. PLEASE. I ONLY GET ONE OF THESE.

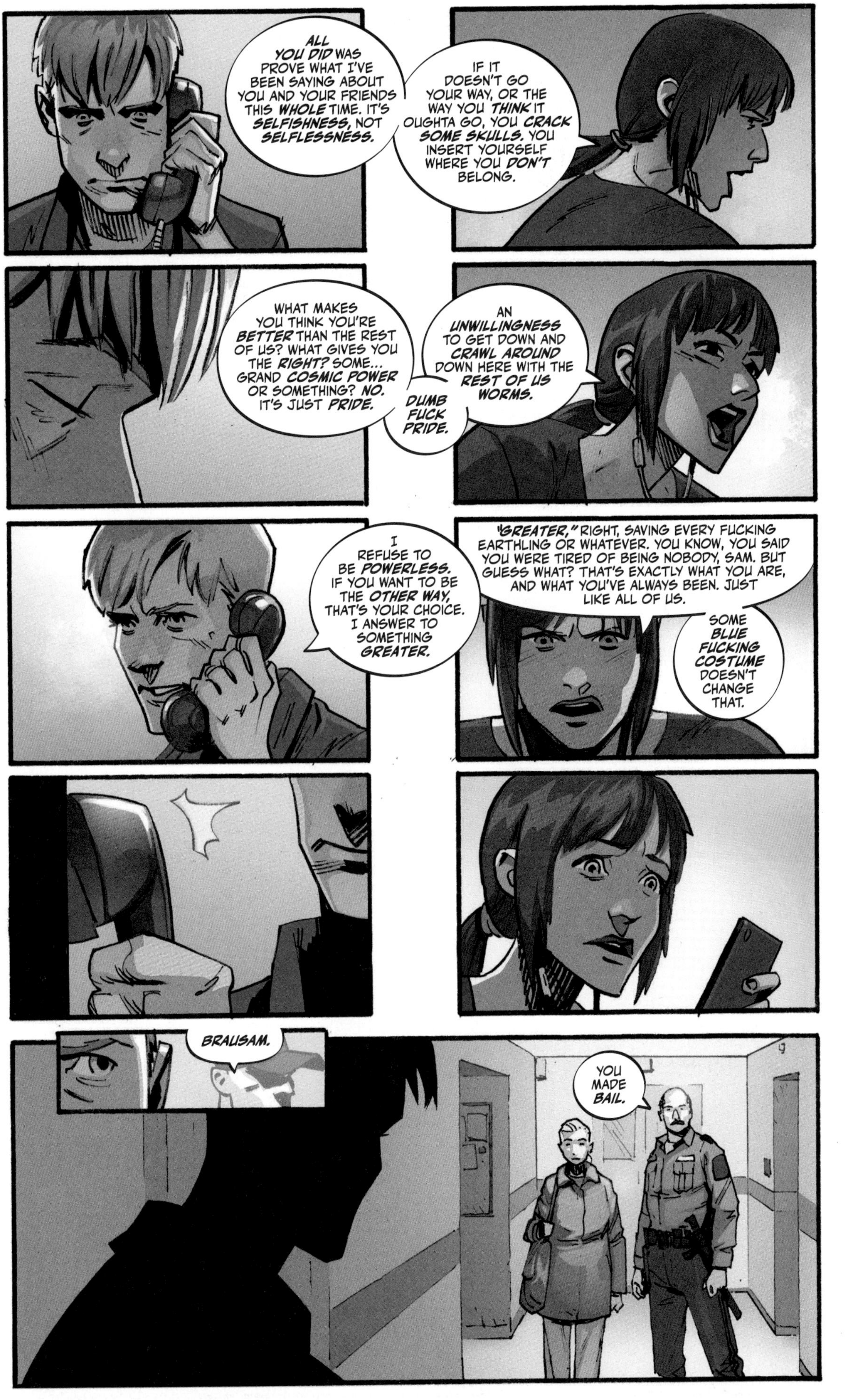
ALL YOU DID WAS PROVE WHAT I'VE BEEN SAYING ABOUT YOU AND YOUR FRIENDS THIS WHOLE TIME. IT'S SELFISHNESS, NOT SELFLESSNESS.
IF IT DOESN'T GO YOUR WAY, OR THE WAY YOU THINK IT OUGHTA GO, YOU CRACK SOME SKULLS. YOU INSERT YOURSELF WHERE YOU DON'T BELONG.
WHAT MAKES YOU THINK YOU'RE BETTER THAN THE REST OF US? WHAT GIVES YOU THE RIGHT? SOME... GRAND COSMIC POWER OR SOMETHING? NO. IT'S JUST PRIDE.
DUMB FUCK PRIDE.
AN UNWILLINGNESS TO GET DOWN AND CRAWL AROUND DOWN HERE WITH THE REST OF US WORMS.
I REFUSE TO BE POWERLESS. IF YOU WANT TO BE THE OTHER WAY, THAT'S YOUR CHOICE. I ANSWER TO SOMETHING GREATER.
"GREATER," RIGHT, SAVING EVERY FUCKING EARTHLING OR WHATEVER. YOU KNOW, YOU SAID YOU WERE TIRED OF BEING NOBODY, SAM. BUT GUESS WHAT? THAT'S EXACTLY WHAT YOU ARE, AND WHAT YOU'VE ALWAYS BEEN. JUST LIKE ALL OF US.
SOME BLUE FUCKING COSTUME DOESN'T CHANGE THAT.
BRAUSAM.
YOU MADE BAIL.

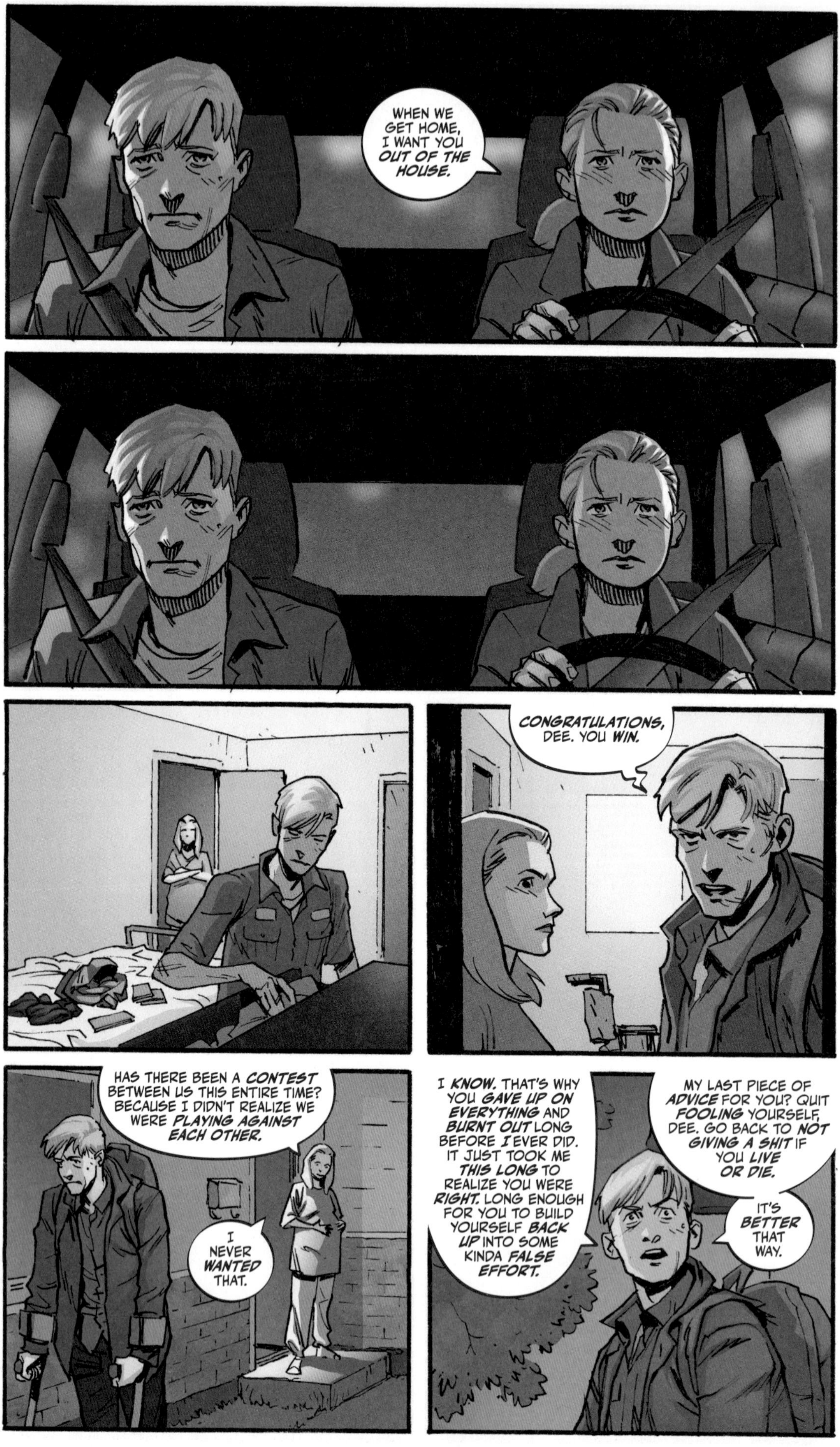
WHEN WE GET HOME, I WANT YOU OUT OF THE HOUSE.
CONGRATULATIONS, DEE. YOU WIN.
HAS THERE BEEN A CONTEST BETWEEN US THIS ENTIRE TIME? BECAUSE I DIDN'T REALIZE WE WERE PLAYING AGAINST EACH OTHER.
I NEVER WANTED THAT.
I KNOW. THAT'S WHY YOU GAVE UP ON EVERYTHING AND BURNT OUT LONG BEFORE I EVER DID. IT JUST TOOK ME THIS LONG TO REALIZE YOU WERE RIGHT. LONG ENOUGH FOR YOU TO BUILD YOURSELF BACK UP INTO SOME KINDA FALSE EFFORT.
MY LAST PIECE OF ADVICE FOR YOU? QUIT FOOLING YOURSELF, DEE. GO BACK TO NOT GIVING A SHIT IF YOU LIVE OR DIE.
IT'S BETTER THAT WAY.

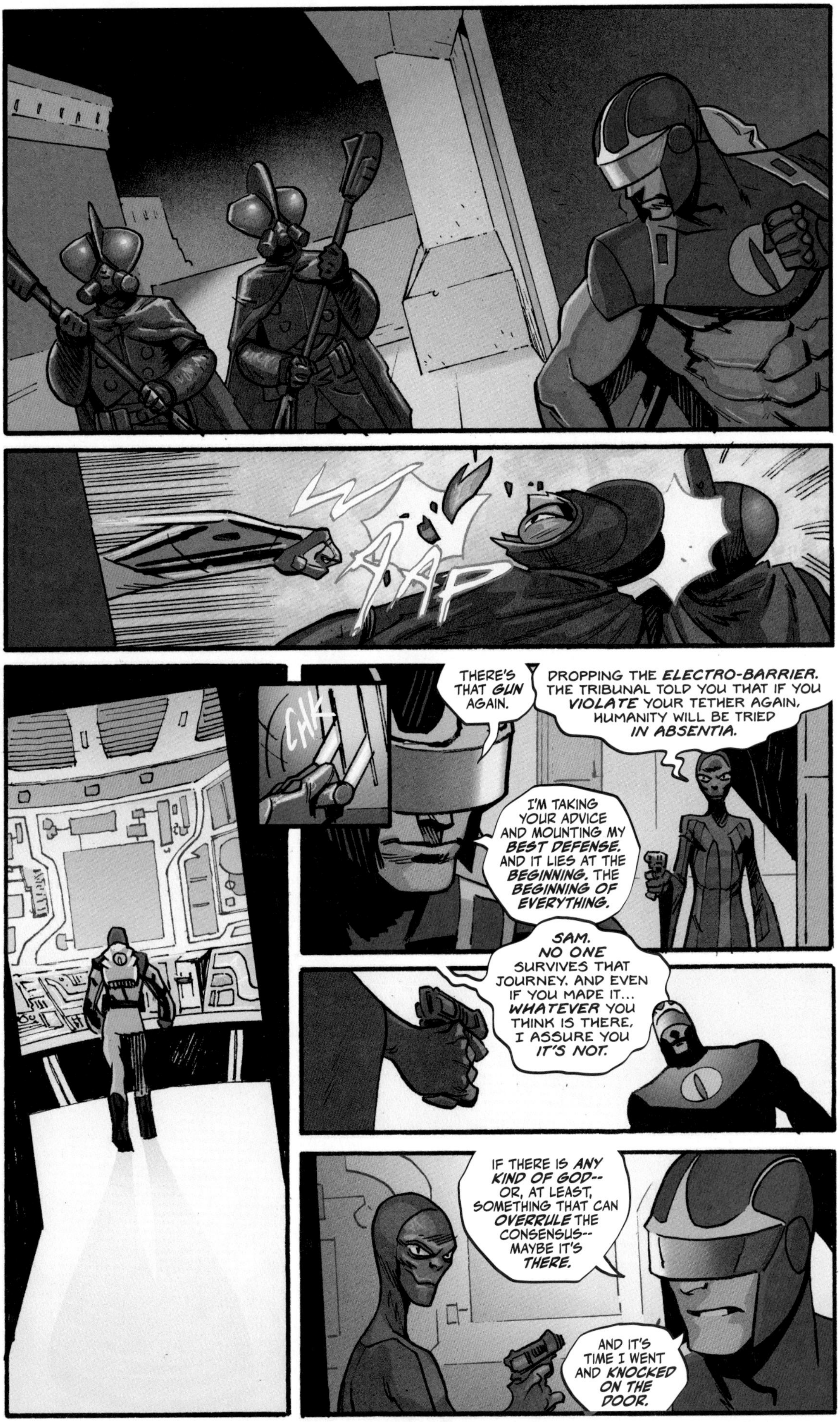

WAAP
CHK
THERE'S THAT GUN AGAIN.
DROPPING THE ELECTRO-BARRIER. THE TRIBUNAL TOLD YOU THAT IF YOU VIOLATE YOUR TETHER AGAIN, HUMANITY WILL BE TRIED IN ABSENTIA.
I'M TAKING YOUR ADVICE AND MOUNTING MY BEST DEFENSE. AND IT LIES AT THE BEGINNING. THE BEGINNING OF EVERYTHING.
SAM. NO ONE SURVIVES THAT JOURNEY. AND EVEN IF YOU MADE IT... WHATEVER YOU THINK IS THERE, I ASSURE YOU IT'S NOT.
IF THERE IS ANY KIND OF GOD-- OR, AT LEAST, SOMETHING THAT CAN OVERRULE THE CONSENSUS-- MAYBE IT'S THERE.
AND IT'S TIME I WENT AND KNOCKED ON THE DOOR.

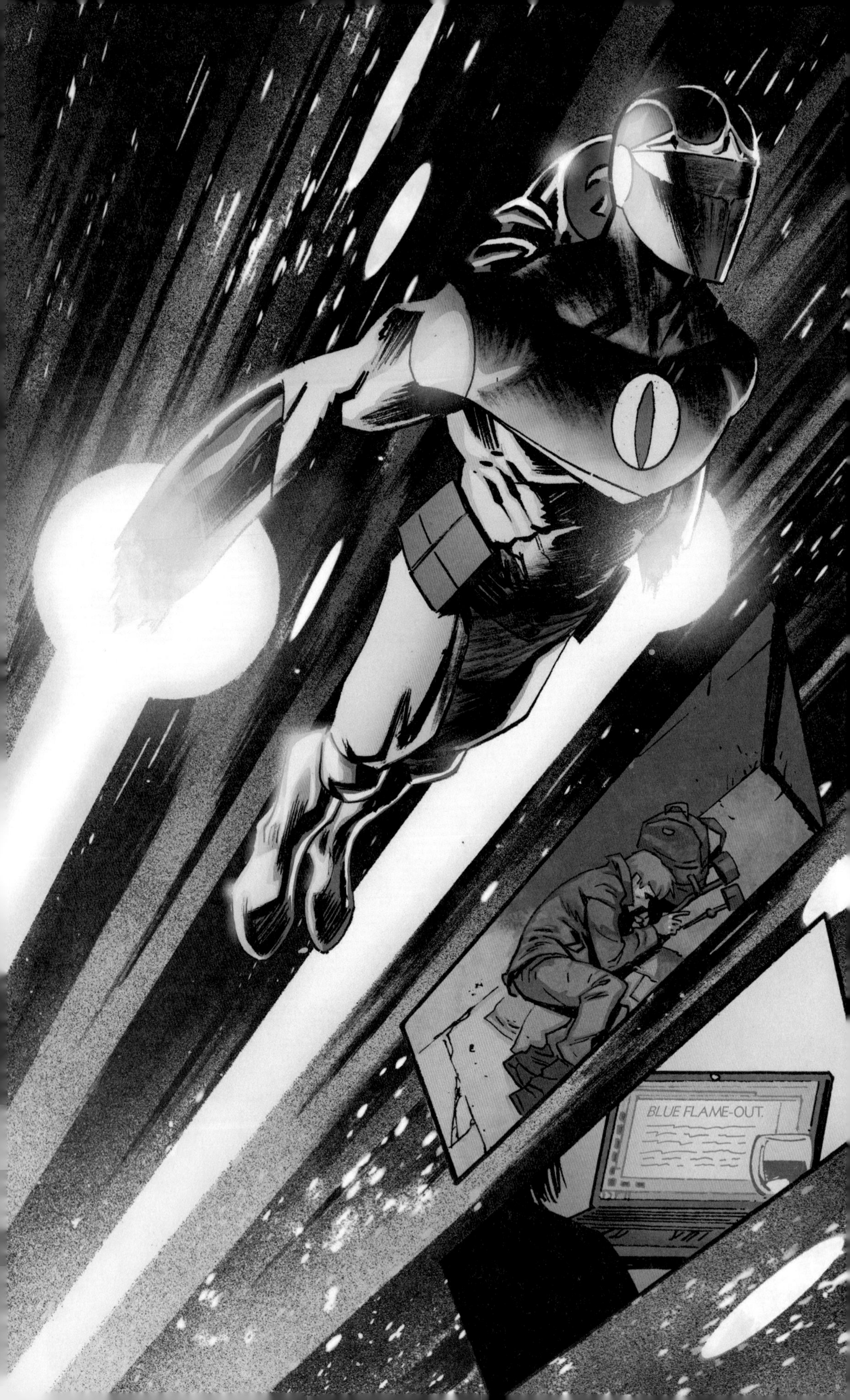
BLUE FLAME-OUT.

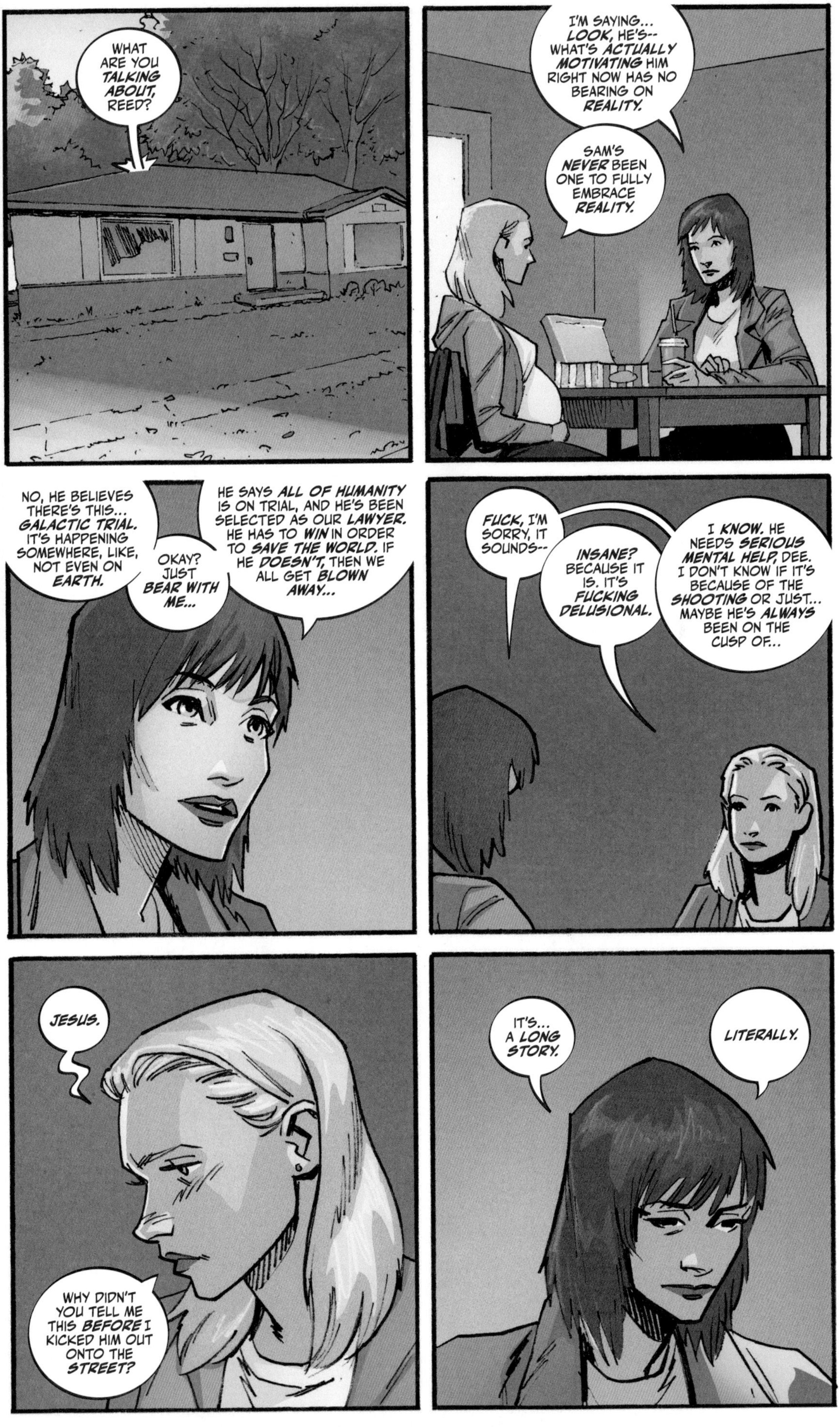
WHAT ARE YOU TALKING ABOUT, REED?
I'M SAYING... LOOK, HE'S-- WHAT'S ACTUALLY MOTIVATING HIM RIGHT NOW HAS NO BEARING ON REALITY.
SAM'S NEVER BEEN ONE TO FULLY EMBRACE REALITY.
NO, HE BELIEVES THERE'S THIS... GALACTIC TRIAL. IT'S HAPPENING SOMEWHERE, LIKE, NOT EVEN ON EARTH.
OKAY? JUST BEAR WITH ME...
HE SAYS ALL OF HUMANITY IS ON TRIAL, AND HE'S BEEN SELECTED AS OUR LAWYER. HE HAS TO WIN IN ORDER TO SAVE THE WORLD. IF HE DOESN'T, THEN WE ALL GET BLOWN AWAY...
FUCK, I'M SORRY, IT SOUNDS--
INSANE? BECAUSE IT IS. IT'S FUCKING DELUSIONAL.
I KNOW. HE NEEDS SERIOUS MENTAL HELP, DEE. I DON'T KNOW IF IT'S BECAUSE OF THE SHOOTING OR JUST... MAYBE HE'S ALWAYS BEEN ON THE CUSP OF...
JESUS.
WHY DIDN'T YOU TELL ME THIS BEFORE I KICKED HIM OUT ONTO THE STREET?
IT'S... A LONG STORY.
LITERALLY.

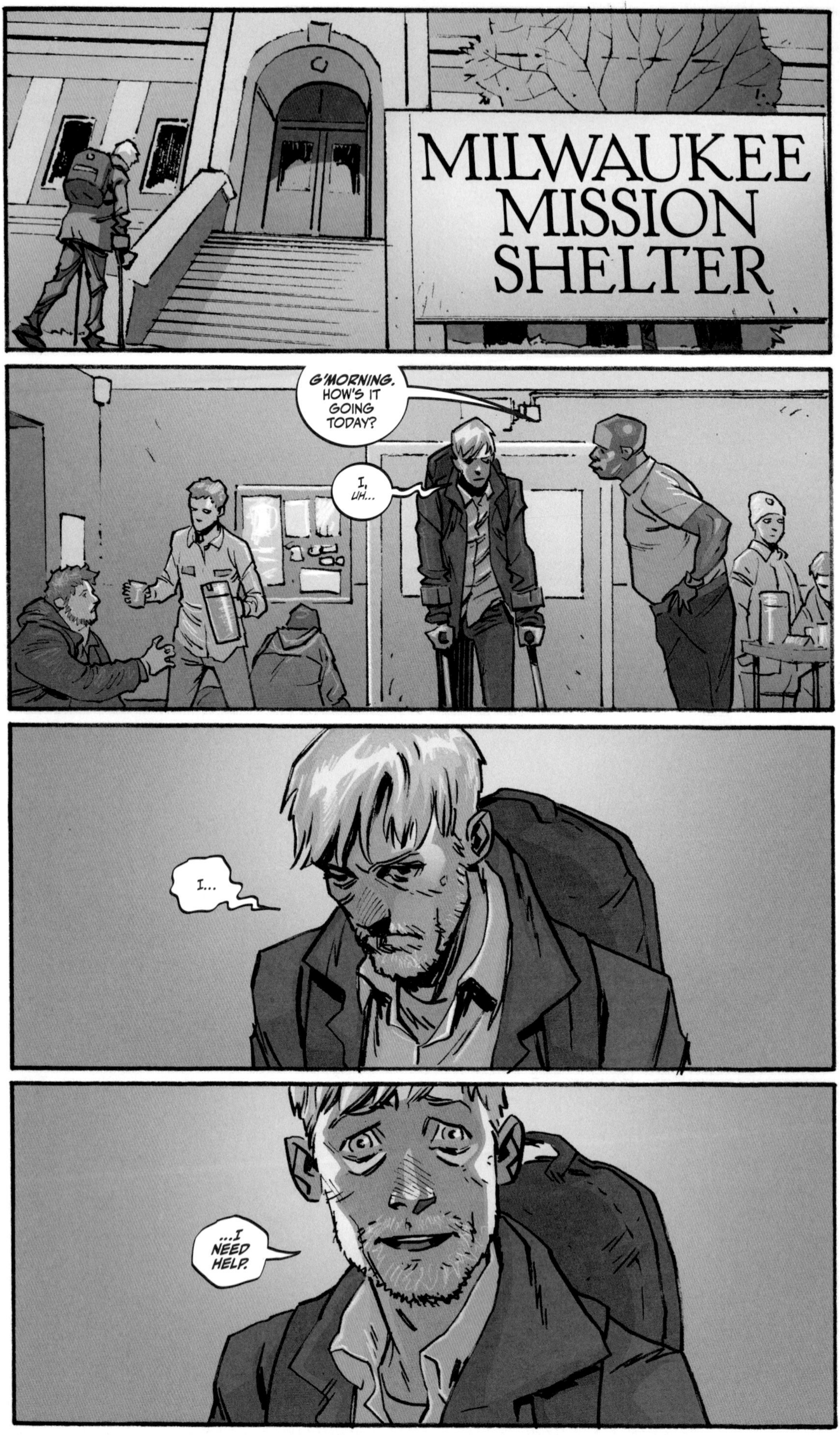
MILWAUKEE MISSION SHELTER
G'MORNING. HOW'S IT GOING TODAY?
I, UH...
I...
...I NEED HELP.

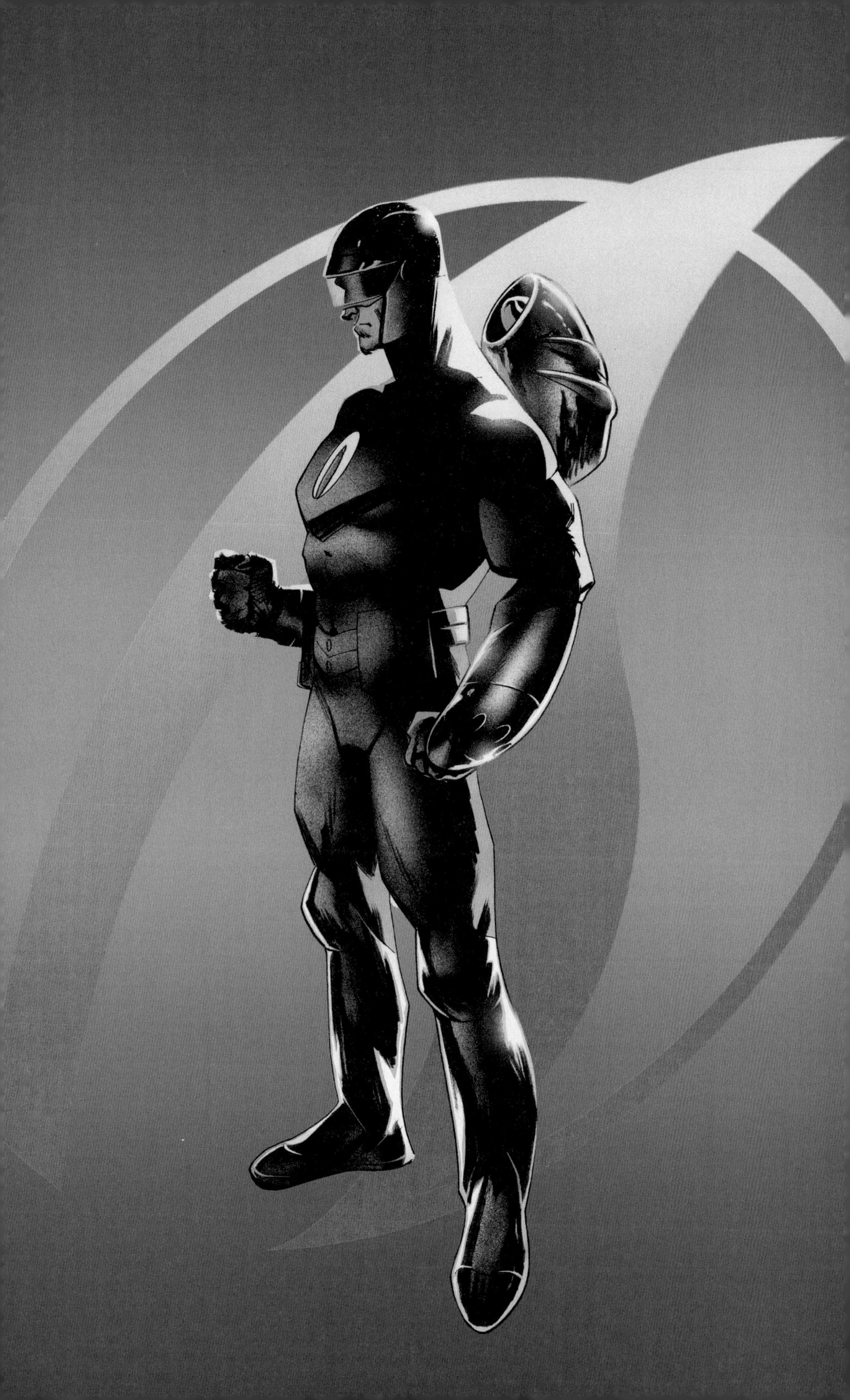

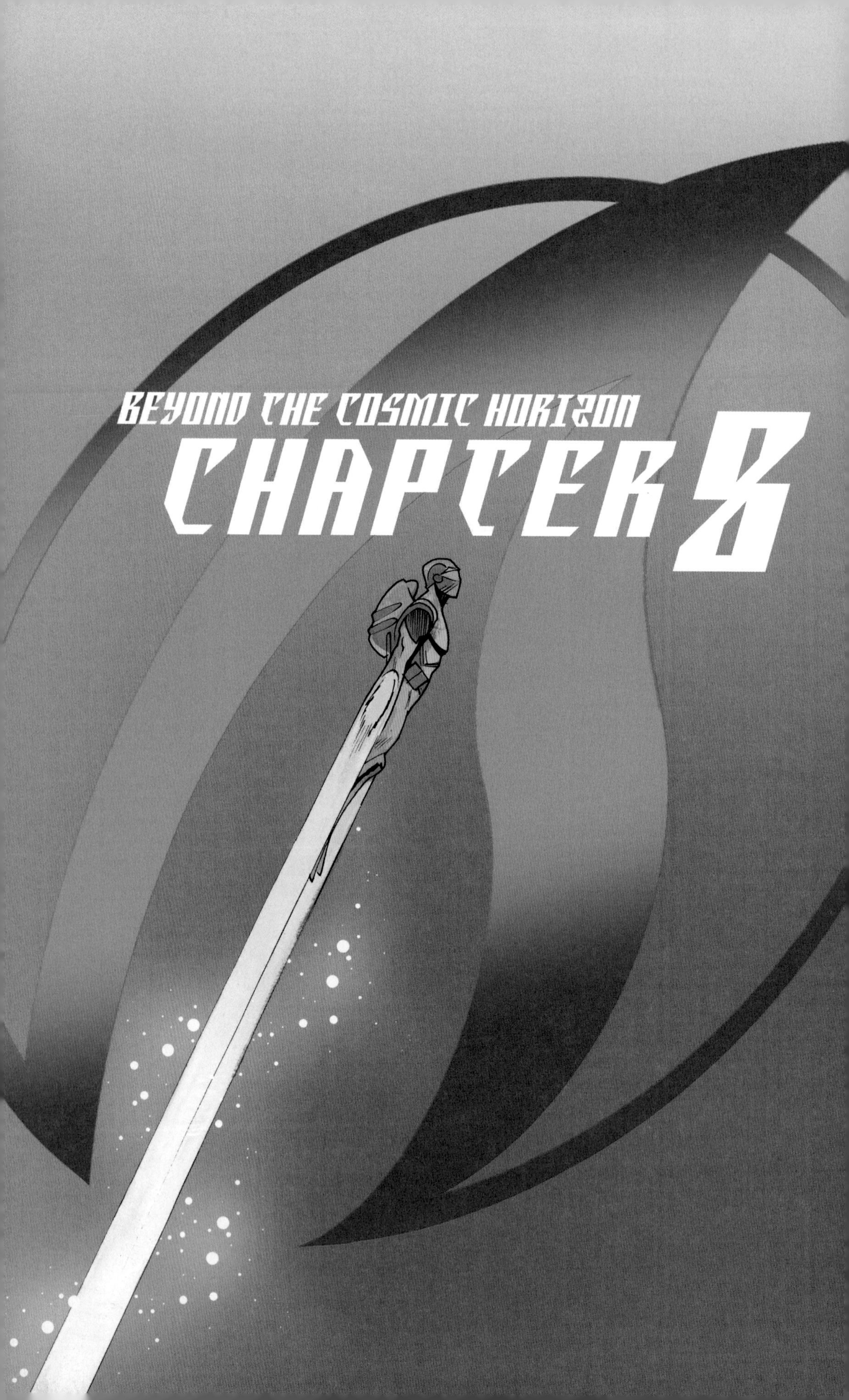
BEYOND THE COSMIC HORIZON
CHAPTER 8

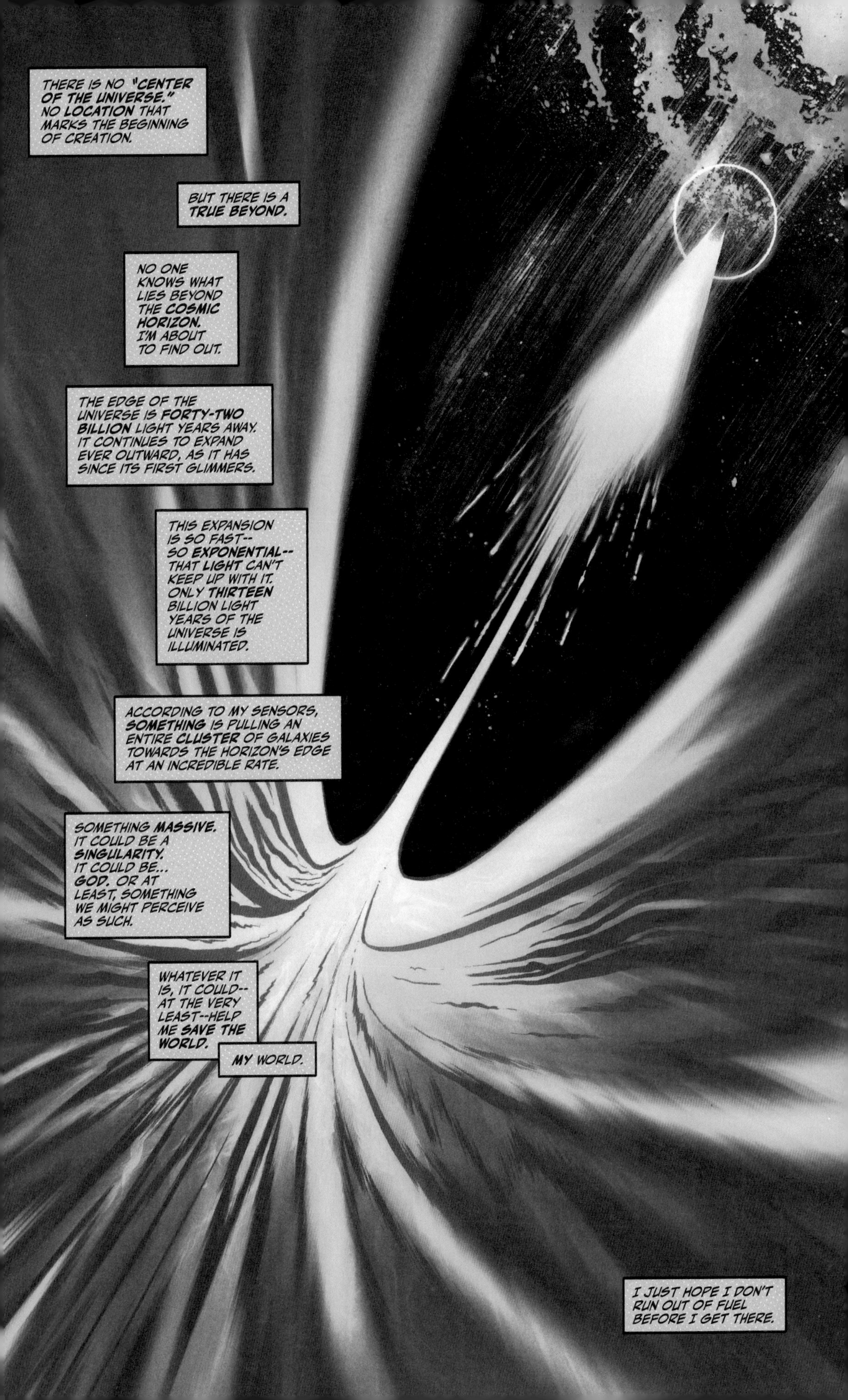
THERE IS NO "CENTER OF THE UNIVERSE." NO LOCATION THAT MARKS THE BEGINNING OF CREATION.
BUT THERE IS A TRUE BEYOND.
NO ONE KNOWS WHAT LIES BEYOND THE COSMIC HORIZON. I'M ABOUT TO FIND OUT.
THE EDGE OF THE UNIVERSE IS FORTY-TWO BILLION LIGHT YEARS AWAY. IT CONTINUES TO EXPAND EVER OUTWARD, AS IT HAS SINCE ITS FIRST GLIMMERS.
THIS EXPANSION IS SO FAST-- SO EXPONENTIAL-- THAT LIGHT CAN'T KEEP UP WITH IT. ONLY THIRTEEN BILLION LIGHT YEARS OF THE UNIVERSE IS ILLUMINATED.
ACCORDING TO MY SENSORS, SOMETHING IS PULLING AN ENTIRE CLUSTER OF GALAXIES TOWARDS THE HORIZON'S EDGE AT AN INCREDIBLE RATE.
SOMETHING MASSIVE. IT COULD BE A SINGULARITY. IT COULD BE... GOD. OR AT LEAST, SOMETHING WE MIGHT PERCEIVE AS SUCH.
WHATEVER IT IS, IT COULD-- AT THE VERY LEAST--HELP ME SAVE THE WORLD.
MY WORLD.
I JUST HOPE I DON'T RUN OUT OF FUEL BEFORE I GET THERE.

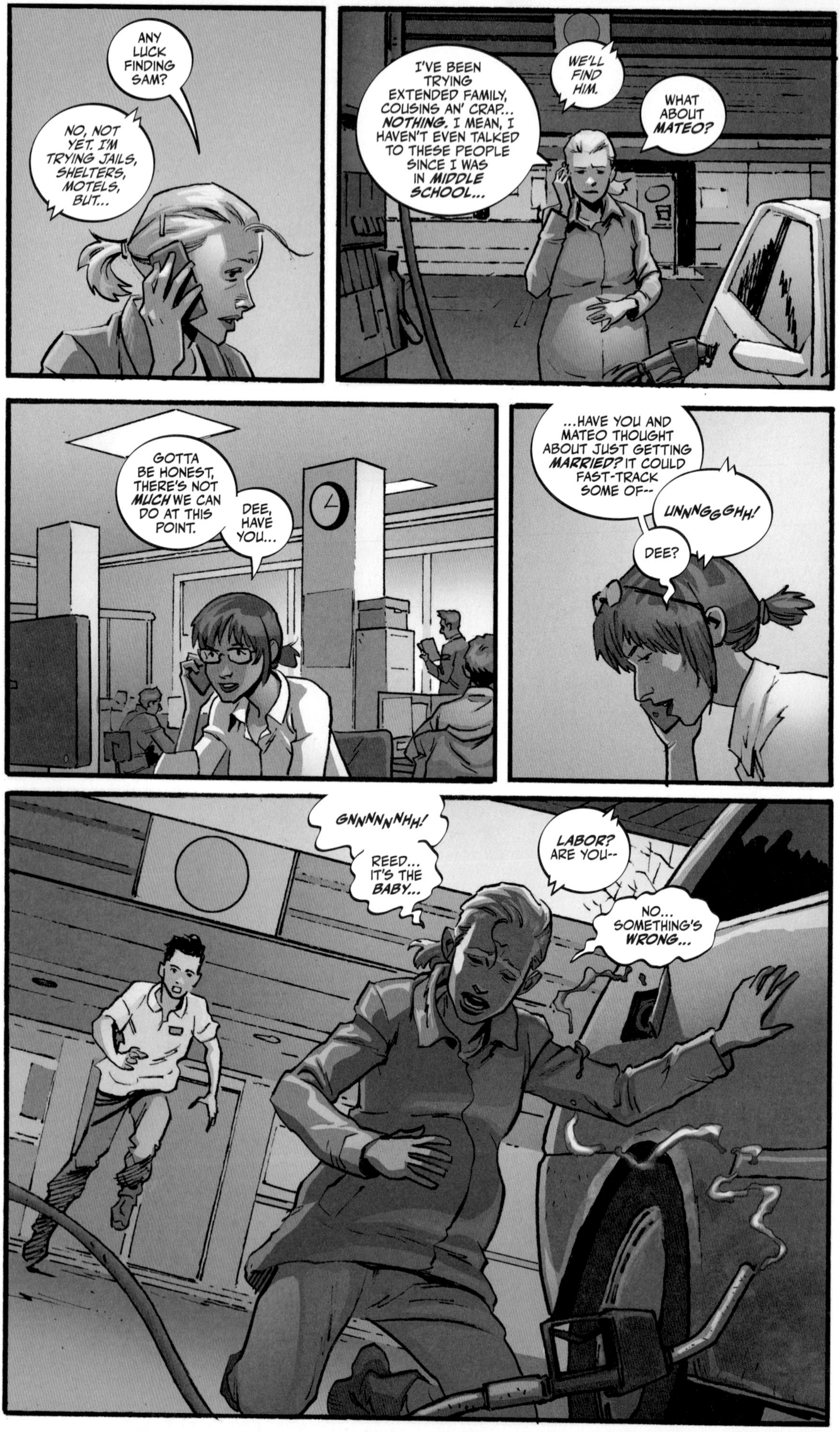
ANY LUCK FINDING SAM?
NO, NOT YET. I'M TRYING JAILS, SHELTERS, MOTELS, BUT...
I'VE BEEN TRYING EXTENDED FAMILY, COUSINS AN' CRAP... NOTHING. I MEAN, I HAVEN'T EVEN TALKED TO THESE PEOPLE SINCE I WAS IN MIDDLE SCHOOL...
WE'LL FIND HIM.
WHAT ABOUT MATEO?
GOTTA BE HONEST, THERE'S NOT MUCH WE CAN DO AT THIS POINT.
DEE, HAVE YOU...
...HAVE YOU AND MATEO THOUGHT ABOUT JUST GETTING MARRIED? IT COULD FAST-TRACK SOME OF--
UNNNGGGHH!
DEE?
GNNNNNNHH!
REED... IT'S THE BABY...
LABOR? ARE YOU--
NO... SOMETHING'S WRONG...

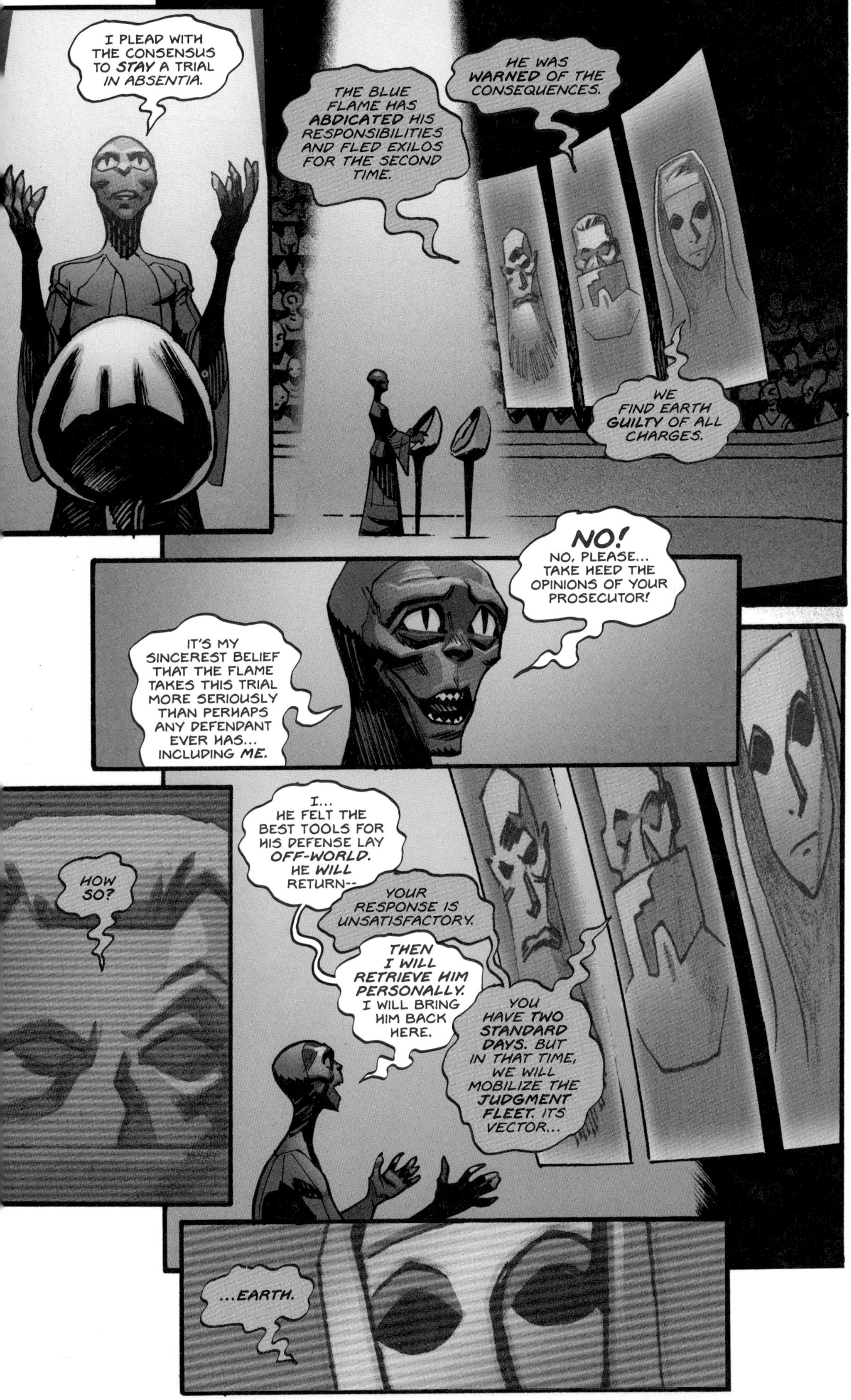
I PLEAD WITH THE CONSENSUS TO STAY A TRIAL IN ABSENTIA.
THE BLUE FLAME HAS ABDICATED HIS RESPONSIBILITIES AND FLED EXILOS FOR THE SECOND TIME.
HE WAS WARNED OF THE CONSEQUENCES.
WE FIND EARTH GUILTY OF ALL CHARGES.
NO! NO, PLEASE... TAKE HEED THE OPINIONS OF YOUR PROSECUTOR!
IT'S MY SINCEREST BELIEF THAT THE FLAME TAKES THIS TRIAL MORE SERIOUSLY THAN PERHAPS ANY DEFENDANT EVER HAS... INCLUDING ME.
HOW SO?
I... HE FELT THE BEST TOOLS FOR HIS DEFENSE LAY OFF-WORLD. HE WILL RETURN--
YOUR RESPONSE IS UNSATISFACTORY.
THEN I WILL RETRIEVE HIM PERSONALLY. I WILL BRING HIM BACK HERE.
YOU HAVE TWO STANDARD DAYS. BUT IN THAT TIME, WE WILL MOBILIZE THE JUDGMENT FLEET. ITS VECTOR...
...EARTH.

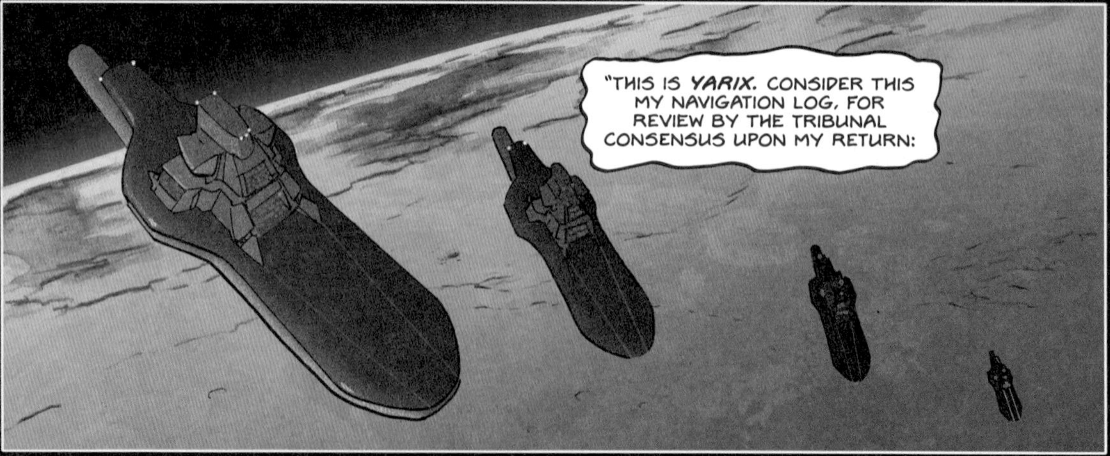
"THIS IS *YARIX.* CONSIDER THIS MY NAVIGATION LOG, FOR REVIEW BY THE TRIBUNAL CONSENSUS UPON MY RETURN:

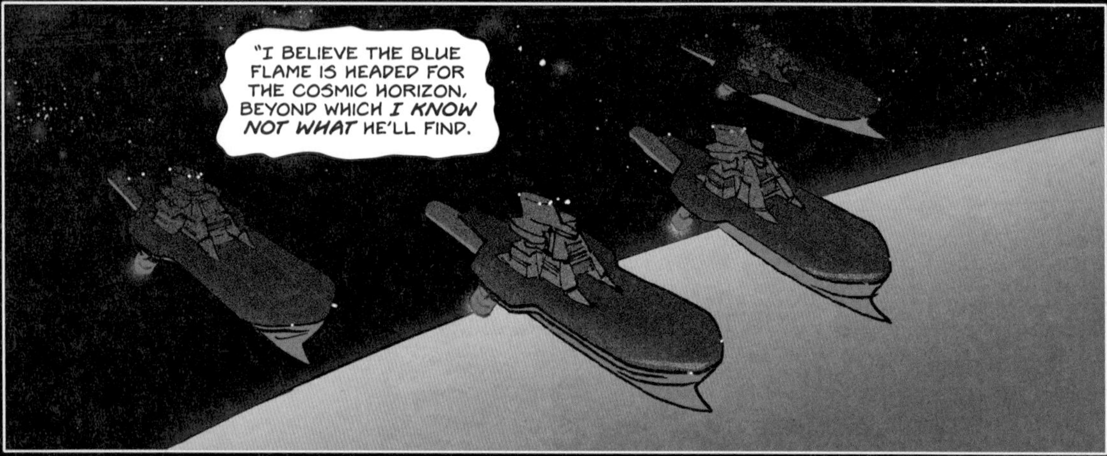
"I BELIEVE THE BLUE FLAME IS HEADED FOR THE COSMIC HORIZON, BEYOND WHICH *I KNOW NOT WHAT* HE'LL FIND.

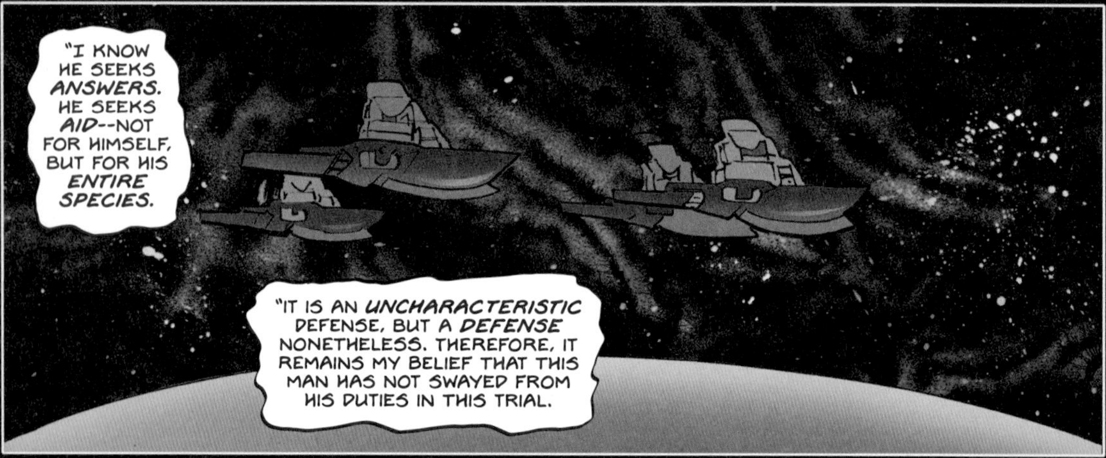
"I KNOW HE SEEKS *ANSWERS.* HE SEEKS *AID*--NOT FOR HIMSELF, BUT FOR HIS *ENTIRE SPECIES.*
"IT IS AN *UNCHARACTERISTIC* DEFENSE, BUT A *DEFENSE* NONETHELESS. THEREFORE, IT REMAINS MY BELIEF THAT THIS MAN HAS NOT SWAYED FROM HIS DUTIES IN THIS TRIAL.

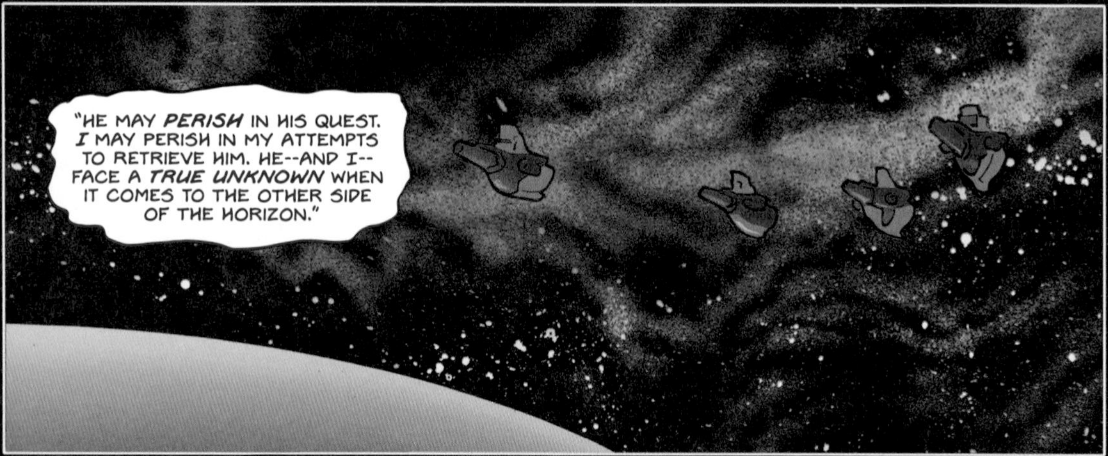
"HE MAY *PERISH* IN HIS QUEST. *I* MAY PERISH IN MY ATTEMPTS TO RETRIEVE HIM. HE--AND I--FACE A *TRUE UNKNOWN* WHEN IT COMES TO THE OTHER SIDE OF THE HORIZON."

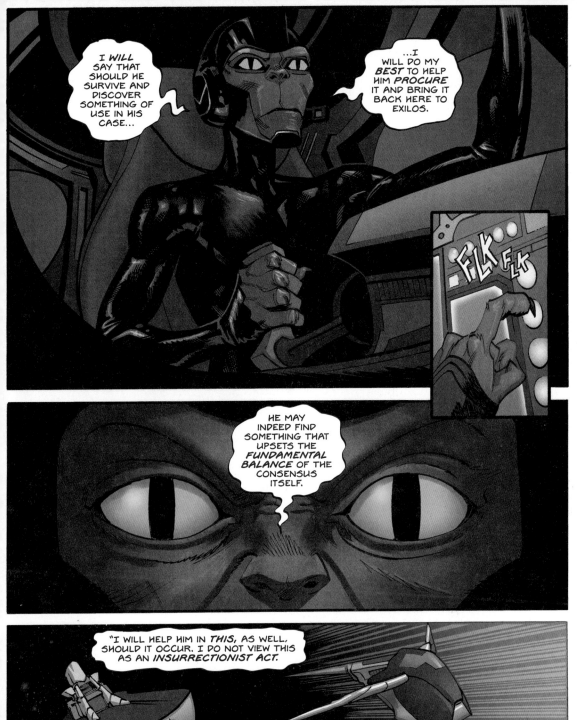

I *WILL* SAY THAT SHOULD HE SURVIVE AND DISCOVER SOMETHING OF USE IN HIS CASE...

...I WILL DO MY *BEST* TO HELP HIM *PROCURE* IT AND BRING IT BACK HERE TO EXILOS.

HE MAY INDEED FIND SOMETHING THAT UPSETS THE *FUNDAMENTAL BALANCE* OF THE CONSENSUS ITSELF.

"I WILL HELP HIM IN *THIS*, AS WELL, SHOULD IT OCCUR. I DO NOT VIEW THIS AS AN *INSURRECTIONIST ACT.*

"I VIEW IT AS AN ACT OF *HONEST INQUIRY*, WHICH IS WITHIN THE PURVIEW OF MY PROFESSION WITHIN THE CONSENSUS.

WHO KNOWS...PERHAPS SUCH A DISCOVERY WILL BREAK UP ANY *COMPLACENCY* WITHIN THE CONSENSUS, AND ALLOW IT TO REMEMBER IT IS NOT THE *ABSOLUTE LAST WORD* ON ALL THAT IS.

YARIX *OUT.*

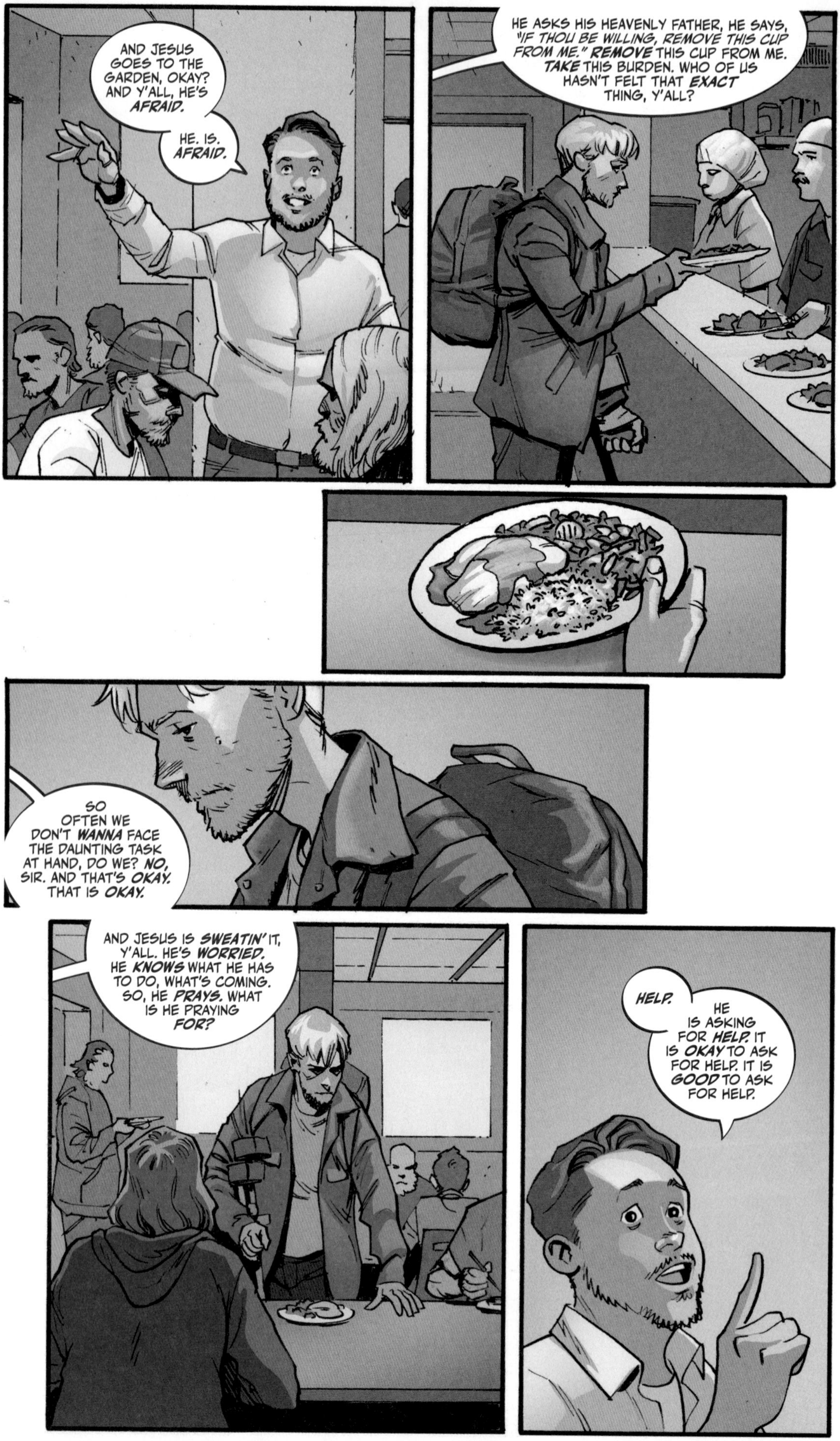
AND JESUS GOES TO THE GARDEN, OKAY? AND Y'ALL, HE'S AFRAID.
HE. IS. AFRAID.
HE ASKS HIS HEAVENLY FATHER, HE SAYS, "IF THOU BE WILLING, REMOVE THIS CUP FROM ME." REMOVE THIS CUP FROM ME. TAKE THIS BURDEN. WHO OF US HASN'T FELT THAT EXACT THING, Y'ALL?
SO OFTEN WE DON'T WANNA FACE THE DAUNTING TASK AT HAND, DO WE? NO, SIR. AND THAT'S OKAY. THAT IS OKAY.
AND JESUS IS SWEATIN' IT, Y'ALL. HE'S WORRIED. HE KNOWS WHAT HE HAS TO DO, WHAT'S COMING. SO, HE PRAYS. WHAT IS HE PRAYING FOR?
HELP.
HE IS ASKING FOR HELP. IT IS OKAY TO ASK FOR HELP. IT IS GOOD TO ASK FOR HELP.

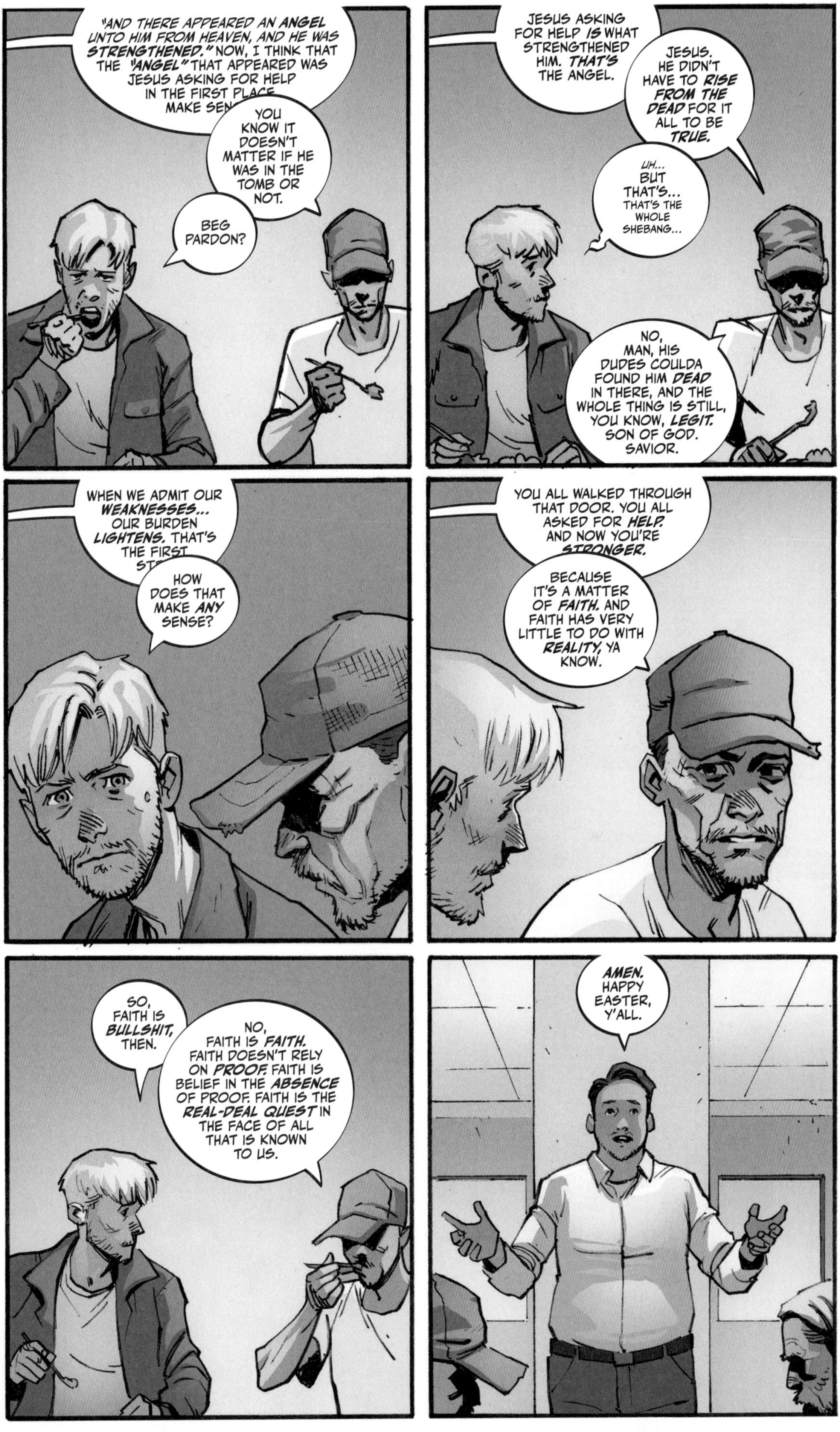
"AND THERE APPEARED AN ANGEL UNTO HIM FROM HEAVEN, AND HE WAS STRENGTHENED." NOW, I THINK THAT THE "ANGEL" THAT APPEARED WAS JESUS ASKING FOR HELP IN THE FIRST PLACE. MAKE SEN
YOU KNOW IT DOESN'T MATTER IF HE WAS IN THE TOMB OR NOT.
BEG PARDON?
JESUS ASKING FOR HELP IS WHAT STRENGTHENED HIM. THAT'S THE ANGEL.
JESUS. HE DIDN'T HAVE TO RISE FROM THE DEAD FOR IT ALL TO BE TRUE.
UH... BUT THAT'S... THAT'S THE WHOLE SHEBANG...
NO, MAN, HIS DUDES COULDA FOUND HIM DEAD IN THERE, AND THE WHOLE THING IS STILL, YOU KNOW, LEGIT. SON OF GOD. SAVIOR.
WHEN WE ADMIT OUR WEAKNESSES... OUR BURDEN LIGHTENS. THAT'S THE FIRST
HOW DOES THAT MAKE ANY SENSE?
YOU ALL WALKED THROUGH THAT DOOR. YOU ALL ASKED FOR HELP. AND NOW YOU'RE STRONGER.
BECAUSE IT'S A MATTER OF FAITH. AND FAITH HAS VERY LITTLE TO DO WITH REALITY, YA KNOW.
SO, FAITH IS BULLSHIT, THEN.
NO, FAITH IS FAITH. FAITH DOESN'T RELY ON PROOF. FAITH IS BELIEF IN THE ABSENCE OF PROOF. FAITH IS THE REAL-DEAL QUEST IN THE FACE OF ALL THAT IS KNOWN TO US.
AMEN. HAPPY EASTER, Y'ALL.

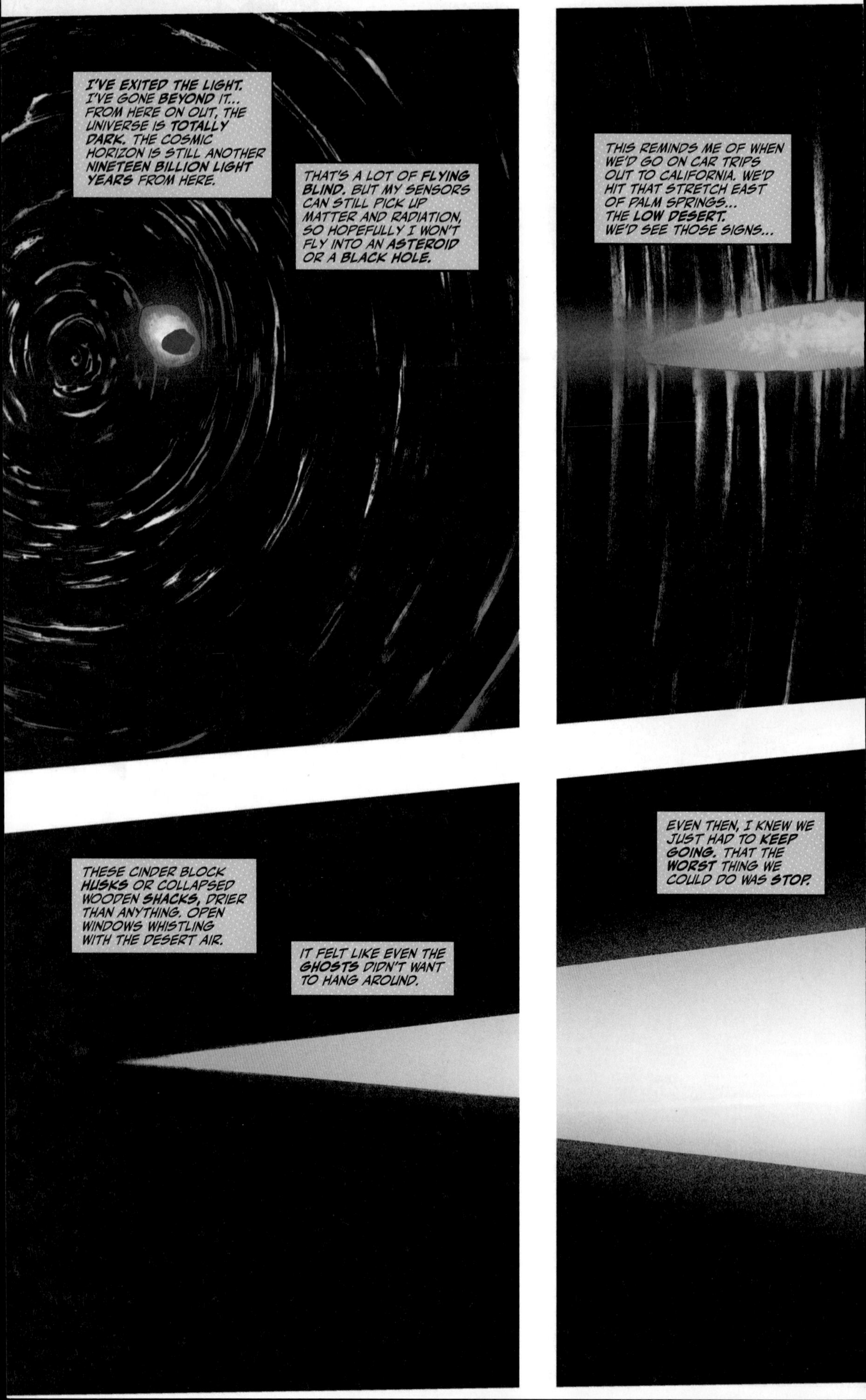
I'VE EXITED THE LIGHT. I'VE GONE BEYOND IT... FROM HERE ON OUT, THE UNIVERSE IS TOTALLY DARK. THE COSMIC HORIZON IS STILL ANOTHER NINETEEN BILLION LIGHT YEARS FROM HERE.
THAT'S A LOT OF FLYING BLIND. BUT MY SENSORS CAN STILL PICK UP MATTER AND RADIATION, SO HOPEFULLY I WON'T FLY INTO AN ASTEROID OR A BLACK HOLE.
THIS REMINDS ME OF WHEN WE'D GO ON CAR TRIPS OUT TO CALIFORNIA. WE'D HIT THAT STRETCH EAST OF PALM SPRINGS... THE LOW DESERT. WE'D SEE THOSE SIGNS...
THESE CINDER BLOCK HUSKS OR COLLAPSED WOODEN SHACKS, DRIER THAN ANYTHING. OPEN WINDOWS WHISTLING WITH THE DESERT AIR.
IT FELT LIKE EVEN THE GHOSTS DIDN'T WANT TO HANG AROUND.
EVEN THEN, I KNEW WE JUST HAD TO KEEP GOING. THAT THE WORST THING WE COULD DO WAS STOP.

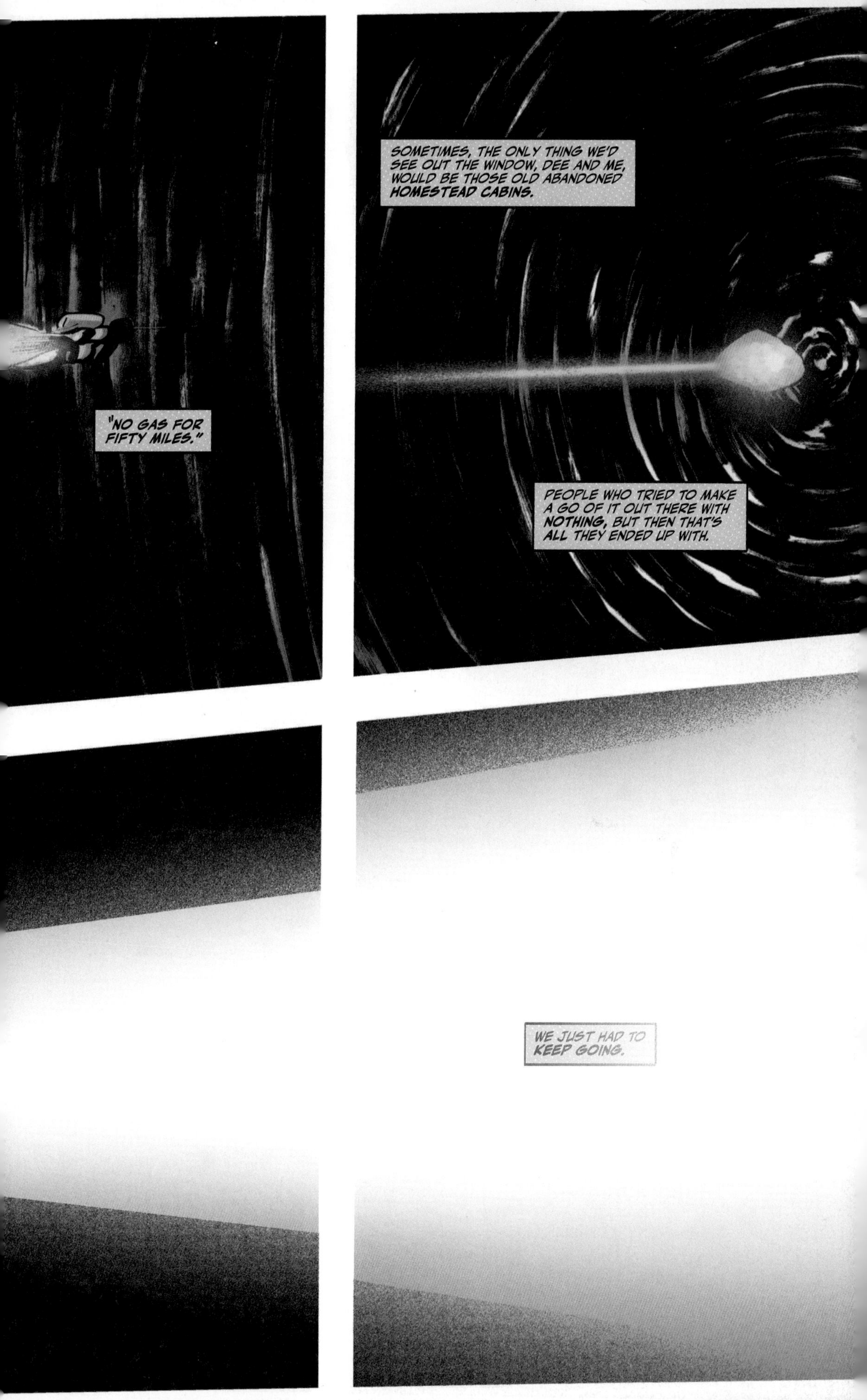
"NO GAS FOR FIFTY MILES."
SOMETIMES, THE ONLY THING WE'D SEE OUT THE WINDOW, DEE AND ME, WOULD BE THOSE OLD ABANDONED HOMESTEAD CABINS.
PEOPLE WHO TRIED TO MAKE A GO OF IT OUT THERE WITH NOTHING, BUT THEN THAT'S ALL THEY ENDED UP WITH.
WE JUST HAD TO KEEP GOING.

IT'S *OKAY.* THE BABY'S OKAY.

OH, THANK GOD--

WHICH IS?

SO LONG AS SHE DOES WHAT I'M SAYING.

BED REST. WE'RE LOOKING AT A PARTIAL *PLACENTAL ABRUPTION* HERE-- MINOR, BUT WE NEED TO TAKE IT *SERIOUSLY.* AND SINCE WE'RE RIGHT ON THE CUSP OF FULL TERM, I WANT THE KIDDO TO STAY PUT ANOTHER *WEEK OR TWO* BEFORE WE INDUCE.

I WAS PLANNING ON *WORKING* ANOTHER TWO WEEKS. AT *LEAST.*

YOU WOULD HAVE IDEALLY *STOPPED* ALREADY. YOU'RE *THIRTY-FOUR WEEKS* AND THAT MIGHT HAVE CONTRIBUTED TO THIS.

YOU CAN WRITE A NOTE FOR THE STORE, RIGHT? EXPLAIN TO HER MANAGER THAT--

IT'LL BE TIME OFF *WITHOUT PAY.* I NEED THE *MONEY.*

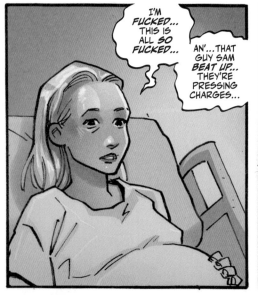

I'M *FUCKED...* THIS IS ALL *SO FUCKED...*

AN'...THAT GUY SAM *BEAT UP...* THEY'RE PRESSING CHARGES...

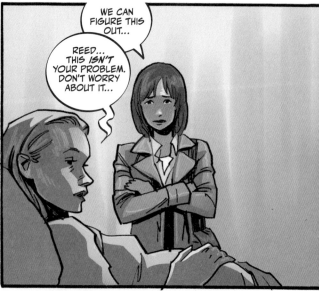

WE CAN FIGURE THIS OUT...

REED... THIS *ISN'T* YOUR PROBLEM. DON'T WORRY ABOUT IT...

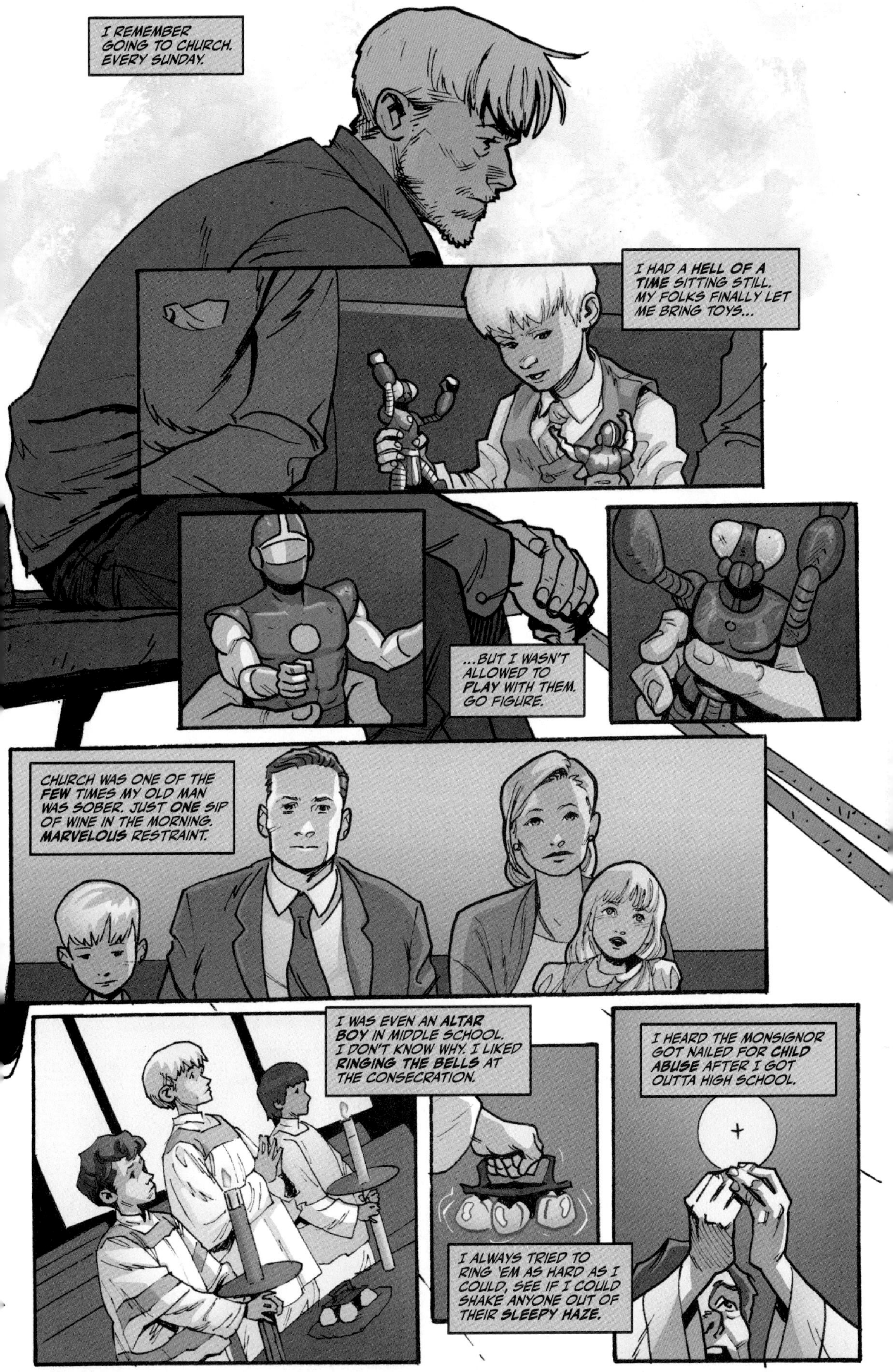
I REMEMBER GOING TO CHURCH. EVERY SUNDAY.
I HAD A HELL OF A TIME SITTING STILL. MY FOLKS FINALLY LET ME BRING TOYS...
...BUT I WASN'T ALLOWED TO PLAY WITH THEM. GO FIGURE.
CHURCH WAS ONE OF THE FEW TIMES MY OLD MAN WAS SOBER. JUST ONE SIP OF WINE IN THE MORNING. MARVELOUS RESTRAINT.
I WAS EVEN AN ALTAR BOY IN MIDDLE SCHOOL. I DON'T KNOW WHY. I LIKED RINGING THE BELLS AT THE CONSECRATION.
I ALWAYS TRIED TO RING 'EM AS HARD AS I COULD, SEE IF I COULD SHAKE ANYONE OUT OF THEIR SLEEPY HAZE.
I HEARD THE MONSIGNOR GOT NAILED FOR CHILD ABUSE AFTER I GOT OUTTA HIGH SCHOOL.

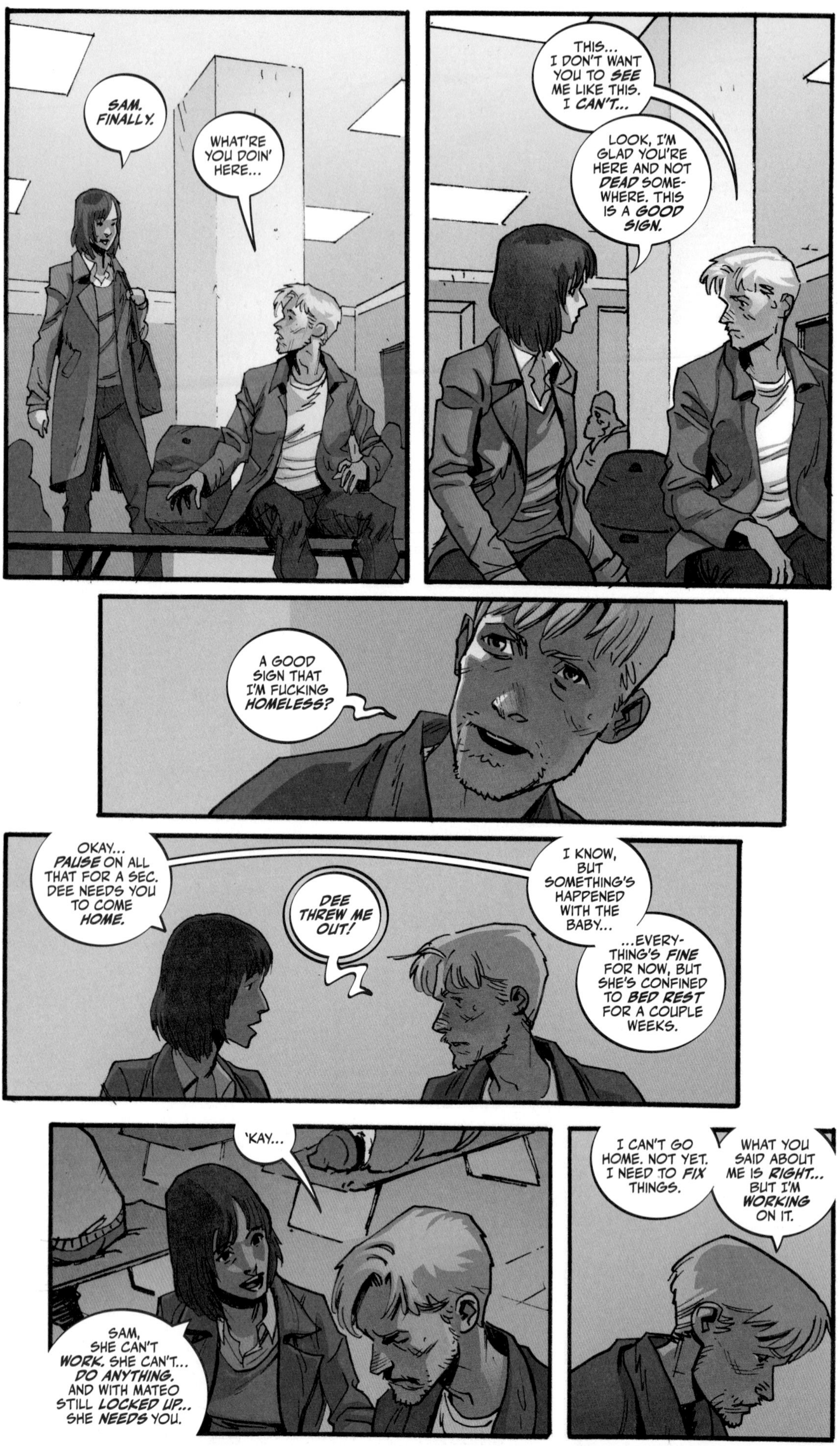
SAM. FINALLY.
WHAT'RE YOU DOIN' HERE...
THIS... I DON'T WANT YOU TO SEE ME LIKE THIS. I CAN'T...
LOOK, I'M GLAD YOU'RE HERE AND NOT DEAD SOME-WHERE. THIS IS A GOOD SIGN.
A GOOD SIGN THAT I'M FUCKING HOMELESS?
OKAY... PAUSE ON ALL THAT FOR A SEC. DEE NEEDS YOU TO COME HOME.
DEE THREW ME OUT!
I KNOW, BUT SOMETHING'S HAPPENED WITH THE BABY...
...EVERY-THING'S FINE FOR NOW, BUT SHE'S CONFINED TO BED REST FOR A COUPLE WEEKS.
'KAY...
SAM, SHE CAN'T WORK. SHE CAN'T... DO ANYTHING. AND WITH MATEO STILL LOCKED UP... SHE NEEDS YOU.
I CAN'T GO HOME. NOT YET. I NEED TO FIX THINGS.
WHAT YOU SAID ABOUT ME IS RIGHT... BUT I'M WORKING ON IT.

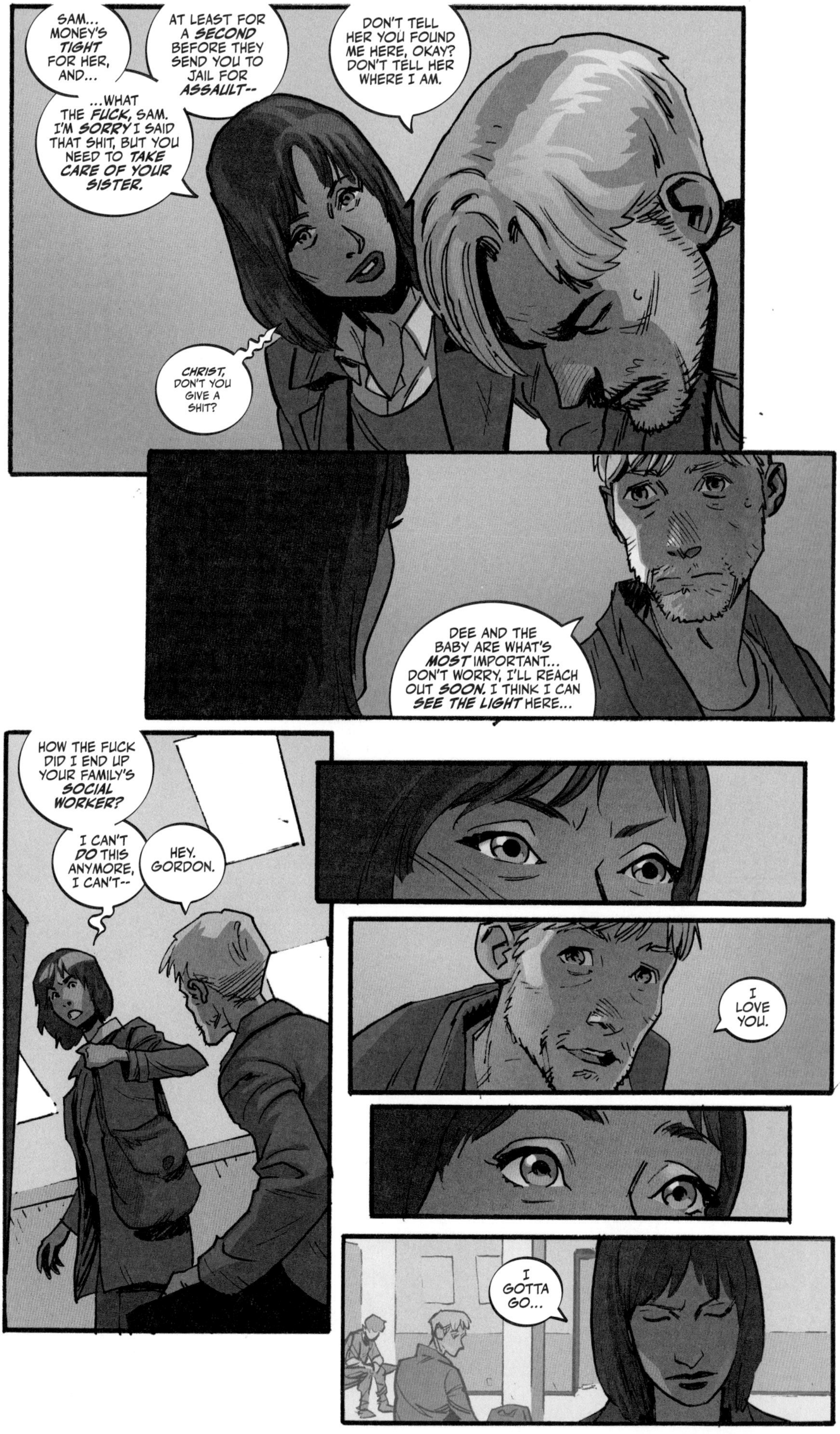
SAM... MONEY'S TIGHT FOR HER, AND...
AT LEAST FOR A SECOND BEFORE THEY SEND YOU TO JAIL FOR ASSAULT--
...WHAT THE FUCK, SAM. I'M SORRY I SAID THAT SHIT, BUT YOU NEED TO TAKE CARE OF YOUR SISTER.
DON'T TELL HER YOU FOUND ME HERE, OKAY? DON'T TELL HER WHERE I AM.
CHRIST, DON'T YOU GIVE A SHIT?
DEE AND THE BABY ARE WHAT'S MOST IMPORTANT... DON'T WORRY, I'LL REACH OUT SOON. I THINK I CAN SEE THE LIGHT HERE...
HOW THE FUCK DID I END UP YOUR FAMILY'S SOCIAL WORKER?
I CAN'T DO THIS ANYMORE, I CAN'T--
HEY. GORDON.
I LOVE YOU.
I GOTTA GO...

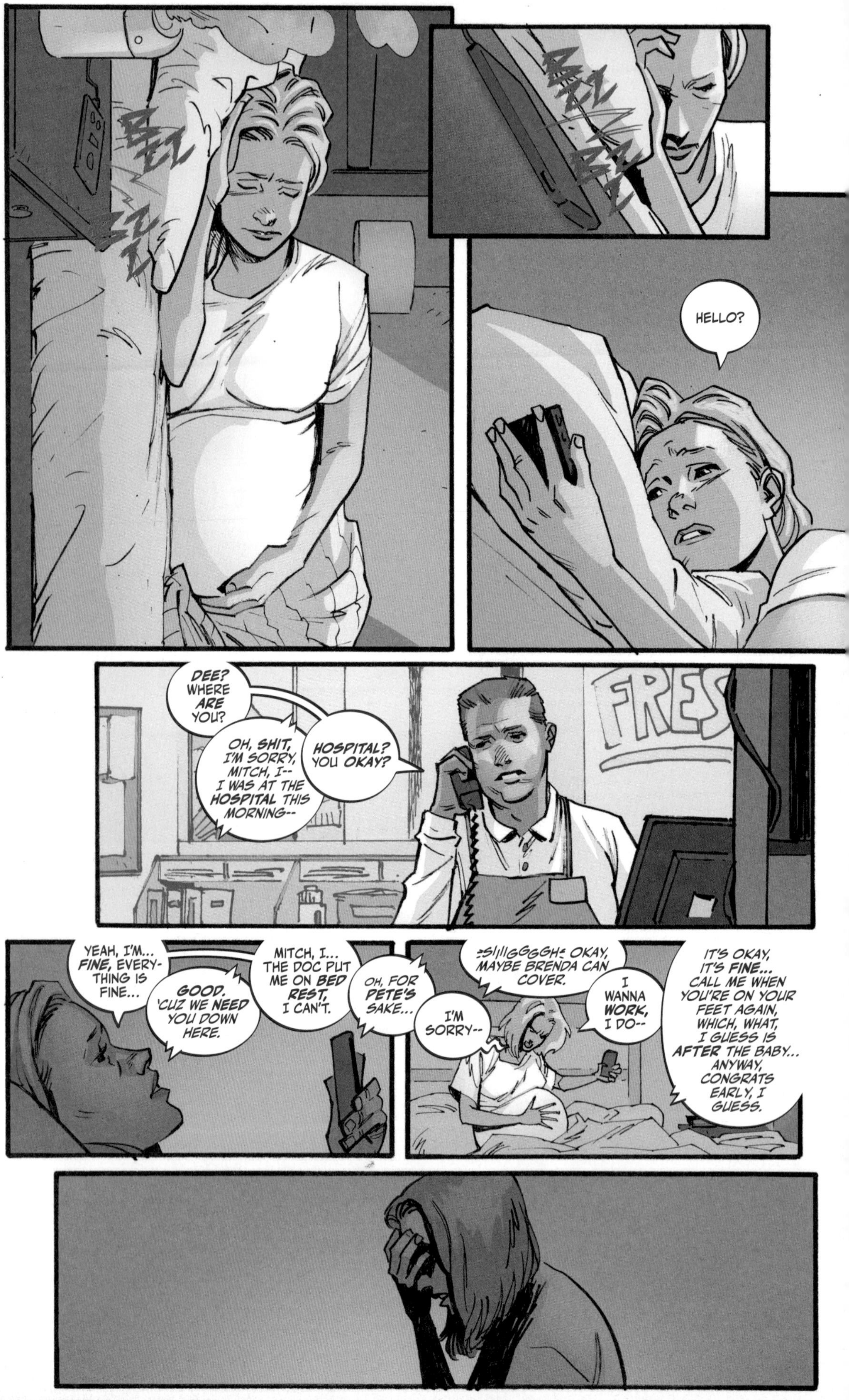
BZZZ
ZZZZ
BZZZ
BZZZ
HELLO?
DEE? WHERE ARE YOU?
OH, SHIT, I'M SORRY, MITCH, I-- I WAS AT THE HOSPITAL THIS MORNING--
HOSPITAL? YOU OKAY?
FRES
YEAH, I'M... FINE, EVERY-THING IS FINE...
GOOD. 'CUZ WE NEED YOU DOWN HERE.
MITCH, I... THE DOC PUT ME ON BED REST, I CAN'T.
OH, FOR PETE'S SAKE...
=SIIIGGGH= OKAY, MAYBE BRENDA CAN COVER.
I'M SORRY--
I WANNA WORK, I DO--
IT'S OKAY, IT'S FINE... CALL ME WHEN YOU'RE ON YOUR FEET AGAIN, WHICH, WHAT, I GUESS IS AFTER THE BABY... ANYWAY, CONGRATS EARLY, I GUESS.

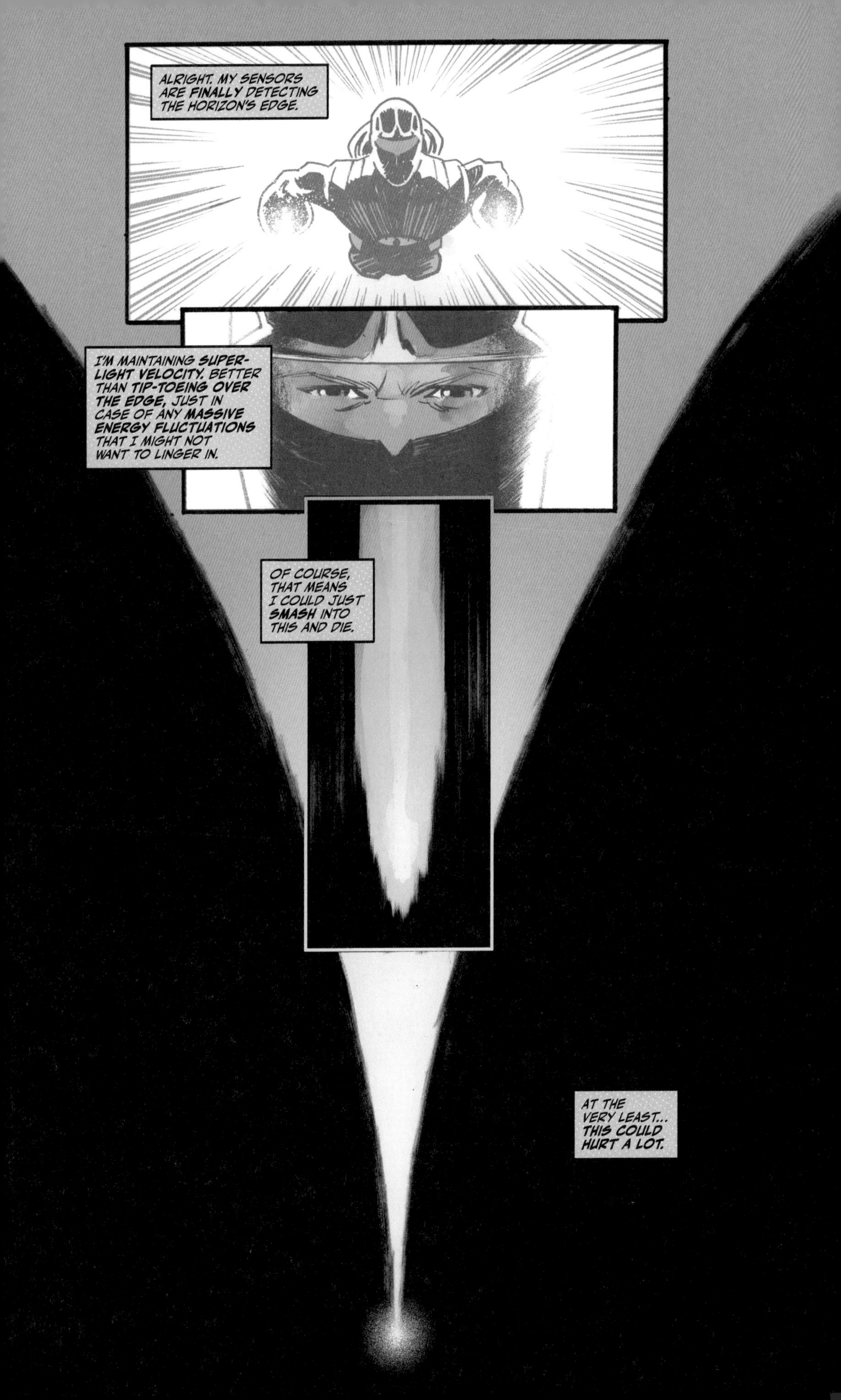
ALRIGHT. MY SENSORS ARE FINALLY DETECTING THE HORIZON'S EDGE.
I'M MAINTAINING SUPER-LIGHT VELOCITY. BETTER THAN TIP-TOEING OVER THE EDGE, JUST IN CASE OF ANY MASSIVE ENERGY FLUCTUATIONS THAT I MIGHT NOT WANT TO LINGER IN.
OF COURSE, THAT MEANS I COULD JUST SMASH INTO THIS AND DIE.
AT THE VERY LEAST... THIS COULD HURT A LOT.

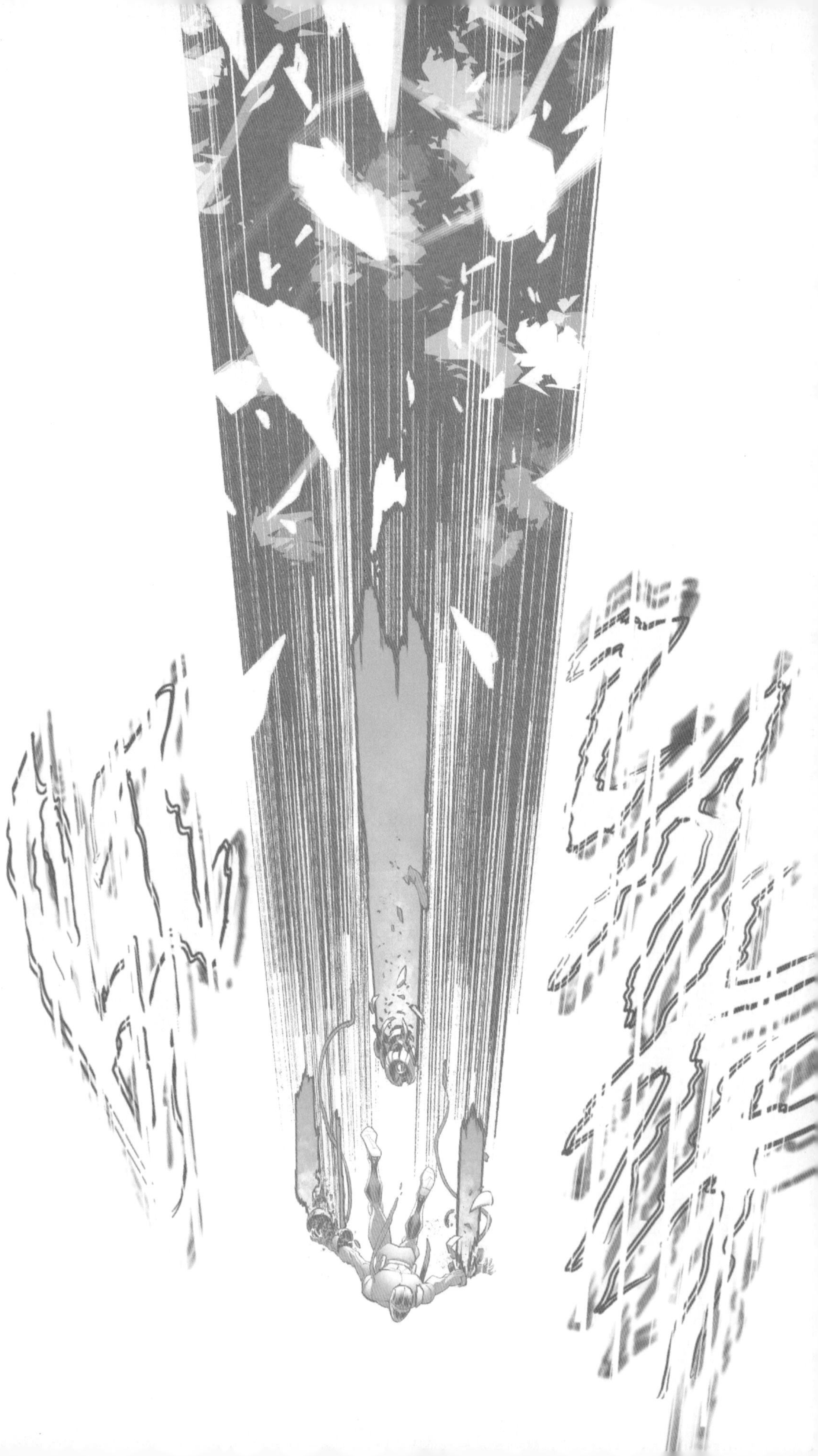

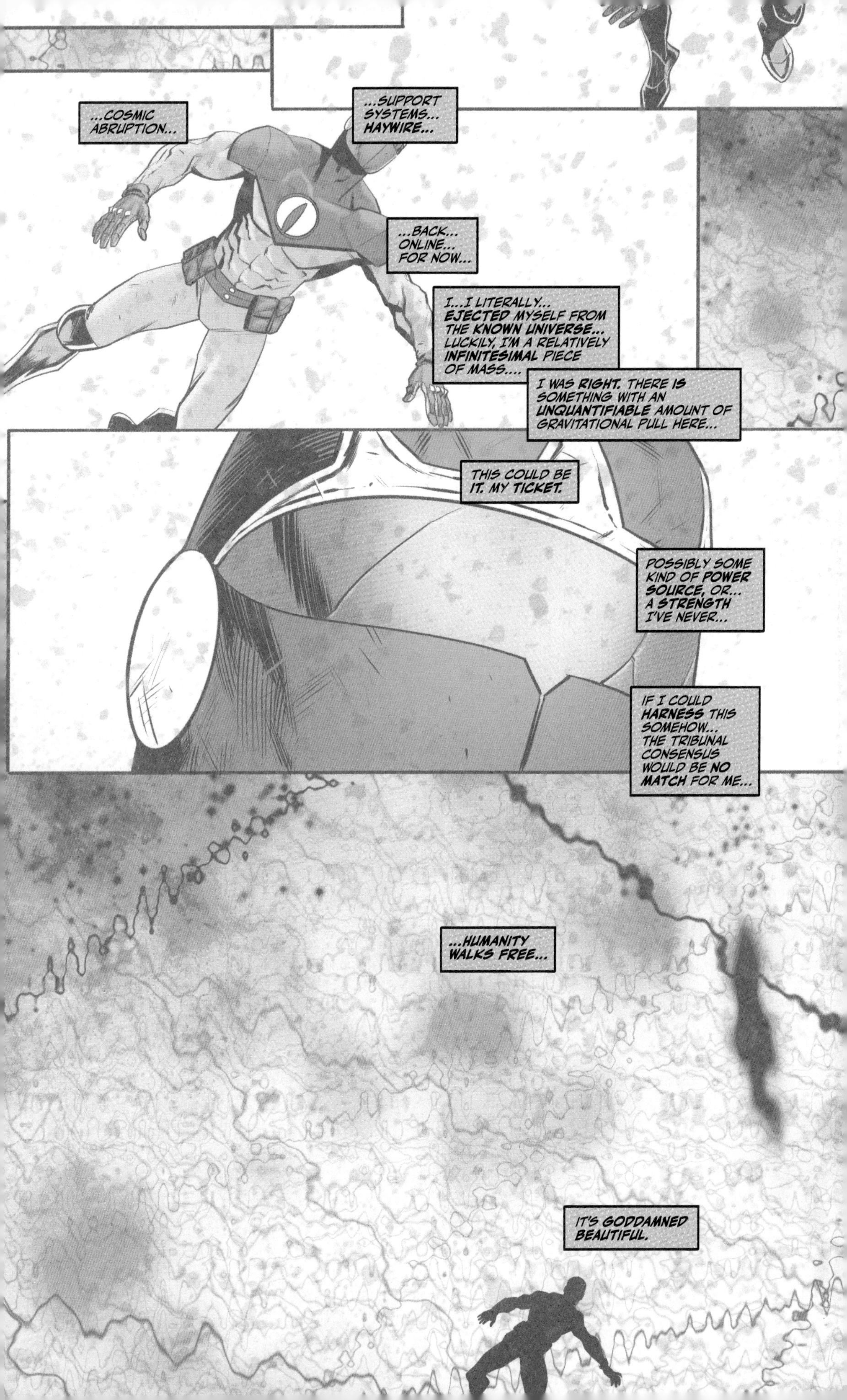
...COSMIC ABRUPTION...
...SUPPORT SYSTEMS... HAYWIRE...
...BACK... ONLINE... FOR NOW...
I...I LITERALLY... EJECTED MYSELF FROM THE KNOWN UNIVERSE... LUCKILY, I'M A RELATIVELY INFINITESIMAL PIECE OF MASS....
I WAS RIGHT. THERE IS SOMETHING WITH AN UNQUANTIFIABLE AMOUNT OF GRAVITATIONAL PULL HERE...
THIS COULD BE IT. MY TICKET.
POSSIBLY SOME KIND OF POWER SOURCE, OR... A STRENGTH I'VE NEVER...
IF I COULD HARNESS THIS SOMEHOW... THE TRIBUNAL CONSENSUS WOULD BE NO MATCH FOR ME...
...HUMANITY WALKS FREE...
IT'S GODDAMNED BEAUTIFUL.

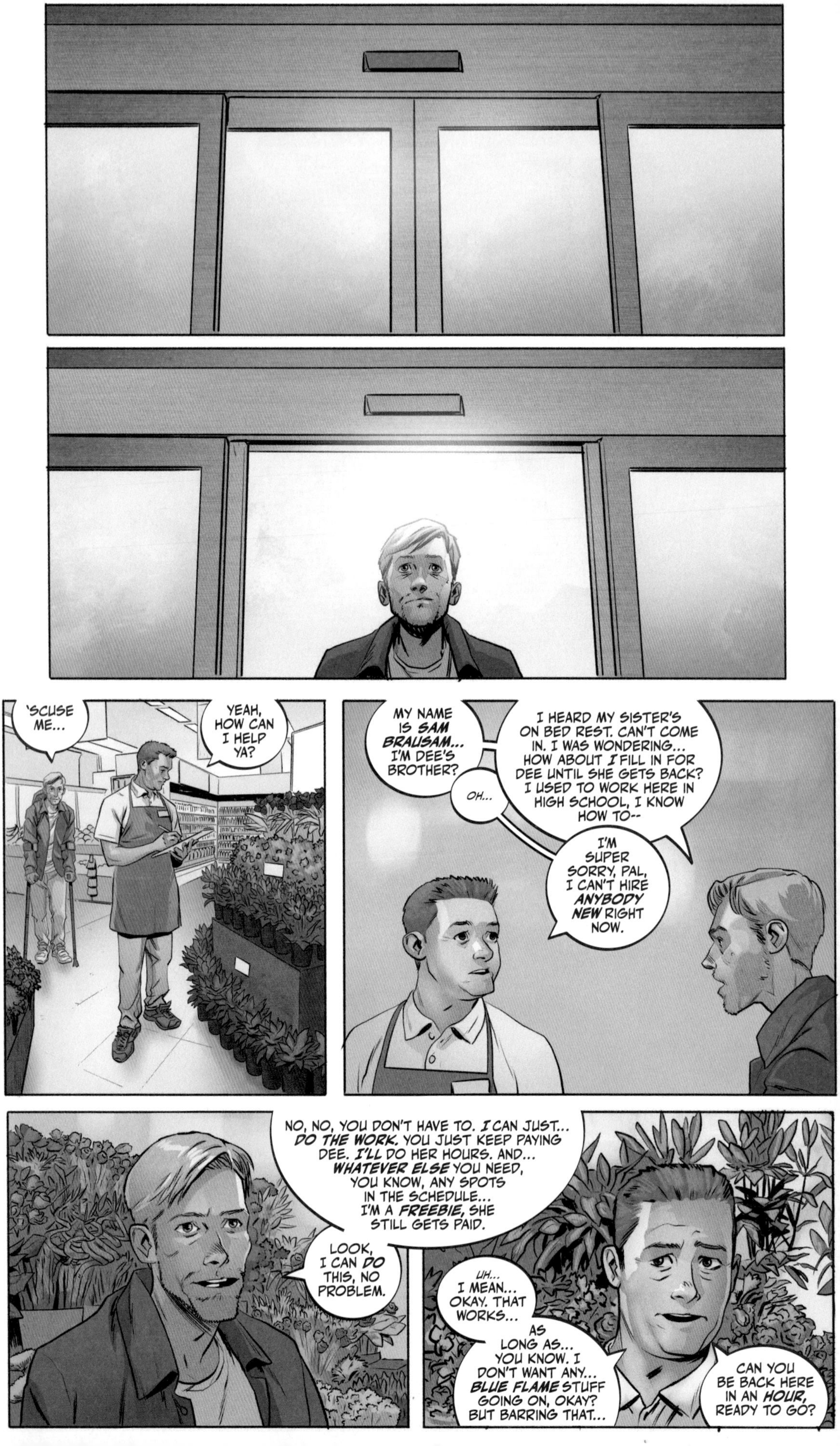
'SCUSE ME...
YEAH, HOW CAN I HELP YA?
MY NAME IS SAM BRAUSAM... I'M DEE'S BROTHER?
OH...
I HEARD MY SISTER'S ON BED REST. CAN'T COME IN. I WAS WONDERING... HOW ABOUT I FILL IN FOR DEE UNTIL SHE GETS BACK? I USED TO WORK HERE IN HIGH SCHOOL, I KNOW HOW TO--
I'M SUPER SORRY, PAL, I CAN'T HIRE ANYBODY NEW RIGHT NOW.
NO, NO, YOU DON'T HAVE TO. I CAN JUST... DO THE WORK. YOU JUST KEEP PAYING DEE. I'LL DO HER HOURS. AND... WHATEVER ELSE YOU NEED, YOU KNOW, ANY SPOTS IN THE SCHEDULE... I'M A FREEBIE, SHE STILL GETS PAID.
LOOK, I CAN DO THIS, NO PROBLEM.
UH... I MEAN... OKAY. THAT WORKS...
AS LONG AS... YOU KNOW. I DON'T WANT ANY... BLUE FLAME STUFF GOING ON, OKAY? BUT BARRING THAT...
CAN YOU BE BACK HERE IN AN HOUR, READY TO GO?

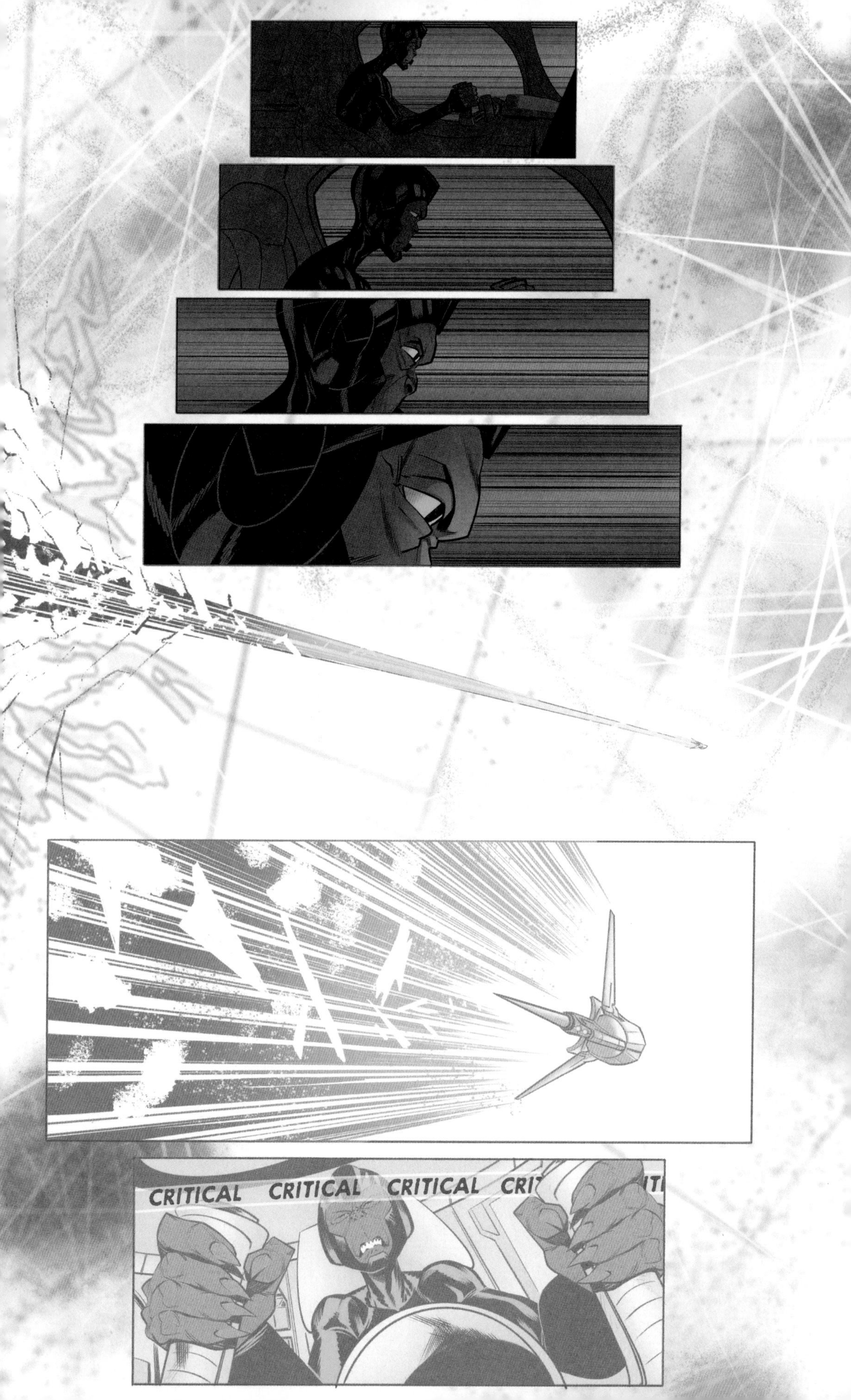
CRITICAL
CRITICAL
CRITICAL

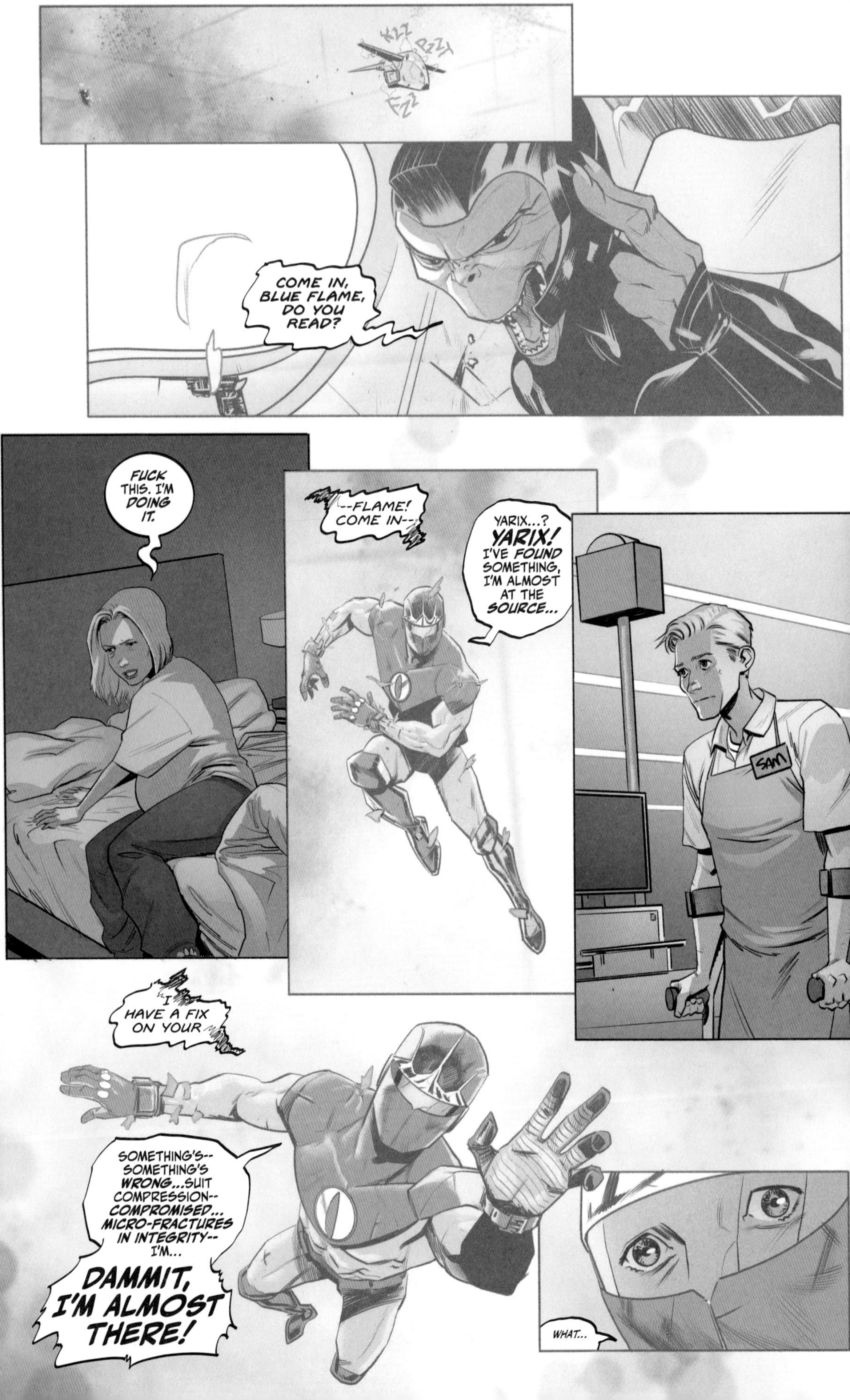
KZZ
PZZT
FZZ
COME IN, BLUE FLAME, DO YOU READ?
FUCK THIS. I'M DOING IT.
--FLAME! COME IN--
YARIX...? YARIX! I'VE FOUND SOMETHING, I'M ALMOST AT THE SOURCE...
SAM
I HAVE A FIX ON YOUR
SOMETHING'S-- SOMETHING'S WRONG...SUIT COMPRESSION-- COMPROMISED... MICRO-FRACTURES IN INTEGRITY-- I'M...
DAMMIT, I'M ALMOST THERE!
WHAT...

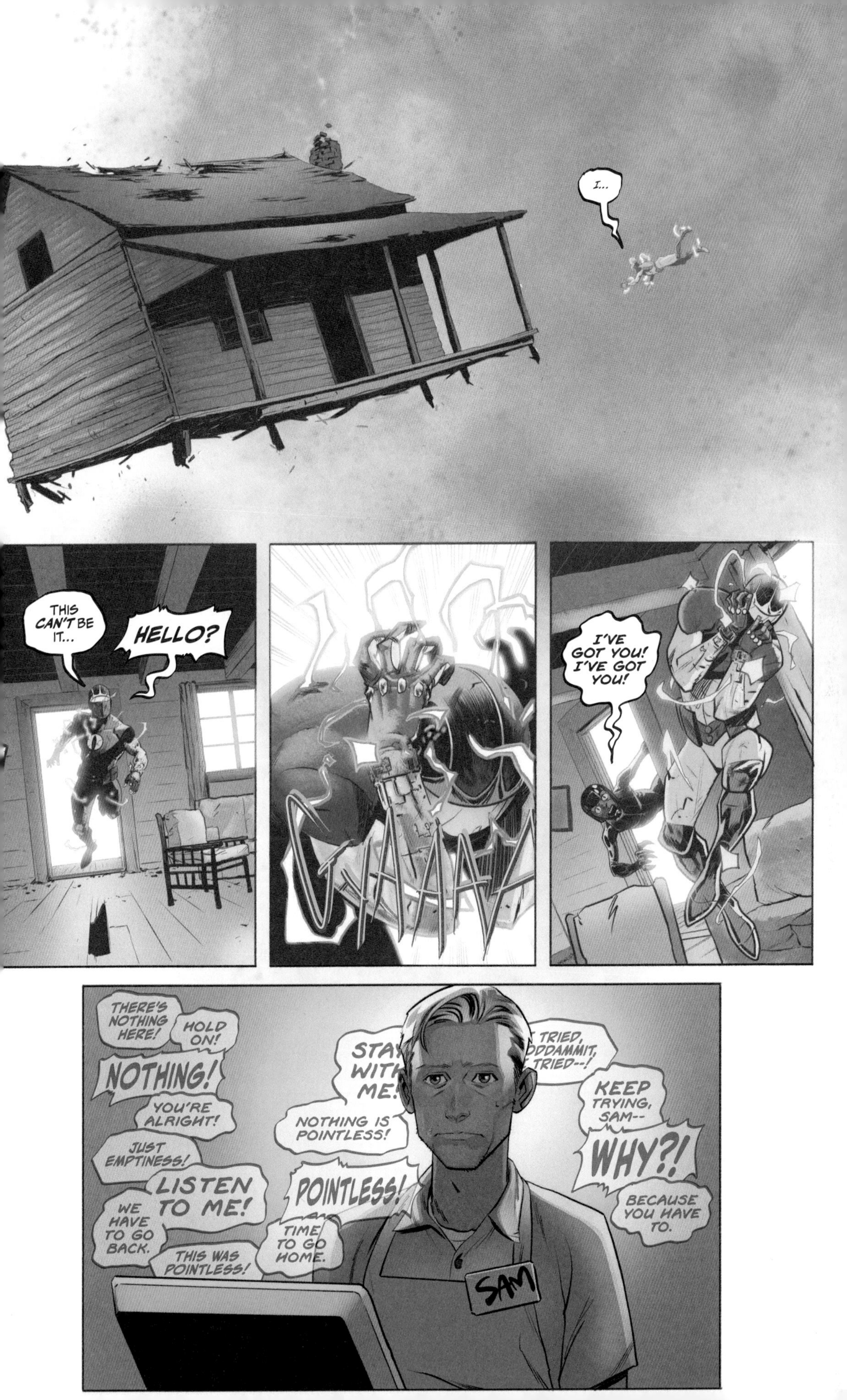
I...
THIS CAN'T BE IT...
HELLO?
AAAAA
I'VE GOT YOU! I'VE GOT YOU!
THERE'S NOTHING HERE!
HOLD ON!
NOTHING!
YOU'RE ALRIGHT!
JUST EMPTINESS!
LISTEN TO ME!
WE HAVE TO GO BACK.
THIS WAS POINTLESS!
STA WITH ME!
NOTHING IS POINTLESS!
POINTLESS!
TIME TO GO HOME.
TRIED, ODDAMMIT, TRIED--!
KEEP TRYING, SAM--
WHY?!
BECAUSE YOU HAVE TO.
SAM

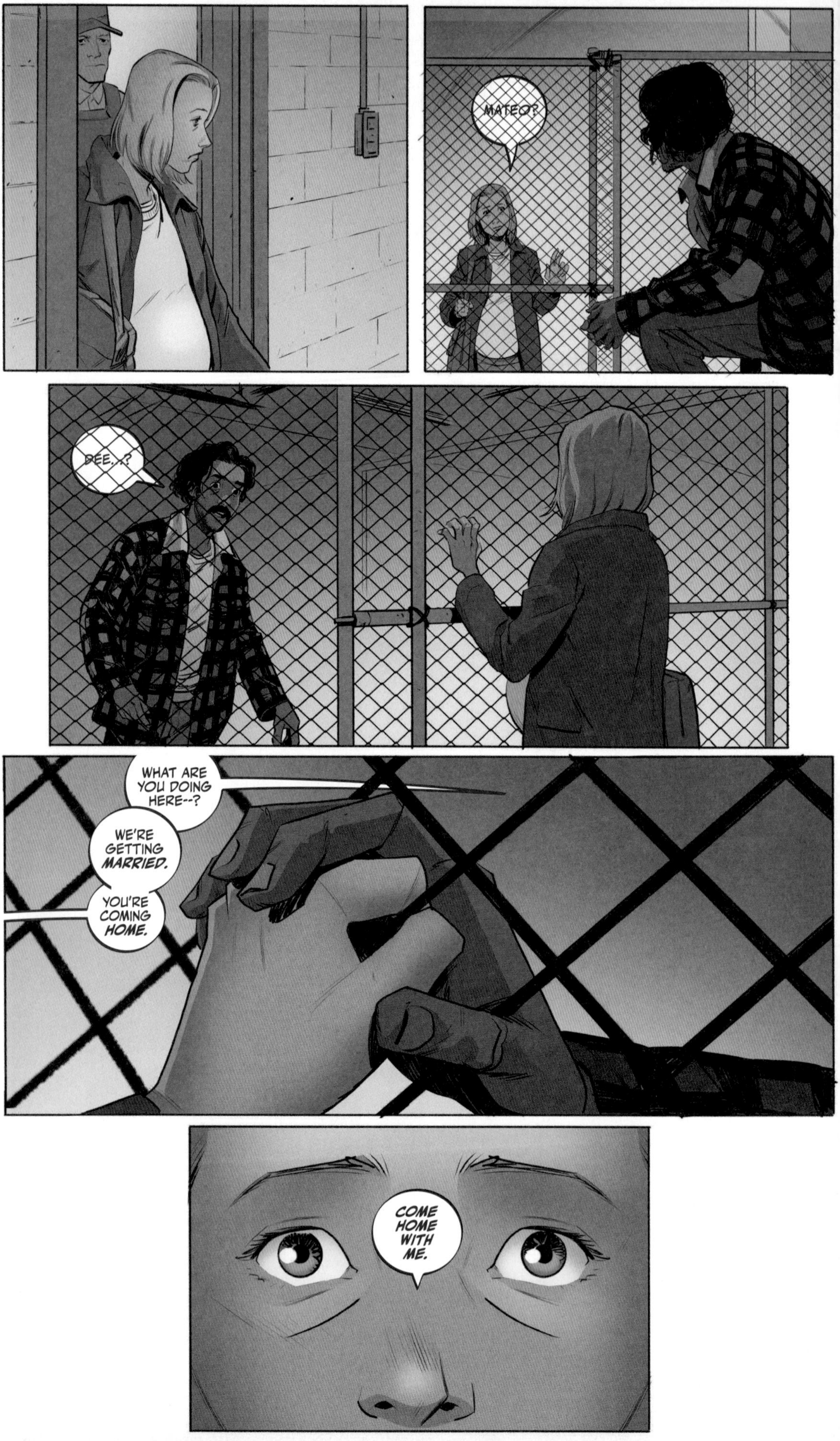
MATEO?
DEE...?
WHAT ARE YOU DOING HERE--?
WE'RE GETTING *MARRIED.*
YOU'RE COMING *HOME.*
COME HOME WITH ME.

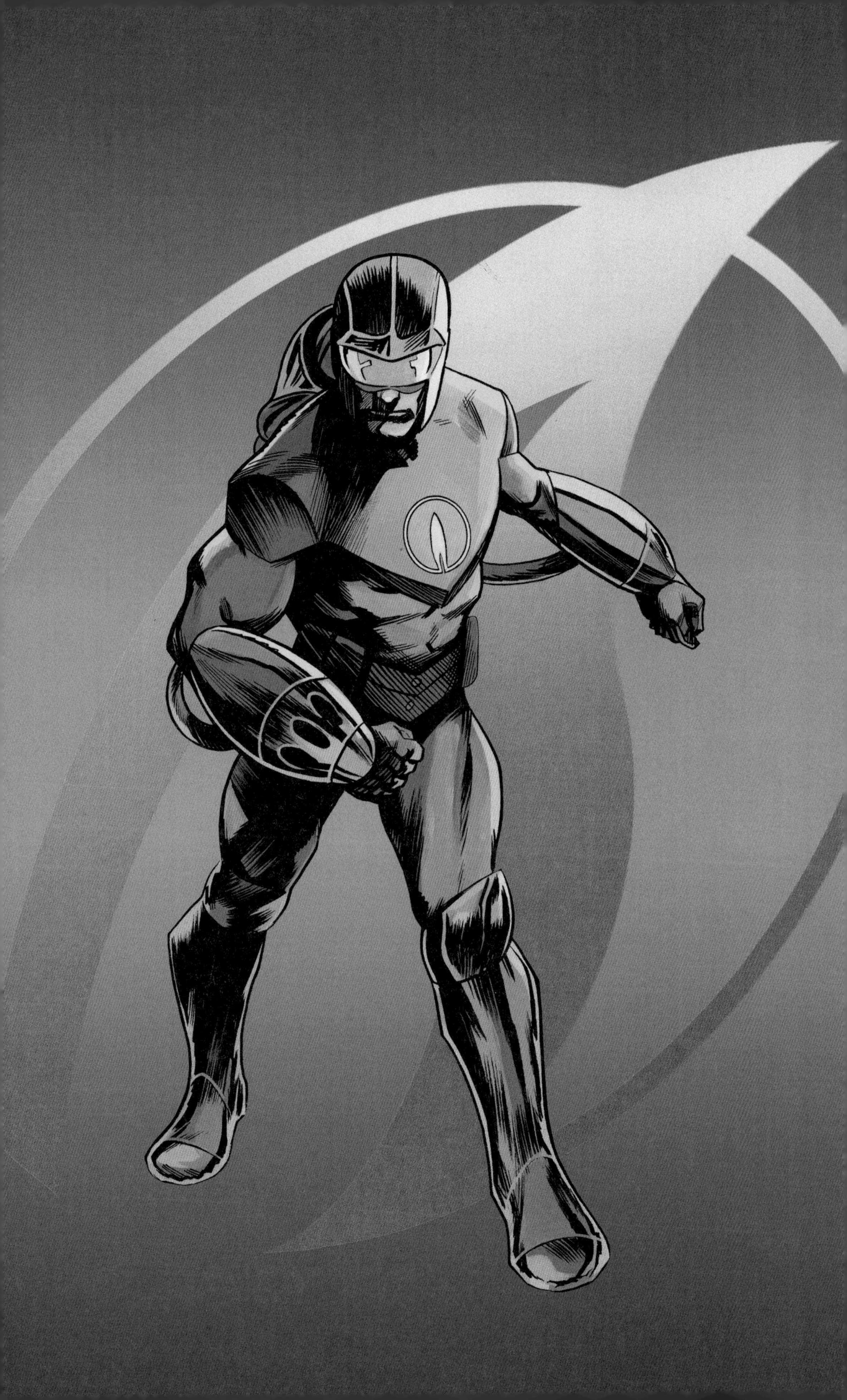

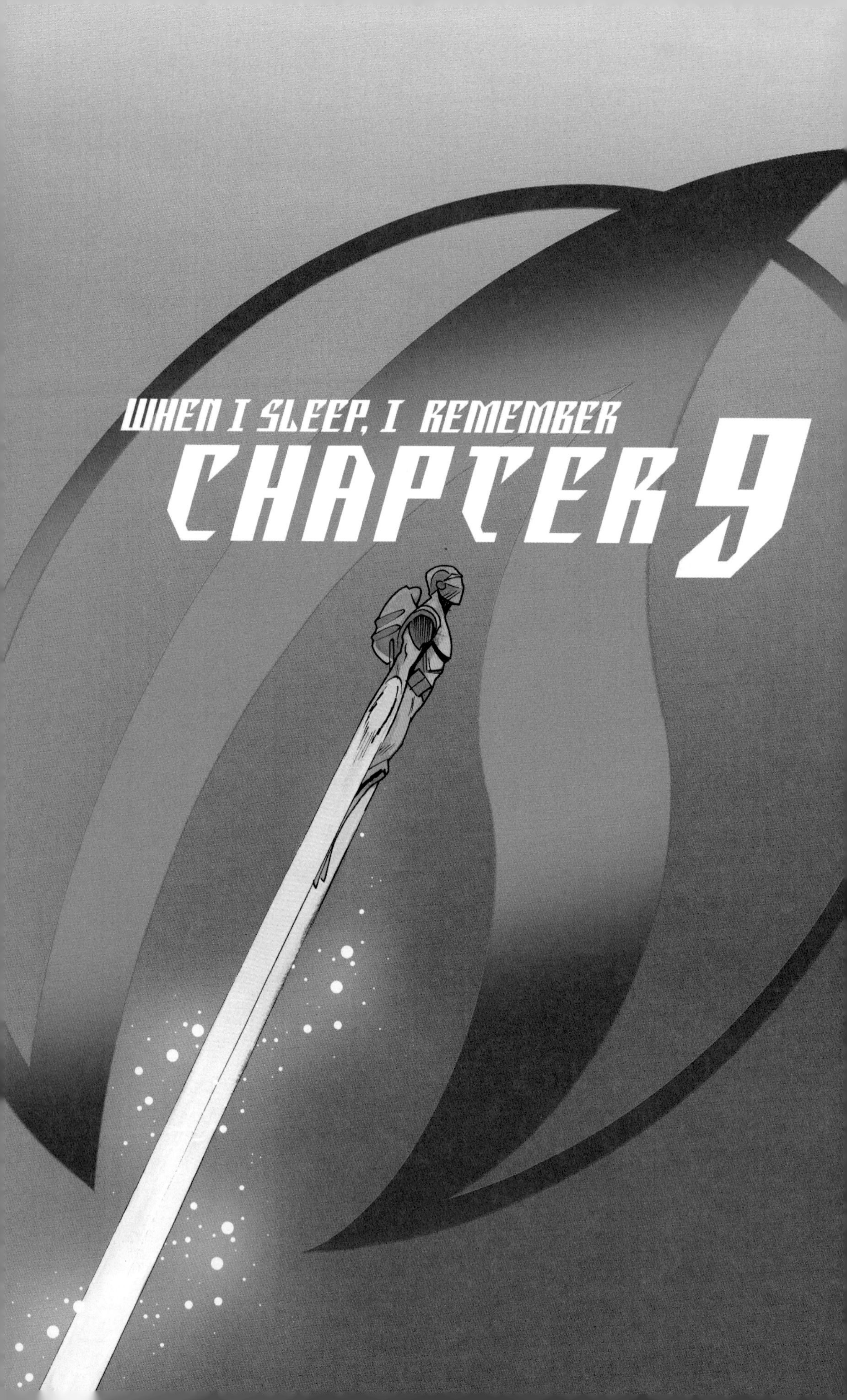
WHEN I SLEEP, I REMEMBER
CHAPTER 9

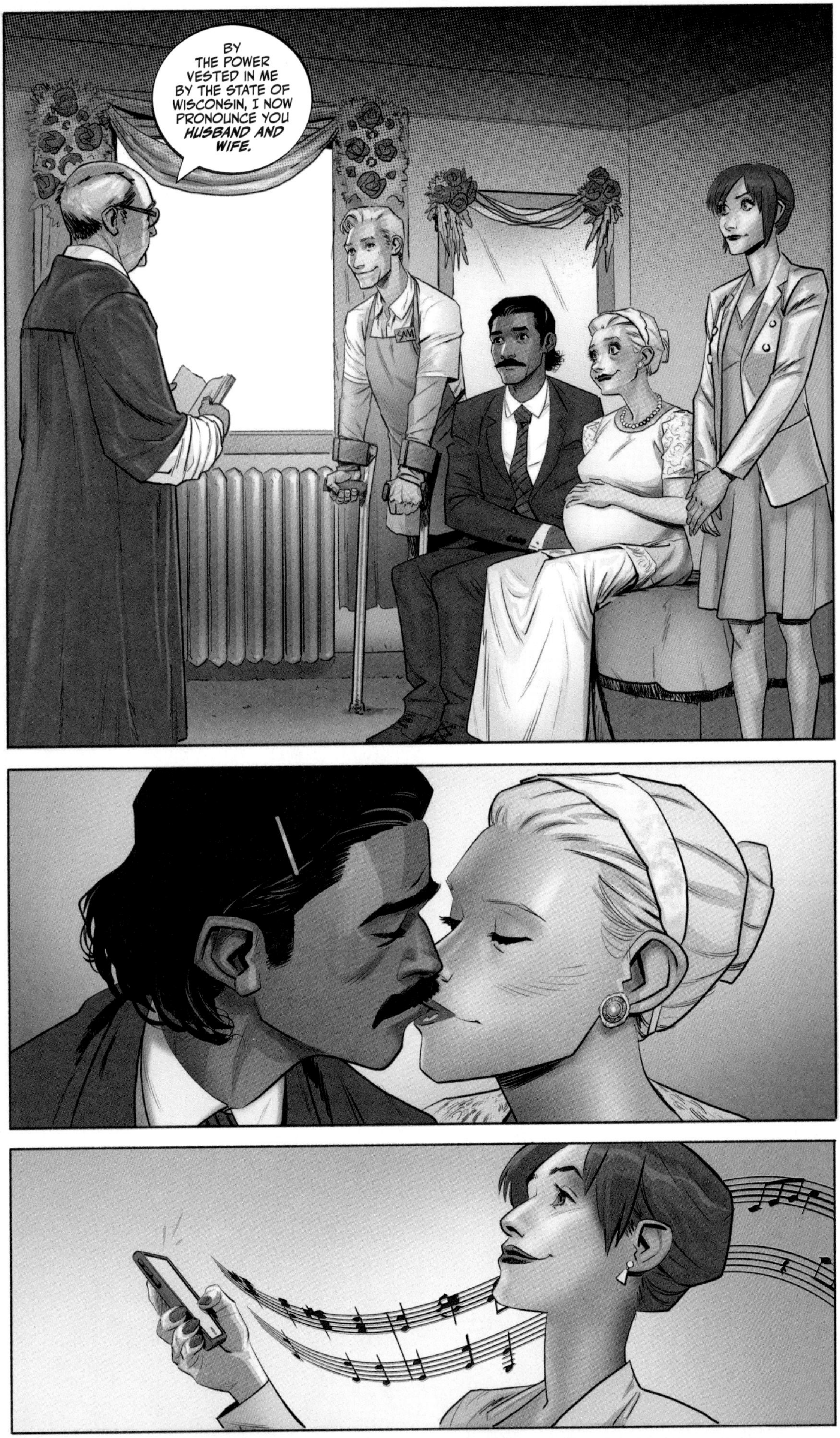
BY THE POWER VESTED IN ME BY THE STATE OF WISCONSIN, I NOW PRONOUNCE YOU *HUSBAND AND WIFE.*
SAM

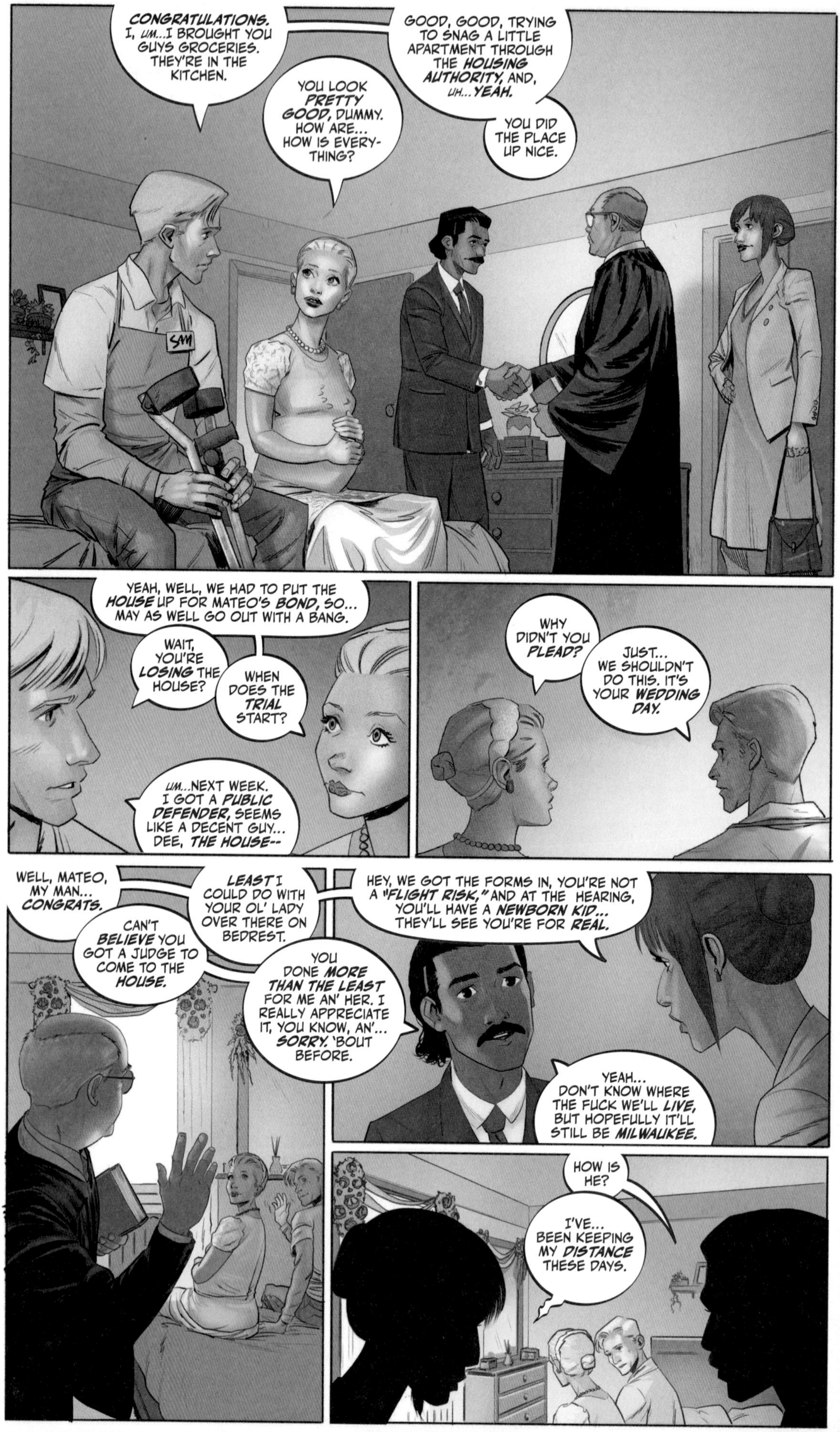
CONGRATULATIONS. I, UM...I BROUGHT YOU GUYS GROCERIES. THEY'RE IN THE KITCHEN.
YOU LOOK PRETTY GOOD, DUMMY. HOW ARE... HOW IS EVERY-THING?
GOOD, GOOD, TRYING TO SNAG A LITTLE APARTMENT THROUGH THE HOUSING AUTHORITY, AND, UH...YEAH.
YOU DID THE PLACE UP NICE.
YEAH, WELL, WE HAD TO PUT THE HOUSE UP FOR MATEO'S BOND, SO... MAY AS WELL GO OUT WITH A BANG.
WAIT, YOU'RE LOSING THE HOUSE?
WHEN DOES THE TRIAL START?
UM...NEXT WEEK. I GOT A PUBLIC DEFENDER, SEEMS LIKE A DECENT GUY... DEE, THE HOUSE--
WHY DIDN'T YOU PLEAD?
JUST... WE SHOULDN'T DO THIS. IT'S YOUR WEDDING DAY.
WELL, MATEO, MY MAN... CONGRATS.
CAN'T BELIEVE YOU GOT A JUDGE TO COME TO THE HOUSE.
LEAST I COULD DO WITH YOUR OL' LADY OVER THERE ON BEDREST.
YOU DONE MORE THAN THE LEAST FOR ME AN' HER. I REALLY APPRECIATE IT, YOU KNOW, AN'... SORRY. 'BOUT BEFORE.
HEY, WE GOT THE FORMS IN, YOU'RE NOT A "FLIGHT RISK," AND AT THE HEARING, YOU'LL HAVE A NEWBORN KID... THEY'LL SEE YOU'RE FOR REAL.
YEAH... DON'T KNOW WHERE THE FUCK WE'LL LIVE, BUT HOPEFULLY IT'LL STILL BE MILWAUKEE.
HOW IS HE?
I'VE... BEEN KEEPING MY DISTANCE THESE DAYS.

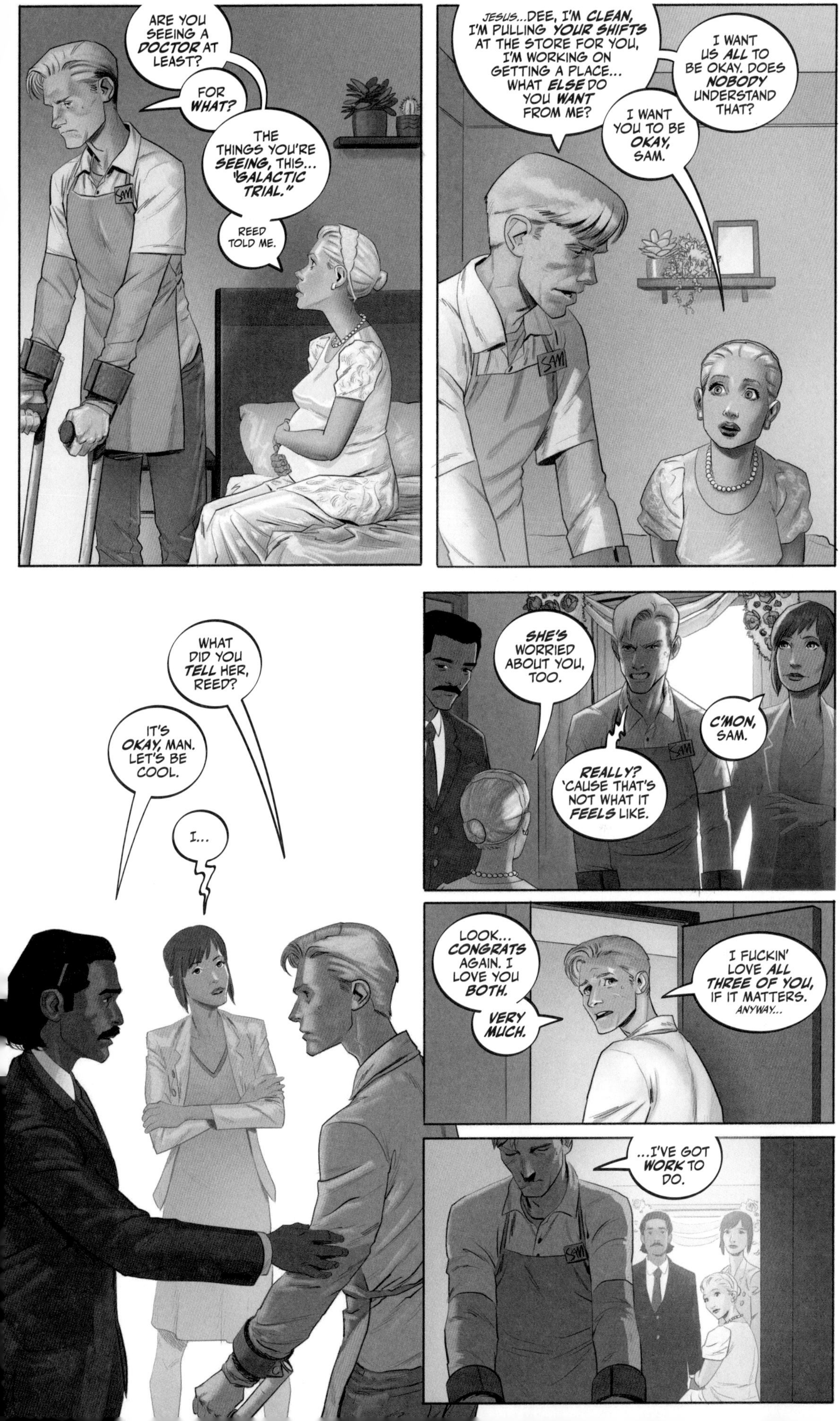
ARE YOU SEEING A DOCTOR AT LEAST?
FOR WHAT?
THE THINGS YOU'RE SEEING, THIS... "GALACTIC TRIAL."
REED TOLD ME.
JESUS...DEE, I'M CLEAN, I'M PULLING YOUR SHIFTS AT THE STORE FOR YOU, I'M WORKING ON GETTING A PLACE... WHAT ELSE DO YOU WANT FROM ME?
I WANT US ALL TO BE OKAY. DOES NOBODY UNDERSTAND THAT?
I WANT YOU TO BE OKAY, SAM.
SHE'S WORRIED ABOUT YOU, TOO.
C'MON, SAM.
REALLY? 'CAUSE THAT'S NOT WHAT IT FEELS LIKE.
WHAT DID YOU TELL HER, REED?
IT'S OKAY, MAN. LET'S BE COOL.
I...
LOOK... CONGRATS AGAIN. I LOVE YOU BOTH.
VERY MUCH.
I FUCKIN' LOVE ALL THREE OF YOU, IF IT MATTERS. ANYWAY...
...I'VE GOT WORK TO DO.

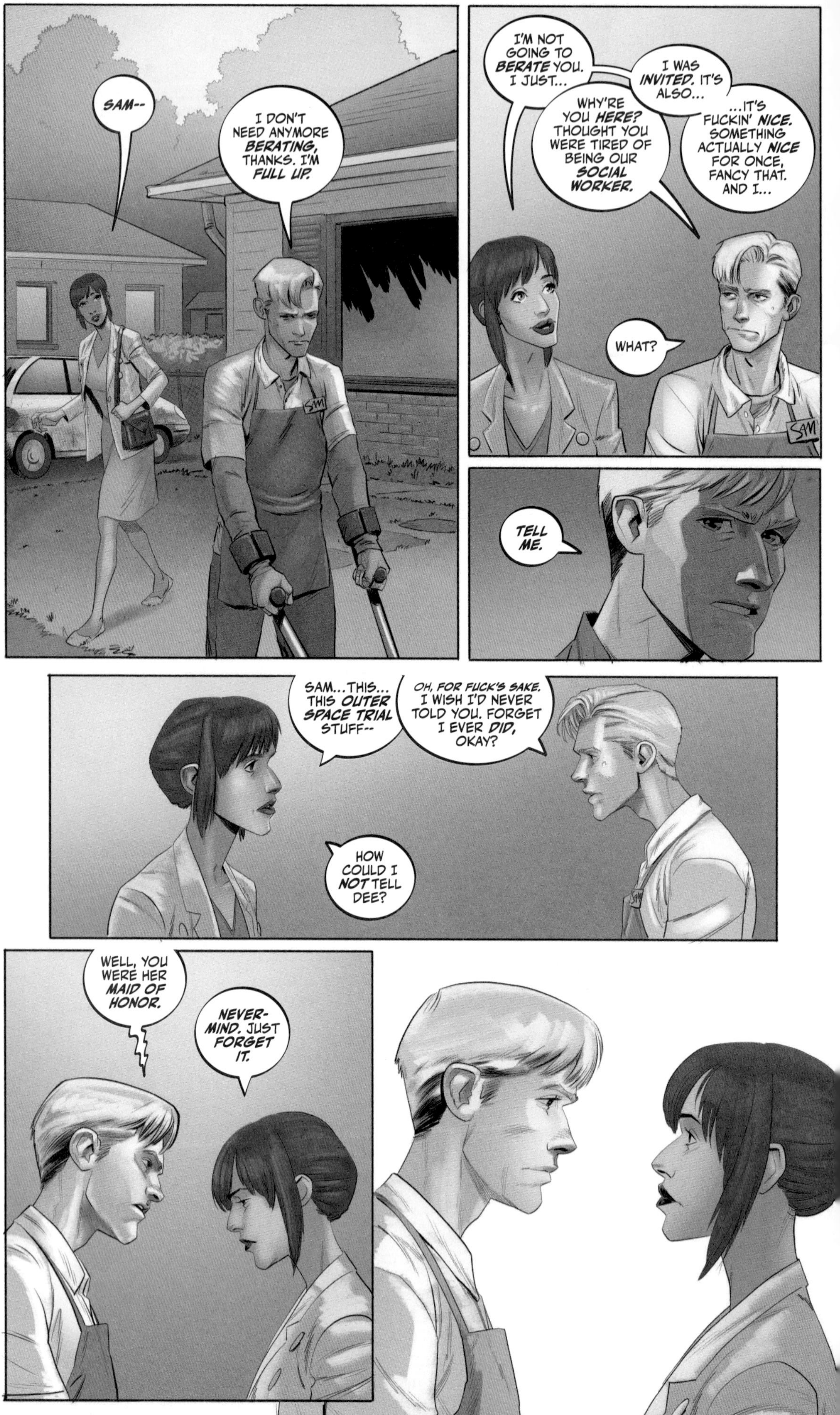
SAM--
I DON'T NEED ANYMORE BERATING, THANKS. I'M FULL UP.
I'M NOT GOING TO BERATE YOU. I JUST...
WHY'RE YOU HERE? THOUGHT YOU WERE TIRED OF BEING OUR SOCIAL WORKER.
I WAS INVITED. IT'S ALSO...
...IT'S FUCKIN' NICE. SOMETHING ACTUALLY NICE FOR ONCE, FANCY THAT. AND I...
WHAT?
TELL ME.
SAM...THIS... THIS OUTER SPACE TRIAL STUFF--
OH, FOR FUCK'S SAKE. I WISH I'D NEVER TOLD YOU. FORGET I EVER DID, OKAY?
HOW COULD I NOT TELL DEE?
WELL, YOU WERE HER MAID OF HONOR.
NEVER-MIND. JUST FORGET IT.

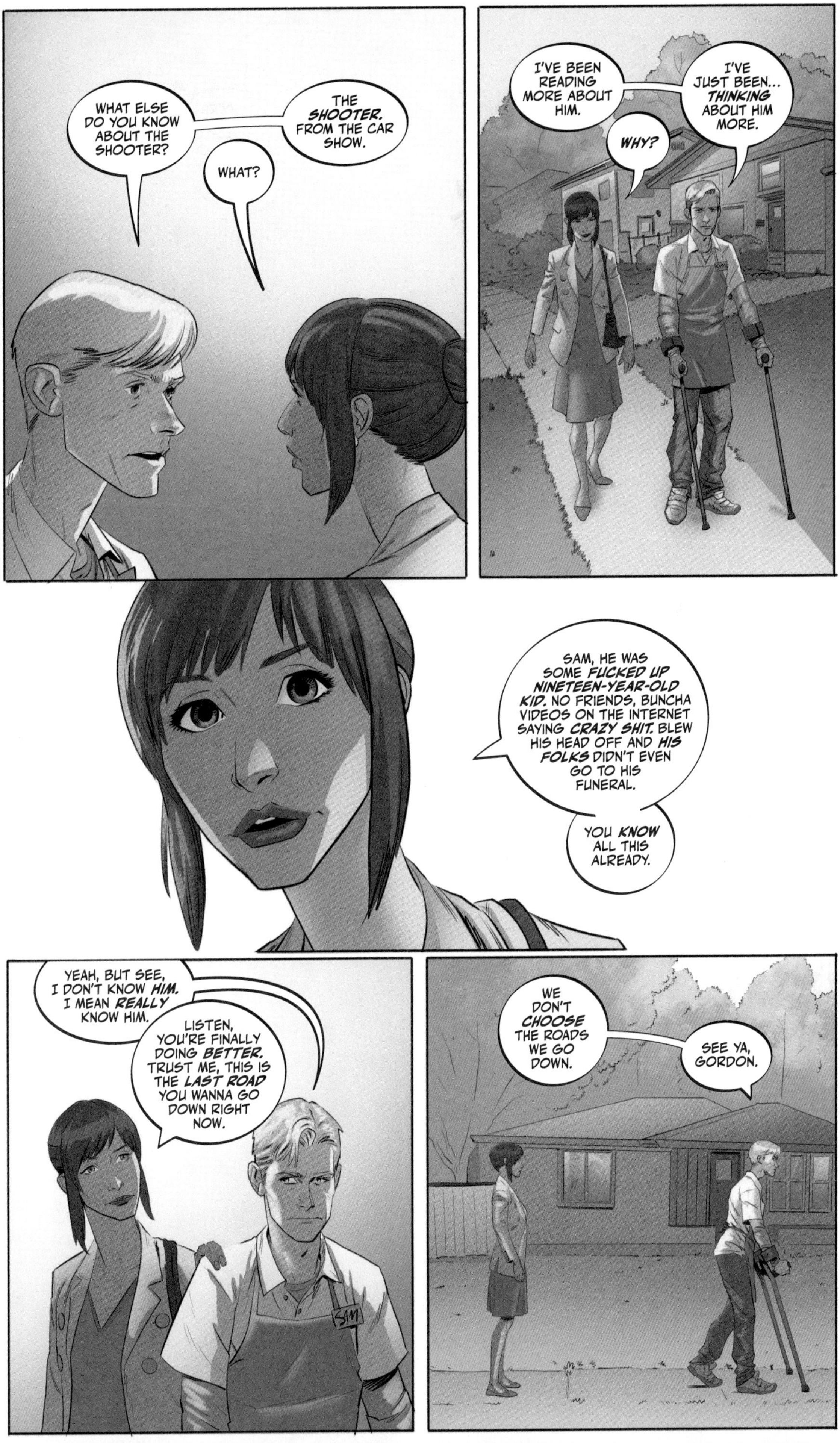
WHAT ELSE DO YOU KNOW ABOUT THE SHOOTER?
WHAT?
THE SHOOTER. FROM THE CAR SHOW.
I'VE BEEN READING MORE ABOUT HIM.
WHY?
I'VE JUST BEEN... THINKING ABOUT HIM MORE.
SAM, HE WAS SOME FUCKED UP NINETEEN-YEAR-OLD KID. NO FRIENDS, BUNCHA VIDEOS ON THE INTERNET SAYING CRAZY SHIT. BLEW HIS HEAD OFF AND HIS FOLKS DIDN'T EVEN GO TO HIS FUNERAL.
YOU KNOW ALL THIS ALREADY.
YEAH, BUT SEE, I DON'T KNOW HIM. I MEAN REALLY KNOW HIM.
LISTEN, YOU'RE FINALLY DOING BETTER. TRUST ME, THIS IS THE LAST ROAD YOU WANNA GO DOWN RIGHT NOW.
WE DON'T CHOOSE THE ROADS WE GO DOWN.
SEE YA, GORDON.
SAM

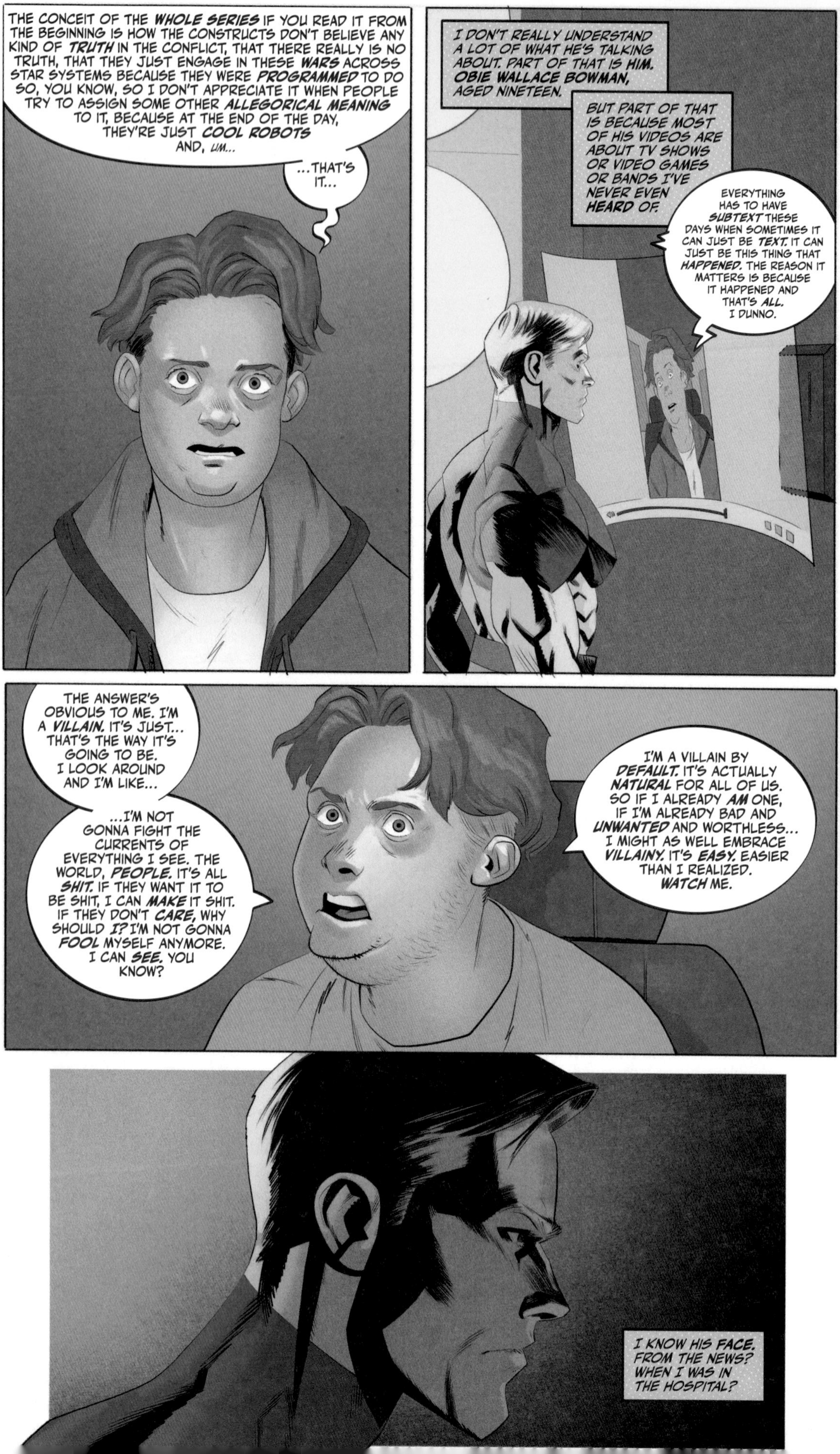
THE CONCEIT OF THE WHOLE SERIES IF YOU READ IT FROM THE BEGINNING IS HOW THE CONSTRUCTS DON'T BELIEVE ANY KIND OF TRUTH IN THE CONFLICT, THAT THERE REALLY IS NO TRUTH, THAT THEY JUST ENGAGE IN THESE WARS ACROSS STAR SYSTEMS BECAUSE THEY WERE PROGRAMMED TO DO SO, YOU KNOW, SO I DON'T APPRECIATE IT WHEN PEOPLE TRY TO ASSIGN SOME OTHER ALLEGORICAL MEANING TO IT, BECAUSE AT THE END OF THE DAY, THEY'RE JUST COOL ROBOTS AND, UM...
...THAT'S IT...
I DON'T REALLY UNDERSTAND A LOT OF WHAT HE'S TALKING ABOUT. PART OF THAT IS HIM. OBIE WALLACE BOWMAN, AGED NINETEEN.
BUT PART OF THAT IS BECAUSE MOST OF HIS VIDEOS ARE ABOUT TV SHOWS OR VIDEO GAMES OR BANDS I'VE NEVER EVEN HEARD OF.
EVERYTHING HAS TO HAVE SUBTEXT THESE DAYS WHEN SOMETIMES IT CAN JUST BE TEXT. IT CAN JUST BE THIS THING THAT HAPPENED. THE REASON IT MATTERS IS BECAUSE IT HAPPENED AND THAT'S ALL. I DUNNO.
THE ANSWER'S OBVIOUS TO ME. I'M A VILLAIN. IT'S JUST... THAT'S THE WAY IT'S GOING TO BE. I LOOK AROUND AND I'M LIKE...
...I'M NOT GONNA FIGHT THE CURRENTS OF EVERYTHING I SEE. THE WORLD, PEOPLE. IT'S ALL SHIT. IF THEY WANT IT TO BE SHIT, I CAN MAKE IT SHIT. IF THEY DON'T CARE, WHY SHOULD I? I'M NOT GONNA FOOL MYSELF ANYMORE. I CAN SEE. YOU KNOW?
I'M A VILLAIN BY DEFAULT. IT'S ACTUALLY NATURAL FOR ALL OF US. SO IF I ALREADY AM ONE, IF I'M ALREADY BAD AND UNWANTED AND WORTHLESS... I MIGHT AS WELL EMBRACE VILLAINY. IT'S EASY. EASIER THAN I REALIZED. WATCH ME.
I KNOW HIS FACE. FROM THE NEWS? WHEN I WAS IN THE HOSPITAL?

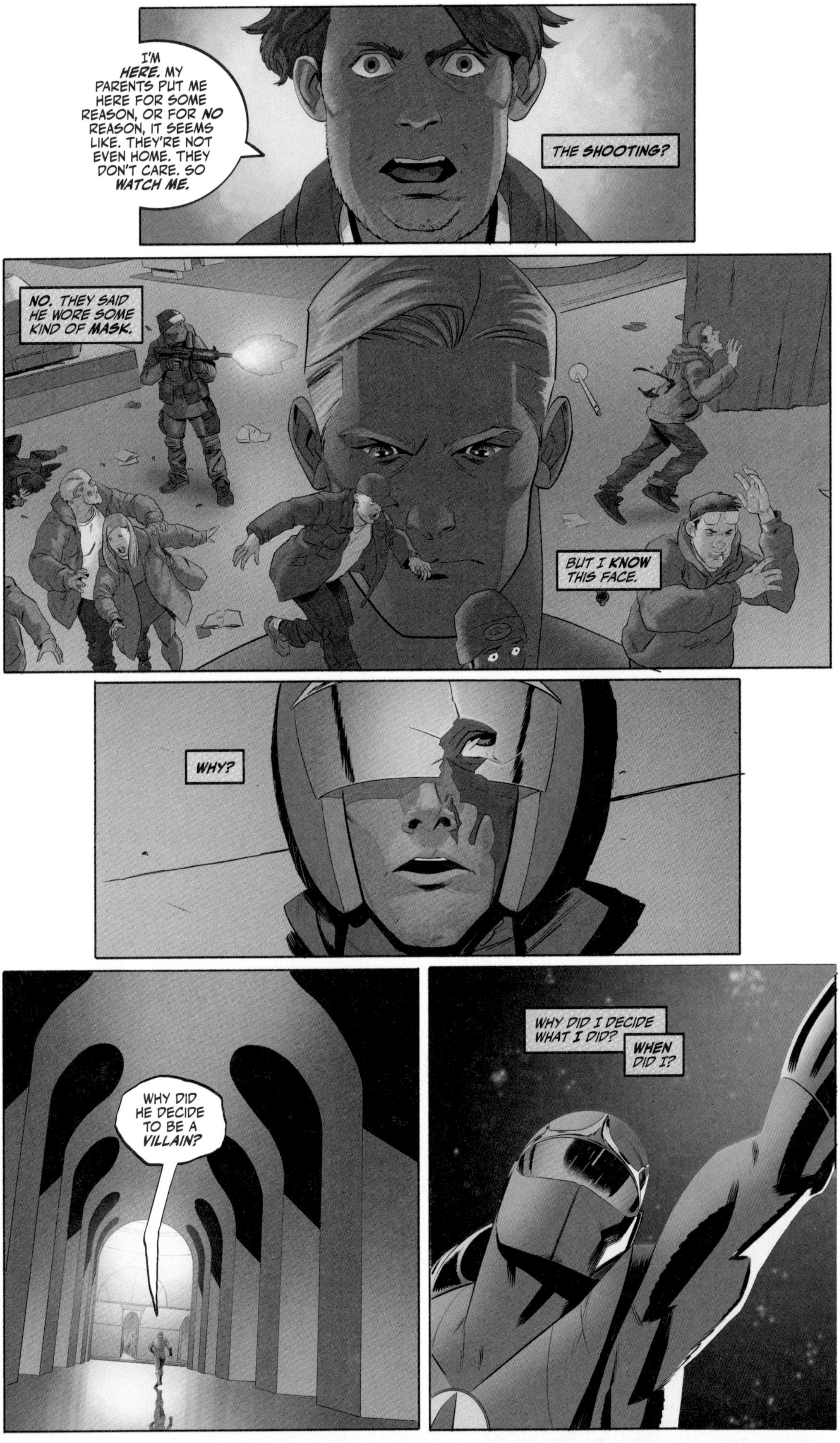
I'M HERE. MY PARENTS PUT ME HERE FOR SOME REASON, OR FOR NO REASON, IT SEEMS LIKE. THEY'RE NOT EVEN HOME. THEY DON'T CARE. SO WATCH ME.
THE SHOOTING?
NO. THEY SAID HE WORE SOME KIND OF MASK.
BUT I KNOW THIS FACE.
WHY?
WHY DID HE DECIDE TO BE A VILLAIN?
WHY DID I DECIDE WHAT I DID?
WHEN DID I?

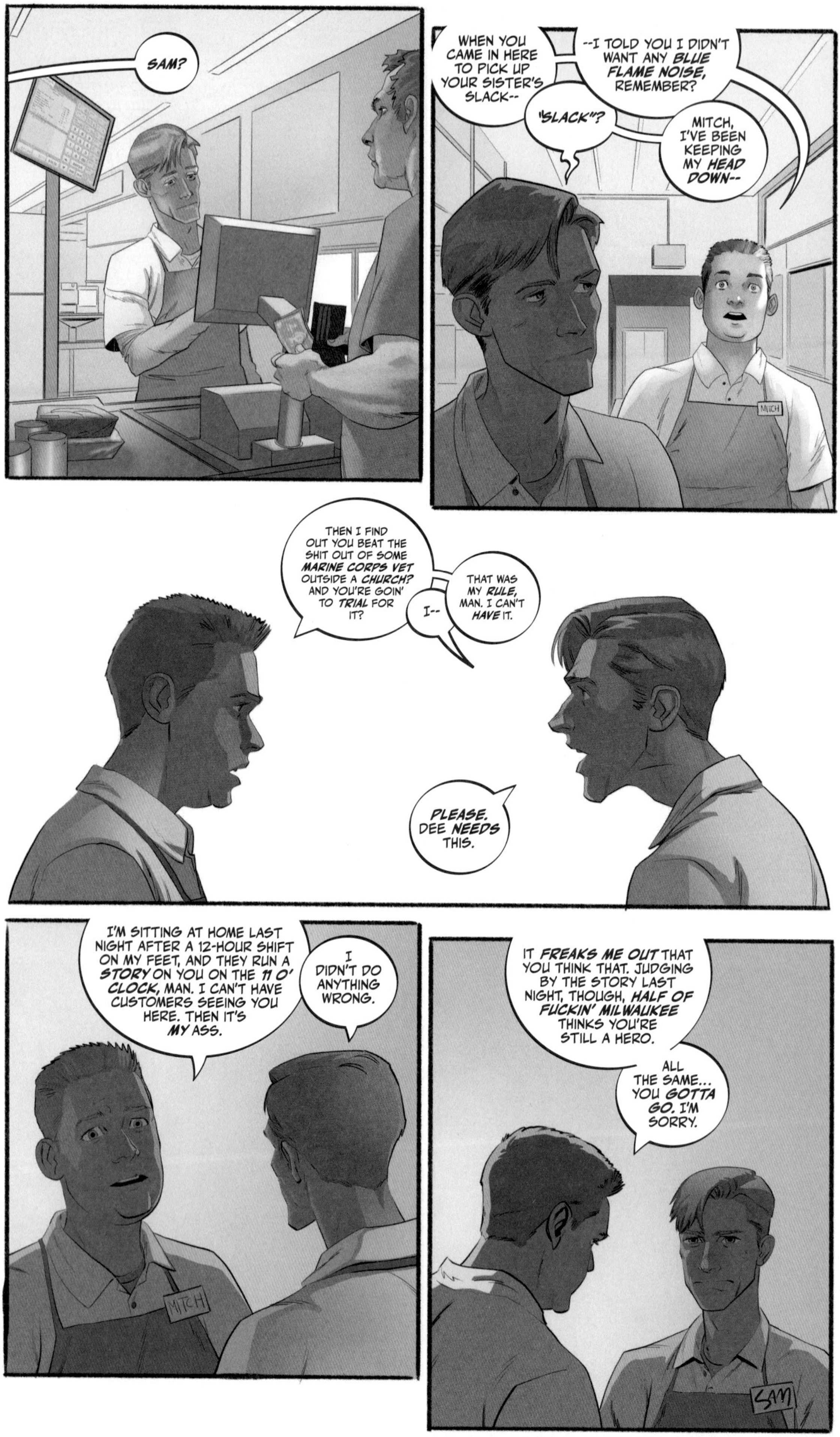
SAM?
WHEN YOU CAME IN HERE TO PICK UP YOUR SISTER'S SLACK--
"SLACK"?
--I TOLD YOU I DIDN'T WANT ANY BLUE FLAME NOISE, REMEMBER?
MITCH, I'VE BEEN KEEPING MY HEAD DOWN--
MITCH
THEN I FIND OUT YOU BEAT THE SHIT OUT OF SOME MARINE CORPS VET OUTSIDE A CHURCH? AND YOU'RE GOIN' TO TRIAL FOR IT?
I--
THAT WAS MY RULE, MAN. I CAN'T HAVE IT.
PLEASE. DEE NEEDS THIS.
I'M SITTING AT HOME LAST NIGHT AFTER A 12-HOUR SHIFT ON MY FEET, AND THEY RUN A STORY ON YOU ON THE 11 O' CLOCK, MAN. I CAN'T HAVE CUSTOMERS SEEING YOU HERE. THEN IT'S MY ASS.
I DIDN'T DO ANYTHING WRONG.
MITCH
IT FREAKS ME OUT THAT YOU THINK THAT. JUDGING BY THE STORY LAST NIGHT, THOUGH, HALF OF FUCKIN' MILWAUKEE THINKS YOU'RE STILL A HERO.
ALL THE SAME... YOU GOTTA GO. I'M SORRY.
SAM

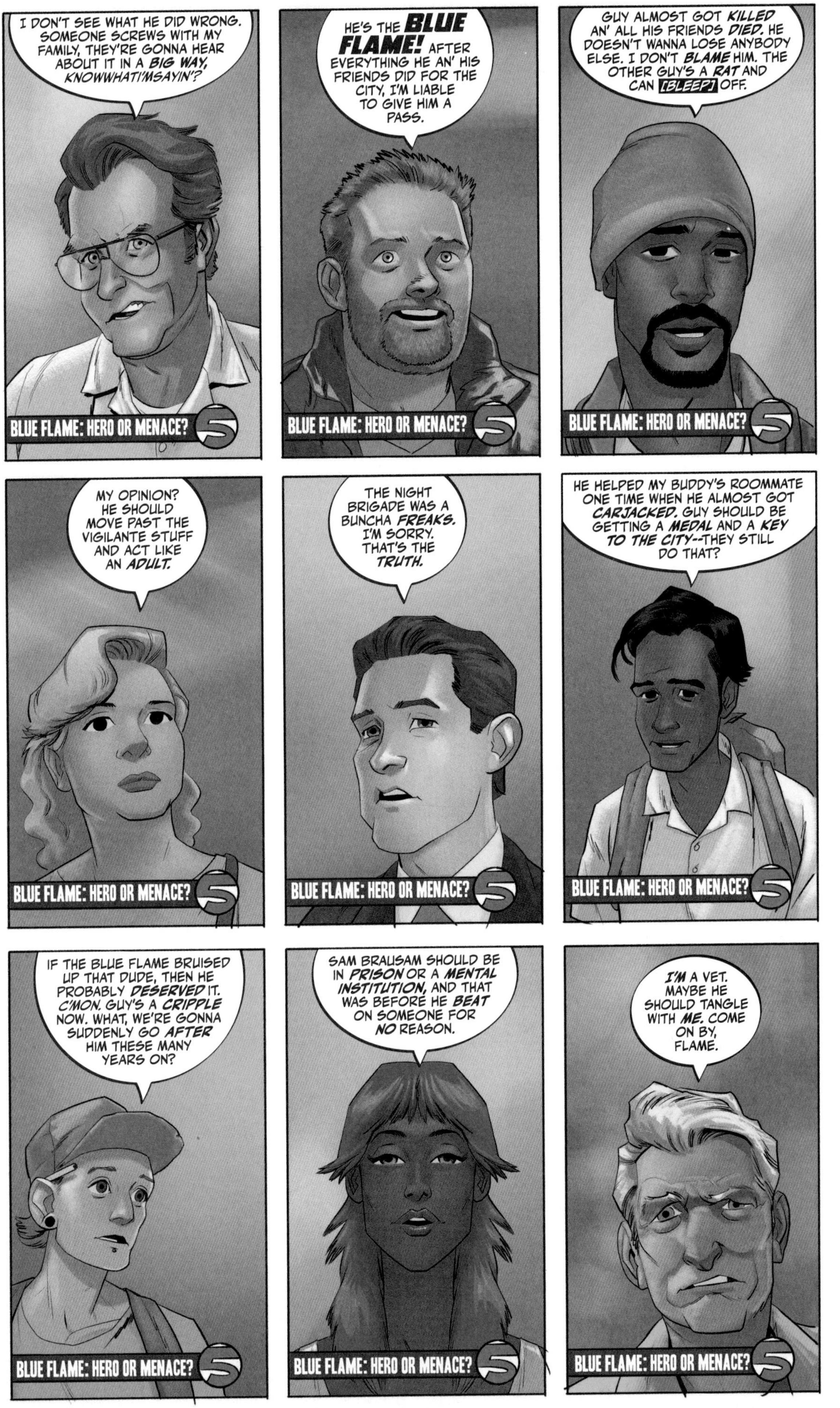
I DON'T SEE WHAT HE DID WRONG. SOMEONE SCREWS WITH MY FAMILY, THEY'RE GONNA HEAR ABOUT IT IN A BIG WAY, KNOWWHATI'MSAYIN'?
BLUE FLAME: HERO OR MENACE?
HE'S THE BLUE FLAME! AFTER EVERYTHING HE AN' HIS FRIENDS DID FOR THE CITY, I'M LIABLE TO GIVE HIM A PASS.
BLUE FLAME: HERO OR MENACE?
GUY ALMOST GOT KILLED AN' ALL HIS FRIENDS DIED. HE DOESN'T WANNA LOSE ANYBODY ELSE. I DON'T BLAME HIM. THE OTHER GUY'S A RAT AND CAN [BLEEP] OFF.
BLUE FLAME: HERO OR MENACE?
MY OPINION? HE SHOULD MOVE PAST THE VIGILANTE STUFF AND ACT LIKE AN ADULT.
BLUE FLAME: HERO OR MENACE?
THE NIGHT BRIGADE WAS A BUNCHA FREAKS. I'M SORRY. THAT'S THE TRUTH.
BLUE FLAME: HERO OR MENACE?
HE HELPED MY BUDDY'S ROOMMATE ONE TIME WHEN HE ALMOST GOT CARJACKED. GUY SHOULD BE GETTING A MEDAL AND A KEY TO THE CITY--THEY STILL DO THAT?
BLUE FLAME: HERO OR MENACE?
IF THE BLUE FLAME BRUISED UP THAT DUDE, THEN HE PROBABLY DESERVED IT. C'MON. GUY'S A CRIPPLE NOW. WHAT, WE'RE GONNA SUDDENLY GO AFTER HIM THESE MANY YEARS ON?
BLUE FLAME: HERO OR MENACE?
SAM BRAUSAM SHOULD BE IN PRISON OR A MENTAL INSTITUTION, AND THAT WAS BEFORE HE BEAT ON SOMEONE FOR NO REASON.
BLUE FLAME: HERO OR MENACE?
I'M A VET. MAYBE HE SHOULD TANGLE WITH ME. COME ON BY, FLAME.
BLUE FLAME: HERO OR MENACE?

GORDON. COME IN HERE!

WHAT ABOUT PAROLE? IT'D BE A SHAME TO PUT BLUE FLAME BEHIND BARS...

YEAH, WALT, WHAT'S UP?

THIS *BLUE FLAME* SHIT. DIDN'T YOU PROMISE ME A STORY ON HIM A HUNDRED FUCKING YEARS AGO?

OH... YEAH, IT WAS GONNA BE A WEEKENDER PIECE, BUT I, *UM--*

BLEW THE *DEADLINE.*

YEAH.

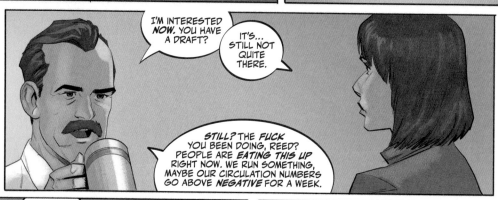

I'M INTERESTED *NOW.* YOU HAVE A DRAFT?

IT'S... STILL NOT QUITE THERE.

STILL? THE *FUCK* YOU BEEN DOING, REED? PEOPLE ARE *EATING THIS UP* RIGHT NOW. WE RUN SOMETHING, MAYBE OUR CIRCULATION NUMBERS GO ABOVE *NEGATIVE* FOR A WEEK.

I JUST NEED A LITTLE MORE *TIME.*

A *DAY.* SPELLCHECK IT AND GET IT ON MY *DESK.*

WOULD I... COULD I STILL HAVE THE *WHOLE WEEK-ENDER?*

WE'LL SEE.

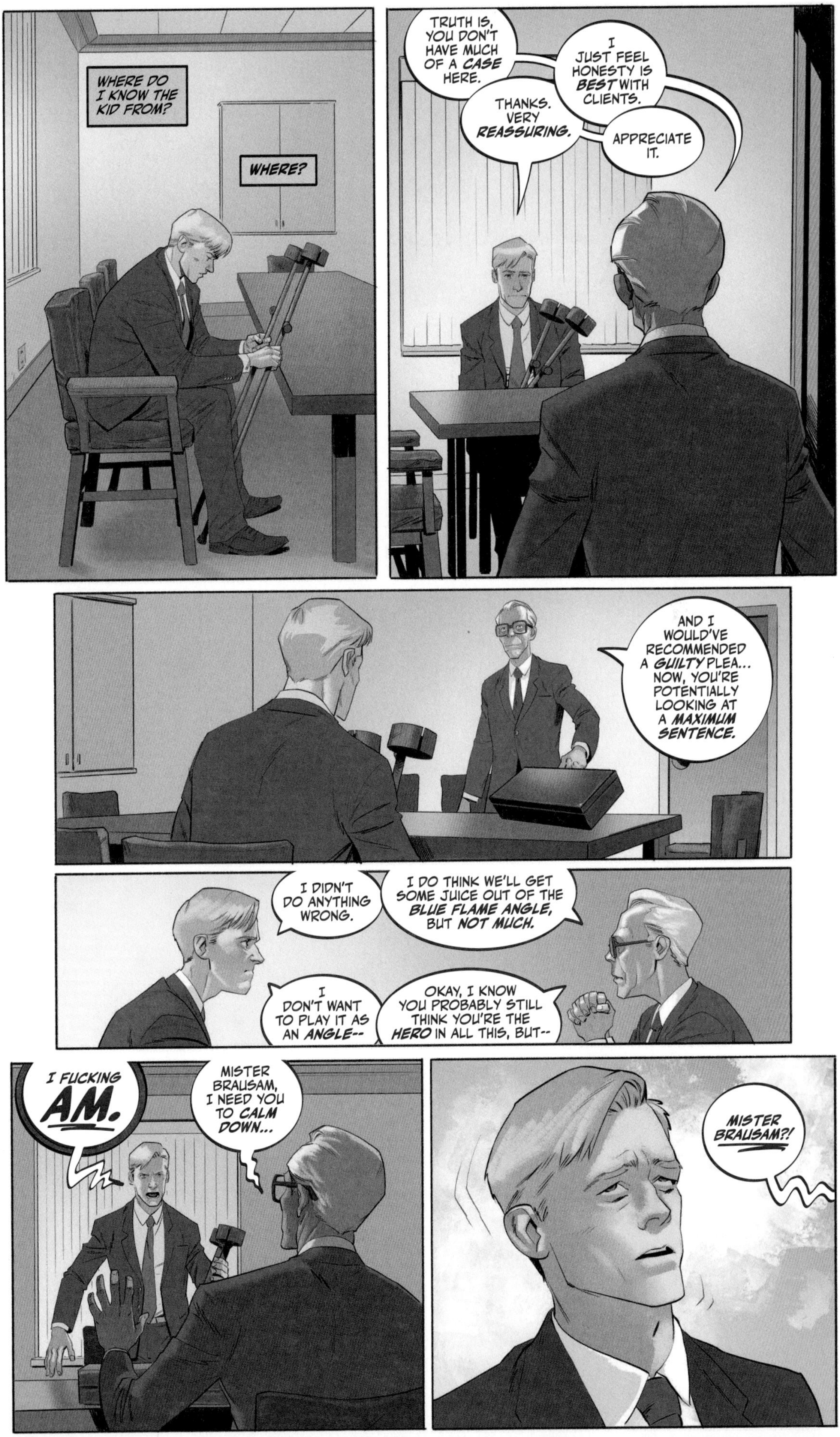
WHERE DO I KNOW THE KID FROM?
WHERE?
TRUTH IS, YOU DON'T HAVE MUCH OF A CASE HERE.
THANKS. VERY REASSURING.
I JUST FEEL HONESTY IS BEST WITH CLIENTS.
APPRECIATE IT.
AND I WOULD'VE RECOMMENDED A GUILTY PLEA... NOW, YOU'RE POTENTIALLY LOOKING AT A MAXIMUM SENTENCE.
I DIDN'T DO ANYTHING WRONG.
I DO THINK WE'LL GET SOME JUICE OUT OF THE BLUE FLAME ANGLE, BUT NOT MUCH.
I DON'T WANT TO PLAY IT AS AN ANGLE--
OKAY, I KNOW YOU PROBABLY STILL THINK YOU'RE THE HERO IN ALL THIS, BUT--
I FUCKING AM.
MISTER BRAUSAM, I NEED YOU TO CALM DOWN...
MISTER BRAUSAM?!

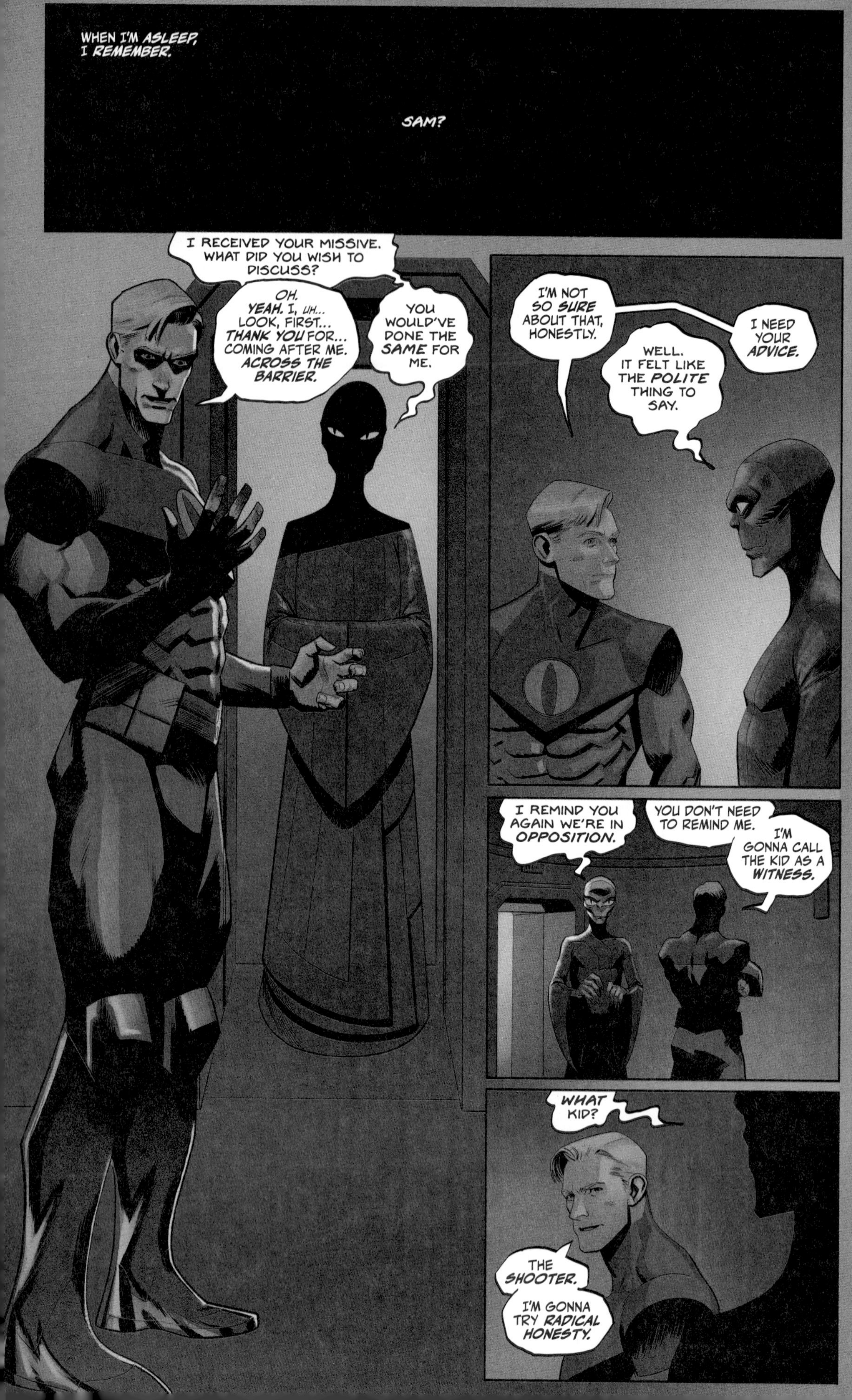
WHEN I'M ASLEEP, I REMEMBER.
SAM?
I RECEIVED YOUR MISSIVE. WHAT DID YOU WISH TO DISCUSS?
OH. YEAH. I, UH... LOOK, FIRST... THANK YOU FOR... COMING AFTER ME. ACROSS THE BARRIER.
YOU WOULD'VE DONE THE SAME FOR ME.
I'M NOT SO SURE ABOUT THAT, HONESTLY.
WELL. IT FELT LIKE THE POLITE THING TO SAY.
I NEED YOUR ADVICE.
I REMIND YOU AGAIN WE'RE IN OPPOSITION.
YOU DON'T NEED TO REMIND ME.
I'M GONNA CALL THE KID AS A WITNESS.
WHAT KID?
THE SHOOTER.
I'M GONNA TRY RADICAL HONESTY.

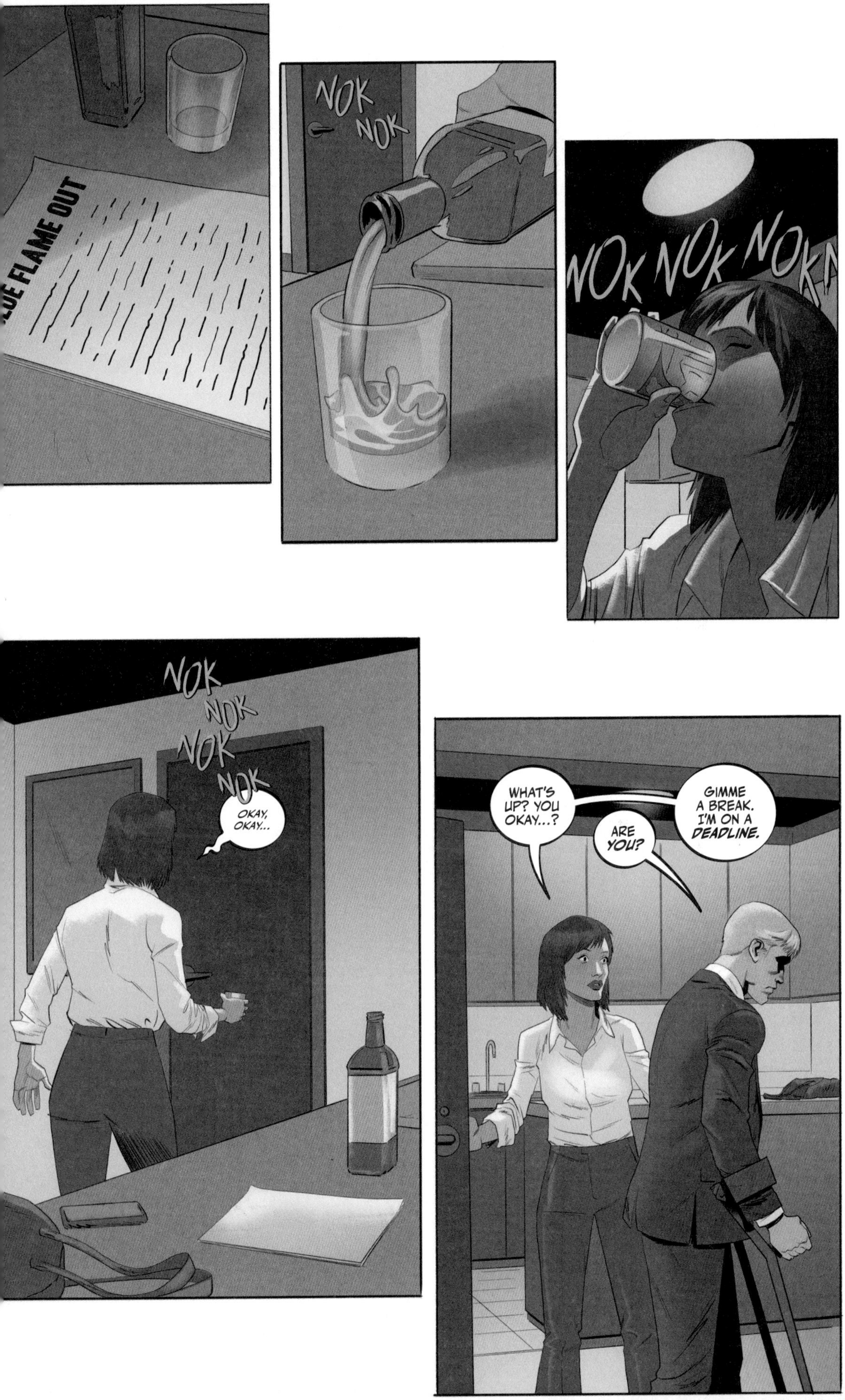
BLUE FLAME OUT
NOK NOK
NOK NOK NOK
NOK NOK NOK NOK
OKAY, OKAY...
WHAT'S UP? YOU OKAY...?
GIMME A BREAK. I'M ON A DEADLINE.
ARE YOU?

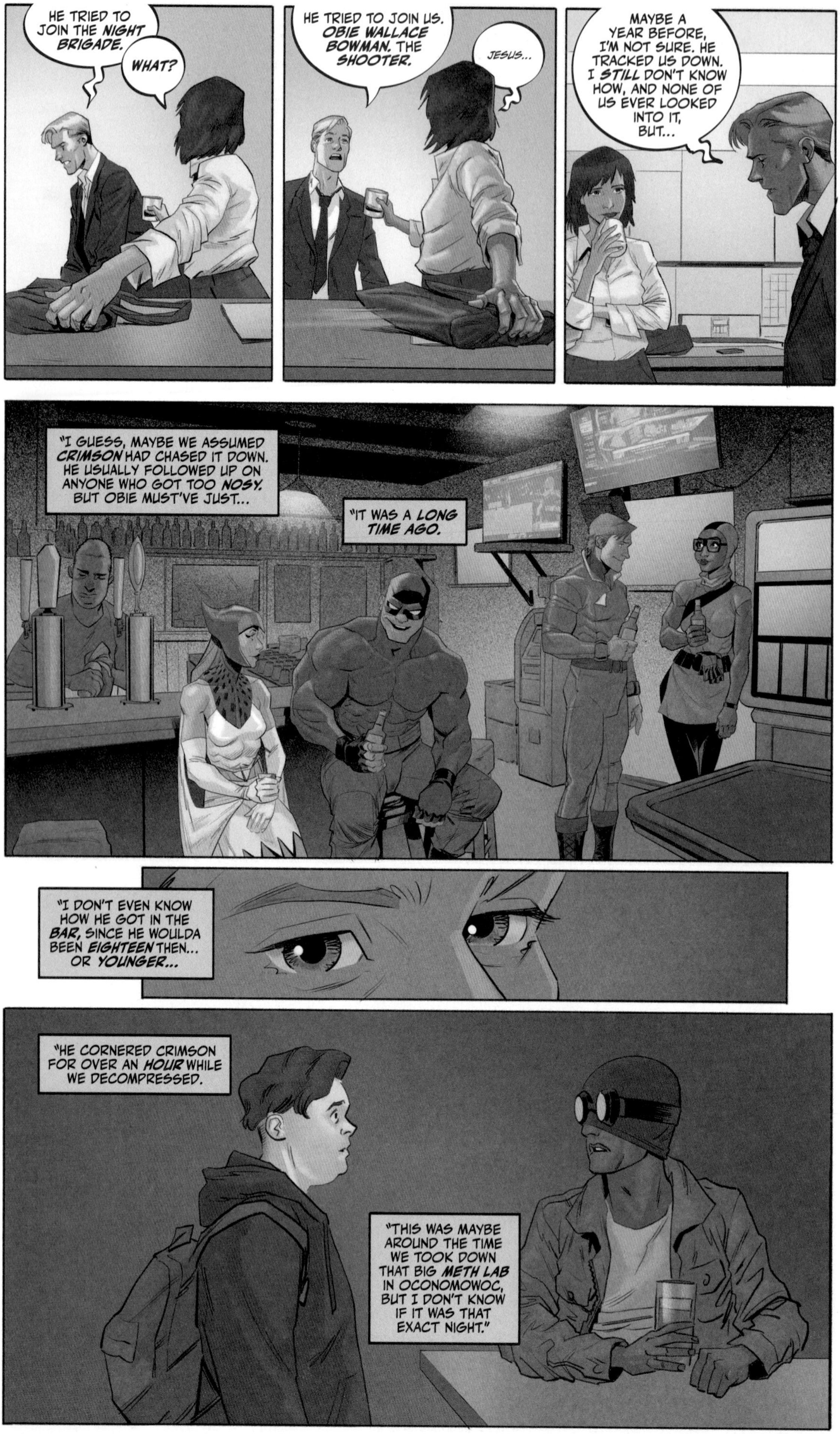
HE TRIED TO JOIN THE NIGHT BRIGADE.
WHAT?
HE TRIED TO JOIN US. OBIE WALLACE BOWMAN. THE SHOOTER.
JESUS...
MAYBE A YEAR BEFORE, I'M NOT SURE. HE TRACKED US DOWN. I STILL DON'T KNOW HOW, AND NONE OF US EVER LOOKED INTO IT, BUT...
"I GUESS, MAYBE WE ASSUMED CRIMSON HAD CHASED IT DOWN. HE USUALLY FOLLOWED UP ON ANYONE WHO GOT TOO NOSY. BUT OBIE MUST'VE JUST...
"IT WAS A LONG TIME AGO.
"I DON'T EVEN KNOW HOW HE GOT IN THE BAR, SINCE HE WOULDA BEEN EIGHTEEN THEN... OR YOUNGER...
"HE CORNERED CRIMSON FOR OVER AN HOUR WHILE WE DECOMPRESSED.
"THIS WAS MAYBE AROUND THE TIME WE TOOK DOWN THAT BIG METH LAB IN OCONOMOWOC, BUT I DON'T KNOW IF IT WAS THAT EXACT NIGHT."

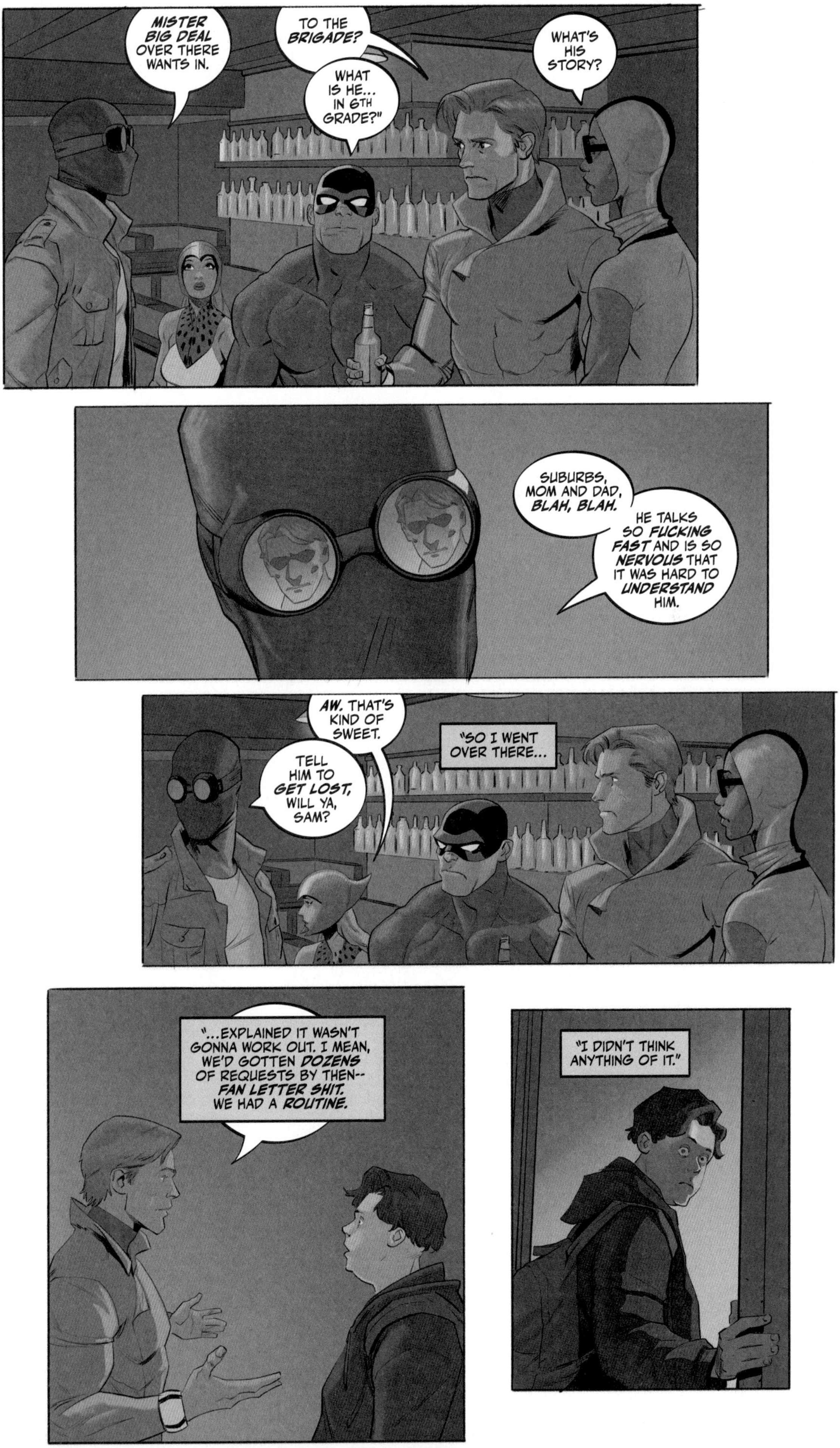
MISTER BIG DEAL OVER THERE WANTS IN.
TO THE BRIGADE?
WHAT IS HE... IN 6TH GRADE?"
WHAT'S HIS STORY?
SUBURBS, MOM AND DAD, BLAH, BLAH.
HE TALKS SO FUCKING FAST AND IS SO NERVOUS THAT IT WAS HARD TO UNDERSTAND HIM.
AW. THAT'S KIND OF SWEET.
"SO I WENT OVER THERE...
TELL HIM TO GET LOST, WILL YA, SAM?
"...EXPLAINED IT WASN'T GONNA WORK OUT. I MEAN, WE'D GOTTEN DOZENS OF REQUESTS BY THEN-- FAN LETTER SHIT. WE HAD A ROUTINE.
"I DIDN'T THINK ANYTHING OF IT."

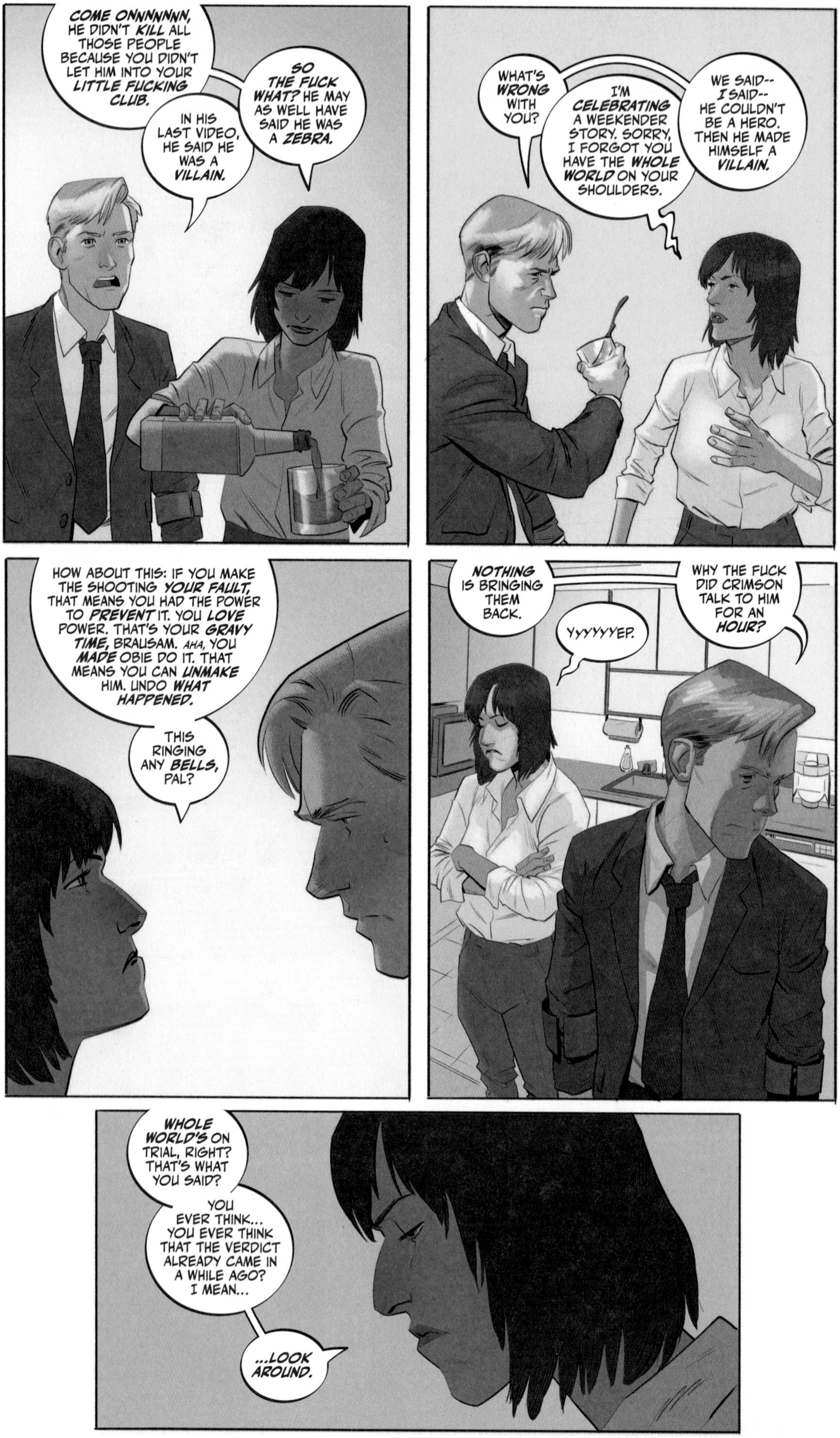
COME ONNNNNNN, HE DIDN'T KILL ALL THOSE PEOPLE BECAUSE YOU DIDN'T LET HIM INTO YOUR LITTLE FUCKING CLUB.
IN HIS LAST VIDEO, HE SAID HE WAS A VILLAIN.
SO THE FUCK WHAT? HE MAY AS WELL HAVE SAID HE WAS A ZEBRA.
WHAT'S WRONG WITH YOU?
I'M CELEBRATING A WEEKENDER STORY. SORRY, I FORGOT YOU HAVE THE WHOLE WORLD ON YOUR SHOULDERS.
WE SAID-- I SAID-- HE COULDN'T BE A HERO. THEN HE MADE HIMSELF A VILLAIN.
HOW ABOUT THIS: IF YOU MAKE THE SHOOTING YOUR FAULT, THAT MEANS YOU HAD THE POWER TO PREVENT IT. YOU LOVE POWER. THAT'S YOUR GRAVY TIME, BRAUSAM. AHA, YOU MADE OBIE DO IT. THAT MEANS YOU CAN UNMAKE HIM. UNDO WHAT HAPPENED.
THIS RINGING ANY BELLS, PAL?
NOTHING IS BRINGING THEM BACK.
YYYYYYEP.
WHY THE FUCK DID CRIMSON TALK TO HIM FOR AN HOUR?
WHOLE WORLD'S ON TRIAL, RIGHT? THAT'S WHAT YOU SAID?
YOU EVER THINK... YOU EVER THINK THAT THE VERDICT ALREADY CAME IN A WHILE AGO? I MEAN...
...LOOK AROUND.

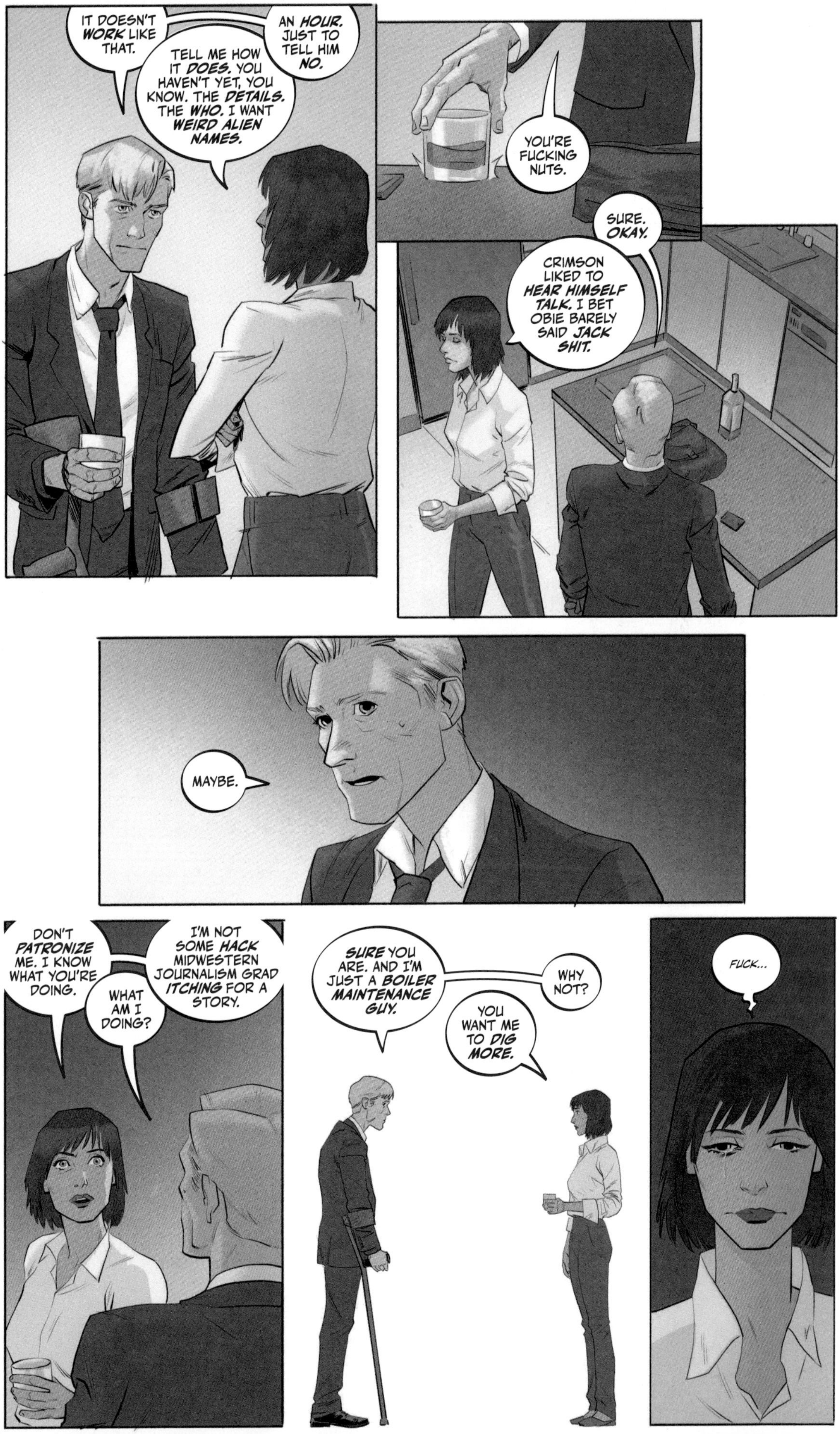
IT DOESN'T WORK LIKE THAT.
AN HOUR. JUST TO TELL HIM NO.
TELL ME HOW IT DOES. YOU HAVEN'T YET, YOU KNOW. THE DETAILS. THE WHO. I WANT WEIRD ALIEN NAMES.
YOU'RE FUCKING NUTS.
SURE. OKAY.
CRIMSON LIKED TO HEAR HIMSELF TALK. I BET OBIE BARELY SAID JACK SHIT.
MAYBE.
DON'T PATRONIZE ME. I KNOW WHAT YOU'RE DOING.
WHAT AM I DOING?
I'M NOT SOME HACK MIDWESTERN JOURNALISM GRAD ITCHING FOR A STORY.
SURE YOU ARE. AND I'M JUST A BOILER MAINTENANCE GUY.
WHY NOT?
YOU WANT ME TO DIG MORE.
FUCK...

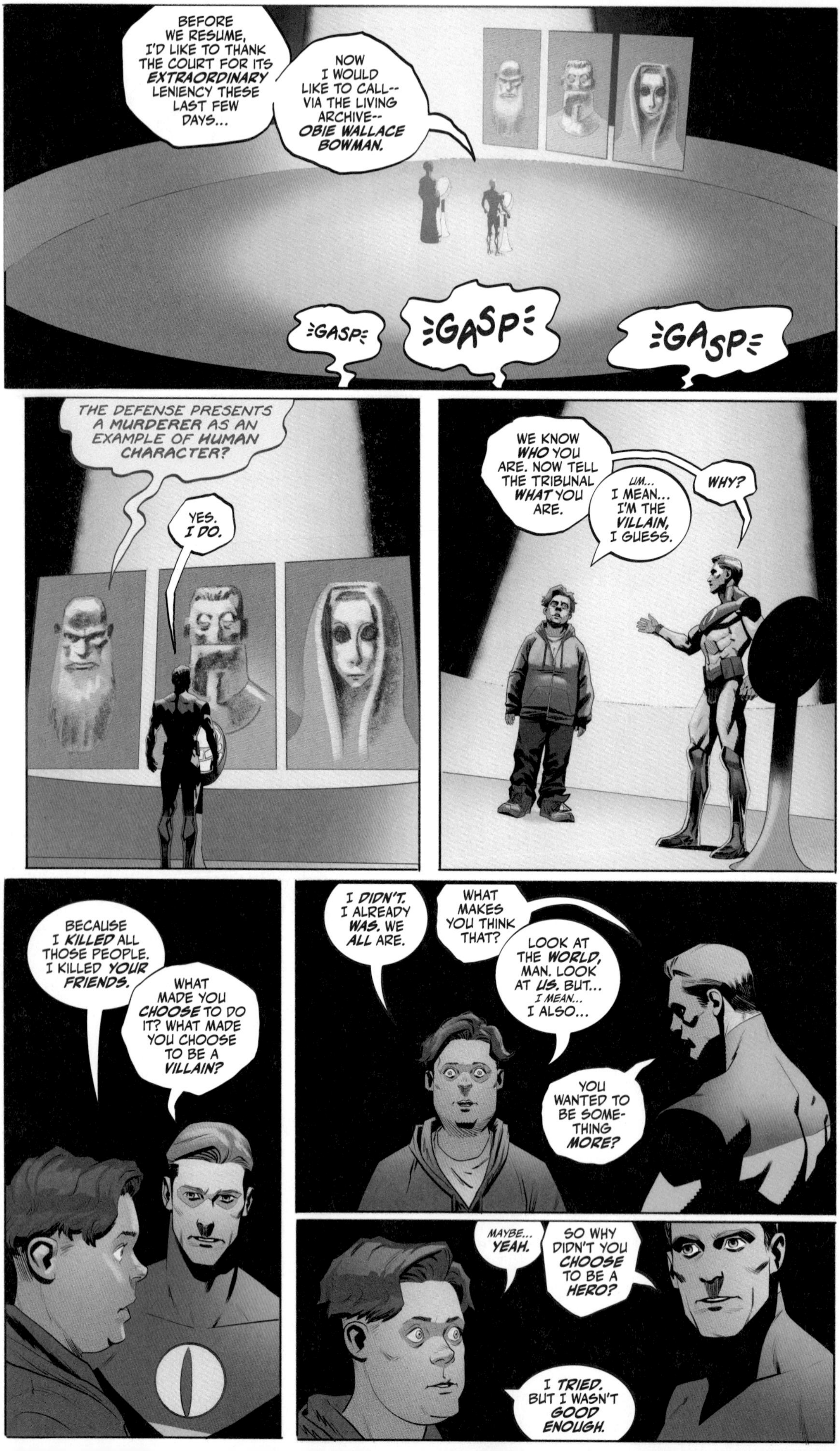

BEFORE WE RESUME, I'D LIKE TO THANK THE COURT FOR ITS EXTRAORDINARY LENIENCY THESE LAST FEW DAYS...
NOW I WOULD LIKE TO CALL-- VIA THE LIVING ARCHIVE-- OBIE WALLACE BOWMAN.
GASP
GASP
GASP
THE DEFENSE PRESENTS A MURDERER AS AN EXAMPLE OF HUMAN CHARACTER?
YES. I DO.
WE KNOW WHO YOU ARE. NOW TELL THE TRIBUNAL WHAT YOU ARE.
UM... I MEAN... I'M THE VILLAIN, I GUESS.
WHY?
BECAUSE I KILLED ALL THOSE PEOPLE. I KILLED YOUR FRIENDS.
WHAT MADE YOU CHOOSE TO DO IT? WHAT MADE YOU CHOOSE TO BE A VILLAIN?
I DIDN'T. I ALREADY WAS. WE ALL ARE.
WHAT MAKES YOU THINK THAT?
LOOK AT THE WORLD, MAN. LOOK AT US. BUT... I MEAN... I ALSO...
YOU WANTED TO BE SOME-THING MORE?
MAYBE... YEAH.
SO WHY DIDN'T YOU CHOOSE TO BE A HERO?
I TRIED. BUT I WASN'T GOOD ENOUGH.

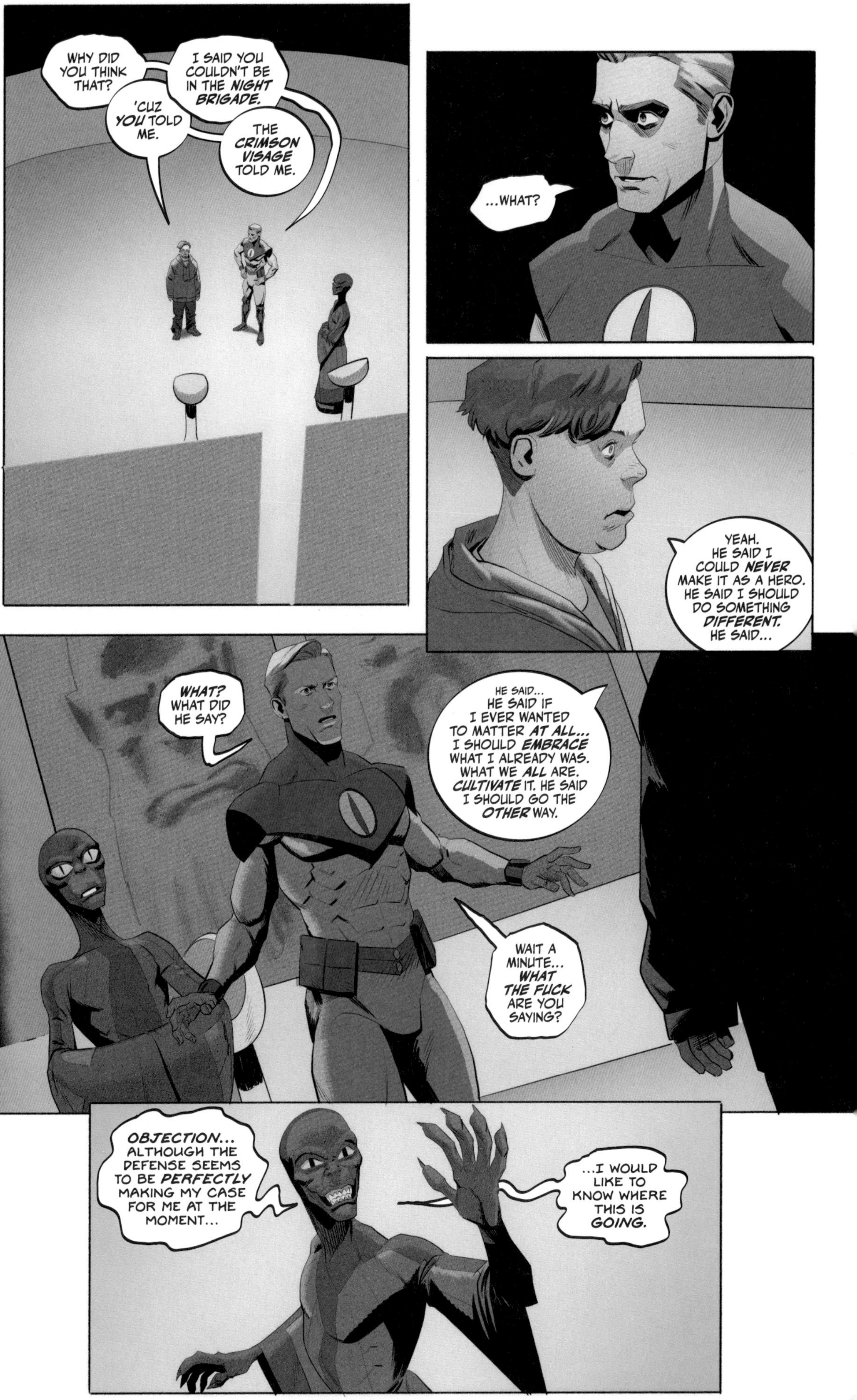
WHY DID YOU THINK THAT?
I SAID YOU COULDN'T BE IN THE NIGHT BRIGADE.
'CUZ YOU TOLD ME.
THE CRIMSON VISAGE TOLD ME.
...WHAT?
YEAH. HE SAID I COULD NEVER MAKE IT AS A HERO. HE SAID I SHOULD DO SOMETHING DIFFERENT. HE SAID...
WHAT? WHAT DID HE SAY?
HE SAID... HE SAID IF I EVER WANTED TO MATTER AT ALL... I SHOULD EMBRACE WHAT I ALREADY WAS. WHAT WE ALL ARE. CULTIVATE IT. HE SAID I SHOULD GO THE OTHER WAY.
WAIT A MINUTE... WHAT THE FUCK ARE YOU SAYING?
OBJECTION... ALTHOUGH THE DEFENSE SEEMS TO BE PERFECTLY MAKING MY CASE FOR ME AT THE MOMENT...
...I WOULD LIKE TO KNOW WHERE THIS IS GOING.

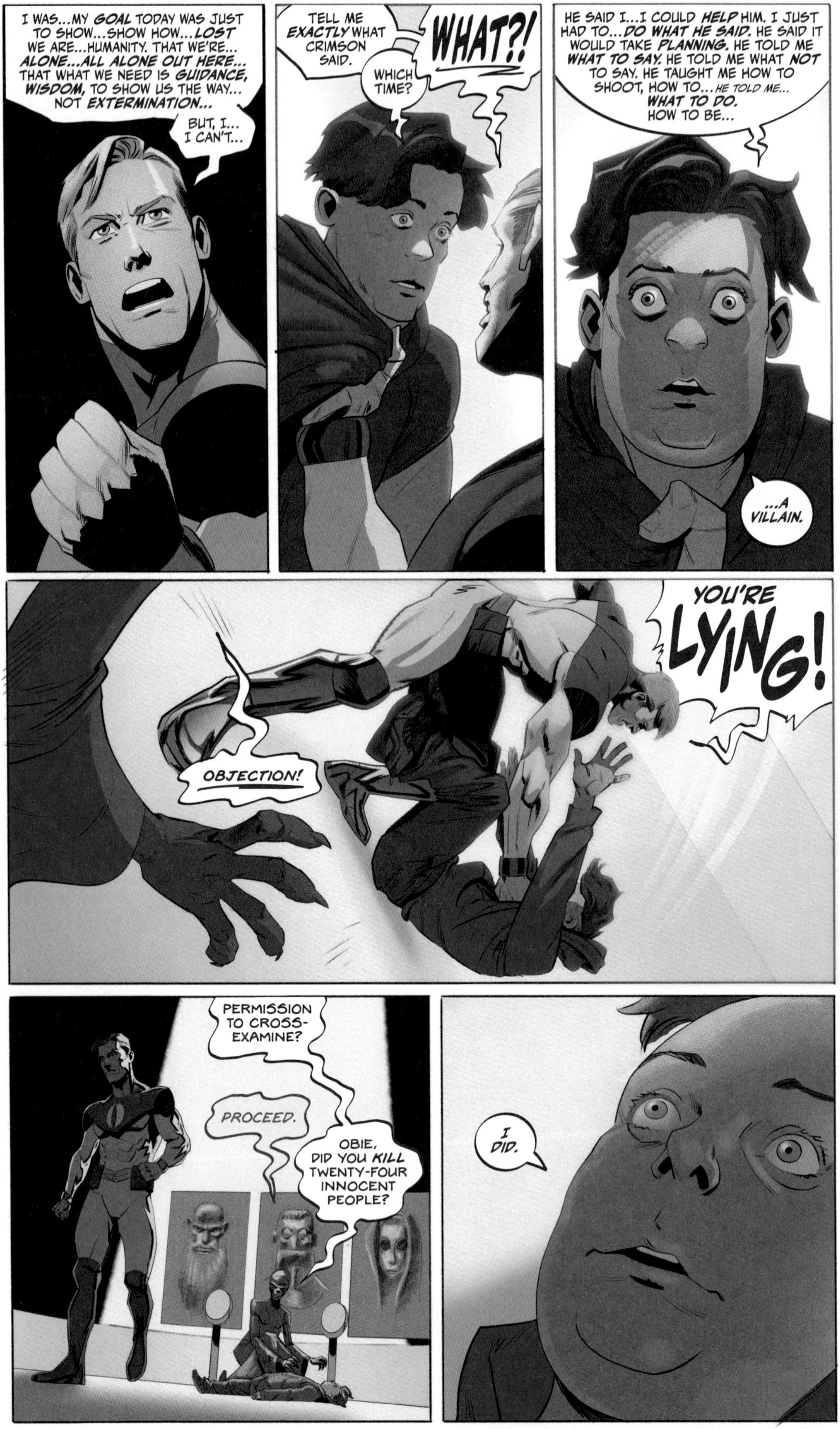
I WAS...MY GOAL TODAY WAS JUST TO SHOW...SHOW HOW...LOST WE ARE...HUMANITY. THAT WE'RE... ALONE...ALL ALONE OUT HERE... THAT WHAT WE NEED IS GUIDANCE, WISDOM, TO SHOW US THE WAY... NOT EXTERMINATION...
BUT, I... I CAN'T...
TELL ME EXACTLY WHAT CRIMSON SAID.
WHICH TIME?
WHAT?!
HE SAID I...I COULD HELP HIM. I JUST HAD TO...DO WHAT HE SAID. HE SAID IT WOULD TAKE PLANNING. HE TOLD ME WHAT TO SAY. HE TOLD ME WHAT NOT TO SAY. HE TAUGHT ME HOW TO SHOOT, HOW TO... HE TOLD ME... WHAT TO DO. HOW TO BE...
...A VILLAIN.
YOU'RE LYING!
OBJECTION!
PERMISSION TO CROSS-EXAMINE?
PROCEED.
OBIE, DID YOU KILL TWENTY-FOUR INNOCENT PEOPLE?
I DID.

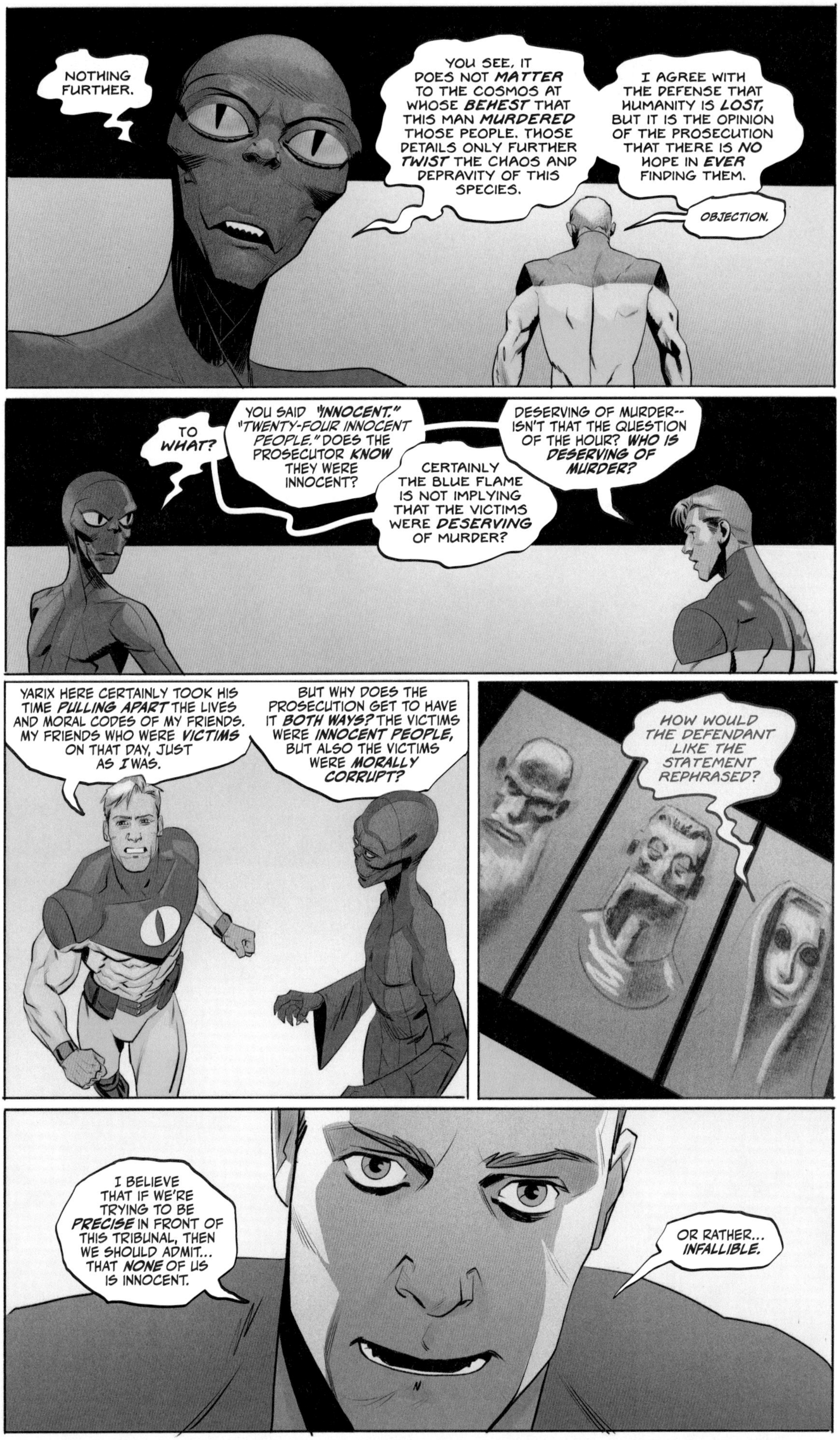
NOTHING FURTHER.
YOU SEE, IT DOES NOT MATTER TO THE COSMOS AT WHOSE BEHEST THAT THIS MAN MURDERED THOSE PEOPLE. THOSE DETAILS ONLY FURTHER TWIST THE CHAOS AND DEPRAVITY OF THIS SPECIES.
I AGREE WITH THE DEFENSE THAT HUMANITY IS LOST, BUT IT IS THE OPINION OF THE PROSECUTION THAT THERE IS NO HOPE IN EVER FINDING THEM.
OBJECTION.
TO WHAT?
YOU SAID "INNOCENT." "TWENTY-FOUR INNOCENT PEOPLE." DOES THE PROSECUTOR KNOW THEY WERE INNOCENT?
CERTAINLY THE BLUE FLAME IS NOT IMPLYING THAT THE VICTIMS WERE DESERVING OF MURDER?
DESERVING OF MURDER-- ISN'T THAT THE QUESTION OF THE HOUR? WHO IS DESERVING OF MURDER?
YARIX HERE CERTAINLY TOOK HIS TIME PULLING APART THE LIVES AND MORAL CODES OF MY FRIENDS. MY FRIENDS WHO WERE VICTIMS ON THAT DAY, JUST AS I WAS.
BUT WHY DOES THE PROSECUTION GET TO HAVE IT BOTH WAYS? THE VICTIMS WERE INNOCENT PEOPLE, BUT ALSO THE VICTIMS WERE MORALLY CORRUPT?
HOW WOULD THE DEFENDANT LIKE THE STATEMENT REPHRASED?
I BELIEVE THAT IF WE'RE TRYING TO BE PRECISE IN FRONT OF THIS TRIBUNAL, THEN WE SHOULD ADMIT... THAT NONE OF US IS INNOCENT.
OR RATHER... INFALLIBLE.

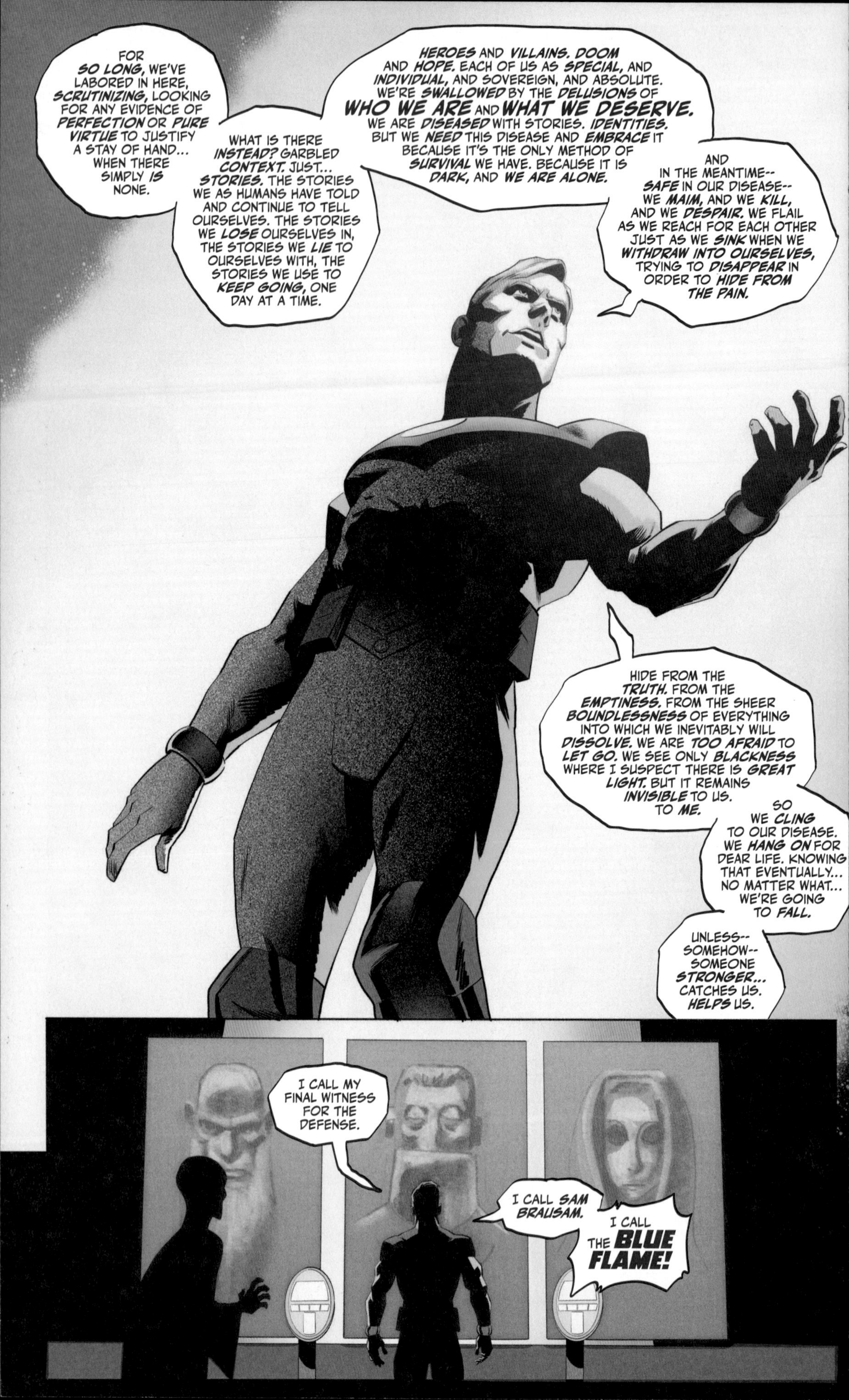
FOR SO LONG, WE'VE LABORED IN HERE, SCRUTINIZING, LOOKING FOR ANY EVIDENCE OF PERFECTION OR PURE VIRTUE TO JUSTIFY A STAY OF HAND... WHEN THERE SIMPLY IS NONE.
WHAT IS THERE INSTEAD? GARBLED CONTEXT. JUST... STORIES. THE STORIES WE AS HUMANS HAVE TOLD AND CONTINUE TO TELL OURSELVES. THE STORIES WE LOSE OURSELVES IN, THE STORIES WE LIE TO OURSELVES WITH, THE STORIES WE USE TO KEEP GOING, ONE DAY AT A TIME.
HEROES AND VILLAINS. DOOM AND HOPE. EACH OF US AS SPECIAL, AND INDIVIDUAL, AND SOVEREIGN, AND ABSOLUTE. WE'RE SWALLOWED BY THE DELUSIONS OF WHO WE ARE AND WHAT WE DESERVE. WE ARE DISEASED WITH STORIES. IDENTITIES. BUT WE NEED THIS DISEASE AND EMBRACE IT BECAUSE IT'S THE ONLY METHOD OF SURVIVAL WE HAVE. BECAUSE IT IS DARK, AND WE ARE ALONE.
AND IN THE MEANTIME-- SAFE IN OUR DISEASE-- WE MAIM, AND WE KILL, AND WE DESPAIR. WE FLAIL AS WE REACH FOR EACH OTHER JUST AS WE SINK WHEN WE WITHDRAW INTO OURSELVES, TRYING TO DISAPPEAR IN ORDER TO HIDE FROM THE PAIN.
HIDE FROM THE TRUTH. FROM THE EMPTINESS. FROM THE SHEER BOUNDLESSNESS OF EVERYTHING INTO WHICH WE INEVITABLY WILL DISSOLVE. WE ARE TOO AFRAID TO LET GO. WE SEE ONLY BLACKNESS WHERE I SUSPECT THERE IS GREAT LIGHT. BUT IT REMAINS INVISIBLE TO US. TO ME.
SO WE CLING TO OUR DISEASE. WE HANG ON FOR DEAR LIFE. KNOWING THAT EVENTUALLY... NO MATTER WHAT... WE'RE GOING TO FALL.
UNLESS-- SOMEHOW-- SOMEONE STRONGER... CATCHES US. HELPS US.
I CALL MY FINAL WITNESS FOR THE DEFENSE.
I CALL SAM BRAUSAM.
I CALL THE BLUE FLAME!

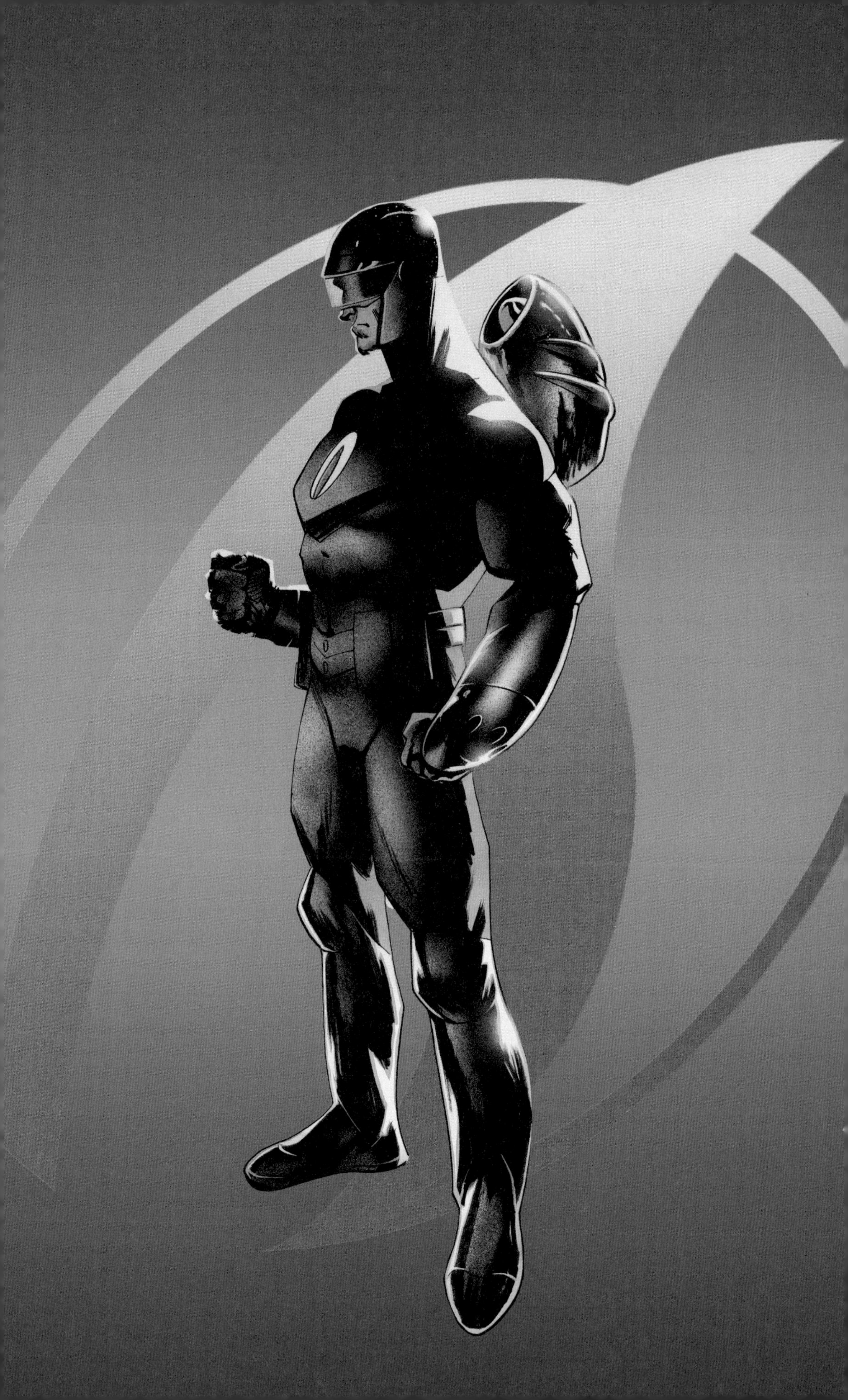

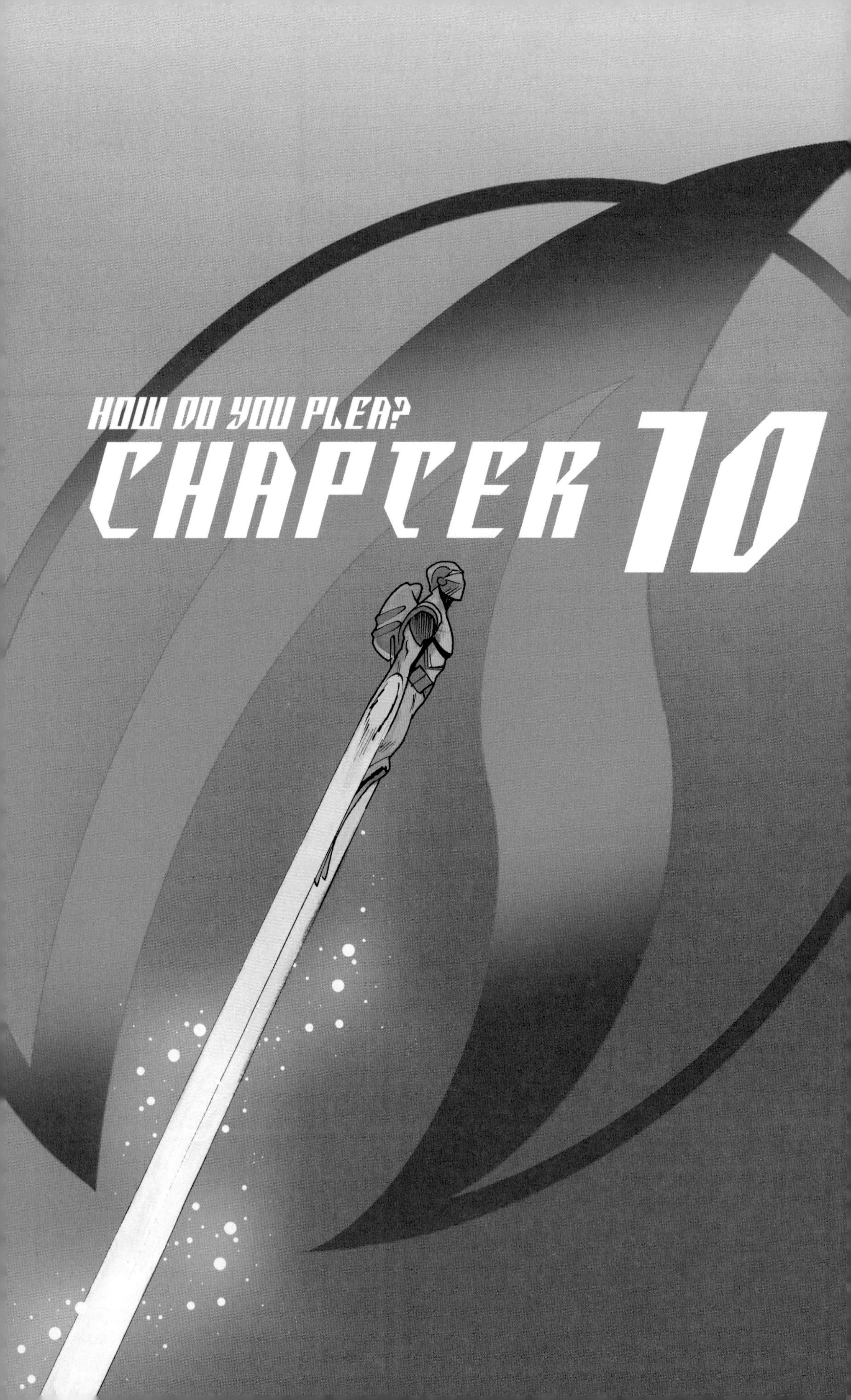
HOW DO YOU PLEA?
CHAPTER 10

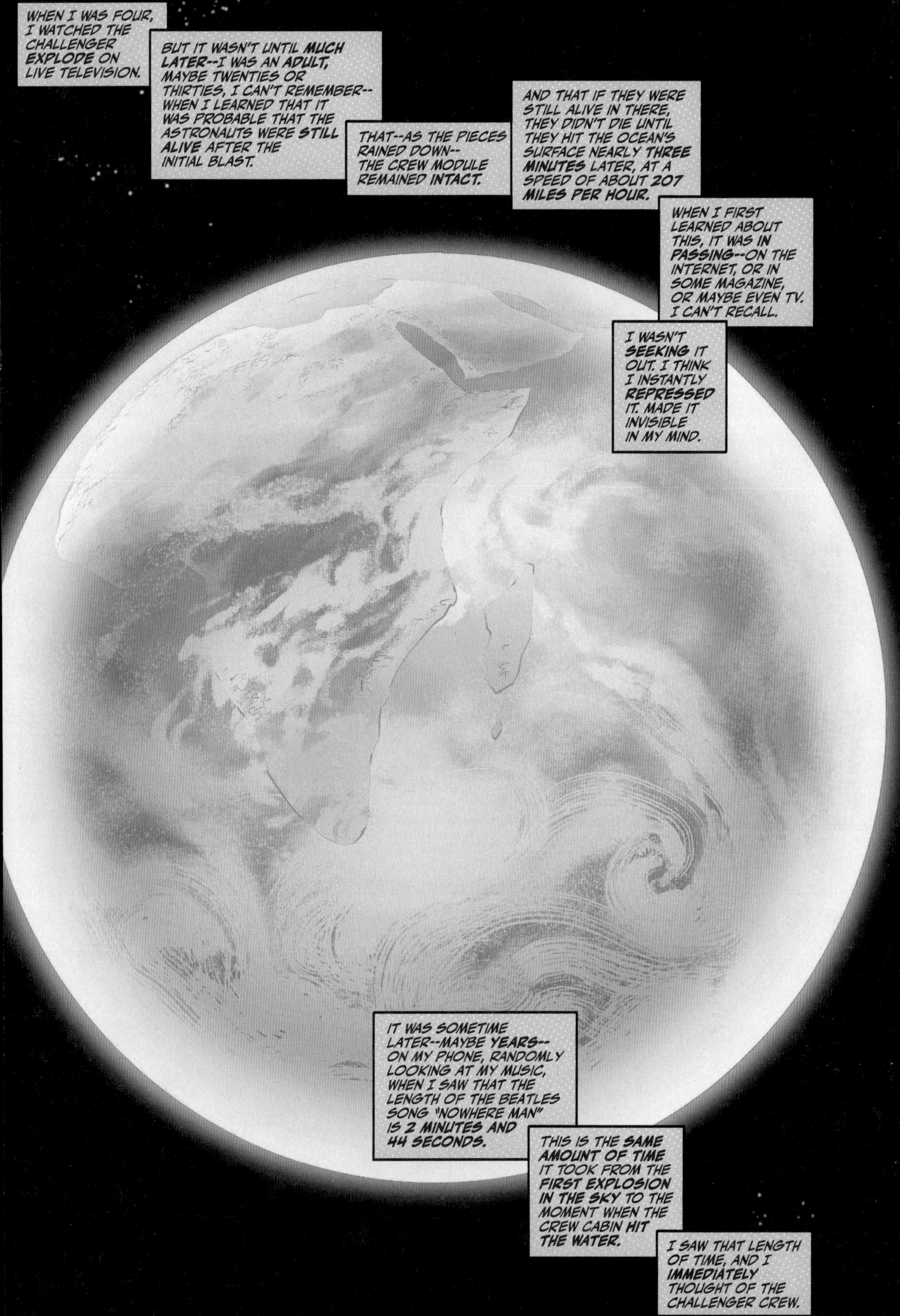
WHEN I WAS FOUR, I WATCHED THE CHALLENGER EXPLODE ON LIVE TELEVISION.
BUT IT WASN'T UNTIL MUCH LATER--I WAS AN ADULT, MAYBE TWENTIES OR THIRTIES, I CAN'T REMEMBER-- WHEN I LEARNED THAT IT WAS PROBABLE THAT THE ASTRONAUTS WERE STILL ALIVE AFTER THE INITIAL BLAST.
THAT--AS THE PIECES RAINED DOWN-- THE CREW MODULE REMAINED INTACT.
AND THAT IF THEY WERE STILL ALIVE IN THERE, THEY DIDN'T DIE UNTIL THEY HIT THE OCEAN'S SURFACE NEARLY THREE MINUTES LATER, AT A SPEED OF ABOUT 207 MILES PER HOUR.
WHEN I FIRST LEARNED ABOUT THIS, IT WAS IN PASSING--ON THE INTERNET, OR IN SOME MAGAZINE, OR MAYBE EVEN TV. I CAN'T RECALL.
I WASN'T SEEKING IT OUT. I THINK I INSTANTLY REPRESSED IT. MADE IT INVISIBLE IN MY MIND.
IT WAS SOMETIME LATER--MAYBE YEARS-- ON MY PHONE, RANDOMLY LOOKING AT MY MUSIC, WHEN I SAW THAT THE LENGTH OF THE BEATLES SONG "NOWHERE MAN" IS 2 MINUTES AND 44 SECONDS.
THIS IS THE SAME AMOUNT OF TIME IT TOOK FROM THE FIRST EXPLOSION IN THE SKY TO THE MOMENT WHEN THE CREW CABIN HIT THE WATER.
I SAW THAT LENGTH OF TIME, AND I IMMEDIATELY THOUGHT OF THE CHALLENGER CREW.

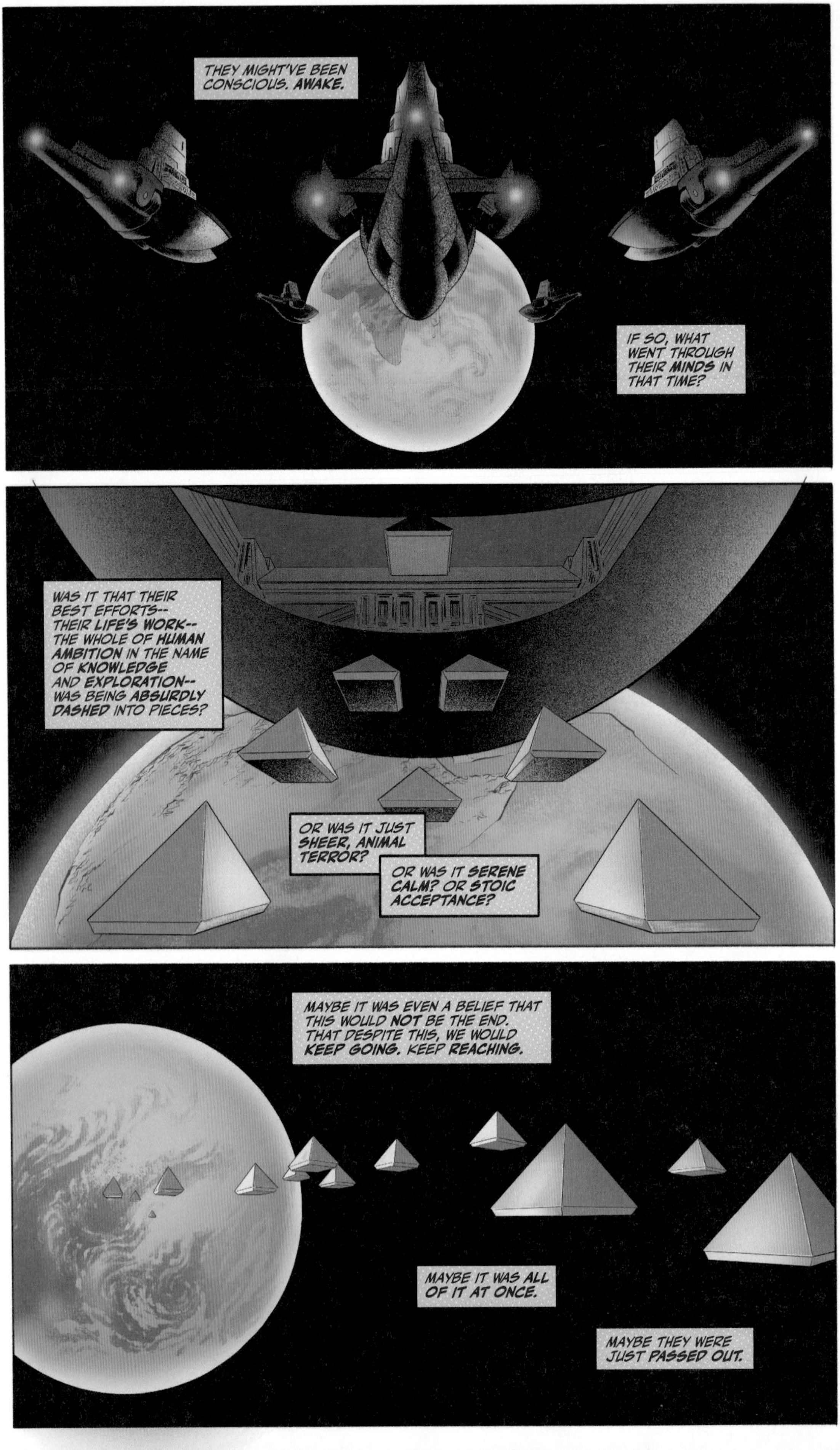
THEY MIGHT'VE BEEN CONSCIOUS. AWAKE.
IF SO, WHAT WENT THROUGH THEIR MINDS IN THAT TIME?
WAS IT THAT THEIR BEST EFFORTS-- THEIR LIFE'S WORK-- THE WHOLE OF HUMAN AMBITION IN THE NAME OF KNOWLEDGE AND EXPLORATION-- WAS BEING ABSURDLY DASHED INTO PIECES?
OR WAS IT JUST SHEER, ANIMAL TERROR?
OR WAS IT SERENE CALM? OR STOIC ACCEPTANCE?
MAYBE IT WAS EVEN A BELIEF THAT THIS WOULD NOT BE THE END. THAT DESPITE THIS, WE WOULD KEEP GOING. KEEP REACHING.
MAYBE IT WAS ALL OF IT AT ONCE.
MAYBE THEY WERE JUST PASSED OUT.

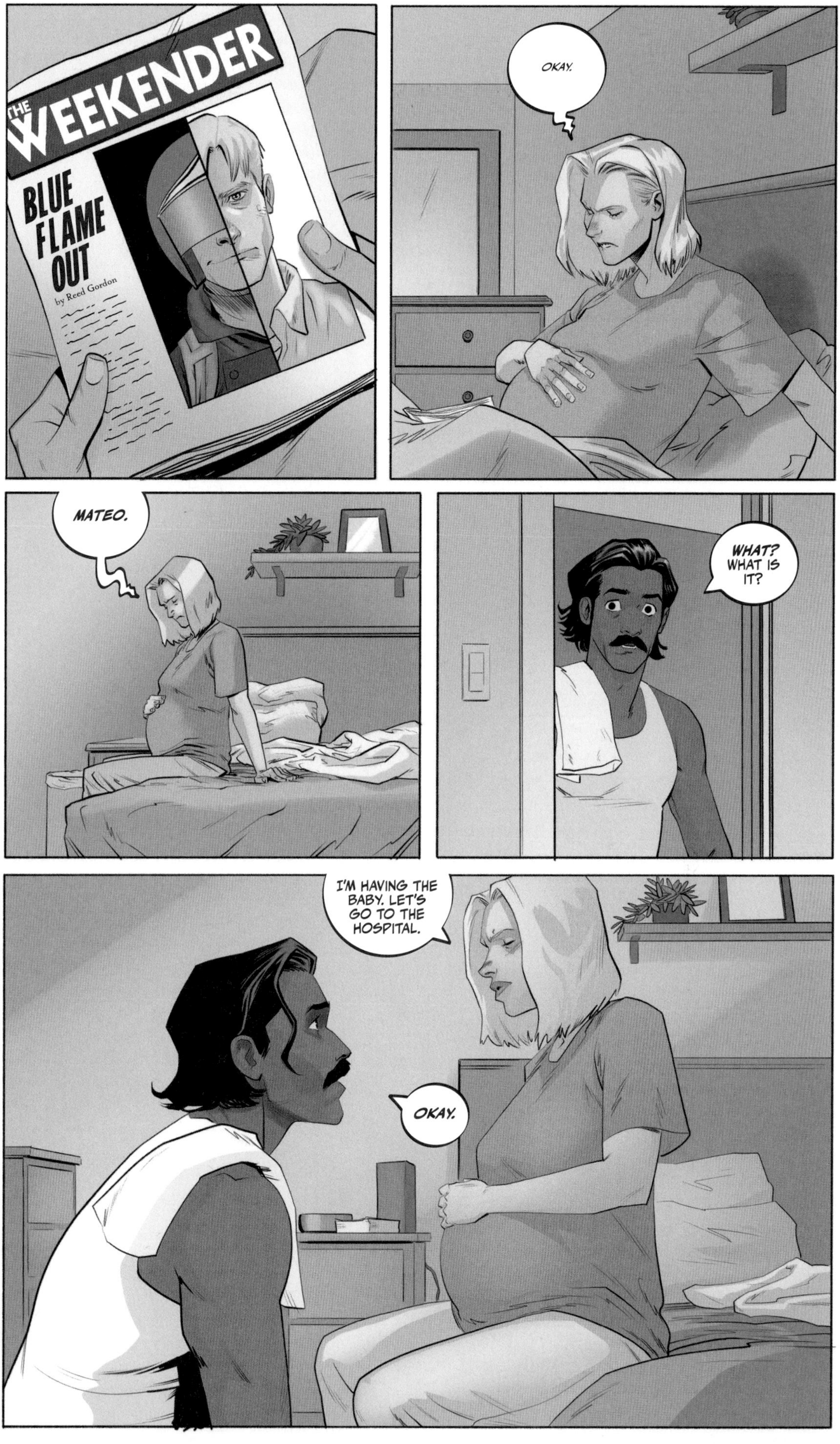
THE WEEKENDER
BLUE FLAME OUT
by Reed Gordon
OKAY.
MATEO.
WHAT? WHAT IS IT?
I'M HAVING THE BABY. LET'S GO TO THE HOSPITAL.
OKAY.

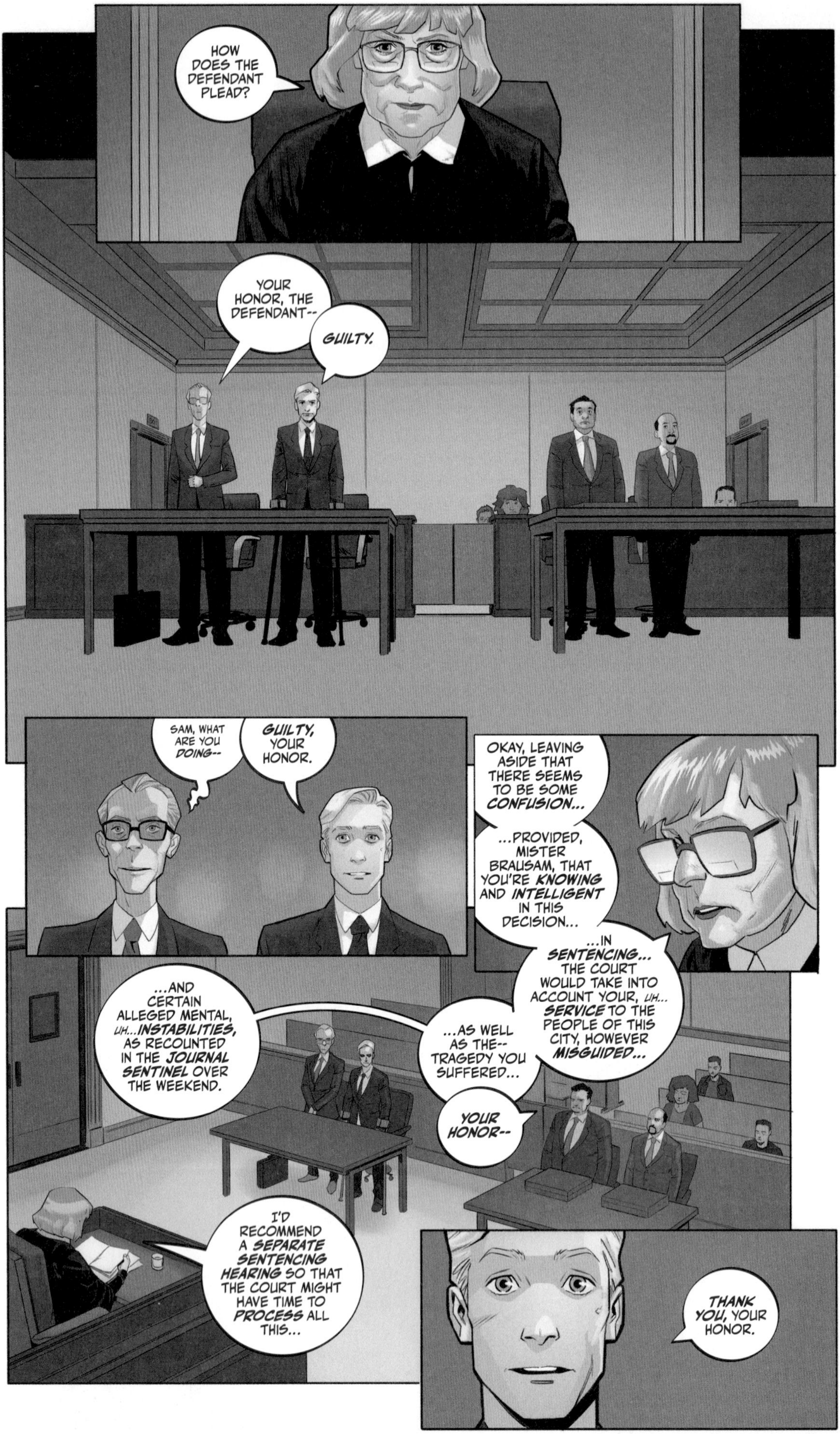

HOW DOES THE DEFENDANT PLEAD?
YOUR HONOR, THE DEFENDANT--
GUILTY.
SAM, WHAT ARE YOU DOING--
GUILTY, YOUR HONOR.
OKAY, LEAVING ASIDE THAT THERE SEEMS TO BE SOME CONFUSION...
...PROVIDED, MISTER BRAUSAM, THAT YOU'RE KNOWING AND INTELLIGENT IN THIS DECISION...
...IN SENTENCING... THE COURT WOULD TAKE INTO ACCOUNT YOUR, UH... SERVICE TO THE PEOPLE OF THIS CITY, HOWEVER MISGUIDED...
...AS WELL AS THE-- TRAGEDY YOU SUFFERED...
...AND CERTAIN ALLEGED MENTAL, UH...INSTABILITIES, AS RECOUNTED IN THE JOURNAL SENTINEL OVER THE WEEKEND.
YOUR HONOR--
I'D RECOMMEND A SEPARATE SENTENCING HEARING SO THAT THE COURT MIGHT HAVE TIME TO PROCESS ALL THIS...
THANK YOU, YOUR HONOR.

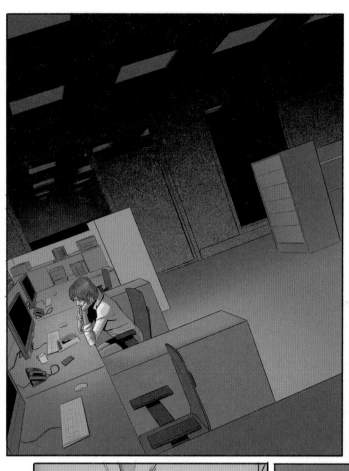

WEEKENDER

BLUE
FLAME
OUT

by Paul Gordon

C'MON.
JUDGE US
ALREADY.

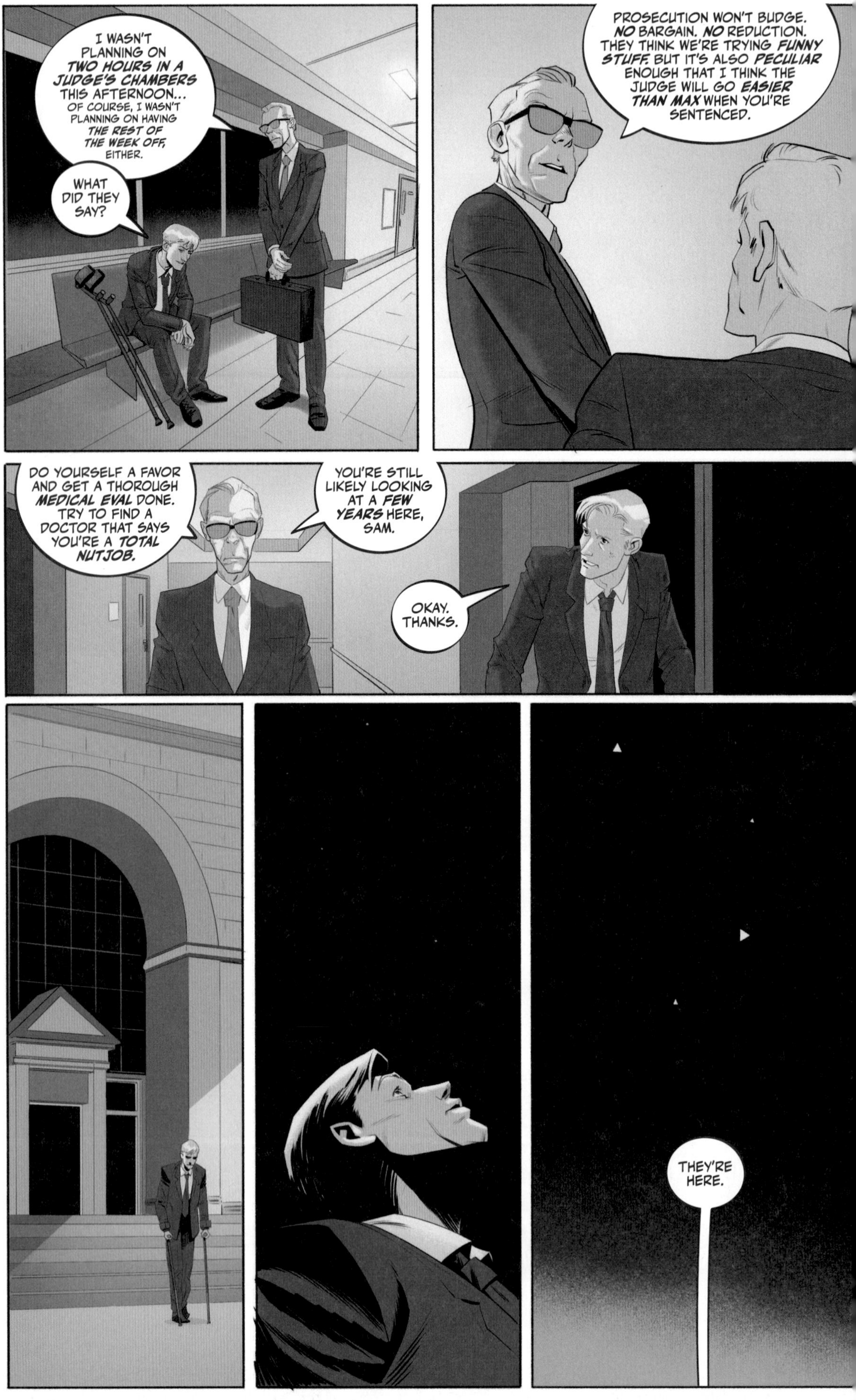
I WASN'T PLANNING ON TWO HOURS IN A JUDGE'S CHAMBERS THIS AFTERNOON... OF COURSE, I WASN'T PLANNING ON HAVING THE REST OF THE WEEK OFF, EITHER.
WHAT DID THEY SAY?
PROSECUTION WON'T BUDGE. NO BARGAIN. NO REDUCTION. THEY THINK WE'RE TRYING FUNNY STUFF. BUT IT'S ALSO PECULIAR ENOUGH THAT I THINK THE JUDGE WILL GO EASIER THAN MAX WHEN YOU'RE SENTENCED.
DO YOURSELF A FAVOR AND GET A THOROUGH MEDICAL EVAL DONE. TRY TO FIND A DOCTOR THAT SAYS YOU'RE A TOTAL NUTJOB.
YOU'RE STILL LIKELY LOOKING AT A FEW YEARS HERE, SAM.
OKAY. THANKS.
THEY'RE HERE.

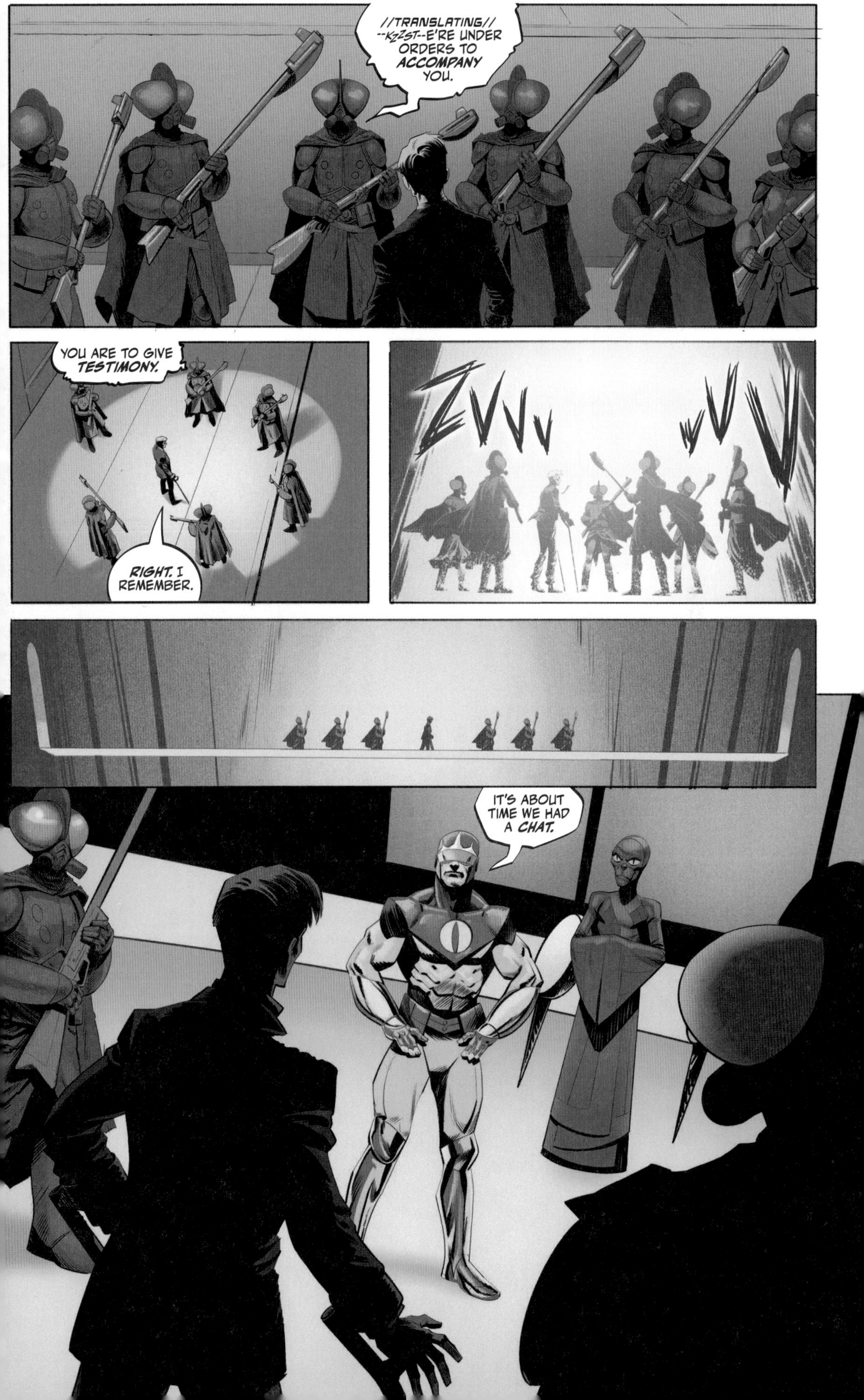
//TRANSLATING// --KZZST--E'RE UNDER ORDERS TO ACCOMPANY YOU.
YOU ARE TO GIVE TESTIMONY.
RIGHT. I REMEMBER.
ZVVV
VVV
IT'S ABOUT TIME WE HAD A CHAT.

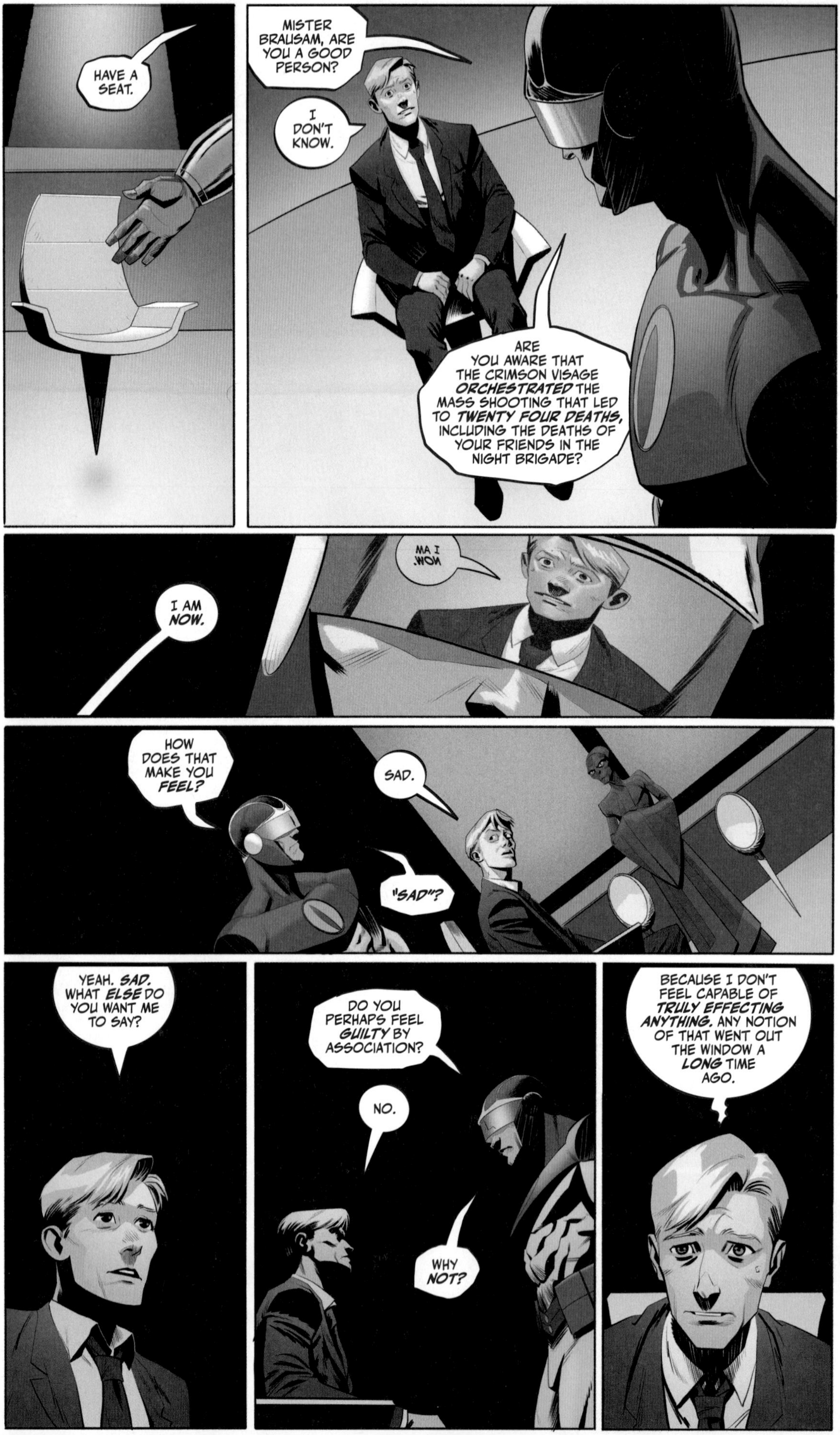

HAVE A SEAT.
MISTER BRAUSAM, ARE YOU A GOOD PERSON?
I DON'T KNOW.
ARE YOU AWARE THAT THE CRIMSON VISAGE ORCHESTRATED THE MASS SHOOTING THAT LED TO TWENTY FOUR DEATHS, INCLUDING THE DEATHS OF YOUR FRIENDS IN THE NIGHT BRIGADE?
I AM NOW.
HOW DOES THAT MAKE YOU FEEL?
SAD.
"SAD"?
YEAH. SAD. WHAT ELSE DO YOU WANT ME TO SAY?
DO YOU PERHAPS FEEL GUILTY BY ASSOCIATION?
NO.
WHY NOT?
BECAUSE I DON'T FEEL CAPABLE OF TRULY EFFECTING ANYTHING. ANY NOTION OF THAT WENT OUT THE WINDOW A LONG TIME AGO.

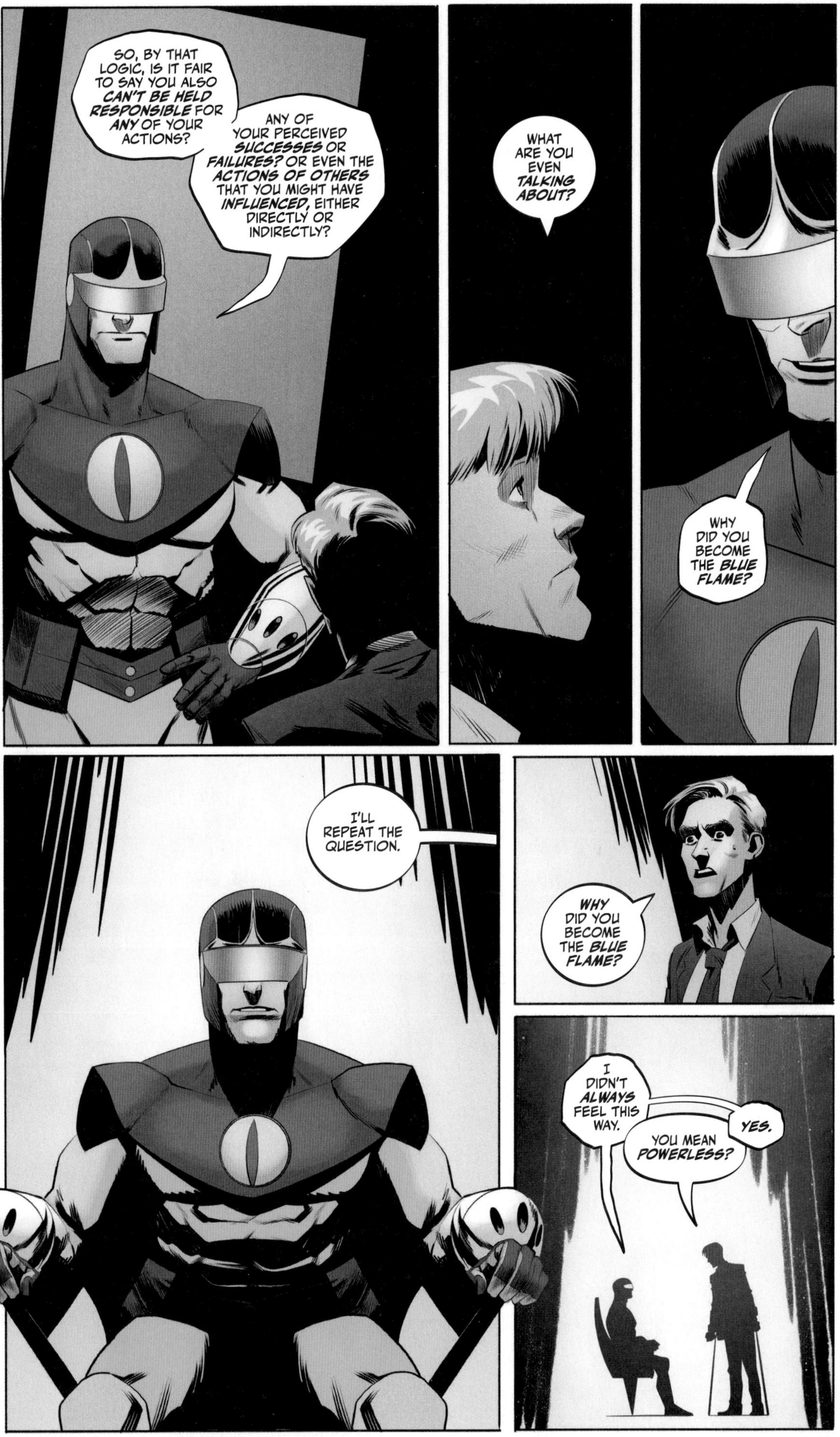
SO, BY THAT LOGIC, IS IT FAIR TO SAY YOU ALSO CAN'T BE HELD RESPONSIBLE FOR ANY OF YOUR ACTIONS?
ANY OF YOUR PERCEIVED SUCCESSES OR FAILURES? OR EVEN THE ACTIONS OF OTHERS THAT YOU MIGHT HAVE INFLUENCED, EITHER DIRECTLY OR INDIRECTLY?
WHAT ARE YOU EVEN TALKING ABOUT?
WHY DID YOU BECOME THE BLUE FLAME?
I'LL REPEAT THE QUESTION.
WHY DID YOU BECOME THE BLUE FLAME?
I DIDN'T ALWAYS FEEL THIS WAY.
YOU MEAN POWERLESS?
YES.

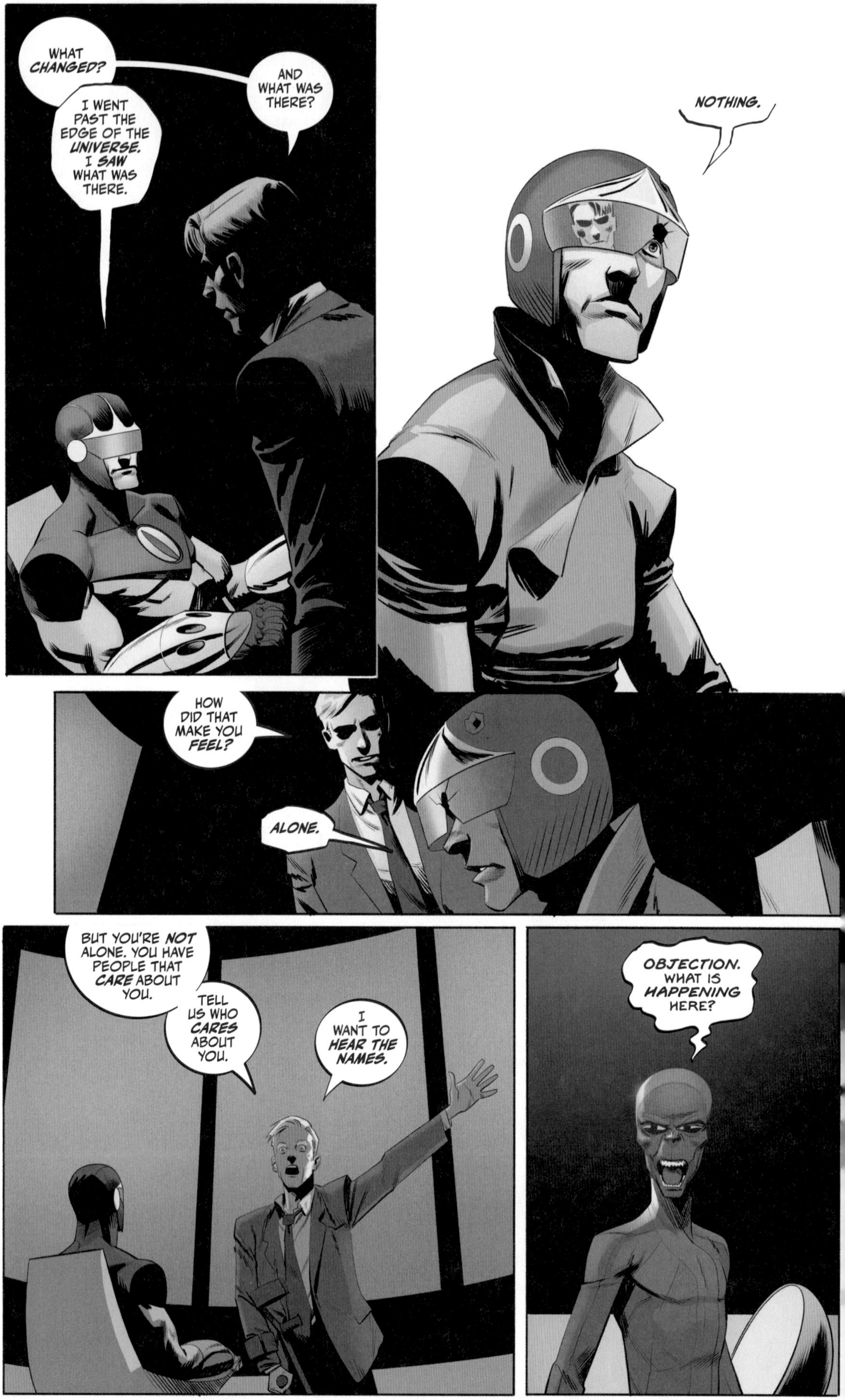
WHAT CHANGED?
AND WHAT WAS THERE?
I WENT PAST THE EDGE OF THE UNIVERSE. I SAW WHAT WAS THERE.
NOTHING.
HOW DID THAT MAKE YOU FEEL?
ALONE.
BUT YOU'RE NOT ALONE. YOU HAVE PEOPLE THAT CARE ABOUT YOU.
TELL US WHO CARES ABOUT YOU.
I WANT TO HEAR THE NAMES.
OBJECTION. WHAT IS HAPPENING HERE?

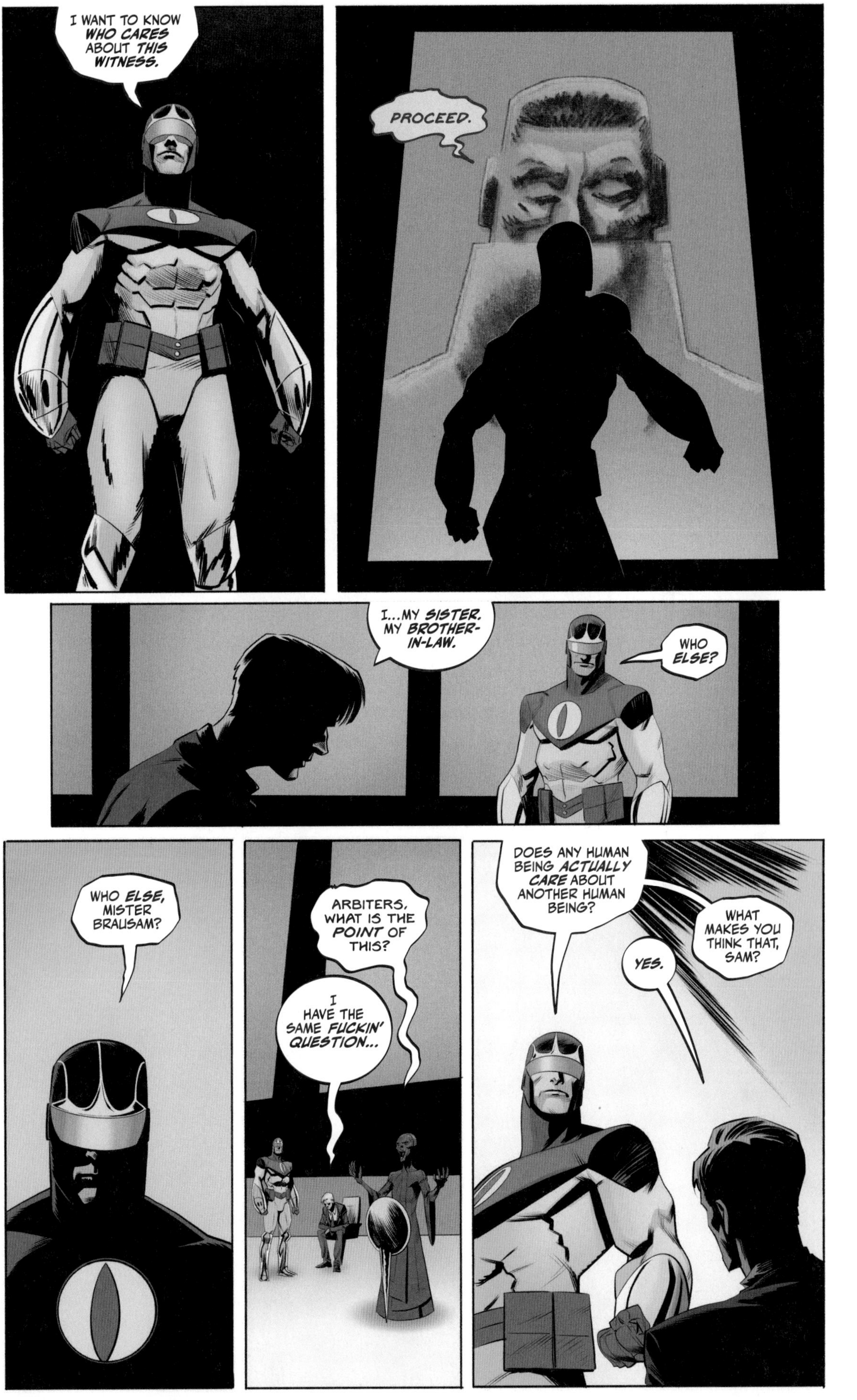
I WANT TO KNOW WHO CARES ABOUT THIS WITNESS.
PROCEED.
I...MY SISTER. MY BROTHER-IN-LAW.
WHO ELSE?
WHO ELSE, MISTER BRAUSAM?
ARBITERS, WHAT IS THE POINT OF THIS?
I HAVE THE SAME FUCKIN' QUESTION...
DOES ANY HUMAN BEING ACTUALLY CARE ABOUT ANOTHER HUMAN BEING?
WHAT MAKES YOU THINK THAT, SAM?
YES.

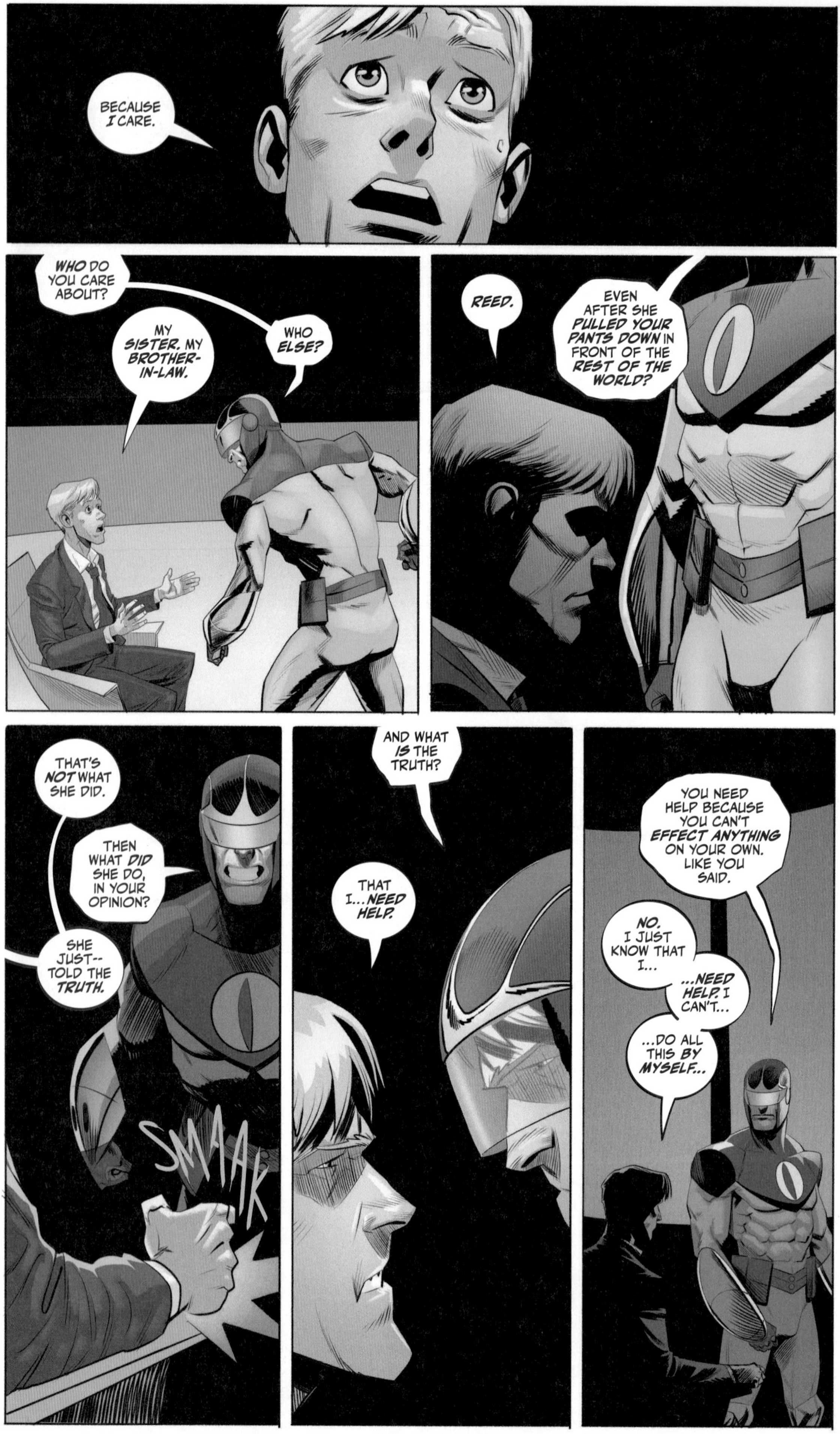
BECAUSE I CARE.
WHO DO YOU CARE ABOUT?
MY SISTER. MY BROTHER-IN-LAW.
WHO ELSE?
REED.
EVEN AFTER SHE PULLED YOUR PANTS DOWN IN FRONT OF THE REST OF THE WORLD?
THAT'S NOT WHAT SHE DID.
THEN WHAT DID SHE DO, IN YOUR OPINION?
SHE JUST-- TOLD THE TRUTH.
SMAAK
AND WHAT IS THE TRUTH?
THAT I...NEED HELP.
YOU NEED HELP BECAUSE YOU CAN'T EFFECT ANYTHING ON YOUR OWN. LIKE YOU SAID.
NO. I JUST KNOW THAT I...
...NEED HELP. I CAN'T...
...DO ALL THIS BY MYSELF...

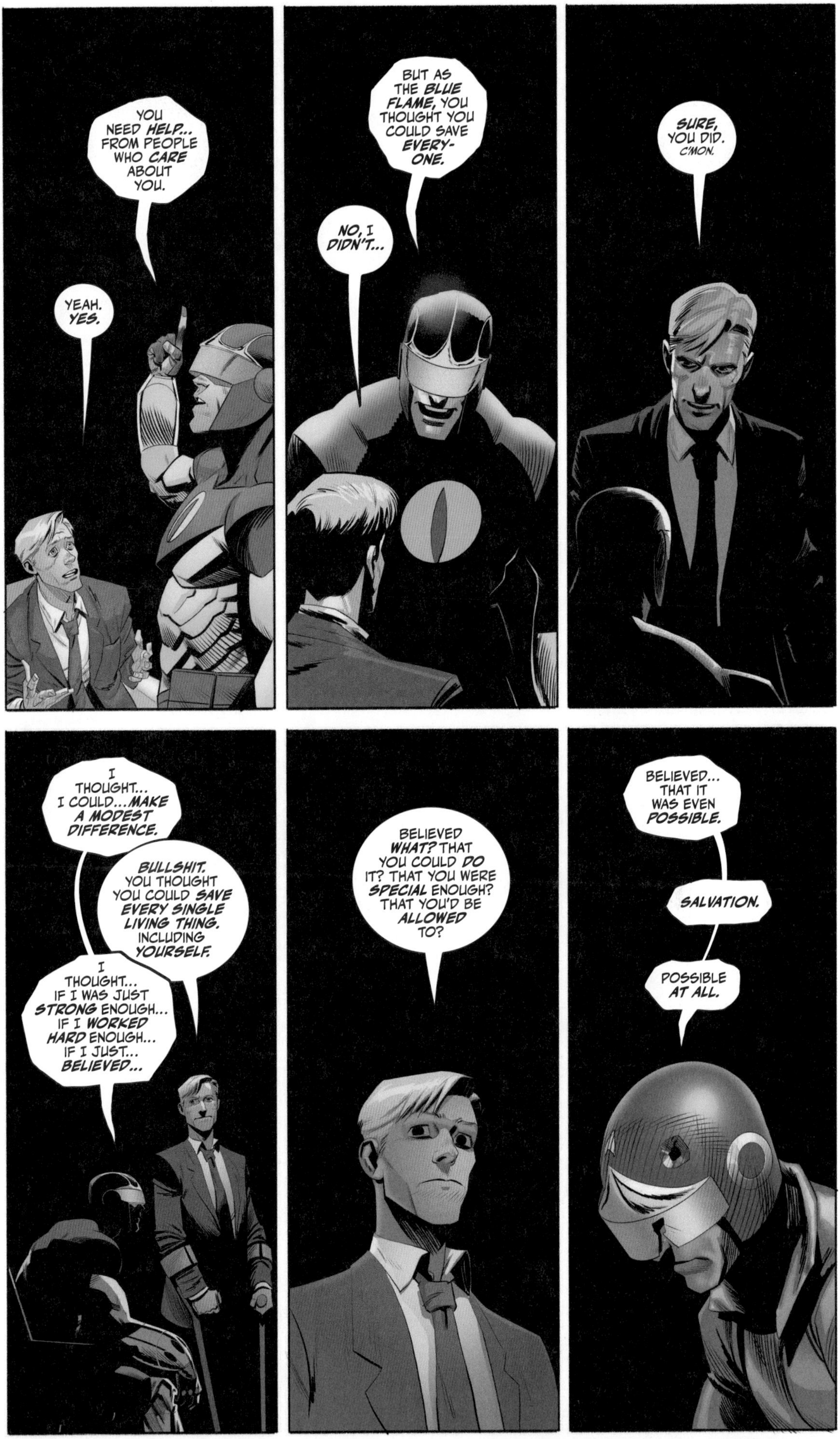
YOU NEED HELP... FROM PEOPLE WHO CARE ABOUT YOU.
YEAH. YES.
BUT AS THE BLUE FLAME, YOU THOUGHT YOU COULD SAVE EVERY-ONE.
NO, I DIDN'T...
SURE, YOU DID. C'MON.
I THOUGHT... I COULD...MAKE A MODEST DIFFERENCE.
BULLSHIT. YOU THOUGHT YOU COULD SAVE EVERY SINGLE LIVING THING. INCLUDING YOURSELF.
I THOUGHT... IF I WAS JUST STRONG ENOUGH... IF I WORKED HARD ENOUGH... IF I JUST... BELIEVED...
BELIEVED WHAT? THAT YOU COULD DO IT? THAT YOU WERE SPECIAL ENOUGH? THAT YOU'D BE ALLOWED TO?
BELIEVED... THAT IT WAS EVEN POSSIBLE.
SALVATION.
POSSIBLE AT ALL.

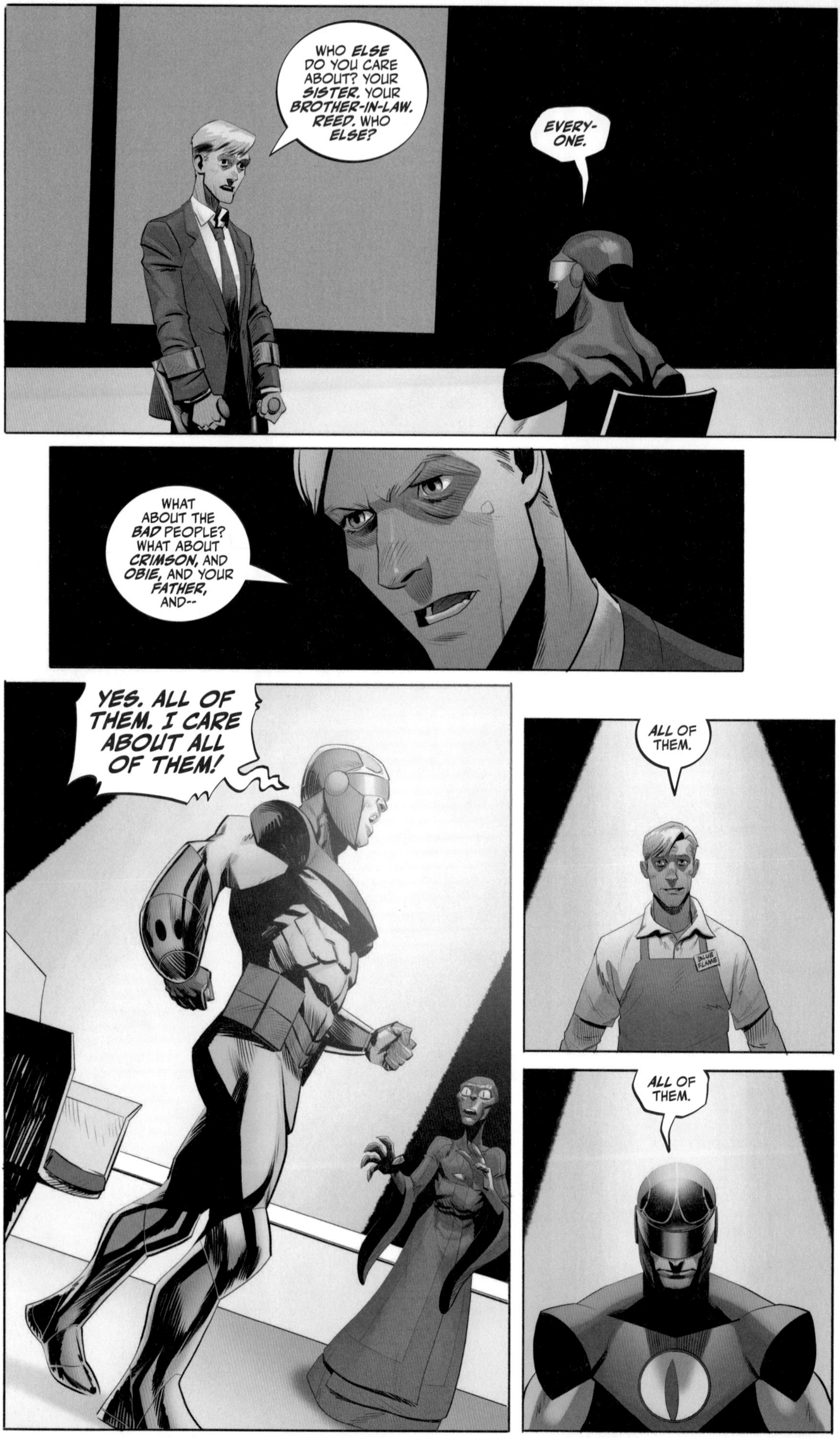
WHO ELSE DO YOU CARE ABOUT? YOUR SISTER. YOUR BROTHER-IN-LAW. REED. WHO ELSE?
EVERY-ONE.
WHAT ABOUT THE BAD PEOPLE? WHAT ABOUT CRIMSON, AND OBIE, AND YOUR FATHER, AND--
YES. ALL OF THEM. I CARE ABOUT ALL OF THEM!
ALL OF THEM.
BLUE FLAME
ALL OF THEM.

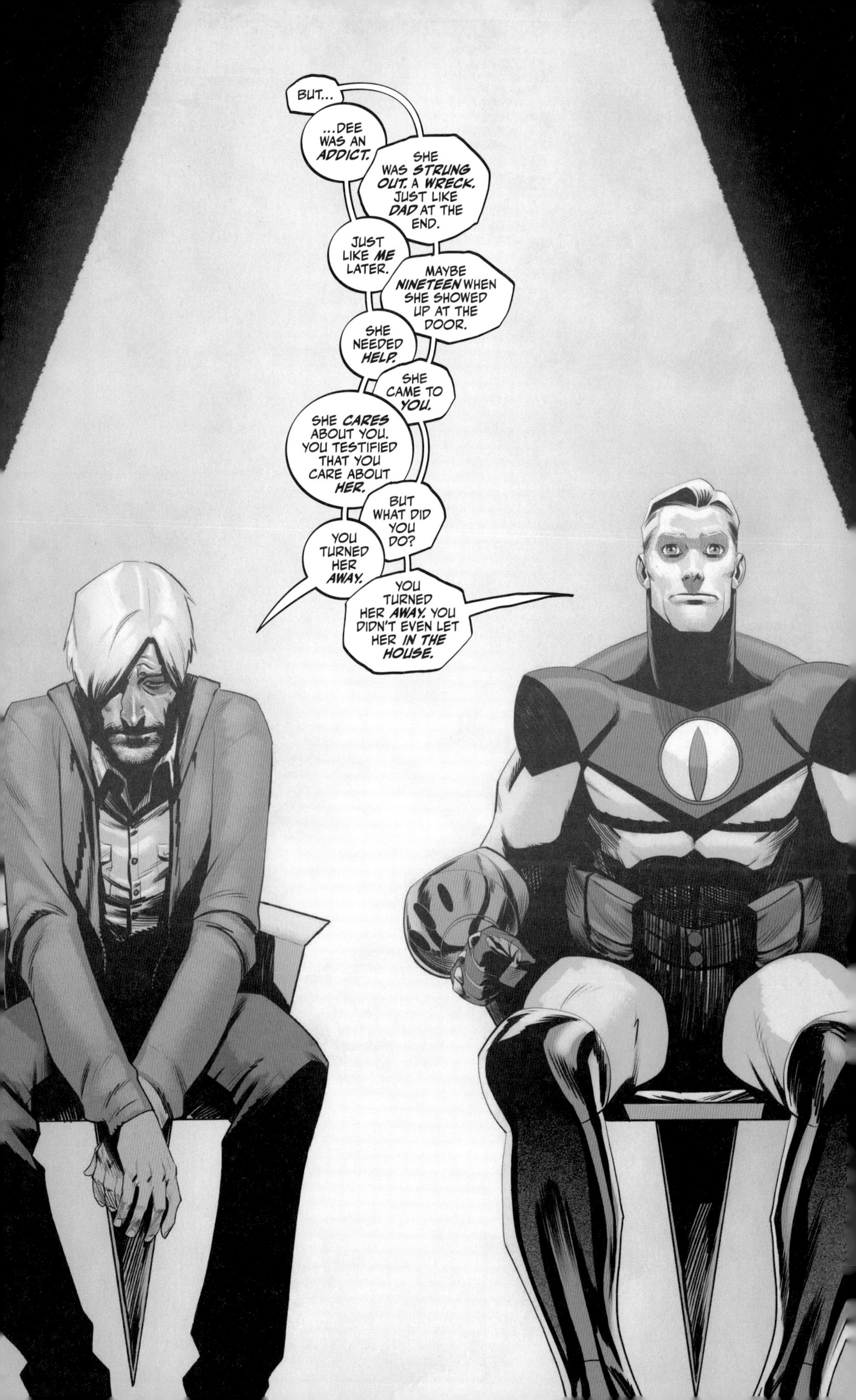
BUT...
...DEE WAS AN ADDICT.
SHE WAS STRUNG OUT. A WRECK. JUST LIKE DAD AT THE END.
JUST LIKE ME LATER.
MAYBE NINETEEN WHEN SHE SHOWED UP AT THE DOOR.
SHE NEEDED HELP.
SHE CAME TO YOU.
SHE CARES ABOUT YOU. YOU TESTIFIED THAT YOU CARE ABOUT HER.
BUT WHAT DID YOU DO?
YOU TURNED HER AWAY.
YOU TURNED HER AWAY. YOU DIDN'T EVEN LET HER IN THE HOUSE.

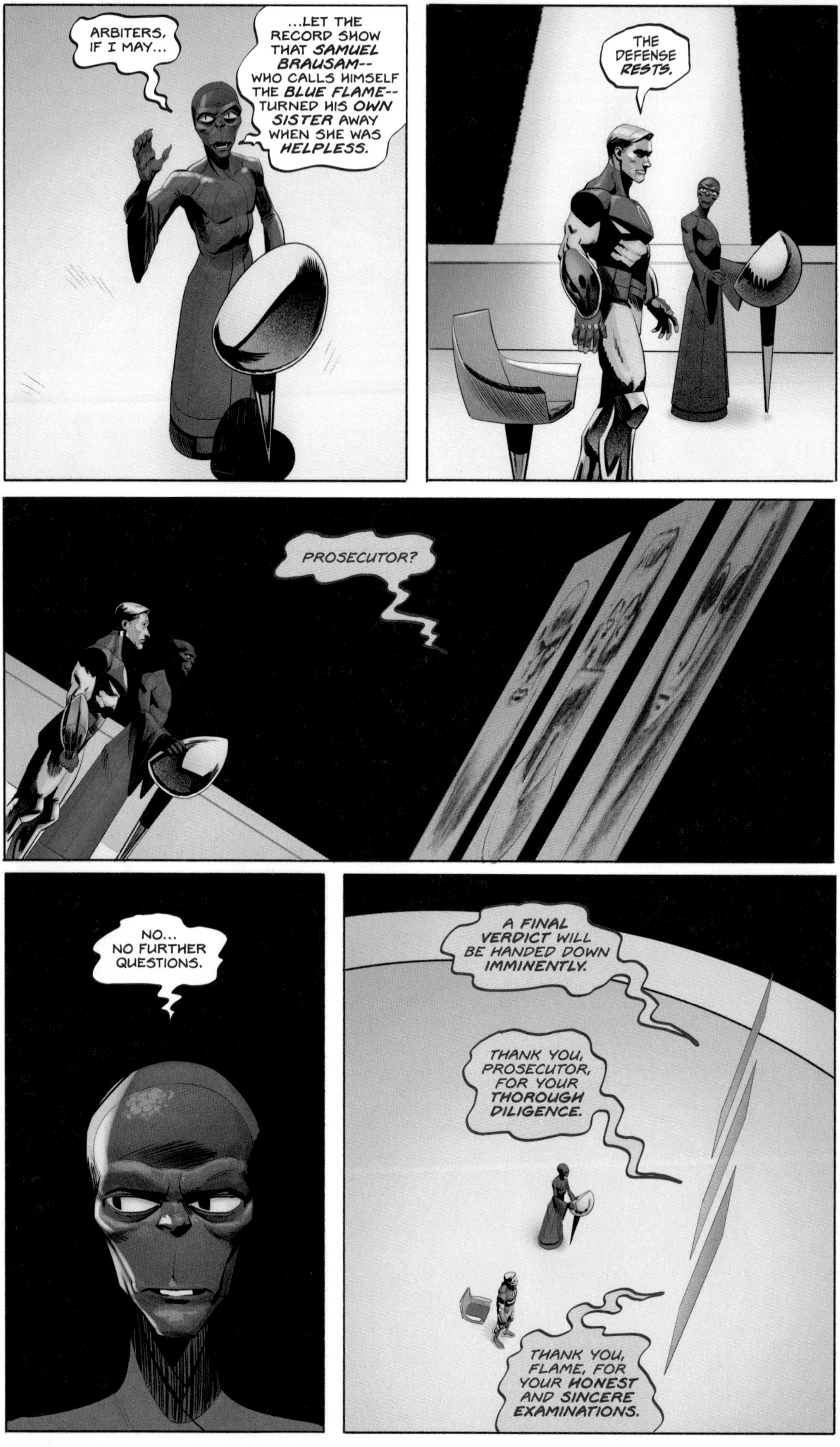
ARBITERS, IF I MAY...
...LET THE RECORD SHOW THAT SAMUEL BRAUSAM-- WHO CALLS HIMSELF THE BLUE FLAME-- TURNED HIS OWN SISTER AWAY WHEN SHE WAS HELPLESS.
THE DEFENSE RESTS.
PROSECUTOR?
NO... NO FURTHER QUESTIONS.
A FINAL VERDICT WILL BE HANDED DOWN IMMINENTLY.
THANK YOU, PROSECUTOR, FOR YOUR THOROUGH DILIGENCE.
THANK YOU, FLAME, FOR YOUR HONEST AND SINCERE EXAMINATIONS.

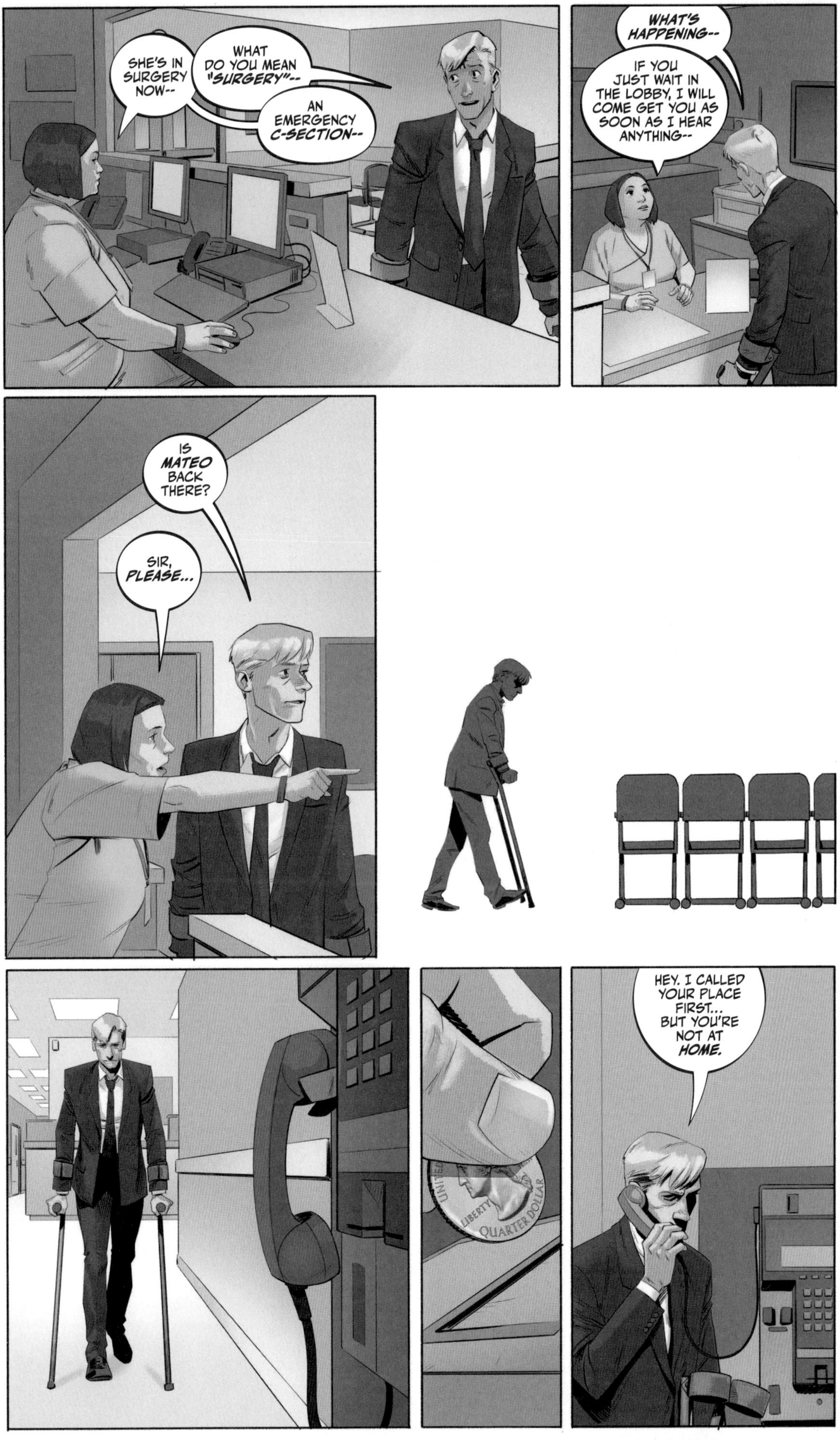
SHE'S IN SURGERY NOW--
WHAT DO YOU MEAN "SURGERY"--
AN EMERGENCY C-SECTION--
WHAT'S HAPPENING--
IF YOU JUST WAIT IN THE LOBBY, I WILL COME GET YOU AS SOON AS I HEAR ANYTHING--
IS MATEO BACK THERE?
SIR, PLEASE...
UNITED
LIBERTY
QUARTER DOLLAR
HEY. I CALLED YOUR PLACE FIRST... BUT YOU'RE NOT AT HOME.

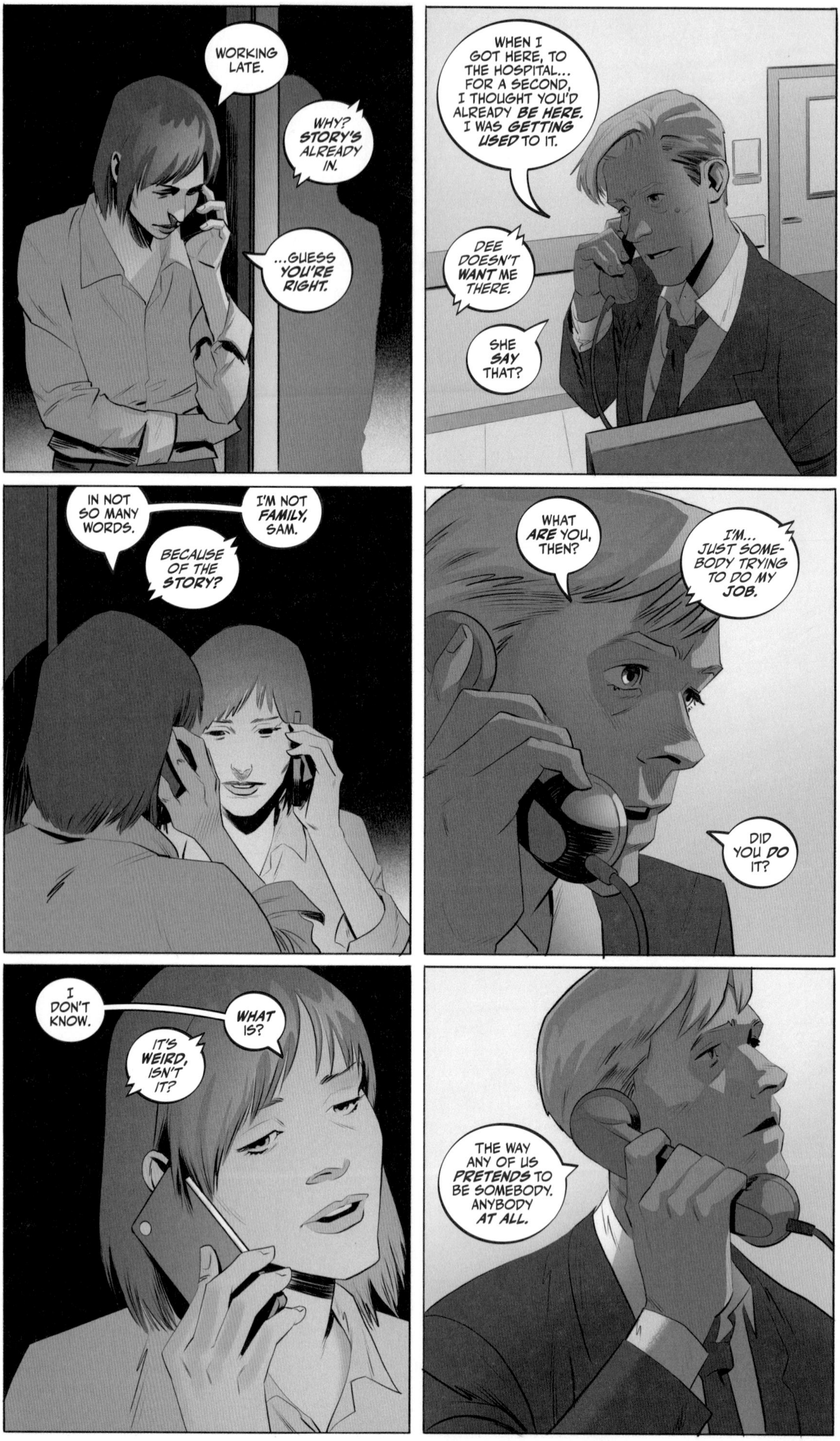
WORKING LATE.
WHY? STORY'S ALREADY IN.
...GUESS YOU'RE RIGHT.
WHEN I GOT HERE, TO THE HOSPITAL... FOR A SECOND, I THOUGHT YOU'D ALREADY BE HERE. I WAS GETTING USED TO IT.
DEE DOESN'T WANT ME THERE.
SHE SAY THAT?
IN NOT SO MANY WORDS.
I'M NOT FAMILY, SAM.
BECAUSE OF THE STORY?
WHAT ARE YOU, THEN?
I'M... JUST SOME-BODY TRYING TO DO MY JOB.
DID YOU DO IT?
I DON'T KNOW.
WHAT IS?
IT'S WEIRD, ISN'T IT?
THE WAY ANY OF US PRETENDS TO BE SOMEBODY. ANYBODY AT ALL.

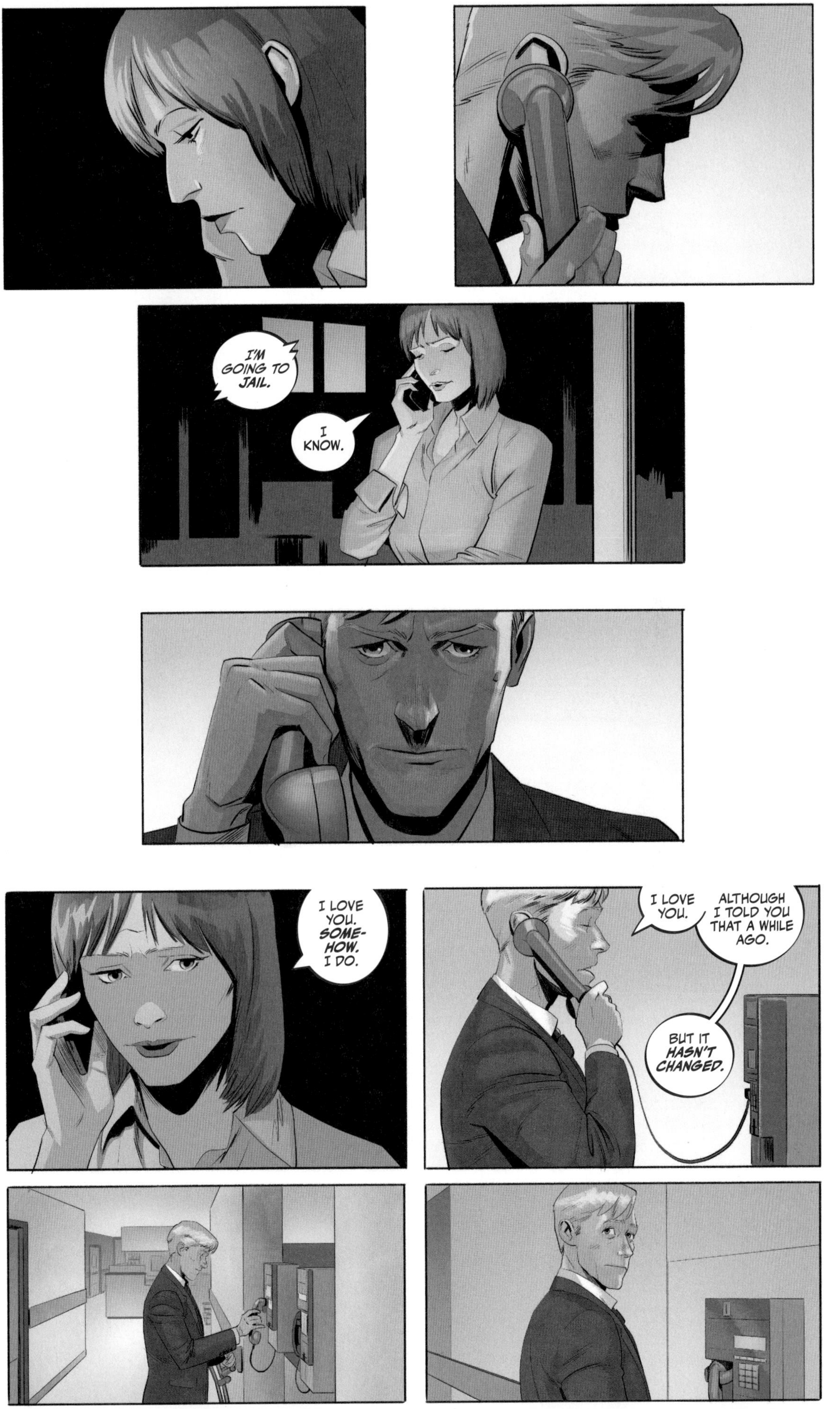
I'M GOING TO JAIL.
I KNOW.
I LOVE YOU. SOME-HOW. I DO.
I LOVE YOU.
ALTHOUGH I TOLD YOU THAT A WHILE AGO.
BUT IT HASN'T CHANGED.

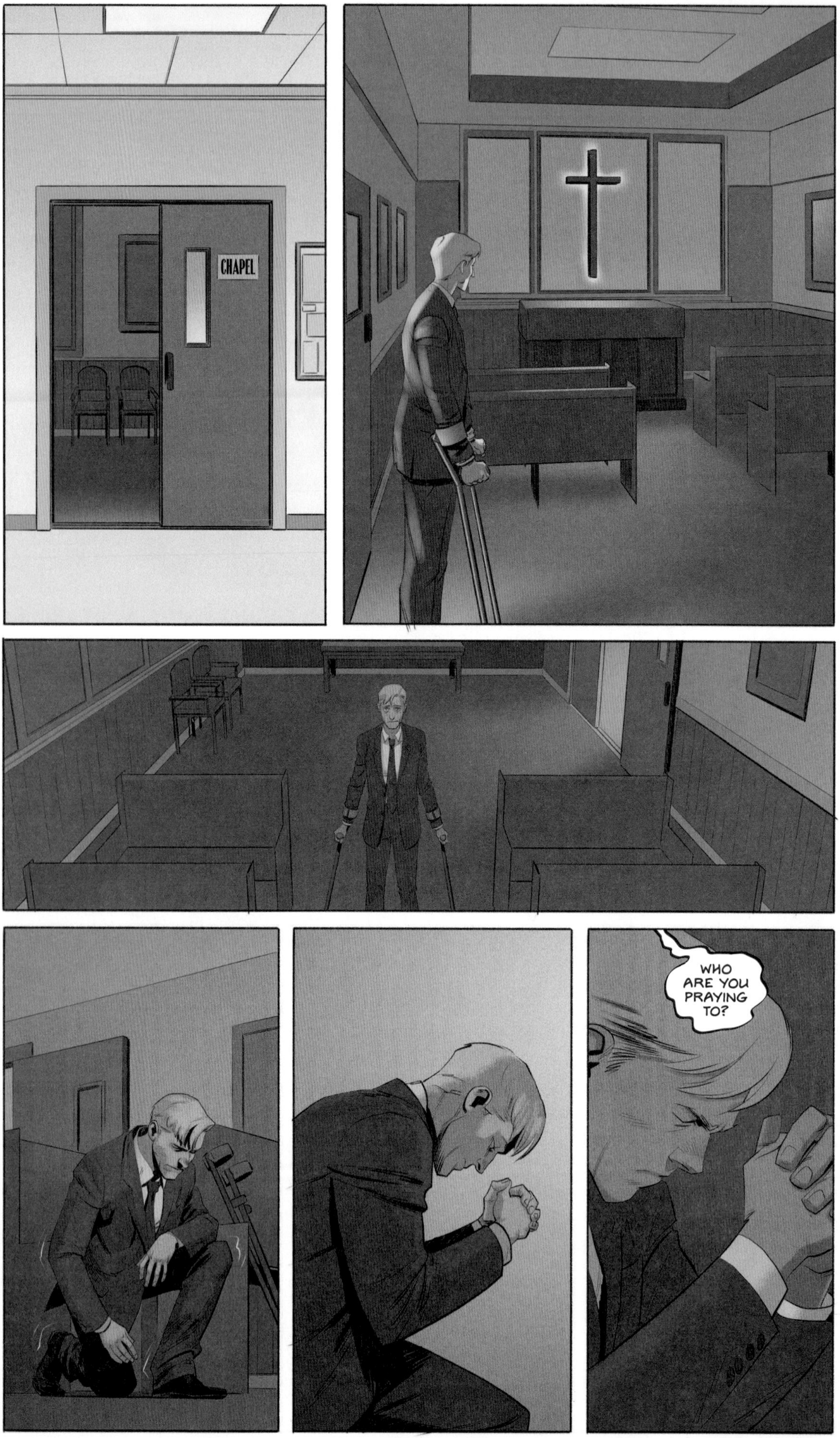
CHAPEL
WHO ARE YOU PRAYING TO?

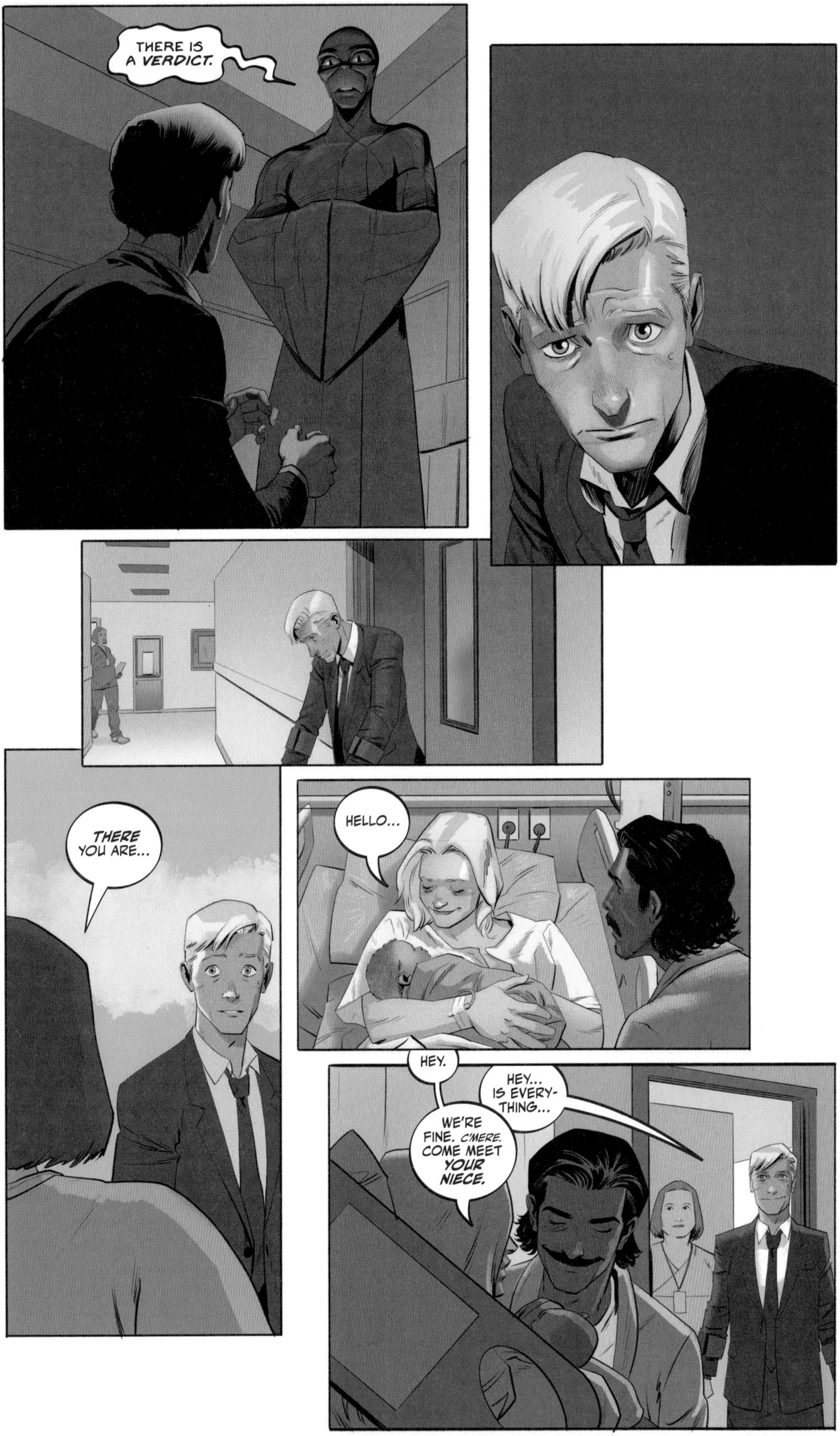
THERE IS A VERDICT.
THERE YOU ARE...
HELLO...
HEY.
HEY... IS EVERY-THING...
WE'RE FINE. C'MERE. COME MEET YOUR NIECE.

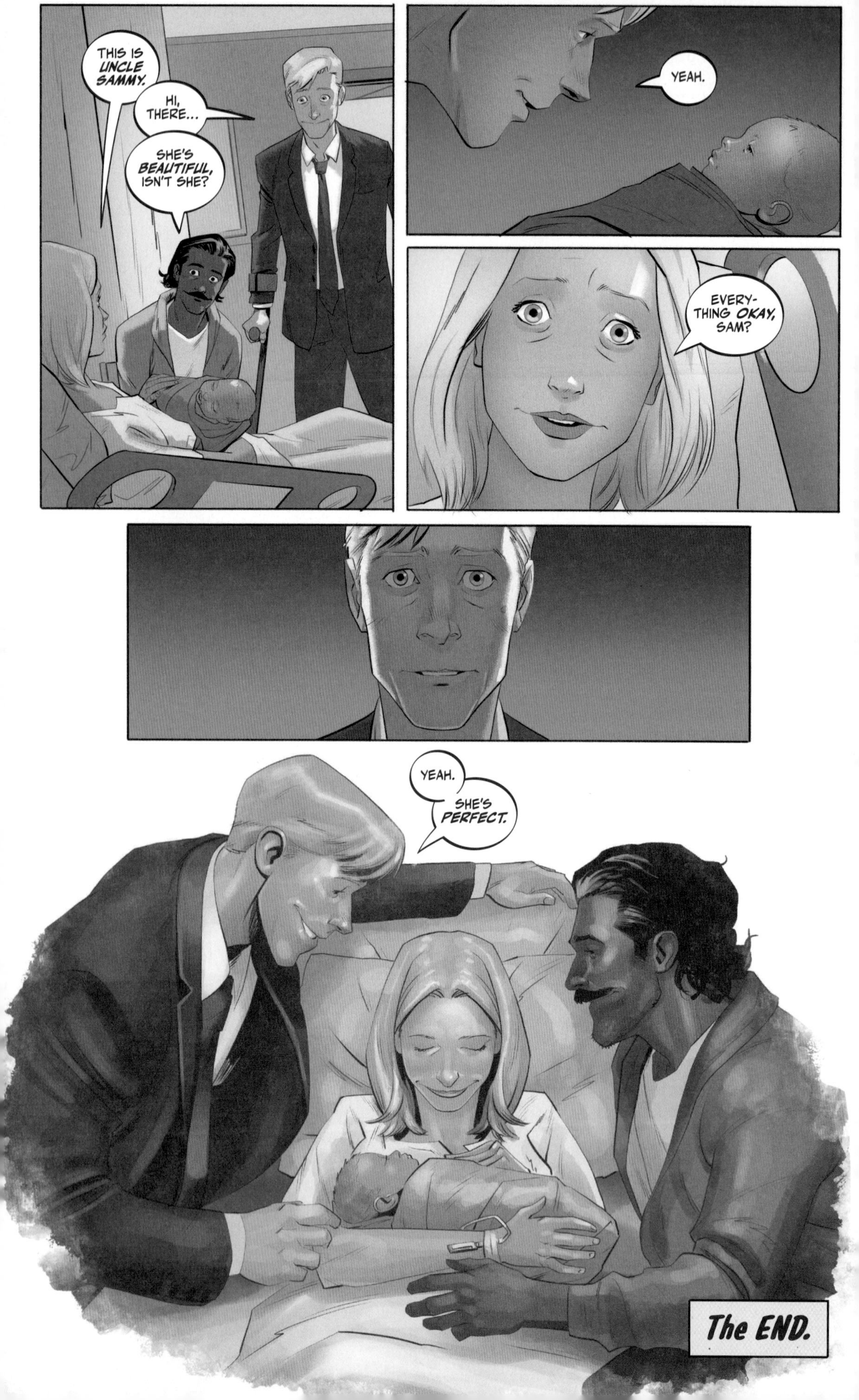
THIS IS UNCLE SAMMY.
HI, THERE...
SHE'S BEAUTIFUL, ISN'T SHE?
YEAH.
EVERY-THING OKAY, SAM?
YEAH.
SHE'S PERFECT.
The END.

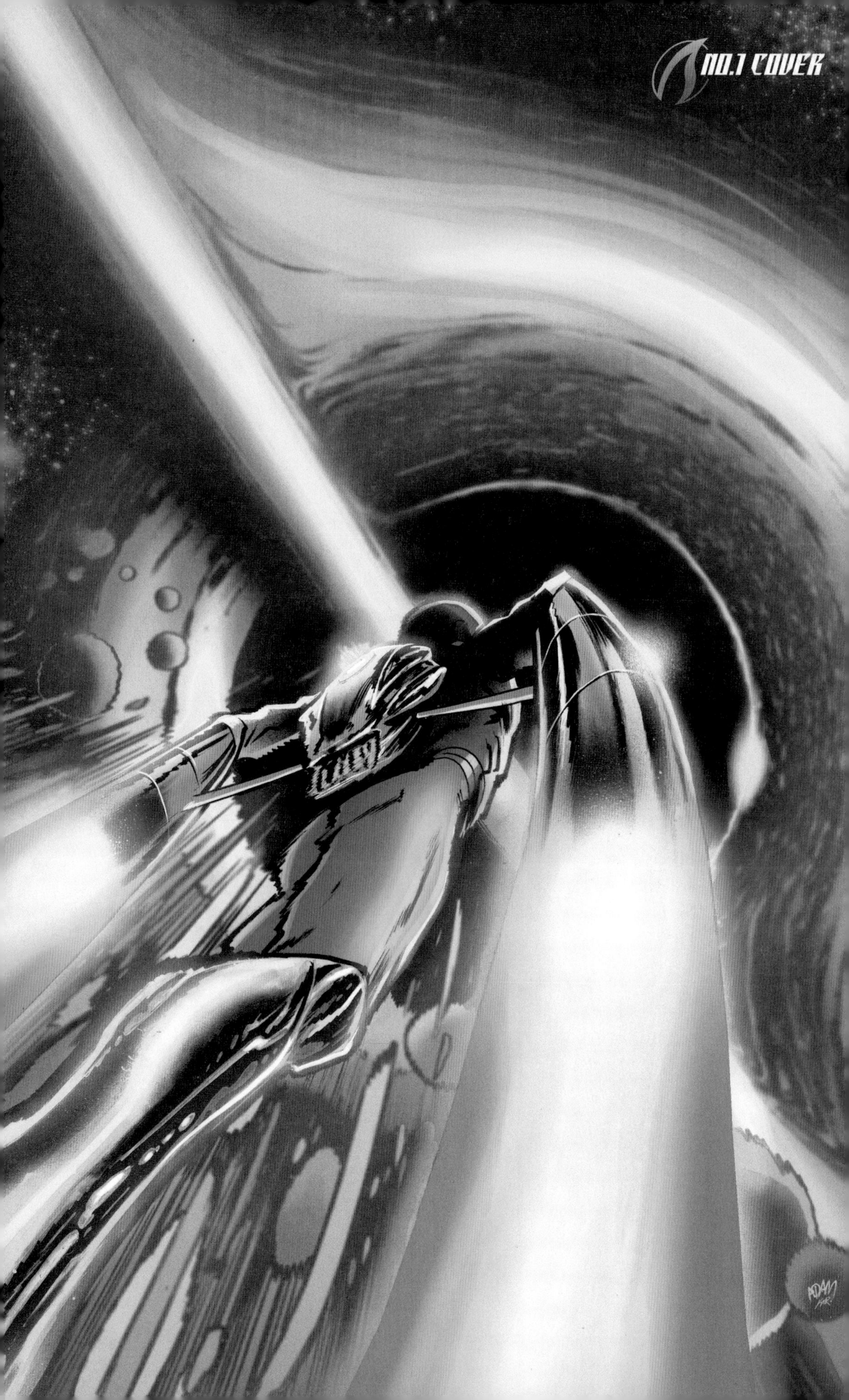
NO.1 COVER

NO.2 COVER

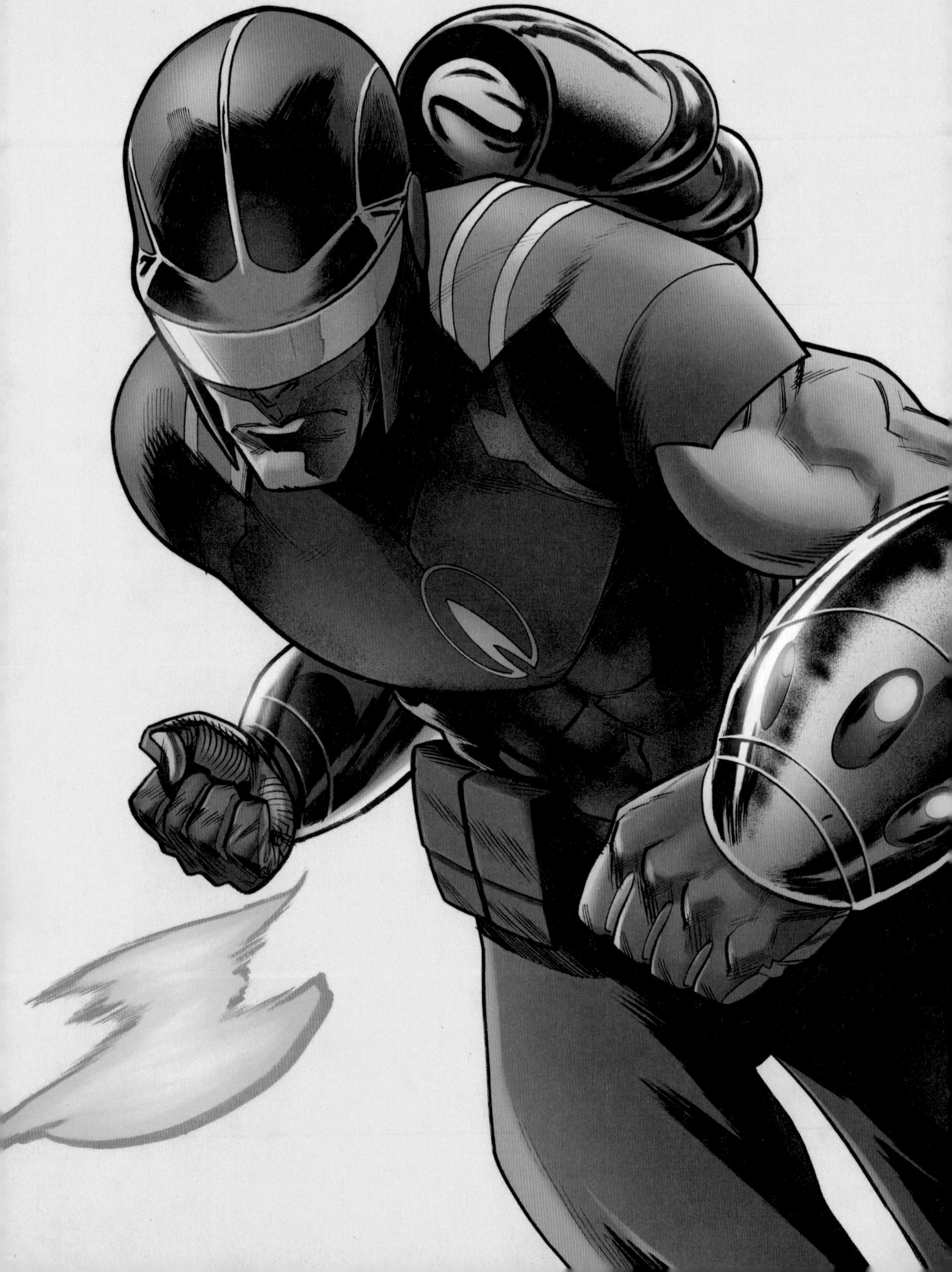

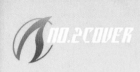

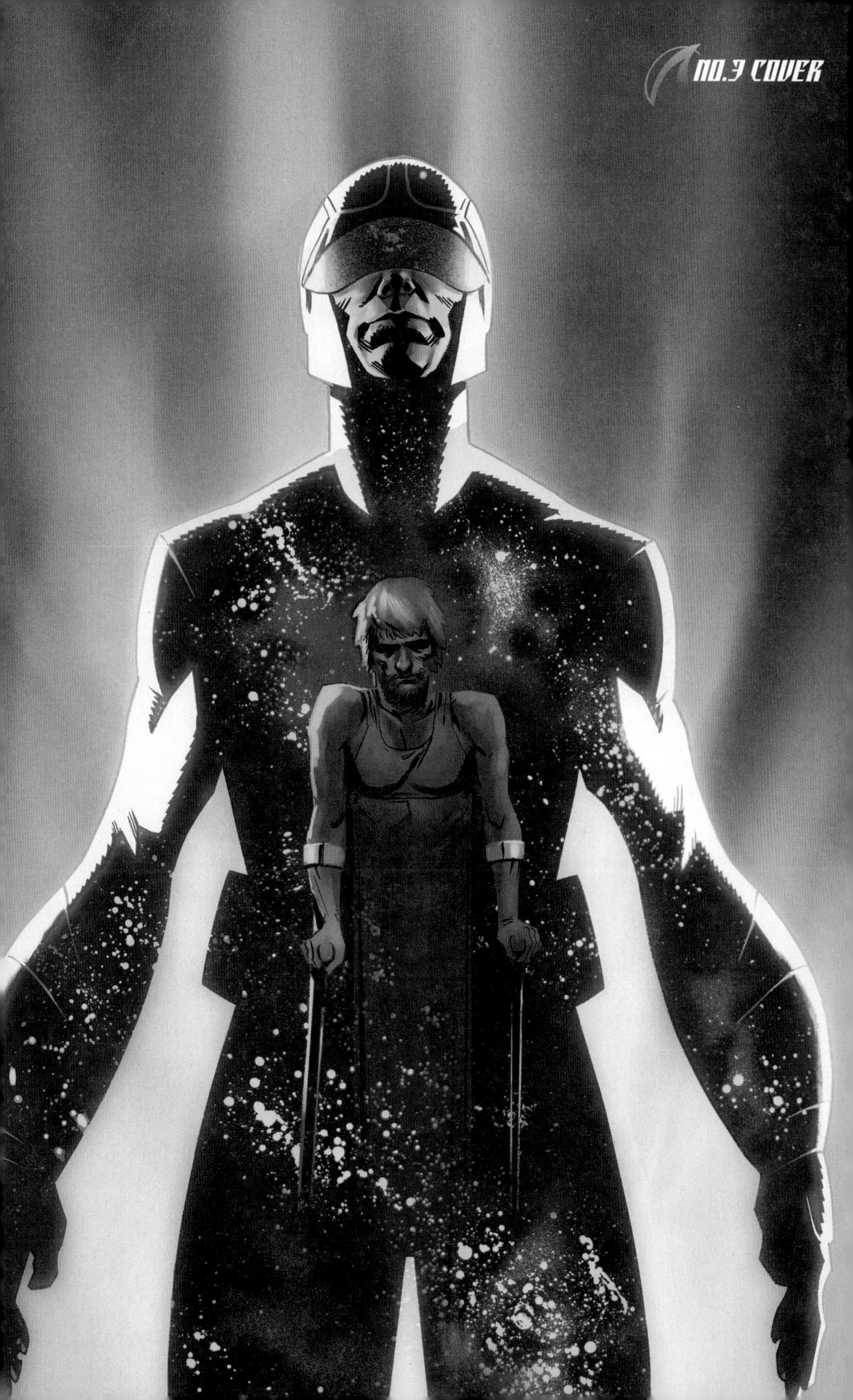

NO.3 COVER

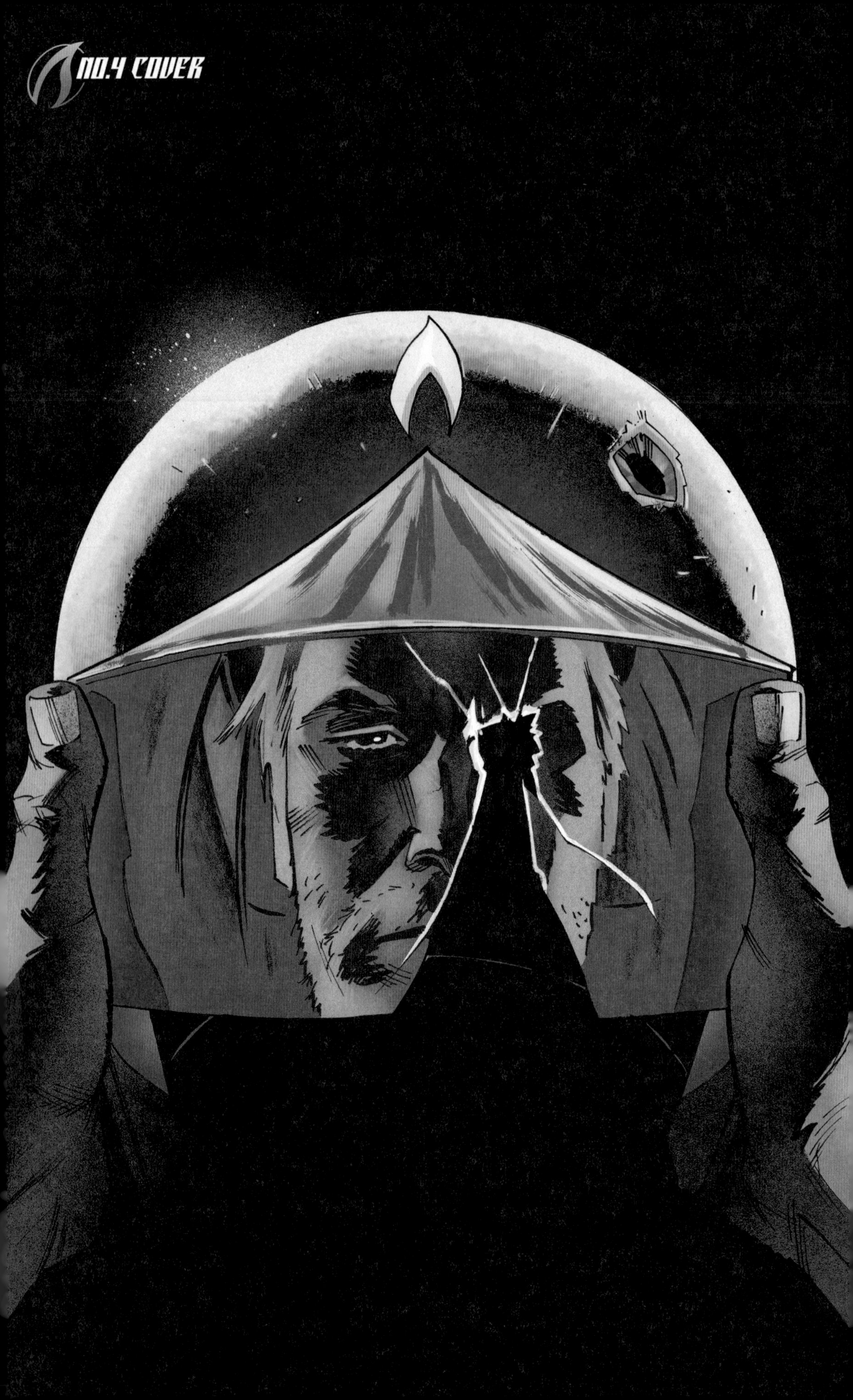
NO.4 COVER

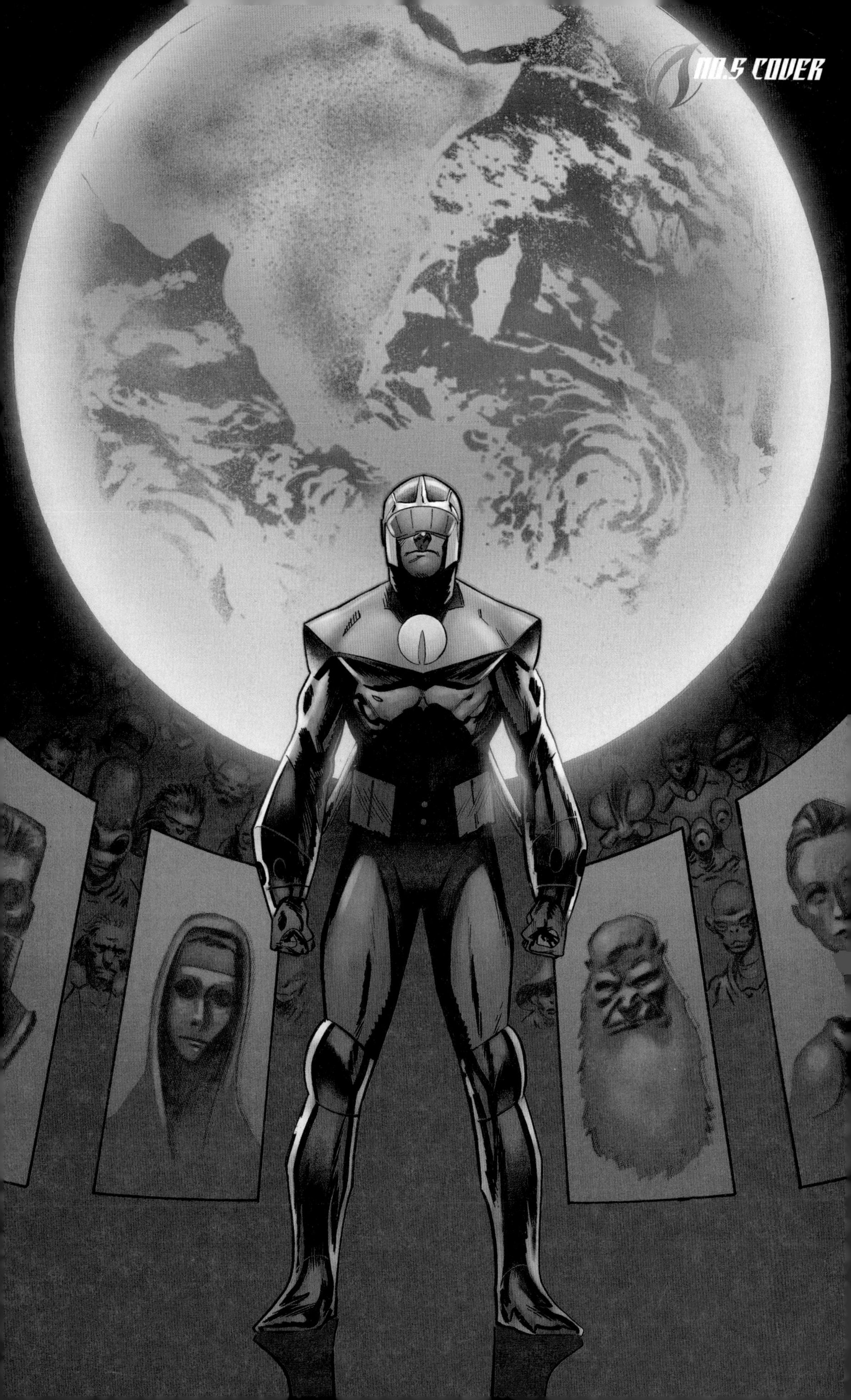

NO.5 COVER

NO.6 COVER

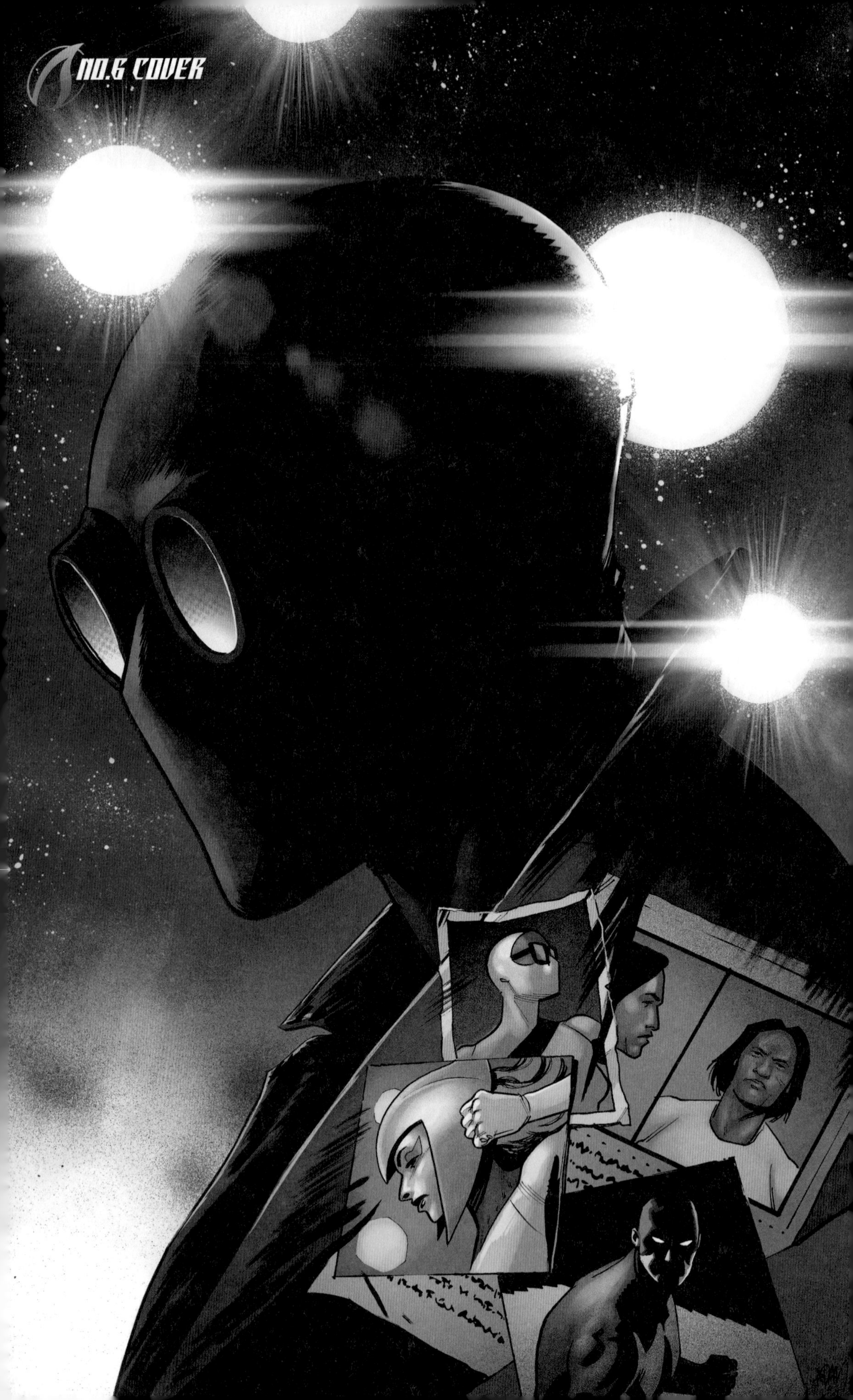

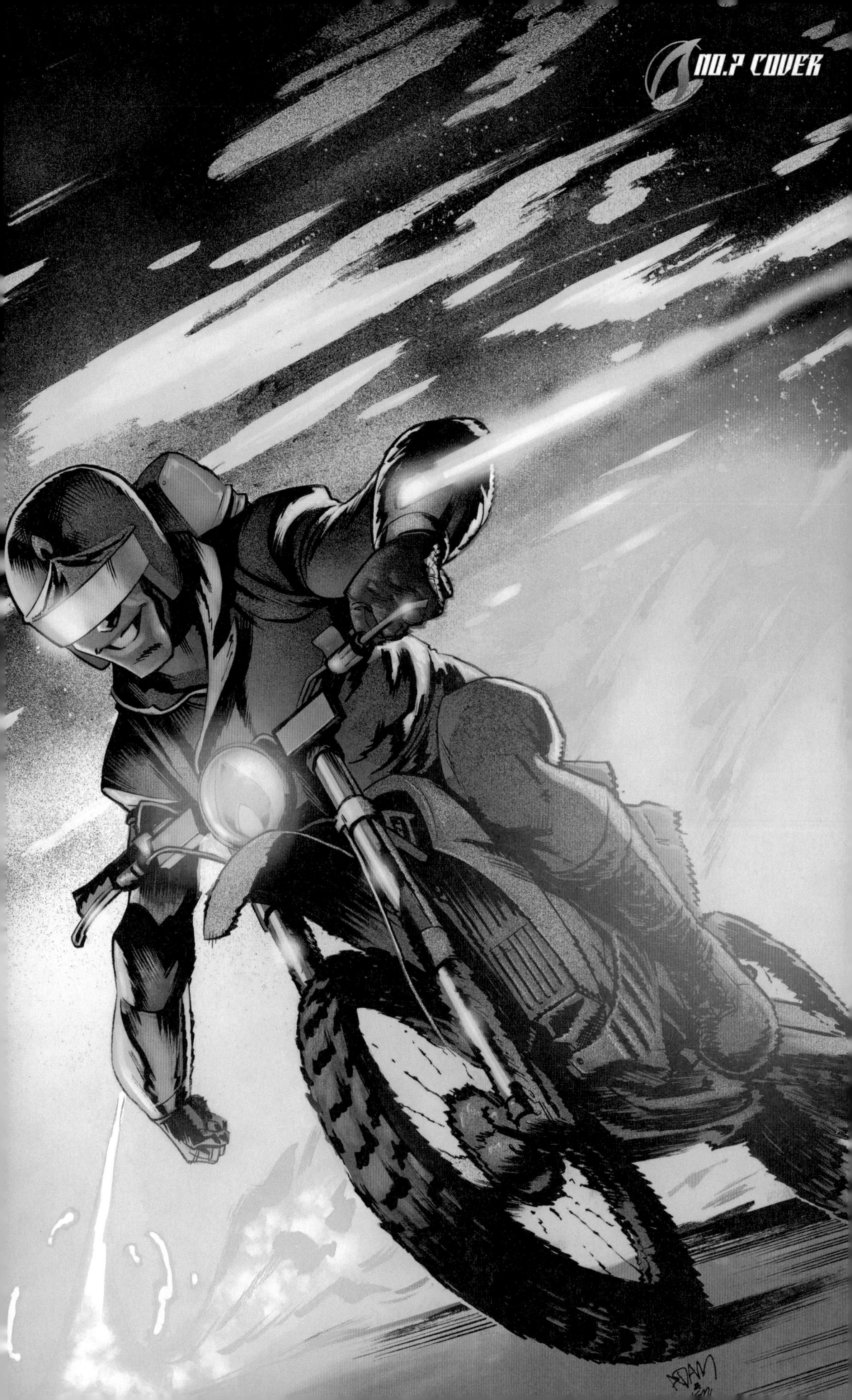
NO.7 COVER

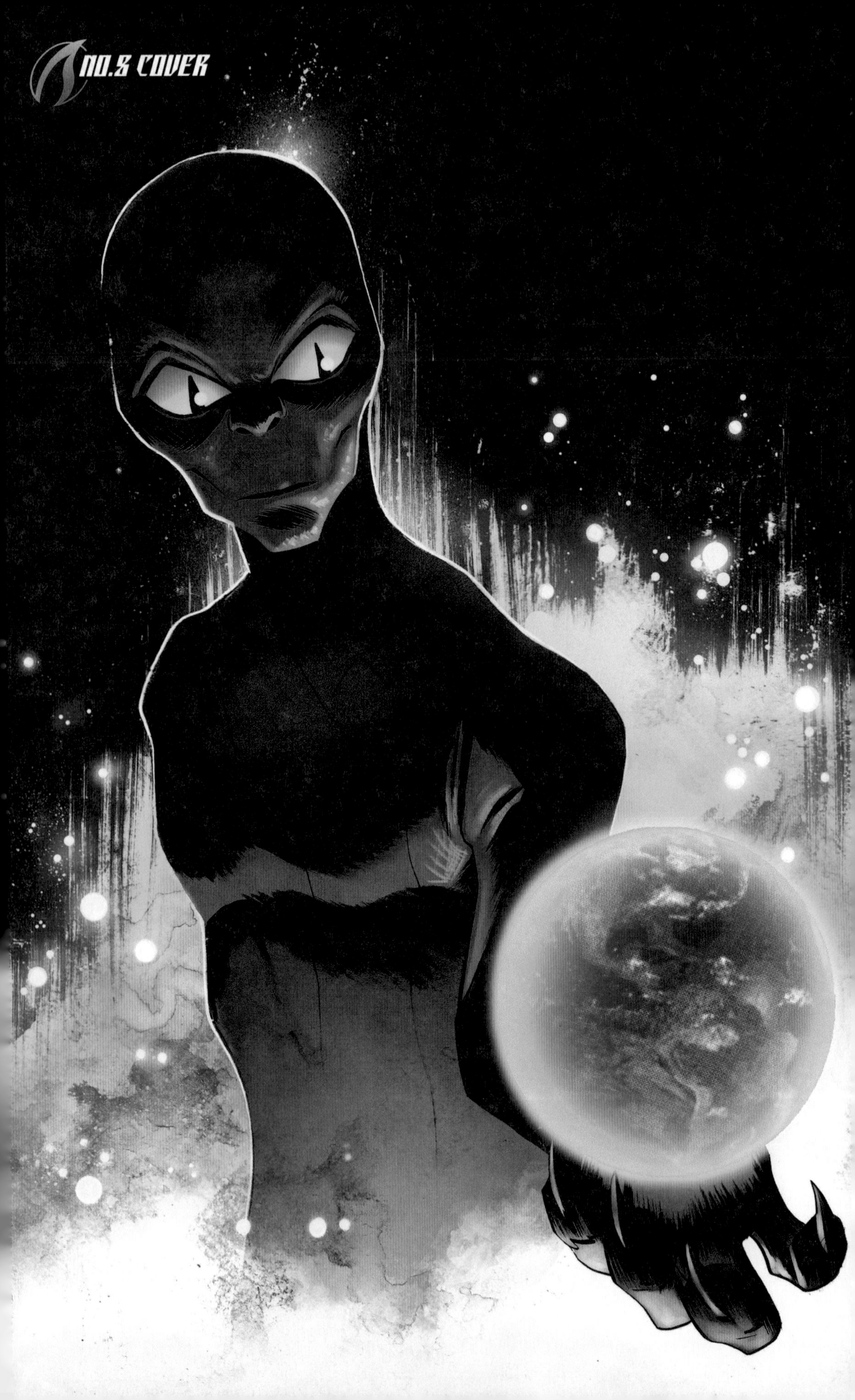
NO.5 COVER